SWEET SURRENDER

Firewalker reached out to touch the cascade of blue-black hair. It was silken and fragrant as he knew it would be. Unable to help himself, he raised a wisp of it to his lips and pressed a kiss on it.

"You are very beautiful, Caldwell the Healer." He stroked her long hair and her face and sought her lips. When they parted for him, sweet and welcoming, he covered her mouth with his.

Everything about him was wonderful: his hardness and strength, and his kisses, so tender at first but growing wilder, more arousing and possessive by the moment. She loved the taste of him and the smell of him—and she loved his hands, strong yet gentle, stroking her face and throat and shoulders and breasts. Fire raced through her, fire and ice. She was heated by his touch but could not stop shivering . . .

Other AVON ROMANCES

SURRENDER TO THE FURY *by Cara Miles*
THE LION'S DAUGHTER *by Loretta Chase*
CAPTAIN OF MY HEART *by Danelle Harmon*
SILVER FLAME *by Hannah Howell*
TAMING KATE *by Eugenia Riley*
LORD OF MY HEART *by Jo Beverley*
BLUE MOON BAYOU *by Katherine Compton*

Coming Soon

SCARLET KISSES *by Patricia Camden*
WILDSTAR *by Nicole Jordan*

And Don't Miss These
ROMANTIC TREASURES
from Avon Books

MY WILD ROSE *by Deborah Camp*
ONLY WITH YOUR LOVE *by Lisa Kleypas*
FIRE AT MIDNIGHT *by Barbara Dawson Smith*

BELOVED INTRUDER

JOAN VAN NUYS

AVON BOOKS NEW YORK

BELOVED INTRUDER is an original publication of Avon Books. This work has never before appeared in book form. This work is a novel. Any similarity to actual persons or events is purely coincidental.

AVON BOOKS
A division of
The Hearst Corporation
1350 Avenue of the Americas
New York, New York 10019

Published by arrangement with the author
Library of Congress Catalog Card Number: 92-90558
ISBN: 0-380-76476-8

First Avon Books Printing: November 1992

AVON TRADEMARK REG. U.S. PAT. OFF. AND IN OTHER COUNTRIES, MARCA REGISTRADA, HECHO EN U.S.A.

Printed in the U.S.A.

RA 10 9 8 7 6 5 4 3 2 1

To my darling Gretchen,
so special and so quiet and so deep—
the most Indian of my daughters . . .

To keep one sacred flame
Through life, unchilled, unmoved,
To love in wintry age the same
As first in youth we loved,
To feel that we adore
Even to fond excess,
That though the heart would break with more
It could not live with less.

—Anonymous

Prologue

Kittanning, Pennsylvania
August 1774

Morning sun searched through the mist and trees, and birds and squirrels chattered as the youth sat, cross-legged, scowling into his fire. These past three mornings, as the hunger of his fast gripped him more intensely, Little Hunter had hoped for a glimpse of his manitou in the flames. So far he had seen nothing, and he chafed with impatience. In his brother's youth vigil two winters ago, the Creator had quickly sent the vision of a fierce fiery cloud. In his father's trial of manhood, a diving eagle had come on the second day, and to his mother's brother, their chieftain, came a towering black thunderhead on the fourth day. From the visions, all three had thus received their adult names and had thereafter received guidance and protection from the totems the Great Spirit had sent them.

But it seemed he himself was not to be so honored at this time. After five days of fasting and testing his fortitude in this woodland far from his village, Little Hunter had seen no vision in the smoke and flames. His nights had been dreamless, nor had he seen any animal or thing that in any way could be considered his totem. He could not suppress his disappointment. Or his anger. He had looked forward to meeting his manitou, and was eager for the strength and protection it would give him throughout the rest of his life. He had hoped secretly that a wolf or a mountain lion would be his link with the world beyond, but instead he had nothing.

He shook his head and sat straighter. It did not matter. If and when the Creator saw fit to bless him, he would be grateful, of course—it was said one was swept with a feeling of security and peace at the sight of one's manitou—but until then, he needed no such symbol to prove his manhood. He knew he was a man. All in the village knew he was a man. He had slain his first buck and hunted with Lenape braves since he was ten winters.

Now he was fourteen, and already he was taller and stronger than his brother, War Cloud, and taller than his father and his uncle. And he was the future Keeper of the Wampum. He was a man, whether the Great Spirit knew it or not, and he was tired of this foolishness and he was hungry. Hunger was a wolf that gnawed his belly. If he left for his village now as the sun rose, he would be there before it stood overhead.

Little Hunter uncoiled his lean, dark-skinned body and got to his feet. He stretched, yawned, and with his tawny eyes narrowed, studied the gray sky. It would rain this day; the sweet damp scent of it filled his nostrils. It was good. Rain was long overdue. As he bent for a handful of earth to smother his fire, he hesitated, his whole being suddenly alert. Why had the forest grown quiet so suddenly? The birds and squirrels no longer talked, and even the breeze had ceased. He withdrew his knife from his belt and moved on silent feet to a great elm. For long moments, he stood, his back to it, gazing warily about him.

Deciding finally that there was no danger even though the silence was a strange thing, Little Hunter returned to his fire with the handful of earth. He frowned. It, too, seemed suddenly strange. He knelt, seeing that the smoke had turned yellow and dense and did not rise but clung to the flames. He stared as, in the thick acrid swirl, an image began to form. His heart pounded. Was his vision about to manifest itself at last? His manitou? He held his breath, waiting for some noble beast or a bird or a snake to take form, but none did. In the yellow flames, he saw a woman. . . .

Embarrassment scorched Little Hunter's naked body. Was she to be his guide and protector and his source of comfort? Was a female to guide and guard a Lenape warrior? He gritted his teeth. It absolutely could not be. Never had a human been the totem of another. It was then that he remembered his last night's sleep had not been dreamless. He dreamt that he had been with a woman whom he had taken many times. His lips curved at the memory. His uncle, Thunderhead, would not approve, for his night had not been one of privation—nor was this vision he was seeing now a spiritual one. *Matta.* This was a continuation of his night yearnings. A waking dream. This was wishing. . . .

Narrowing his golden eyes, he tried to discern her features. He could not. But he was sure in his heart that she was beautiful. Her hair was long and night black, and she was slender—slender yet rounded in all the proper places. She held her head high and carried herself proudly. . . . But enough of such foolishness. He carefully scattered his small fire and smothered it with the earth. Maybe someday he would have such a woman, but for now, his thoughts were on things of more immediate importance—home and his bed and food . . .

As Little Hunter girded himself, the forest again found its voice. The stream nearby once more talked noisily as it paddled west toward the Alligewi Sipo, and from afar, a dove called low. He looked about him. Satisfied that he was leaving all as he had found it, he slipped into the woods and soon was deep within its green shadows.

He was nearly home when he realized that the mist through which he had been running since sunup was no longer mist, but was now smoke. It had been many days since the earth had had enough to drink, and now something was afire. Hearing the nearby crackling, he knew it was that part of the forest which lay between him and his people. The smoke grew dense so quickly, he was stopped even though he reckoned his village was within ten bow shots of where he stood.

He dared not go straight ahead. It would be too easy to lose his way and perish, for he had no manitou to protect him. *Matta,* he must find a path where the smoke was thinner. But as he turned south, a sound from the woods stopped him in his tracks. He froze, his ears straining, his eyes on the now-billowing smoke. When it came again, his heart thudded. It was the voice of a child calling for help.

"Ho, you!" Little Hunter gave a great shout. "I am coming! Keep calling so I can find you!" Plunging into the eye-stinging haze, he heard nothing but the distant roar of the fire. "Cry out, little friend, else I cannot find you. Call to me—quickly now!" His anger leapt. What ailed the little one? Without a voice to follow, all was lost.

"I am by the twin birch," came a small cry finally. "W-which way shall I go?"

The breath fled Little Hunter's lungs as he realized it was his own small sister. "It is Little Hunter," he yelled. "Keep on calling—I must hear your voice! I, too, will call out and you must walk toward me, Flower. Quickly, now!"

" 'I weave my blanket red,' " Flower cried. " 'I weave my blanket blue—' "

" 'I weave my blanket all my life—' " Little Hunter bellowed, his heart galloping.

" 'Until I come to you—' "

" 'I bring my blanket red—' " He had begun to cough, and his eyes and his lungs stung and burned.

He knew if the two of them did not soon depart this inferno, they would depart this life.

" 'I bring my . . .' " The little voice wavered, ceased.

Little Hunter knew terror. She was close by; she was so close he could hear her coughing—but where . . . ? Suddenly he saw her. She was crumpled on the ground, her black eyes huge and her pretty little flower face tear streaked and pale with fright. When he lifted her up into his arms, she smiled, whispered: " 'I—I bring my blanket blue—' "

Little Hunter held her close, his heart swelling. " 'They are the story of the wife—' "

" 'The gray chief sold to you . . .' "

He said softly, "Well done, my sister."

With that, he slung her firmly across one wide shoulder and ran back whence he had come. But the fire was now behind him as well as before him, and he did not know if it bound him from the south and the north as well. He had little time to decide on which direction to go; his sister was gasping for every breath, and his own lungs were protesting. He closed his burning eyes and asked the Great Spirit for help. Flower was far too young to leave this good earth, nor was he himself ready to hunt in the world beyond.

When he opened his eyes, she was the first thing he saw—*memedhakemo*. The turtledove. In the midst of the fire storm, she sat unconcerned atop a nearby larch preening her soft gray feathers. Even as he gazed on the bird, she gave her soft mournful call, spread her wings, and flew toward the south. Taking it as an omen, Little Hunter turned south. As he ran, walls of fire on either side of him, he knew a peace and a well-being he had never known before. He was filled with wonder, for he knew he had met his manitou. And she was a dove. A brave little gray dove—and she had saved them . . .

Upon crossing the stream and entering his village, Little Hunter heard the weeping of the women. But when he was seen with Flower over his shoulder, there were shouts of joy. Only after he had placed the child in the arms of their mother, Walks Alone, did his father speak.

"Your feet are badly burned, my son. You must let your mother tend them."

Little Hunter looked down at his raw singed flesh in astonishment. "I did not feel the flames . . . I did not know they were underfoot even. Father, I—do not understand."

Diving Eagle drew him aside. "Did your manitou come to you?" he asked quietly.

Little Hunter's face grew hot. He considered saying nay, for how would it look, a warrior of the Lenape guarded by a dove? But he would never deny her.

"*Kehella,*" he said low. "She—is a dove, Father. She led us out of the fire."

Diving Eagle nodded. He saw well the boy's dilemma and was greatly pleased with this son of his. He had not denied his manitou, but would revere and honor it. He would always hold it in his heart. It was that which was most important. He need not bear its name also. He placed his hands on the strong shoulders of the boy who now stood taller than did he himself.

"I am proud of you," he said, his voice raised for all to hear. "Welcome home, Firewalker."

Chapter 1

Pittsburgh, Pennsylvania
March 1788

Hope yearned to close her eyes, but she dared not. She forced herself instead to sit straighter and study the quiet, elegantly appointed bedchamber in which she kept watch over the sick child. Hearth fire was reflected on the polished floor and on the brass-bound mahogany tallboy and wardrobe that stood side by side against one wall. Her gaze next moved over the brocade settee, the graceful mahogany looking glass and richly hued Oriental rug underfoot—and to Laura sleeping fitfully in the great carved canopy bed. She rose and felt the girl's flushed forehead. Finding her skin drier and hotter than it had been moments before, Hope knew she must take drastic measures soon.

She went to the window, parted the draperies, and peered anxiously at the thickly falling snow. What on earth could be keeping her father so long? He should be here by now. Laura was his patient, not hers. He had sent for her in the middle of the night when he was called to an unexpected birthing, and now the morning was half over. She shivered, drew her woolen cloak about her more snugly, and tried not to think of his being trapped in some icy ditch in his gig. But if that were the case, he would simply leave it where it was and ride in on horseback. So where was he, then? The Anderson twins should have arrived hours ago. As she dipped a cloth into a basin of cold water and began bathing Laura's hot face, she heard the rustle of silk and turned.

"We were able to sleep a bit as you suggested," Caroline Thorpe whispered, lifting her daughter's hand to her own pale lips. "How is my baby?"

"I'm concerned, Caroline."

The mother's eyes widened. "Oh, nay—please—"

"I must say," Charlton Thorpe said stiffly, "I find it strange that Thomas has not returned."

"I'm sure he has good reason," Hope replied, her thoughts flying on ahead. She could not wait for her father any longer. Once more she felt the girl's forehead and placed her ear against the fragile chest. Laura was burning with fever, and her heart fluttered thinly. She said quietly, "I must bleed her."

The banker looked at her in complete astonishment. "Without the doctor here?"

Hope's eyes flickered, but she forced herself to be coolly civil. "I, too, am a physician, Mr. Thorpe."

Charlton Thorpe was an old friend of her father's and the employer of her fiancé. He was a powerful force in the town, but Hope had never liked him. He was an unsmiling, ungenerous man who always smelled of spirits. She had long suspected that he abused his wife.

He flushed. "Of course you are a—physician, but the point is—"

His wife cried suddenly, "Bleed her? With leeches? Hope, I'll not have those slimy things on my baby!"

Hope said crisply, "Not leeches, Caroline." As she knelt by the hearth, holding a scalpel to the flames, the woman began to weep.

"S-surely you are not going to use that thing on her?"

"See here," the father rumbled, "you cannot possibly be serious. I cannot possibly allow you to—"

Hope got to her feet, firelight glittering in her gray

eyes and her face pink with anger. Damn them both to hell and back. She would not allow their prejudice and ignorance to jeopardize Laura. She knew what had to be done and she was going to do it. There was no time for politeness.

"Listen carefully, both of you," she said softly, but with undeniable command. "Your daughter has a dangerously high fever, and unless I can bring it down quickly, her heart could fail."

Caroline stared. "Do you mean—she'll die?"

Compassion overcame Hope's fury. She put an arm around the woman's shoulders. "I mean to see that she does not," she said gently. "You might say a prayer for us both . . ." She quickly gathered the things she needed and placed them before her on the bed. "Do you have more quilts? And I would like a hotter fire, please. I want her to sweat." As the two frantically summoned servants to do her bidding, Hope put the girl's hand into the small porcelain basin of water and lightly nicked a vein in her wrist. The blood trickled out.

The fire hummed, the clock on the mantel ticked, and the wind screamed beyond the great stone house. Caroline Thorpe wept softly into her handkerchief while her husband paced the bedchamber. Hope neither saw nor heard any of it. Her whole being, her eyes and ears, her sensitive fingers—all were attuned to the sounds and movements of the child's body: the soft, rapid in-and-out sighing of her breathing, the steady dripping of her life's blood into the basin, the temperature of her skin, her heartbeat. Soon Hope detected the lowering of heart action and a deepening of breathing—signs she'd been waiting for. She was rapidly binding the wound to staunch the bleeding when Thomas Caldwell arrived. He hurried to Laura's side, the breath of winter still clinging to him, and felt her damp forehead.

"How is she?"

"Much better. Her fever just broke and her heartbeat is strong and steady now."

"Much congestion?"

"Aye, during the night she was choking badly. I tickled her throat with a goose quill, and she coughed it all loose. The new syrup you made seemed to soothe her then." Hope watched as her father bent and put a practiced ear to the child's chest.

"She sounds good now." Noting the scalpel and basin on the washstand, he said crisply, "I see you bled her."

"Aye, but most of that is water. I was bathing her earlier."

Tom nodded. "It looks like you have things well in hand."

Charlton Thorpe said stiffly, "I find it reprehensible that you saw fit not to be here, Thomas."

Tom looked at his old friend in surprise. "Man, it wasn't by choice. I couldn't leave a woman who'd have died without me. She was birthing twins, and the first was breech and wouldn't budge—"

"I believed my daughter was your responsibility also."

Tom drew a deep breath. "Laura was in hands as capable as my own. I'm sorry if you don't understand that. Now if you'll excuse me, I'd like to look at her more closely. We can talk about this later if you want."

He examined Laura thoroughly, discussed her with Hope and her parents, and then he and Hope both watched over her while she slept. He examined her a final time before leaving. It was nearly dinnertime before the two departed the Thorpe mansion and drove through the still-falling snow to the stately brick Caldwell residence on Seventh Avenue. Charlie Watson, Tom's apprentice, took their horse and gig to the stable and inside, the housekeeper took over.

"Sich weather!" She halted them in the mudroom and swept the snow from their cloaks and their feet. "I'm jist so glad ye're both home safe an' sound, an', ma'am, afore I forgets, Mr. Kendall dropped by this noon an' will stop agin after dinner." She bustled them out of their cloaks and hung the garments up to dry. "When'll ye' be wantin' to eat, ma'am?"

"We'll change first."

"Fine. There's nothin' that won't keep, an' I've the fires goin' in yer bedchambers so ye'll be warm when ye bathe. I'll have yer water fetched in no time."

"Wonderful—and you're wonderful, Sally, and dinner smells wonderful. My mouth is watering." Hope was unbuttoning her gown before the fire when Sally hurried in with a kettle of steaming water and poured it into the washbasin.

"There! And here's a fresh tablet o' soap and a nice fluffy towel." Seeing Hope's long luxurious yawn, she shook her head. "I doubt ye'll stay awake long enough to enjoy me food or yer young man's company. I'll say it agin, ma'am, it ain't fittin' that a fine lady like yerself should work so long and hard ter—"

Hope laughed. "You know I love my work. Dr. Tom and I both do. We'd better, considering there's not money enough in all of Pittsburgh to pay us for the time and worry we put into it."

As she stepped out of her clothing and began lathering her tired body, Hope thought how blessed she was to have so much: her practice, her father, this comfortable home, and Sally to take care of it and cook and fetch for them. And she had friends, and she had places to go and interesting things to do. And she had Sam. Above all she had Sam. Her heart did a flip at the thought of him. Strong and handsome and bright, Sam Kendall was the best thing that had ever happened to her.

"Will ye want th' gray wool, ma'am?" Sally asked. "It's sich a bitter night an' wool's so nice and warm agin th' skin."

"I think I'll wear my new gown," Hope answered.

"Ye'll freeze in silk!"

Hope smiled. "I doubt it." Her blood heated just thinking of how Sam's eyes were going to glow when he saw her in it.

* * *

Thomas Caldwell was reflective as he studied the young woman seated at the candlelit dinner table opposite him. She was growing more beautiful by the day if it were possible. Long shining hair black as ebony, clear gray eyes, good skin and teeth, a straight back, long strong legs. And she had a mind like a man, this daughter of his. He frowned. Nay, that was poor thinking. There were men out there practicing medicine who were no more capable of it than a barber was. Hell, his barber *did* practice medicine, much to his own disgust. But this girl, this girl was keen. She had the gift, and his patients would be in good hands when he left for Twin Oaks. He sighed thinking of it. He really should tell her his plans so she could make some of her own.

Hope leaned forward laughing, tapping her goblet with her fork. "Hello, hello! Come back from wherever you are."

Tom grinned and sipped his wine. "What did I miss?"

Hope grew serious. "I was just asking what you thought about Laura's chances."

"As of two hours ago, I'd say damned good."

But his mind was not on Laura, it was on Hope. Why wait any longer to tell her? The transferral-of-property papers were signed, and he could take possession of the place whenever he chose. And he had no real worries about Hope. She was set in her practice, she was about to marry, and her financial future was taken care of. She was the sole beneficiary of her mother's estate in addition to his own, and would be a very wealthy woman one day.

"You're so far away," Hope murmured. "Are you all right?" She felt a pang, noticing for the first time the abundance of silver that frosted her father's black hair. Why, he was growing old, and she had been too busy with her own life to even notice. It seemed she scarcely saw him anymore except at mealtimes.

"I'm fine, princess, but we have to talk." Tom took

a deep breath. "Do you remember my telling you about the Donation Lands?"

"Aye, but I—didn't pay much attention. What are they?"

"It's land the Pennsylvania legislature promised us veterans for fighting the British. The good Lord knows, I did my stint."

Hope frowned. "What would you do with land if you were to claim it?"

"Work it." He could already feel the grass beneath his feet and smell the rich black new-plowed earth. "You wouldn't be forgetting, would you, girleen, that I'm an old farm boy born and bred?"

"I—guess I did . . ."

Suddenly she was uneasy. When her father got an idea in his head, he never let go. It was how she had gotten her certificate to practice medicine. No other woman in the country had one nor, more likely, wanted one. It was her father who saw her interest and gave her the chance to apprentice under him; Father who had copious notes of the lectures he had attended in Philadelphia. And after training her, he had convened his colleagues to examine her and sign her certificate. He had then taken her into practice with him so that Pittsburghers eventually gave her their trust. Now he had that same look in his eyes again.

"Princess," Tom said quietly, "I've been waiting for the right time to tell you this—I already have the land. A thousand acres. An old army friend of mine, Con Mackey, got his plot in eighty-six, and he's done quite a bit with it. He's built a house and barn, a smokehouse and springhouse and he managed to clear and fence a lot of the land. He calls it Twin Oaks. But his health is failing now and—"

Hope's heart was beating faster. "Just where is this land?"

"A hundred miles or so north of here."

"A hundred miles!" She stared at him, disbelieving. "Father, that's wilderness! Why on earth would you want land there when you can buy it here? Pittsburgh is surrounded by farmland. Up north you'll run into Indians."

Tom chuckled and poured himself another sip of wine. "This thousand acres is coming to me, sweetheart. I earned it. In fact, as an officer, I can have as many as two thousand, and I might just do that. As for Indians, we've got them right here. Yesterday I treated Guyasuta himself over in Sharpsburg."

"That's another thing," Hope protested, getting to her feet. "Your practice. Anyone can farm, but you're a doctor. How could you just give it up like that?"

"Did I say I'd give it up? Hell, I'd say doctors are in demand there. I expect I'll be busier than I am here, and I'll be able to smell the honeysuckle and hear the birds and watch my own corn sprout, too." Seeing her eyes glisten, he went over to her, pulled her to her feet, and put his arms around her. "Little girl, it's what I want. I'm tired of mud and drunks and rowdiness, and you have your own life ahead of you. You have your patients, and you'll be marrying young Kendall soon and giving me some grandchildren one of these days." He shook his finger at her affectionately. "You're to let me know ahead so I can trek down and do the deliveries. D'you hear?"

Hope nodded and tried to swallow the lump that had come to her throat. "When will you go—and will you be taking Charlie?" It worried her to think of losing both her father and his apprentice, too.

"I wouldn't do that to you. Charlie stays. He'll be certified any day now." Tom settled her in the wing chair by the fire, pulled up a straight chair, and sat opposite her. "As for when I leave, I'm waiting for the others who are going there so we can travel together." He didn't add that it was for protection against Indians as well as convenience.

Hope managed a smile. "Well, my goodness, it seems all settled. I'll get used to it soon enough. Actually, I think it will be—wonderful for you. I really do. What is the house like?"

Tom grinned. "Not like this one, that's for sure. It's just a four-room log cabin, but then I don't need anything fancy." He looked at the clock on the mantelpiece. "We can talk more later, but right now I want to check on Laura. I want Charlie to have a look at her, too."

Sally hurried into the room just then. "Dr. Tom, sir," her eyes were big and she spoke softly, "ye'd best come t' th' door. It's Mr. Thorpe. . . ."

Tom strode rapidly to the foyer. He frowned. "What is it, Charlton? I was just about to ride over and visit our girl."

The banker's lips worked for some moments before he rasped: "My daughter is dead, Caldwell."

Tom's jaw dropped as he stared at his old friend. "God almighty . . ."

Hope emerged from the dining room just then, black hair shimmering down over the low neckline of her vermilion gown, and her gray eyes wide and questioning. Seeing Charlton Thorpe's white angry face, her heart nearly stopped. "Mr. Thorpe, w-what is it?"

"Hope, Laura's dead," Tom muttered.

She swayed, feeling the room spin. She whispered, "What happened?"

"You dare ask," the banker hissed, "after removing a whole basin of blood from her veins?"

Hope gasped. "But I didn't! Don't you remember? The basin had water in—"

"Listen to me and listen well, you damned quack." He pointed a finger at her. "You will never—"

"Charlton, my God, I know you're in pain, but be reasonable."

Charlton Thorpe ignored him. In a voice that shook, he continued to lash Hope, "You will never treat another soul in this town, I promise you. As for you, Caldwell, I hold you equally responsible with this bitch. You're murderers, both of you."

Tom strode past him and jerked open the front door. He spoke gruffly through stiff lips. "Man, believe me when I say we're grieving with you—but I think you had best leave now."

"I'm leaving, never fear, but you've not heard the last of this."

After Tom had ridden off raging into the snowy night to sign the death certificate, Hope collapsed into the wing chair by the fire. She was trembling and too shocked to weep as she thought about Laura. The poor, poor baby . . . What could have happened? And why had she not told Charlton Thorpe how sorry she was? Except he'd not given her the chance. His accusations sickened and outraged her. The more she thought about it, the angrier she became. She was so deep in thought, she jumped when Sam entered the room. She had forgotten entirely that he was coming, but she was so glad he was there, so glad. She went into his arms.

Sam laughed softly. "Well, now, that's the kind of welcome a man likes to receive." He kissed her warm lips and murmured, "Hope, you're a vision." Tantalized by her lilac scent and the whiteness of her flesh against the deep red gown, he lightly cupped her breasts and tried to kiss her again. When she turned her head, he frowned. "What is it?"

"Sam—Laura Thorpe . . . died . . . this evening. . . ." With his arms about her, she was finally able to weep. "Her father . . . is blaming me."

Sam hid his shock as he held her trembling body close. It was some moments before he said easily, "Now, sweetheart, that simply cannot be." He took a linen handkerchief from his pocket and dabbed at the tears streaming down her pale cheeks. "Shh, you mustn't cry so. I'm sure there has been some mistake. He could not possibly think such a thing."

Hope gulped, shook her head. "There's no mistake. He thinks it." Seeing that Tom had just returned, she cried, "Father, what have you learned? What happened to her?" His face was so drawn and ashen, she knew to expect the worst.

"Suffocation," Tom muttered. His legs were trembling so they would not hold him. He sat down heavily in the wing chair.

"Oh, God . . . oh, the poor baby. . . ." She sagged in Sam's arm. "I don't understand. Didn't they give her the cough syrup? It should have lessened the congestion."

"Thorpe swears they did."

Seeing the strange look in his eyes, she whispered, "He's still talking about the blood in the basin, isn't he?"

"Aye."

"Father, I swear most of it was water. I'd never lie about such a thing. . . ."

"I know that, princess."

"And did you tell him my treatment was standard and that you approved?"

"Sweetheart, you heard me tell him that this afternoon." He had never lied to her and he was not about to start now. She needed to know exactly how things stood. "Thorpe thinks I said it to protect you."

"The other doctor in town will tell him the same thing—he'll speak out for me."

"Don't count on it," Tom muttered.

"Father, he knows me!"

"How bad is it, sir?" Sam asked, his arms still about Hope.

Tom shook his head. "Not good. Thorpe's mind is fixed on that damned basin. I fear the word will spread like wildfire."

"But the other doctor—"

"Girl, forget the other doctor," Tom snapped. "Thorpe's a power. No one will buck him because he holds their purse strings."

"Well, he doesn't hold my purse strings!" Hope cried. "I'll buck him, and I'll win, just watch me. I have friends, and I have patients who trust me. I have the two of you and Charlie. . . ."

Tom said gruffly, "Hope, we have to be realistic.

The first thing we'll do is just sit back and see if things calm down."

But Tom knew they would not. This was a catastrophe as far as Hope's practice was concerned. It would destroy her credibility, and he would go down with her, for he meant to defend her. As for Kendall, the fellow was a rock: confident, calm, soothing. Tom had never felt closer to him. He watched appreciatively as Sam held Hope close, smoothing back her hair, stroking her, talking to her firmly and reasonably as he would a frightened child. Tom was damned glad she had him. Damned glad. Because if worse came to worst as it doubtless would, the two of them could go away somewhere and start anew. God knows, young people had done it before. . . .

Chapter 2

Shenango Valley
July 1788

Hope had finally accepted the fact that she was not going to awaken from her four-month-long nightmare. She was not asleep. She was, God forbid, in the Donation Lands with her father, and there was not going to be any message from Pittsburgh saying the whole thing was a terrible mistake and would they please come back. This was reality. She tasted the rabbit stew simmering over the hearth fire, grimaced, added salt, and then walked aimlessly about the cabin built by her father's friend.

It was nice enough as cabins went, she supposed, but she would never think of it as home. Never. Not here in this wilderness where animals howled the night long and where, beyond the windows, there was that soul-crushing blackness and the sound of Indian drums beating when the sun went down. What on earth went on there? she wondered, but she did not really want to know.

She hugged herself as she gazed about at the crude chinked-log walls of the living room and at the hearth that yawned so black and empty. And those lace curtains she'd hung at the lone window—how sad and out of place they looked. Everything looked sad and out of place: the desk and chair from home, her grandmother's beautiful rocker, the Oriental rug that covered the rough wide-plank floor. In his wood shop, Tom had made the deacon's bench that stood against one wall. It was the only thing that truly belonged there.

Hope returned to the kitchen. She liked it best of all for its coziness. Here the curtains were red calico, and the trestle table, benches, and corner cupboard were of a warm, glowing pine. The copper pans, too, glowed from the wall shelves where they sat. Little by little she was learning to contend with implements she had never used before: kettle hooks and stirrers, graters and whisks and the awesome log mortar with a pestle that was three feet long and as heavy as lead. Thinking longingly of the ease with which Sally had prepared their delicious meals, Hope shook her head. She had a long way to go, but at least she was learning; and she was somewhat efficient. It was still morning, and already she had a rabbit in the kettle—poor thing—she had washed up the dishes, swept the floor, and finished the book she had begun yesterday. Now what?

Aye, now what indeed? She blinked back the tears that were always there when she thought of the life she had left behind—her work, her friends, her beautiful home, civilization. It was not that she missed Pittsburgh itself. She had never cared for its filth and rowdiness and the drunks in the streets, but she missed the shops and the convenience and social events with her friends—the parties and dances and outings. And she missed Sam. A blanket of anger and emptiness smothered her every time she thought of him and of what had happened between them—a thing more terrible because of its total unexpectedness.

At first it had seemed everything was going to be all right despite Charlton Thorpe's threat. She had continued to work and live her life as she had done before the tragedy, and Sam was always there. He was as attentive and loving as ever, and they were eagerly making plans for an August wedding. And then one morning, the words "bitch" and "quack" were found scrawled across their stable door.

Hope trembled thinking of it, and of how quickly everything had changed from then on. That same evening, stones were hurled at her gig from unknown hands as she drove home from a sick call. The following morning, she was turned away by a patient she was treating, and Tom himself was refused admittance when he went to demand an explanation. Other patients soon dropped away from them both.

It was as if the city itself had been poisoned by Charlton Thorpe's venom. More stones were thrown, a window in their house was broken, fingers were pointed, and shouts of "murderers" reached Hope's ears as she went shopping. For over a week, she maintained a calm dignity, certain the madness would pass. She finally broke down in Sam's arms when it did not.

"I hate this!" she wept, "and I hate seeing Father suffer so. If they can turn on a good man like him when I'm the one they think is a murderess, they don't deserve a good doctor. They're certainly not going to have this one!" She took his grave face between her hands. "Darling, let's go somewhere else. Let's marry now, not in August but now, this week, and let's move to Philadelphia or Boston!"

He had removed her hands, gone to a window, and stood looking out into the spring darkness, his fingers drumming on the sash. When he turned, his expression was so grim it frightened her. "Sam, what is it?"

"I'm sorry, Hope, but this has to be said. I heard today that Charlton Thorpe is considering taking you to court."

Feeling the room closing in on her, Hope clutched the back of an armchair. "Court? How can he do that?"

He gave her a disbelieving look. "Is it really so surprising? The man thinks you killed his daughter."

Hope stared at the dark red flush suffusing his face. She had the sudden strange feeling that they were not merely on different sides of the room, they were in two different worlds. He was unchanged, as blondly handsome and elegantly dressed as ever in a ruffled cambric shirt, slim gray breeches, and patterned stockings. An up-and-coming young banker with the world at his feet. She, on the other hand, was an evil woman. A bitch, a quack, a murderess, and her own world was falling to pieces.

"I didn't realize you were so angry with me—"

"I am not angry," he said angrily, "but do you really expect me to be overjoyed at the way things are going?"

"What you seem not to understand," she said through clenched teeth, "is that my father and the other doctor agree completely with my treatment of Laura. I did the only thing that could be done."

"And what you seem not to understand is that it doesn't matter. No jury will care."

"This is unbelievable!"

"It is, I agree. Hope"—he made no move toward her but remained stiffly at the window—"I think for now it would be wise if you went to the Donation Lands with your father. As soon as possible."

Hope was so stunned she could not speak. Eons later, when she found the heart to answer, she asked, her lips trembling, "Is that what you want, then? For us to part?"

"You make it sound like the end of the world." He began to prowl the room as if he were caged. "It's not, you know. And it's not that I want it, believe me. It's just that I think it's best for now."

"Best for whom?" Her throat was so constricted, her voice sounded as high as a young girl's.

Sam, this is Hope! she wanted to cry. This is the same Hope you wanted to make love to last night because we were "nearly married." And she had nearly yielded because she loved him so. Now he was looking at her as if she were a stranger.

"Best for us both, of course," he answered, "and for our future." He came to her then, a smile on his handsome face and his blue eyes as tender as ever. He pulled her easily into his arms. "Darling, you can see, can't you, that to go running off without some idea of how I can support us is folly?" He brushed a kiss across her lips and wiped away her tears. "Surely you see that. And surely you see by now that Pittsburgh is a dangerous place for you to be at the present. If you stay and there is a trial—" He shook his head and held her close. "It doesn't bear thinking about. . . ."

Hope closed her eyes and leaned her head against his chest. She listened to the unhurried beating of his heart. All that he said was true, but it crushed her that he seemed so cool and reasonable about it whereas she felt as if she'd fallen into a deep, black hole. More tears crept from beneath her closed lids.

"If I do go, when will I see you again? It's so far away. . . ."

"Darling, darling, what a question. You'll see me again soon. This parting is just temporary. Right now, the most important thing is your safety."

But the following morning, a messenger had brought his unexpected letter whose every word was still seared into her brain.

My dear Hope,

I know I can trust you to understand why we must postpone our marriage plans indefinitely. I dare not at this time jeopardize all that I have worked for. It has taken me years to establish the fine position and reputation I now hold in Charlton's bank. I'm sure you can see that losing either would be a catastrophe which I must avoid at all costs. When this difficulty is resolved, then, my darling, we can resume our plans. Until then, I remain,

Your loving Sam

"Liar, liar, liar!" Hope shouted to the empty kitchen.

She lowered herself to a stool before the fire, buried her face in her hands, and wept long and noisily. She remembered all over again her first fury: how she had stormed through the house, snatching from tables and shelves and drawers all of the gifts Sam had given her and hurling them furiously into one large box. She had then tossed on top of them her diamond and emerald engagement ring. She had sent the box by messenger to Sam, and had not bothered to include a message.

The days that followed were filled with such grief and emptiness, she was sure her heart would never stop aching. The house had never seemed so big and dark and devoid of warmth. And on her subsequent journey with her father by pack train, she had sat astride her mare in a numbed daze, scarcely aware of the others who accompanied them. Her eyes never saw the narrow Indian trails they followed, nor did she hear the birds that sang along the way announcing that spring had come to the northwestern woodlands.

But little by little, day by day, her anger had mounted, and now it was flaming up to scorch the ugly self-pity in which she had wallowed for so long. The bastard! How could she have misjudged him so? A man who had not even possessed the common decency, the common courtesy to face her when he broke their engagement. It would be a long, long time before she trusted another man with her heart—if ever.

She stood, shook the wrinkles out of her skirt, and tossed back her long braids. Her bout of weeping had left her exhausted and completely disgusted with herself. She had had enough of self-pity to last her a lifetime. As of this instant, all of it was behind her. It was time to move ahead. She was twenty-three years old, and she had blessings aplenty if she but looked for them. Her father was strong and healthy and happy here, they had this snug cabin and an abundance of food and fresh water, and she'd been able to bring her dog as well as her mare with her. She had even made a close friend—Maybeth Springer, a young newly wed woman from eastern Pennsylvania.

As for medicine, she and her father had discussed her work at length and plotted their course. The settlers knew vaguely that she was a doctor, and on that inevitable day when her father was temporarily ailing or on another call, she would take his place. It was the slow way, but it was the sure one. Cheered by the thought, she carried a book out to the stoop, a porch sheltered by a shake roof, and settled herself in a rocking chair.

She was deep into volume I of *Tristram Shandy* when she felt the hair stir on her nape and arms. Someone was watching her, she was sure of it. Pretending to read, she slowly raised her eyes. Oh, Lord. At the far edge of the clearing was a mounted Indian, silent, motionless, and watching *her.* So far, she had not met any of them. She had just heard their drums in the night. She rose and was moving shakily toward the front door and the safety of her house when a high, musical voice suddenly called out, "Greetings, my friend, I come talk. . . ."

Hope spun, her eyes widening. What in the world? It was not a warrior at all; it was a young woman! As her pinto drew near, Hope smiled warmly and stepped off the stoop to greet her.

"Hello. Welcome. My name is Hope."

"My name is Flower," the girl replied. "Long have I—" Her words ended in a shriek.

Hope watched, horrified, as Joshua, her big hound, raced out of nowhere to charge snarling and snapping at the pinto's hoofs.

"Josh, nay!" she cried. "Joshua!!" She grabbed his collar, but it was too late. The frightened pinto had reared, hurling the girl to the ground. Hope was by her side in an instant.

"Oh! I'm so sorry!" she exclaimed. "Are you hurt?" The girl's eyes were closed, and blood streamed from her right temple. Hope knelt. She caught and patted the small hand. "Flower?" When Joshua drew near to sniff, she pointed a finger. "Go, you miserable hound!"

Seeing that Flower had lost consciousness, Hope examined her swiftly, but found only the head wound. She raised her skirts and, braids flying, ran back to the cabin. She fetched a blanket, water, clean rags, and her father's new mash of black byrony root. Hurrying back, she covered the girl to keep her warm and then quickly cleansed and dressed the wound.

"Flower. Come, honey, wake up." She was patting the girl's cheeks when she heard approaching hoofbeats. Good. It would be Father, and he could carry the Indian girl to one of the beds so she would be comfortable.

But it was not Thomas Caldwell, and it was no woman again either. It was an Indian brave. A bow was slung over one lean dark shoulder, and he was naked but for the smallest scrap of loincloth. And as he galloped across the clearing on a lathered black horse, a wild cry exploded from his throat. His feet hit the ground even before his mount came to a halt.

Fear drained the strength from Hope's body. She had heard terrible tales of Indians stealing women and children and adopting them into their tribes. Was that why he was there? Or was his purpose a far worse one? Terrified and trembling, she nonetheless put herself between him and the helpless girl. She had not the slightest idea how she could protect the two of them from such a savage. She knew only that she must try.

Firewalker's annoyance with his sister had fast turned to apprehension. Where was the little fox? He had gone to all of her favorite places, he had ridden up one side of the Shenango Sipo and down the other, over and over making the sound of the whip-poorwill, but Flower had not come forth. He had then ridden up to the highlands, quietly scouting the properties of the white men, but she was not in sight. The fact that his mother had interrupted him in the sweat house as he prepared for a hunt did not hearten him, for Walks Alone did nothing lightly or in haste. It would seem now that he must consider the possibility that the Mengwes had her.

Firewalker's eyes, coppery against his dark skin, slitted at the thought. The day was a dark one when those devils had settled nearby in Ohio. His people would have welcomed any other tribe as neighbors, but the Mengwes were enemies as ancient and treacherous as were the whites themselves. Thinking of them, he tightened his legs about the barrel of his mare, causing her to move more swiftly along the trail. He had one more place to look: the cabin where the white healer was said to dwell. If he did not find his sister there, he would return home for a scouting party to ride to the Mengwe village.

He shook his head in exasperation. That his sister was forever in need of rescue had always been a source of amusement to him, but the truth was, he admired her boldness and bravery and great spirit. This time, however, she had gone too far. He grew cold thinking of his soft, pretty little sister in the hands of enemy braves.

It was at that moment that he rode out of the woods and into the clearing. On its far side, he spied his sister's mare, and saw the small blanket-covered figure lying at the feet of the enemy. Not the Mengwe, but a slim white girl. By the Eternal, what had she done to Flower? He emitted a war whoop, gave Nightwind his heels, and galloped toward them at breakneck speed.

Hope had never been close to a brave before, and she saw instantly that this one could snap her in two with one big hand. He was tall—well over six feet of hard lean power—and as he drew near, she saw that his eyes, like a panther's, were a strange tawny gold. They were in striking contrast to his dark oiled skin and black hair; when his eyes moved over her, the leashed fury and savagery within them made Hope fear for her life. When his gaze next went to Flower, Hope stepped between them, her arms outstretched.

"What do you want?" When he ignored her, moving past her to kneel by the girl's side, anger overcame Hope's fear. "Don't touch her!" she cried, looking about for something, anything to use as a weapon.

It was then that Flower opened her black eyes and sat up. She murmured, "Is all right, Hope. Is only Firewalker. My brother."

Relief washed over Hope in a lovely warm wave. She stepped back and dropped her arms to her sides. "I'm sorry," she told him. "I thought you were about to harm her and—" She tightened her lips, seeing that she was being coolly ignored.

Firewalker tilted up his sister's small chin and studied her bandaged temple. "What is this?" he asked gruffly in Lenape.

Flower gingerly touched the dressing and grimaced. "I do not know. My head hurts. It must have happened when I fell."

A muscle moved in his jaw. "Fleeing the Mengwes?"

Flower gave him an impatient look. "There were no Mengwes. I have been here all morning waiting for Hope to come outside. I wanted to see her. And when I did, Timkin bucked me, the stupid thing."

Hope. So already she called her Hope. "It is you who are stupid," Firewalker spoke softly, but his anger seethed. His fear for her had been so great, he would have gone to war to retrieve her. Now, seeing that she was safe and had never been in any danger, he wanted to put her over his knee and pound her rump. "Why were you here at all?" he demanded.

"Long have I wanted to meet this girl and—"

His voice was a rumble. "It would seem you have forgotten a white killed our father."

"Well, Hope did not kill him!" Flower retorted, but she was frightened by the look in his eyes. She had rarely seen him so angry.

"She is the enemy," Firewalker said low. "She lives on this land which was stolen from us, and now you hang about like a dog waiting to be kicked while—"

"That is not so!" Flower cried, and got to her feet.

"While our mother fears and grieves for you."

Firewalker gripped her slim shoulders so roughly she whimpered, but he did not release her. He himself was gripped by thoughts that were whipping him to fury: the senseless slaying of Diving Eagle, the ongoing theft of Lenape land by the white government, the recent coming of the Mengwes to dwell nearby, and now this small foolish sister of his. She would never acknowledge the threat posed to her by Mengwe braves. She had the spirit of an eagle in the body of a kitten. He shook her suddenly, such a shake that her coiled hair lost its red ribbon and spilled down her back. No word passed her lips, but tears filled her eyes. She lifted her small chin and glared at him defiantly.

"Hear me well, woman. I tire of being summoned by our mother to hunt you down. It was foolish and selfish of you to risk capture by coming here alone. You will not do it again. Do you hear?" When she did not answer, he muttered, "You would not like being the squaw of a Mengwe brave, my sister."

Hope had not understood one word of the argument between the two, but she resented Firewalker's harsh treatment of Flower. At the same time, she could not take her eyes off him. As a doctor, her professional opinion of his tall lean body was that she had never seen a more perfect specimen of manhood. And her feminine eye admired his exotic panther eyes, arrow-straight nose, and long hair, as thick and black as the mane of his mount. It was kept from his eyes by a beaded headband from which hung two long white feathers.

Studying him, she felt a flare of excitement. It neither surprised nor dismayed her, for he was magnificent. But he was also a savage who thought nothing of manhandling a woman. Were she looking for the company of a man, which she most decidedly was not, she would not be stirred for long by such a one as Firewalker. Even Sam, despicable as he had turned out to be, had never laid a hand on her in violence. Flower's doleful voice interrupted her simmering resentment.

"I—sorry. Not come again, Hope. Not allowed . . ."

Hope bristled. "Really? Not allowed? I'm sorry, too, Flower. How old are you, if I may ask?"

"Twenty winters," Flower murmured.

"Indeed." She turned accusing eyes on the brave and was met by the full impact of his golden gaze.

Firewalker hid his surprise as he looked on the white girl, for he saw now that she was not a girl at all. He had been deceived by the gleaming black braids hanging down her back. She was a woman, and a beautiful one. He had never seen such silky white skin nor such eyes, the silver gray of a stormy dusk. Her mouth was a woman's mouth, soft, full, pink, moist. Thinking of her body beneath the ugly white woman's garb she wore, he felt regret that she was the enemy, but it was fleeting.

"You are the daughter of the healer?" he asked.

Hope lifted her chin. "I am." She was surprised his English was so superior to Flower's. The very air seemed to vibrate with the resonance of his voice.

"Bring him to me," Firewalker ordered, "that I may thank him for his help." He indicated Flower's bandaged head.

Hope felt as if she were standing next to a bonfire, such life and vitality radiated from him. And did she dare admit that her father was not there and she was alone? But she doubted she could lie even to save herself with those strange eyes burning through her.

"My father is not here," she said. "It was I who treated your sister."

Firewalker turned to Flower, who stared glumly at the ground. "Is this so?" he asked in English.

"She was not conscious at the time," Hope said coolly, "but I assure you, it is so. I have given her the best of care. I am a doctor also." Seeing his mouth twitch, she flared, "I fail to see why that would amuse you. Perhaps you will explain . . ."

Firewalker saw anger, like heat lightning, flicker in her gray eyes. His own anger moved through him once more—not with her but with himself. It had been wrong of him and unlike him to reveal to anyone, especially a woman, how deeply his feelings ran. He had been as undisciplined as a wild boar before them. He did not doubt she had treated his sister with skill and kindness. Was not his own mother the medicine woman, the *meteinuwak,* of the Shenango Lenape? But for this Hope-woman to claim she was actually a doctor made her generous act small. Did she think he was so ignorant as to believe her? He knew well how little respect the white devils had for their women. No white man alive would accept a female as a doctor.

"It's all right," Hope snapped. "You needn't answer. It's quite obvious you don't believe a word I said. You think your sister cleansed and dressed her own wound though she was unconscious at the time!"

Now Firewalker smiled. He shook his head, the feathers stirring against his black hair. "No, lady, I think it was as you said."

Hope did not answer. Why on earth had she made such an issue of it? What did it matter what he believed? He was only a savage, after all, and there was no telling what he might do if she provoked him. She shook her head.

"It's unimportant." She would never see him again, and for that she rejoiced, but she regretted that she had found a new friend and already lost her.

Watching Firewalker lift Flower onto his sleek long-legged black mare, she said, "It would be best for her wound if you kept your mount to a walk."

"I will do that," Firewalker answered politely. He fastened one end of a rope to the pinto's bridle, and wound the other end about the broad palm of his hand.

"And it would be helpful if you did not shake her again," Hope added crisply. "At least not so violently." The tawny eyes, locked on hers, seemed to smolder as he mounted behind his sister.

Firewalker's tongue fought to tell this she-devil to take herself and her people and leave these Lenape lands and never come back, but he subdued it. He would not heap his wrath on her. She was only a woman; she must follow where her men led. And she had shown kindness.

"I thank you for your concern," he said tersely, "and for tending my sister so carefully."

Hope gave him the briefest of nods and extended a hand to Flower. When the girl caught it, she said, "I am glad you came, Flower. I pray we'll meet again someday."

"Hope come visit?" Flower asked suddenly, eagerly. "Aye?"

Hope laughed, pleased. "Thank you so much. Perhaps someday I shall." But as the brave turned his mount toward the valley, she knew she would not. The look in his eyes warned that she would not be welcome.

Chapter 3

Jacques d'Arcy had just finished unloading his last mule when he heard hoofbeats. Shading his eyes from the afternoon sun, he watched with grudging admiration as War Cloud thundered up the dusty trail toward his trading post. It was incredible, the grace and command with which these devils rode. It seemed an inherent part of every Indian he had ever known.

"Welcome, *n'tschu,*" he called. "Come and sit awhile. It has been a long time since we talked and I would hear news of my friends the Lenapes."

War Cloud dropped lightly to the ground and approached the tall Frenchman, his right hand raised. "Welcome back, *n'tschu.* You have been gone many nights."

"*Oui,* and I have traveled many miles and brought back many treasures. You must come again tomorrow when everything is unpacked. Make sure to bring your kin and friends with you."

"I will do that."

Jacques stared, intrigued by the slight trembling of the brave's hands and the way his black eyes darted over the assortment of bales and bundles stacked on the ground. He felt a leap of triumph. *Nom du Nom,* it had happened. It was not baubles or flints that War Cloud was interested in, it was whiskey. He had feared he would never instill in him a craving for it, but he'd finally succeeded. Now he had the red devil by his scalp lock. He might be tall and strong as an ox, but Jacques had him in his power just as surely as if he'd bound him with chains. It was an important step in his own plans, for War Cloud was the future chieftain of the Shenango Lenapes.

Jacques mopped his face with a red kerchief and tied it about his head, pirate fashion, to tame his thick crop of brown curls. He then lowered himself to the grass with his back against a maple.

"Sit, my friend. Rest with me in the shade while we talk." His brown eyes narrowed, watching the brave assume a straight-backed cross-legged position opposite him. "I pray that Thunderhead still breathes," he continued. In truth, he had prayed while he was gone that the old devil had finally departed for the happy hunting grounds.

"My uncle, the chief, does well enough despite his old man's bones," War Cloud answered. Helldamnfire. Why did this devil, d'Arcy, not stop his talking and offer him whiskey as he always did? His thirst was like a grizzly gnawing his belly. He licked his dry lips and tried not to look at the newly arrived packages. Was there whiskey among them? He half hoped there was not, for he hated and feared the terrible new weakness that had come upon him. He did not need the devil's brew and his head was happier without it—but it made the rest of him feel braver and stronger.

Jacques forced a smile. "It pleases me greatly to hear of Thunderhead's continuing health. He is a veritable lion, that one." But his eyes did not smile with his lips. The old chief was exactly what his name implied. He was a storm and a threat to Jacques's own success in this valley.

Three years earlier, Jacques d'Arcy had arrived in Pittsburgh for the sole purpose of buying a small but thriving trading company called Allegheny Furs. He had left France already a wealthy man, but he was still hungry. He wanted more, much more, and he knew that in this wild young country a clever man could build an empire. And if he was anything, he was clever. He had given himself five years in which to succeed.

After hiring a competent man to run his business in the city, he had set about wooing and winning the fur trade of the various woodland tribes by lavishly gifting their chieftains. And when he found a sachem with an ungovernable weakness for guns or whiskey, he made sure to keep him well supplied. Eventually, he paid far less for their peltry than what the furs were actually worth. But the sachems did not complain. They could not. He had seen Conestogas and Shawnees strip the clothes off their backs in return for rum. What he did was illegal, of course. Laws had been enacted to prevent the sale of spirits to Indians, but such things did not concern him. And the other traders had quickly learned not to interfere with Jacques d'Arcy's routes and methods. It was rumored that the dark, handsome Frenchman with the winning ways had left France with the blood of more than one man on his hands.

But Jacques had found the work tiring and lonely and never ending. And beneath him. He brooded constantly that, even at the end of the five years, his dream of retiring to a life of great wealth and leisure might never come to pass. To give himself the strength to go on, he thought constantly of the mansion he would build and the lofty position in society which he would occupy. Not least, he dreamt of the beautiful and wealthy woman he would one day marry, for wealth must marry wealth, after all.

But at the end of three years of drudgery, he felt he would go mad if he did not pull up his woodland stakes and leave. He could not bear two more years of the sight and sound and smell of savages. It was torture. He was sick to death of hiding his scorn for them and sick of pretending a friendliness he would never feel. He decided to sell Allegheny Furs and seek his fortune elsewhere, anywhere as long as it was within the bounds of civilized society and away from Indians.

Thus, October had found him leading his pack train south, back toward Pittsburgh and into a part of western Pennsylvania he had not seen before. The air was hazy with wood smoke and the thickly wooded forests blazed with the reds and golds of autumn. A blue green river slipped placidly through a valley that was lushly green and of exceptional breadth and beauty. The settlers who welcomed and fed him and eagerly bought his wares told him he was in the Donation Lands. They were veterans of the war with the British, and their acreage was payment for their services. He learned that the river was the Shenango, and that Ohio was no more than two leagues into the setting sun. He learned, too, that the woods teemed with fox and beaver and mink, and that the Indians who lived there, the Lenni Lenape, were great hunters.

Examining the pelts shown him, Jacques's excitement had burned anew. He did not understand why it should be, but the furs had a luxuriant thickness and richness he had seen nowhere else. Realizing they would bring top prices and that he could reap in one year a profit it would take two or more years to garner elsewhere, he decided on the spot to stay. *Mon dieu*, the riches of this land could be his. All his! He could tolerate one year of *anything*, even savages, for such a reward.

But things had not gone as he'd planned, for the Lenape sachem, Thunderhead, had taken a strong and unreasonable dislike to him. While the old man had no objection to his people's buying cloth and knives and trinkets from Jacques, he had rejected outright the idea of opening a fur trade and stubbornly resisted every effort to change his mind. Jacques maintained an amiable front, but so deep was his fury and disappointment, he would have slain Thunderhead had there been the slightest opportunity.

But all was not lost. The old chief was not a well man, and Jacques had set out immediately to befriend his nephew War Cloud, the next chieftain.

He rose now, stretched, and gazed down upon the Indian who sat staring at the boxes which held the whiskey Jacques had brought back. It was to laugh, seeing the devil looking so strong and iron masked and pretending no hunger gnawed his belly. Jacques yawned and stroked his beard.

"I feel the need of some refreshment, *mon ami*. Will you join me? I have a new shipment of very fine whiskey from Pittsburgh."

War Cloud frowned, as if considering the offer, but already he was tasting it, feeling the heat scorch all the way down to his gut. He said gruffly, "I will join you." He watched, his black eyes unblinking, as Jacques went into his small storeroom and returned with two tin cups and a bottle. He watched, his mouth watering, as the cups were generously filled, and received his with hands that trembled. He raised it too quickly and eagerly to his lips, swallowed, felt the sting of the sweet fire, and drew a deep breath of satisfaction.

Jacques nodded. "Did I not say it was fine?" Once more he lowered himself to the grass, his back against the maple.

"It is indeed fine."

"My friend, you can have all you want whenever you want," Jacques said softly. When the brave's black eyes flickered but he did not reply, Jacques added, "And now I would hear of your honored mother, the medicine woman. Does it go well with her?"

"*Kehella.*" There was no need to tell this devil that Walks Alone grew more sour with him by the day. Even his manitou could not protect him if she ever discovered him with whiskey.

"And I trust Firewalker fares well?" Jacques murmured, nonchalant, not wanting his keen interest in the brave known.

He had swiftly discovered War Cloud's feelings of inadequacy toward his younger brother and discovered his belief that he would always be second to him in the eyes of his mother and his people. Jacques could see why he was worried. Firewalker was indeed a force. He could well wrest power from War Cloud once Thunderhead was gone; and what was worse, Firewalker disliked him, Jacques, even more than did the old chieftain.

And so gently, cleverly, Jacques had begun to play upon War Cloud's weakness as a musician plays a harp. With subtle words and whiskey, he constantly fanned the flames of the brave's jealousy of his brother, hoping it would turn to hatred. For if he were to succeed with his plan to be the sole trader with the Lenapes and have their rich furs for himself, War Cloud must never look to his brother for advice when he became chief.

"My brother fares well," War Cloud muttered, draining his tin cup of its last drop.

Jacques's scorn swelled. The damned fool pig savage, gulping the best Scotch in the land as if it were water, and in return giving him no information worth knowing. He hid his annoyance as he refilled the cup.

"That is all? He fares well? Come now, *n'tschu*, I cannot believe Firewalker has done nothing remarkable in the long time I was gone. In truth, I had no idea he was so widely admired until this last trip I made. The Wyandots and Senecas both know of his bravery and his wisdom." He lowered his voice. "I confess, it was not to my liking that they thought he was the next chieftain. How can this be? They should know by now it is you."

War Cloud laughed, for his body felt good now. He was feeling the firewater. "They will know in due time, and I will not disappoint them. As for my brother, his most recent feat was a tame one. He rescued Flower from the new white woman."

Jacques's dark gaze narrowed. "What white woman is that?"

"The daughter of Caldwell the healer."

Caldwell . . . He remembered vaguely that a family named Caldwell had indeed come there in April from Pittsburgh. It was just as he himself was departing for the city to look into his affairs, and he had forgotten them completely.

"How large is the family?"

War Cloud looked bored. "None but the father and daughter."

"Where do they live?"

"The place called Twin Oaks that belonged to the man called Mackey."

Jacques nodded. He knew it, and already he was wondering what the wench looked like and how old she was. That she lived with her father was good, for it meant she was unwed or widowed. *Mais alors,* it mattered little. All he asked of her was that she be white and had not the face of a horse. Here in this damned wilderness, there were no fair-skinned women to bed, and he was hungry for her already. After ceremoniously presenting War Cloud with an unopened bottle, he bade him good-bye and reminded him to return the next day to trade.

After stowing away his goods and washing up, he dressed in his cleanest clothes and headed for Twin Oaks. He would be leaving the valley again on the twentieth, so he had not a moment to lose.

Hope was still thinking about the Lenapes' visit when the sound of hoofbeats and Joshua's joyful barking told her that her father had arrived home. He had been gone all day, and this time she actually had news of her own to tell him over supper.

He came in after unsaddling his mount and washing up. "Evening, princess. How's my girl? Your day all right?"

Hope gave him a hug and a kiss after he deposited

his bag in the living room. "I'm fine, and my day was—interesting." Her eyes danced.

Tom did not notice; he was sniffing the air. "Is that so? I'll want to hear about it. Supper smells good. I hope you don't mind that I brought home company . . ."

"Of course I don't mind." It was nothing unusual for him to bring home visitors. Hope fetched a plate and bowl, a goblet, and another knife and spoon from the corner cupboard.

Tom went to the door. "Come on in, neighbor." He grinned at Hope and half whispered, "Fellow's shy. He didn't want to impose, but I insisted."

Hope's eyes widened as a tall dark stranger appeared in the doorway, a look of uncertainty on his face. His garb was ordinary—a blue plaid shirt, brown breeches, and tall brown boots—but he had about him an intriguing foreignness which was not at all ordinary.

"Hope, this is Jacques d'Arcy. He has a trading post down on the flatlands. Jacques, this is my daughter, Hope."

So, a Frenchman. She gave him a welcoming smile and her hand. "I'm so glad you could come, Mr. d'Arcy."

Jacques's brown eyes gleamed in admiration. "*Mademoiselle,* the gladness is mine."

"Please, call me Hope."

"*Merci,* and you must call me Jacques."

Jacques raised her hand to his lips with practiced charm, but in truth, she had stolen his breath away. She was so ravishing that he was stunned, and as he gazed on her, he knew that he was going to bed her. *Sacre,* this one he might even wed.

Hope gently retrieved her hand. "Supper is ready," she murmured, knowing that her father would be famished. "We're quite informal here, so please, just help yourself. . . ." As Tom poured the burgundy, she indicated the kettle suspended from an arm now swung away from the hearth. In it was the rabbit stew which had been simmering all day. "Use the potholder please, the spoon is hot." She lit two candles on the table with a spill.

As they talked and ate, Hope studied Jacques d'Arcy. He was tall—at least six feet—and he was handsome—a mass of tightly curled long brown hair, a neatly trimmed beard, black arched brows, a wide sensuous mouth. He might have been roguish looking had he not been so obviously shy and eager to please. In addition, he had manners fit for a king, and his accent was charming. In fact, he seemed such a catch, Hope could not imagine why he had not been snapped up by some woman long ago.

"Your cuisine is *magnifique,*" Jacques declared, gratefully accepting more applesauce and biscuits.

Hope laughed. "It's limited. I'm a—a new cook."

"Never would I have suspected it." He noted with interest the almost guilty glance she exchanged with her father. "I wish there were some way, other than mere words, that I could show my appreciation."

"You can," Hope said promptly. "Tell me about the Lenapes. You say your trading post is near them?"

Jacques frowned. "That is so. What would you like to know about them?"

"Where is the village, for instance?"

"On the west bank of the Shenango roughly one league from here." He hoped to God she did not plan to go there.

"What's this all about, Hope?" Tom asked, buttering a biscuit.

"It's my interesting day I was going to tell you about. A Lenape woman named Flower came to visit me, but she no sooner got here then her brother galloped up with a whoop and a scowl and took her home."

Jacques's mouth curved. "Firewalker."

"Aye . . . Firewalker." Hope recounted the whole tale, afterward asking, "Is he really as fierce as he looks?"

Jacques sipped more of the very excellent burgundy while he pondered his answer. It would not look good were he to show his true animosity toward the devil, yet he could not pass up this chance to do Firewalker some very real harm.

He said carefully: "He is held in high esteem by his people, but I try not to cross his path. One hears stories . . ."

Hope's skin tingled thinking of the brave. His chilling cry, the feathers in his long black hair, the savage beauty of that powerful nearly naked body. She murmured, "What sort of stories?"

Jacques shrugged. "Do not misunderstand, I like the fellow. I like all Indians. One cannot blame them for being born heathen savages, for after all—"

Tom chuckled, but his eyes glinted. "Heathen savages? Hell, man, I've met Thunderhead, the sachem, and talked with him, and I like him. He's a clever old boy who speaks better English than I do." And he thought the chief was damned wise in not allowing his people to have guns or whiskey or wanting them to be dominated by the fur trade. The Lenapes took from the forest only what they needed to live on. "I can say for a fact," he went on, "that he's a damned sight more civilized than some whites Hope and I know." He shot a meaningful glance at her.

Jacques saw it and was intrigued. What was this mysterious secret the two shared? There were, in fact, many things about them he did not understand. It was natural for the doctor father to be educated, but he saw that the daughter, too, was highly educated. That mystified him. And his curious eye had spotted numerous items of great worth in the two rooms he had seen. Even the wine was of the highest quality, and he recognized the goblets as French. Thomas Caldwell seemed to be a man of considerable wealth. *Mais alors,* now was not the time to dwell on such things. The good doctor was waiting for his response and looking none too pleased.

"*Mon ami,* you are right, of course," he replied easily. "My words were poorly chosen. The Lenapes are deeply religious—they have one god and much ancient wisdom. Also, if you are their friend, there is nothing they will not do for you. But if you are their enemy, you had best beware. Firewalker hates whites. It is said he nearly killed a man in Kittanning some seven years ago."

Hope blinked. "You mean—just because he was white?"

Jacques shrugged. "It appears reason enough for Firewalker." He would not arouse her compassion by telling her the real reason: the white had slain the brave's father in cold blood. He continued, "It took ten men to pull Firewalker off the poor fellow. It is why the Lenapes are now in this area. They fled what would have been a just retribution in Kittanning." He looked thoughtful. "I must admit, Hope, I find the man dangerous."

Recalling the brave's smoldering copper eyes, Hope felt her flesh prickle. "I can see why. . . ."

Tom said brusquely, "Take it with a grain of salt, girleen. These tales grow with the telling, and I don't want you afraid to step outside the door while I'm gone." He said to Jacques, "What of Flower? Is she supposed to be bloodthirsty, too?"

Seeing that to retreat would be wise, Jacques laughed. "The little Flower? *Mais non,* Thomas, she is merely high-spirited." His brown eyes moved, teasing, over Hope's face. "And like this daughter of yours, she is very beautiful. *Très belle.*" He added contritely, "Hope, forgive me if I have frightened you. I assure you, it is quite safe for you to go outside your door."

Hope smiled. "Good, then let us have our pudding and cream on the stoop."

After dessert and coffee, they talked far into the evening, and Hope decided that she liked Jacques d'Arcy. He was amusing, he was not afraid to speak his mind, and it was pleasant to be teased again by such a handsome man. She noticed he'd gotten over his shyness—or had she only imagined it? For as he bade them good night, she sensed that the Frenchman was the least shy man she had ever known.

The next afternoon, Hope was weeding her small herb garden when Flower trotted her pinto across the clearing. She watched, astonished, as the woman dismounted, fastened her reins to the hitching rail, and brushed one hand against the other, a symbolic dismissal of a problem. Her brother.

"Now we talk," she declared.

Hope was tickled. "You're not afraid Firewalker will come for you again?"

Flower grinned. "He not know. Is hunting."

"I see." She must remember to tell Jacques he'd been right. Flower was definitely high-spirited, and she was honest. Hope saw that she herself could be honest. "I've been quite curious—why was Firewalker so angry with you yesterday?"

"Mengwes. He feared Mengwes had me. He hates Mengwes—and whites." She blushed. "It sorrows me. . . ."

"It sorrows me also."

The girl was so very lovely, Hope found herself staring. She was small and delicately built with soft, dark gold skin and long-lashed black eyes. Her black hair was dressed in a gleaming ribbon-bound coil at her nape, and her doeskin clothing was wonderfully outlandish—a fringed shirt, leggings, and butter-soft moccasins, all gaily decorated with porcupine quills and brightly colored beads. Hope coveted all of it, for it seemed so much more practical and comfortable than her own cumbersome gown with its yards of cotton.

"I come here many times," Flower said softly, unexpectedly. "I watch you. . . ."

"You watch me? But why?"

"I watch you read."

"Read?" She was astonished.

"*Kehella.* I want learn. Could I learn?"

"I—I suppose. If someone taught you—"

"You," said Flower, promptly.

"Me?" Taken aback, Hope laughed. "Oh, nay, not I. I know nothing about teaching anyone to read."

"Read and write," said Flower firmly.

Oh, Lord. "Flower, I'm a doctor, a—a healer, not a teacher." Read and write? Why would she want such a thing?

"We barter. I give in return."

Hope shook her head. "I would be a terrible teacher. I would be awful!" But there was such pleading in those black eyes, she felt a twinge of guilt. "Why do you want this so badly? How would you use it?"

"I want—read talking papers. Want learn about more than this . . . place." She waved an arm that encompassed the woods, the sky, everything. "Want learn—"

Hope sighed. " 'To learn,' " she said. "I want 'to learn,' not 'I want learn.' "

Flower's eyes widened. "I want *to* learn about seas and cities and other people. I want to know how they live."

Hope could not speak she was so touched. And then she thought, why not at least try? What else had she to occupy her time? It was not as though she had twenty patients a day to care for, and it certainly would do no harm. If she knew nothing of teaching, she could learn, couldn't she? She might even get a pair of doeskin leggings or moccasins out of it, so why not? She knelt, took up two sticks and handed one to Flower. She drew a letter in the soft earth.

"This is the letter *A*," she said, "and *A* is for 'ant.' Say it after me."

Flower looked at her with huge eyes. She, too, knelt and with a hand that shook in her eagerness, bent to her task. "This is the letter *A*," she said, her voice hushed, "and *A* is for 'ant.' "

The trail stretched arrow straight through green and shadow, and the damp aroma of pine and rich black soil hung heavy in the air. Hope was so intoxicated by the sights and smells and the sounds of insects and birdcalls, she slowed Beauty to a walk. She did not want to return to the four walls of the cabin and the boredom of chores she had neglected in order to meet Flower. They had met at *meechek achsinik,* the big rock, for her second lesson, and Hope was thrilled by her promise. Flower had remembered everything. From *A* ant to *H* hand, she had carved in the earth for Hope those letters she had seen only once seven days ago.

Hope thought it was remarkable, but she was also apprehensive. What would the brother, Firewalker, do were he to discover their secret? But then she already knew—he would be angry. Was he ever anything but angry? Her own resentment still simmered remembering his smirk when she'd said she was a doctor. And she had not forgotten that he had tried to kill a man in Kittanning. She shook her head and tossed back her heavy braids. Nay, her father was right. Such tales grew with the telling. She of all people should know that. She could not assume he was guilty of attempted murder or capable of it merely because there were stories about and she did not like him.

She drew back on her reins as a horse and rider appeared suddenly on the trail ahead of her. Oh, Lord, speak of the devil. Firewalker, on his glossy black mount, had come out of the woods and was blocking her path. As he sat quietly, his strange golden eyes studying her, Hope's heart beat harder. She tugged down her skirts, which had been pulled halfway up her thighs for easy riding, and shot him a blazing look.

He appeared as he had before: dark and polished, wide shouldered, those long lean arms and legs, the same fluttering feathers white against his black mane. But the bonfire of anger and vitality she had sensed earlier was gone. Now his face and eyes were masked, and she did not know which frightened her more. But he would never know she feared him. She, too, could wear a mask.

"Greetings." She did not smile.

Firewalker nodded. "Greetings."

He had been stalking small prey when there before him suddenly was the daughter of the healer. The breath fled his lungs at his brief sight of her soft white thighs pressed against the mare's dark barrel. Filled with a hunger that threatened to overwhelm him, he forced his gaze upward to her pink cheeks and flashing gray eyes, and prayed to his manitou to deliver him from this temptation. Never had he craved a white woman before, nor would he hunger for this one now. She was as beautiful as the night and the dawn combined, but she spoke with a forked tongue and he had sensed earlier that a storm raged within her.

"Let me pass, please," Hope said crisply.

Firewalker remained where he was. "Your father shows little wisdom, Caldwell's-daughter, in allowing you to roam these woods alone."

"Allowing me?" Hope laughed sharply. "I need no permission to ride these woods—or to do anything else for that matter. My father is not so foolish as to treat me as a child when I am a woman." Her cheeks burned as his gaze measured her, slowly and insolently, from the top of her dark gleaming head to her small leather boot tucked into the stirrup.

"It would seem the Lenapes guard their women more carefully than do white men," he said drily. "But perhaps the healer is unaware the Mengwes have moved into this area. You will tell him." He turned his mare about. "Come, I will take you home."

Indignation quickened Hope's breathing. Never in her life had she met such an arrogant, overbearing man. "Hear me well, Firewalker." Her voice and eyes were wintry. "You can order your sister and your Indian women about, but don't tell me what to do. I'll take myself home, thank you." She collected Beauty's reins. "Now if you will kindly allow me to pass . . ."

Firewalker shrugged and moved aside. Gazing after her dust and her flying black braids, he shook his head. After tomorrow, his debt to her would be paid. He would give her a portion of the day's hunt in return for tending Flower's wound, and that would be the end of it. Returning to the woods, his thoughts were of how much he disliked her and everything about her—her boldness and sharp tongue and free ways. Yet it disturbed him to think of her in the hands of a Mengwe brave. Belonging to such a one, she would soon learn that her free ways and her boldness were a thing of the past. . . .

Chapter 4

One week had passed, and Flower was having her third lesson. Hope watched with the greatest of pleasure as, carefully and neatly, Flower drew her letters in the earth, named each, and pronounced the word accompanying it.

"There. Is done," she said, finally. "*A* for 'ant' to *P* for 'pot.' Is not"—she blinked up at Hope—"I mean, are they not good?"

"Not good? Oh, Flower, they're very good." Hope traced the lines and curves with wondering fingers. "In fact, they're very, *very* good. I'm thrilled that you've remembered everything so well." She meant every word, and gave Flower a big hug to emphasize it.

Flower beamed. "There is more," she said, smoothing away the old marks. "You want *Q-R-S* and *T*?" Without waiting for an answer, she bent forward again, frowning and chewing her lower lip.

Hope looked on in complete astonishment as Flower continued on to the final letter, a beautiful tall *T* for "top."

Hope shook her head. "I can't believe it! You've learned twenty letters in two weeks! How did you do that? How did you remember so much and so well?" She was completely delighted and bemused. "Flower, you're so clever!"

"Is easy," Flower said, her cheeks pink. She grinned then. "It is easy. . . ."

As Firewalker marked the strongest and straightest dogwood shoots to cut for arrow making, his thoughts were of his mother. It was unlike Walks Alone to tell him her worries, yet this morning she had heaped them all upon him—the Mengwes, Thunderhead, War Cloud. He could do nothing about any of them. He could not order the Mengwe chieftain to move his people farther west. He could not improve the failing health of Thunderhead, his mother's brother, nor could he change the ways of his own elder brother.

Besides, he felt in his heart that when War Cloud became chief, he would rise to his responsibilities. He was well liked, he led council meetings with authority, and he was an impressive representative of their tribe at conferences. All of this Firewalker had told Walks Alone that morning. He had told her also that there the matter rested. He would not waste further thought on it.

As he made to cut the shoots, he was surprised suddenly to hear the silvery sound of womens' voices. Stealing forward on silent feet, he gazed in disbelief upon the sight before him. Sheltered beneath *meechek achsinik*, the great outcropping of rock, their heads close together as they murmured and laughed softly, were Flower and Caldwell's-daughter.

Firewalker's anger leapt. By the Eternal, this sister of his! He had never known a maid so contrary or with such indifference to danger. She deserved to be taken home in disgrace for such disobedience. But first he would find out what it was the two did with such intensity and enjoyment. Noiseless as a cat, he crept closer. Observing that each of them held a stick with which they took turns drawing in the earth, his lip curled. It was unbelievable. They had actually risked coming into this forest where Mengwes and rattlesnakes lurked to play games. How foolish women were. How foolish and childish.

Creeping still closer, he was able to hear his sister's low murmurings—"*D* is for 'dog' . . . *E* is for 'egg' . . . *F* is for 'fire' . . ." He listened in grim astonishment, and when she was finished, he lowered himself silently to the forest floor. With his back against a broad maple, he sat musing over what he had just seen and heard. The maid was learning to write. The healer's daughter was showing his sister how to write English letters. But why? Whose idea was it?

He felt envy. It was quickly replaced by suspicion as he dwelt on the warmth he had observed between the two. It was not good. Whites could no more be given one's trust or friendship than could a wolf be given sheep to guard. And his sister was willful and rebellious enough without that sharp-tongued female teaching her secrecy and deception, too. That the woman had brought Flower there to the woods to teach her made his blood boil. He would put an end to this here and now. But as he got to his feet, he heard his name mentioned, and stayed his step.

"Firewalker is much clever, too," Flower said.

"Firewalker is very clever," Hope amended, covering her instant irritation. Damn, why did Flower talk of him so constantly, and why could she herself not think of the man without growing hot and weak inside?

"Aye, he is very clever," Flower agreed eagerly. "Is Wampum Keeper of Shenango Lenape."

"He is *the* Wampum Keeper of *the* Shenango Lenape," Hope corrected, not knowing what it meant nor did she care. The less she heard about the great Firewalker and his doings, the better.

It was because of him that they met in these woods in secrecy instead of having their lessons in comfort at Twin Oaks. Flower was certain he would be watching the house and would drag her home if he found her there. Yet she remained all forgiving and bursting with pride. Hope sighed. It would be heartless not to make some show of interest in the wampum thing.

"I've not heard of a Wampum Keeper before," she murmured. "What does it mean?"

Flower's eyes glowed. She said, carefully choosing her words, "The Wampum Keeper must know the past of the Lenni Lenape. He must know *the* times and *the* places"—she stressed each "the"—"of every battle and every treaty and the movements of every tribe. All things, from the beginning, are woven into the wampum belts and are learned and remembered by the Wampum Keeper. By Firewalker." She gave a small squeal and clapped her hands. "I said it good, *kehella?*"

Hope laughed, delighted by her delight. "*Kehella.* You said it correctly and beautifully." She was so proud of her, but she had doubts about the tale itself. She could not help but ask, "Honey, are you sure Firewalker knows all of that?"

It was as if the sun had gone behind a cloud. "I am sure, *n'tschu.* My brother is a good Keeper of the Wampum."

Hope said quickly, "I'm sorry, I was just a bit confused. I've never heard of such a thing. . . ."

She had never given a thought to how a people with no written language might remember their history. Handing it down through the generations by word of mouth, even with reminders from wampum belts, seemed an enormous feat. She remembered well her own difficulties in memorizing the work for her degree. It explained Flower's quickness. It was in her blood.

"He is clever, aye?" Flower asked, shy now.

"He is more than clever," Hope assured her. "He is remarkable and—and special. It's right that you should be proud of him." She still did not like him. She would never like him, but she would not deny the brilliance of such a feat nor deny that she admired him. And she envied him.

* * *

The shadows were lengthening and the night insects had begun their evening songs as Firewalker rode out of the pines on the western edge of the highland forest. Sitting astride Nightwind, he gazed across the clearing toward the small cabin of Caldwell the healer. Its lone occupant sat at one end of the stoop, the sun's last rays slanting over her black hair and onto the book she was reading.

Firewalker drew a long breath. He had practiced over and over what he would say to her. Now if only his wits and his breath did not flee and leave him looking like a fool. He nudged his mare, and she responded with a smooth canter that carried him across the clearing. He saw the woman's gray eyes open wide as she rose from her chair, the book clutched tightly to her fine breasts.

"Good evening," Hope called.

"Good evening."

His morning's anger with her was gone. It had flown, he was shamed to admit, upon the wings of her praise of him. He had been touched deeply by his sister's eagerness to learn, but it had not changed anything. He disapproved of it, she had disobeyed him, and this woman was of the enemy. But throughout the day, his thoughts had moved along a new and exciting path. If Hope Caldwell wanted to teach, he would give her someone to teach. He would give her his three young cousins, kin from his father's side of the family.

"I am so glad you came by," Hope said, leaving the stoop and approaching the black mare. "I wanted to thank you for the fresh meat. My father and I both appreciate it. I saw you leave it, but by the time I ran out, you were gone."

Realizing that she was babbling, Hope bit her lip. She could not meet those inscrutable panther eyes, and she dared not look lower, for then she would see that expanse of dark gleaming skin stretching over his chest and those long legs and arms. Damn, she could not even think, let alone speak intelligently.

And when she remembered all of the history stored in his brain, she grew more flustered than ever. She stroked the mare's beautifully shaped head.

"He's lovely," she murmured. "What is he called?" He? He??? Aghast, she heard herself giggle. "Believe it or not, I do know she's a mare . . ."

Firewalker laughed. "She is called Nightwind. And the venison is but payment of my debt to you." Her blooming cheeks reminded him of cherry blossoms.

"There was no need, really . . ." Hope was taken aback by his laughter; she had thought he never laughed. And his eyes were moving over her, appreciative, exploring . . . When he raised one leg over his mount's black neck and dropped lightly to the ground, close to her, facing her, she blinked. Again, she did not know where to look. Certainly not at his faintly smiling mouth nor those hard shoulders. Heat swept over her body in waves. She could not stand there blushing and tongue-tied like some silly young girl. She murmured: "Did you come for some—special reason?"

"Aye. For talk." How strange were these whites. The July days and nights steamed like the inside of a sweat house, yet she wore that long ugly dress which clung to her legs and arms and was buttoned up to the small shadowy hollow at her throat. Why did she not do as his people did and remove her clothing and be comfortable? His eyes were drawn irresistibly to the moisture beading the downy skin above her upper lip and to the wisps of black hair clinging to her temples. Feeling a familiar stirring in his loins, he decided it was best she was fully clothed.

He stared at her so long, Hope grew uneasy. "Is there some problem?"

"Aye. This morning I chanced upon two women in the forest. I found their talk about tops and pots and quills very strange."

Hope lifted her chin and kept her face as impassive as his own. "I was teaching Flower the alphabet."

"Why?"

"She asked me to."

"The forest would seem a strange place for such a thing."

Hope felt a small leap of triumph. "The forest *is* a strange place for such a thing, but she feared you would be watching this house and take her away." She enjoyed that, but she did not forget her manners. "Would you care to sit down?" She indicated the two rockers on the stoop.

Firewalker seemed not to hear. He said quietly, "I do not want my sister hurt, Caldwell's-daughter."

Hope was astonished. She laughed. "Hurt? I'm trying to help her, not hurt her. Perhaps you don't know that her dream is to read books. She wants to learn about places and things and people she will never see."

"Ah." The air resonated with the sound. "And these people she will never see—will they warm her at night and provide her with food and protection?"

Hope crossed her arms. "What you are saying hardly makes sense."

"What I am saying is that no brave of worth wants a woman whose head is filled with dreams of things he cannot give her. And a woman without a man has neither meat nor protection nor does she have children. I do not want such a life for my sister." Once again, he saw the flickering, the heat lightning, in those gray eyes.

"Then you are also saying"—Hope was trying to keep her temper—"that the things which make Flower happy don't matter. What matters is that she must please a man." Suddenly she was remembering Sam and his letter about his position and his reputation and his loss. Was there no unselfish, giving man in this whole world except her own father?

Firewalker's patience was fast disappearing. "Among our people," he said, "a woman's happiness and well-being depend upon a man. Her man and her children. There is nothing more. She asks for nothing more."

"Indeed. And who is it that decides that, pray tell?" Hope asked hotly. "I doubt it is the woman!"

He expelled a long breath. "Our women are content. They do not concern you. There it will end."

She yearned to lash back at him, but she saw that it was a time for silence. He spoke English almost as well as she, but she had just glimpsed the savage beneath that handsome face, the angry god of a primeval forest. She stepped back, flesh tingling and the hair standing on her nape. Nothing had changed since their first angry meeting. No matter how much he infuriated her, she must placate him. She shrugged.

"If that's all . . ."

"It is not all." Firewalker saw that she clutched her book so tightly, the knuckles of her fingers were white. He was sorry, for he had not meant to frighten or anger her. He said gently, "You have given me much cause for thought this day, Hope Caldwell. Your teaching of letters interests me greatly."

Hope felt new dismay. "Do you mean—for yourself?" She could not teach him. Not with those eyes burning through her. She was relieved when he shook his head.

"I myself have no need for such a thing."

In truth, there was nothing he wanted more. He had craved as a youth to know the tongue of the enemy and had learned to speak it well. He had craved also to read and write it. He knew that only with education would his people be treated fairly by whites. But there had been no one to teach him. Not until now. And for it to be a woman, and this woman in particular, was intolerable. What she could give him was as precious as air and water, but even so he could not submit to her. He could not put himself in a position of such weakness with a fork-tongued, enemy female. It would shame him among his brothers to put his neck beneath her heel. But for his young kin, it was a different thing. They were ruled still by women.

"There are three youths," he said. "I would have them read and write."

Hope could hardly believe what she was hearing. "You want me to teach three boys?"

"Aye. Each has the ability to become a Keeper of the Wampum, but they lack the interest and the patience."

"I really don't—"

"In return, I will supply fish and game for you and the healer."

She wanted to refuse outright, but she feared antagonizing him. She murmured instead, "And Flower?"

"It is not for Flower," Firewalker said firmly.

Not for Flower? Flower who was doing so well, and was receiving so much joy over the new world opening up to her? After the lesson this morning, Hope had been so excited about her prospects, she'd made out an order for school supplies for the next pack train to take to Pittsburgh. But, nay, it was not for Flower. Heaven forbid she learn more than some stupid brave who might want her for his squaw. But of course it was all right for the boys to learn. . . .

She felt such a rush of anger, she had to bite her tongue to contain it. But she knew what her answer would be. She was not going to teach any arrogant Indian males. Not now, not ever. She said softly: "You have given me cause for thought also, Firewalker. I need time to consider this."

"I will come again tomorrow night."

"I will give you your answer."

It was the middle of the night and the village slept. In the four great longhouses of the Shenango Lenape, only Walks Alone of all her tribe was awake. She sat before the cook fire in front of her own small compartment gazing at the flames, and although the night was hot, it was as if ice water ran in her veins.

It was the way she had felt before the death of her mate. No vision had foretold that the shot of a vengeful white would plunge into the chest of Diving Eagle on his solitary hunt. She had felt only this same cold emptiness.

None knew that she missed him as much now, seven years later, as she had on that first terrible day when he was torn from her. Her heart was still a raw gaping wound. She yearned to go to him, yearned to let her soul slip away and join him, but she could not. Not until War Cloud was chief and all was well with him and their people could she go to her beloved. It was the promise she had made Diving Eagle as he lay singing his death song, and it was a promise she would keep. She would hold this headstrong son of theirs on a path that was straight.

Walks Alone crossed her legs, folded her arms across her bared breasts, and lifted her chin. She closed her eyes. A vision was coming although she had not sought it. This was not a fire of purification burning before her; it was but her dying cook fire whose smoke was suddenly making her head swim. Behind closed lids she watched the coming of a dazzling white light. She drew a deep breath and filled her lungs to their fullest as a tall figure moved through the brightness. Firewalker . . .

Eyes still closed, she looked with pleasure on his tall figure with its wide shoulders and slender waist. He was fiercely strong and brave, this younger son of hers, and he was comely. Broad cheekbones, a straight well-shaped nose, his black hair long and gleaming against his dark skin, and those unforgettable eyes. The eyes of his father . . .

Now a second brave moved through the white light. The image had begun to shift and fade, but there was no mistaking the heavy muscular body, the scalp lock, and the handsome hawk nose of War Cloud, her elder son. What was this about? she wondered, dread stirring. Why was she seeing her sons as she experienced this icy premonition of doom?

Even as the thought came, the two locked in violent combat. It was brief, but when it ended, only one remained standing.

Walks Alone knew in her heart that the other was dead, but the light was now too faded for her to see either the victor or the vanquished. Discerning a third figure—a young woman with long black hair—moving in the haze, her breath caught and her heart fluttered in her throat. Was it her daughter joining them? *Matta! Matta!* came her silent cry as her body began to tremble. Let it not be so. She prayed to the Great Being to spare all three of her children, and then willed herself, steeled herself to strength and to wisdom and understanding.

She was Walks Alone, *meteinuwak* of the Shenango Lenape, sister of the great sachem, Thunderhead, and mother of the future chief, War Cloud. She was depended upon by her people to keep a level head so that she could lead them in the ways of the spirit and in any other way she could. She forbade herself therefore to leap to any frightening imaginings and conclusions from this vision she had not sought. She had not fasted, nor was this fire purified; it was doubtless a waking dream involving her many worries. She would think no more of it. With that, she rose, banked her fire, crawled into her bunk, and lay down on her skins beside Flower. She turned her face to the wall and closed her eyes, but it was a long time before she slept.

Chapter 5

It was a late golden afternoon in the last week of July as Tom Caldwell stood admiring his cornfield. It stretched in a gleaming green swath from the end of his south meadow to the edge of his woods, and it would soon be ready for harvest. He took off his wide-brimmed hat, wiped the sweat from his face, and gave Hope a grin.

"Did you ever see anything prettier?"

Hope chewed on a long blade of grass and grinned back. "I guess you knew what you were doing after all. It's beautiful."

"Next year, I'll let this field lay fallow, put corn in the north meadow, and add a new crop. Maybe wheat or oats." He put an arm around his daughter's shoulders and hugged her. "Son of a gun, Hope, I love it here. It's quiet and peaceful, the water's good, the food couldn't be fresher." He pointed to Josh chasing a squirrel. "Dog's happy." He grew quiet then, seeing her suddenly pensive face. "Hell, princess, I'm sorry. I know things could be better for you. It's my one and only regret about being here."

"Well, don't give it another thought." Hope tucked an arm inside his as they walked to their mounts. She laughed then. "And don't look so grim. I'm fine; I mean it. We both know the day will come when I'm needed."

"You're needed right now. I need you, Flower

needs you—in fact, I've been wanting to hear more about her. I know how much you like the lass."

"She's amazing, that's all. She's quick and eager and there doesn't seem to be any limit to what she can learn. It's Firewalker who's the problem." Hope shook her head, recalling his stubbornness. "He's so unfair about her that I just want to shake him!" Considering the brave's height and those wide dark shoulders, she might as well try to shake an oak. "At any rate, Flower won't be stopped. We'll work something out."

"I wouldn't aggravate the man," Tom warned, seeing the obstinate set of his daughter's jaw.

"Believe me, it's the last thing I want to do. Actually, I'd be happy if I never saw him again." She gathered up her skirts and mounted Beauty.

Tom, too, swung into the saddle. "You say he's coming this evening for your answer?"

"Aye. I should have refused him last night, but plain and simple, I wasn't brave enough. He's—a bit frightening. I'm glad you'll be home tonight."

Tom nodded. "I'll be interested in meeting him."

As they rode the short distance back to the cabin, his thoughts were troubled. This girl of his was going to be a long time getting over the hurt Sam Kendall had dealt her—if she ever did. And Firewalker's plan would suffer because of it. It was too bad, for he thought the brave's idea of stuffing some learning into young Lenape heads was a good one. And it would be a good thing for Hope. He hadn't a doubt she would learn the teaching knack fast enough. She was quick, and it would give her a feeling of worth that didn't come from cooking and sewing. More important, it would help keep her mind off what had happened in Pittsburgh. He gave her a cautious sidelong glance, his gray eyes shaded by the brim of his hat.

"I think this Firewalker has a sound idea, Hope. And he's paid you a high compliment."

"What do you mean?"

"I mean his willingness to put three young bucks under your thumb. Whether you agree or not, and whether he knows it or not, he's honored you, girleen."

Hope gave him a baleful look. "It's one more reason for refusing, as far as I'm concerned. I'd be living a lie, pretending to be something I'm not. Teaching Flower is one thing—I'm doing it out of friendship—but struggling with three bratty boys—" She shook her head. "Nay, Father, I'll not do it, especially since Flower isn't important enough to be included."

Tom shrugged. "Whatever you say." But he had a hunch she'd change her mind before long. The pack train was leaving on the morrow for Pittsburgh, and he meant to add on to the order she'd already given. He'd get extra primers and slates, tablets, quills, and ink.

His thoughts were interrupted when he spied a neighbor galloping hellbent toward him across the clearing. He reined and waited.

"What's wrong, Jim?"

"Doc, thank God ye're home! Johnnie's fell out o' the hay mow an' done somethin' to 'is shoulder. He's a-screechin' so loud I fear it's broke. Can ye come?" Finally noticing Hope, he tipped his hat respectfully. "G'day, mistress. 'Scuse my manners . . ."

"Let me fetch my bag," Tom said. "You go on back and try to keep him calm—and warm."

Hope watched as her father collected his things and left at a gallop, Joshua racing after him. Remembering their neighbor's belated "G'day, mistress," her resentment simmered. She was a nonentity up here. A nonperson. She gave herself a mental shake. She was not going to start that miserable self-pity again. It was all right. There was a time for all things, and now was her time to do those chores she would be too busy for later on. This month, for instance, she was dipping candles and making clothes for the two of them. Putting the practice of medicine from her mind, she went into the kitchen and tested the meat and vegetables with a fork. Good, everything was done. She slid the kettle along the iron arm away from the heat, and recalled her father's words about Firewalker's honoring her. She grew thoughtful.

If Firewalker hated whites so much, and if he considered women as mere chattels to be ordered about, it was rather an amazing thing that he was willing to put three young males into her hands. She had not looked at it that way, and now she wondered what he would do when she refused. Remembering the way those coppery eyes of his tended to smolder, she felt a small shiver of dread. Lord, she certainly didn't want him for an enemy. . . .

She brooded over the possibility as she took candles from the candle safe and carried them to the living room. She was about to insert them into the candleholders on the mantelpiece when she sensed someone watching her. She turned, eyes wide, one hand to her breast, fully expecting to see a tall near-naked form in the doorway. But it was not Firewalker; it was the Frenchman, Jacques d'Arcy. She laughed, vastly relieved, as he knocked.

"Hello. You're back!"

"*Oui, ma belle.* Happily, I am returned." His smile turned to a frown. "But I see I have frightened you."

Hope shook her head. "Only for an instant."

"A thousand pardons."

"Jacques, for goodness sake, I'm fine. Don't stand there—do come in. I'm so glad to see you."

When she held out her hand, he took and kissed it, and pulled her into his arms. The warning look in those cool gray eyes caused him to change his tack. He laughed, gave her a quick brotherly hug and a kiss on the cheek, and released her.

"Forgive me, *mon amie.* It is just that I am so delighted to be back." While he was gone journeying, he had decided absolutely that he would wed her. And having reached the decision, he was constantly overheated thinking of the many tantalizing things he would do with her when she was his. For a start, they would live in bed the first month or so, and then he would—*mais non,* he was doomed if he thought of it now. She would sense it. *Sacre.* Seeing that she held a pair of fresh white tapers, he took them with a flourish. "*Mademoiselle,* allow me." He inserted them into the tin holders for her. "*Voilà.*"

"Thank you," Hope answered politely, but she was flustered. "May I offer you something to eat or drink?"

"Water would be fine." He followed her to the kitchen and watched hungrily as she dipped it from the bucket into a tin cup.

Mon dieu, such skin and eyes. The wench was a hundred times more ravishing than he had remembered, but she was a veritable fortress. Cannon bristling from every battlement and a high stone wall erected about her. If he was to have her, he must do it subtly and without storming her defenses, or she would shoot him down. She was an educated woman, a physician, not some ignorant maid who would believe his every lie. She would be a challenge, but one well worth the effort.

"There you are." Hope handed him the cup. "Let's go onto the stoop for a bit."

She felt guilty as they moved outside and sat down. It was ridiculous the way she had stiffened when he'd embraced her. It was only a hug and a kiss on the cheek, for heaven's sake, and common sense told her he had meant nothing by it. His warmth and lack of restraint were just his French way. But his beard brushing against her face reminded her of Sam's beard, and his body against hers had felt like Sam's—big and strong and solid with a slight thickening about the waist from too much good food. The dark curls visible in the open neck of his red shirt reminded her of the mat of blond curls that covered Sam's chest.

Suddenly she was reminded of Firewalker's chest and belly, and of how smooth and hard muscled they were. Only then did she realize why the coppery skin stretching over the long clean lines of his bones and muscles looked so polished. It was unmarred by the crisp hair that white men had. She bit down hard on her lip. What a stupid, stupid thing to be thinking . . .

"Is all well with you and Thomas?" Jacques asked, contemplating the lessons of love he would soon be teaching her.

Hope nodded. "Everything's fine. Jim Slater just came to fetch him, but I expect him back for supper. Will you join us?"

Jacques shook his head. "Alas, I cannot." He did not dare. His hunger for her was such that he would be hard-pressed not to give her a first lesson tonight. He dug into his shirt pocket and fished out a small beribboned packet. He placed it in her hands. "I just came by to bring you this."

"How sweet of you." She prayed it was something she could accept, for she truly liked him. She was charmed by his Gallic shrug and the way "will" and "this" turned into "weel" and "theese" when he spoke. But if he should ever want more than friendship from her, she could not give it to him.

Jacques watched her, hotly aware of everything about her. The long shapely fingers carefully untying the ribbon, the rosy pink touching her cheeks, the rise and fall of her breasts. He stared. *Sacre,* how soft and full they were. He wet his lips and struggled to subdue his hunger.

Hope's eyes widened as the wrapping fell away. It was a simple Indian headband of bright multicolored glass beads, and it made her feel happy just to look at it.

"Oh, Jacques, thank you!"

"C'est belle, n'est-ce pas?" he asked, softly. *"C'est* Wyandot."

He had known better than to gift her with anything of value just yet. The thought caused him to wonder about the man she had left behind. For there was a man, of that he had no doubt. Some calamitous *affaire de coeur* had befallen her, and if she did not eventually tell him of it freely, he would discover it from his many contacts in Pittsburgh.

"I love it!" Hope laughed, slipping the band over her hair and centering it on her forehead. "There. How does it look?" She struck a pose, chin high, face masked, lids lowered over her gray eyes, hooding them. It was the way Firewalker looked at her.

"You are Indian, I swear." Jacques, too, laughed, but he was not as amused as he pretended by her uncanny transformation.

"Speaking of Indians reminds me," Hope said, "there's something I've been saving to tell you! But first, you must have some sherry."

"You have convinced me."

He felt an ugly sweep of resentment as she hastened inside to fetch it. How damnable that it should be savages and not himself that made her eyes sparkle so.

When she returned with the wine and he had taken a sip, he said: "*Mais allons*, let me hear this news that has made you so happy." He wished she would take the damned headband off—it made him uncomfortable.

"It's about Flower. You were right, you know, when you said she was high-spirited. She came back after Firewalker forbade it, and, Jacques, you'll never believe this—she wants me to teach her to read and write!"

Jacques chuckled. "*C'est incroyable*. But I trust you will not."

"But I am! I've given her several lessons already."

Seeing his amused disdain, Hope did not tell him about Firewalker and the youths he wanted her to teach. It would be a betrayal somehow to repeat his words for Jacques to ridicule.

Jacques took another sip of wine and studied her thoughtfully. "You are a remarkable woman, Hope Caldwell. I think it is admirable that you desire to help the maid, but I fear she will disappoint you."

"I can't imagine how. She's a good student."

Jacques shook his head. "Perhaps for now, but I assure you, she will not be interested for long. Indians do not like to work. They are happiest when they are painting their bodies or playing games or going to war. Or dancing. Do you not hear the drums at night? They can dance away half the night. They are children. . . ."

Hope's lips tilted. "Not heathen savages?"

Jacques did not smile. He said softly, "I regret that I led you to believe I do not like or respect them. You should know that my very close friend is the brother of your fierce Firewalker."

"War Cloud?"

"You know of him then?"

"Aye. Flower says he will be the next chief."

"And he will be a good one."

"Does he—hate whites also?"

Jacques's teeth gleamed in his dark beard. "All Indians hate all whites, although some pretend they do not. The Lenapes hate us especially, and Firewalker hates us most especially of all. War Cloud, however, is—open to reason." He drained his goblet and got to his feet. "And now, *ma chère*, I will thank you for the excellent sherry and be on my way."

Hope, too, rose. "Why?" she asked.

Jacques was pleasantly surprised. "Because I have been gone for some time and I have much to put in order."

Hope flushed. "I'm sorry, I meant—why do the Lenapes hate us? And why Firewalker especially?"

Damn the wench. He had had enough talk of savages, yet her own interest seemed insatiable. He would explode in another moment. "You must ask him. I know only that they hold much bitterness for both whites and Mengwes. Since Firewalker is the so-called historian of his tribe, I suspect he is steeped in every treachery, real or imagined. *Maintenant*, I depart." Observing that she was staring up at him, frowning, he asked, *"Qu'est-ce que c'est?"*

"Your forehead—there's blood on it." Hope moved

closer and pushed back his hair for a better look. "Jacques, it's a rather nasty gash! Don't you feel it? How did it happen?" She gently probed the area about the wound with skilled fingers.

Jacques himself touched it, felt the stickiness of dried blood, and shrugged it off. "It is nothing. I recall now it was a branch I did not see. I was more concerned with the wolf who was hungry for my mules."

Hope took his arm. "Come, *m'sieu*, inside with you. I'll cleanse it for you and give you a salve that will hasten the healing."

He laughed. "I tell you it is nothing. I will tend it myself."

"Hush, you're being very male and very silly. It could become infected. You brought me a lovely gift. Now for goodness sake, let me do something in return."

Jacques sighed. "You are right, of course. *Eh bien, mademoiselle le docteur,* I am in your capable hands." He allowed her to draw him back into the cabin.

Firewalker's thoughts dwelt on Caldwell's-daughter as Nightwind forded the shallows of the Shenango Sipo and trotted toward the eastern highlands. Soon he would have an answer from her, but he knew that whatever her decision, he would be dissatisfied. He wanted her to say aye, yet he wanted no further dealings with her nor with any white. And if she said nay, he would resent it. It was a weakness he could not conquer, this inability of his to meet whites with equanimity despite his hatred for them. He could act only as he felt, he could not pretend, and he was sometimes moved to envy when he saw the easy ways of his brother, War Cloud, with the enemy.

He gazed about him, taking no pleasure in the familiar sights of the woodlands in midsummer: green acorns shining on the oaks, tender green cones on the pines, fireflies dancing among scrub and saplings in the evening heat. He wiped his face and wished for the cooling breath of the wind, but there was none. His discomfort was of his own doing. He had foolishly donned a doeskin shirt and leggings because of the woman. He had seen that she was embarrassed by his nakedness, and now his body's moisture, trapped by the clothing, streamed down his back and chest.

Firewalker forgot his discomfort, seeing his mount's ears prick. She whinnied, and from the woods to his right came an answering call. He reined, wondering who would be there this late in the day. A prowling Mengwe? He quickly took his bow from his back, drew an arrow, and readied it.

"*Kou-e!*" he shouted. When no one answered, he frowned. Perhaps someone was in trouble. He was about to go into the brush when he spied War Cloud astride his stallion. He called, "Is all well?"

"*Kehella.*" Though War Cloud's eyes were dimmed with rum, he saw his brother, Firewalker, as he always saw him. With envy. It disappointed him. He had hoped that were he drunk enough, the battle raging within him so constantly over Firewalker would surely cease. But it was still there, pushing him first one way and then the other. Loving him, *kehella*, loving him as he loved himself, but hating him, too. It was the way it had always been.

War Cloud's losses to his younger brother in the competitions of childhood had given way to even greater losses as they encountered the everyday trials of manhood. The fairest women favored Firewalker, the largest bucks presented their hearts to his arrows willingly, even the woodland trails grew level and broad for his passage. Or so it seemed.

To War Cloud's jealous eyes, Firewalker was taller, stronger, fleeter, and wiser than he. His face and form were of a striking beauty, and he was possessed of a natural sureness and confidence and an innate fearlessness that War Cloud could not match. He would never surpass nor even equal this perfect brother of his who stood tall in the eyes of his tribe and their mother. He was a failure by comparison, and over the years, he had grown wild and impetuous in order to hide it. Now, as he approached Firewalker, his teeth grated against each other. Helldamnfire, why did this devil not have some doubts and needs and frailties like other men?

Firewalker's gaze narrowed, noting that his brother's black eyes were overbright and his face flushed. It would seem he had been trysting. It was one of their mother's many worries concerning War Cloud, his overfondness for women. He was newly joined with a young maid whose heart belonged to him alone, and he had immediately gotten her with child. Now here he was, toying with another and acting as though nothing had happened.

War Cloud laughed. "Such a face, my brother! Have you been eating sour apples? And where do you go in such fine garb on such a hot night?"

Firewalker's heart froze, hearing War Cloud's slurred speech. It was not a woman; it was worse. He was drunk. Firewalker had had a suspicion of it several moons ago, but had refused to believe his brother could be so foolish. Thunderhead's ruling against alcohol was ironclad and could mean banishment from the tribe if War Cloud were caught. Yet there was no denying the vacant look on his face nor the fumes emanating from him. And Firewalker knew exactly who had given him the brew. He had observed the return of the trader d'Arcy, the friend of War Cloud. Such a friend his brother did not need.

"Why have you done this thing?" he asked quietly.

War Cloud sought scorn and disgust in Firewalker's words and found them. Once again he had failed in the eyes of the one who could do no wrong. He forced another laugh. "You are indeed fortunate to be so pure, my brother." He received a long chilling gaze from those strange gold eyes.

"You of all people know my faults," Firewalker

muttered, for it was War Cloud who had helped prevent his killing a man in a hot rage. "But then my faults are not the issue. I am not the future chief. If I were, I would not be such a fool as to drink d'Arcy's whiskey. Man, he wants only to use you. . . ." No sooner had the words left his lips than he regretted them. Criticism always made his brother more rebellious.

War Cloud's black eyes glittered beneath lowered lids. So, yet another pronouncement from the throne. "You will betray me, I suppose?" he asked softly. Now he hated him; there was no room for love here. He would be betrayed, banished, and Firewalker would be voted sachem when that time came. It was his worst nightmare.

"You know I will not," Firewalker answered gruffly, "but surely you see this must end."

War Cloud bristled. "*Matta!* It will not end. It gives me pleasure, and I suffer no evil consequences. There it stands. You will not interfere."

Firewalker's first angry reaction was to shake some sense into him. But this was not his foolish young sister; this was a man, his proud elder brother and the future chieftain. He shrugged. "It will be as you wish. If you want to destroy yourself, I will not prevent it." Nor would he warn him against returning home in such condition. Let what would happen, happen.

War Cloud watched, glowering, as Firewalker continued on his way, but beneath his anger he felt a sick emptiness. He hated and resented that his brother was a mountain in the path of everything he had ever done or thought or sought. But why, then, did he believe it to be such a magnificent mountain? And why did he berate himself so for fighting against it and wish that he, too, might soar above the clouds? He shook his head. It was as it was, and always would be. He loved and admired Firewalker more than he could ever hate him, but he had no defenses, no barriers against the bitter jealousy he felt toward him.

As Nightwind carried him uphill, Firewalker seethed, pondering his brother's easy careless ways and the growing conflict between them. As boys they had been close and constant companions, comrades who had made a covenant to remain together always and share all. As men, they no longer understood each other, and the gulf between them was widening by the day. He had always believed that War Cloud would change when he held the scepter of a sachem in his hand, but now he was not so sure. Perhaps their mother was right to worry.

Reaching the highlands, Firewalker branched off the main trail to the left, following a path that overlooked the cornfield of Caldwell the healer. The corn stood tall and green within the rail fencing, and Firewalker admitted grudgingly that the man had done well for a white. But the fact remained that it was on land stolen from the Lenapes that he grew his corn.

This all had been theirs, this vast Pennsylvania woodland. And when the whites began to come as they always did, his people had been resigned to sharing it with them. In truth, there was plenty for all. But then five winters ago a treaty had been drawn and signed in which they'd had no part, and suddenly this land to which they had title was no longer theirs. Now it was being taken from them, chunk by chunk, and given to the enemy.

It was a constant fire burning within him, but he damped it as he approached the clearing and turned his thoughts to the woman. His decision was made. He wanted her to teach. And if she agreed, he would be politeness itself, no matter how sharp her tongue. The boys' learning must come before any pride he might have. Seeing her on the stoop, he frowned and reined. She was not alone. The trader d'Arcy was with her. He watched grimly as she touched one small white hand to his hair and smoothed it off his forehead. And then she drew him back into the cabin. Firewalker was not prepared for the arrow of jealousy that pierced him.

Chapter 6

Hope was relieved that Jacques's wound was less serious than she had first thought. After cleansing it and applying the salve, she followed him back outside. "Make sure you put the salve on twice a day."

"*Merci*—I am grateful."

"You're sure you won't stay and eat with us?"

"I am sure. My work awaits me."

"The next time, then, and thanks again for my gift. I do love it." She patted his arm. "It was thoughtful of you."

"I am pleased." Suddenly he was looking beyond her, his lips tightening into a grim line. "You have a visitor, I see. The fire breather. What does he want, I wonder?"

Turning, Hope saw Firewalker riding across the clearing. She watched as he slid to the ground, tethered his mare beside Jacques's roan gelding, and came toward them. She sensed the storm within him even though he appeared placid. Perhaps it was the widening of his pupils as he looked from her to Jacques and back to her. She put on a smile although a shiver stole through her.

"Good evening."

She had never seen him fully clothed before. His pale butter-soft shirt and leggings made his hair and skin seem swarthier than ever, and she was astonished by how ordinary, how almost insignificant, the tall Frenchman seemed in contrast.

"Good evening." Firewalker's gaze went to the Wyandot headband on the black hair of Caldwell's-daughter. Despite her white skin, she had an Indian look about her. Perhaps it was because she moved like an Indian in her ugly garb: tall, straight, and with her shoulders back and her head held proudly on her slender neck.

"Bon soir, n'tschu," said Jacques, interrupting the locked gaze between the two.

A muscle moved in Firewalker's jaw at the "my friend." He acknowledged the trader's presence with a barely perceptible nod.

Jacques asked low, "Hope, do you—wish me to stay?"

Hope wanted very much for him to stay, but she knew it would not be wise. Firewalker would be annoyed enough when he learned she was not going to teach, without the added irritation of Jacques's presence. She shook her head. "Thank you, but Firewalker and I have business to discuss."

Jacques did not reveal his displeasure. "Well, then, *adieu, ma belle.*"

"Good-bye."

To Hope's great relief, her father returned as soon as Jacques was out of sight. She quickly made introductions, and Tom gave the brave a strong handshake. "I'm glad to meet you, son," he said. "I've met your uncle and I admire him."

"Thunderhead will be pleased," Firewalker answered politely, but he doubted the man's sincerity. Whites gave freely of their friendship and praise, but quickly forgot they had given them.

Tom turned to Hope. "I'll go on in and let you two get on with your talk."

Hope nodded. He had been gone longer than expected, and she knew he was tired and hungry. She knew also that he would be there if she needed him. She looked up at Firewalker. "We can sit on the stoop if you like." She watched as he complied, folding his tall body into a rocker that seemed suddenly small. She herself felt small as his eyes moved over her. Small and soft and very female.

"I have given this further thought," Firewalker said gruffly, still feeling the jealousy that had pierced him when she had touched the Frenchman. He told himself to look only at her eyes, not at her soft pink mouth nor the curve of her cheeks nor her glorious white skin.

Hope swallowed. Her throat was suddenly dry. "I have thought about it, too—as I said I would."

"I will hear your words first."

When he had first seen her with d'Arcy, he had wheeled Nightwind about and started for home, but then he had thought better of it. Why should he be the one to leave? Let the Frenchman go. And as he waited in the trees for them to reappear, he knew that he did not want his young cousins in her hands. Not if she were under the influence of such a one as d'Arcy.

"Very well," Hope answered. "I'll be very honest. I have only a vague idea of what I would have taught Flower had you allowed her to continue. After the alphabet, that is . . ." It was the truth. He needn't know she had sent for books which would tell her exactly what to do. "I just don't feel capable of any serious teaching." She could not resist adding, "As I mentioned, I am a physician."

Firewalker kept the muscles of his face smooth, but his scorn burned hot. So she was still insisting on that, was she? If she did not want to teach, why did she not just say so? He asked coolly: "Then you do not recall your own learning?"

Hope flushed. "Certainly not enough to teach anyone."

"I see." He found it unbelievable. He remembered every milestone in his life.

Hope knew exactly what he was thinking behind the mask he wore. Not wanting her father to hear, she said low but heatedly, "I resent very much that you never believe a word I say. Who do you think you are to judge me so? God?"

It was enough. Wordlessly, Firewalker unwound himself from the rocking chair, a true instrument of torture, and got to his feet. The woman was a shrew. No squaw ever spoke with such a forked waspish tongue to a warrior. None would dare. He felt sudden sympathy for Caldwell, but then a man who ruled his wigwam no better than this deserved whatever he got. And the fact that she was sweet as honey with d'Arcy and sharp as salt with himself stung Firewalker deeply. He wanted to tell her that even if her answer had been aye, he would not have placed Lenape youth in her hands under any circumstances. But he kept his silence. The only purpose in saying such a thing would be to hurt her, and he hoped he was above such smallness.

"Thank you for your time," he muttered, and strode abruptly to his mount.

Hope stared after him, wanting to call him back, but for what? What was there to say? She watched until he disappeared into the woods, and then she went inside. Damn! Their meeting had ended almost before it began, and now he was furious with her. He hated her. Damn . . .

Riding homeward, Firewalker chewed over his clash with the woman and his behavior these past few days. What had come over him? It was not like him to approach the enemy, and a woman at that, for help of any kind. And then to be jealous of her . . . And it was not like him to turn his back on War Cloud. From the time they drew their first arrows, they had watched over one another and their mother and sister. Yet now that War Cloud had become his own worst enemy, Firewalker actually thought to desert him. He was disgusted with himself. He would not. He would never desert him. *Matta.* His brother was going to be a chieftain worthy of the

Lenapes even if he had to push and guard him every step of the way. . . .

Jacques d'Arcy set his lantern on a shelf in his storage room and contemplated his booty. All told, he had a hundred and fifty beaver peltry, six bales of fox, otter, and deerskins, a parfleche containing many wide pewter bracelets and rings, and several bales of good heavy Indian blankets. His pack mules had been laden down. In return he had parted with glass beads, calico, flannel, cheap knives, mirrors, and metal tools.

It had been child's play. But then after three years of dealing with Wyandots, Mengwes, Lenapes, and Senecas, he should know how to come out ahead. He had become very adept at keeping the chieftains happy. When he catered to their secret yearnings, it followed as night followed day that the rest fell into place. In fact, everything was falling into place for him now. He but needed a bit of luck in regard to Thunderhead. Perhaps the same luck that had placed Hope within his grasp would strike the old man dead one of these days . . .

Hope . . . Heat swelled in his loins as he thought of her, but then his memories of her never did her justice. She was exquisite. Matchless alabaster perfection. Even if it were not apparent that her father was a man of great means, he would still covet her for her beauty. But how long should he wait before he proposed? How long could he bear to wait? It was a quandary, for she was as skittish as a mare being led to her first stallion. The thought of a stallion jolted him, for it brought Firewalker to mind.

He had pushed away the ugly thought of the two of them together, but now the image would not leave his head. What, in God's name, kind of business had a savage to discuss with a white woman of culture? And why had he himself not stayed to protect her? But then she had sent him off. He had gone, *oui*, but certainly not willingly. He had departed only because he thought Thomas was due to return at any moment. But had he? Damnation, if he had not, and if that dark devil had laid one lustful finger on that delectable white body, the body that was going to be his . . .

Sensing suddenly that he was not alone, Jacques spun. He nearly jumped out of his boots seeing Firewalker standing in the doorway. In the flickering dimness, he felt the quiet menace in those strange tawny eyes. The fellow was a devil, there was no doubt. No ordinary man had eyes like that. . . .

"Can I help you, *n'tschu?*" His voice sounded strangled.

Firewalker said softly, "You can cease calling me 'my friend.' "

Realizing that he was not about to be scalped, Jacques managed a smile. "As you wish. I trust you concluded your business with *mademoiselle.*" Intrigued to see scorn flare in the brave's eyes, he added cautiously, "It would appear your meeting did not go happily. Perhaps if I were to—"

Firewalker growled, "I did not come here to discuss your woman, Frenchman. I am here to warn you, do not give my brother any more of your whiskey."

"Pardonez moi?" Jacques stared at him. He did not believe it. The savage thought Hope was his woman—was that why he was so angry with her?

"No more whiskey," Firewalker rasped.

Jacques smiled. *"Mais alors,* War Cloud is my friend and I think I must let him decide that. It gives him great pleasure, after all." He was rocked backward by the sudden painful stab of a steely finger against his chest.

"Matta. Here it will end. I know that you have managed to bribe certain sachems, and I see well that it is your plan for War Cloud."

At that moment, Jacques considered slaying him. Then and there he could slay him, but that was the easy part. The difficulty was what to do after. How to hide the fact. *Mais non,* there could be no slaying. He would keep his head, but the devil did not know how close he had come to his great hunting ground in the sky.

He said smoothly: "Am I not allowed, then, to show gratitude for their friendship?"

"Your 'friendship' could better be shown by giving them fair trade instead of whiskey," Firewalker muttered. He shook his head. "It is a fine game you play, d'Arcy, but you will not play it with my people. Thunderhead sees it and I see it. So will War Cloud. It is a promise." As abruptly as he had come, he departed.

"How you frighten me," Jacques shouted after him. "You are as fierce as the tales I have heard of you. . . ." Seeing him turn, his eyes slitted, Jacques blustered, "Tales from Kittanning . . ." He wanted to cow him, to have some hold, any kind of hold over him. But when Firewalker returned to loom over him, a wolf smile on his lips, Jacques was sorry he had spoken.

"If it is said I nearly killed a man," Firewalker replied quietly, "it is true. I have never hidden the fact. And if I ever meet the devil again, he will not be so lucky."

The parting look in those unholy eyes chilled Jacques despite the hot wind that was blowing from the west. But as the brave sprung easily onto his mare and loped off under a small high moon, his outrage grew. Where was the law when the near killing took place? It was not safe for decent folk to carry on their business with such savages free to roam at will. Thinking of Firewalker having War Cloud under his thumb outraged him further. It was intolerable that the fellow was as highly regarded as God himself. If only he would have a fall from grace. But he was so perfect it would never happen unless—his heart pounded—unless he were helped along.

Considering the thought, Jacques carried his lantern into the other room, dimmed it, and sat down on the edge of his bed. *Nom du Nom,* why not? Why not help him along? In fact, he had the glimmering of an idea even now. He stretched out to mull it over, not bothering to take off his boots, for he suspected he would be going out later this night . . .

The next morning, Hope had cleaned up after breakfast and just set the bread to rise when her father returned unexpectedly from the fields. When he came into the kitchen and took off his hat, she was shocked. His face under its sunburn was sheet white. He sat down heavily at the table, his head in his hands.

"Father, what is it?" She quickly covered the bread and went to him. "What's happened?"

"Our corn's gone . . ."

"Gone? What do you mean, gone?"

"Everything's down," Tom muttered. "It looks like a tornado went through it."

"I don't understand . . ."

He drew a long breath and let it out. "Someone's ridden through it."

She blinked. "On—purpose?"

"It would seem so."

She sank to the bench beside him, hardly knowing what to say, but her thoughts were flying. His wonderful corn. His pride and joy, and his very first crop on his own land. She was hit by fury. "Who would do such a thing—and to you of all people? You've given so much!"

Seeing his pain, she wanted to stamp her feet and scream and throw things the way she had when she was a child and life did not go her way. More than that, she wanted to learn who had done such a vicious thing and hold them up to shame. In addition, they should be made to clear the field and plant next year's crop.

"Who hates you enough to have done this?" she choked.

"No one that I know . . ."

"Well, obviously someone does!" It brought back the horror in Pittsburgh all over again. The ugly words smeared across stable doors, the broken window, and the stones hurled at their gig as they drove along the streets. Cowardly malicious acts from unknown hands so that they could not defend themselves. But who up here hated them so . . . or hated *her* so? Who? Her breath caught. . . .

"Firewalker!" she cried.

Tom raised his head from his hands. "Hope, for God's sake."

"Why not? Who else is angry with us—with me? Oh, damn him!"

"Hope, this kind of talk is foolish and it's dangerous. We have to live with those people, and I'll not have you stirring up trouble with unfounded accusations. My God, girl, you have nothing to go on!"

"I know him." She was breathing fire. "He hates whites, and he hates me especially."

"That may be so, but we've no proof he did it. Keep such thoughts to yourself. Trust me in this, princess."

Hope's eyes filled. He was so good and fair and honest and he worked so hard, and she was so angry and vindictive and hateful. He didn't deserve such a daughter. She put an arm around him and leaned her head on his shoulder.

"We still have the garden, and we won't go without corn once people know."

"That's so." Tom got to his feet and clamped on his hat. He went to the hearth, took down his rifle from where it hung over the mantelpiece, and in silence slung his powder horn over one shoulder. He emptied a box of lead balls into a pocket of his vest. Meeting Hope's wide eyes, he said grimly, "I don't expect trouble. This is just in case. You'll be safe here, princess, I haven't a doubt of it. You've got Josh and your own lady musket's always loaded and primed.

If anyone should need me, I'll be chopping wood in the north meadow."

After he left, Hope tucked her small dagger into her belt, put Joshua in the house, and marched to the barn. As she saddled Beauty, she told herself she would obey her father. Oh, aye, she would not tell a soul of her suspicions, but she certainly meant to tell Firewalker himself what she thought of him. She would explode if she did not. She cantered south across the clearing and alongside the poor ruined cornfield, staring in shock at the carnage there, before turning due west. Finding the great rock where she had once met Flower, she looked out over the heavily wooded slope stretching off toward the west hill and Ohio. In between was the valley of the Shenango where, on a broad river meadow between the east and the west hills, the Lenape village lay.

What she was doing was foolhardy, she knew it, but she had to talk to Firewalker himself about their cornfield. And she would know if he spoke the truth or if he lied. Brooding over the coming confrontation, she did not see the three mounted braves who had come out of the woods and were waiting on the trail ahead of her. When she realized her danger, she tried desperately to turn Beauty about, but it was too late. One seized the reins while another dragged her roughly from the mare and stood her on her feet.

With her heart in her throat, Hope managed to gasp, "Wh-what do you want?"

They made no answer, but gathered around her closely to stare. Hope stared back. She tried to appear unafraid, but her heart grew faint at the sight of their near-naked bodies glistening with red and ochre paint, and the long oiled scalp locks springing from their shaven heads. A sickening reek of bear grease, sweat, and alcohol filled her nostrils, nearly overcoming her. But what frightened her most of all was the cruelty she saw in their dark eyes.

She swallowed, and said again, "What do you want?"

She held her head high, instinct warning her not to show her enormous fright as one brave reached out a long sinewy painted arm and touched her hair. He laughed. His attention was then drawn to the dagger at her belt. He removed it, tested the blade, and returned his gaze to her.

"It's all right"—her mouth was dust dry—"take it if you want. I—I'll just be on my way then . . ." She turned to go, but he roughly caught her wrist and yanked her back. He smiled at her.

"Woman stay." He grasped her gown at the neckline, punctured it with the point of her dagger, and proceeded to slit it down the middle, exposing her thin cotton chemise and petticoat to their curious eyes. All three laughed at her yelp of outrage.

Hope struck out, charging and swinging at her surprised attacker with both fists. "Bastard!"

The brave leapt back while the other two hooted, but his retreat did not last. Returning and catching Hope's long black hair in his painted fingers, he twisted it about his hand and cruelly jerked her head back.

"Woman be quiet," he growled. "No make big noise."

Hope gritted her teeth against the pain, trying not to let terror overcome her, but she knew what her fate was going to be. They were going to rape her. It was not all clear what would happen after that. She shuddered as they tore off her ruined gown and eagerly ran their dark fingers over her arms and shoulders and squeezed her breasts.

"You—can't do this." Her teeth were still clenched. "My people will—" Her head was forced back further still. There was a flash, sun on the blade of her dagger, and then she felt a hot, raw, stinging sensation on her throat. Oh, God have mercy . . . he had cut her . . . he was going to slit her throat. When she opened her mouth to scream, the brave tightened his cruel grip on her hair. She could not suppress a moan.

"Woman be still," came the guttural command. "No make big noise." The blade was pressed against her throat once more.

Hope saw clearly that if she disobeyed, she would be slain. Perhaps they would kill her afterwards anyway. Thinking of her father and how he would grieve, she wanted to weep. What would he do without her? And why had she not listened when Firewalker warned her not to ride alone in the forest?

Wondering suddenly if they were Lenapes, she grasped at this unexpected straw. She cried: "I—I know Firewalker!"

"Woman no talk."

Her captor released his grip on her hair only to shove her to the ground and abruptly pull her petticoat and chemise up over her head. She was smothered as her body was bared to them. When she struggled to pull the garments off her face, her arms were pinned above her head, and rough hands grabbed at her breasts. There was more laughter as her legs were brutally forced apart.

She tried to pray, but she could not. She was too terrified. Every sense, every cell, every part of her was waiting for the first terrible bloody thrust and the fiery torment to begin. And her father would blame himself for this. He would never get over it and never be the same. A silent prayer came: oh, God, be with him . . .

It was then that Hope realized the cruel hands forcing apart her legs and grabbing at her breasts were no longer on her. They were gone! She did not know why, nor did she take the time to wonder. Pulling her skirt down off her face, she quickly righted her clothing and scrambled to her feet. Her heart soared at the sight that met her eyes: Firewalker, tall, savage, glowering, truly the god of the forest, stood not more than forty feet away, his great bow drawn and an arrow aimed, unwavering, at her tormentors.

"Woman," his voice rang out, "come to my side. Quickly!"

Chapter 7

Hope stumbled toward Firewalker. "My mare is here somewhere . . ." she murmured. But she knew she was too dazed to find her, and shaking too badly to ride her.

"I will return for her," Firewalker said, his arrow still aimed at the three. He asked low, "Did they harm you?"

"You—came in time. . . ."

His quick glance saw that she was shaking. Her blue gown lay in a heap on the path, and her flimsy upper garment was torn, revealing the inner curves of her breasts. They were full and tempting, and he knew these Mengwe devils would come back seeking her—unless they thought she was his.

He called to them in his own tongue, his deep voice shattering the quiet. "I am Firewalker. You are on Lenape land and it is my woman you have soiled with your filthy hands. I can kill you where you stand—or you can go back to your chieftain and tell him no Mengwe is to set foot here henceforward. The choice is yours. Decide now."

Firewalker's mouth tilted in scorn as they scrambled toward their horses. After their hasty retreat, he helped Caldwell's-daughter to mount and then leapt up behind her. Anger scorched him as he urged Nightwind to a canter—anger with the Mengwes, anger with her, and anger with himself. He resented the beauty of her slender body and the fragrance of her gleaming hair taunting his nostrils; he resented her softness and the heat her closeness stirred within him. What a fool she was to have come here alone, yet he would have known real anguish had they raped her. One moment more and he would have been too late—and had there been a band of them; he could have lost his life defending her.

Hope was hotly aware of him as they rode—the strength of his dark arms around her and the hard warmth of his naked torso pressed against her back. She also was aware of his fury boring through her. She was afraid to speak, but she must. They would be at Twin Oaks soon, and she wanted him to know that, never in this life, would she forget what he had done for her.

"I thank you, Firewalker," she said quietly. "I'm grateful."

He did not answer immediately. When he did, it was to ask sharply, "Why were you there?" He reined as a terrible thought suddenly struck him. "Is my sister back there hiding? Were you in these woods to meet her?"

"Oh, nay, I would have told you! Nay, I was alone. I—was coming to see you."

Her words surprised him. "So. I am here."

Hope wanted nothing so much as to disappear. If only she had kept silent, but there could be no turning away from the unpleasantness of the cornfield, and no going around it. She had to go through it.

"Th-the whole thing is ridiculous, I see it now." She took a breath, and blurted, "It's—really quite silly. I—I thought you had destroyed our cornfield. Someone, maybe those three, rode through it last night and trampled everything." She expected him to explode, and when he did not, she babbled on. "We lost the entire crop, and I was so furious, I—I wanted to hear what you had to say a-and—"

Firewalker was attempting to contain his fury, but he could not. He reined, slid to the ground, roughly grasped the woman about the waist, and stood her on her feet facing him.

"Why me?" It was a soft growl.

The top of her head came to his chin, and she was so close he could see the flecks of green in her gray eyes and the ripeness of her mouth. His fingers could have slipped between the white curves of her breasts and stroked them, but he clenched his hands into fists at his sides. He had never touched a white woman before, and now he was seared by the faint flower fragrance which clung to her skin and by the passion which had so suddenly gripped him. Fighting his way free of it and reminding himself he was furious with her, he said thickly, "Answer me, woman."

He saw the color drain from her face. She was attempting to hold together her torn garment so he would not see her shame, but he felt no pity for her. "I am not Mengwe," he said sharply. "I will not harm you, but you will answer me. Now."

Once more Hope felt as if she were standing beside a bonfire, as if she could stretch out her hand and touch a flame. She gasped. "I thought since you were so angry with me last night th-that you had—"

He glowered down at her as her meaning became clear. By the Eternal. "You thought I sought revenge? Because you would not teach?"

"Aye," she answered faintly. "I'm sorry. . . ."

He gave a harsh laugh. "Lady, I would not have you even had you agreed."

It was as if he had slapped her. "You *asked* me!"

"It was a mistake."

Hope felt the blood rush to her face. "I see. You took my refusal as an insult, and now you think you are insulting me. Well, you are not!"

Firewalker ignored her outburst. His hands formed a stirrup for her small booted foot. "Mount," he said coolly. "I will take you home."

"Take yourself home!" she cried, and then bit her lip. Dear God, she was so angry she was not thinking clearly. She did not dare walk home alone. She was afraid to. Face flaming, she allowed him to help her mount. She was still seething when Nightwind came to rest at the hitching rail at Twin Oaks.

"In case you did not know, those were Mengwes," Firewalker said as he helped her down.

"As I said, I am grateful." She bit off the words.

"Since I was certain they would return for you"—he heard her indrawn breath, saw her small hand fly to her heart—"I told them you were my woman. I doubt they will risk war with the Lenapes over you"—his golden eyes swept her—"although it is possible."

Despite the terror his words aroused in her, Hope managed an air of bravado. "I don't know which is more appalling, being thought your woman or having them return for me. And if you are trying to frighten me, Firewalker, I resent it very much!"

Firewalker shook his head, and the feathers stirred against his black hair. His smile was mocking. "I would never try to frighten you, Caldwell's-daughter, but you live among savages now. We take special delight in ruining white men's crops and raping their women. You must be more careful." He was surprised to hear himself saying such words. He was more surprised when he reached out suddenly, inexplicably, and traced her mouth with his fingers. Her lips were so warm and soft, a bolt of pleasure tore through his body. He said roughly, "Perhaps you should return to that place whence you came . . ."

Hope had seen the devil dancing in his eyes, but when he touched her mouth, they grew veiled. She quickly veiled her own feelings—her shock at the fiery tingling his fingers had produced and the unexpected stirring of passion. And to think, she had just stood there meekly allowing such boldness!

She said icily: "It does not suit me to return, but you're right, I must be more careful. To begin with, I intend to go down on my knees and pray that I never have to see you again!"

He smiled at her spirit. "Then you do not want me to return your mare?"

"There's the barn," she snapped, pointing to it, "and here is the hitching rail. Is my presence necessary?"

Noticing for the first time the scarlet ribbon of blood about her white throat, Firewalker's heart lurched. The bastards. He knew she had been close to death, but he had not known how close. "You are bleeding. Are you all right?"

Hope gave a bitter laugh. "Of course. I've never felt better in my life!" Feeling the sting of tears, she caught up the skirt of her petticoat and ran into the cabin. He would never see her weep. . . .

When Tom returned at noon from the north meadow, Hope was at the kitchen table mending clothes. It was as if she had never left the house. Firewalker had returned Beauty to the barn, and her father never noticed that she now wore a gown of green sprigged cotton instead of the blue one. When he reminded her again to say nothing to Firewalker about the ruined corn, Hope said she would not. She did not even want to think about the corn or the Mengwes or Firewalker.

It was Tom who later told Jacques of the damage when he came by after supper, and Tom who told the Greens, a family Hope had never met, when the whole noisy clan of them trooped by unexpectedly. They were properly outraged, of course, but it was clear that their interest lay elsewhere. It seemed that Tom had told them that Hope was teaching Flower, and now they wanted her to teach their own children. She refused as gracefully as possible, but after the good-byes were said and the three of them, Jacques included, had gone back inside the cabin, Hope lost her temper.

"Why have you told everyone about Flower?" she flared at her father. "You know it's a special situation." And as far as she knew, one which was now ended.

Tom's gray eyes widened. He said easily, "Well, now, princess, the subject just seems to come up when folks ask about you."

"Then please come up with something else. Tell them I'm dipping candles or baking bread or—or knitting socks! For goodness sake, Father, I have no intention of teaching flocks of children!" Seeing his quiet surprise, Hope was instantly regretful. She had never in her life been so sharp with him. "Daddy, I'm sorry. I didn't mean to snap."

Tom patted her shoulder. "It's all right. I see I've said more than I should."

"Nay, it's not your fault. . . ."

She felt guilty and hateful. And resentful and frightened and confused. She could not push from her mind the three Mengwes grabbing at her and forcing her legs apart—and she could still feel Firewalker's fury pounding through her, and feel his hard warm arms around her. If only she were away from all of this. If only she were still in the city where it was safe and where she could do the work she was trained to do and wanted to do. But there was no city where she would be accepted without her father's being with her, and he loved it here. And she would never ask him to leave.

Tom kissed the top of her head. "I'll say no more about it, Hope, I promise. And now I'd better catch some early sleep. I figure to be up with a delivery tonight." He lit a candle from the hearth fire and then grasped Jacques's outstretched hand. "G'night, d'Arcy. Stop by again. You're always welcome."

But he was perturbed as he climbed the steep, narrow steps to his bedchamber. Something was troubling his daughter, and it was something beyond the cornfield. More than likely it was that her talk last evening with Firewalker had not gone well. But he had gone ahead and ordered extra school supplies anyhow. The way he figured it, she was going to teach someone someday. Whether Lenapes or white, he didn't know nor did it matter.

Jacques gazed thoughtfully at Hope as she sat at the table, clasping and unclasping her hands before her. He sat down across from her, and immediately imagined her in his bed. It was a thing he dwelt on many times a day now. He had known her three whole weeks, and it galled him that he had not bedded her. *C'était incroyable.* Never had any woman treated him with as little romantic interest as did this one. Or was the wench but waiting for him to master her and cover her with kisses and tell her she had been put here on this earth for him alone? He was tempted; *mais non,* it was too risky. He must continue being her friend and confidant, and nothing more. He gave her a rueful smile.

"You look so sad, *mon amie.* Can I not help in some way?" When she shook her head, he asked, "Is it those fools, the Greens? Or your poor cornfield? Is it the—business you discussed with Firewalker? Come, *ma petite,* tell Jacques, for it pains me to see your sorrow."

Impulsively, Hope reached over and covered his hands with hers. It was all of those things and more, and she wished she could confide in him, but she could not. "It's something I must work out alone, but you're so kind to offer. So very dear . . ."

Feeling her soft hands on his and seeing the warmth in her eyes was all he needed. Caution be damned, he no longer cared. He would hold and kiss her this instant. He murmured, "And you are so very beautiful. Hope, let me take care of you."

Hope stared at him. Take care of her? She stiffened as he caught her hands and raised them to his lips. His hungry kisses covered them and her wrists and then crept up her arms.

"Jacques!" She pulled away.

"*Ma chère,* marry me. I know this comes as a surprise, but not an unpleasant one, I pray."

It was as if he had hurled a bolt of lightning at her. She got to her feet. "You can't mean it."

He moved quickly to her side and put his arms around her. "Never have I meant anything more." The softness of her body and her breasts caused his manhood to stiffen and his breathing quicken. "Say you will be my wife, Hope."

"Jacques, I—I cannot!" She wondered wildly if this were her fault, if she had somehow led him to believe she cared for him in such a way. Seeing that he meant to kiss her, she turned her head and whispered, "Jacques, nay! I'm sorry, but nay. Now please, do let me go." She did not want her father to hear.

Jacques held her tightly as he battled his fierce arousal. He yearned to take her there on the floor and flood her with the hot seed he had been withholding these many days. But she would scream and he would be a dead man. Thomas Caldwell was a war veteran who knew how to handle his fists and a musket. Nay, he could not do with her as he wished. *La belle* Hope must remain unsullied until she was legally his, and then he would make up for his deprivation. He dropped his arms reluctantly to his sides and gave her a sad smile.

"Ah, Hope, it would seem I have chosen the worst possible moment to make known my love for you."

His love? Oh, Lord. "Jacques, I'm deeply honored, but I'm not going to marry for a long, long time, if ever."

"*Ma chère,* let us talk of it later . . ."

"My answer will be the same later as it is now."

"Then I will ask again and yet again." He kept his voice easy and a smile on his lips although he yearned to shake her, the damned stubborn wench.

Hope followed him out to the hitching rail and watched in silence as he mounted and collected the reins. What more could possibly go wrong this day? She had treasured this man's companionship and now, suddenly, all of that was ended. It was as if she didn't know him. He was a stranger in her eyes.

"I have almost forgotten to tell you," Jacques lowered his voice. "In addition to the wanton destruction of your own field last night, the Jacksons on the west hill had a field and barn burnt."

"That's terrible . . ."

"It is not good. I said nothing to Thomas for I know he does not like ill said of the Indians."

Hope blinked. "Indians did it?"

"A brave was seen in the area shortly before the fire was discovered."

Something in his eyes chilled her. "A Lenape?"

"It is not known."

"I think it is, and you're not telling me."

"Now, Hope—"

Her heart went harder. "It was Firewalker, wasn't it?"

"I must admit, it is he who was seen. I'm sorry."

It was another thunderbolt striking Hope, and it took the wind out of her. Why would he do such a thing? And now she was worried about Flower. This would crush her.

"Hope, in truth, because the man was seen in the area is no proof of his guilt." He was pleased by his performance. He was defending the devil, yet the damage to him was done. He asked quietly, "Does Thomas think, then, that it was Firewalker who destroyed your field?"

"It was I who thought it . . ."

She had been so sure at first that he was guilty, and then just as sure that he was not. Now it seemed her first instincts had been right after all. She felt empty thinking about it, and she was hugely disappointed.

"Doubtless you are right," Jacques said grimly. "This now causes me to fear you are in jeopardy when Thomas is absent. I advise you to keep your musket handy at all times."

Hope tried to smile. "I do."

"*Très bon*. It will give me peace of mind when I am

away. Tomorrow I fear I must make another trip—a short one this time. I am forever coming and going."

But as he rode homeward past the tattered ghost of the cornfield and through the black woods, his peace of mind was already gone. What he had told Hope was God's own truth. Firewalker had indeed been seen before the blazes started on the west hill. But it was not the Lenape who had come here last night and quietly, mercilessly trodden down every proud green stalk of Thomas's corn. It was Jacques's own work.

Having seen Firewalker's anger with Hope the night before, he was certain they had battled, and equally certain that she would think him guilty of such an act. And so she had. And now word would spread, and Firewalker would be discredited among whites and Lenapes alike. But what this other was, this burning on the west hill, he had no idea. How ironic, and how frightening if the devil actually was involved in some vendetta against the settlers of the Donation Lands. The very thought of Firewalker on a rampage chilled him to the bone, for he himself could well be his next target. The brave hated him. . . .

The moon was already high when Tom left Twin Oaks to spend the night with his patient in labor. Hope sent him off with a smile and a wave, but afterward, she looked about uneasily. Her worried gaze went from the barn to the springhouse and then to the forest which stretched without end beyond the clearing where the cabin stood. What if the Mengwes knew that Firewalker had lied and that she was not his woman? What if they knew she lived here and even now were in those woods watching and waiting for her to be alone? And Firewalker—would he return tonight to trample another field as he had last night? Or would he burn the house and barn?

She wished suddenly, desperately, that she had gone with her father. She shook her head then. Nay, she could not begin at this late date to be afraid of the darkness and of being alone. After all, some night soon she herself would be setting out to attend a patient. With one last glance at the woods, she called Joshua to her side, went into the cabin, and bolted the door. The fire in the living room hearth was a comfort, and soon she was seated in a rocker before it, a candle by her side and a book in her hands.

She had not read more than a page when she heard hoofbeats, and saw Joshua's hackles stand up. He growled. Hope froze at the sudden sharp rapping on the door. Should she pretend she was asleep, or better still, pretend she was not there? But what if someone were desperately ill and needed her? Her knees a-tremble, she took down the primed musket from above the mantelpiece and called out: "Who is it?"

"Firewalker," came the deep voice.

She immediately thought the worst, but her good sense prevailed. If he were up to no good, would he come galloping up for all to hear and bang on the door? She drew it open after putting down her weapon and collaring the dog. There he stood, taller than tall, frowning, torch in hand, hair and skin gleaming in its light. He was so magnificent, her heart turned over. She had to remind herself fiercely that she could not abide the man.

"What do you want?" she asked. Hope noticed then that he was not alone; another Indian stood behind him. Frightened by the savage looks of the second brave, she was grateful for Joshua's snarling and barking. She felt safe until Firewalker stretched forth his arm and pointed a long finger at the dog.

"Go, my friend," he commanded. "Lie down."

"Josh, stay!" Hope snapped. She watched in disbelief as Joshua pulled free, went to the hearthstone, and lay down. He looked up at Firewalker with melting eyes and thumping tail.

With quiet restored, Firewalker turned his attention to Hope. "We seek the healer."

"He's not here," Hope answered tautly. And he might as well have taken that faithless hound with him!

The unknown brave growled: "Where is he?"

"With a patient. He expects to deliver a baby this night." She spoke firmly, but her skin crawled at the sight of him. The man was comely but not as tall nor as lean as Firewalker, and his long oiled scalp lock and glittering black eyes reminded her of the Mengwes.

"You will tell us where so we may fetch him," he ordered.

Despite her fear, Hope retorted, "My father will not leave a woman in labor!"

"Woman, you dare to—"

Firewalker spoke to him sharply in Lenape, and then turned to Hope. "My brother has grave concern for our uncle. Thunderhead has not eaten nor passed food in four days. We fear he is dying. . . ."

"I'm so sorry." She meant it with all her heart. If that brute was War Cloud, the future chieftain, she wished earnestly for Thunderhead's speedy recovery. In fact, she would offer her own services except they would laugh in her face. But if she did not, how could she call herself a doctor? She met Firewalker's worried gaze. "I will go to Thunderhead if you wish."

Their reaction was exactly as she expected. War Cloud gave a groan and shook his head. Firewalker's mouth twisted. She said quietly, "You have me or nothing."

The two brothers spoke rapidly to each other in their own tongue, and then Firewalker said, "You will come. I will saddle your mare."

As Hope wrote a note for her father and flew about the kitchen gathering the things she would need, her wiser self warned her not to go. If Thunderhead died, she would surely be blamed. But if he lived, how wonderful to have saved him. And when her head spun with those tales of heathen savages and of Firewalker's destroying property, she thought of Flower, and how gentle and clever and beautiful she was. She was frightened nonetheless as she mounted Beauty and, between the two braves, their torches lighting the way, galloped through the black woods and down the hill toward the river.

Firewalker was consumed by misgivings as they neared the village. What authority could this frail white-skinned female possibly have over sickness and death? He began to fear that she had bewitched them into bringing her, and that Thunderhead's weakened body and spirit would be further harmed by her. As the three of them galloped into the torch-lit village, he determined to stop this foolishness before she could even lay a hand on his uncle. But something told him not to interfere, and he stilled his tongue and his hand. Even so, he was filled with foreboding as they released their horses in the paddock and he led her toward the royal wigwam.

Hope tried not to shrink away as the Indians pressed close to stare. The women wore little more than the men, being clad only in cotton skirts, and she felt every eye upon her as she was escorted to a dome-shaped dwelling and through the door. Inside was bedlam. Wailing women, the stench of smoke and sickness and bear grease, shadows dancing on the rush-covered walls and flickering over the throng whose moans now beat against her ears so loudly, it was dizzying. Thunderhead, ghost pale, lay on a pallet beside a central fire with his eyes closed. As Hope made her way to his side, she swayed, stifled by the crowd pressing in upon her. She said to Firewalker, "Who are these people and why are they wailing so?"

"They are mourners."

Gazing down on the sick man, Hope's anger replaced her fear and revulsion. It was not fair to the man to already have him dead and buried. She said crisply, "It is too soon to mourn. Get them out of here."

Firewalker straightened. He resented the command in her voice, and her gray eyes held an authority he had never before encountered in a woman—except his mother. But he saw that she was right. The air was foul enough in itself to kill his uncle. As he and War Cloud ordered their kin to leave and the woman knelt by Thunderhead's side, he prayed for them both, and asked wisdom for himself. He was going to need it when Walks Alone learned of this. She had not been herself in recent days.

Hope's concern grew as she studied her patient. His skin was pale and cold to the touch and his pulse was weak. When he opened his eyes, she saw that he was without sight.

"Who is there?" he asked in Lenape, his voice strong despite his infirmity.

Firewalker answered in English, "It is a healer, Uncle. The daughter of Caldwell."

Hope took Thunderhead's hand. "Sir, I have come to help you."

The sachem's face, drawn with pain, was transformed by a smile. "Your voice is a dove song, Caldwell's-daughter, I feel better already. Are you fair?"

Hope smiled. "I fear you'll have to ask another." It was a good sign that the old man still had his humor, but she had just noticed that he spoke through clenched teeth. He could not open his jaws. No wonder he had not eaten.

"Is she fair, my nephew?" Thunderhead persisted.

Feeling Firewalker's golden eyes studying her, Hope's face grew hot.

"*Kehella*, my uncle. She is fair."

Again Thunderhead smiled. "You may proceed, Caldwell's-daughter." Closing his sightless eyes, he began to sing, and through his clenched jaws came the rise and fall of the same words over and over, like the murmuring of the wind.

Firewalker, arms crossed and his face and eyes impassive, stood gazing down on his uncle as the old man's eerie crying filled the empty wigwam. War Cloud, his own face inscrutable, sat cross-legged in the shadows rocking back and forth.

"Why is he singing?" Hope whispered.

"It is his passing song," Firewalker answered. "He sings to the spirits that it is a good night to die."

Shaken, Hope got to her feet. How could she help a man who was already reaching out toward the next world and who could not even take nourishment? This was hopeless. But if she thought that way, she was defeated before she ever began. She must get busy, and she had not a moment to lose.

"I happen to think it is a good night to live," she said firmly, "and I would like to speak to whomever has been treating this man. Is he here?" She frowned, seeing the panther eyes shutter. "He has been treated by someone, has he not?"

"*Kehella*," Firewalker muttered. "Walks Alone, the *meteinuwak*, has treated him. I will fetch her. . ."

Chapter 8

Firewalker found his mother asleep in her bunk in the longhouse. She had cared for Thunderhead so constantly these past three days, he was glad she had finally gotten some rest. He touched her shoulder.

"Mother . . ."

Walks Alone was instantly awake. She sat up. "Is he here?"

"The healer is here," Firewalker answered, "but it is not Caldwell. It is his daughter."

Walks Alone rose. She took in hand her medicine bundle and *Ohtas,* the doll being who possessed great healing power, and in silence led the way to her brother's dwelling. Observing the crowd milling outside, she frowned.

"What is this? Why are you not inside?"

"Your sons ordered us out," several muttered.

Walks Alone drew aside the door covering, entered the royal wigwam, and stared at the woman who stood there. She was young and slender and of startling fairness, and she had about her the look of an Indian although her skin was white and she wore a long pale green gown. Perhaps it was the directness of her gray eyes beneath those straight black brows, Walks Alone mused. Or perhaps it was the black as night hair which fell to a waist slim as a wand. But it was not her beauty which stunned Walks Alone to speechlessness. It was the fact that she breathed and that she was there in the royal wigwam. For Caldwell's-daughter was the woman in her vision.

Walks Alone had seen it thrice now. She had also dreamed it. There was no longer room for doubt that one of her sons was going to die, or that this woman was somehow involved. But why? How could such a thing be? What had she to do with either of them? Walks Alone almost swayed under the assault of her shock and bafflement. She caught herself.

"This is my mother, Walks Alone." Firewalker addressed Hope. "She is the sister of Thunderhead and the *meteinuwak*, the medicine woman, of our people."

"I'm honored," Hope answered gravely, not allowing her gaze to go to the woman's bare breasts.

She could not judge her age, but the *meteinuwak* was beautiful still. She was small, fine boned, and held herself proudly, and the long hair framing the dusky oval of her face seemed as thick and black as her daughter's. In the firelight, in her bright red skirt and beaded moccasins, she looked much like Flower, but her almond-shaped brown eyes were not laughing and friendly. They burned with such hostility, Hope felt withered by its intensity. She saw that she must tread carefully while she was there, for she could be in great danger from these people, and from this woman especially.

She said quietly, "Please, I must know how the chief's illness came about and how you have treated it."

Walks Alone gazed unblinking at the intruder. So this was the Hope woman of whom her daughter chattered so constantly. The woman who called herself "doctor." For the first time, she realized what the forthcoming tragedy involving her sons must be about. Of course. Because of the extraordinary fairness of Caldwell's-daughter, they would fight over her. Because of her, one of them would meet his doom. At the thought, she was filled with such bitterness she could scarcely think or make her lips move.

"I fear we have little time," Hope said when the *meteinuwak* did not reply.

"Why did the healer himself not come?" Walks Alone rasped.

"He is with a woman in labor," Hope answered, startled by the look of hatred hurled at her and by Thunderhead's singing anew his death song. "I, too, am a healer. I—healed in Pittsburgh before we came here. Please"—there was urgency in her voice—"what medicines have you given the chief and how did he respond?"

Walks Alone studied her sourly. "I do not trust you, white woman, but because you might do some small good for my brother, I will tell you what you ask. But know that I will be watching you with the eyes of a hawk to see that you do him no harm."

Hope squared her shoulders and stood taller. Some small good? And she was to be watched with the eyes of a hawk? Just who did this woman think she was?

"I have no trust in you either," she replied crisply, her eyes moving to the buckskin bag and the small carved wood Indian doll which Walks Alone held clutched in her hands. "For all I know, it was your treatment that put your brother in the deplorable condition he is in. I pray I can do more than 'some small good' for him. Now"—she crossed her arms—"either you want me to begin or you don't. Which will it be? You had best decide quickly." She was surprised to discover a quickly hidden smile on Firewalker's face.

Walks Alone pursed her lips as she gazed on the other's defiant stance and manner. This was indeed a brave woman, but even so, she yearned to drive her away. But it would accomplish nothing. Fate was in command. Nothing would change the fact that one of her sons was going to die. Nor was it in her heart to deprive Thunderhead of any help the woman might give. She would therefore tell her of the medicines she had concocted from the special roots in her medicine bundle. But the sacred articles in it—the bird claw and eagle feather, the piece of bone, the bear tooth, and her medicine stone—those precious things and her uses for them would remain secret.

She said glumly, "I would have you begin. His illness came about in this way . . ."

Hope listened carefully, afterwards thanking the *meteinuwak* with cool politeness for the information. "Eventually, I will be attempting to feed the chief," she said, "so please make a broth of whatever vegetables you have—also a broth of goose or chicken, if possible. Bring me the vegetable broth first."

"My brother has no will to eat," Walks Alone muttered, "and these past two days his jaws have stiffened."

"Nonetheless he must have nourishment," Hope said firmly. If he received none, all was truly lost. The wailing from beyond the wigwam did nothing to hearten her.

"I will have my daughter do your bidding," Walks Alone replied. Turning to Firewalker, she said, "Fetch your sister."

As Firewalker departed, Hope knelt and lay her hand on the chief's bare shoulder. "You are going to eat, my friend." She tried to sound reassuring.

"Alas, I cannot."

"You will. I will help you."

From Walks Alone, she had learned that Thunderhead was susceptible to a tightening of the bowels, but never before had it been so severe. Perhaps it was because he had lain abed these many days with a knee injury. As for the stiffening in his jaws, she had seen such a thing in malnourished children, but nowhere else. And that he had lost his sight just this day was another mystery. It made her uneasy that she understood so little, and she wondered, did this man crave death so strongly that he was willing it to happen? She had heard tales of those Indians who, wishing to die, went off alone and commanded Death to claim them. And Death obeyed. She would be wise to learn Thunderhead's wishes before she went any further.

When Firewalker returned with Flower, Hope had only an instant to exchange a smile with her before Walks Alone drew the girl outside. Hope seized the chance to speak with Thunderhead alone.

"My friend"—she took his hand and placed her mouth to his ear—"do you want to live?"

Thunderhead smiled. "*Kehella, n'tschu.* I would see and hear the wild geese fly over this land of ours one last time."

The tears came to Hope's eyes. How kind and noble his face was, how venerable, even in suffering. "Then you shall. You shall see and hear them many times yet." It was a promise she made to herself as well. "Can you open your jaws at all, *n'tschu?*" The unfamiliar Lenape word for friend seemed to come effortlessly when speaking with this noble chieftain.

He shook his head. "*Matta.*"

Walks Alone returned to the wigwam as Caldwell's-daughter was removing a small crock from her bag of medicines. When it was opened, filling the air with a sweet winy fragrance, she asked, "What is that?"

"It is conserves, a mixture of various fruits. It has great cleansing powers." Taking a jackknife from her bag, Hope carried it and the conserves to the chief's side and knelt on the mat there. She prayed for God's help and that her hands would not shake as she used the knife.

Walks Alone moved to her brother's head and her sons to his feet. "This seems very strange," she muttered. "What is the knife for?"

Hope felt as if a sword were hanging over her by the thinnest of threads. "I must pry open his jaws." She gave Firewalker a look of appeal. "I need the help of one of you."

War Cloud made a threatening rumble, but

Firewalker moved swiftly, kneeling opposite Hope at his uncle's head. "It is all right, my brother," he said gruffly, "I see that this must be done. I will help you, lady."

Hope was surprised by his support. She whispered, "Thank you."

With the eyes of the three upon her, she delicately sought, with the knife blade flat, a wide enough opening between Thunderhead's clamped teeth to insert it. Heart racing, sweat starting out on her forehead, she gently probed for endless moments to—Oh, God, there! She had found a place for the blade to slip in—there . . . Now if she could just use it as a lever. She lifted the handle slightly, felt the resistance, gently applied more pressure, and then more, more, more until finally, miraculously, Thunderhead's jaws begin to yield, slightly at first and then there was an opening that could actually be seen. He startled her with such a piercing wail, her heart nearly stopped.

Walks Alone hissed, her dark hand instantly grasping Hope's wrist, but when Firewalker uttered a warning, she withdrew. Thunderhead's cry, Hope had realized, was not the result of pain. He was beginning his death song once more.

"Firewalker, now!" Hope ordered. "Can you get your fingers between his jaws and pry them open?"

"*Kehella.*" His uncle's jaws, rigid as they were, were no match for his own great strength. Thunderhead's mouth yawned wide.

Hope laughed at the wonderful sight. "Keep them open!" she cried, and hastily spooned a bit of the juicy fermented fruit into the old chief's maw. Seeing that he was able to swallow it, she gave him more, murmuring under her breath, "Thank you, God, thank you. Oh, thank you . . ." She smiled at Thunderhead, relief swimming over her. "That's right, my friend, swallow it down. Chew it a bit if you can." To Firewalker she said, "You can release him now. The tetany—the tightening in his jaws—is leaving." It was a blessing. A beautiful blessing.

Firewalker obeyed, and then moved into the shadows against the wall where he sat, watching, waiting to be called upon again.

War Cloud joined him. "What do you think?" he muttered.

Firewalker waved off his question. His head was filled with what he had just seen, and he was in no mood to talk.

War Cloud was disgruntled. He did not crave his uncle's death, but in these past few days, he had come to accept it as an accomplished fact. Now, seeing that Thunderhead would surely live, he feared it was an unwise thing that this woman had done, interfering with both their destinies.

Walks Alone, seated on the mat at her brother's head, the *Ohtas* still clutched tightly in her hands, felt a grudging admiration for Caldwell's-daughter. Why had she herself not thought of prying open her brother's jaws to feed him? She covered her eyes. She well knew the answer.

Since the death of Diving Eagle, she had perceived the present only dimly and without interest. For seven years, she had given only half of herself to her people and her family, and now her selfishness had nearly caused her to lose her brother. She was shamed. From this moment forth, she would put her own cares behind her. She would think no more of leaving this earth until Thunderhead himself was laid to rest and she was certain her people thrived under their new chieftain—whichever of her sons it would be . . .

She watched in silence as Caldwell's-daughter tended her brother, carefully feeding him the remainder of the conserves, and afterwards gently bathing his face and cleansing his furred tongue with a damp cloth. Her small white hands were competent and rock steady as she spooned into him the vegetable broth into which she had measured out her healing herbs.

Suddenly Thunderhead said in a ringing voice, "You may return to your people, Caldwell the healer. I will live, although I doubt these eyes will ever see again."

Pleasure warmed Hope. Caldwell the healer . . . They were the most beautiful words she had ever heard. But she must not be too pleased with herself, for Thunderhead was still in danger. And she feared he was right about his sight. In all likelihood, he would not see again, but she would never tell him that. She placed her hands atop his big ones folded on his chest.

"Are you the Great Spirit, then, that you know so much, my friend?" she asked. He did not answer, for already he had sunk into a peaceful sleep.

Hope sat quietly by Thunderhead's side in the smoky half darkness, while outside the muffled wailing of the mourners continued. She fretted over her rudeness toward Walks Alone. She should not have said to her what she did—it had been retaliatory. She herself was the enemy, after all, and she had come there, unexpected, and taken over. She understood the *meteinuwak*'s resentment and why she had lashed out. She even contemplated apologizing. But the woman sat so stiffly, her face and eyes closed to any overture, that Hope knew it would be futile. When Walks Alone rose and went outside, Hope followed her, but they did not speak. She was grateful to find Flower there, and to be shown where to tend to her personal needs.

When she returned to the wigwam, Walks Alone sat in the shadows with her sons. The three murmured in low voices the remainder of the night, and when the sun rose and streamed in through the smoke hole, Thunderhead awakened and the hot rich chicken broth was brought. Hope fed it to him after first explaining to all of them exactly what she hoped it would accomplish. And it was successful. Thunderhead was taken outside where he vomited and evacuated mightily. The crisis had passed. Afterward, freshly bathed and wrapped like a babe in his bearskin, he slept for hours. When he awakened, he gazed on Hope thoughtfully as she bathed his face.

"Either I dream," he whispered, "or these eyes can see, Caldwell the healer."

Hope grew still as she saw that indeed, his gaze did seem to meet her own. "Are you—teasing me, Thunderhead?"

"*Matta*, I do not tease. These eyes see. You make powerful medicine . . ."

"*N'tschu*, follow my finger." She tried to remain calm as she moved her forefinger from right to left and then in circles. His brown eyes followed it. She was filled with such joy and astonishment, it bubbled out in happy laughter. She clasped her hands, almost prayerful. "Oh, Thunderhead, how wonderful—your sight has truly returned!"

"Because of you, Caldwell the healer." Now his eyes glowed. "I thank you."

"I didn't do it," Hope protested, "nor do I know how it happened. It seems—a greater power has touched you . . ."

"Then I will thank the Great Creator also," the chief replied solemnly, but he smiled. Looking on Hope, he nodded. "My nephew was right. You are indeed fair, Healer." He took her small hand between his. "This is my promise, *n'tschu*. You are ever welcome here with us, either to visit or to lay your head. And until I am laid prostrate at your feet, you and yours can walk these lands unafraid. None will harm you."

Hope was overwhelmed by her joy and relief, and filled with wonder for what had just come about—it could only be a miracle. And now these beautiful words of Thunderhead's. She wanted to hug him, kiss him as she hugged and kissed her own father. She wanted to blurt her thanks for his friendship and his generosity, and, aye, for getting well for her. But he was a chieftain, and she was a stranger, an outsider. She knew instinctively that she must answer with all the decorum she could muster.

"You please me greatly, *n'tschu*," she began, searching her brain desperately for the appropriate words. "In return for your kindness, know that—I am yours to command in sickness and in health. Until there is no breath left within me . . ." She blinked. Where on earth had *that* come from? She did not know, but she saw that Thunderhead was nodding, well satisfied.

The sun was high as Firewalker escorted Hope Caldwell back to Twin Oaks. Riding behind her in silence, his thoughts were alive with his memories of the night just passed. He was shamed that he had been so wrong about her, and grateful that she was exactly what she had claimed to be all along. A doctor. She had performed with great skill and compassion and gentleness, and she had been fearless. Thinking of her sharp confrontation with Walks Alone, he smiled. But he was baffled by his mother.

Normally the most reasonable of women, Walks Alone had been a witch woman last night. He did not understand it. But Hope Caldwell had downed her, and had proceeded to act with calm precision under the critical eyes of the three of them for those long hours on end. She was like no woman he had ever known, and because of her, Thunderhead lived. Now he was at war with himself.

In all fairness, he should admit to Caldwell's-daughter that he had been wrong about her. Had she been a man, he would have done so by now. But because she was a woman, his jaws were clamped as tightly as Thunderhead's had been. His brain could find no words for his tongue to speak, and the venom from their earlier encounters still ran in his veins. He steamed over her refusal to teach and her thinking it was he who had trampled their cornfield. And her closeness to the Frenchman remained an arrow in his heart. Over and over he saw her drawing d'Arcy into the dim reaches of the cabin, and over and over he felt the same fierce sting of jealousy. Remembering lifting her off her mare, standing close, feeling his own blazing heat, he clenched his teeth and held back a groan. It was clear that the less he saw of her and the fewer the words spoken between them, the better.

He felt disgust with himself then. Was he so small that he would deny her his apology for such a reason? It was not her fault that he lusted after her, or that he feared being ensnared in a net of his own weaving. He was behaving like the most addled of young bucks. He scowled, seeing that her cabin had come into sight. If he was going to say anything, it had to be now. He cleared his throat.

"I—would speak with you, Hope Caldwell." Drawing abreast of her, he saw that fatigue etched her face and had put faint purplish shadows beneath her gray eyes. It made her more beautiful than ever.

Hope had been nearly asleep in the saddle when Firewalker spoke. After giving her his help last night, she had scarcely looked at him nor thought of him again. All of her attention had been on the old chief. But now Firewalker's face held such a dark look, she suspected he had some complaint or criticism to heap upon her. As usual.

"What is it?" she asked quietly.

Firewalker glanced about, for he wanted no ears but their own to hear his words. He forced himself to mutter, "I have—been wrong about you, Caldwell's-daughter. I would not have this day grow older without telling you."

Hope was instantly wide awake—and astonished. She had never expected to hear such humbling words from him. She took keen pleasure in the triumph they gave her, but only for a moment. Her victory seemed not as important as the fact that he had cast aside his pride to admit his mistake. Firewalker, the great hunter and runner and Keeper of the Wampum, was suddenly a shamefaced boy. She was tempted to say that it was all right, that she understood why he had not believed her, but why should she? Nay, the man had been arrogant and overbearing and he deserved to suffer a bit.

She said simply, "Thank you, it's kind of you to tell me. And thank you for your support and help when I needed it. I appreciate it."

"I accept no thanks. It is you who have given my uncle life for yet a while longer."

The admiration in those golden eyes warmed Hope, and she wondered, was this a new beginning for them and would they become friends? She hoped so, for no matter what Jacques said, she now knew for certain that this was not the man who had destroyed her father's cornfield and torched another's field and barn. Nay, Firewalker was a man of honor, and she intended to tell Jacques the first chance she got.

As he galloped homeward, Firewalker's spirits soared. Thunderhead lived, and it gladdened him to have admitted his wrong to Caldwell's-daughter. She was of the enemy and she was but a woman, but she deserved his deepest respect. No longer would he think of her as Caldwell's-daughter. His uncle had called her Caldwell the healer, and so she was. She stood alone, apart from her father, and her beautiful face had glowed when he had apologized. She cared about what he thought. It made him want to do something special for her, to give her something apart from the fish and game he would provide for her and her father from now on. But what? What would make her glow like that again?

Chapter 9

After her return from the village, Hope had eaten ravenously of the huge delicious breakfast her father prepared for her, and told him everything from beginning to end. She had done her usual chores then, but after making supper she had fallen asleep and not awakened until this morning. Tom was gone when she finally crawled out of bed. He had cleaned up every crumb and spatter, swept, washed the dishes, and left her a note. He was in the east meadow mending fences, and he'd found a nice cut of venison suspended from one of the oaks in front. He'd hung it in the springhouse. Firewalker, he reckoned. Hope smiled. Aye, Firewalker for certain.

As she bathed and dressed and combed out her tangled hair, she mused over how delighted her father had been upon learning that while he was delivering a baby, she, too, was on a sick call. It was happening exactly as they thought it might, although neither of them had foreseen that the patient might be Indian, and a chieftain at that. And for Thunderhead to have awarded her and hers tribal protection—and then for Firewalker to have apologized . . .

Hope hugged herself and enjoyed the exhilaration sweeping over her. Remembering the admiring light in those lion eyes and the flush touching his dark face, she chuckled. He had been shamefaced. Downright shamefaced. And he'd deserved to be. He had needed to be taken down a peg, and she had thoroughly enjoyed seeing it. But she knew the price he had paid, and it touched her deeply. That he was the bravest of the brave, and fleet as the wind, and of remarkable intelligence was all wonderful, but admitting he had made a mistake showed her the true mettle of the man. She was still eager for Jacques to stop by and learn of her change of heart until she remembered that things were no longer the same between them. Why was her life always filled with so many complications?

She made breakfast while her many thoughts were turning over, and then seeing how lovely the morning was, she placed her food on a tray and carried it out to the stoop. She nearly collided with the small, smiling figure in doeskins who had just arrived.

"Good morning to you, Hope, my friend."

"Flower! My goodness, what a wonderful surprise. I never expected to see you!" The two exchanged a hug. "Does Firewalker know you're here?"

"*Kehella*. I came with him. He is looking at your cornfield."

Hope's feeling of well-being was instantly dampened. Why could he not just forget about the cornfield and her stupid accusation? "Did he—give some reason for wanting to see it?"

Flower's eyes danced. "I did not ask, O great Caldwell the healer."

Seeing that her friend was about to burst with her news, whatever it was, Hope grinned. "All right, tell me. And come in and let me make you some breakfast in the meantime."

As she sliced and buttered more bread and got out another teacup and the jam, Flower chattered, scarcely stopping to take a breath.

"—and so my uncle not . . . I mean, my uncle does not talk now of dying, but of hunting." She frowned with the effort of speaking correctly. "And he makes big talk of your great powers and of how fair you are. And he grumbles to my mother that he is too ancient to tryst with you."

Hope's laughter pealed out. "Tryst with me!" The old rogue. He was recovering far faster than she had ever thought possible. "I can well imagine how your mother likes that."

"My mother smiles, *n'tschu*. She sees that his rainbow arches over you. She calls him a wicked old goat, but she smiles. She is pleased."

"I couldn't be happier." Happy was not the word. She was thrilled. Relieved. Delighted. Perhaps Walks Alone did not hate her after all.

"Lenapes all pleased. Firewalker, too."

Hope felt her cheeks grown warm. "I'm glad . . ."

They sat on the shaded stoop rocking, eating, laughing, talking, drinking cups of sweet dark tea as a breeze laden with the scent of summer cooled them. But Hope grew quiet when she saw Firewalker cantering across the clearing. Something fluttered deep within her, seeing his dark body framed against the sky and grass. Teak against cobalt and emerald. It was a sight she would never forget—sun glinting off his black hair, his long bare legs gripping the mare's ebony barrel, his bow slanting across his back, a frown on his face as he glanced toward them with the sun in his eyes. Hope forgot Flower was there even as she rose, smoothed back her hair, and shook the wrinkles out of her skirt. Her heart pounded.

Flower stared, seeing her friend's white skin turn pink and her breathing quicken. What was this? Did Hope actually like her brother? She nearly laughed aloud in her delight, realizing that it was so. In fact, it was plain to see that she more than liked him. Now if only her favorite brother would behave himself in front of her and not act so stiff and stern and stupid. But it was too much to ask . . .

"You have come too soon," she called to him from the rocker. "I want to stay longer."

"I must get back," Firewalker answered, his eyes

on Hope. He dismounted, inclined his head. "Greetings."

"Greetings, Firewalker."

Studying her pink face and smiling lips, he found it difficult to believe she was the commanding woman who had confronted Walks Alone with such boldness and snatched his uncle from the hands of death. This woman was so soft and slender, so girlish in her long gown with its small pink flowers . . . As he gazed on her, a puff of wind lifted her black hair and blew it against her cheeks. Her hands flew to it and tucked it behind her ears, hands that were so small and white he craved to cup them between his own and hold them, raise them to his lips. He reined his thoughts sharply.

Hope scarcely dared breathe. Things were different between them. She saw it instantly in his face and eyes, and felt it within herself, in her heart and in every bone of her body. Things had changed.

"My father and I thank you for the venison," she said.

"I will take no thanks."

"If you wish—but it was kind of you."

Her heart thudded harder. She forced her eyes down, away from the beautiful rough planes and angles of his face, only to be confronted by that glorious expanse of polished skin and his wide shoulders. Her gaze flew back to his face. This was ridiculous. She was a physician, for heaven's sake. She had seen ungarbed men without number. But she was also a woman with a normal healthy appreciation for masculinity and virility. Now she was imagining how those long hard arms might feel slipping about her, pulling her against him, his unsmiling mouth taking hers in a kiss that was at first gentle and then growing more hungry and demanding. Growing savage . . .

A shiver rippled through her, excitement tinged with guilt. What a fool she was. She had rejected and hurt Jacques who wanted her, and now she was daydreaming about a man she could not have and certainly did not want. He was Indian! He lived in a world completely different from hers. A world that was primitive and alien and frightening, and their two peoples would always be enemies. She blinked, realizing that he was speaking to her.

"—and if it is what you both want, I will not interfere."

Hope looked up at him, embarrassed. She had not heard one word he'd said. She saw that Flower was gaping at him.

"What?" Flower cried. "Hope teach me again? You allow?"

"*Kehella.*" Firewalker was not prepared for her squeal or for her arms flying around his neck in a death grip.

She kissed him on both cheeks and crooned in Lenape, "You are the dearest and the sweetest of brothers . . . the best of brothers . . ."

He scowled and attempted to disengage himself. He had known she would be excited, but he had not expected her to be silly. He answered sternly in their tongue, "Come now, little fox, we are not alone. Also, you are choking me."

Flower released him and turned, smiling to Hope. "He says you can teach me again! Oh, Hope, he is best of brothers, *kehella?*"

Hope saw that Firewalker was genuinely pleased by his sister's joy, yet she sensed there was more to his offering than wanting Flower's happiness. Meeting his eyes, she saw their message. This was for her. For her . . . She smiled, and knew she was beaming.

She said softly, "I must agree, Firewalker, you are the very best of brothers . . ."

"You will teach her, then?"

"Aye." Embarrassed by his long, openly admiring gaze, Hope blushed and laughed.

It was a low happy sound, music to Firewalker's ears, and the sight of her delighted his eyes. The wind lifted her hair just then so that once more it was caught in her long lashes. A gleaming black tendril lay across her lips. He commanded his hands to remain at his sides, not reach out and smooth it back into place. He watched greedily as her own small hands did it.

"When can I come, Hope? Tomorrow?"

Flower's words jarred Hope back to reality. She had been caught in another web of make-believe, imagining that she saw hunger in those golden eyes. She lifted her chin. It was not so. His eyes held respect and admiration, and he was pleased that she would be teaching Flower again. It was nothing more.

"Hope, when?" Flower persisted.

"Any time tomorrow is fine."

"Firewalker?" Flower turned to her brother and asked in Lenape, "Is all right? You do not have to bring me—I am well able to come alone." She sighed and made a face. He would never allow it, not with the stupid Mengwes about.

Firewalker considered his young sister thoughtfully. She knew nothing of the Mengwe attack on Hope, nor that Lenape braves had been patrolling both the highlands and the flatland ever since. She could indeed ride there in safety now, but he wanted to bring her. But only the first day, he told himself. Only the first day.

"Tomorrow is satisfactory," he said. "I will bring you in the morning—but you must promise me you will not pine for those things you read about in books. I would have a good man and a good life for you."

"I promise." Seeing that he was satisfied, she climbed onto her pony's back, ready for departure.

Firewalker also mounted. He asked Hope, "Is your father here?"

"Nay." Hope's heartbeat had returned to normal, and she was able to look up at him with detachment.

"He's in the east meadow mending fences. You're welcome to go there if you want."

"There is no need. Tell him I will help clean up that cornfield and plant it when the time is at hand."

It was as if he had thrown cold water on her. "I've told you—we don't blame you."

Amusement glittered in his eyes. "I would no longer protest if you did. It is said I am on a rampage."

"A rampage?" She was remembering Jacques's words—a field burned, a barn torched, and Firewalker seen in the area. It was impossible. This man in front of her was not the one who had done those things. She shook her head. "I can't believe it."

Flower added hotly, "They come yesterday with guns and call him hot-spur horse thief!" Gone was her careful English. "No find horse. Was stolen same night you save our uncle."

Hope's outrage was immediate. "Who are these people? I will go to them and tell them we were together the whole night!"

Firewalker's lips curved.

Flower giggled. "Hope, that—not sound too good . . ."

"What do you mean, not sound good?" Hearing suddenly what she had said, Hope grinned. "I admit, it didn't sound quite the way I intended. But you needn't fear, *n'tschu,* I'll not disgrace your brother. I'll simply tell those folk exactly what happened, but first I must know who they are. Father and I will go to them today, I promise you."

"Nay, Hope." Firewalker's heart filled as he listened to her. His gesture of friendship toward her father, a small offer to help with his cornfield, had become a thing he would never forget. She was defending him.

Hope blinked. Did he realize he had just called her by name for the very first time? She asked quietly, "Why not, pray?"

"I have already told them I did not steal their

horse. If they cannot believe it, they must deal with me, not you. I will not hide behind a woman's skirts."

"You will not be hiding behind my skirts," she reasoned. "It simply makes sense to tell them that Thunderhead was ill and I tended him the night long and that you were there, too."

"I will not involve you."

"Why are you so stubborn? I can help you. They'll believe me more than they will you. It's a natural thing for people to believe their own kind."

"I forbid it."

He was entranced as she gazed up at him angrily. Her eyes, as she shaded them from the sunlight, were molten silver, and her face was suffused with glorious color. By the Eternal, why was she not Indian?

Flower said suddenly, "Our mother has already told the white men of Hope." Seeing his look of angry disbelief, she nodded. "I sorrow, but is true. She say whites believe whites, not Indians."

Hope saw the storm coming. Firewalker's eyes fairly crackled as he looked down on her from the back of Nightwind.

"If they come to you," he ordered, "you will send them to me."

She gave him a teasing smile, a thing she had never dared do before. But then he had never called her Hope before. "You'd have me lie?"

"I would have you say nothing. You will send them to me."

"He not always so sour," Flower muttered. "He—"

"Enough!" Firewalker turned Nightwind's head to the south. "We go."

Flower shrugged and threw Hope a cheery wave. "Until tomorrow, my friend."

"Until tomorrow, *n'tschu*. Good-bye."

Hope watched pensively as the two cantered across the clearing. When they had disappeared into the woods, she carried the breakfast tray inside.

Would she really see them tomorrow? she wondered, for she had displeased Firewalker again. The two of them could not be together ten minutes without clashing. She recalled with some surprise that she and Sam had never argued.

Sam. The banker and gentleman, the essence of politeness and honor, the man with the speckless reputation destined to have the world at his feet. The man who had not had the decency to face her when he had abandoned her. But Firewalker, the heathen savage and hater of whites, would not hide behind her skirts. She knew instinctively that he would never, never, never turn his back on her. . . .

Walks Alone had been two days in the deep woods gathering herbs and roots for her medicines. After talking as a friend to those plants she had chosen, she had sung to them, plucked them, placed them in carefully prepared bags and baskets, and then carried them back to the village for drying. She had returned with her bounty just as her brother was emerging from the sweat house by the river. Observing him wade into the cool water to bathe and refresh himself after his steaming, her mouth tilted into a smile of tenderness.

Already Thunderhead looked his old self, and he walked with such a spring in his step she knew she could put her mind to other concerns. There were so many of them, she was ashamed to ask the Creator to intervene. Nor would she. She had been raised to make her own way and solve her own problems. Nor would she beg Him to change that which already had been decided concerning her sons. If one was meant to leave this earth, she would accept it. But she could not bear the thinking of it . . .

Entering the longhouse, she drew the curtain across her compartment, and in privacy removed the doeskins she had worn into the woods. She donned her red cotton skirt, leaving her breasts bare, for the day was hot. After oiling her skin against sun and insects, she took her basket outside, lowered herself to the earth, and began to sort its contents. As she did, Hope Caldwell came to her thoughts. She sighed. The woman was ever in her thoughts nowadays.

Walks Alone regretted having behaved toward her with rudeness, and she did not enjoy hating her—but she could not help herself. She begrudged and resented this stranger's becoming so involved in her sons' lives that she would be present for the dying of one of them—and perhaps be the cause of it. Walks Alone gritted her teeth. She could not prevent that which had been predestined for her sons, but her daughter was still under her command. A daughter whose sun rose and set upon Hope Caldwell.

Now it would end. From this moment forward, she would permit no further friendship between Flower and Caldwell's-daughter. That much at least was in her hands. As she spread the sorted piles of roots, bark, bulbs, and flowers on a great flat rock for drying, Flower appeared in a breathless rush.

"My mother, I have good news!"

The *meteinuwak* saw that her daughter's cheeks were flushed and her eyes bright with excitement. "Where have you been?"

"At Hope's." Seeing her mother's suddenly veiled gaze, she added gently, "Mother, I was in no danger. I went with Firewalker. He had business there."

Walks Alone held herself stiff so she would not tremble. "What manner of business was that?"

"The cornfield. He told Hope he will help clear and plant it when the time comes." She added quickly, "It is but payment of his debt for our uncle."

"I see," Walks Alone answered quietly. Even her lips felt stiff with the outrage that stung her.

So. Her son was above clearing the fields and planting the corn of his own people as was every other Indian male. It was woman's work. But he was not too proud to do it for the white man and his beautiful daughter. Remembering Hope Caldwell's soft, milk white skin and her eyes that looked like the dawn, Walks Alone knew her first instincts regarding the woman had been correct. Her sons were bewitched and, like two great bulls, would fight to the death over her. She thrust away the dreadful image.

"And what is the good news of which you speak?" she asked.

"Hope is going to teach me again. Firewalker told her he would not interfere. I go tomorrow." In her joy, Flower did not notice that Walks Alone made no answer, but continued to spread out her bits of bark and leaves to dry. "Oh, Mother, I am so happy! It is a dream come true, to learn to read and write. I must go now to tell my uncle and my friends." As an afterthought, she asked, "Am I needed for anything now?"

"*Matta,*" Walks Alone said brusquely, and waved her off. She simmered as she finished her work, and afterward grimly sought Firewalker. She found him repairing the fish dam on the river, and watched in silence for some moments before she spoke.

"Flower has told me her good news."

Seeing his mother's taut face and pale lips, Firewalker waded ashore. "Why are you displeased?" He thought her anger towards Hope Caldwell had vanished upon seeing her competence.

"Why have you done this thing without asking me?" Her voice quivered in her fury. "I have lived forty-three winters and treated and guided our people and received their respect without reading or writing. Not even Thunderhead has learning. Why then is it so necessary for Flower?"

Firewalker was surprised by her vehemence. He answered calmly, "She craves it, and I no longer see harm of it. It will be to the maid's good, not her detriment."

"Pah!" The brown eyes flashed. "And for you to plant the corn of those people—it is foolishness. It will be thought you did it out of guilt."

Firewalker was disturbed by the unhappiness he

saw in his mother's usually serene face. More and more she was becoming a woman he did not know. "What is all of this, Mother? What worries have you not told me yet?"

Walks Alone shook her head. She had not told either son of her terrible vision, nor would she. Why blight their lives with a thing that might happen tomorrow or not for ten winters yet? She answered, "It is that I—fear for you. It is said you have laid waste a cornfield, started two fires, and stolen a horse. I know none of this is true, but the white man thinks it is so, and that is bad. For the first time in my memory, my worries for you ride yoked with those I feel for your brother."

Firewalker laughed. "Then lighten your heart. I promise you, nothing will come of this. As for War Cloud, I am watching over him." So far as he knew, he had drunk no more whiskey.

Walks Alone said dully, "I doubt watching over him is enough. Your brother is adrift. It is as if I were maneuvering a boat with neither paddle nor rudder. He will not be steered. His mind does not go beyond the next hunt or the next meal or his next pleasure. I am failing him." And failing her beloved. "More and more I fear for our people if he becomes sachem."

Firewalker clasped her shoulders. "You are tired after your gathering. You have forgotten a chieftain is moved only by the breath of his people. He can lead them nowhere without their consent."

"It is that which I fear. Your brother is well liked, and many will gladly follow his careless ways. A life of sloth is easier to live than any other. . . ."

"Do you trust me, my mother?"

"You know I do." Walks Alone lay a hand to her son's dark face. It was a comely face, but more than that, she saw such kindness there.

"Then you will not worry. I will be by his side. War Cloud is going to be a fine chieftain."

Walks Alone nodded, but in a black corner of her

mind was the fear that War Cloud would be dead before that time ever came. Her greater terror was that if he did indeed become chieftain, it could mean only one thing—that Firewalker, her best loved, had been slain by his hand. In a voice strange to her own ears, she murmured, "Let us not talk of it further just now, my son. . . ."

Chapter 10

Hope could not stop smiling. It seemed everything good was happening at once. After fearing Flower would not come for her lesson, she had had four of them in the past two weeks, and this morning—this morning, she, Hope Caldwell, had treated a second patient!

Her father, just returned from a late morning visit to a patient of his own, studied her curiously across the kitchen table as he ate. He grinned.

"All right, let's hear it. You look like Christmas morning and your birthday all rolled into one. What's put that look in your eyes?"

Hope gave him a mysterious smile and pushed a skillet of cornbread and a small crock of molasses toward him. "Something happened while you were gone."

Tom stroked his beard, eyes teasing. "Well, now, let's see—you finished knitting my sweater?" He had a damned good idea what it was.

"Father, I set a broken finger!"

He beamed. "Go on!" Sonofagun, he'd been right. He knew it wouldn't be too long before the news about Thunderhead got spread around. "Who came?"

"Luke Springer. The right forefinger. Maybeth came with him, and she's invited us over for supper tonight."

"Good." He slathered a wedge of hot cornbread with butter and molasses.

The Springers had arrived from the east shortly after they themselves had gotten there. Hope had met Maybeth then and liked her, but she'd not had the heart for any socializing—so this supper invitation was another breakthrough. They were coming fast now. Thunderhead, Flower's lessons, and now the first neighbor coming to Hope to be treated. It was all good. He hadn't seen her looking so healthy or happy in a long, long time.

"I've been wondering," Hope added, "since Firewalker is allowing Flower to come, do you think maybe I should offer to teach those boys he mentioned earlier?"

Well, well, that, too . . . She was finding her teaching legs sooner than he'd expected. Tom covered his amusement with a serious face. "I think maybe you should. You'll recall I liked the idea all along."

"Aye. But I recall that Firewalker changed his mind about it overnight. Flower says he may come with her this afternoon, and if he does, I'll ask him. And if he agrees, and if the boys show any interest and aptitude, I'll order books. In the meantime, I could copy lessons for them from Flower's book when it gets here."

"Sounds reasonable."

He poured more molasses on the surprisingly good cornbread, and debated whether or not to tell her he'd already ordered a crate of school supplies. He decided not. He'd do as he planned. If the lads wanted to learn, then he would confess. He took a bite of cornbread, chewed, and gazed on her contentedly. What a pretty thing she was—sun-kissed face, the roses in her cheeks matching her pink dress, her eyes dancing like a dawn full of stars, her hair two gleaming black Indian plaits. All of this country living was good for her. But then he suspected it was more than sunshine and fresh air. He had seen more than once that she was affected by Firewalker.

He asked nonchalantly, "Is Firewalker pleased with Flower's progress?"

"Aye. It's why he might come today. To see how she's doing." Hope was clearing the table when she heard Joshua's frantic barking. "It seems they've arrived."

Tom finished his tea, rose, and stretched. "That was a good meal, girleen." He kissed her cheek. "It seems the happier you are, the better the vittles get around here."

Hope put her hands on her hips. "Are you suggesting that my cooking has been less than perfect?"

His eyes crinkled at the corners. "It's been—just dandy. It's certainly kept me from starving—"

"You hound! Who told Sally to keep me out of the kitchen all those years because I had to study? Who told me I was going to be a doctor, not a housewife?" They were both laughing as she chased him into the living room and hurled her balled-up napkin at him. He ducked.

Firewalker, looming in the doorway, caught it. Seeing her pink and laughing and looking like a young maid with her black braids tumbling down her back, he forgot himself. He captured her small hands and pressed the colorful square of calico into them. Clever words formed in his brain, but never reached his lips, for he was stunned by the velvety softness of her skin and the startled widening of her eyes as she gazed up at him. He heard himself mutter stupidly, "I believe you dropped this . . ."

Hope was still laughing. "I was pretending it was a rock! This man insulted my cooking."

He freed her abruptly, but she was astonished. He had touched her. He had actually caught and held her hands, and his were big and hard and warm and protecting. And that look in his eyes . . . She knew now that she had seen it there once before. She had dismissed it then, but now she could not. It was hunger.

Lord. She enjoyed her fantasies of being held and

kissed by him, and she enjoyed the sense of danger she felt in dreaming of the forbidden, but it was all make-believe. She did not want him to want her. She looked away in confusion, but his image was burned in her mind: his towering darkness dominating the small living room, white feathers in his black hair, silver bands on those long arms, his small breechclout—so indecently small. He was of another time and another place, a dangerous time and place. He did not belong in a room with lace curtains, an Oriental rug, and a Chippendale desk. In a daze, she watched her father greet him warmly, watched Tom next turn to Flower and request that she recite her alphabet for him. Hope reached out for the safety of it, putting her whole attention on it, but she still felt the heat of Firewalker's gaze upon her.

As his sister eagerly complied, Firewalker's pride in her swelled, as did his disgust with himself. He craved this woman so fiercely he'd had to forbid himself to think of the coming of this day and of seeing her again. His entire mind and body would have been consumed by it. Now, here he stood in this enemy dwelling, this dark, hot, closed-in place built on stolen Lenape land, just so he could look at her and hear her voice. It was madness. The only thing that seemed real was the big hound joyously baying at him and waving his tail.

"Joshua, hush!" Hope said sharply.

"It is all right." Firewalker softly snapped his fingers and the dog came. Standing on his hind legs, his huge paws on Firewalker's chest, Joshua gently lapped his face, his brown eyes adoring. Cradling, stroking the dog's head, Firewalker gravely touched noses with him. "You are a good dog, my friend."

A shimmer of fire and ice brushed across Hope's flesh as she watched them. How beautiful and how graceful the brave's big hands were. She wondered, scarcely breathing, how those long dark fingers might feel stroking and caressing her. When Firewalker looked down at her, his golden gaze capturing and holding hers, she sensed she had but to say aye and she would know. She fought free of his eyes and the mesmerizing thought, and as Joshua padded to the hearth and settled down, content, she hurriedly collected paper, quills, and ink.

"It's time you two left us," she said briskly. "Flower and I have work to do."

When the men returned, Flower was bubbling over with all she had learned.

"She is progressing satisfactorily then?" Firewalker asked.

"Aye, she is very quick. She's printing sentences already. Come, I'll show you." Hope led him to the kitchen with Flower trailing after. She took several papers from the table and handed them to him.

Studying the pages and seeing only meaningless scratches, Firewalker felt envy. What foolishness it was that the maid was learning this precious thing and not himself. He reminded himself again that he could never accept teaching from a woman. Certainly not this one whose gray eyes had cast a spell upon him, and whose voice was the low music of running water. His heart roaring, he returned the papers to her and wrapped himself in dignity.

"I am pleased." He turned to Flower. "My sister, it is time we left."

"May we talk first?" Hope asked quickly. All throughout Flower's lesson, she had worried and wondered—should she still offer to teach the boys? Was it wise now, considering the way he had looked at her? She cringed thinking that he might somehow have sensed her ridiculous fantasy about him, but that was foolishness. Besides, this was a thing she felt strongly about. She wanted to do it for him. When Tom drew Flower outside, leaving them alone, she said, "I wanted to discuss the boys you mentioned earlier."

"What about them?"

She hesitated. He was his aloof, distant self once

more, but if she did not discuss the matter now, it might be another whole week before she saw him again, if then. She swallowed. "I was wondering if you . . . might want them to come a time or two with Flower. Just to see if—"

He frowned. "You would teach them?"

"I would like to try," she answered quietly. "It doesn't seem as impossible as it once did." When he remained silent, her face grew warm. "Of course, if you would prefer I didn't . . ."

"That is no longer true." It was difficult to think about anything but the small dimples he had just discovered on either side of her mouth. He wanted to press his lips to them, press kisses on them. He clenched his teeth. He had known it would be painful to see her again, but not this painful.

"Good." Hope could not meet his eyes, not when they burned over her like that. She busily neatened Flower's small stack of papers on the table and placed the ink and quills beside it. "I know I've taken you by surprise, so don't feel you must answer right away."

Firewalker's mouth tilted. "I am not taken by surprise." Nothing she did from now on would surprise him.

"I see." She felt a stab of disappointment as an unexpected thought occurred to her. Of course . . . he had foreseen that she would feel grateful and would relent and do exactly what she had just done. She laughed. "I—suppose that's the real reason you brought Flower back." She moved the things to another spot on the table.

Firewalker abruptly caught her shoulders and spun her to face him. "Stop fussing with those things and look at me!" Seeing her eyes widen in astonishment, he growled, "I did it for you. . . ."

She felt the power in his hands, and a fire storm of excitement and terror swept over Hope. What was happening to her? She had never felt this way when Sam touched her and had never wanted him as much as she suddenly wanted this man. But she dared not let him know. He must never know. Calling on the strength she had summoned so often these past months, she managed to say quite calmly, "I'm glad. I—rather thought you did, and hoped you did." She even managed a smile. "Thank you again."

Firewalker expelled a deep breath and released her. He was not pleased with himself, grabbing her that way and saying what he had. It told him, more strongly than ever, that he should not see her again. She was destined to go one way in life and he another. But how could he not see her again when she had just given him the prospect of a new beginning for his people? The choice between darkness and dawn. Thinking of his young kin, even one of them, being able to read and write the tongue of the enemy, made his spirits soar. He could not turn down such a thing.

"I accept your offer," he said.

"Very good." Fresh terror clutched Hope at the prospect of seeing him more often. How long could she hide that one look from his eyes and one touch from his hand destroyed her? But perhaps she was fretting needlessly, for the thing mightn't work out at all. "I would like a trial period to make sure of their interest."

"It will be so."

"And you realize I have no books yet. I'll just teach them the alphabet and some simple words as I have Flower."

"That is fair."

"Yes, well—" Her heart pounded. "Is tomorrow morning all right to start?"

"Tomorrow is satisfactory. And they will be interested, I promise you. I will tan their hides if they are not."

Hope had to smile as she led the way to the front door. "I thought Indian children were never punished."

"These three are not children. They will soon enter manhood."

Flower, still chatting excitedly with Tom on the stoop, looked up as they appeared. "Who will enter manhood?"

"Your cousins."

"They will be joining you in class," Hope added. "At least for a while."

"Then it will be a real school! Can I help teach?"

"Perhaps . . ." Hope put her hands to her cheeks. Oh, nay! Oh, Lord. A thought had just struck her, a thing she had forgotten completely. How could she be so stupid?

Tom scowled, seeing the wild look in her eyes. "What is it?"

"I can't believe this. I've told the Greens and Johnsons I wouldn't teach their children, and now when they hear this—"

Tom said abruptly, "Don't tell them."

"Don't tell them? How can I not with folks coming at all hours to fetch you to some sickbed? The word will spread."

"Hell. Teach their young'uns, too, then. It seems simple enough to me."

Hope said hotly, "I assure you, teaching eight or ten children is not simple if one bears in mind I have no supplies and I've never done this before!"

Tom stuck a blade of grass in his mouth. "Well now, let's see. One reckons you'd have two Johnsons at the most, but the four Greens you can forget. Jeb's varmints will never sit still for learning. Add four Lenapes and I count six. Is that too many? As for supplies, now is as good a time as any to confess they're already ordered." He grinned sheepishly. "I figured something like this might happen."

Hope stared at him. "I don't believe it—you've ordered school supplies?"

"Aye." He looked like a cat filled with cream.

Hope shook her head, and grinned back at him. He'd always had a knack for simplifying things and rescuing her. She threw her arms around his middle, lay her head on his broad chest, and hugged him. She whispered, "How come you're so clever?"

Firewalker was not amused. There was nowhere his people could go and nothing they could do without the constant intrusion of whites. He should have known this would be no different, and he would not have Lenape youth mingling with them. He moved quietly to where Nightwind stood waiting for him.

Hope saw his stormy eyes. "I'm sorry, I didn't plan it this way. I hope it won't change your mind."

He was about to inform her that, aye, his mind was certainly changed, when he heard the familiar fluttering of wings. Looking up, he saw *memedhakemo*, the dove, his totem, alighting on a branch, and looking at him with her bright eyes. He hid a smile. By the Eternal, if she approved, who was he to protest?

"Nay, Hope, I have not changed my mind. It is all right."

Jacques d'Arcy had not expected to be gone so long from the valley on his jaunt north. He had made a longer, wider loop than usual, met with tribes he'd not known were there, and had, in fact, to buy another mule to carry back his booty. Now, in great high spirits, he sang bawdy songs as he unpacked his goods and stored them on the shelves in his storeroom. Since it was still early in the day, he could bathe leisurely, change clothes, and arrive at Twin Oaks in time for an invitation to supper. He meant to propose again to Hope this night, and this time, he felt in his bones that she would be ready to accept. She would have missed him. *Mais alors*, now was not the time to think of her and grow overheated. He had much to do.

Unstrapping a bale of peltries from his new mule, he mused on what news might await him. He hoped Firewalker had gotten himself into more trouble and that Thunderhead was planted in the ground. The old devil had seemed not long for this world when he'd last seen him. As Jacques heaved the bale to one shoulder, he heard hoofbeats, and turned. *Bon,* it was War Cloud. He would hear of the goings-on in the valley sooner than he had anticipated. Depositing the peltries in his storeroom, he returned to greet the brave.

"*Bonjour, mon ami,* it is good to see you."

"You have been gone long," War Cloud muttered.

"Twenty-one days to be exact. Of course, if Thunderhead would but give me the furs I seek, I would not need to venture so far to earn my keep." He fetched the tin cups, splashed rum into both, and offered the fullest one to the brave. "Sit, *n'tschu,* and drink."

War Cloud hesitated, but only for an instant. He was angered, frightened even by how fierce his craving for alcohol had become. But when it was offered to him like this, the Creator himself could not have stayed his hand. He took the cup, lowered himself to the grass, and tried not to gulp down the fiery brew but to sip it discreetly.

Jacques seated himself on a log close by and did not allow his amusement to show. He said gravely, "I am almost afraid to ask—does your uncle still breathe?"

"*Kehella.* He was near death, but the woman healer came and worked great magic on him." Thinking of her, War Cloud gave up all pretense of sipping and gulped half the rum.

Jacques stared, halting his cup halfway to his lips. He asked carefully, "The white woman healer?" The sounds of August—the hummings and whirrings of insects and the chatterings of bobolinks in a nearby meadow—pressed in on his ears as he waited for an answer.

"*Kehella,*" said War Cloud finally. "The Hopewoman. Because of her, my uncle lives. He is his old self. I rejoice as do we all."

Jacques gaped at him. What? Hope had saved the

old devil? Hope? *Sacre,* it was not to be believed. He saw by the brave's sour countenance that he was not rejoicing, but then one did not contradict War Cloud.

"How is it"—he pretended only faint interest—"that the woman treated him rather than the man?"

"The healer was not there. My brother and I went for him, but only she was there, and my uncle lay dying."

"Ah."

At the thought, War Cloud tilted back his head and drained the remainder of his rum in one swallow. He could no longer contain his bitterness. "But for that damned female," he muttered, "I would be chief. My uncle was singing his passing song."

Jacques's eyes glittered. *Mon dieu,* what a damnable thing. But he must not brood; he must think, for what was done was done. To the good, the brave was confiding in him for the first time. He refilled War Cloud's cup.

"I understand well how you must feel, *n'tschu.* I know you are pleased that Thunderhead breathes, but on the other hand, it is unfortunate that you have been deprived of the honor you so richly deserve. You will make a fine chief. . . ."

War Cloud shot him a burning black gaze. His brother was right. This devil was just waiting for him to become sachem, and was plying him with alcohol for his own gain. He had suspected it all along, but ignored it. He would continued to ignore it. Never would a white man have a hold on him, nor would his brother, Firewalker, nor would this damned brew. He was young and he was strong and he was in command of himself. At least most of the time.

"You are right." He took another swallow and licked his lips. "I will make a fine chief if that day ever comes. . . ."

"It will come, *n'tschu.*"

Jacques's skin crawled as he wondered what was going on in the brain beneath that ugly greased scalp lock. One never knew what these savages were thinking. He moved to another subject. "Does all go well with the rest of your family? With Firewalker?"

War Cloud gave an ugly laugh. "The damn fool whites on the west hill say he stole their damned horse."

Listening to the tale, Jacques noticed the brave's tongue was growing thick. He could learn many things now if he but probed gently enough. "It seems odd, does it not," he ventured cautiously, "all of these recent happenings tied to Firewalker? The cornfield, the fires, the horse. What do you make of it, and how does he defend himself?"

War Cloud's eyes flickered resentfully. He grunted. "Defen' from what? He is not guilty. If it was my brother who took their damn horse or started fires, none would've seen him. Ghos' in the night . . ." He spoke slowly so his tongue would work.

Jacques smiled. "You are right, of course. He would indeed be a ghost in the night. I forgot but momentarily that I spoke of Firewalker who is perfect in all ways."

The two sat in silence for a long time, and then the big brave sank his head in one hand, covering his eyes.

"I wish—I pray to all the spirits he will—fall. . . ." War Cloud's world had never seemed so bleak. He told himself he was young and strong and in command, but in truth he was not. It was Firewalker who was in command while he himself was weak and growing weaker. Before d'Arcy had begun supplying him with this damned brew, he was reasonably happy and confident and clever. Now he was a hog. He would do anything to quench his thirst for it. He would give his clothes and his weapons . . . he would give his wife . . . he would give his own mother. . . .

He shuddered and drank more deeply, loving yet hating the warmth it gave him. He yearned to kill this devil Frenchman for enslaving him, but he dared not, for then he would have no more liquor. He held out his cup.

"I would have more, white man. . . ."

Jacques had been astonished by the brave's confession, but he said easily, "Of course, old friend." He poured out the remainder of the bottle, and clapped his shoulder. "I understand well that brothers can be troublesome. Did I ever tell you, I have a brother who is so high and mighty, he thinks he is king of France?"

It was a lie, but it served its purpose. War Cloud actually smiled. But Jacques was uneasy. He hoped to God the devil would not remember any of this. If he did, he would be enraged at revealing so much, and there was no telling what he might do. Jacques doubted if anyone, dead or alive, had ever seen him so vulnerable.

War Cloud looked at the Frenchman with glazed eyes. "Did I ever tell you, *n'tschu*"—he spoke slowly for his tongue was numb—"that my brother craves the Hope-woman? My mother does not know. S'good, for she hates her. . . ."

Jacques sat very still, the sounds of the cicadas whirring filling his ears. He said softly, "You jest." Thinking of his enemy, a naked savage, lusting for the woman he had chosen as his own, caused murder to stir in his heart.

War Cloud shook his head. His scalp lock swayed. " 'S no jest. He says nothing, but he is my brother. I see that he burns for her. My sister goes for lessons, my young cousins go, and he goes to see their progress." He put down the cup, sank his head heavily into his hands.

Jacques felt as if a tomahawk had cleaved his skull. It was too much. Hope had interfered with Thunderhead, she was teaching savages at Twin Oaks, Firewalker craved her. . . . What more could happen? "When did this all happen?" he rasped, but the brave seemed not to hear.

"I am doomed," War Cloud muttered.

"You are not doomed," Jacques snapped. "You are drunk."

"*Kehella,*" he said thickly, "a thing my brother will never be. Drunk. He will make a far better chieftain." He shook his head, gave a short wild bark of laughter. "Man, I am doomed even if he joins with th' woman and c'n never be sachem. None listen t' me when he speaks, and th' damn woman'll be underfoot meddling, teaching, ruining everything. . . ."

Joins? Firewalker intended to wed her then? The veins in his temples swelled. *Mais alors,* it would never be. Never. He would kill the devil before he would allow such sacrilege to happen.

Chapter 11

Hope carried her mending to her favorite spot under one of the front oaks, and lowered herself to a blanket. As she darned one of her father's hose, she thought back on the morning. It had not gone well. In fact, she was surprised that Firewalker had not arrived by now to see why she had sent his three young kin packing. It was what she had feared might happen, and it was a shame because, like Flower, they were quick and capable.

They had had three good productive lessons in the past week, but yesterday, Tuesday, they had been bored and refused to finish learning the alphabet. She had promised that they would soon have books and paper and quills of their own, but they had stared right through her with their coal black eyes. When Flower had given them a tongue-lashing, they laughed at her. She was a woman, what did she know? Hope had been ruffled, but kept her dignity. She made Flower promise not to tell Firewalker, for she wanted to give them one more chance. This morning they had taken and destroyed it.

Rowdy from the moment they had galloped up whooping on their pintos, the three had then proceeded to ignore her. They had wrestled one another, raced and chased each other around the outside of the cabin, and they had played ball. And although they were only boys, all three were taller than Hope, and when they began teasing and taunting her and she saw the full extent of their disrespect, that was the end. She sharply ordered them to leave and told them not to come back unless they could behave themselves and wanted to learn.

She sighed, thinking of how they had galloped away, still laughing and whooping. It had been maddening, being so helpless. And she was sorry to have failed Firewalker. He would be disappointed. Hearing hoofbeats, she quickly got to her feet, wondering what he would say and what would happen next. But it was not Firewalker riding out of the woods and into the clearing. It was Jacques d'Arcy. It had been ages since she had seen him, and as he tethered his horse and strolled toward her, Hope's stomach knotted. She wondered if he were going to propose again and try to kiss her.

"Hallo, *chérie.*"

"Hello, Jacques." She gave him a friendly smile and put down her mending. "It's been a while. It's good to see you."

"It is good to be back." As he had hurriedly bathed and changed into presentable clothing and ridden there, he had raged over Firewalker's wanting to join with her. But did Hope want to join with him? It was a thing he meant to find out. Forcing himself to calm nonchalance, he returned her smile and gazed about him. "So, how are things at Twin Oaks?"

"We're doing well. As usual, Father is gone. Quite a few babes are being born up here."

He nodded. "It is the same everywhere." It reminded him of the delicious thought he had entertained frequently while he was gone: planting his children within her. It was going to happen, he vowed it would, and soon.

"Can I offer you anything?" Hope was hugely relieved that he was not in a romantic mood, but he was behaving so differently from what she had expected, so distant and doleful, she was almost concerned. Was she the cause of his gloom? For if she were, nothing could be done about it.

"I need nothing, *chérie,* and do not let me keep you from your work. My only need is for a friendly face and a bit of news." When she took up her darning again, he lowered himself to sit cross-legged in the grass beside her blanket. "I am eager to hear all that has happened in the valley while I was gone."

Hope's gray eyes danced. "Actually, there is some interesting news, at least to me. You're not going to believe this . . ."

He managed a smile. "Now you mystify me."

"Jacques, I treated Thunderhead two weeks ago. He was extremely ill and I was able to help him."

He pretended amazement and delight. "Thunderhead? *Mon dieu,* Hope, you are right, I do not believe it."

"Well, it happened."' She had known he would be pleased.

"C'est incroyable. I want to hear it from the beginning to the end."

He seemed so truly interested, Hope excitedly told him the entire tale: the braves' night visit and the torch-lit ride through the black woods, the wailing of the mourners, and Thunderhead singing his death song.

Listening, Jacques felt a grudging admiration for her courage in riding off into the night with those two savages and in confronting Walks Alone. The witch frightened even him with her medicine bundle and that small sinister-looking doll that she carried. *Oui,* he was impressed, for a certainty, but he resented it that this woman who was going to be his wife should succeed so outstandingly on her own. A woman had no business doing that. She should depend completely on her man, in all things and in all ways. Seeing the brightness of her eyes, he said gruffly, "It would seem all goes as you had planned."

"Aye. Very much so." Hope frowned, seeing that

his fingers drummed one knee. "You seem worried. Is anything wrong?"

It was to laugh. Was anything right? Yet there was nothing he could say, nothing he could do about it for the present. He mustered a sardonic smile and cocked one eyebrow. "I admit to feeling quite sorry for myself. Soon you will be so busy doctoring, I will have to break a leg to see you."

Hope giggled. She liked him when he was this way. "Never. A nice sprain or a cut will suffice."

"How kind . . ." He got to his feet and stretched. "Perhaps I will accept your hospitality after all. Perhaps a bit of your excellent sherry to celebrate your success?"

"Of course. But do come inside to drink it. These past few days, we've found that the bees love it, too."

Jacques followed her into the small kitchen and sat in Thomas's chair at the head of the table. Hiding his hunger, he watched the graceful way in which she took the decanter from a corner cupboard, filled a goblet, and handed it to him. His fingers brushed hers.

"*Merci.* Will you not join me?"

Hope shook her head and sat on the bench, chin in hands. "It makes me sleepy. I'd never get my mending done."

"*Mais oui,* your mending . . ." He took it as a subtle hint. It was expected that he should soon depart, but he was damned if he would until he had his questions about Firewalker answered—but how to bring up the subject? He raised the goblet, sniffed the vapors, took a swallow, and asked casually, "Are you still teaching *la petite Fleur?*"

"Aye, and she's doing beautifully." She was tempted to add that Flower was more interested than ever, but held her tongue. He would not appreciate it. Nor would he like the rest of her news, but it was best he hear it from her rather than War Cloud. "I've been teaching her cousins, also. Perhaps you know them—Little Bear and Otter Pup and Stargazer."

His temples began to throb, but he continued to pretend surprise. "*Mais oui*, I know them well, but *mon amie*, I thought you did not want to teach. Now I fear you will truly be disappointed."

"You said that about Flower."

"So I did, and it appears I was wrong, but those three—they are clever enough, but they are lazy as sin." In the name of God, what had prompted her to do such a stupid thing?

"Then I will have made a mistake, won't I?" Hope answered sweetly. "And since nothing will have been lost but a few hours of my time, I hope you'll not concern yourself over it." She was not about to tell him he was right. They were lazy, and she had made a mistake, and aye, she was disappointed.

He shook his head and raked a hand through his thick thatch of dark curls. "I must admit, Hope, it baffles me that you would teach Indians and not your own people."

"That's not quite the case. I'll be teaching the Johnson's twin girls just as soon as the supplies arrive from Pittsburgh. As for my teaching the Lenapes, Firewalker asked me earlier, but I refused. After I helped Thunderhead, it all seemed to fall into place."

"I see."

So that was the business Firewalker had gone there to discuss and why he had been so angry with her? Teaching. It was amazing. And how unfortunate that the bastard actually had the wits to realize the value of education. But then perhaps that was his main interest in Hope—as a teacher. The thought alleviated his fears only for a moment, for War Cloud had said Firewalker burned for her. What red-blooded man would be interested in only the brains of such a wench? And Firewalker was red-blooded, if he was anything. Damnation, but he was confused. It was intolerable that in the three weeks of his absence, so much had gone awry. Thunderhead should have been in the ground and War Cloud the new chief, thus paving the way for a lucrative fur trade. Instead, Thunderhead thrived, and Jacques foresaw a multitude of difficulties confronting War Cloud if those damned young bucks learned to read and write. It was better by far that savages be kept ignorant.

"What reason does Firewalker give for this sudden thirst for knowledge for his cousins?" he asked.

"He says they have the potential to be wampum keepers, but have no interest in memorizing the Lenape history."

Jacques gave a snort. "As I said, they are lazy. But actually, I cannot blame them. Lenape history is dull stuff from what I have heard. They are a bunch of women as warriors go."

Hope was indignant. "Why on earth would you say such—" She bit off her words seeing that Firewalker was standing in the kitchen doorway. Her heart sank. How much of what Jacques said had he heard? She rose and gave him an uncertain smile. "Come in . . ."

Jacques sprang to his feet, a deep flush spreading across his face. "The way you creep about, my friend, you need a bell around your neck."

Firewalker's tawny eyes passed over his enemy without the slightest acknowledgment of his presence. But with every sense he possessed, he was aware of the Frenchman's dangerous mood: his narrowed eyes and quickened breathing, the hand that slid to his belt where his knife was held. It would take little to ignite him, whereas he himself was always in a dangerous mood where this one was concerned. His thoughts ran wild. He imagined Hope in Jacques's arms, imagined the trader in her bed with his greedy hands moving over her.

He muttered, "Hope, I would talk with you."

Hope nodded. "I've been expecting you." Feeling the heat of Firewalker's hostility, she glanced uneasily at Jacques. How awkward it was with the two of them standing there glaring at each other. She said gently, "Jacques, will you excuse us, please?"

Jacques's temples throbbed harder. Hope . . . He had called her Hope, and War Cloud had said he burned for her and had been coming there regularly. And now she said she had been expecting him. What in God's name was that about? Lovemaking? Did they use her bedroom? Had they some secret forest glade where they trysted? Thinking of those dark hands moving over her body, he savored the sweet thought of murder. And he knew exactly how he would accomplish it. He had an affinity for the dagger. . . .

"Are you saying you wish me to leave?" he asked in icy disbelief.

Firewalker smiled. "That is what she is saying."

His hatred flaring, Jacques stepped forward. "I did not ask you."

Firewalker stretched his spine and towered. "I am telling you, Frenchman."

"I am not your brother that you can order me about."

Firewalker's eyes glowed, the eyes of an eagle about to dive. "Nor am I my brother that you can bribe me with your whiskey and your crooked tongue."

"You had best leave." Jacques choked. For if he did not, he would slay him there in that small kitchen.

Firewalker gave a ghost of a smile, and spoke softly, "Do you think you can make me?"

Hope was frightened. She had known they disliked each other, but this raw, hissing violence between them was far more than dislike. This was hatred. She could almost hear the war drums beating. She slipped between them. "Please, I want you both to stay, but not if you fight. Jacques, I only meant that Firewalker and I would step outside for a moment to talk."

"It is I who will step outside." His voice shook in

his fury. "I doubt you could budge this bull from where he stands."

Watching the trader leave, Firewalker yearned to follow and thrash him. But he would not have stopped with a mere thrashing. He wanted to destroy him. It was why he did not trust himself to touch the man. He turned his smoldering eyes on Hope, wanting to ask, to demand why Jacques d'Arcy was there. He locked his lips. This woman did not belong to him. She could see whomever she chose and do whatever she wanted, and he dared not forget it. He could not afford to anger her; he needed her.

"What on earth is the matter with you two?" Hope asked hotly when they were alone.

"It is not your concern."

She faced him, chin high and her hands on her hips. "When two men want to kill each other in my kitchen, it's my concern."

"I would not have laid a finger on him."

She stared. He was breathing hard, nostrils flaring, pupils wide and black. "You wanted to."

"Aye. But I would not, nor will I ever."

"But why did—"

He shook his head. "There it stands."

It was maddening, the way he just cut things off in the middle, and now she must deal with the other thing while he was still angry about this. Well, she'd best get it over with. It was not going to go away.

"I—suppose you've come about your cousins. I'm sorry. They seemed so interested at first, and they really are quite capable, so I thought it was going to work out."

Firewalker frowned. "I don't understand."

She stared. "Firewalker, why are you here?"

"I have been hunting. I stopped to see how things went this day."

"Oh." She sank into her father's chair. She had expected, she had hoped that Flower would have supplied him with a full outraged account of the event, but instead it had fallen to her. Oh, dear. And now she was the mean teacher, the overstern taskmaster. She drew a fortifying breath, released it, and began: "Well, what happened is that—well, the three of them—"

"Were devils?" he asked quietly.

"Aye." She felt as contrite as if it were her fault. "I'm sorry. They were so good at first, and they were learning so well and so quickly and then—then this morning they just went wild. I had to send them home." She added softly, "I hate disappointing you. . . ."

Firewalker held up his hand. "They will apologize."

"Oh, please, nay!" She did not know what she had expected, but not that. She could not imagine anything worse than having grudging apologies forced from them. "Please, let it pass."

"*Matta.* I will bring them tomorrow."

"But—"

"Tomorrow." Firewalker could not prevent his hungry fingers from brushing lightly across her cheek. He marveled at how silken her skin was, and when she gazed up at him, her silvery eyes wide and wondering and her pink lips parted, he felt a stab of regret. What was he doing, touching her this way and delighting in her softness and her closeness when nothing could come of it? He said gruffly, "It will be all right, Hope, I promise you."

Hope's tongue and mind would not work. She could only nod woodenly as he left and wonder what was happening to her. Dear Lord, she had yearned for him to hold and kiss her. Kiss her all over . . .

As Firewalker moved toward his mare, he was still savoring the sweet rush of heat that had filled him when he'd touched Hope. It faded when he saw d'Arcy pacing in the clearing. As he mounted and took Nightwind into a gallop, the Frenchman's look of hatred went with him. He left his enemy with a black glance of his own. This land was too small for the two of them.

Jacques watched as Firewalker rode off, as swiftly and silently as he had come. The damned sly sneaky devil. Seeing Hope emerge from the cabin, he said curtly, "I protest strongly leaving you with him. I deplore it. Are you all right?"

"Of course." Her cheek was still tingling from Firewalker's caress.

"Did you see? He wanted to kill me."

Hope gave him a level look. "I would have said the same was true of you."

Jacques's brown eyes glittered. "Why was he here exactly?"

"He came to see how the class went today." Not that it was any of his business. "He frequently stops by to check on the boys."

Of course that was what Firewalker would tell her, Jacques brooded. He was not such a fool as to say he lusted after her. But at least this day the savage would not have dared lay a finger on her while he himself waited outside.

"I don't understand," Hope murmured, seeing that he was still furious. "What is it between the two of you, and what was that about War Cloud?" She had not understood any of it—the talk of whiskey, a crooked tongue, a bribe.

"War Cloud is my friend, and that devil cannot stand the thought."

"It's a shame you can't work something out."

Jacques grunted. "With a madman? Impossible."

Fetching her sewing basket from under the oak, Hope speculated on how she might calm him. She did not want him riding off in the murderous rage he now felt toward Firewalker. "Your wine is in the kitchen where you left it." She spoke softly. "Why not finish it while I finish my mending?"

"I had forgotten it," he muttered. But it mollified

him that she had thought of it, and obviously wanted his company.

He had long since abandoned his earlier plan to propose to her this coming night. It would wait. But as he sipped and she sewed, he could not resist preparing her for it. He regaled her with his sweeping dreams for the future. He told her of the grand mansion he meant to build and the luxuries he would give that woman who would be his wife. And when he finally said his good-byes, he was content, convinced that Firewalker was nothing to her. The look in those beautiful gray eyes of hers was one of admiration for himself alone.

The next morning, Tom had already left to see a patient when Hope heard Firewalker and his young kin galloping out of the woods. She waited uneasily while they dismounted and tied up at the rail. And since she did not know what to say or do, and since it was Firewalker's idea, she decided to follow his lead. Observing his unsmiling face, she said coolly, "Good morning."

"Good morning, Hope Caldwell. We have come for talk."

"Very well." She folded her arms.

She saw that the bucks' faces were sullen and when they avoided her eyes, Hope wished the whole thing were over—or that it never need begin. She watched as the three, at an imperceptible command from Firewalker, lined up before him, and were questioned by him one by one. She understood none of it, but suspected that he was hearing, for the first time, what had happened there yesterday. The last one to be questioned was Stargazer.

"Why were you sent home, my cousin?" Firewalker asked.

"For the same reason as the others," muttered Stargazer.

"But now I am asking you. Why were you sent home?"

"I—did not want to learn."

"What did you do instead?"

Stargazer shrugged his fine dark shoulders. "I guess I played—"

"You guess?"

Stargazer did not flinch. "I played games and ran races with the others. And wrestled." His black eyes went to the woman and then returned to Firewalker. Not knowing how much she had told him, he added, "We teased her. . . ."

Firewalker studied the three in silence before returning his attention to Stargazer. "Why did you tease her?"

Stargazer drew himself taller. "She is a white, my cousin, and she is but a woman. What does she know?"

Firewalker felt the sting of his own guilt. It was the way he himself had felt not so long ago. Even now, he was not completely without such feelings. He said gruffly, "If you had in your empty heads one speck of what she knows, I would be proud of you—but you do not. But you are going to learn, and you are going to learn quickly, for much time has been lost. For our people you will learn. It will require great discipline and sacrifice. And if you are moved instead to tease and run races and wrestle, you will tease and run races and wrestle with me. You will then return to your studies. Is that understood?"

Forgetting to mask their faces, the three gaped up at their tall kinsman. Stargazer was the first to compose himself. "I—understand, my cousin." The other two muttered assents.

Firewalker gave a short nod. "I expect to have pride in you someday—pride which I do not have now." When their faces flamed, he said to Hope, "My young kinsmen have told me what happened. They have shamed me and themselves and our people before you, but they will give you no further trouble. They will return for teaching if you will still have them. . . ."

Hope continued to follow his lead. She studied the three with unfriendly eyes before answering sharply, "I don't think I want them. I know that you wish for them to learn, but I doubt they themselves are interested." She shook her head. "Nay, I see well that it would be a waste of my time."

At that, Stargazer spoke. "Lady, I sorrow. Not tease again. I want come back and learn. Want Firewalker be proud of me." His intelligent eyes were pleading.

"I want, too," said Otter Pup, "and I sorrow. Not tease again."

"And me," Little Bear muttered. "No tease. Want learn."

Hope felt herself warming to them. They were good boys, she knew they were, and she liked all three of them. It was why she had given them a second chance and why she was so hurt and disappointed when they'd behaved so rudely. Now her wintry eyes moved over them and she compressed her lips.

It was a long time before she said finally, "Very well. I will give you one chance to prove you mean what you say. Do you understand?"

"*Kehella.*" Three shining dark heads nodded.

"I will expect you tomorrow morning, and by the end of the week, I expect you to know the alphabet."

"We will know it," said Stargazer.

"I hope so. You may go now."

Hope watched as they rode off, considerably subdued and respectful. She turned to Firewalker. He was leaning against Nightwind, his arm draped over her silky black neck. He was laughing softly.

Hope gave him a grin. "Did I do it right?"

"You did it right." It was what he would have expected from the one who had snatched Thunderhead from death and confounded Walks Alone. "They will perform well for you. They understand strength and bravery. They but needed reminding that you possess both."

Seeing that glorious pink suffusing her face and

throat, Firewalker thought again how beautiful she was, and how it would feel to pull her into his arms and press her softness against him—and taste those rosy lips and that silky skin. But he had touched her for the last time.

Hope could not move nor breathe nor speak. She knew by the way his eyes were searching over her face and hair and mouth that he was going to kiss her. And she wanted it, oh, aye, she wanted it. And then the moment was gone and he had not kissed her at all. Somehow he was on Nightwind gazing down on her.

"I will stop by tomorrow—just in case." He added a smile.

Hope nodded. "Aye. Till tomorrow, then." She watched until the woods swallowed him, and then sat on the front step, her chin in her hands. Something was happening between them. She didn't know what. She knew only that it was something wonderful and that she was not going to fight it. . . .

Chapter 12

Hope looked about at her small brood of students with a warm sense of satisfaction. The school supplies had arrived two weeks earlier, and now the six of them sat under the sheltering boughs of one of the twin oaks with their slates on their laps and chalk in their hands. While Flower helped speed Emma and Amy Johnson along, Hope taught the boys simple words. How right it seemed, having them here together, white and Indian, and it seemed right, too, for her to be here in these northern Pennsylvania woodlands that she had so hated and feared at first. She loved them now, and she loved what she was doing. She was needed here. These children needed her, and Flower needed her, and she needed them. Out of the tragedy in Pittsburgh had come a new life she had never dreamed possible.

"Have you finished your words?" she asked the boys.

"I have." Otter Pup held up his slate and waved it.

Hope examined it. "*Bat* and *cat* are correct. Very good. But what letter gives us the *H* sound? *Hat* does not begin with an *F*, Otter Pup. Think again."

Otter Pup frowned. "*G*? Is it g-a-t?"

"Is *H*," said Stargazer with a disdainful look at his cousin. "H-a-t, hat. F-a-t, fat. M-a-t, mat. R-a-t, rat. S-a-t, sat." His black gaze moved lazily to Hope. "Is right, teacher?"

"That is correct." Hope did not allow herself to smile. Stargazer was by far the brightest of the three, but he was also the cockiest and the most unruly.

He shrugged. "Is simple."

"Say it correctly, please." He spoke English well when he chose, but he rarely chose to. Now she saw the devil dancing in his eyes.

"*Matta*, no talk fancy. Reading and writing, *kehella*, but no talk fancy."

"Speaking good English is not talking fancy."

"Is fancy," he said stubbornly.

Hope never had the chance to reply, for suddenly Firewalker stepped out from behind the oak under which they sat. He startled her. She had neither seen nor heard his approach, nor had the others. Sensing danger behind him, Stargazer sprang from the spot and turned, crouched and ready for battle. He laughed seeing who it was.

"Ho, it is only you!" he said in Lenape.

"*Kehella*, it is only I," Firewalker growled.

Stargazer's laughter turned to an indignant yelp as he was upended and tossed over the brave's wide shoulder. His cousins, gleefully shouting jibes, danced about Firewalker as he made his way a short distance east of the house.

Firewalker stopped at the spot where a spring bubbled out of the ground to form a small sparkling pond. His anger toward Stargazer had already cooled. He cared for this young kinsman of his more than any of the others, but he must be punished. His disobedience could not be tolerated, for it was he who would be the next Keeper of the Wampum. Of that there was no doubt. He grasped the boy's ankles and dangled him headfirst above the water. Stargazer made no sound nor did he struggle.

"Do you understand why I am doing this, kinsman?" Firewalker asked low.

"*Kehella*. I was—disrespectful and disobedient." Grateful that the females had not followed, Stargazer crossed his arms, closed his eyes, and stoically awaited his fate.

Firewalker lowered him into the water. Only when air exploded from the boy's lungs did he raise him and set him on his feet beside his laughing, taunting cousins. They did not laugh for long. Firewalker seized and dunked them both.

Afterwards, as they choked and coughed, he said quietly, "You will return now to your studies."

Hope found it impossible to ignore Firewalker's presence as she completed the remainder of the lesson. He sat under the other oak, his back against its trunk and his golden gaze never leaving her. Numbly she gave the assignments for the class two days hence. In a haze, she saw the Johnson twins collect their belongings, climb onto their ponies, and jog off, their adoring eyes fastened upon the tall brave.

Firewalker got to his feet and addressed his kin: "Ride on ahead, you four. I would speak with your teacher."

Hope knew it was Stargazer he wished to discuss, but her blood would not stop racing. She sat down on the thick carpet of grass beneath the tree, shook out her skirts, and looked up at him.

"They're doing well, all of them. Extremely well."

Firewalker sat down beside her. He plucked a foxtail and studied it, frowning. "Stargazer?"

"Especially Stargazer. This was a passing thing." His sitting close beside her was so intoxicating Hope's heart was running away. It was flying, and there was nothing she could do to stop it. "He's been fine, believe me. Usually he's polite and respectful and he works hard. I'm pleased with him. . . ." She pulled her gaze from his dark face and looked down at her hands in confusion. He was beautiful. How could any human being be so beautiful?

"I did not like what I saw," Firewalker said.

He wanted to believe her, but he could not. The damned young hot spur. It was because of Stargazer that he came there, visiting briefly every class so far, inspecting the meaningless scribbles on slates and papers, meting out swift discipline when necessary, and then departing. It was torture. Seeing this woman and not being able to touch her left him as drained and aching as if he had been downed in battle. Looking at her now, he felt the pain anew. It was a fire scorching his vitals and spreading its heat throughout his body. He yearned to hold and kiss and taste her, to inhale the scent of that soft white flesh—but instead he held himself, body and soul, in a vise of iron. He would not touch her.

Seeing the grimness of his face, Hope said gently, "Firewalker, believe me, the boy is fine. He's cocky, but then that's Stargazer. I'd not have him any other way. . . ." Her head was swimming . . . he was looking at her so strangely. "He'll not disappoint you, I promise. He'll read and write. . . ." The words trailed to a whisper.

Firewalker forbade himself to touch the cascade of blue black hair so close to his fingers, but suddenly his resolve vanished. He must. He reached out, stroked it, and raised a wisp of it to his lips, to his nostrils to inhale its scent. It was as silken and fragrant as he knew it would be. Unable to help himself, he pressed a kiss on it.

Hope's breath fled in a soft gasp as pleasure swept her. She could not believe it—he had kissed her hair, and now he was going to kiss her lips. She knew by the way he was gazing at her mouth. It was what she had yearned for, and feared, and yearned for again, yet now she told herself that she dared not let it happen. She must rise, smile, laugh even, and above all say something, anything, to make light of what was happening. And quickly, quickly, before it was too late.

She did not move. She asked herself why she was fighting the powerful magnetism drawing them together when Firewalker was now her friend. She honored and respected and admired him, and she had been intrigued and excited by him since her very first sight of him. Who better to kiss than Firewalker? She smiled, seeing the heat in those golden eyes. Heart pounding, soaring, she lay her fingers on his lips, gently tracing their beautiful sharply carved lines. She felt a thrill of shock at her own boldness and the startling contrast of her white skin against his darkness.

Her breathing was shaky as she whispered, "Oh, Firewalker . . ."

Firewalker, his golden eyes locked on hers, caught her hand and raised it to his lips. He kissed her palm and the inside of her wrist and each slim white finger, all the while telling himself this was madness—and it was wrong. But was it? He had fought his growing hunger thinking that no good could come of it, yet if it pleased Hope and it pleased him, and it hurt no one, what else mattered?

Wordlessly, he put his arms about her and, lying back in the deep grass, cradled her against his bare chest. He stroked her long hair and her face and breasts, and gently sought her lips. When they parted for him, sweet and welcoming, Firewalker touched his tongue to hers in a brief greeting before covering her mouth with his.

Hope was swept into a warm ever-deepening spiral of pleasure. Everything about him was wonderful. The hardness of his tall body, his lean strength, his mouth on hers, so tender at first but growing more wildly arousing and possessive by the moment. She loved being crushed against him so tightly, she loved the taste of him and the smell of him—as if he slept on a bed of pine boughs—and she loved his hands, strong yet so gentle and sensitive, stroking her face and throat and shoulders, her breasts. Fire raced through her, fire and ice. She was heated by his touch, yet she could not stop shivering, nor could she get enough of his hungry kisses—she who had so feared growing close to another man.

Firewalker kissed her deeply again and again, and then afterwards, brushed his lips lightly across hers, teasing over the delicate curve of her jaw, down her throat, and thence to her shoulder. Baring it, he bit into the soft flesh ever so gently. He said low, "You are very beautiful, Caldwell the healer. These many weeks I have wanted to kiss you . . ."

Hope was pulsing with the fire his lips and hands had aroused within her. She had almost forgotten what such sensations felt like. She chuckled, "I confess, these many weeks I've wanted you to kiss me . . ."

"Now you are teasing me."

"Nay, I am not."

As he caressed her shoulder, touching the tip of his tongue to it to taste its enchanting sweet saltiness, she reached out and entwined her fingers deeply in his hair. Seeing her rosy and excited, her breath coming in soft pants, Firewalker felt the hot hardening of his body. He wanted her so fiercely, his heart roared and his leashed muscles ached; sweat beaded his temples. If they continued on in this way, he would take her. It was the logical consequence of such passionate kisses and caresses. Yet he wanted to be very sure that she wanted him, for he would not harm her. He must give her every chance to withdraw.

"You resented and feared me," he reminded her.

"That's true, but it seems so very long ago . . ." She loved the feel of his hair between her fingers, so strong and silky and alive.

"It was not long ago. My kinsmen and I are still feared by your countrymen. Hope, our people are still enemies." He would not have her remember it suddenly after giving herself to him.

Seeing the grimness of his face, Hope sat up. As her reason returned, she pulled up her gown to cover her bared shoulder. Remembering his hands and his lips moving over her, she knew they had come very close to making love. She shivered. She had wanted him to consume her, to possess her completely. She still did. She wanted him as much as ever; inside she was trembling for him. She climbed unsteadily to her feet. He rose also.

"You're right"—she smoothed back her hair—"thank you for reminding me. Our people are still enemies. . . ." There was far more to consider than any brief pleasure they might give each other. This land, for instance. How could she make love with a man on land her country had stolen from him! For she knew now that the rights of his people had been overlooked when the Donation Lands were formed. "And while we're on the subject of enemies—I'm sorry about this land! We have no right being here. . . ."

"It is done," he said gruffly. He had been watching her inner struggle and was sorry at its outcome—there would be no lovemaking this day. But he could wait, for he knew now that she was going to be his woman. "As for you yourself being here, it is a blessing. You were brought here and you are treasured. Never forget you have been invited to dwell among us."

Hope smiled. "I won't forget."

Having held and tasted her, Firewalker knew that she was all he had ever desired in a woman. She was beautiful and she was brave and her heart was tender. But one thing chilled him: d'Arcy. How much did she care for him? Were they only friends or was it more, and how often did he come there, drinking her wine and sitting close, talking with her in that dim, dark cooking room? He recalled, as he often did, her stroking the devil's hair and drawing him back inside the cabin. Had she kissed d'Arcy as hungrily as she had just now kissed him? Had that man some claim on her? It would seem, if she were going to be his woman, that he needed some answers.

He asked abruptly, "Do you belong to the Frenchman?"

His words were so unexpected, Hope's laughter rang out. "Belong? To Jacques? Heavens, we're friends. Even if we were affianced, which we are not,

I wouldn't 'belong' to him. I don't belong to anyone but myself, I assure you."

In that instant, Firewalker vowed that when she was his, she would in truth belong to him and not herself. His eyes flickered over her. "I sense he is more than a friend."

"Then you sense wrong." She rested her hands on her hips. "I said he was a friend, and I meant it."

Seeing the sudden angry flush on his face, she was warned. She knew that he hated Jacques, but this was different—this involved her. She saw well that he was jealous, wildly, furiously jealous, and although she was still experiencing the warm afterglow of his kisses and the exciting memory of his hands moving over her, she resented his possessiveness. She was not bound to him.

She asked quietly, "What is this about, Firewalker?"

He was not ready to admit that he wanted her to join with him. The idea was too new and too precious to reveal to anyone, even Hope herself. And the thought stung him that the kisses they had shared might have meant more to him than they did to her. But if that were so, it would change.

"Why don't you answer?" Hope persisted. "Or perhaps I know already. Perhaps you are thinking that since I have kissed you, I cannot now be friends, or more than friends, with other men."

Seeing the gathering storm in her eyes, Firewalker said, "What I am thinking is that you should choose your friends more carefully. The Frenchman is dangerous. You should not encourage him."

Hope raised an eyebrow. "That's very interesting. Jacques says the same about you. He says you are dangerous and should not be allowed to come here." Seeing his flush deepen, she added more gently, "It's not that I don't appreciate your concern. It's just that you both are my friends and—"

Firewalker lay his fingers over her lips. "It is all right." Having experienced her loyalty, he knew she would not turn away any whom she called friend. He would ask the Creator to watch over her, and his manitou would give him the swiftness and strength to guard her if danger came. "It is all right. . . ."

Hope had been thinking about what had almost happened between Firewalker and herself ever since he had left. She was still savoring it when Maybeth Springer galloped up on her big chestnut gelding and tied up at the hitching rail.

Hope hurried out to greet her. "You've actually come for a visit!"

"Aye." Maybeth dismounted and the two hugged. "I've left Luke t' fend fer hisself in th' fields fer a while."

Seeing the streaks of sweat on Maybeth's dust-covered face, Hope said quickly, "Come up and sit on the stoop where it's cooler and let me get you something to drink."

Maybeth was happy to comply. "A nice swaller o' water'd be lovely." As she sipped it from a crystal goblet, she studied her friend with placid blue eyes. "I've heard sich tales about ye at the general store, Hope Caldwell, I just had t' hear 'em wi' these two ears."

Hope laughed. "What tales are those?"

"They say y'r teachin' school."

Her gray eyes twinkled. "It's true, I am."

"An' they say y'r teachin' savages. . . ."

Hope grinned. "Well, now, I guess they mean the Johnson twins. I admit they're a bit wild, but my four Lenapes are a calming influence."

Maybeth hooted and tucked a strand of flyaway blond hair behind her ear. "That's a good un, that is—but I know what thee means. They're twin terrors, those two. How do thee keep them in hand when their own paw can't?"

"Do you promise not to tell their folks?"

"I promise."

"They're in love."

Another hoot. "Go on wi' ye. Wi' one o' them young Lenape bucks?"

"Nay," Hope said, "with Firewalker, their kinsman. He usually stops by during every class to—check on their progress."

"Ah . . ."

Maybeth had seen the brave just once when she and Luke had first come to the Donation Lands, and she'd never forgotten it. The two of them had been clearing the south field for planting when all of a sudden she'd come all a-prickle. She'd turned, and there he was on his big black mare, half naked, and those gold eagle eyes of his all wise and seeming to read her very thoughts. He'd nodded, all of half an inch, and disappeared into the woods. Maybeth sighed thinking of it, for he'd been the most splendiferous man she had ever seen in all her twenty-five years. Her darling Luke, God bless his gentle soul, was a scarecrow in comparison.

"The girls are so eager to impress him," Hope was saying, laughing, "that they're behaving like lambs for me."

"Tch! Well, count yer blessin's, I say, but it do start early, don't it? They can't be mor'n ten or eleven."

"Ten," Hope said.

Maybeth noted with surprise that her friend's beautiful face had grown pink at the mention of Firewalker. That fretted her. Not because she thought it was wrong for a white woman to be charmed by a brave, but because other folk would see it as wrong. *Tch,* should she warn her? But then it was none of her business. She didn't relish folk telling her what to do, so she'd not butt into this. Nay, not for the world. But speaking of love, it seemed her friend had a bad case of it. . . .

Hope reached over and caught Maybeth's small rough hand. "I'm so glad you came. We live too far apart."

"And I'm glad ye're up here in this wilderness wi'

me, lovey, fer come November, I'll be birthin' me a babe. Will y' deliver it f'r me?" Her blue eyes shone.

Hope's mouth fell open. So that was why she had come. A babe in November! She carried it so well, no one would ever guess—and she wanted her to deliver it? "Oh, Maybeth, how happy I am for you! And aye, I'll certainly deliver it—I'll be honored . . ." Suddenly they were in each other's arms, laughing and weeping.

Maybeth dried her eyes and rose. "Well, then, I'd best be gittin' along now. I told Luke I'd be right back. We're cuttin' barley."

Hope stared after her, dumbfounded, as Maybeth moved toward her horse, gathered up her skirts, and lifted herself up easily into the saddle. Cutting barley? Lord, she had seen her father cutting barley, swinging his heavy scythe for hours on end with the sweat pouring down his bare chest and arms. She was horrified, thinking of Maybeth doing it. Not only that, the riding could not be good for her. Six months pregnant and all that jogging . . .

Seeing the disapproval on Hope's face, Maybeth shook her yellow head. "Nay, don't ye say it. I'll work an' ride alongside Luke till the end, jist like th' other women i' my family."

"Maybeth, it's not safe. . . ."

"Nay, lovey, I'll not do less than them." She gave Hope her placid smile. "This babe sh'll work alongside its daddy an' me an' we'll all three be the better f'r it." She patted her belly. "Ye'll see."

"I admit, you seem to be thriving—but I think we'll talk more about it later."

Maybeth shrugged. "If ye insist, but I'll not be changin' m' mind. . . ."

Chapter 13

Jacques d'Arcy sat on a log before his cook fire eating the remains of his supper and staring into the flames. He was tired. He was sick to death and tired of this miserable existence—his own wretched cooking, sitting in a saddle for hours on end, sleeping on a straw pallet, haggling with stinking savages, and fighting heat and cold and wind and loneliness. And he was tired of waiting. *Sacre,* it seemed he was as far as ever from the life of leisure and pleasure which he craved and so richly deserved.

He bit into the last of the rabbit with his strong white teeth, hurled the bone into the fire, and thought bitterly of Hope. Damn her beautiful eyes, it was all her fault. Thunderhead had been so close to death and he himself so close to success that he could taste it. But nay, she had to go and save the old devil, and she had added insult to injury by refusing to wed him.

He ran his hands through his mane of dark curls and stroked his beard. *Mais alors,* adversity had always served to make him more determined, and this was no different. He would have the Lenape fur trade eventually, no matter what the cost, and he would have Hope Caldwell for his wife. He must simply cultivate more patience. He wondered then, as he had wondered many times, about the mystery surrounding her.

That she was a medical doctor like her father was intriguing enough in itself. But why would Thomas Caldwell, so obviously wealthy a man, have brought her to this godforsaken wilderness in the first place? He could understand Thomas's own desire for a challenge—but Hope? Why Hope, when she could have remained in comfort in civilization? More than comfort, he mused, thinking of the costly and exquisite objects and furnishings in their cabin. And those odd, secret looks he glimpsed between them from time to time and the cryptic things said—what were those about? He had tried to question her subtly about her life in Pittsburgh, but had learned nothing. Now he was awaiting word from a friend there who was looking into it for him.

Hearing a soft noise, and sensing suddenly that he was being watched, Jacques froze. The hair rose on his scalp as he imagined Firewalker behind him. He leapt up, drew his knife, and then relief flooded him seeing the big muscular brave who stood there. War Cloud's black eyes glittered in the firelight and his oiled body and scalp lock gleamed.

"*Mon dieu,* why do you creep up on me that way! I might have slain you."

War Cloud's lip curled as he looked about. "Where are the other ten it would take, Frenchman?"

"You have come here to insult me, then?"

"I have come for talk," War Cloud muttered, "but I see it is a bad time. You are skittish as a woman."

Jacques's hand trembled on his dagger. What pleasure it would give him to show this devil just who it was he likened to a woman. Damn his black soul. But of course he could not. That was the way of it in this accursed place—pretend and more pretend. God willing, they would see, all of them, the true Jacques D'Arcy before he made his departure. And God willing, it would be soon. Until then, he must remain smiling, amiable, giving . . . He sighed and sheathed his knife.

"I am not skittish, *mon ami,* I am cautious. I had to

drive off a bear earlier. Wolves I do not mind, but bears concern me."

"Then you must summon me if it frightens you again, *n'tschu.* I took my first bear when I was eleven winters old."

Jacques gritted his teeth. "I will do that, *n'tschu.* And now let us talk. First, let me fetch a tin for you."

"Matta!" It was like the crack of a whip. "No more liquor." War Cloud had seen finally with terrible clarity why his uncle had forbade their people alcohol. He himself could think of nothing else, and looked for any excuse to swill it. But now it was ended. He had sworn it.

Jacques shrugged. "As you wish, but I have a thirst myself. You do not mind?" He sat back down on the log and reached for his cup and the bottle.

"Why would I mind?" War Cloud sat on the log opposite, and shuttered his senses to the sound of the pouring and the smell that reached his nostrils. His mouth watered. He spat, and then said, "I have come about the Hope-woman."

Jacques kept his face composed. "What about her?"

"You will do something about her."

"Now you mystify me."

"You will stop her meddling. It is enough that she has interfered with my destiny, but now this teaching of hers—" He scowled at the flames before giving Jacques a sharp look. "It seems I have talked to you before of her teaching those damned cubs. . . ."

"Never," Jacques lied. "Hope herself has told me of it, but this is the first you have mentioned it."

He held his breath, and then seeing the uncertainty in those unholy black eyes, he rejoiced. Thank God, the devil did not remember the night he'd spilled his guts and almost wept in his envy of Firewalker.

War Cloud grunted and threw a twig into the flames. "Do you yourself read and write, Frenchman?"

"I?" Jacques laughed, seeing at once where this

was headed. He lied again. "Nay, not I. What need has a man for such a thing when he has his strength and wits to rely on?"

"It is my own belief. Thunderhead does not read or write, so why should any other?"

"Why, indeed?" The poor ignorant stupid bloody fool.

But the Frenchman's words did not stop War Cloud's brooding. He could not cease thinking that, if the old man had been educated, if any of them had been, these woodlands might still be theirs. And if he himself had had a good brain, and there had been someone to teach him, he might have welcomed learning. But there had been no one, and he had not the head for it. Wisdom was not his; it belonged to Firewalker. And now Firewalker, himself too proud to submit to the woman for teaching, had dragged their young kin to her. Helldamnfire, but he hated Hope Caldwell. First she had robbed him of the early claiming of his heritage and now she was robbing him of his peace of mind. And he would not have it. He would not have those damned cocky snot snivelers knowing more than he himself did.

"I suppose your young bucks are feeling quite important these days," Jacques said softly. He had seen they were arrogant, those three, and liked nothing better than to taunt and show off.

"The classes will cease," War Cloud ordered. "You will see to it."

"How am I to stop them? You give me powers I do not possess, my friend."

"Wed the woman. I have seen that you crave her. Wed her and control her. Forbid her to teach."

Jacques blinked. It was not to his liking that such a one as War Cloud had observed his deepest feelings. He replied as calmly as he was able, "Even were I moved in such a direction, these things take time."

War Cloud got to his feet and began to pace. "My

brother should have let the Mengwes have her," he muttered. "He should have turned his back."

Jacques sat riveted. "What do you mean," he asked softly, "he should have let the Mengwes have her? I have heard nothing of this. When did it happen?"

"Weeks ago."

It knocked the wind out of him. The Mengwes . . . He had been planning a visit to them to open trade. Now his wrath rose that Hope had had a bad encounter with them and not seen fit to confide in him. Did Thomas know? he wondered.

"What happened?" he asked.

"What do you think happened? She was half naked with her legs spread when my brother found them crawling all over her."

Jacques hissed in a breath, thinking of it. Damnation, it was his woman the bastards had spoiled with their filthy red bodies. *His*. "How many?" He could barely croak it out.

"I do not know, nor do I care. But for her, I would be sachem."

Jacques wanted to throttle him. He took a great gulp of rum and got a tight hold on his fists and tongue. "What else did Firewalker tell you?"

"My brother told me nothing. I overheard his talk with our uncle." War Cloud's eyes crackled over the trader. "We stray from the point, Frenchman. You will stop the meddling of this woman or I will."

"My friend"—Jacques smiled through his clenched teeth—"your help will not be necessary. I will take care of the matter, but as I said, this will take a bit of time."

"Seven days."

Now Jacques got to his feet. "Impossible. I need at least one moon. No less." He would propose again at the earliest opportunity, and if she refused him—but he would not entertain that possibility. He would anticipate success, and not accept defeat.

War Cloud gazed at him through lowered lids. "So

be it. I give you one moon, and then I myself will take the matter in hand."

"I promise you, all will be well. And now let me give you a small gift before you depart." He strode into his storeroom.

"No devil-water," War Cloud called after him sharply.

Jacques's hand was already on the bottle. He carried it outside. "*N'tschu*, I admire greatly your ability to resist the devil's brew—I myself am not so lucky. But since you are so very strong, it is all right to take it. You can save it. Who knows, you might need a small sip when the snow flies to warm your bones." He offered it. "Only to warm your bones . . ."

War Cloud shrugged, the muscles rippling under his polished dark red skin. To protest too strongly would alert this bastard to his struggle. "What you say is so, Frenchman. I am strong, and soon the nights will grow cold, and a small sip will warm me." He took the bottle, vowing that it would never touch his lips. As soon as he was in the woods, he would dash it against a tree. "One moon," he said, and moved toward his mount.

"One moon," Jacques agreed. The devil had not even thanked him.

Hope knelt by the second pond below the spring and gingerly lowered her head into the water. She gasped. It was icy, but how wonderful it felt once the first shock was over. She quickly soaped her hair, working it into a fragrant, foamy lather, and then rinsed her hair again and again until it squeaked. As she twisted out the water and wrapped a towel about her head, she decided she would wash clothes next—but first she would shake the bedding and pillows and hang them on the line to air. The day was so sunny and blue skyed, it was making her feel quite domestic. As she hurried back toward the house, she stopped in her tracks. Jacques's horse was at the rail, and there he was, seated in his favorite rocker on the stoop.

"Good morning. What a surprise . . ." She could not imagine what had brought him there at such an early hour. In fact, she was lucky she was dressed.

Jacques got to his feet. "*Bon matin*, Hope."

He did not permit his eyes to feast on the wet pink gown clinging to her breasts, but he had seen that the nipples were small and hard. Succulent buds thrust against the thin fabric. He realized with a shock that she wore only her gown and no chemise beneath it, and he wondered—was this how she had been dressed when the Mengwes found her? At the thought, desire raced through him, followed by regret that it was they who had had her and not himself. *Sacre*, what a bastard he was, but his callousness did not disturb him. Any conscience he'd ever had, he left at his mother's knee.

Hope saw instantly by his grave face that this was not a social visit. She said quietly, "What brings you here so early?"

Jacques had determined, after brooding most of the night, that it suited his purpose to be truthful. He replied, "I had news last night that disturbed me greatly. I nearly came to you then but I"—he looked about—"I thought we should have privacy. I trust Thomas is not here?"

Hope stepped onto the stoop. "He's cutting barley." She dabbed at the trickles of water trailing down her cheeks and gazed at him, concern in her eyes. "Jacques, what on earth is it? You look as if you didn't sleep all night.

"In truth, I did not." He sank into the rocker again.

She sat in the other, frowning. "You're not ill, are you?"

"Hope, I know about the Mengwes."

Hope felt the blood drain from her face. Even though the woods were being patrolled by Lenapes now, she still jumped at strange noises, and she kept Joshua and her small musket close by on those nights when she was alone. Aye, even some days she kept them close. But at least no one had known of her shame but Firewalker—or so she thought.

Seeing the question in her eyes, Jacques said quietly, "War Cloud told me. He overheard Firewalker and Thunderhead talking."

"I see." She began to rock, tracing with a finger the tiny daisies on her dress. She could not look at him.

"Hope, *mon dieu*, why did you not come to me?"

"What good would it have done?"

"What good? Why, I—I would have gone there," he blustered. "I would have gathered a band and gone there and laid waste their village, the damned devils."

Hope was touched by his indignation, but it seemed the ultimate in foolhardiness. "I appreciate it, but I wouldn't want a war started. As it happened, Firewalker arrived before I was harmed a-and put the fear of death into them."

Jacques breathed hard through his nose. If he heard much more about that devil he would go mad—and it infuriated him further that she was lying to him. War Cloud had said they were all over her, and had her legs spread. He wanted to slap her, berate her for getting herself into such a disgusting situation. He jumped up and paced the stoop.

"Can you not see I will go out of my mind with you in such danger?"

"I'm not in danger. Not anymore. The Lenapes are patrolling everywhere."

He threw up his hands. "Have I not told you they are all savages? You need a white man to protect you."

Hope said quietly, "I have a white man to protect me."

Jacques muttered, "An old man who is gone most of the time."

She laughed. An old man? "I doubt very much you'd enjoy a battle with my father. And he's home more than you might think. If I rang that bell"—she pointed to where it hung from a roof post—"he would be here within minutes. With his musket."

"Damnation, you know well what I am saying, Hope. You need a husband to protect you."

"A husband who is gone more than my father is?"

He cursed himself for not having thought farther ahead than wedding and bedding her. "I will take you with me part of the time," he amended quickly. "You will greatly enjoy meeting the various tribes, liking Indians as you do, and then in a very short time, we will return to Pittsburgh or Philadelphia or wherever your heart desires, and I will build our home. I have told you—it will be a mansion, a castle fit for a queen. For you . . ."

He was keenly aware that he was babbling and pressing her too hard, but all he could see, all he could hear in his mind was War Cloud. He had been given one month, one miserable month to win Hope and her father's riches before the devil acted. He had no doubt that War Cloud meant to slay her then. Thinking of it, he caught her hands and pulled her up from the rocker. "You will wear silks and satins, *chérie,* and I will adorn that lovely throat with diamonds and pearls. . . ." He traced with one dark finger where it would lie against her white skin. "Marry me. I will give you the world." He kissed her, briefly and passionately, but released her before she could struggle.

"Jacques, for goodness sake!" Hope was laughing; she could not help it.

Jacques did not appreciate her merriment. "Forgive me. I am acting the impassioned clown, I know, but the very thought of you in danger . . ."

Listening to his pleading, Hope was astonished by her own lack of enthusiasm. She had friends in Pittsburgh who would have adored Jacques d'Arcy. Died for him. Here was a man who was charming, caring, handsome, and who wanted to shower her with riches, yet his touch and his kisses gave her no pleasure at all. He turned her to ice. He smothered her.

All that she could give him in return for his love was hurt and rejection. She felt bad about it, but what else could she do? How did a woman refuse such an offer without completely breaking the heart of the man who had given it?

"Hope . . ."

"Jacques—" She saw that he was still annoyed, and with good reason. "I wasn't laughing at you. I was laughing at myself. You honor me."

He grimaced. "That was hardly my purpose."

"I'm sorry. . . ."

He tightened his lips. "There is someone else?"

Hope shook her head. "Nay, there is not."

"Is it Firewalker?"

It was some moments before she trusted herself to speak. "Why would you think such a thing?"

"I have seen how he looks at you."

"Then your eyes must be better than mine. I never noticed it . . ." She removed the towel from her head and began calmly to dry her hair, but her thoughts were spinning. She had feared this might happen someday, and it was frightening. The two hated each other enough as it was.

"He lusts for you," Jacques grumbled. "I cannot believe you are so blind that you cannot see it."

"And I can't believe you would think such a silly thing. Please, put it from your thoughts, for it's not so."

Jacques's need for her was growing painful. She was tantalizing, her damp hair streaming over her breasts and down her back, and its lilac scent tormenting him, but War Cloud's poisonous presence cast a pall over him. "Hope, for the love of God, I fear for you."

Hope's eyes widened, seeing his very real despair. How on earth did one handle such a problem? She'd never had to reject anyone before. She herself had been the rejected one, and she knew exactly what he was feeling.

She put the towel around her shoulders, crossed

her arms, and said, gently chiding, as if he were a small boy, "Jacques d'Arcy, what am I going to do with you?"

"Wed me."

She shook her head. "Nay, my friend. I care for you, you know I do, but I've already told you—I won't wed you. I've never given you cause to think I would. You know I haven't."

"You have not allowed yourself to," Jacques answered stiffly. "You have been hurt too badly."

Hope grew still. "Who told you that?"

"No one needed to tell me." He saw in her eyes that his arrow had hit the mark. There was some ugly *affaire de coeur* in her past. "Why else turn away a man who loves you unless it is not to be hurt again? God knows I will never hurt you, Hope, I want only to love and take care of you."

She gazed up at him thoughtfully. Perhaps it was best after all to tell him the truth, or at least part of it. Maybe then he would understand why she felt as she did, and would not be so hurt. Aye, she would do it. Contemplating what to say, she wound a strand of damp hair about one finger.

"Maybe I should have told you this before—" She unwound the tendril, wound it again. "I have been disappointed. Deeply disappointed. I was engaged, but it—didn't work out. It's one reason I'm not eager t-to get deeply involved with anyone again. Not for a long time. Maybe not ever . . ."

"I knew there was a sadness."

"Yes, well—it's over now, and I'm not at all eager to open myself to such a thing again. I'm content with my life just as it is."

He said quietly, "I see. I am grateful to be told this."

If she were a normal female, he would embrace her now. He would whisper gently into her ear that when she was his, and she saw how deeply he cherished her, she would wonder why she had ever said nay to him. He would cradle her face, tenderly kiss her lips, and she would melt into his arms. But this wench was no normal female. She was an educated, sophisticated woman with a mind of her own. *Sacre*, but she had a mind of her own. It would only enrage and disgust her if he lay one finger on her now after she had confided in him. She would think he was a boor and a clod.

He cringed. She might already think it, for he had been relentless. But he was at his wits' end. He was not used to pursuing recalcitrant women. It was Jacques d'Arcy who usually was the pursued, and he was in a quandary he had never faced before. Pleading and flattery and sweet talk had gained him nothing, and she cared nothing for mansions nor jewels nor the fact that he'd said he loved her. Seduction was out. What in God's name did that leave? But even as the question loomed in his mind, he knew exactly what was left. Trickery. Some sort of trickery. He had not the vaguest idea what, he knew only that he had to be quick for the clock was ticking. . . .

"Jacques . . ." Hope touched his arm. He had been standing there for so long staring into the distance that she was concerned. "Are you all right?"

He pulled himself back to the present and ran a hand through his hair. "Of course. I was, how do you say it, daydreaming. And as usual, I have kept you from your work." He gave her wet hair a little tug. "Forgive me."

"Don't be silly. It was important that we had this chance to talk. I'm sorry now that I didn't tell you sooner. . . ."

"Give it no more thought."

She watched him mount, and seeing how he slumped in the saddle, she felt a decided pang. She hated hurting him. She hated it. Should she tell him again that she was sorry? Should she ask if they were still friends? Lord, what could be worse—being friends when he wanted to wed her. Damn, she had to say something. She could not just let him ride off in dead silence.

"Jacques!" When he reined and turned, she called, "Come again soon." She saw him smile and touch his fingers to his forehead.

Chapter 14

It was a hot Friday morning in the last week of August. Hope was seated under the cool green canopy of one of the twin oaks at the small desk Tom had made for her. She was grading papers while around her the children sat in the grass diligently working at their slates. Orioles sang, robins scolded, and bees hummed among the asters and goldenrod. It was still summer, but fall was on its way. And after fall, winter would soon follow and what was she going to do with all of these children then?

She mused that her kitchen would not hold them all, for there were nine of them now. In addition to the four Lenapes and the Johnson twins, three new children had come to her last Friday. The Goffs—Samuel, Millicent, and Lemuel. They were wildly eager to learn and had fit right in. This week for the first time, Hope had taught daily classes of two hours each. It had gone well, especially with Flower helping to correct papers. As she pondered it, Millie Goff gave a shriek and jumped to her feet. Hope was by her side immediately.

"Oh, ma'am, I been stung!" The child danced up and down holding her left forefinger, blond pigtails flying and her blue eyes filling with tears. "Oh, ma'am, it do hurt."

"I know it does, honey, I know, but I have something that will make it all better."

Hope removed the stinger, then hurried to her medical bag. She kept it nearby ever since she had discovered that children, even when they were not at play, mysteriously and regularly got splinters, cuts, and nosebleeds. Now she shook a bottle of amber-colored liquid and removed the stopper.

Millie drew back. "What is't?" she whimpered.

"Nothing but goldenrod, love. Pretty flowers. I dry them, powder them with a mortar and pestle, and then add a bit of spring water. Here, let's put some on the hurt." She took the girl's chubby brown hand and smoothed on the lotion. "There, it will feel better in no time—and the next time I make it, you can help me if you like. You can crush and powder the petals. Would you like that?"

Millie wiped her eyes and nose on the hem of her skirt. "A-aye."

"Me, too," Amy Johnson hollered, waving her hand above her head. "I want to make medicine, too."

"And so you shall," Hope replied. "When you had a cold last week, I gave you wintergreen tea. When fall comes, you can collect the leaves for me, and then all of you can learn how to brew it. But for now, let's get back to the alphabet. Amy, can you recite the letters up to Q?"

"Yes'm."

The child was halfway through when Hope observed the leisurely arrival of Firewalker from the north. As he was tethering Nightwind in a shady spot with deep grass, Amy, too, spotted him and raised her voice. Hope hid her concern. The little imp. She wanted his attention and praise, but so far he had paid no heed at all to the white children. It was as if the five of them did not even exist. This time, however, he watched the girl intently, his golden eyes fastened upon her until she had finished. Hope was further amazed and delighted when he nodded his approval and gave her a wink.

"Amy, that was very very good," she told the

blushing girl. "I can see you've worked hard." She moved among the others, looking at their slates. "You've all done well, and I'm pleased. Remember now," she addressed the Indians, "you'll be having a spelling test on Monday, so study your words. Amy and Emma, please be more careful with your printing when you do Monday's assignment, and you three"—she smiled at the Goffs—"this has been a good first week for you. Review your letters and learn the new ones and you'll catch up with the others in no time. Does anyone have any questions?"

There were none, and within minutes the nine had packed up their belongings and were on their ponies and gone. Hope noted that Firewalker's kin no longer waited for him. She felt a tug of embarrassment recalling Flower's knowing smile as she bade them good-bye. Exactly what did she think the two of them did after everyone left? For the truth was, they had done nothing but talk since that magical day last week when they had kissed and lain in each other's arms.

Hope had thought about it endlessly, and it frightened her. The attraction between them was not only enormous, it was hopeless. How could anything ever come of it when it was thought by everyone that Firewalker was a renegade, and when whites and Lenapes were still attacking and killing each other in distant places? The infrequent news that reached them from afar was all bad, and most folk did not distinguish between the Lenapes living miles away and those in the valley. Indians were Indians and they all were the enemy.

Last week when the Goffs showed concern about their children's future classmates and Firewalker's daily visits, Hope had spoken up. She assured them that the four Lenapes were excellent students and that she believed completely in Firewalker's innocence. Now as he came toward her, his muscles shifting, rippling under his polished skin, and his hair shining blue-black with the sun on it, her heart pounded. She wondered if he were going to kiss her again, and if she should allow him. She wanted it, aye. It was a thing she had been dreaming about, a stolen moment of pleasure without any consequences—but she feared they could not stop with kisses as they had before.... She looked up, suddenly shy and so uneasy she could not even smile.

"Hello, Firewalker."

"Good morning." Firewalker clasped his hands safely behind his back.

Studying that beautiful face with its somber green-flecked eyes, white brow, and small straight nose, he marveled at how he had felt about her not so very long ago. Hostile, resentful, scornful, suspicious. She had been the enemy. He had never touched a white woman before nor had he wanted to or planned to. He had prayed to his manitou for the strength to resist the temptation. Now, he gave his humble thanks to the Creator for putting such a perfect creature on this earth and bringing her there for him. This was his woman....

Suddenly, like a knife in his heart, he was remembering her on the forest floor, her gown pulled up over her head, her legs forced apart, the Mengwes' dirty hands grasping and cruelly squeezing her. He was jolted by the fury that swept him still, but then he told himself that all was well. She was safe now. No Mengwe dared venture onto these lands, and when she was his, he would let nothing and no one harm her.

"How was school?" he asked, more gruffly than he intended.

"Fine." Hope wondered at the odd wild look that had suddenly come into his eyes and left just as quickly. "By the way, it was nice of you to notice Amy."

He shrugged it off. "Did those bucks behave?"

"Aye. Your four are rapidly building a nice vocabulary of nouns and verbs."

Vocabulary . . . nouns . . . verbs . . . His anger toward the Mengwes turned inward toward himself. The words made no sense to his ears at all, but he was not about to reveal his ignorance by asking what they meant. He nodded wisely.

"Of course everything is very simple still," Hope went on. "The fat cat runs . . . the big dog sits—that kind of thing, but then you have to remember they've been at it such a short time. Frankly, they're amazing. Especially Flower and Stargazer." Her heart went harder, seeing those golden eyes lingering on her mouth.

"They are special, I know it well," Firewalker said low.

This day he was going to hold her and kiss her and nothing was going to stop him. He had been hungering for her, yearning to touch his lips to hers again. . . . By the Eternal, she was glorious. Unclasping his hands gripped so tightly behind him, he reached out and lightly stroked her cheek. He smiled. The texture of her skin was as he had remembered. Satin, white satin, and her hair was a gleaming ebony veil spilling over her breasts and down her back. He saw her lips part and the black centers of her eyes widen, nearly hiding the gray. He heard her breathing quicken, matching his own.

Wordlessly, his arms slid around her, drawing her close and lifting her off her feet to clasp her against his bare chest. He covered her mouth with his. She tasted so fresh and sweet and returned his kisses so hungrily, his head swam. She was his, was there any doubt? Never would a woman kiss a man in such a way if she did not feel in her heart and soul that she belonged to him.

Molding her to him more closely, Firewalker pressed kisses over her face and throat, over her hair and her slender shoulders before hungrily claiming her lips again. Her soft moans brought him to the limit of his endurance. He wanted her, but he would not dishonor her. He would first ask her to join with him, to become his wife. He cradled her face.

"Hope—"

"Oh, Firewalker . . ." Released from his kisses, Hope gasped air into her lungs. She was on fire, her body filled with hot flickerings and pulsings and yearnings she had never experienced before. This was no stolen moment of pleasure . . . this was the center of an earthquake . . . the flaming maw of a volcano.

Noting her glazed, half-closed eyes and quickened breathing, Firewalker knew that the time for talk had passed. For now, all that mattered was that she wanted him as much as he wanted her. When he tightened his arms about her, she melted into him, her pink lips parting and eagerly accepting his searching tongue. Lowering her to the grass beneath the oak, he kissed her mouth thoroughly and deeply, kissed the soft full swell of her bosom beneath the rough cotton of her gown.

Hope's thoughts were swept into a swiftly moving spiral of delight as Firewalker's mouth and hands moved over her, gentle yet commanding and possessive. She wanted him to make love to her, her entire body cried out for it, but she knew she must not. She dared not, for nothing had changed—yet body and soul, she wanted him. She was flowing into him, liquid flame, ready and eager for him to thrust within her and ignite her and make her his—and never let her go. Oh, God, it was madness, wanting a man she could not have and a thing that could never be. She pulled away from him, put her hands to her flushed cheeks.

"Firewalker, we mustn't . . ."

But her eyes and body belied the words. She did not protest his arms slipping around her, sealing her to him again as his mouth sealed hers with his kisses. She did not protest when he unbuttoned the front of her gown, and his mouth sought her bared breasts. And when he lifted her skirts and his gentle teasing fingers found the soft darkness between her thighs, pleasure shot through her, and tears came to her eyes. In a haze of delight, she thought how handsome he was, how dark and strong, and yet how careful and gentle he was being with her. How could anyone think him savage . . .

Firewalker gave a soft groan seeing those long white legs again. They were as smooth and flawless as the rest of her. Tenderly caressing, he slid his hands up and down them and brushed kisses over her knees and the curve of her belly. When his fingers went once more to that hidden place of her maidenhood, it was hot and wet, beckoning him, enticing him, yet he saw that tears stole down her cheeks.

He asked softly, "Hope, do you still say we must not?"

"Nay, I want you . . ." He had never seemed more dear nor beautiful nor more exciting than in his concern for her. He was what she wanted. Why had she ever doubted it, and why should anything matter but that? Her arms went around him to pull him close, closer, ever closer. "Oh, Firewalker, I want you so much. . . ."

He smiled at her eagerness. Doffing his breechclout, he knelt beside her in the grass and parted her legs. He saw her eyes widen as she gazed on his manhood which was fully extended. Seeing her uncertainty, he whispered, "Nay, little fox, I will not hurt you." He ached with the sudden fierce surge of desire that filled him as he bent to taste her lips again and to suckle her hardened nipples.

Hope's answer was another hungry kiss. She had been shocked by his size, aye, but he was a big man, and she must expect a certain amount of pain. As she thought it, his fingers were between her thighs, fluttering, easing, opening her maidenhood to him, and then, like lightning striking, he was within her, and she felt a part of herself separate. The rending brought a small involuntary shriek from her, and then the long smooth length of him was plunging slowly, slowly in and out, stroking, rubbing against her passageway to touch the very entrance to her womb.

A flame had been lit when Firewalker entered her, and now it was burning deep inside her. Heat filled her body, and colors—red, orange, purple, white—dazzled the dark reaches of her mind; searing, soaring, expanding, matching the white-hot sensations that soared and seemed to explode in the very center of her. Time stretched out, boundless, endless, as if the paradise in which she walked with him would last forever. Hope heard herself cry out as Firewalker carried her to the pinnacle with him, heard her whispered thanks to God for this strong gentle man He had given her.

Afterwards, Firewalker donned his breechclout and righted Hope's clothing, tenderly tucking her skirts about her legs, and buttoning the small buttons at her neckline. He then wrapped his arms around her and they lay quietly as the sun crossed the sky. He was in a daze of contentment. He had never known such fierce hunger or sweet release, and he kissed her hair and her closed lids over and over as she slept, and listened to the beating and the soaring of his heart. He had been the first. She had not known any man before him. He was the first. . . .

Hope fought her way up from her deep sleep and the wonderful dream she'd been having. She and Firewalker had been making love, and she could still feel the way it had been. She sighed, pressing her thighs together to prolong the exquisite sensation of having him held so tightly within her. She opened her eyes then, and—oh, nay . . . It had not been a dream at all. She was in the deep grass under the oak, and she lay in Firewalker's strong arms. Oh, Lord . . . She sat up, remembering fully her disgraceful behavior. She had actually begged him to make love to her. Worse, she was feeling the hot stirrings all over again just looking at him. Her face flamed.

"What must you think of me . . ."

Firewalker had heard her small shocked intake of breath. He had seen her hand fly to her mouth, and then to her heart. He gave a low chuckle. "I think you have pleased me greatly."

Hope got to her feet. She was mortified. "I don't know what to say. . . ."

He rose, took her shoulders, and turned her firmly to face him. "Hope, I will not dishonor you."

She folded her lips tightly. "I have dishonored myself."

"Join with me," he said quietly.

She gazed up at him, astonished. He was willing to join with the enemy? It was a thing she had never expected, and she could not suppress a small laugh. "What a sacrifice . . ."

Firewalker chuckled. "Sacrifice has nothing to do with it." His head was filled with the smoldering memories of their lovemaking.

"We are still enemies. Nothing has changed. . . ."

He slid his arms around her and pulled her close again. "You and I are not enemies. Your father and my uncle are not enemies. You and my sister are not enemies. . . ."

She was weary suddenly. "You know well that's not what I meant. There is fighting still. We hear of it."

"There is peace in this valley, and for many leagues around." His eyes held a devilish glow. "There is great peace between the two of us. . . ."

And if a man and woman truly loved each other, Hope told herself, nothing else mattered. Love would overcome all. But this was not love. This flame burning inside her, so sweet and bright and tantalizing, was the age-old call of the wild, the siren song that had nothing to do with love. His hard arms around her had her melting again, wanting to make love again, but for certain now she would not. She refused absolutely to give in to it and compound her wrongdoing. She expected more of herself than that, and aye, she wanted more.

Mere desire for a man who was wonderful to look at was not enough. She wanted a man with whom she could share life and children, a man who would laugh and cry with her and grow old with her, a man who would die for her as she would for him. For such a man she had meant to save herself, that faceless, nameless man she would wed someday. Thinking of it, she felt cold regret. She doubted she would ever wed, feeling as she did—afraid to trust herself and her happiness to someone who might hurt her as Sam had. And as for saving herself, that part of her dream had ended this day.

Firewalker was impatient for her answer, but she seemed to have fallen under a dark shadow. The closeness and the passion they had shared was gone, and she was a stiff, icy stranger in his arms.

"Do my own people frighten you?" he asked.

Hope shook her head. "Nay." Her head swam she was so confused. How could she have fallen so quickly from that paradise she had found when this was the same man who had taken her there?

"What is it then? Why do you tremble." He tucked a silky tendril behind her ear and kissed the side of her throat. "How beautiful you are . . ."

Hope willed herself to be strong. "Please, don't . . ."

"Don't what?" His arms about her tightened. He was not going to give up.

"Say that I'm beautiful, or kiss me, or hold me like this. And please don't think you need to make an honorable woman of me. . . ." She pushed against his chest and was surprised when he actually released her. She felt disappointment. She wanted him to kiss her again—and again, and again. And she loved his saying she was beautiful, and the way it made her all hot and weak inside.

Firewalker stood scowling down at her. She was being totally, ridiculously female. She wanted him.

He saw it in her eyes and felt it in her soft yielding mouth and in the way she allowed him to hold her, yet she refused to admit it. He knew also that there was no woman alive more stubborn than this one. He stepped back, crossed his arms, and regarded her with quiet amusement.

"It will be as you wish. I will not hold you, nor call you beautiful, nor kiss you again. Nor will I make love to you—not until you beg me." His lips twitched at the surprised look on her face. "There is one more thing—you are my woman, Hope Caldwell, and we will join."

Hope stared up at him, dumbfounded. However he had come to such a conclusion, it was impossible. She heard herself murmur, "I'm honored. . . ." The words had a familiar ring. First Jacques, now Firewalker. In fact, he was behaving like Jacques. Bringing this up so suddenly and without warning, overwhelming her, deciding for her . . . She tried to stay calm. "I am honored, Firewalker, believe me, but—"

"We will talk of it tomorrow. I but wanted you to know—you are my woman, and we will join."

"We cannot." Hope raised her voice, her calm forgotten. She was completely confused. She had never before experienced those feelings he had kindled within her—ecstasy, excitement, and, aye, contentment—but she was not in love with this man. She scarcely knew him; it was that she had been swept off her feet by his glorious appearance and his gentleness. But when all was said and done, she would not just be joining him, she would be joining his entire family, his people. And their two peoples were blood enemies. . . .

Firewalker held up his hand. "Tomorrow."

He was not concerned. Not when he thought of how she had given herself to him, slim and soft and warm in his arms and kissing him more hungrily than any woman had ever kissed him before. He understood her worries about their two peoples, but he was determined it would not keep them apart. *Matta*, he was not concerned. She was his.

Hope was surprised and relieved when Firewalker did not return either Saturday or Sunday. She hoped desperately it was because he had changed his mind about her, but on Monday she learned from Flower that he and War Cloud had been summoned to a Lenape village to the south to help settle a dispute. It was not known when he would return.

Only the Lenapes were in class that day, and when Tuesday came and went without the five whites appearing, Hope feared they might be ill. On Wednesday, when they still did not come and sent no word as to why, she told Flower of her worries.

"Something must be wrong," she fretted. "I'm going to ride over after class and see what's going on."

"I will go with you," Flower replied.

They stopped at the Johnson cabin first. Seeing the door open, and two horses at the hitching rail, Hope called out a hello. When no one answered, she dismounted, crossed the stoop, knocked, and called again: "Hello? Anybody home?" She was puzzled. It was clear there were visitors, yet the living room was empty, and no one answered.

"Can we stop on the way back?" Flower asked.

"Aye. I'm sure they're close by." Riding next to the Goff homestead, Hope found Mary Goff, in apron and bonnet, bent over her kitchen garden.

"Good afternoon," Hope called from the saddle. "I've come to see how the children are." She had brought her medical bag just in case she could be of help.

Mary Goff straightened her back, shaded her eyes, and gazed up at Hope with a frozen unsmiling face. She did not even acknowledge Flower's presence. "They be fine," she answered shortly, and returned to her weeding.

Hope did not show her surprise at such rudeness.

"I'm so glad. Since they haven't come to class, I thought perhaps they were ill."

"They be fine." This time the woman did not bother to look up.

"I—don't understand . . ."

"They'm ull not be seein' ye again. They'm lost interest."

Hope felt a leap of unnamed dread. "Mistress Goff, I never saw children more interested in learning than your three. How could this happen so suddenly?"

"Wull, it happened, so don't thee be lookin' fer 'em. They'll not be back, my three."

When she flashed a look of active dislike at Flower, Hope felt a flare of resentment accompanying her dread. "I would like to speak with them, please," she said crisply.

"No need, mistress. They be wi' their father i' th' fields. They've no time fer thee er fer learnin' now." She straightened again and fixed Hope with a hostile blue glare. "I'll thank thee now ter excuse me." She marched toward the cabin, stiff backed and her head high.

Hope stared after her in angry astonishment and then met Flower's eyes. She murmured almost to herself, "Something very strange is going on here." Strange and terrible. It seemed almost as if Mary Goff hated her. She wondered then, had the Johnsons and their visitors been there after all and avoided her? Damn, what was happening?

Flower said quietly but firmly, "She is not a nice woman, *n'tschu*. I don't like her. Will it—be the same at the Johnsons?"

"I don't know." Hope was not sure that she wanted to stop there again. The confrontation with Mary Goff had shaken her. Yet how else could she learn what this was all about? She gave Beauty's ribs a gentle kick. "Let's find out."

They arrived just as Maud Johnson and her two visitors walked out onto the stoop talking and laughing. Hope smiled despite her racing heart and greeted them, but they stared back in chilly silence. Anger constricted her throat and then sank, leaden and sickening, into her stomach. Pittsburgh. It was Pittsburgh all over again. She wanted, childishly, to accuse them of having hidden when she was there earlier. Instead she gazed down on them coolly.

"What is your problem, Maud?" Her cheeks flamed when the other two women sniggered and retreated into the cabin.

"Th' problem's not mine, but yours, mistress. Actin' so big with yer doctorin' an' yer teachin' an' all the while—" She shook her head pityingly, and gave Flower a scornful look.

"All the while what, pray?" Hope demanded, so fury filled she could scarcely choke out the words. "Do tell me, Maud."

Maud Johnson rested her hands on her ample hips. "We're decent women here, mistress, an' as sich, I'll jist ask ye nice t' move along now, an' not cause no trouble. I wunt want t' fetch m' man . . ."

Hope stared at her, too crushed and angry to reply to the insinuation. Decent women—meaning, of course, that she herself was not. What in God's name . . . Had they somehow heard about Pittsburgh and thought she was a murderess? She was shaking as she spun Beauty about, gave the mare her heels, and galloped hard toward Twin Oaks with Flower close behind. Once home, she could only pace, white faced and silent, before the cabin.

Flower watched gravely for a long time before she spoke. "That one you do not need as a friend, *n'tschu*. Nor the other."

Hope shook her head. "I just don't understand. I can't imagine what has happened. . . ."

Flower fell into step beside her. "Will the other women act the same now?"

Hope pressed her pounding temples. "I don't know." She was so hurt and confused, she wanted to weep. But not with Flower there.

"Hope . . ."

"Aye?" She noticed for the first time her friend's pained face, and it tugged at her heart. "Honey, please—I don't want you to worry! I sure it's some misunderstanding that can all be worked out." In truth, she thought no such thing, but she put a smile on her face and gave Flower's hand a squeeze.

Flower made a face. "Those two are women of salt. They tried to make you small, and I don't like them. Come and live with my people, Hope."

Hope's eyes filled. "You honor me, *n'tschu,* but this is where I belong. Here in my own home with my father. As I said, I'm sure this is all a misunderstanding that will work itself out."

Flower caught both her hands. "But if you are unhappy, you will come to us. Promise me."

Hope pulled in a deep breath and released it. "I will come to you, I promise it."

She had counted on her father's making sense of the whole dreadful affair when he came home for supper. As it happened, he stopped by only long enough to collect his medical bag. One of his patients on the west hill needed him. She poured out her worries instead to Jacques d'Arcy when he came for an evening visit.

Chapter 15

Sitting on the breeze-swept stoop beside Hope, lending her his support while he enjoyed her tea and cakes, Jacques reveled secretly in her distress. It had been five days since he had last seen her, and in that time, he had managed to bring about her downfall. The Goff and Johnson women had responded exactly as he'd intended they would. His desire for Hope, and his jealousy of her obvious feelings for Firewalker, had led him to conceive and put into motion a reckless plan which had borne fruit so easily and so swiftly, he wished he had done it sooner. He suspected Hope might be his wife even before the month War Cloud had allotted him was ended.

Ma foi, but it was a clever plan—and diabolical. But then all was fair in love and war. And now it was time his future bride learned the worst. He patted crumbs from his mouth and beard with a calico napkin and gazed at her dolefully.

"Hope, I must tell you—your strange confrontation with Madame Goff may be connected to a thing I heard this afternoon."

Hope put her teacup on the floor beside her rocker. "What did you hear?"

"It will grieve you further."

"Jacques, for heaven's sake, tell me!"

"Know that I would bear this burden on my—"

She could have shaken him. "Are you going to tell me or not?"

Jacques, too, set his cup carefully on the floorboards. He leaned forward, elbows on his knees. "It is said you are an Indian lover."

Hope's defiance welled. "Well, good, I plead guilty."

He gave her a dark look. "It is said also that you are Firewalker's squaw."

It was as if a hand had closed around her throat. "I see."

She wanted to die, thinking of someone's lurking in the shadows and spying on their nakedness and their lovemaking. But as for the accusation of being Firewalker's squaw, it did not faze her. She had been truly honored by his asking her to join. But she was well aware that no white man on earth would consider it an honor. A white woman who chose to live with a brave, with or without wedding vows, was an object of scorn and contempt. And while anyone who looked could see that she was not living with Firewalker, they had chosen to condemn her anyway. So be it. Recalling the paradise she had felt in Firewalker's arms, sharing his kisses and belonging to him however briefly, she wondered if perhaps she was exactly what they thought she was: a fallen woman. She lifted her chin.

"Who told you this amazing thing, and how does he or she come to know so much?" She felt almost sorry for Jacques, he looked so wretched.

"Several men came to my trading post, and as they looked over my wares, they were laughing and joking about it until I ordered them to still their venomous tongues. I regret to say you know them all"—he named their names—"but as for where the devils heard such a tale, God only knows. It is vicious and I deplore it." He shook his head. "How I regret being the bearer of such a tale. . . ."

Hope could have wept, but it would not help matters to make a scene. Not when Jacques was already so distressed. She stepped off the stoop and began walking across the clearing, long furious strides, her gown whipping about her ankles and the wind lifting her long hair.

"How dare they?" she said finally, breathless with the exertion and her anger. "Firewalker would never use me in such a way nor would I allow him to. I have a mind to confront every one of them and demand to know who told them such slanderous rot. In fact, I'd like to wring it out of them!"

She was furious. But she was also powerless. No one would tell her anything. At the thought, her head began to pound. She put her hands to her temples and squeezed her eyes shut. Dear God, it *was* going to be another Pittsburgh—and she had been so happy here. . . .

"You are hurt and furious as well you should be," Jacques said quietly, walking beside her. "Be assured that I told them in the sternest words possible that you are a gentlewoman, and not one to consort with braves."

Hope gave a wild laugh. She wanted to fling out that she was indeed one who consorted with braves. With one special brave. Oh, God, who had spied on them? Who? And how had it happened when she almost always heard the approach of hoofbeats? Had someone come on foot especially to spy on her? But it was useless to speculate. Somehow and in some way, someone had seen them or guessed about them. Someone who wanted to hurt her . . .

"If I may advise you . . ." Jacques offered. When she gave a vague nod, he went on, "I think it would be a grave mistake to go to them. I think you should behave judiciously in this matter. Keep your dignity and ignore what they say. Put yourself above it . . ."

"I suppose you're right," she murmured. "If I went to them, I would tell them exactly what I thought of them. . . ." She snatched up a stone and flung it as far and as hard as she could. "But it would give me such huge satisfaction."

"And make you their enemy."

"I already am." She began walking slowly back toward the cabin.

"It need not be for long."

"It can be forever as far as I'm concerned." She found another stone and sailed it off into the blue.

Jacques shook his dark head. "I think you have forgotten, *mon amie,* that these are simple folk for whom the red man is the Great Enemy. They hate and fear him for good reason." Jacques knew little of Lenape history, but for a fact, he knew that in the recent war they had committed to the Americans but had fought against them in the end. "Massacres and abductions are still carried on, and surely you can see how it looked when you began teaching the Lenapes. . . ."

Hope's resentment bubbled. "The Lenapes are no threat, and I resent very much being ostracized for my friendship with them. How can people be so cruel to other people? Have they nothing better to do with their time?"

"It is most unfair," Jacques agreed calmly. "But the minds of these farmers are small, and they thrive on gossip. It is their entertainment to speculate on the doings of a woman who is so superior to them in all ways."

Hope frowned. "Superior? I'm certainly not superior. I'm not clever at sewing, I don't knit beautiful garments or bake bread that melts in your mouth."

Jacques smiled. "But you set bones and sew up torn flesh and a hundred other things. You are superior, *ma chère.* Never doubt it. And never forget that the dullards of this world like nothing better than to see such folk fall. I am surprised you have not experienced such a thing before."

Seeing those gray eyes shutter and a flush brighten her pale cheeks, Jacques was intrigued. So, it was more than an unfortunate love affair that had driven her from Pittsburgh. Sensing suddenly that it was something scandalous, he was heartened. He would use any means he could to win her. It was a pity that she did not confide in him, but if something was to be learned, his eyes and ears in the city would discover it soon enough.

"If they want to see me fall," Hope said quietly, "they'll have a long wait."

Jacques's eyes gleamed. "You are as courageous as you are beautiful—and I will sing your praises at every opportunity." But she would fall. For a certainty, she would fall and he would catch her.

"Then they'll hate you, too," she murmured. And they would hate her father. It killed her that she was hurting him all over again.

"If I cannot help you in such a small way, what manner of man am I?"

Hope remembered the ice in Mary Goff's eyes and Maud Johnson's insulting words. "I think it's too late for anyone to help me."

"It is not. I have a sixth sense about this, and I perceive that the best thing for you now is to cease your teaching. Just for a time, *savez-vous?* Just long enough for them to see that you are no Indian lover and—"

"I hate that word!"

And she hated feeling helpless, and she hated those who so carelessly and eagerly hurt others with never a thought for the consequences. She was consumed by hatred, and she hated her hatred most of all. Tears filled her eyes and streamed down her cheeks.

"Ah, *ma foi,* now see what I have done. I am a wretch. Forgive me."

"It's not you. . . ."

It had not been his plan to touch her on this visit, but now he seized the moment. He cupped her face, and gave her mouth a light kiss. "All will be well, I promise you." He was pleased that she did not draw away.

Hope did not respond, but neither did she resist the brief touching of his lips to hers. She knew it was his attempt to comfort her, and it was not in her heart to hurt and reject him just then as she herself was being hurt and rejected. But suddenly his arms were around her and his tongue was probing her mouth in a deep kiss which left her gasping for breath. She twisted her head to one side and tried to free herself.

"Jacques!"

"*Ma belle,* listen while my heart speaks."

She said through clenched teeth, "Let me go, Jacques."

Her defiance made her irresistible. Pink cheeks, flashing eyes, her small white teeth showing. Jacques smoothed back a long shining strand of hair from her cheek and held her more tightly. "Come, come, admit you enjoyed that as much as I."

"Now!" Hope's voice and eyes crackled.

Jacques ignored the command. He said stiffly, "It would seem that vile rumor is true. You prefer the kisses of a bloodthirsty heathen to mine—and prefer disgrace to respectability."

Hope's palm connected with his cheek in a resounding slap. She was furious—and she was disappointed. She had been blind! Jacques d'Arcy did not care about her or her wishes at all. He only cared about himself. His desires, his needs, his beliefs. How could she have been so stupid about him for so long?

Jacques reddened, and released her. As she strode back toward the cabin, he followed her. "Hope—I am sorry. I spoke in anger, but can you not see this is absurd? All of this squaw foolishness will cease if you let it be known you will wed me. These men know that I am a respectable man. They know I would not marry a woman who had soiled herself with a brave."

She clenched her teeth. There it was. *Soiled.* They all thought she was soiled, and yet when she thought of Firewalker's gentleness, and his arms about her and his making love to her, he was all that she cared about on this earth. She felt so tired suddenly, she wanted only to crawl into bed and sleep. Just sleep. She continued plodding toward the cabin.

"Hope . . ."

Hope shook her head and kept walking. Nothing he could say would erase her rage and her disappointment with him, and she was tired of arguing with him. He had a wall around him. He thought he knew what was best for her but he did not. He absolutely did not. He only knew what was best for Jacques d'Arcy.

Jacques's concern grew as she marched on in frigid silence. She was neatly ensnared in the trap he had set for her, but somehow she was slipping from his grasp. He caught her arm as she stepped onto the stoop. She shook it off.

"Hope, again—I am sorry. Forgive me. It was wrong of me to kiss you." And stupid. *Sacre,* but it was stupid. It had never been his intention, not today. The wench was an iceberg; he had known he must thaw her a bit first.

"I'm very tired, Jacques."

"Let us not part on such an unpleasant note. I know I do not deserve it, but say that you forgive me."

Anything, she thought. Anything to send him on his way. She said crisply, "I forgive you."

"*Bon.*" Seeing her sway as she stepped onto the stoop, he would have steadied her, but for the steeliness of her eyes. His own narrowed. "Are you all right?"

"I'm fine."

"Thomas will be returning soon?"

"Aye."

"Then I will depart and let you get some rest. But I will return tomorrow, for we must certainly talk of this further."

"Very well." She thought bitterly that he could talk all day and all night, aye, all week if he wanted, but it would do no good. She would never wed him. And he had touched and kissed her for the last time.

"Adieu then."

"Adieu."

Jacques's spirits lifted slightly when she actually gave him a smile before going inside. He mounted, but then sat gazing pensively at the house for some time before he forced himself to be on his way.

Riding across the highlands, Jacques felt scattered. Had she really forgiven him? He doubted it, except she said she had and he had never known her to tell a lie. She was the most truthful woman he had ever known, and yet— He shook his head recalling how furious she had been when he kissed her. But she was so docile when she'd bade him farewell. Damn the woman, she had him so confused, he did not know what to think. He could only pray that tomorrow those beautiful eyes would be opened, and she would see that her very honor depended upon their moving ahead swiftly with marriage plans.

His confidence grew as he thought of her dilemma. What woman could stand up to the scorn and ridicule facing her? There was nothing more disgusting, *nothing*, than a white woman who had given herself to a brave. The shame from that gossip would surely make her back down; she was not that strong. And Thomas liked him, and for a certainty would not want his daughter to live in disgrace. What father did? Tomorrow he would have a man-to-man talk with him. *Bien.* Thomas would be on his side.

He sighed and wondered, did the world actually look brighter or was he a fool for thinking it did? *Mais alors,* he would not be negative. It was brighter. He felt in his bones that it all would work out to the good. Perhaps even within the week, *la belle* Hope would be his. Her body, all of her earthly goods, aye, even her soul could belong to him if all went as it should.

Tom had worked the whole afternoon clearing a neighbor's field of rocks and boulders, and then spent more time than he'd planned comforting an elderly patient. He returned home at sunset to find Hope on the stoop in the fading light, a small pile of mending in her lap. He kissed the top of her head. "Still busy, I see."

"I wanted to get it done." Hope caught his hand and squeezed it. "Are you hungry?"

"Nay, I've had plenty. Peg kept the food coming all day." He pulled off his boots, stretched and yawned. "I'm tuckered out. I hope no one gets sick tonight. Maybe you'll go if they do. . . ." He did not miss the muscles tightening about her soft mouth.

"Girleen, what is it?"

Hope tried to smile. "My day has been somewhat of a disaster."

Tom took off his hat, sat down on the step, and frowned up at her. "Tell me about it."

"Well, it started when I—was worried about the children who haven't been to class this week. I went to enquire about them, and I—I was snubbed by Mary Goff and insulted by Maud Johnson."

After hearing the whole tale, Tom shook his head, in angry bemusement. "Sonofagun. It makes no sense, does it? Damned silly old hens." He hadn't a clue as to what ailed them or why they would have treated Hope so badly. But then life here in the north was hard for a woman. Working from sun to sun with none of those things available that were dear to a woman's heart—shopping, parties, dancing, and such. It made tempers short. He said, with more confidence than he felt, easily, "Don't get too riled just yet, princess. It's probably some kind of misunderstanding." He watched as Hope lay down her mending and was shocked by the dullness of her eyes.

"It's more than that. There's trouble, Father."

Tom got to his feet. "What sort of trouble?"

Hope found it hard to meet his eyes. "Jacques says that the men are—calling me Firewalker's squaw."

Great God almighty. He pulled in a long breath, let it hiss out, and forced a smile. He'd not have her see his concern, but for the love of God, was there to be no peace for this girl of his?

He said finally, "Well, now, no one mentioned it to me today."

"Who would dare with your being a good neighbor and helping clear fields?"

Tom felt the heat rising into his head and steaming out of his ears. "Jacques was sure, was he?"

"Aye. A group of them were laughing about it at his store. Scott and Fielding and Kestner—" She named the others and watched his face darken.

"The bloody bastards. And to think I was there working with them . . ." He slammed a fist into his palm, and shook his head. He got up, pulled his daughter into his arms, and gave her a long silent hug. "If I ever find who started such a rumor . . ."

"I'm so sorry," Hope murmured against his chest. "It seems I keep hurting you."

"Lord, girl, if that's not just like you, worrying about me when you're the one under fire."

Hope smiled. "Who else can I worry about? You're all I have." She gathered her mending and carried it inside.

Tom followed, his heart almost bursting with the love and sorrow he felt for her. It wasn't right nor fair for her to have had such burdens twice in her young life. And neither of them warranted. Thunderation, if he ever caught the bastard responsible for this latest outrage, he'd horsewhip him within an inch of his worthless life. And what was saddest of all, he'd have welcomed Firewalker gladly into his family if Hope wished it. There was none finer.

But he knew he was alone in his approval. Except for a few, including the Springers, this was as skittery a bunch of whites as he'd ever come across. There was no telling them that Firewalker could not be accused of wrongdoing without proof, and no telling them that the Shenango Lenapes were not out to scalp them in their sleep. He turned up the lamp and laid another log on the fire. The kitchen seemed as dark and damp as a grave suddenly. Watching Hope sitting quietly at the table, folding and stacking the mended clothes in a neat pile, he ached for her. He hadn't done well at protecting her.

"Father . . ."

"Aye, darlin'?"

Hope could not look at him. She clasped her hands and gazed down at them. "You can see, can't you, why I must leave here? Why I want to leave?"

After Jacques left, she had not collapsed into bed and slept as she thought she might. She had instead fought a fierce battle within herself, warring back and forth over the various things she might do. She could retaliate, she could turn the other cheek, or, as Jacques had suggested, she could ignore what was said and rise above it. But the truth was, she did not want to fight, nor turn the other cheek, nor ignore her accusers and rise above the situation. Very simply, she did not want to live among folk who would drag her down gleefully and then wipe their feet on her and shun her. Folk who scorned Firewalker and his people. She played over and over the words of those hateful women and the scathing looks they had hurled at her. And she could well imagine the leers and the coarse jesting of the men as they laughed about her and Firewalker. They disgusted her, all of them, both the men *and* the women . . .

Tom frowned. "Damnation, Hope, what foolishness is this?"

"I haven't forgotten that Thunderhead invited me to live with the Lenapes if I ever chose, and Flower was with me this afternoon. She wants me to come."

"For the love of God!"

Seeing his gray eyes shimmer suddenly, Hope nearly wept herself. But she would not have him think she was anything but confident about her decision. She smiled up at him.

"Will I be any more miserable there than here among women who shun and insult me and men who laugh at me?" When he did not answer, she went on: "Firewalker has often told me that his people treasure my skills. And I love Flower—she's the sister I never had. . . ." But thinking of the hostility of Walks Alone, and of War Cloud's fierce painted face and greased scalp lock, she was apprehensive. She pushed it aside. She could not be fearful about her plan, or she could never go ahead with it.

Tom muttered, "I can't let you do it. In fact, I forbid it." He had been in Indian villages aplenty, and the thought of his beautiful, gently-bred daughter living under such hardship shook him right down to his roots. He had not raised her for such a life. But then neither had he raised her to be the butt of slander and scandal.

Hope had not expected him to yield easily. "Then you'd rather have me live among folk I'll never see nor talk to because I'm an Indian lover? Folk whose children aren't allowed near me for fear I might soil them?"

"Not the Springers. Maybeth and Luke aren't that sort, and I can think of several others. As for the rest, you're best off without them." But he knew in his heart she could not live that way.

"I've not forgotten Maybeth and Luke, believe me. I'll come and visit—and there's her babe to deliver. But, Father, I want to live with the Lenapes. They need me, and I need to be needed. I want to do more in my life than cook and sew." He looked so old suddenly and so sad, she got up and threw her arms about him in a fierce hug. It broke her heart to see him looking that way, and now she had to hurt him further. She had to tell him everything. "Papa, I—want to be near Firewalker. He's asked me to join with him, but in truth, I'm confused. I want to be near him, but I—I hate hurting you and—" She stared, seeing that he was laughing. He was shaking his head and laughing and laughing. She whispered, "Wh-what is it?"

"Ah, girleen . . ."

His laughter was so contagious, Hope began to

giggle there in his arms. Pounding his chest with her fists as she had when she was small, she demanded, "Tell me! What is it?"

He shook his head again, marveling to see that the light was back in her eyes again. "So it's Firewalker, is it?"

"Aye . . ."

"To think, I was worried damn near to death about you, and you've gone and caught yourself the finest buck in the northland." He hugged her until she could scarcely breathe and gave her a resounding kiss on the cheek.

Hope was astonished. "You're—not angry?"

"Angry? Little girl, I welcome him. With open arms. I've always wanted a good man for you, and there's none finer than Firewalker. I couldn't have picked anyone I like more if I'd searched for years. Hell, he's dependable, hardworking, honorable."

"I can hardly believe this."

Tom chuckled and gave her another hug. "Believe it. If my approval is all you need to wed him, you've got it."

It was not all she needed. She needed to be sure in her own heart—but she did not want to think about it just then. "I want you to know I'm not deserting you. I'll come back often to visit and wash your clothes and cook. . . ."

"Nay, lass, I'll not have you waiting on the old man," Tom said with mock sternness. "Don't forget, I never intended for you to be here even. I can fend for myself just dandy. On second thought, I've half a mind to go and live with the Lenapes myself. Let these folks doctor themselves for a while and see how they like it."

"Tom Caldwell!"

He grinned down at her. "It's damned pleasant to contemplate, but, nay, I haven't forgotten my oath." He yawned, stretched. "Like I said, I'm going to turn in early, then in the morning after I bring in the hay,

I'll take you down. There's rain on the way and I want to beat it."

"Take me down?" Hope protested, laughing.

"Aye, take you down. I'll see you safely in Firewalker's hands and that's that."

"But no one knows about us—only you."

"Then I'll put you in Thunderhead's hands. And that, my chick, is that." When he got that look in his eye, Hope knew better than to argue. "All right, if it will make you happy. But I want to get there early—before Flower and the boys can leave for here." And before Jacques came. Her stomach knotted, imagining how he would react when he learned what she had done. Perhaps he would finally believe that she was not going to marry him.

Chapter 16

During Firewalker's five-day sojourn south in Kuskusky with War Cloud, he thought constantly of Hope Caldwell and their lovemaking. He had allowed his spirits to soar with the birds, for she was the fairest thing he had ever seen in his life, and she was his. He knew instinctively that she was not a woman who would give herself to a man lightly, yet she had given herself to him. They would join, he had not a doubt of it, and every night she would lie in his arms.

As he and his brother rode homeward, his thoughts were still alive with her. He would ride directly to Twin Oaks, for he could not allow another day to pass without seeing her. His heart swelled as he considered that this very night she could be his.

War Cloud was immersed in his own glum thoughts of the woman who had disrupted his life. In the five days he had been gone, he could not shake them. But then much could happen in five days. Perhaps d'Arcy had moved swiftly for a change and wed Hope Caldwell.

Seeing his brother's sudden grim smile, Firewalker said, "Something pleases you finally. You have been under a cloud these many days."

And it was Firewalker's doing, thought War Cloud bitterly. If he had not gotten the woman to teach their cousins, he himself would be walking under sunny skies now instead of within the gray cloud that was smothering him. It was clear that Firewalker hungered for her still. He had said nothing to anyone, but War Cloud knew his brother. He lusted after Caldwell's-daughter more deeply than ever.

Giving in to the malicious spirit that touched him suddenly, he said, "I *am* pleased, *kehella*. I am thinking that my good friend, d'Arcy, will soon be wedding the Hope-woman. She has long teased him, but has promised finally to yield. Doubtless he will have tasted her by now." He stole a sidelong glance at his brother and was gratified to see the sudden granite cast to Firewalker's profile. "Even now they may be one," he added.

War Cloud's unexpected words brought the sky crashing down upon Firewalker. They roared, whirling, in his head, as he tried to grasp them and understand them. But what was there to understand? They were simple enough: d'Arcy was going to wed Hope or had already—and they had made love while he was gone. And he himself was the fool of all fools.

He completed the remainder of the journey in silence, overwhelmed by his hurt and fury, yet trying to deny the terrible image spread across his mind. His enemy claiming the woman he had thought was his own. Over and over, he told himself his brother's words could not be true—yet what reason had War Cloud to lie? And when he told himself Hope could not have made such sweet hungry love with him had she meant to wed another, he reminded himself that she had refused outright to join with him. Was it because, as she lay in his arms, she knew she was going to wed that devil d'Arcy? Once more he felt such rage that he trembled, and felt the blood drain from his face. He had to know the truth. . . .

He did not stop in his village, but rode directly to the highlands and through the woods toward Twin Oaks. As he approached the clearing, he reined sharply. D'Arcy was there, and Hope had just gone into her dwelling. Firewalker watched, his eyes blazing, as the trader mounted and then gazed at the cabin for an endless time before departing. Had they just made love? he wondered, and was he lusting for her still? Scorched by the thought, he wanted to send an arrow into d'Arcy's black heart, wanted to seize Hope and carry her home with him, heedless of her wishes, but shame stung him. Not for his murderous thoughts, but for his stupidity.

When he had asked her to join and seen her hesitation, he ignored it. And when he'd pressed her, and she had insisted that she could not, he'd not believed her. He had been so filled with himself and the fire of their lovemaking, so certain that she craved him as he craved her, he had actually forbidden her to answer him. With the assurance of the ignorant, he had known he could overcome any fears or objections she might have.

Now, sitting beside the river and chipping at the leaf-shaped form of a cache blade, he pondered again what a fool he was. Because she had kissed him with hunger and looked on him with shining eyes, he had believed she cared for him and wanted him. She did not. It seemed clear to him now that she had given to d'Arcy the same treasure she had given to him. In this hurt, he wanted never to see her again and wanted to forbid his young cousins and his sister from continuing their lessons. He wanted to wound her as he was wounded. But he could not afford such luxury. She was too important to his people to take so drastic a step, and as much as he resented it, things must continue as they were.

He reminded himself that he had been warned. He had seen her with d'Arcy, stroking his hair, drawing him back into the cabin—and he had let himself forget. Now, imagining their bodies pressed close and her kissing him hungrily as she had kissed him, Firewalker threw down his blade and chipping tool and got abruptly to his feet. He was too angry for such delicate work. It required patience as well as skill to make an arrowhead, and of patience he had none. Heated by his anger, he waded out to the middle of the river where it was deep and green and plunged in.

Swimming cooled his body but not his torment. The blue of the sky was the color of a gown she wore . . . the rain-dark clouds on the horizon were the gray of her eyes . . . the scent of summer flowers wafting across the water was the fragrance of her skin—sweet, fresh, wildly tantalizing. He was bewitched. He saw her everywhere, especially in the depths of his mind where again and again he saw her hungrily kissing his enemy.

As he came ashore, he knew he would not go to her this day, nor would he see her tomorrow, nor the next day nor the next. He did not want to look at her again nor hear her voice, knowing she was not his. He could not. He was strong, but not that strong. Next week would be soon enough. He would stop by Twin Oaks on Monday, but only to see if his kin were behaving themselves properly. And if she did not bring up the subject of joining, neither would he. And if she spoke of it to refuse him, as he now knew she must, he would tell her that— He hissed in a deep breath. In truth, he did not know what he would say or do.

He wrung the water from his hair and breechclout and then sat, cross-legged, gazing at the river and feeling his emotions seething through him still. Resentment, jealousy, humiliation, hatred for the Frenchman, confusion . . . He did not understand the woman. Could she not see beyond d'Arcy's smoothness and polite smiling ways? Or worse, did she see those things and not care, as did those foolish chieftains the trader bribed? By the Eternal, why did he even waste time wondering about it when he had better things to do? He had arrows to make, and he was in need of a new bow.

Firewalker gazed about him, opening his eyes and ears to the sights and sounds he had shut out in his anger. He had felt betrayed and alone; now he reminded himself he was not. Everywhere were those spirit-friends who had warmed and fed and healed him since he was put on this earth. They were in the river, the sun, and the sky; they were in every creature and in the wind and the earth, in the very grass beneath him. And he had his people. He thanked the Creator for them, and for the familiar comforting sounds coming from his village—the snapping of dry wood in the cook fires, the pounding of corn in mortars, the hack of hoes working the earth. As he listened, every dog in the village began to howl. He rose, frowning, his eyes slitted against the morning sun. He had best see what was happening.

Riding into the Lenape village with her father by her side, Hope tried to hide her uneasiness. Everything looked so strange and different from the way she had remembered it. But then she had arrived at night, and when she left the following morning, she'd been so drained she could hardly hold her eyes open. The Lenapes, gathering to stare at her and her father, were so silent and unsmiling that she felt further misgivings. Where were Flower and Firewalker? She had expected them both to come forth when they saw her. But perhaps Firewalker was not yet back from his journey.

Looking at the naked children and the half-naked women and barking dogs, Hope was convinced that she had made a terrible mistake. Why had she ever thought that coming here was the solution to her problem? She was grateful that Father had insisted on accompanying her.

She had turned to him suddenly and whispered, "I—think I want to go home. . . ."

Tom grunted. "Good. We'll tell Thunderhead we're just paying him a friendly visit."

"At this hour?" It was then that she saw the old chief emerging from the royal wigwam. He approached them with measured dignity, his long gray hair streaming.

Tom dismounted. He raised his right hand. "Greetings, *n'tschu.*"

"Greetings, my friend Caldwell, welcome," said Thunderhead solemnly. When his eyes lit on Hope, still astride her mare, a smile cracked his face into a thousand wrinkles. "It gladdens me to see you again, Caldwell the healer." He reached up, caught her hands, and grasped them tightly.

The gesture was filled with such genuine warmth and affection, Hope basked in it. "And it gladdens me to see you, *n'tschu.*" She knew she had reached a haven.

"Come and sit," Thunderhead offered. "Stay awhile."

Holding her blue gown close, Hope slid to the ground. She now saw the shy grins on the faces of the women and children, and suddenly Flower was there, her pretty face wreathed in smiles. The two women embraced.

"Hope! How grand, you have come to visit! And Dr. Caldwell, welcome!" But Flower was concerned. This was not just a visit. She knew that Hope had come to stay and that it had to do with those two salt women.

Tom saw that Thunderhead was about to offer them hospitality which would take hours. They would be seated in his wigwam, the tobacco pouch would be passed, victuals would be prepared and served, and Hope would be dying inside the whole while.

He bent to the old chieftain's ear. "*N'tschu,* our visit is an—unusual one. We would speak with you quickly and alone, if we may."

Seeing his friend's taut face, Thunderhead nodded. "Come." With no further word spoken, he beckoned them to follow him to his wigwam.

As she stepped inside, Hope was struck by the memories of her earlier visit: the heat and noise and the stench, the blazing eyes of Walks Alone, Thunderhead singing his passing song. Now everything was serene and orderly. On the two bed shelves, she saw several brightly colored blankets, and beneath the shelves were Thunderhead's weapons, clothing, and his snowshoes. In the fire pit, a small well-behaved fire burned quietly. Thunderhead threw down three pelts upon the hard-packed earth.

"Sit. We will talk."

As the three settled themselves cross-legged before the fire, Tom tried to collect his wits. He knew well what the Indian thought of the white man: he talked too much, he talked too fast, he was loud, and he never listened. He was as bad as a woman. It behooved him, therefore, to speak sparingly in a quiet, unrushed voice—and he must remember to hide the truth about Hope and Firewalker. It was a lot to ask of a man before breakfast. He cleared his throat.

"*N'tschu*, yesterday my daughter and I came under a black cloud. It is spoken falsely among our people that she is the squaw of one of your braves."

The muscles of Thunderhead's face did not move, but his eyes flickered. "Which?"

"Your nephew Firewalker."

For long moments, the old man sat with his eyes closed. When he opened them, they twinkled. Turning to Hope, he said, "You would do well to be the squaw of such a one, Caldwell the healer."

Seeing Hope's face turn pink, Tom spoke for her. "It is my thinking also, *n'tschu*, but my daughter is not of a mind to marry anyone just now."

"And your people do not approve of the joining of white and Indian."

"*Matta*."

"Nor do mine." The old chieftain's eyes again twinkled over Hope's black cape of hair and her beautiful face. "But your blood, Great Healer, mixed with that of my nephew, could only bring us good."

Hope was flabbergasted. The last thing in the world she had expected to hear was such talk as that. She smiled. "You are kind."

Thunderhead regained his grave demeanor. "*Matta.* I am not kind; I am practical. But we will continue. You did not come here to talk of joining my nephew. I assume you have come for sanctuary."

"Aye," she answered quietly. She wondered if he could see into her heart as well as her thoughts, and if he knew that she and Firewalker had lain together. "But I want to come only if it is no trouble. I would never disrupt your lives. . . ."

"I made you welcome once, Caldwell the healer, and since then nothing has changed. This is your home for as long as you wish."

"Thank you. . . ." Hope was deeply touched. Feeling tears gathering behind her eyes, she quickly blinked them back. Indians deplored weakness. She did not know who had told her that, she knew only that it was so.

Thunderhead's serene gaze moved from Hope to her father. "Was there more you wished to say, Caldwell?"

"Only that I thank you for your help."

"I accept no thanks. It is an honor."

Thunderhead got slowly to his feet, after which the other two rose. Outside, he spoke to a brave, and within moments, the beat of a drum began to reverberate up and down the valley.

Hope was embarrassed as the entire village gathered around the three of them. She had not wanted any attention at all, and now she was the center of it. Among the throng she spied Walks Alone and War Cloud, as well as Flower. The only one missing was Firewalker. She thought it strange that he was not there, seeing that War Cloud had returned. Her thoughts were broken by Thunderhead's voice.

"My friends and kin," he spoke in English, "the sun shines upon us this day. Caldwell the healer, she who brought me back from the dead, has come to live among us. I know you will welcome her as I have."

After repeating his message in Lenape, he gave Hope a warm fatherly embrace.

Next Flower hugged her and spoke in her ear: "Hope, this gladdens me, but I know you are sad to leave your grand house and your people. We will try to make you happy."

Hope whispered, "Can we talk later?"

"Aye. And now here comes my mother to greet you."

Hope braced herself to meet the dark eyes of the *meteinuwak*. She said politely, "Greetings, Walks Alone. I thank you for allowing me to come here."

Walks Alone nodded her head a fraction. She was stunned. What did her brother mean, allowing this woman to come here? But of course, he did not know that she brought Death with her, for Walks Alone had not told him. None but herself knew that one of her sons was going to die, and that this one would cause it. She yearned to drive her away, but she dared not defy the Great Manitou.

Weighted by her anger and despair, she nonetheless addressed the visitor respectfully: "I welcome you, Hope Caldwell. We will try to make you comfortable." To her daughter, she said, "Perhaps you and the healer should have your own wigwam."

Flower's eyes lit. "*Kehella*, we want a wigwam!"

"There is no need," Hope protested. "I will live as you live. I want no special favors."

"You don't understand," Flower explained. "We live in the longhouses, except my uncle. That one is ours—" She pointed to the nearest of several large rectangular lodges. "We could never ask you to live there; it would not be right."

"I agree," said Walks Alone. "The men can drive in the saplings this day, and the rest of us will prepare the rush mats."

"I'm causing extra work," Hope protested.

Walks Alone said firmly, "My daughter wishes it, therefore it will be done." But the truth was, she could not bear to share air with the woman.

* * *

After Hope bade her father good-bye, she was led by Flower and an excited group of girls and women toward one of the longhouses.

"Our wigwam will not be ready until tomorrow," Flower said, taking her inside. "Until then, you will share space with my mother and me."

Hope blinked to accommodate her eyes to the dimness and to the strange sight that greeted her. The dwelling, well over one hundred feet in length and a fourth as wide, was constructed of poles and covered with sheets of elm bark. On either side of a central corridor were wide shelflike platforms piled with bearskins and partitioned with curtains for privacy. Banked fires, spaced every ten feet or so along the corridor, sent smoke curling up to the open smoke holes far above.

"How interesting!" she murmured, looking about and feeling every eye upon her. She was reminded suddenly of her own comfortable bedchamber at Twin Oaks, and of her cozy kitchen with its many conveniences. Flower had thought them both large and grand, and she had been thrilled to sit at a table to eat. Now Hope understood why. These small curtained bunks were for both living and sleeping, and the fires for cooking.

"No other Lenapes live like us," Flower muttered as she stored Hope's medical bag and her small bundle of belongings under one platform. "Nor do they call themselves Lenapes anymore. They are Delawares now and have been for many years. It is such a pretty name, Delaware."

Hope smiled. "So is Lenape a pretty name. I like it."

Flower sniffed. "My elder brother says our people in Ohio even live in fine cabins like yours. I would love to live in a fine cabin with a bed and table and chairs, but my mother says *matta*. She allows nothing white here and my uncle agrees. I think the Shenango Lenape will live with the old ways forever."

"Well, I happen to like the way you live," Hope declared. "It's fascinating. I'm glad it's different from my own. I can see that I'm going to learn a lot of new things."

Flower laughed. "Oh, aye, my friend, you will."

Hope was eager to ask about Firewalker's whereabouts, but surrounded as they were by women and children, she did not dare. Suddenly it was as if Flower had read her thoughts. She spoke in Lenape, and the entire group quickly vanished.

"What did you tell them?" Hope asked.

Flower gave her a mysterious smile. "You will see." As she bent to neaten the small space they would share, she lowered her voice: "Are you here because of those salt women, Hope, or is there more?"

It was the moment Hope had been dreading. How could she admit to Flower that she was being shunned by her people because of Firewalker? How could she possibly hurt her like that when her brother was her pride and joy? She hardly knew where or how to begin. "Those women—" she murmured.

"Aye?" Flower's brows drew together.

Hope said a silent prayer. "It seems that they a-and everyone else think that Firewalker and I—well, they think that I'm, ah—"

"His squaw?" asked Flower bluntly.

Hope was taken aback. "Aye." She had expected tears or outrage or embarrassment, almost anything except such calm matter-of-factness.

Flower nodded gravely, "I have heard, for a white woman, this is a terrible thing. Now you are dirtied."

"Now I am furious," Hope declared. "And ashamed and disgusted that grown people should behave so childishly." Recalling Jacques's words on the subject, she murmured, "But I'm sure it's only because they fear your folk and don't understand them. Not that it excuses them . . ."

Flower shrugged. "They hate us. They laugh at us

and call us heathen pig savages." Seeing Hope's face, she laughed. "My friend, why are you shocked? You know it is so. They hate us, and we hate them. They talk big and loud and are stupid. Hope, they are so stupid! Our men laugh at them. They dirty the woods; they cannot build a fire; they lose things all over; they kill our animals for sport." She made a face. "We laugh at them. Not at you, *n'tschu*," she added quickly, "never do we laugh at you nor your father. Only at them. They are fools." She covered her mouth and blinked. "Heavens. I think I said too much."

Hope had been chuckling for some time, and now her laughter was full-blown. Her own pet word on Flower's lips tickled her. "I think you said exactly enough, and exactly what I needed to hear." She gazed contentedly on her friend's lovely face and the ribbon-bound coils of hair. She hardly noticed that Flower, like the other women in the village, was naked above the waist. She caught her hand. "Thank you, *n'tschu*."

Flower giggled. "I will take no thanks." She was jubilant, thinking how perfect everything was.

Because of those stupid, stupid whites, Hope was here. She was actually here with them, and while she did not yet know it, she was going to join with Firewalker. The very morning Flower had prayed to the Creator for it, she had asked for a sign—and had seen a rainbow. She was musing on it when the women, laughing and chattering excitedly, returned with a great heap of clothing.

Hope gasped as it was piled at her feet. "What is this?"

Flower said sweetly, "Perhaps you will find something that fits you from among these things."

Her eyes shining, Hope fingered a butter-soft tunic decorated with beads and fringe and feathers. She murmured, "You'll never know how I've wanted clothes like these."

For the next hour, she tried on shirts, skirts, and

leggings before choosing one of each. She donned them, and to the slim maid whose garb it was, Hope gave her own blue gown and petticoat. It was not until the others had returned to their chores that Flower shyly handed her a pair of beaded moccasins.

"For you, my sister. They have been long in the making, for I am slow. I am better at reading, I think."

"Oh, Flower . . ." Hope hastily pulled off her black slippers and, as Flower watched anxiously, tried the moccasins on. She took several steps in them.

"Is—all right?" Flower asked, forgetting her hard-won English in her concern.

"It feels like I'm walking on a cloud. . . ."

"Is not—beautiful like yours."

"But they are!" Hope exclaimed. "They're wonderful. I like them better—and since you like mine, take them. They're yours."

"Ohh!" Flower stroked the slippers, held them to her bare breasts, and donned them finally. The fit was not perfect, but she padded happily in them up and down the corridor. She looked about before whispering behind her hand, "No tell my mother, but—I feel white."

Hope laughed softly, happily. "And I feel Indian." She fetched the Wyandot headband from the bundle she had brought and settled it over her forehead and her long hair. "What do you think?"

Flower stared, admiring. "*Kehella*. You are Indian. . . ."

"Good." Eyes dancing, she repeated the word in Lenape: "*Wu lit*." Seeing Flower's surprise, she said, "You are not the only one learning a new language, *n'tschu*."

She was going to learn a whole new way of life, and this was a wonderful beginning, shedding those yards and yards of heavy cloth. How light and unencumbered and unburdened she felt! Relishing her new freedom, she raised her arms and spun around.

Realizing suddenly that Firewalker had entered the longhouse and was silently watching her, she stopped, pink cheeked and laughing with her long black hair a-tumble. A greeting came to her lips but fled when she saw the ice in his eyes.

Chapter 17

"Where have you been, my brother?" Flower asked. Seeing that Firewalker's hair and clothing were wet, she added, "I guess you were emptying the fish baskets." Only then did she notice that his mood was stormy and that his gaze locked on Hope was a wintry one. She was shocked, but she said brightly, "Hope has come to live with us!"

Firewalker tossed his bag of cache blades and his chipping tool onto his bunk. "Welcome," he said crisply. "And now I had best help with your wigwam." He strode out.

Flower saw that Hope's face had turned white. "What happened between you?" she gasped.

"I don't know. . . ."

FLower nearly wept in her disappointment. She had thought Firewalker would be overjoyed to see Hope. Instead he looked as if he would have slain her gladly. She whispered, "He is very angry with you, my friend. Something has happened."

"If you learn what it is, do tell me," Hope answered tersely. "He was perfectly fine on Friday. In fact, he—" She tightened her lips.

"He what?"

"It's not important." As much as she loved and trusted Flower, she did not want to reveal that Firewalker had asked her to join. And now it seemed no longer true. "I didn't mean to be so sharp," she murmured. "I'm not angry with you; I'm angry with him. Believe me, nothing happened that could have led to this." She felt betrayed. She had done nothing to deserve such fury—unless he now regretted their lovemaking. Trying to push the awful thought from her mind, she said, "Shouldn't we be outside helping with the wigwam?"

"Aye."

They found the braves driving tall elm saplings into the ground in a circle. The women were gathering rushes and grasses and weaving them into long thick mats which would cover the conical skeleton of saplings. Hope's dextrous fingers soon learned the pattern, and as she bent to the task, her eyes sought and remained on Firewalker as he helped to sink the saplings. She could not put his terrible anger from her mind. What had happened? What on earth had happened? She sensed then that she herself was being watched. It was Walks Alone staring at her, her hands all the while working the long grasses; Walks Alone who wielded great power and who allowed nothing of the white man in her village. Hope wondered how long she herself would be allowed to remain.

The men's work was done swiftly, and Firewalker disappeared from Hope's sight. For what seemed like hours, she sat under a steadily graying sky with Flower and the women, lulled by the weaving and their laughter and chatter. Flower kept her informed.

"They talk of men," she said, and then, "They talk of babies," or "They talk of the joining of Bear-Claw and River-Song. She is a Mengwe."

Mengwe. Hope's interest was piqued. "Is she one of these women?"

"Nay. Bear-Claw is of her family now. And because she is of the enemy, he is dead to us. His moccasins have been buried." Seeing Hope's confusion, Flower said, "That is the way of it. Also it is the way of Indian men to go to the families of their wives. Even if

River-Song was not Mengwe, he would not be here. He would be with her."

Hope was amazed. Had Firewalker intended to live with her at Twin Oaks then? It hardly seemed likely, and now she would probably never know. Her body tightened, remembering again how furious he had been. In addition, her neck and shoulders were aching and so were her fingers from the unaccustomed work. And her belly was protesting. Did these people never eat? She had lost all track of time, but surely it was nearing suppertime.

"Here comes the rain!" Flower shrieked, suddenly, pointing to the sky. As they scrambled to their feet, raindrops spattering the ground, she cried, "Hurry, Hope, bring your things!"

The sky was filled with swirling black clouds, and as Hope and the other women quickly gathered their rushes and mats, wind roared through the valley, driving the rain before it and bowing the trees. Day turned to night as they fled to the longhouses. There, in the smoky dimness, the women continued their weaving and chatting before the fires. The men, already sprawled sleeping or resting on the skin-covered bunks, now teased and played with the younger children who romped over them.

Hope sent a furtive glance toward Firewalker's bunk, and froze. He was staring at her, his coppery eyes hooded and unblinking. Seeing that he was raging still, she looked back quickly to her weaving. She had been trying, ever since that morning, to discover what had made him so angry. What could she possibly have done? She could think of nothing, nothing whatsoever except their lovemaking. She trembled, remembering his kisses burning over her flesh, and the hot sweet excitement of his crushing her against him. She could still feel his hands caressing and gentling her, feel his manhood sliding within her, slowly, languorously at first and then moving faster, deeper, each thrust bringing her closer to such a wild peak of excitement that she had cried out in her pleasure.

The memory made her warm and breathless, even as she felt terror that it was their lovemaking that had caused her to lose him.

"Do you still like the way we live?" Flower whispered, bringing her back to reality.

"I find it—very interesting. . . ." She felt ill with Firewalker's hostile gaze burning through her. But then perhaps part of her nausea was related to hunger. Lord, but she was hungry. . . .

When the supper hour finally approached and the cook fires were stirred, Hope was dismayed to see that the smoke holes were still closed against the rain. As Walks Alone and the other women began to prepare the food, thick smoke filled the lodge. It stung Hope's eyes as it mingled with a miasma of other odors: sweat, soot, venison, grasses, babies, tobacco, bear grease.

"*N'tschu,* are you all right?" Flower asked.

Hope nodded. She would not lose the contents of her stomach before them all. She would not! Please, God, nay . . . She swallowed, murmured, "I'm fine. . . ." Desperately she put her attention on her aching fingers and the things about her. "Those wolf symbols painted above the doors—have they a meaning?"

"They have," Firewalker answered brusquely from his bunk. "We are of the *Munsees.* The Wolf Clan. The wolf is our totem."

Turning, Hope met his molten eyes. So. After all of these many hours, he had finally deigned to speak to her. Despite her flare of outrage, she said coolly, "Thank you so much for telling me."

Firewalker held his anger close. Never in his worst dreams had such a thing as this ever happened. To have her here living among them, seeing her, eating across from her, sleeping where he had but to stretch out his hand to touch her—and instead of wanting her, he hated her. He took up his tool and blade and began chipping again. *Matta,* he did not hate her at all. It was that he was hurt. Furious. Stabbed to the heart.

The ecstasy he had found with her still burned inside him. She was a fire in his veins, a shiver up his spine, a vision that would not leave his fevered brain day or night. She was the woman he had wanted to share his life, to give him sons. He could still taste her soft mouth, feel her body under his. The frantic beating of her pulse beneath his lips was a part of him forevermore. . . .

As he gazed on her brooding, a heavy lethargy moved over him. He saw her as if she sat alone within the red-gold fire glow, darkness about her and the storm's growl muffled. As if only the two of them were in the longhouse . . . in the village . . . *kehella,* in the whole northwest woodlands. It was as he always dreamt it, the two of them alone together in the world. He willed her to look at him. She did, her gray eyes widening and secret pleasure flushing her beautiful face. And when he held out his hand, she came to him, a knowing smile curving her soft lips.

"I have been waiting for you, my husband . . ." Her voice was low, husky with desire.

As he drew her into his bed and into his arms, she arched her body against him, the sensuous movement pressing her soft belly against his hardened shaft, and thrusting her breasts upward toward his hungry mouth. He felt her nails delicately scoring his shoulders and neck, raking through his hair. He smiled, hearing her small moans. She craved him, his woman, as hotly as he craved her.

He removed her clothing, and she, with trembling fingers, drew off his breechclout. She touched the tip of her hot little tongue to his naked skin, tasting, licking, kissing. . . . He uttered a growl of pleasure, brushed his lips over her breasts, and saw, hot eyed, that her nipples had become tiny pink pearls. Fire flamed through his veins as he thought how beautiful she was, so smooth and gleaming, so pink and white. She was his treasure—pearls and satin and stars in her eyes. She was his woman. His . . .

Firewalker shuddered. He pulled himself back to the present, and felt the emptiness, the hollowness that his body had become. It was not so. She was not his woman. He had known well that the deep trancelike web in which he had been so deliciously trapped was not reality—but he had willingly allowed it to consume him. Now he forced himself back to the sights and sounds of the longhouse. His dreams and plans for her, his sweet memories of her were ended. Now he had another memory, this one bitter. The memory of his brother's words: she had promised to give herself to Jacques d'Arcy; she had teased him long enough. That devil, too, had tasted her sweetness by now, and had intended to wed her.

After seeing her that morning, twirling and dancing about, bright eyed and laughing as a young maid in her doeskins, Firewalker had stormed to Thunderhead and had learned why she was there. He thought darkly that the Frenchman had probably turned her away upon hearing she was his squaw. Why else would she have fled here rather than to him? He snorted, scornful. Had she actually thought he himself would want her after she had lain with that bastard? Contemplating it, a soft growl vibrated in his throat. Never. Never would she be his woman. Not now. Doubtless she was more than eager to explain to him her behavior with d'Arcy, but he did not want to hear it. He no longer cared.

Hope felt Firewalker's eyes boring through her as she and Flower continued to weave and chat. She was filled with resentment, and she was no less angry than he. Her fury, in fact, had made her feel ever so much better. Observing Walks Alone preparing the meal, she decided that it would actually be quite appealing if only the smoke would disappear. She studied with interest the bunks lining the walls of the longhouse. They held entire families: children, braves, pet dogs, and the women going between the cook fires and their small apartments. The Lenapes' brown near-naked bodies no longer shocked her, and she marveled at how content they all seemed, crowded in with each other as they were.

Hope's interest was caught also by the young woman in the next compartment. Flower had said she was War Cloud's squaw, and as she stirred her kettle, Hope guessed that she was far along in her pregnancy. She was curious. Had they, did they make love with only a curtain separating them from the eagle eye of Walks Alone? And if she herself had joined Firewalker, would the two of them be living where he now sat glaring at her? She shivered. It was unthinkable.

"The food is ready," Walks Alone said finally. From the shelf above their bunk, she took down clay bowls, bark plates, spoons, and knives.

Hope's heart lurched as Firewalker slid his long dark gleaming legs from his bunk. In silence, he lowered himself to the mat before the fire and in silence was served soup and cornbread by his mother and sister. When he not so much as glanced at Hope, her blood began to boil anew. Damn him. How long was his frigid punishment of her going to continue? For she could ignore him forever if that was his wish. Two could play the game. Silently she ladled soup into her bowl, cut her cornbread, and lowered herself to her mat before the fire. She was hungry, and the food tasted good, but she was too annoyed to enjoy it. She was being roundly and soundly ignored by mother and son, and it was mortifying. If lightning had not been crackling outside and the wind still howling, she would have left the longhouse then and there. She could be shunned among her own people.

Flower leaned toward her and said softly, "Tomorrow we will be in our own dwelling, my friend."

Seeing her concern, Hope smiled. "That will be very nice."

"My cooking is not so good. How is yours?"

"Not as good as this, I fear."

Flower spoke suddenly to her sister-in-law in their tongue, "Sings Low, where is my brother?"

"I do not know, my sister." Sings Low had no appetite, but sat aimlessly stirring her kettle.

Flower frowned. "I thought he was sleeping."

"*Matta.* He left after the Hope-woman's arrival without even bidding me good-bye. He has been gone ever since."

Walks Alone, mired in her own thoughts, cut a piece of cornbread and offered it to the girl. "Here, my daughter, you must eat."

Flower could have kicked War Cloud in her anger. Why was he not there with Sings Low? Had he not been absent enough days already when he and Firewalker journeyed to Kuskusky? As for Firewalker, she wanted to kick him, too. Why was he behaving so stupidly, sitting there scowling into his bowl and talking to no one? He had scarcely looked at Hope since he had crushed her spirits this morning. And there across the room sat Glad Tidings, staring and smiling at Flower herself. He was tall and handsome, he gave her fine courting gifts, he was clean and gentle and praised her cooking, and had even said that he loved her. But he laughed at her learning. He had said he would forbid it when they joined. For that reason alone, she would not have him. Flower gave him a frigid gaze and continued chatting with Hope. Men. Sometimes she hated them all.

War Cloud was drenched to the skin as he slid from his horse and staggered to the front door of the Frenchman's trading post. He thumped on the door, and shouted above the wind, "It is War Cloud, let me enter!" He banged again, almost falling into the small storeroom when the door opened suddenly.

Jacques, lantern in hand, stood scowling at him. It was not his wish to entertain a wet Indian who reeked of bear grease and whiskey. *Sacre.* Whiskey? That was a change. Was War Cloud back on the bottle, then, after turning up his nose at it? Studying him closely for some moments, he saw that it was so. It was the only good thing to come of this day.

"Come in," he said, and led the brave back to his small bed-sitting room. As he set his lamp on the table, he noted with distaste the other's streaming-wet body, soaked breechclout, and the limp soggy rope of his scalp lock. He noted, too, that War Cloud's black eyes glittered. "What brings you here in such weather, *n'tschu?*"

"You have failed me, Frenchman." War Cloud's heart was roaring in his ears, and when the room seemed to spin, he planted his feet far apart.

"Failed you?"

"Failed."

The breath caught in Jacques's throat seeing that War Cloud's hand rested on his dagger. When would he learn to keep his own weapon on him at all times when he was among savages? After he was scalped? But he knew better than to show fear. He shook his head and said boldly, "You are mistaken."

"Then know this," War Cloud hissed. "The Hope-woman has left her people to live with the Lenapes."

Jacques nearly laughed aloud. It was absurd, but his heart grew faint when those glittering eyes said it was so. He knew that Hope had not been at Twin Oaks when he had gone early that morning to talk again of marriage. But he thought she and Thomas had been on a sick call together. And when he'd returned later and they still were gone, he had been annoyed but not concerned. Now this.

Damnation, he could kill her. Why had the Lenapes he had seen throughout the day not told him of this? But Indians, unlike whites, were a close-mouthed lot. He told himself then that it did not matter. In fact, one night in a Lenape longhouse might be a good thing after all. It could well cure the wench of this latest insanity of hers. But he knew he was grasping at straws, and he jumped when War Cloud growled.

"I have told you, Frenchman, rid me of this female or I will do it myself."

Jacques's face showed nothing. If he had learned anything from red men, it was to hide his emotions. "I trust you would not take back that which you have given?"

War Cloud swayed ever so slightly. "What have I given?"

"Time. You have given me the length of one moon to work my will with the woman, and only a short time has passed." The wind keened and shadows danced on the walls as Jacques saw the brave battle with this.

War Cloud said finally, "I will not take back what I have given. I am a man of honor. But when the time is up, she goes, trader. By your hand or by mine."

Because of her, War Cloud had this morning dug up the bottle of whiskey he had buried and drunk the whole thing. He who thought he would never again be enslaved by that devil's brew was as enslaved as ever. And then the rains came and he had sat, blind drunk in the downpour with the lightning crashing about him. Not daring to go home reeking, he had sat there the day long hating himself, hating d'Arcy, and, most of all, hating the woman. It was intolerable that she had come to them and been welcomed with open arms by all. Excepting his mother. Walks Alone was not happy about it, but Walks Alone was not happy about anything anymore.

"When the time is up, she will be gone," Jacques said. "I promise it. You must not fear, *mon ami.*"

"Fear?" War Cloud laughed. "I do not fear, Frenchman."

Carrying his lantern, Jacques followed him to the front of the cabin. In the small storeroom, he took a bottle from one of the shelves. "Here is a little something for you." He did not mind when War Cloud took it, giving him no thanks, and returned to the storm.

* * *

Night had come. Hope lay in the bunk fully garbed with a bearskin pulled over her against the damp and the chill of autumn's coming. Flower lay beside her, breathing softly in her deep sleep, and beside Flower lay Walks Alone. Hope did not know if the *meteinuwak* slept. She knew only that the woman lay unmoving and her breathing was regular. Hope herself was wide awake. She was too tired to move, yet too agitated to sleep. She was grateful for her warm welcome from Thunderhead, and she was grateful for Flower's loyalty and for her wonderful new clothing, but those things paled when she thought of Firewalker.

Remembering his hostile gold slit eyes and that he had scarcely looked or spoken to her the entire day, she felt lost. She had been counting on him, certain he would be overjoyed to see her. Instead he had left her broken. And then there was that dreadful meal during which he and his mother had both ignored her. She grew hot just thinking of it. She heard him tossing in the bunk to her left and knew he was awake. She felt his wrath pointed at her still, and from her right came the soft weeping of Sings Low.

Hope's heart went out to her. The girl could be no more than fifteen, yet she was with child, and joined with a man whose fierce appearance frightened Hope herself. She wanted to draw back the curtain separating their two apartments and comfort her, but she hesitated. The girl spoke little English, and she feared War Cloud might return and find them together.

The storm had departed, and now the vents in the ceiling were open. Hope lay quietly, gazing through the fine smoky haze at the banked cook fire and the shadows dancing. Outside, owls hooted close by and wolves called in the distance. She heard the stifled yip of a dog, then, and knew that someone was moving softly down the center corridor. A man passed between her and the fire glow, and she saw that he was tall and wore a scalp lock. War Cloud? Hearing the low angry complaint of Sings Low, she knew he had returned.

Hope smiled. Good. Big and fierce looking as he was, his young wife was not afraid of him. Sings Low lashed out furiously in her soft voice. But then War Cloud gave a gruff command, and she fell silent. Hope held her breath hearing the maid's small cry, instantly smothered, and then came sounds that she recognized instantly. Wet sucking noises, growls, groans, scufflings, and eventually the fast raspy breathing of the brave and the maid's small whimpering moans.

Hope was horrified. He was raping her, although it would never be called rape between man and wife, and she could do nothing about it. Nothing. She lay there, her hands gripped into fists—but then Sings Low giggled. It was followed by a soft slap, a low chuckle from War Cloud, and more wet noises. Many more. Hope felt her taut nerves relax. She had been wrong, and stupid and nosy. It was nothing but a lover's quarrel which was now made up. Perhaps War Cloud was not as bad as she thought. Relief made her warm and relaxed and sleepy, and as she was drifting off, she knew that she was going to relent towards Firewalker. Tomorrow, even if he were still angry, she would swallow her pride and go to him and try to learn what had happened. She wanted nothing so much as for everything to be right between them.

The next morning, she awakened to an empty longhouse. She was embarrassed to think that she had slept through everyone else's arising and eating and now they were already at work or play. After quickly brushing her hair and slipping into the nearby woods to tend her needs, she found Flower and several other women hard at work on the mats for the wigwam. They smiled at her approach, and Flower jumped up.

"Hope! Good morning!"

"Good morning. I didn't mean to sleep the morning away."

Flower waved off the apology and took her hand. "Come, I saved you food." She drew Hope back inside the lodge and lowered her voice. "My brother is not here. He left before we ate breakfast, and looked like a thundercloud still."

"When he returns, will you please tell me? We must talk."

"I will tell you." Looking beyond Hope's shoulder, she added quietly, "You have a visitor, *n'tschu.*"

Hope knew even before she turned who would be there—Jacques.

"Hope, Flower, *bon matin.*"

Flower murmured a good morning and fled. She knew that Firewalker did not like the Frenchman and neither did she. She did not like anything about him, especially the greedy way his eyes slid over Hope when he talked to her. And if Firewalker, stupid man, was not here to protect her from him, why then she must. Perhaps if she fetched some of the children—and the dogs . . .

Hope was surprised, not that Jacques had come, but by his mild demeanor. She had expected him to be indignant, but instead he seemed tired and resigned. She felt a twinge, just a twinge, of guilt for her behavior.

"I know I've disappointed you. . . ."

"*Oui,* I am disappointed."

After pacing the floor all night, he had decided to face her calmly. Surely, with his facile tongue and quick mind, he could outwit one silly woman and a tribe of savages. But when he entered the longhouse and saw her in her heathen skins and with the Wyandot band on her head, his blood turned cold. Did the woman *want* to be Indian? From a distance, she looked as savage as any damned squaw he had ever seen save for that luscious white skin of hers. He wondered suddenly, shocking even himself, if he wanted her after all, for surely she would drive him out of his mind. But he quickly decided he was being foolish. He'd had no sleep and he was out of sorts.

"I think we might have talked before you did this," he muttered.

Hope folded her arms. She said firmly, "We have absolutely nothing to discuss. This was my decision and really, Jacques, it had nothing to do with you."

"Hope, you cannot have thought this through. You are an educated woman." He looked about pointedly at the primitive living quarters and the ever-present smoky haze hanging over the room. "How can you even contemplate—" He stopped as the lodge erupted suddenly with yapping dogs and little naked boys chasing each other up and down the corridor and between the cook fires. "I said, how can you even—" He could not even hear himself what with dogs howling, brats screaming—and this confounded stubborn female. He grasped Hope's arm and marched her outside to where the woods crept close to the village. It did not help his mood to see that she was laughing. But she would not laugh for long.

"Do you not see how it will look," he said stiffly, "if you are here, with Firewalker now on another rampage?"

"Another?"

"The military will doubtless be brought from the nearest garrison to take him into custody." He was pleased to see her blink.

"Pardon me," Hope retorted, "but you're mistaken. He was never on any rampage, let alone another one!" Firewalker's strange silence had wounded her, aye, but she could not let him go undefended from such a ridiculous accusation. "As I'm sure War Cloud has told you, he was in Thunderhead's wigwam that night he—"

"I see you have not heard of the latest small but vicious incidents these past few days," Jacques interrupted. "Dogs killed, fruits trees mutilated . . ." It was God's own truth. "Hope, let me take you home. I fear for you here."

"He didn't do it," Hope said stubbornly. "He's not a destroyer." Besides, he had been away. Or had he? she wondered suddenly. She wondered too—was Firewalker's rage really with her, or was it with himself for having done things he was ashamed of?

She shook her head. Now she was being foolish. She knew this man, and angry and disgusted though she was with him, her heart would never allow her to believe he would do such ugly things as kill dogs and destroy fruit trees. Nay, not Firewalker. It simply was not possible.

Chapter 18

The sun was shining the next afternoon when Hope and Flower moved into their new wigwam. Flower had quickly made it cozy—bull rush mats on the tamped earth floor, decorated mats brightening the walls, and skins and colorful blankets were heaped on the two sleeping platforms opposite each other. In the center of the floor was the shallow pit for their cook fire.

Hope had just stored her few belongings beneath the bed shelf when a shadow fell across the floor. Looking up, she found her best student, Stargazer, in the opening.

"Greetings, teacher." He looked about, nodding. "This is good. This is very good."

"Thank you." Hope got to her feet.

"Will you teach today?"

"I plan to."

"Good," he said again.

It was his favorite word, but Hope did not allow herself to smile. She had learned that sternness went farther with Lenape bucks than lenience. But what a far cry this was from those early days when he had been like an unruly puppy and Firewalker had dunked him in the spring behind the cabin. Those early happy days . . .

"Tell your cousins we will meet at the river by the willows. I will be there shortly." She summoned

Flower, quickly gathered books and her slate, and soon the five of them were seated in the willow shade beside the Shenango.

It was September, and it was hot. Locusts shrilled, bees hummed in the goldenrod, and sweat beaded Hope's face and streamed down her body beneath her skin clothing. As she led her charges through their lessons, she grew aware of the sounds of the village: the constant pounding of corn in mortars and the chink of hoes striking earth and stones in gardens and fields. It was the women at work.

That morning alone, she had seen them making pottery, fetching water, baking bread, and gathering the firewood that would keep the soup kettles bubbling throughout the day. From Flower, she had learned that they tanned the hides, made the clothes, dressed the game, and plowed, planted, cultivated, and gathered the corn as well as ground it. It was no wonder Flower wanted sometimes to escape into a make-believe world through books.

That night when the drums were quiet, and the dancing was over, they lay talking on their fur-covered beds. Hope said softly, "Your women work very hard. . . ." In the moonlight streaming through the smoke hole, she saw Flower rise on one elbow to gaze over at her.

"It is to save our men."

"So I hear."

"They must be strong and rested for their hunts."

Hope nodded. She had heard before from Flower of the rigors and dangers of the hunt, and how fit the men must be for it. "I just wanted you to know—I admire all of you very much." She saw her friend's large black eyes blink.

"Thank you. We admire you." Flower lay back down.

She had been thinking of Glad Tidings, and of Firewalker. She was furious with both of them. Glad Tidings was pressing her to join, and while she loved him with all her heart, he would forbid her to learn.

Could she really wed such a man? And as for her miserable brother— She raised on her elbow again to peer across at the other bed.

"Hope—"

"Aye?" Hope was gazing drowsily at the moonlight streaming through the open smoke hole.

"I am so shamed. . . ."

Hope sat up. "Shamed about what?"

"My brother. He has never been this way. Never. And my mother— I do not know my mother. She is not herself. Last night—"

Hearing the catch in her voice, Hope got up and stepped around the fire pit. She sat down on the edge of Flower's bed. "It's all right."

Flower gave her head a vehement shake. "It is not. It is terrible that they sat like logs and did not talk to you or make you welcome last night—your first night among us. They shamed me."

"Your mother made me quite welcome with this lovely wigwam," Hope responded quietly. She patted Flower's hand. "It's all right, really it is."

"Firewalker was a bear."

"He was, I agree, and when he returns, we will talk. . . ." She stared at the banked fire. "Is he still hunting, do you think?"

"Aye, he is hunting." And doubtless he would stay away for days to show his displeasure. It was the way of Indian men.

"Well, we had best get to sleep." Hope returned to her own bed and lay back on the furs again. The quiet was wonderful, and it felt good to be in a nightdress instead of her day wear. She smiled, seeing that a star now twinkled through the opening.

Flower's voice came again: "I pray you have a good night in our new home, *n'tschu.*"

"I know I will. I love it already. I pray you have a good night, too."

"I will. . . ." But Flower knew she would not. She had a decision to make about Glad Tidings. And she knew that no matter which choice she made, it would be the wrong one.

The day after his ill-fated meeting with Hope, Jacques d'Arcy loaded a pack mule and headed for Ohio. He told himself he had been intending to visit the Mengwes ever since their move to the area. The truth was, he had to get away from his many problems, and away from Hope especially. He would go mad if he did not. The sun had traveled a quarter of the way across the sky when he finally glimpsed the palisades surrounding their village. He had felt himself observed long before that, and it sent a chill up his spine. He had dealt with Mengwes before. He did not like them, but he had respect for them. They were a fierce lot who took what they wanted and let no one stand in their way. Not unlike himself.

Meeting a small band of braves outside the village, he said to the biggest, "I am d'Arcy, the trader, *mon ami.* I am interested in Mengwe furs and would see your chieftain."

"I am Red Buck," came the gruff reply. "Stands Tall sees no one."

Jacques studied the brave with practiced calm, noting his painted face and greased scalp lock. He saw the authority in those black eyes as well as the cruelty and decided that the man was a subchieftain. He shrugged. "It is a great pity, for he will not see the treasures I carry. I have brought just a small sampling, *savez-vous?*"

"I look. Tell Stands Tall if good."

Jacques smiled. "*Très bon.* I am sure you are a man of taste and quality."

With that, he was led within the palisade where his quick glance took in five longhouses and another under construction. It seemed this was a prosperous place and could be profitable for him. If each dwelling held sixty persons or thereabouts, he reckoned the number in this bustling village to be three hundred and sixty or so with roughly a third of them braves. It would be a grand *coup* if he got their fur trade. He began to unload his mule.

"Where from Frenchman?" asked Red Buck.

"Pennsylvania—near the river Shenango south of the Cuyahoga Path." Jacques lay his bales and cases and pouches on the grass and began opening them as the men jabbered among themselves. It was the same as always. These devils, fierce as they were, were agog over his bolts of cheap cotton, knives, mirrors, and jewelry. They were children. It never ceased to amaze him.

Red Buck loomed over him, watching. "You know Lenapes? Shenango Lenapes?"

Jacques continued to spread out his goods. Knowing the Lenapes and Mengwes were blood enemies, he said carefully, "One cannot dwell in the area and not know the Lenapes. I know every tribe thereabouts."

"There is white woman among them. Hair like night . . . pretty . . ." Red Buck moved his hands to form her breasts and buttocks, bringing forth much laughter. "We want. Is still squaw of brave named Firewalker?"

Jacques's shock was so great, he swayed. He replied tersely, "There is a white woman, but she is no squaw."

"Is strange. We return to Firewalker. He say she his woman."

Rage swept him so suddenly, it left him sweating. He himself had invented that damned tale, or so he thought. Or had Firewalker bedded her even before the idea was a gleam in his own eye? Was that why she would not marry him and why she had fled to the Lenapes? Was that why she always defended Firewalker? Was she, in truth, his squaw? She had denied that she cared for him, but Jacques had always sensed she did. It revolted him so that he felt almost ill.

He mopped his face with a red kerchief, and said thickly, "It seems you know more about it than I." He was so overwhelmed by his feelings of betrayal and disgust, he could think only of revenge. Gone was his desperate desire to wed her. He could not possibly wed such a deceitful wench, and one soiled by a savage. Not for any reason. *"Mon ami"*—the thudding of his heart almost drowned the sound of his voice—"if you want this woman, you have but to let me know. She will be yours. But I am a trader, I must have something in return for such a valuable item." It would not be the first time he had supplied white women for braves, or squaws for white men. He tried to please all who could pay his price.

"Name it," muttered the big Mengwe.

"Your furs," answered Jacques promptly. "She is much woman. The three of you can share her." The whole damned tribe could share her as far as he was concerned.

"I talk with Stands Tall. . . ."

"*Bon.* Talk with Stands Tall. I will return in two days for your answer."

"Too soon."

"Two days, no more." He was damned if he would put it off longer. He would not have War Cloud doing something stupid to be rid of her if he himself could receive Mengwe furs in exchange for her. Seeing the approach of several squaws, he thrust the whole matter to the back of his mind and, with a flare, unfurled a fresh bolt of crisp red-print cotton. "Ladies, see this fine fabric. *C'est très belle.* You can make fine skirts with this. . . ."

Firewalker had lost count of the days he had been living in the forest. He had made himself a lean-to shelter, and hunted only enough to eat. All of his time he spent on weapon making—searching for arrow wood and the straightest shoots of dogwood, forming arrowheads, and finally beginning work on a new bow. But as he stripped the bark from a likely piece of wood and began shaping it, his thoughts were not on the bow. They were on Hope Caldwell.

Since he had been there in the woods—*matta*, since his brother had told him of her and d'Arcy—he had not put away the hurt. He could not, and it angered him that he was still so torn in his heart and spirit over a woman.

He had stayed away from his village, not wanting to see her and wishing her gone, yet his curiosity was getting the better of him. His feet wanted to carry him to her, and his tongue yearned to ask her those questions his heart craved to know. The most important being, was she all right? But his will was an iron trap. He would not let her see his interest and concern nor his ever-present hunger for her. It was beneath the dignity of a Lenape warrior even to look at a woman who had deceived him.

But he remained grateful for her teaching his kin. He had stolen near the village one day and, from across the river, saw her sitting under a willow with the four of them. Watching Stargazer poring over his books and writing on paper with a quill, Firewalker's heart had gone faster. An old dream came to life to torment him—the thought of himself reading and writing. But it meant yielding to her, and that he could not do. He could not humble himself so.

He brooded, imagining that his cousins were quicker at learning than he, and that he would be dull and slow in comparison. Even as the thought turned his blood to ice, he felt scorn for himself. Not only was he stiff with pride, he was arrogant. What made him think Hope would even consider teaching him? She was a proud woman, and he had not treated her well before he left. But in truth, she had not deserved to be treated well. . . .

As he greased his roughly shaped bow and hung it from a tree to begin seasoning, he felt his emptiness and hollowness. Why did he not admit what this whole thing was about? He yearned to be taught, *kehella*, but that was only part of it. The other part was that he wanted an excuse to be near Hope again. Any excuse. He wanted to see and touch her again, even if it was just the merest brushing of her fingers over his. He wanted to hear her low voice, and he wanted to inhale the faint mysterious flower fragrance of her skin. He wanted to taste and kiss her again. . . .

Hope was uneasy as she and Flower sat husking the corn they had just harvested. Nay, she was more than uneasy. She was terrified. Her menses were three days overdue, and she feared she was carrying Firewalker's child. The thought was forcing everything else from her mind. She loved children and had always wanted babes of her own, but not like this—not out of wedlock with a man who, suddenly and without reason, hated her. Firewalker still had not returned from hunting. He had been gone six days now, and Hope had concluded that he hated her so much, he was never coming back. At least, not as long as she was there. Maybe it would be best for everyone if she returned to Twin Oaks. Firewalker certainly would not care, and her father would be happy—except it would break Flower's heart.

"You are quiet, *n'tschu,*" Flower murmured.

"So are you. You've not said one word all morning." She was sunk so deeply in her own problems, she'd not even noticed her friend's quietness until now. "Flower, is something wrong?

Flower had finally made her difficult decision concerning Glad Tidings and she was miserable. Her only wish now was that it would hurt him as much as it did her. She shrugged. "Everything is fine—except that my life is over."

Hope's own worries vanished on the instant. She placed a half-shucked ear of corn back into the basket. "What on earth are you talking about?"

"Soon I will be old and ugly and a burden to my people," Flower murmured. And she hoped Glad Tidings would be satisfied.

Hope bit her lip so as not to laugh outright. No other woman among the Shenango Lenapes was as beautiful or as hard-working as Flower. "Is it possible you're wrong?"

Flower's black eyes flashed. "I am not wrong. I will never join, and a woman without a man is said to lose her bloom quickly. I will be one of those toothless old women that Firewalker protects and cares for among our people. But at least I—I will read and write—and I will teach as you do!"

So. This was about Glad Tidings and his disapproval of Flower's learning. Hope said with a confidence she did not feel, "I'm sure things will work out."

"I am sure they will not." Flower's face was dusky pink in her anger. "He insists we join, and when we do, he will forbid me to learn." She took out her wrath on the corn, furiously shucking a fresh ear. "I want only two things in this world, but if I have the one I cannot have the other—and I cannot live without either. . . ."

Hope considered and savored the thought of finding Glad Tidings and telling him exactly what she thought of such bullying, but it was wishful thinking. She was a guest among these people, an outsider.

It was some moments before she trusted herself to say carefully, "Perhaps you should join with another."

Flower looked at her, stricken. "Another? *Matta!* If I cannot have him, I will have no one. I love him. I have loved him forever. I loved him when I was a maid and he looked on me with the eyes of a brother. Now, finally, he sees me as a woman, and he loves me. When we lie together, I want nothing more than him—"

Hope did not show her surprise. Flower's open mention of a thing that whites frowned upon was but one more way in which their two peoples differed greatly.

"But then I look at my books, and I know my life would be empty without them. I cannot give them up. I—I will not."

But she was suddenly terrified by the thought of never holding Glad Tidings again, and if he joined with another, she would die—if not of grief, then of rage. After being so sure of herself, she was not sure at all. She hurled the corn to the ground and covered her face.

"I am so confused. I think I am not a good woman."

"Honey, don't . . ."

Flower rocked back and forth, her face still buried in her hands. "I should want to please him. I should think only of him. He loves me. He is a good hunter and he will care for me a-and do all in his power to please me."

Except give you the thing you want most, Hope thought resentfully. She watched in angry silence as Flower recovered the corn from the ground and continued listlessly to shuck it. It was not right that she should have to give up her dreams. She remembered then how Flower had defied Firewalker to come to her for those first lessons. If she wed Glad Tidings, would she defy him the same way? It worried her. Firewalker was a loving brother, but Glad Tidings would be a husband. There was a difference. A husband would expect obedience.

"If you join, and you displease him," Hope asked, "what will he do?"

Flower shrugged. "I suppose he will put me aside."

Hope laughed. "You don't mean it."

"Why would I not mean it? It is the way of it. If I behave well, he will keep me. If he himself does not behave well," she made a motion with her thumb, "he is out."

Hope's mouth had fallen open. "Now you are teasing me."

"Is it not the same among your people?"

"It's not at all the same. We strive to keep the vow which we take when we wed." Her head was spinning. Did joining mean nothing more to the Lenapes than that?

Flower frowned. "What is a vow?"

"A promise. A man and woman promise, in a wedding ceremony, to love and honor each other until death parts them. Among my people, marriage is meant to be forever." Thinking suddenly of Sam, she was pleasantly shocked. His face was hazy, not burned in her mind as it once was, and she felt nothing, absolutely nothing except relief that they had never spoken those vows.

"I have never heard of such a thing. . . ." Flower breathed. It was what she wished for herself and Glad Tidings, a marriage that was forever. And she wished it for Hope and Firewalker. Except that hardly seemed possible now. She had to remind herself that she had seen a sign when she prayed for their togetherness. She had seen a rainbow. . . .

As Hope worked in the fields the remainder of the morning, she grimly considered all that Flower had told her. She had learned that some marriages did last—usually after the arrival of children. But no one ever joined with high expectations; only to stay together as long as they pleased each other. It seemed a trial to be won or lost, and if love came, it was accepted quietly and little was made over it. Was that what Firewalker had planned for the two of them? Hope wondered hotly. A trial marriage? Of course it was, for he knew nothing else. And wouldn't that have been a fine thing, living with the man, sleeping with him, thinking she was wed to him only to discover herself put aside. The more she thought of it, the angrier she became.

She had been willing, aye, she had been eager to put things right between them when he returned—if he ever returned. Now she was not so sure. Why should she be the one to make the first move? Let him make it. He was the one who had started this whole unfortunate thing between them, snapping and glowering at her and going off for days on end.

Let him come to her. At this point, she no longer wanted things to be smooth between them. In fact, she didn't care if she never spoke to him again. Except—oh, Lord, except if she were carrying his child . . .

She had been so caught up in Flower's problem and the talk about joining that she had actually forgotten about it. And now she felt so disheartened, so completely bereft that she yearned to sit down in the middle of the field and sob. It was then that she felt the familiar dull cramping deep inside and felt the warm flow. She gasped. Oh, please, let it be what she thought it was. Please . . . She knew soon that she was not mistaken—her blessed glorious menses had come. She had been spared. Everything was all right, and never in her life, never again would she tempt fate again in such a stupid way.

Chapter 19

Firewalker's inner battle was won. Day by day it had volleyed back and forth until he had decided finally that he would not ask Hope Caldwell to teach him. He told himself that it was not in him to be a taker instead of a giver, even for a cause as grand as this one. But when he saw that it was his pride, nothing more, which had won the contest, the protector within him was ashamed. How could he not make an attempt at least to help his people when it would mean the difference between darkness and dawn for them? He thought of the endless treaties in the past and of those to come in the future. Treaties which left his own people and all other Indians with less and less land and which pushed them farther west. Treaties which cheated them and were misrepresented to them because they could not understand what was happening. Because they could not read . . .

It was then that Firewalker knew he was going to go to Hope, crawl to her if need be, and ask for her help. He shrank at the thought, for he had told her he needed no learning. He had encouraged her to believe he could both read and write. How his kin and friends would laugh, and how fitting they would think it that a brave whose *manitou* was a dove should sit at the feet of a woman for teaching. But perhaps he deserved to be shamed for such deception. He needed to learn, once and for all, that smallness and softness did not mean a lack of spiritual strength or wisdom. *Memedhakemo* was small and soft, yet never once had she failed him or steered him in the wrong direction. He had lived a strong protected life.

Firewalker stopped in his tracks, hearing a familiar mournful call above his head. Looking up, he saw her—his small gray dove. She sat looking down on him from a tall oak before spreading her wings and fluttering off to the west. Toward home. He laughed. She was always far ahead of him, that one. She had given him a sign he had not even asked for. But he could not yet make himself return home to the painful chore he had set himself. Not yet. He would hunt for several more days.

Hope rejoiced as she walked with Flower back to their wigwam. She was free at last! And of all the things that had happened to her these past months, this was easily the strangest.

"Hope, I am so sorry. . . ."

"Don't be. When I came here, I expected to live as you lived."

"But that!" Flower protested, and made a face. "I should have told you so you could be prepared." Except she had been so unhappy about Glad Tidings that she had forgotten.

"I'll not hear another word," Hope said. "It's over."

She had just regained her freedom after being hidden away for five whole days because of her menses. She had been confined with several other women in a wigwam at the edge of the forest as if she had some dread disease. They were sequestered far from the braves and forbidden any contact with them. To touch a man or his weapons or food or clothing, or God forbid, breathe on him, would put his hunting and his very manhood at risk. But it was over, and now she was striding along with Flower in the warm

September sun. Seeing Flower's continuing glumness, she laughed.

"Honey, believe me, the only thing hurt is my pride."

"We women feared you would leave us."

"Leave you! I'll certainly not leave you." But the next time, she would go home for the terrible event. Her indignation had been greatly softened by the fact that she was not carrying Firewalker's child. Not a day had gone by that she did not give thanks for that. As they reached their dwelling, she asked, "Has Firewalker returned yet?"

"Aye, just this morning. I have not talked with him."

Good. Now she was going to enjoy ignoring him. She stored away the books she had read and the things she had used in her enforced vacation. "I'm ready to start work. Where am I needed most?"

"Will you teach? I have so missed you and our classes."

Hope was tickled. That glow on Flower's face was every bit as satisfying and rewarding as sewing up a cut or putting on a splint. "How about your cousins?"

"All of us have missed you and our classes. We did every lesson you gave us. We have worked hard."

"Then fetch the boys." Nothing else was so important that it could not wait a bit.

"Shall we meet at the willow?"

"Aye, I'll be there right away." She had just collected her things when she heard a familiar voice.

"Hope—I am back," Firewalker called softly through the door.

Hope's heart was bounding as she went outside, but she managed to give him a blank gaze. "Oh—were you away?" She bit her tongue after the words slipped out.

"I have been away several days."

She was disgusted with herself. She had planned exactly how she would act if he ever appeared again.

Polite yet distant. Friendly yet aloof. She would never let him see how deeply he had wounded her. And now, now she had gone and said such a stupid thing as that, a thing that practically screamed he had broken her heart. Naturally he would know that she knew he was gone. Damn.

Firewalker saw well that she wanted to slay him. She was hurting deeply, but it was of her own doing. He would not apologize. He said only, "Have you been well?"

"How kind of you to ask. I've been just fine." While he was away, she had forbidden herself to think of those golden eyes and of that inexorable, exciting pull of her body toward his. Feeling it now, she planted her feet firmly on the ground. "Are you here for any special reason? I was just about to leave to teach a class."

Firewalker reminded himself that was the only reason he was there. Her class. He said, "We must talk." He scarcely recognized his own voice.

"Yes, we must," Hope agreed sweetly. "But right now I must gather up my things and go. They're waiting for me. Will you excuse me, please?"

In an agony, he watched her go back inside the wigwam. He had vowed not to think of how she had felt in his arms, or think of the wild love they had made to each other, but seeing her again, he knew that never in this earth-life would he forget either of them. It filled him with such a sense of loss that he gladly would have sung his death song then and there. Instead, he must humiliate himself before her.

"I guess I have everything." Hope had reappeared, her arms laden with school supplies. "Come by later—any time." She frowned. "On second thought, I'll probably be in the fields, but I'm sure we'll get together eventually."

"Hope—"

"Aye?"

If he did not speak here and now, this moment would pass and his courage would be gone. By the

Eternal, death would be preferable to this. He said gruffly, "We will talk now."

All of the hurt and anger she had felt for him these many days was still simmering inside Hope. He had thought nothing of snarling at her, ignoring her, and then going off without a word and staying as long as it suited him. Now he expected her to drop everything to satisfy his whim. She did not hide her annoyance.

"I can't see what is so important it cannot wait a bit."

"It is important."

He told himself to speak, yet he could only gaze at her. The morning sun glittering on her black hair, the way her breasts filled the beaded doeskin shirt she wore, her mouth—so soft and pink and perfectly shaped. He was staring, and his tongue would not move. He closed his eyes and sent a silent prayer to *memedhakemo*.

Hope's impatience was blossoming. If he wanted to talk, why did he not talk? "We're having our class by the river. Walk with me there, and we can talk on the way."

"I will carry your things." He took them, fell into step beside her, ordered his miserable tongue to move. . . .

Walking through the center of the village with him so tall by her side, Hope felt small and protected. It was a lovely sensation, and one she had forgotten. Now she told herself she had best forget it all over again. Firewalker's protection was not a thing to be counted on. Glancing up and seeing the grim slash of his mouth and the small muscle twitching in his jaw, she wondered what it was that he wanted to talk about. Lord—was it an apology? Was that why he looked as if the end of the world had come?

Firewalker was suffering an agony of denial. He could not do this thing after all. His courage, constant in the face of bears, pumas, and enemy braves, had left him. Even so, he commanded himself to speak. Now . . . now!

He drew a breath, released it, and made himself force the shameful words out: "Hope, I would—join my kin for their lessons." If she consented, he would sit like a child at her feet with his little books and write little letters on his little slate. His face flamed as he awaited her laughter.

Hope shrugged. "Of course. Come by any time. They're always eager to show you their progress." They were walking along the river, and ahead was the grove of willows. Hope saw the four seated figures, their black heads bent over their slates. "Here we are. It seems we'll have to have our talk another time after all. . . ."

Firewalker stopped, caught her arm, and muttered, "Hope, you do not understand. I want to learn."

Hope frowned. Learn? She was shocked, aye, she was dumbfounded by his request and the flush spreading over his dark face. While they had never discussed it, she had assumed he was educated. He had never indicated he was not.

"Are you saying you—want to come to classes with the others?"

"Aye." He also wanted to sink into the earth. He could never hold up his head again.

Indeed. Hope crossed her arms and studied him with cool eyes. So he wanted her to teach him, did he, without so much as offering an explanation or an apology for behaving so monstrously after she had given herself to him? It seemed he needed to learn a thing or two or three about courtesy and friendship and the betrayal of trust before he learned reading and writing. But not from her. If he was too blind and too arrogant to see that he'd crushed her, she certainly was not going to tell him. Nay, if he cared no more than that about what had happened between them, God forbid that she say anything. If he wanted to be taught, why then she would teach him. To refuse would only reveal how much he'd hurt her.

She said politely, "You're more than welcome to join us, but I fear you'll find it boring. You're so far beyond us. . . ." It was a jab she could not resist.

Firewalker smiled. He deserved that. "I will not find it boring, and I thank you for your kindness." He gazed toward the small group under the willows. "If I might be the one to tell them. . . ?"

"Certainly."

"I will come later."

"Whatever you prefer."

The lesson was nearly over when he arrived. He was shown their work and told of their progress. Stargazer, however, was in a state of despair.

"I grow dumber, not smarter," he grumbled. "You are lucky, my cousin, to know this already."

Firewalker was euphoric, a great weight's having been lifted off his shoulders. He smiled. "I confess, I do not know it."

Stargazer frowned. "It is true, you never said you did, but I just thought . . ." He waved it off. "It does not matter. With your great memory, you do not need it."

"That is not so, kinsman. It matters. I need it and I want it." He met Hope's eyes. "This day I have asked Caldwell the healer if she will teach me also."

"And I said I would. . . ." Hope had been leaning against the tree trunk looking down on them.

Flower squealed, and the boys stared. "You will learn with us?" Stargazer asked. "You, who know everything?"

Firewalker gave a low chuckle. "You know more than I, all of you. Who will show me how to write the letter *A*? I know already that *A* is for ant. . . ."

As the four clamored to help him, he felt Hope's curious gaze upon him. Nothing had changed. He wanted her as much as he had ever wanted her, but he would not have her. And he doubted she wanted him. What was between them now was of the mind, not the heart. . . .

* * *

War Cloud's mood was black as he accepted a cup of whiskey from Jacques d'Arcy and squatted before the trader's smoky cook fire. It was night. Fall was in the air, and far off a wolf howled. He had much to say to this devil, but first things came first.

He asked gruffly, "What are you doing about the woman?"

Jacques chose his words carefully. "Since we last talked, I have made great steps. It will not be long before she is gone, I promise you."

After much thought, he had decided not to reveal what he was doing. War Cloud might well protest his dealing with the Mengwes, or worse, in his haste to be rid of Hope, he could demand Jacques give her to them instead of using her for bargaining. It was a risk he could not run.

"You will wed her then?"

Jacques stoked his beard. "I am superstitious, *mon ami*. I prefer to keep my plans quiet."

War Cloud was on him like a hawk. He lifted him up from the log where he was sitting and gave him a shake that rattled his teeth. "It will be best for you I hear them now," he said softly. "*Comprenez*, Frenchman?"

Jacques showed his teeth in a smile. "You are right, of course. It is quite proper that you know." *Sacre*, how he hated this stinking bastard. He would slay him for a certainty before he left these parts, but for now, he must tell him what he wanted to know. But only half of it. Only half. "I have offered her to the Mengwes. To those braves who found her in the woods."

War Cloud quickly covered his shock, but his black eyes flickered as he thought of Sings Low in the hands of Mengwe braves. "This is the woman you thought to wed?"

"It would seem I have changed my mind."

"You are a blacker bastard than I thought."

Jacques shrugged. "One must adapt." Not an easy

thing when all was in such turmoil, he thought resentfully.

He had returned to Ohio on Monday for Red Buck's answer, only to be told that Stands Tall himself was interested in the woman. He insisted on seeing her first, but before he could journey to the Lenape village, he was called away. One excuse had followed another so that all told, eleven days had passed since Jacques had first made his offer. He knew no more now than he had then, and he yearned for the thing to be done, for he was having pangs of guilt.

What if the story he had heard from the Mengwes got twisted? Or what if Hope were not Firewalker's lover at all? Yet it fit, it fit too well. When he had seen her last, she had been positively wallowing in her Indianness. What did it matter what became of her when she had made it perfectly clear he himself would never have her? And if he got a new source of furs in exchange for her—furs of the same luster and richness as those from this area . . .

War Cloud stirred his whiskey with his finger, licked it, and gazed across the flames at the trader. "What will the Mengwes give in return for her?"

Jacques looked at him blankly. "Trade, of course."

War Cloud looked gloomily into the flames, wondering if they would exchange furs for guns. It was the sort of trade his own people would be engaged in if he were chieftain instead of his uncle. "If they refuse?" he asked.

"My friend, they will not refuse. They want her." Even if Stands Tall did not want her, Red Buck and his comrades did. He was bound to profit from it.

War Cloud looked at him sourly and shook his head. "Man, you are slow. Had I taken this matter in hand, she would have been long gone." The accidents that could befall the unwary in the woods were many: poisonous snakes, deadly berries, deep waters. . . .

Jacques reddened. "I am doing my best."

"It is not good enough, Frenchman. This day my brother became one of her 'pupils.' "

It took some moments for Jacques to absorb this remarkable news. He gave a grunt of laughter. "Then he is a fool. He will be a laughingstock."

"It is you who are the fool if you think that. Every brave, every young buck in the village wants to be like Firewalker. It has always been so. Now they will all clamor to learn."

Jacques swallowed. "She cannot teach the entire village, I promise you."

War Cloud leaned forward. "She will not teach any, white man, I promise you." For one terrible moment, he feared he would weep. No one knew the humiliation he was suffering because of that female. His young cousins were impossible in their arrogance. Just this afternoon, that damned young hot spur, Stargazer, had declared if he, War Cloud, could not read and write, he'd best learn or be left behind.

"It will end, d'Arcy," he growled, "and it will end soon. Tell the Mengwes the Senecas want the woman—or the Wyandots. Build a fire under them."

Jacques blinked. He had never thought the devil would take his Mengwe dealing in such a spirit. He felt so magnanimous, he said, "My friend, you are right. If they are still undecided when I go tomorrow for my answer, I will tell them that. For a certainty, it will build a fire beneath them." Seeing that War Cloud was mollified, he refilled the brave's cup and the two drank into the night.

The next morning Walks Alone sought Firewalker and found him greasing a new bow he was making. "Good morning, my son."

Firewalker looked up from his work. "Good morning."

Her heart sometimes flew into her throat when he looked at her with those beautiful panther eyes of his. How like his father he was. Tall, lithe, and with his father's walk and his father's deep, resonant voice. None would ever doubt from whose seed this one had sprung. She tried to smile but she could not, for she was wondering, Was he the one who would depart this earth when the time of her vision came to pass? What irony it would be, knowing what she now knew about War Cloud, and considering that she loved Firewalker best. It was so. Why deny it to herself when even the Great Creator knew it was this one of her two sons she loved the most.

Firewalker got to his feet, suddenly concerned. Walks Alone looked old with her lips folded so tightly and her eyes gazing off onto some sight he could not see.

"My mother, what is it?"

"I would talk with you—away from the others." When they had walked in silence some distance into the forest, she glanced about and then said low, "I was up and about when War Cloud came home in the night. He did not see me." She lay a hand on her thudding heart. "He was drunk. So drunk he staggered and fell."

She looked up at her second son, expectant, wanting him to tell her that she was wrong, or to have some explanation. But Firewalker did not speak. He stood stiff as a pole with his eyes veiled. It was the way he had looked when he was very young and had seen his brother shoot a doe with a fawn by her side. It had been a sad accident, all were certain of that, but Firewalker's lips had been stubbornly sealed. Walks Alone sighed. He had been Little Hunter in those younger, happier days.

"I think there is much you are not saying, my son."

"Mother, don't ask me . . ."

"I must. You know that I promised his father—" she faltered but Firewalker had not noticed. "I promised your father I would guide War Cloud on a straight and narrow path. It is for Diving Eagle you must answer, and for our people. Now—have you ever seen your brother drunk?"

Firewalker stiffened. It was an impossible thing she

asked of him. He could not betray War Cloud, but neither could he lie. And not to answer condemned his brother as surely as if he had told the truth. At that moment he wanted to slay Jacques d'Arcy, but he knew that the fault did not lie with the Frenchman. He had merely brought War Cloud's weakness to light. If not d'Arcy, then another would have done it, and better now than when War Cloud was already sachem. He gazed at his mother, silent and sick at heart.

The face of Walks Alone was closed as she straightened her shoulders. She had learned what she wanted to know. She said quietly, "It is all right. You need say nothing. This day I will tell Thunderhead what I think we must do. If he agrees, I will tell War Cloud that the Twelve must be summoned."

Firewalker felt as if his legs had been cut from beneath him. The Twelve were the advisors to the chief and were called together only for matters of the greatest importance.

"Is my brother not to be given a second chance, then?" But he knew War Cloud had had his second chance. The first had been his own warning.

"The Twelve will decide."

Firewalker nodded glumly and imagined his brother standing before that grim tribunal. The Twelve had the power to detect untruthfulness and to prophesy, and their decision would be final and irrevocable. He wanted to shout a protest and shake his fists at fate, but it was not fate that had brought things to such a pass. It was War Cloud himself. Why had he been such a fool?

Chapter 20

Stands Tall was well satisfied. From his hiding place in the woods, he watched the woman harvest corn, and she was as his braves had said. Her beauty was great. Her skin was as white as the petals of a lily, and her form was pleasing. His eyes rested on her breasts. Even though they were hidden by her clothing, their shapeliness enticed him more than did the naked breasts of the squaws. Perhaps it was this one who would finally bear and suckle a son for him. Perhaps she would give him many sons.

He had not been blessed when it came to wives and children. The one woman he had truly loved would not have him, and his first wife, with his child in her belly, had been stolen by Senecas. The two wives he had now gave him only daughters, and had grown unsightly with the effort. It was time he took another and started over. He turned as his kinsman Red Buck glided toward him, a silent sun-dappled shadow.

"What do you think?" Red Buck's voice was a wind whisper.

"I will have her," said Stands Tall. Though the corn was high and she was beyond sight of the others, wisdom told him that it was best to wait until no one else was about to capture her. "When she bathes in the river at dusk or goes into the woods briefly, we will seize her."

Red Buck gave a soundless laugh. "The Frenchman will be coming tomorrow for your answer. . . ."

"The man is a snake," Stands Tall muttered. He had heard of d'Arcy, and would never allow such a one to get his hands on Mengwe furs. And if the fellow should happen to guess what had become of the woman, he could not prove it. He would never again be taken within the stockades of their village. "He will give us no trouble, but these devil Lenapes are another matter. They will suspect us."

Stands Tall thought then of the one called Firewalker whose woman she was, the one who had driven off three braves in rut for her. That feat had impressed him, for he admired bravery, even in a Lenape.

"I hope to see this Firewalker," he whispered to Red Buck. "Return to our mounts and make sure of their safety." The success of this venture depended not only upon their own skills but on the well-being of their horses. "Bring them to me at sunset. I will be at the spot we agreed upon."

After Red Buck departed, Stands Tall moved deeper into the woods. He glided silently and invisibly from tree to tree, his almost naked body and scalp lock painted with the colors of the dying summer. He froze when he heard the murmur of voices, and soon saw that it was a man and a woman. When it became clear that they had not the slightest suspicion he was there, he drew a deep breath and relaxed his taut body.

Cautiously, his movement so slow as to be imperceptible, he gazed around the trunk of the maple behind which he stood. It was a good vantage point, for he could see them well and not be seen. The two were in profile facing each other, and at first he thought they were lovers seeking privacy. He saw then that the woman, a fine-looking squaw, was much older than the brave. Her voice, a deep rich voice for a woman, caressed his ears. The golden eyes of Stands Tall narrowed and his heart gave a mighty leap. He could not believe it. It was Walks Alone of the Lenapes—his first love. His only love . . .

He stared at her, overcome by the memories streaming over him. He had been strong and bold and young when his people had come from the east to a gathering of many tribes in Kittanning. It was there he had met a slim soft brown-eyed maid, and had held her within his blanket. They had laughed and kissed and talked, and he had known she was the only woman for him. But her father would not give her to him, for he was the enemy.

In the months that followed, he had thought only of Walks Alone. He was wildly, deeply in love with her, and she loved him. He knew it by the way she had kissed him and looked into his eyes. He vowed he would have her despite her father's objections, but when he returned for her, he found her wed, and the mother of a boy babe. He ordered her to leave her husband and join with him, but she would not. He cajoled and gifted her, he demanded, he begged finally on bended knee that she leave the brave, Diving Eagle, and join him, but she would not. She said she loved her husband, and would never leave him.

It was then, in desperation, that Stands Tall claimed her. There in the dark on the grassy banks of the Alligewi Sipo, he had had his fierce angry will of her. She fought him in silence, but there was no turning him away as he proved to her his own undying love and hunger. She made no sound, nor did she weep, but when he left, he saw in her doe eyes her shame and her hatred for him. It tore his heart, and after twenty-seven winters, he remembered it still. Feeling hollow as a log, he leaned against a tree and listened to the pounding of his heart.

She had changed little. There were streaks of white in her black hair, but her skin was still golden and her breasts were small and shapely. And so these were her people, these Shenango Lenape. His head whirled with questions. How long had they been there, and was she still with Diving Eagle? It would be an unusual thing if she was, but then Walks Alone was an unusual woman. Filled with curiosity, he strained to hear the low voices of the two.

"—so drunk he staggered and fell—"

He held his breath, not wanting to miss the brave's answer but there was none. Instead Walks Alone added, "I think there is much you are not saying, Firewalker, my son."

Stands Tall was intrigued. It grew more interesting by the moment. So the tall brave was Firewalker—and he was her son? Was it Firewalker, then, who had been a babe when Stands Tall saw her last? His heart hardened thinking of how he had shamed himself with his begging her, and how she had rejected him. How he had hated her that night. He had never stopped hating her. Or loving her . . .

Bending his ear to their low voices again, he learned that Diving Eagle was gone from this earth, and the drunk was the elder of her two sons and would be sachem. The ever-noble Walks Alone was distraught and the advisors were to be called. Stands Tall smiled. Excellent. Most excellent. Let her suffer for her insanity, for the woman had been mad not to go away with him. Let the bad seed of that fool, Diving Eagle, plague her. She deserved it, and he was glad for her misery. But he resented deeply that she had sons and he did not. Had she been his woman, they would have been his.

Stands Tall peered cautiously around the trunk for another look at Firewalker, but jerked back as the brave turned, facing him. Firewalker did not see him for his eyes were raised to the skies in supplication before he strode off at the side of his mother.

Stands Tall sagged against the tree. He felt his body trembling, and a roaring like a great wind was in his ears. A great triumphal wind. He was stunned. He had just seen himself as he had been long ago. He had been young and handsome then with a brooding craggy face, a body that was lithe yet powerful, but it was his eyes, his beautiful golden panther eyes, that had beguiled the women. He threw back his head and silent laughter filled his throat. They were the eyes of Firewalker. By the Eternal, he had a son. . . .

Stands Tall raised his arms and made a silent prayer to the Great Creator, for the prayer of his life had been answered. It had been answered these many years had he but known it. He had a tall strong son—for there was no denying from whose seed that one had sprung. The white woman for whom he had come no longer mattered. He had no need for her now that he had found Firewalker. For there was no doubt in his mind that the brave would come to him and would walk by his side the rest of his days. . . .

The day following Firewalker's first lesson, two braves came to Hope in the field as she was harvesting squash. She straightened, brushed back a wisp of hair from her damp forehead, and gazed up at them. Recognizing one of them, she smiled. "Greetings, my friends."

"Greetings, lady." It was Glad Tidings who spoke.

Seeing the two grinning at one another, shamefaced, Hope knew exactly why they were there. Four other braves had come to her the night before for the same reason. They wanted to be taught. When the two remained tongue-tied, she asked, "Can I help you in some way?" She waited while Glad Tidings kicked the earth with a moccasined foot.

"We want to learn," he muttered finally.

Hope felt a thrill as she thought of Flower and what grand news this would be for her. But she had not forgotten her hard-won lesson in dealing with Firewalker's young cousins. She must show sternness instead of the delight she felt. She said crisply, "You may join us for a trial period. I teach only those who will work hard."

"Lady, I will work hard," replied Glad Tidings.

"And I," said his friend.

"I will be the judge of that," Hope said. "We meet by the river under the willows every morning. Come when you see the others gathering."

Since that morning, seven days had passed and Hope found it hard to believe all that had happened. When her father paid her his weekly visit, they strolled about the perimeter of the village talking about it.

"And that makes ten braves and five more boys in class now," Hope said. "Father, that's twenty. Twenty!"

"How are your supplies holding up?" Tom studied her as she strode long-legged by his side: doeskins, moccasins, a beaded headband, her long black hair streaming—and Lenape braves coming to her for teaching. He was so proud of her he was fit to bust a gut.

"Can you order more paper when the next pack train comes? And chalk and ink?"

"Aye." He grinned down at her. "Twenty, eh? And all wanting to be like Firewalker, I expect."

"I guess so. . . ."

"I'm not surprised."

Hope had told him nothing of her break with Firewalker. She knew from experience that anything which upset her would only upset him. And since he'd said nothing of any new rampaging, she let well enough alone and did not ask any questions. But in truth, she was still furious with Firewalker. He was absorbing her teaching rapidly, practically drinking it in, but he was as distant as ever. He kept his eyes hooded and looked right through her when she spoke to him. It was as if he had forgotten their lovemaking entirely, whereas it was all she could think about when she was near him. She dared not let her eyes linger on him for long.

"Twenty's quite a crowd," Tom drawled. "I remember when you thought six or eight were too many."

"Flower and Stargazer help tremendously. . . ." She plucked a foxtail and nibbled the stem.

"Uh-oh."

Hope laughed. "You're right, it wasn't popular. The first day, everyone got up and trooped out. Silently and politely, of course, but they trooped out."

"Firewalker, too?"

"Nay, not Firewalker."

He had noticed a shadow on her face when the brave's name was mentioned. But if she wanted to tell him about it, she would.

"After they all marched off," Hope continued, "he said Lenape braves wouldn't place themselves under a maid and a boy. And I said they hadn't a choice, for I wouldn't do it alone. If they wanted to learn, it was that or nothing." She gave him a grin. "And guess what?"

"The next morning they all came back?"

"Aye." She giggled, remembering, and what a grand sight it had been.

Tom gave her a bear hug and kissed the top of her head. "You're something, girleen. Hell, but I'm proud of you. I just wish your mother could see you. . . ."

Hope returned his kiss and hug. She was just as glad her mother could not see her. Her father was the only one in the world who was proud of what she had become. It reminded her, to her great relief, that she had not seen Jacques recently. He was probably on one of his frequent trips.

"Well, it's time I was getting back." Tom walked to where he'd tethered his horse. "I'll reorder those supplies when the pack train comes. It should be any day now."

"Good, and when you see Maybeth, please tell her I'll be stopping by again soon. And tell her not to work too hard in the fields. I worry about that."

Tom mounted. "I'll make it a point to see her."

"Is—Josh all right?"

"He's fine. I think he misses you."

"And I miss him." She sighed, thinking of cuddling and playing with him and kissing his soft brown ears. Indian dogs were just not the same; they reminded her too much of wolves. She remembered suddenly how Josh had adored Firewalker, and remembered the brave's big dark hands moving over him, stroking, so gently stroking him. . . .

Tom frowned, seeing her eyes glisten suddenly. He said softly, "Princess, I'll not meddle, but any time you want to come home, you come. You hear?"

"Aye . . ."

After he was gone, Hope walked slowly toward her wigwam thinking how strange it was that she could feel so empty and lonely when every minute of every day was filled. When she had come here, she had expected to take on the work of a Lenape woman, and had done so willingly. There was none busier, herself included. They hoed the crops, they were regularly yoked under great buckets of springwater and bent under firewood, they pounded corn and tended children and wove mats. And then there were the men . . . Those who were not sleeping in their bunks were sprawled under trees, or were playing ball or cards or dice. She knew for a fact that Lenape men could play dice the livelong day.

She was pleased to note that "her" braves were not occupied in such fruitless activity. They would not dare. Not unless their lessons were perfect, which so far had not happened. Later, as she worked in the herb garden, yanking weeds and thumping the rich earth from them, her anger toward men and Firewalker in particular magnified.

She had sought a haven here and Thunderhead had provided it, and for that she was thankful. But she had had every reason to expect friendship and courtesy from Firewalker. She had received neither, nor had he ever apologized or given her any explanation for his rude behavior. In return for his boorishness, she was teaching him to read and write, teaching his friends and kin to read and write, and doing work the braves could at least help with if they ever dragged themselves away from their beds and games. It was interesting that they were never too tired to eat or to dance the night away!

The more she thought of it, the angrier she grew. Where on earth was her backbone? When she spied Firewalker leaving his longhouse, she got up, brushed the earth from her hands, and marched over to him.

"I want to talk with you," she said sharply.

Ever since his return, Firewalker had seen the storm signals within her. Now the dark centers of her eyes were enlarged and she spoke through clenched teeth. Her breasts rose and fell with her quickened breathing. He said easily, "Then we should go where we will not be disturbed."

Hope followed him into the woods until the sounds of the village were muted. He led her to a small grassy bower pressed in by evergreens and berry bushes, and gazed down on her calmly. He crossed his arms.

"So, what is it?"

Hope, too, crossed her arms. She shot him a blazing look. "You have no idea?"

"I know you are angry."

And he knew he was in torment. From dawn to dusk he was in torment, being in the same village with her, breathing the same air she breathed, and walking the same ground her small feet trod without being able to touch or hold her. He was parched for want of her, and scorched when their eyes met or when her hand brushed his to correct a stroke he had made on slate or paper.

"You might well say I'm angry!" Hope retorted, trying to keep her voice down.

"Yet if anyone has cause to be angry, it is I," Firewalker rumbled.

"You!" Hope gazed up at him in astonishment. "You who have ignored me from the first day I arrived and who won't speak to me or look at me outside of class? You have cause to be angry?" She gave a burst of wild laughter. "Come now, Firewalker." She blinked back tears. She would not cry in front of him, but she was not going to hide how she felt either. It had been stupid to hide it this long. "You had best tell me right here and now what this is all about or I'll never understand. We made love, you and I, and I thought you cared for me. I would not have given myself to you otherwise. . . ."

Firewalker grated: "As you gave yourself to d'Arcy?"

Hope stared at him, unable to believe what she had just heard. Given herself to Jacques? The words were so unexpected, so preposterous she didn't know whether to laugh or cry. And then she felt angry tears streaming down her cheeks. She choked, "What a cruel thing to say. . . ."

Firewalker held himself rigid and glowered at her. If he spoke, if he moved, it would be to take her in his arms and comfort and kiss her. Never had he known that a woman's weeping could so wound his soul.

Hope grew quiet, gazing at his face. For just an instant, she thought she had seen anguish burning in his eyes before it was quickly doused. How wonderful if he were hurting as she was. But more wonderful still would be to discover what all of this was about. And the only way to find out was to ask him. Now—but carefully. He was proud and he was wounded. But so was she. She dashed the tears from her cheeks, and glared up at him.

"Whoever gave you such information lied—or you misunderstood."

Firewalker said drily, "There has been no misunderstanding. On the contrary, I have had an awakening."

She realized suddenly that he must have seen Jacques kissing her. Of course. He must have returned from his journey, gone to Twin Oaks, seen them in the clearing, and departed in a rage before seeing the outcome. There could be no other explanation. And now he hated her, and she had no defense. Only the truth.

She said with feeling, "I have never made love with Jacques d'Arcy."

"Do not lie to me, Hope."

She was about to lash back when his golden eyes flickered over her. Her heart trembled. So it *was* anguish she had seen in them. There it was again. He looked for all the world like a great wounded panther.

She said softly, "If you saw Jacques kissing me, you couldn't have known how furious I was with him. If you had waited one instant longer, you'd have seen me slap him." When his mouth tightened and he made no answer, she shook her head. "You disappoint me, Firewalker, if you think I make love with every man who kisses me. Other men have kissed me, you know. I didn't live in a cave in Pittsburgh with a bag over my head!"

"Hope . . ."

"I saw other men, I kissed other men, I was even engaged to another man when I lived there. Oh, aye, strange as it may seem to you, other men *have* wanted to marry me. Jacques is one of them. But you are the only one I ever made love with. You are the only one I ever wanted to make love to me. . . ."

She had won. His face wore its familiar mask, but now his eyes were like the sun dancing. Pretending not to notice, she shrugged, lifted her chin. "But of course, if you won't talk and you don't believe me, and there is to be no trust between us"—she threw up her hands—"well then, I should go back to my father's house."

Firewalker caught her shoulders. "You will not go back to your father's house." He added quietly, "I did not see Jacques kissing you."

Hope stared. "You—didn't?"

"Nay." He laughed softly then and, pulling her close, buried his face in her neck and hair. "Hope . . . Hope . . ." For certain he was the fool of fools—for ever doubting her and for believing anything d'Arcy said, with his own mouth or through War Cloud.

"Then why did you think I—"

"So he kissed you, did he?" he growled.

Hope grinned. "And got walloped for it. But you haven't said how—"

"I could kill him for that," Firewalker said low. "For touching you and looking at you—for knowing you before I did." He kissed her, a long deep hungry kiss to make up for all of the days and nights of loneliness. "I am so jealous, little fox, I am eaten alive by it, night and day."

Hope slipped her arms around his neck and pressed her body close to his. "There is no need. Believe me, there is no need. . . ." She had always detested jealousy and possessiveness in a man, but how lovely it suddenly felt. How lovely . . . And what did it matter how the misunderstanding had come about? It was ended now.

Chapter 21

Firewalker's arms tightened about the soft body pressed against his. He had never dreamt he would hold her again, yet here she was, smiling up at him, hot eyed, her small hands stroking his face, tracing his lips, smoothing back his hair. . . .

"I thought you hated me," Hope murmured.

"Never." He drank in hungrily the sun's faint speckling across her nose and cheeks, and the way it tipped her long black lashes. Bending to give her another kiss, a memory stirred. He released her and, smiling, put her firmly from him.

Hope's heart was flying, having him in her arms once more. Now she frowned. "What is it?"

"You have no idea?"

She recognized the words she had spoken earlier. "Are you teasing me?"

One straight black eyebrow lifted. "Were you teasing me?"

"When? What do you mean?"

"You ordered me not to call you beautiful, nor hold you nor kiss you. I would never go against your wishes."

Hope's cheeks turned pink seeing the devil dancing in his eyes. She remembered the incident in the keenest detail. After their first wonderful lovemaking, she had had misgivings—and he had vowed not to touch her again until she begged him.

He nodded. "You remember, I see."

"Aye." She could not believe he would hold her to such a thing.

"I pray you do not tarry." The fire was building within him, but he gazed at her placidly. He stood taller and crossed his arms, the very essence of patience.

Hope laughed. "This is so silly. . . ." He knew she wanted him. Her body was heating, weakening, wanting to melt into his, but to beg him to make love to her? It was too silly for words. She teased, "I will be more than happy to kiss you if you wish. . . ."

Firewalker gave a low laugh. "You little fox, what is your wish?"

She was swept suddenly by those hot deep throbbings and pulsings which she felt only when she was with him. Just to look at him set her afire, and she saw his own hunger. She whispered, "I wish you would hold me and kiss me."

Firewalker cradled her face in his hands, and lowered his head so that his mouth neared hers. Golden eyes still dancing, he murmured, "How much do you wish it?"

Hope felt his warm fresh breath on her face and his lips brushing hers, a whisper of silk. But he did not kiss her. She could not believe his stubbornness—and his cleverness. Unable to hold back any longer, she laughed softly. "Very well, I beg it. . . . What a heartless brute you are. I beg it. Are you satisfied?" She was still laughing as his mouth covered hers, warm and firm, and greeted her tongue with his in a slow gentle kiss.

She shivered with the delight of it as he drew her close, his arms enfolding her and his kisses deepening and growing hungrier and more urgent. This was what she had yearned for. How she had missed it, and missed him—even when she was furious with him. She returned his kisses hungrily, sliding her hands across his wide shoulders and down his back, searching over his hips and hard buttocks. She knew then that she could not be parted from him again. She could not bear it. She wanted him, not just now, but forever. And she wanted more than a mere joining with him; she wanted to marry him. She loved him. The thought was a white-hot thrill coursing through her, shocking her. Surely it was not love—but aye, it was. She had no idea when or how it had happened, she knew only that, God help her, she loved him.

But she did not want to think now of the pain it might bring her. Now she wanted to think of how dark and hard and tall and strong and beautiful he was. She wanted to see the pleasure-pain that was already transforming his face, and to feel her own blossoming arousal. His hands burned her already-heated flesh as he slipped her doeskin shirt up over her head and cupped her naked breasts. She gasped, sheer delight, as he pressed his lips and then the tip of his tongue to her nipples, circling them, teasing the velvet to hard little buds, and then nipping them until she writhed in his arms.

Firewalker removed his breechclout then, and kneeling, drew down Hope's leggings. He helped her step out of them, pulled her close, and, still kneeling, rained kisses over the curve of belly. His breathing grew heavy as he looked on her slim long-legged perfection. How unbelievably beautiful she was, and how soft and fragile seeming—yet what bravery and strength of will she possessed. She was a marvel, and she was his. He knew it now with all certainty.

Hope's breathing quickened, feeling his hands caressing her buttocks, molding and pressing her closer as his warm lips and his tongue moved over her abdomen, kissing her, gently licking, tantalizing, teasing. She stroked his wide wonderful shoulders, stroked and smoothed his thick black hair, and cradled his face, tilting it upward as she bent to kiss his mouth again and again.

"I—I want you," she whispered. "I want you so."

Firewalker gave a low chuckle as they kissed. It

was sufficient. He would never make her beg for lovemaking. Drawing her down to the grass beside him, he then lay her back and stretched out beside her, one long arm under her to pull her closer. He was tempted to devour her, but instead leashed his hunger as he kissed and tasted her parted lips and the sweet delicate hollow of her throat. Cupping, molding her breasts to their fullest, he touched the tip of his tongue to her hardened little nipples, fluttering it against them before kissing them and taking them in his mouth and gently sucking them. A stream of fire was racing through him, searing him, and when he heard her moan and saw that her half-closed eyes were glazed and dreamy and that she was panting, he knew it was time.

He thought again how beautiful she was, his woman, as he parted her smooth thighs and gently, gently touched the head of his shaft to the pink valley glistening there. He saw her eyes widen and a smile lift her lips, heard her husky whisper: "Firewalker, please, I want to be yours. Make love to me—I beg you. . . ."

Firewalker lay drowsy and content, his woman still in his arms. He lazily studied the blue canopy of sky and the clouds drifting overhead, and in the woods, he heard squirrels chattering and birds talking to one another in the treetops. Bees hummed, working their way through wildflowers that were gold and white and purple, and locusts sang of winter coming. He sighed and stroked the silken flesh beneath his fingers. He was warm and drained and happier than he ever remembered. He looked down at Hope as she slept, at the thick fringe of black lashes brushing her pale cheeks and the tender curve of shoulder and bosom. He drew a deep breath. This was his woman. Unable to help himself, he tilted her chin and kissed her soft parted lips.

Hope opened her eyes and smiled up at him. "Hello. . . ."

Firewalker kissed her again. "Hello, my wife."

Hope laughed. "Wife? When did that happen?" She caught his hand and covered it with kisses, front and back, and inhaled the intoxicating scent of his skin—pine, earth, wintergreen, wood smoke. "Ummmmm. You smell so good—like the forest. . . ." She buried her face in his neck, kissed it, and breathed in his wonderful male aroma once more.

He clasped her chin and planted a hungry kiss on her lips. He felt his manhood stir. "And you smell like flowers and the sun and the wind." He smoothed back her hair from her warm sleep-pink face. "You are summer, my wife."

Hope sat up. It was the second time he had called her his wife. She smiled. "I don't think I'm your wife quite yet."

Firewalker pulled her back down beside him, her neck in the crook of his arm. His hands moved over her breasts, caressing and exploring. "You would have my mother go to your father, then, and barter for you?"

She grinned. "Maybe. What would she offer?"

"You would command many horses, Hope Caldwell."

"I guess we should pass on that. My father doesn't need horses. . . ."

"Then you are mine. We are joined, and tonight you will sleep in my arms."

Hope tried to sit up, but he held her firmly by his side. His sensuous kneading of her breasts was sending sparks through her again, and he was kissing those places that made her shiver—beneath her ear, her throat, her neck where it curved into her shoulder. She firmly removed his hands from her breasts and covered his lips with her fingers.

"I think we should talk." She sat up again.

Firewalker rolled onto his side, propped his head on his hand, and studied her. "About what?" How gracefully she sat, his woman, with her dimpled knees bent, her small perfect feet tucked beneath her, arms crossed over her beautiful breasts. Breasts that would one day suckle his sons . . . He drew a long breath of satisfaction.

Hope said gently, "We're not really wed, you know. I will not be sleeping with you tonight."

Now Firewalker sat up. "Twice I have made you mine. You asked me to make you mine. Now we are one."

"I—do want to be one with you, but—"

He said tersely, "Then we are joined."

Hope could not help but think of her talk with Flower, and of being on trial and put aside if she were found wanting. Like an old shoe.

"Among my people," she said, "we are not wed unless we are joined by a man of God. A preacher of the gospel." The suddenly dark look on his face chilled her.

"But you are not among your people now," he said quietly. "You are with my people, and we have no preachers here." His tribe had not been among those who went to live with the Moravians and attend their churches. Never his tribe. He studied her with narrowed eyes. "You think we live in sin, then?"

She was embarrassed. "Of course not. It's just that, when your people join it seems so—temporary somehow. . . ." She wished she had not said it, but it was the way she felt.

"I see." So she was content to be sheltered and protected by them as long as she did not have to follow their ways.

"Please understand, I mean no disrespect to your people."

It was not that which stung him. It was her lack of faith and trust in him. "Do you doubt that I care for you?"

"Nay. I see well that you care for me now." But what of next month, or next year? "It's just that I—would not feel wed without speaking vows. It's the way I was raised."

Firewalker pulled on his breechclout and got to his

feet. The heat he felt was no longer that of passion but of anger. By the Great Manitou, was he never to have this woman? Did she hold him in no higher regard than to think he would toss her away after using her? He muttered, "Perhaps you had best wed d'Arcy at that. You say he wants you."

Hope furiously tugged on her shirt and leggings and climbed to her feet. "You dare say that to me now? After this?"

He shook his head. "Why do you not trust me?"

"I—"

"Do you think I will discard you if your biscuits are hard?"

"You might. I just don't know. And is it so wrong to fear being put aside? When I wed, I want it to be forever. Not for a week or a month or a-a year."

Firewalker said stiffly, "Death alone parted my father and my mother. Death parted my uncle from his first and only wife. Had you but asked, I would have told you our joining will be forever. You will be mine until the world stands still."

Hope was momentarily charmed. It sounded beautiful—if he meant it. But the most important thing of all was missing. She said quietly, "You've not mentioned love. You tell me I'm beautiful and that your people cherish my skills, and that I'll be yours until the world stands still, but you've never said you love me."

Firewalker felt a rush of impatience. It was not the way of the Indian to talk of such things. It showed weakness. "A warrior shows his woman his love," he said. "He does not speak of it. He protects her, he brings her meat, and gives her his children."

How lovely, Hope thought, looking at his suddenly masked face. Was there not even one small I love you for those poor women slaving from morn till night? Was their only reward meat and babes to care for? Oh, aye, and protection . . . She gave him a cool smile. "That's very nice. I'm sure your women appreciate it. And now I think it's time I got back to ought harder for her as he now meant to do. an heiress for a wife, he would not have to about Lenape furs or any other furs. He could p this entire miserable business and never lift er again. He was savoring the sweetness of it he arrived at the village and discovered Hope ing water from the river.

onjour, mon amie."

reetings, Jacques."

s mouth twisted. He actually had thought she a squaw bearing the two buckets suspended the heavy wooden yoke across her shoulders. quickly dismounted.

Ma belle, this should not be. Permit me."

Hope allowed him to be gallant, and afterwards, urned to the river with him where they sat under willow. She toyed with the beads on her moccasin, d wondered why on earth he was there. He'd been furious with her when she saw him last, and no wonder. Remembering how Flower, intent on saving her, had fetched all of those little boys and their dogs, she bit her lip to keep from laughing.

"How have you been?" she asked politely. "You're oking well."

He shrugged. "I manage to keep myself busy."

"I'm glad."

'And you?" He saw that she was as much of an berg as ever. "Is all well with you?"

Everything is very well, thank you." She smiled, king of Firewalker's making love to her, and ting to share his life with her. Aye, everything going very well indeed, thank you. . . .

Hope—"

ye?" She had felt him scrutinizing her.

ques said softly, "Forgive me, *ma chère*, but I t keep still. Look at yourself . . ." His pained moved over her beaded doeskins and moccasins er long black braids with the feathers tucked em. "What has become of you—dressing like a and—"

work." She pushed through the narrow path between the bushes.

"I don't recall hearing the word from your own lips," Firewalker muttered, close behind her.

Turning, Hope met his eyes and saw his anger. She felt her body's own angry trembling. "The truth is," she said quietly, "I do love you. I would not have given myself to you otherwise." She had to be mad, telling him that, but then there was a touch of madness in her going to live with them in the beginning. "Perhaps I've loved you from the first day I saw you—I don't know. But I do know you were furious with me then, as you've been furious with me most of the time since. You've not made it easy for me to speak to you of love." She pushed on through the bushes.

Firewalker gazed after her in astonishment. She loved him? Love?? He felt a surge of elation, but he dampened it instantly. Love meant nothing. It was unimportant and it was a nuisance. It was a thing he neither knew how to give nor show, and he resented it that females forever brought up the subject. And he was not going to permit something so vague and inconsequential to come between himself and Hope. He strode after her and caught her hand.

"We are going to talk."

"About what?"

"About love and why it is so important to you. I want to understand."

Hope felt sorry for him. She felt sorry for all of them if they did not know what love was. She replied gently, "There's little to understand. I'm no different from any other woman. We all want to be loved and cherished a-and to be the only woman for our man."

"Then my lovemaking did not make you feel loved and cherished? It was not enough?"

Her color deepened. "It was wonderful, but—" How on earth could she explain? "But loving someone and making love are two different things."

"Then I understand even less." His golden eyes were brooding. "I doubt I am in love—I have never been in love—but I want a lifetime of making love with you. I want your face to be the last thing I see before I close my eyes at night, and the first thing I see when I open them at dawn. I want to give you sons. I want to share life with you, and joy and sorrow. I want to care for you and protect you for as long as I walk this earth, and I will do my best to give you all you crave." He raised her hands to his lips and kissed them. "I will be a good husband, Hope Caldwell. Is that not enough?"

Hope's heart had grown so full as he spoke that for some moments she could not answer. She could only smile, stunned and overcome by her pleasure. She whispered finally, "Aye, it is enough. It is more than enough."

He said he had never been in love, but he was. He was in love with her! And the fact that he wanted to join, and she wanted to be wed was a minor thing and unimportant—it would be easily settled. She was jubilant. He loved her! And he had seen, better than she, that the mere saying of those three small words was not important. But silly as it was, she still yearned to hear them whispered from his lips. Suddenly, bell clear, she knew she would. Oh, aye, someday Firewalker was going to be on his knees telling her of his love. He would be whispering it, laughing and shouting and crying it. Oh, aye, he would, she could see it. He just did not know it yet.

Firewalker was watching her intently. Something was happening inside that beautiful head, but what? He almost feared to know. He took her shoulders. "Hope, what is it? Talk to me."

She touched wondering fingers to his face and his hair. "You're wonderful, and I love you. . . ." She wanted to laugh and cry and sing. She wanted to dance through the woods like some wild thing shouting to the sky and the trees that she loved him. But in truth, she did not want to do any of those things

now. Nay, not now. Slowly, seducti
dering, she slid her arms around his
her breasts to his chest, and kissing, t
his warm lips. She whispered, "Do yo
talk . . . ?"

Firewalker chuckled, seeing the hung
and feeling her softness against him. H
his arms. "Do you?"

"Nay. . . ." It was muffled, for his m
ready claimed hers.

Jacques d'Arcy relished his startling
galloped up the river trail toward the Len
He had not seen Hope for over two week
he care ever to see her again—except when
ered her to Stands Tall. But the pack train
brought him a long-awaited letter from P
and its contents boggled his mind. He had
there was money in the Caldwell family, but Hope
was wealthier than he had ever dreamed possible.
She was a veritable heiress. Her mother, one of the
Philadelphia Cartwrights, had left her a considerable
fortune which she would claim when she reac
age of twenty-six, three years from now.

Even without it, she and Thomas had wall
luxury in a splendid mansion on Seventh
And now he understood why they had left
had fled Pittsburgh to avoid being tried fo
Murder! It was so incredible as not to be
She had been accused by the banker
Thorpe, of gross negligence in the death
child. Thinking of this positively sensatio
tion, Jacques smiled and patted his poc
small pewter ring lay. For a certainty, h
such news to good use.

As for Stands Tall, Jacques thanked
had not wanted Hope. The three bra
consequence; he could forget them. Of
but known then what he knew now,
have offered her to them in the first

"These clothes are the most comfortable I've ever worn," Hope answered pleasantly.

"And I suppose you enjoy being yoked to those buckets like an ox while these devils play their games and sleep?"

"Nay, I don't enjoy it, but I no longer mind." She was slowly coming to understand that if the men were not fit to hunt, there was no meat, no furs for warmth, and therefore no survival.

He shook his head, breathed through his nose. "It is an abomination seeing you this way. A sacrilege."

Her lips curved. "Perhaps you shouldn't look at me then."

"Hope, you are an educated woman. A physician. Why remain here when you can have the world at your feet?"

She got to her feet. "The world is not ready for me, Jacques. And now I'd best get back to work." Her eyes widened as he caught her left hand and slid a ring onto her third finger.

"Jacques, what are you doing!"

He smiled his boyish shamefaced smile. "Did you really think I could stop loving you or give you up? This is in lieu of the diamond I will give you someday. . . ."

She could not believe his persistence. Her anger flared, yet she could not bring herself to lash out at him. She had someone wonderful to love, and he had no one, and she knew how terrible it could be. He was desperate for someone to share his life.

"I'm sorry. It seems I'm forever hurting you." She took off the ring and handed it back. "Some lucky woman will love wearing it someday."

Jacques returned it to his pocket. "It is yours alone, Hope. I will keep it until you change your mind. Which brings me to a subject that—"

"I'll never wear it, Jacques—please believe me. I'm sorry. And I really must go now." She began moving away from him. "This is a busy time."

"You must hear what I have to say, *mon amie,*" he said between clenched teeth. "You really must."

"The next time, perhaps? We're trying to get the harvest in and I've dallied long enough. There's Flower beckoning me." She tossed him a wave. "Good-bye. . . ."

He wanted to strangle her. He wanted to follow her, wrap his fingers about that soft white throat, and squeeze until she begged for mercy. And he would. When she was his, he vowed he would, the damned wench.

Riding home, he anticipated with great pleasure his next visit to her. He would tell her in exquisite detail all of his news, and then he would tell her exactly what he expected of her. Unless, of course, she preferred that everyone in the valley, Indian and white, learn why she had fled Pittsburgh.

Chapter 22

That night, Jacques d'Arcy paced his small bed-sitting room by the light of a guttering candle. His disgusted gaze moved over its cramped interior and meager furnishings: the let-down rope bed with its straw mattress, a splintery chair and table holding two tin cups and plates, the half-log shelves holding his possessions—and in the storeroom in front, more such shelves holding his trading goods. *Sacre.* It was intolerable that he should continue to live this way, and intolerable that he should be so thwarted.

First there was Thunderhead—he should have slain him in the very beginning. And then there was Firewalker. Perhaps the devil would eventually destroy himself with his off-and-on rampages against the whites—it was a fatal flaw in him, his hatred for whites—but until he was caught redhanded, he could not be jailed and would remain a constant thorn in his side. And then there was Hope. Damn her beautiful eyes, why was she not a simple pliable female instead of another Jeanne d'Arc? It was maddening.

Hearing hoofbeats, he took up his candle and lit his way through the black storeroom. He unbolted the door, opened it, and gaped at the ashen-faced brave who stood there huddled beneath his blanket. *Nom du Nom.* He had never seen War Cloud in such a sorry state.

"N'tschu, what has happened?" When the brave did not speak, Jacques felt a premonition of doom. He led him back into his miserable chamber, offered him the chair, and poured him a whiskey. After pouring another for himself, he sat down on the edge of his bed, elbows on his knees. "Man, speak to me. What has happened?" And how did it affect himself? Jacques wondered, his heart roaring.

War Cloud said nothing. He tipped the tin cup and took a swallow. He sat stiff and straight backed, his head high and proud, but he was dying. He was dead already, in fact, having been stripped this day of his birthright by twelve old men who had foreseen that he would not rule wisely. Twelve snot-sniveling old men and his mother. Bitterness gnawed him. To think, his own mother. But it was so far a private matter. None in the village knew what the meeting had been about. They would not know until the death of Thunderhead when Firewalker would almost certainly be voted chief.

It was the nightmare War Cloud had always feared, and after leaving the tribunal, he had sat the day long in the deep woods overwhelmed by his grief and rage. He could not bear the disgrace of his younger brother ascending a throne he did not even want while he himself was cast down. By day's end, he had decided if he could not be chieftain, neither would Firewalker. He decided also what must be done, but without whiskey, he did not have the courage even to think about it let alone order it done. Draining his cup, he silently, imperiously, held it out to the Frenchman for more.

Jacques was incensed by the brave's arrogance, but he kept his peace. He had seen men lose an eye or a nose or an ear when a savage was in such a mood. He refilled their cups, mended the fire, and sat back down to simmer in silence. He prayed to God this was not about Hope. Not now when he had just learned about her fortune.

He cleared his throat. "My friend—"

"Silence." War Cloud's black eyes glittered in the light of the one candle. "Tomorrow, Frenchman, you will go to the Mengwes."

Jacques swallowed and felt the blood drain from his face. So it was about Hope—and if he confessed now that Stands Tall did not want her, he would lose his scalp for a certainty. . . .

"You will hire a brave," War Cloud continued, "to kill the whites' livestock in the highlands. I will pay for the whiskey you will give him in return." He sipped and slitted his black eyes at Jacques. *"Savez-vous?"*

Jacques gaped at him. "I am listening." He felt his courage returning as he realized this was not about Hope. This was about Firewalker—but what in the name of God had happened between them?

"Tell the devil to kill as many animals as he wishes," War Cloud muttered, "but for two of his kills, he must use the arrows I will give you."

Jacques rose. He leaned an elbow on the mantelpiece and drummed it with his fingers. "There may not be any who will take such a risk even for whiskey."

War Cloud detested him and the eagerness he saw in his eyes. The devil knew well that this was about the betrayal of Firewalker. He was reveling in it while his own heart was torn into bloody pieces at the thought. But his pride demanded nothing less. Firewalker had to fall. Maybe then the two of them would be close again if neither was ranked above the other. Maybe then they would recapture the old camaraderie they'd once had. In truth, he missed it.

"The arrows are Firewalker's, as you well know," he said thickly. "Since the Mengwes fear him, you will easily find some bastard to do your bidding."

An idea flickered on the edge of Jacques's mind, and he muttered, "But I no longer trust them. They are dangling me still about the woman, although they swear they want her." It seemed a safe enough thing to say. He was certain the three braves would take her gladly if he sought them out.

War Cloud grunted. What became of Hope Caldwell no longer mattered to him now that he would never be sachem. All that mattered was Firewalker's downfall.

"You will go to them nonetheless." No other tribe in this part of the land would betray Firewalker.

"I saw white captives when I was there last," Jacques lied.

War Cloud gave a ghost of a smile. "You have little cause for worry. You are neither woman nor child, nor are you a warrior."

"That is so, but—"

War Cloud held up a hand. "Do you think I cannot see that you make these protests to enhance your own miserable worth?"

Jacques allowed the insult to slip by. He said softly, "You understand I must ask a price for what I consider to be a dangerous request."

"Name it."

"Furs. I would have the assurance of Lenape furs when you are chief. And you will deal only with me."

War Cloud smiled. When he was chief . . . There it was, all spread out finally for him to see. The thing Jacques d'Arcy had craved all along. Furs. Firewalker had warned him, and he himself had known in his heart it was the only reason the devil gave him such fine whiskey. He wanted Lenape furs when Thunderhead was in the ground. He nodded.

"It will be so."

"You are wise. You will not regret it."

War Cloud showed his teeth. "I know I will not."

"Regarding the woman"—Jacques had lost his fear of the brave, and now his mind raced as he poked the fire and added another log—"should the Mengwes dally too much longer, I may take her myself after all. But I need more time. . . ."

War Cloud looked at him with disgust. He sickened himself, but this Frenchman sickened him more. "She would be better off with the Mengwes."

Jacques chuckled and smoothed his crisp brown beard. "I think not, *n'tschu,* for I have many skills under the blanket. I am very good." His teeth flashed white in his dark face. "And have no fear regarding her teaching. I have promised it will cease, and it will."

War Cloud made no answer. He did not care where or how Hope Caldwell spent her days, and he was surprised to discover he almost wished her well. He wondered if she knew what a bastard d'Arcy was, and decided he would tell her one day. He climbed heavily to his feet. "You will go tomorrow?"

"*Oui,* at dawn."

War Cloud removed his blanket, and removed two arrows from the quiver on his back. He caressed one beautiful leaf-shaped arrowhead. When the enraged whites brought them to the village seeking the killer of their livestock, everyone would recognize them as Firewalker's. No one else made such cleverly wrought blades. He could not meet the Frenchman's eyes as he placed the arrows in his hands. He was as low and treacherous as the Mengwes. Not until he was mounted and about to leave could he bring himself to speak.

"There will be no murder, Frenchman. Tell the Mengwe I will not have men killed—and no horses. Only cattle and sheep."

"I will make it clear, my friend. Have no worry."

Jacques gazed after him thoughtfully as he rode away. Had the devil seen in his eyes that he was thinking that very thing? For when, after all, would he have another such chance to make an end of Firewalker?

Hope could not sleep for thinking of Firewalker. Body, mind, and soul, she was filled with tantalizing memories and the thought that she could have been sleeping in his arms that very night. She could have been his wife, as quickly and easily as snapping her fingers, and they might have been making love this instant. She was thrilled by the thought, but remembering those telltale erotic sounds made by War Cloud and Sings Low, she knew she could never make love with Firewalker with Walks Alone in the next apartment. She could not possibly. It would be too mortifying. And, too, she still felt it was wrong, living as man and wife without being wed in the church. She shook her head then. Nay, how could it be wrong when an entire people thought it was right?

Hope tossed, and stared up at the faint sky glow beyond the smoke hole. She knew she was going to give in and join with him. There was no longer any reason not to. She was burning to be with him. Aye, she was dying to be with him, and she was completely secure in his love now. But she stood firm on one thing: she would not go to him in that apartment beside his mother! Her breath caught, thinking that perhaps they could live here. . . .

She gazed over at Flower with sudden concern. She was so happy about the two of them living together, she might not want to move back in with her mother. Or why couldn't she continue to live here and Firewalker could build them a wigwam of their own? Anything would do, anything so long as she did not have to live in that longhouse! For she sensed the *meteinuwak* hated her still. Walks Alone was polite and showed her every courtesy, but that terrible icy hatred was there in her eyes. Hope sighed. Doubtless it was because she was white, and whites would always be the enemy. . . .

"Hope, are you awake?" It was a whisper from Flower.

"Aye. Are you—all right?" It was the middle of the night.

Flower came over and sat on the edge of her bed shelf. "Everything is all right. Finally. This morning Glad Tidings asked me for help with his letters."

"Flower!" Hope caught her hand.

Flower beamed. "It is so."

Hope sat up. "That's wonderful news. Tell me about it."

She had been deeply concerned about Flower's impasse with the man she loved. When he came to class, she had thought the problem would solve itself, but it had not. Glad Tidings would not accept Flower's need for learning and neither of them would yield. Now perhaps this was the first step.

"He came to see you," Flower bubbled, "but you were not here. I said I would help him, and he looked down his nose at me. I said I would kick him if he walked off like he did before, so he stayed."

Hope laughed, imagining the two of them glowering at each other over the firepit. Flower, pink faced, black eyes flashing, a defiant finger pointing at the big brave, and Glad Tidings, scowling, taken aback, not quite sure what to do with the hissing kitten confronting him.

"And so all morning we worked together, and tomorrow he will have a good lesson. He is quick. . . ." She wanted to tell Hope the rest of her news, but she feared it would hurt her since things were not good for her and Firewalker. But then Hope must learn of it tomorrow anyway. . . .

"His yielding is no small thing," Hope said.

Flower nodded, her long unbound hair gleaming where the moon rays touched it. "He has pleased me greatly."

"Maybe it's time some other changes were made."

Flower took a breath and plunged. "They are made. We are joining tomorrow." She watched, eyes wide, heart thudding for Hope's face to crumple. She would be so lonely. . . .

"Tomorrow! Flower, why that's wonderful!"

Seeing Hope's very real joy, Flower threw her arms around her. "I am so glad you are not sad. I love him so much and I am so happy! He—is proud of me, and he vows I will be his woman forever. It is what I prayed for—a vow. Like your people . . ."

"Flower, Flower . . ." They were hugging, rocking back and forth, and Hope's eyes were unashamedly damp. "I'm happy for you, and pleased and proud of you both."

Flower was suddenly subdued. "I have one sadness still. You are not my sister."

"I've been your sister since the first day we met."

Flower tossed her head and her long hair flew. "*Matta*. That is not what I mean. I mean you and Firewalker. Hope, it is so stupid, this anger between you. I know my brother, I see his face and eyes. He loves you."

"Indeed."

"But he will not tell you, for he is proud and he is a warrior. And he holds his head so high he does not see what I see in your eyes—I know you love him. But you must not worry." She herself, on the other hand, was so worried about it she could scarcely think straight. "I have prayed to the Great Creator that you will join, and I asked for a sign, and—"

"Did you see one?"

"*Kehella, n'tschu*. A beautiful rainbow." She stared, seeing that Hope's eyes danced. "Why are you looking at me like that?"

"Your prayer has been answered, *n'tschu*."

Flower's hands flew to her mouth. She giggled behind them. "You are teasing me."

"*Matta*. I would not tease you about such a thing. Firewalker and I are going to join. He asked me nearly a month ago."

"A month? Why are you not together then? Hope, I do not understand."

Hope laughed. "And I'm not sure I can explain. All that matters is that we'll be together soon now. Very soon."

The next morning, Hope was gathering firewood when, without warning, Firewalker slipped out of the woods and joined her.

"Good morning, Caldwell the healer."

She jumped, and then laughed. "Good morning. I didn't hear you." Her gaze moved over the tall bronzed form that was now so very familiar to her. "You move so quietly."

"You move in a way that pleases me greatly. . . ."

Seeing the heat in his eyes, Hope put down her bundle. She had only to look at him to want him and to feel her breathing quicken. She had decided to tell him she would join with him as they were making love—or perhaps afterwards. She whispered, "I'll not be missed if I'm gone for a while. . . ."

Firewalker shook his head. "You know I want you, but we are about to go on a hunt."

"Oh . . ." Disappointment swept her. In her mind, they were already lying in some grassy bower, whereas they could not even touch one another now if he were ready to hunt. He would have just come from the sweat house and rubbed his body with sweet ferns to remove its human scent.

"I came to say good-bye," Firewalker said.

"I'm glad you did." She gave him a quick smile and retrieved her high spirits and her firewood. Before, he had always come and gone mysteriously. She had never known where he was nor when he left. Now he had sought her out in the woods to say good-bye. She touched her fingers to her lips and gently blew him a kiss. "I'll miss you. . . ."

"And I will miss you." He added low, "I will show you how much when I return."

A hundred thoughts were in his mind and she was in all of them. The way the silken smoothness of her body pressed against his, fitting it so perfectly; her full rose-tipped breasts, so sweet under his lips; those long creamy legs, and the deep valley and honeyed sheath between them—and there was her hunger for him. Her almost childish eagerness for him to make love to her. It told him that she would soon abandon the thought of a preacher's wedding them.

"Will you come back tonight, do you think?" Hope asked.

"*Matta*. Not tonight."

Hope nodded. She had learned that if a deer or bear were wounded, it had to be followed for days sometimes. She feared for him suddenly. "Please, be careful."

He smiled. "I am always careful."

As he turned to leave, Hope knew she had to tell him. She could not keep such a thing from him another moment. "Firewalker—!"

"Aye?" He saw well that she did not want him to leave.

Hope drew closer, hands clasped behind her back so she would not be tempted to touch him. "It occurs to me that we never finished our last conversation. We were discussing wedding each other. Or joining . . ."

Firewalker crossed his arms and regarded her rosy face and the stars in her gray eyes from a safe distance. "I recall there was an interruption." A pair of soft white arms about his neck . . . soft breasts pressed against him . . . a soft mouth lifted for his kisses.

Hope murmured, shy suddenly. "Do you—still want to? Join, I mean?"

The golden eyes flickered. "Do I still want to breathe?"

She smiled. No white man in the world would have thought of saying such a lovely poignant thing as that. Only a heathen savage. Oh, Lord, but she loved him, and now he was hers. He was hers and she was his and nothing had ever felt so right. She wanted to hold him, feel the hard warm strength of him, cover his face and mouth and those wonderful hands with kisses, but she could not touch him. She clasped her own hands more tightly behind her, and declared, smiling: "Then we are joined. We even have a dwelling to ourselves. Flower is going to Glad Tidings."

Firewalker gave a low chuckle. "My cup is running over."

In the space of a heartbeat, he had been given two of the things he desired most in this world. A good life for his sister, and the possession of this woman. One thing remained: he wanted peace for his brother. But there were bad times ahead for War Cloud. When Thunderhead died, his private shame would be made known. But he would help him in every way he could, and he would free him from d'Arcy. He vowed it. But now was no time to be brooding over War Cloud and d'Arcy. Not when his woman stood gazing at him with glowing eyes. His own slid over her hungrily.

"I regret I cannot carry you into these woods now, my wife."

Hope's mouth curved. My wife. How strange and wonderful it sounded. "There will be other days, my husband—and other nights." She could not contain her delighted laughter nor her wonder. She tried the word again, felt it on her lips—"Husband . . . my husband . . . Firewalker, I can't believe it. Are you really my husband now, just with the saying of it?"

His tawny eyes danced over her. "Aye, lady. You will believe it when this hunt is ended and I return, I promise you." He glanced up at the sun. "It is growing late. I must leave now." Having thought of the Frenchman, a worry now nagged him. "I saw d'Arcy talking to you yesterday."

Hope straightened her shoulders as a warning bell sounded. "He visited me, aye. Just a short visit to see how I was."

Firewalker nodded, his eyes distant. "Let it be the last time. I do not want you to see him again."

She could not believe he said it. "Perhaps I didn't hear you correctly."

Firewalker met her eyes. "Then I will repeat it. You will not see d'Arcy again."

"Firewalker, I'm your wife! I have no interest whatsoever in the man. In fact, I don't care if I never see him again, but it should be my choice. You can't just—forbid me to see him!"

"I can and I do. It is because you are my wife that I forbid it. You are mine to protect now, and you never have seen that he is a danger. You do not know the devil as I do."

Hope shook her head in angry wonder. "I can't believe this. I'm a woman, not a child. You can't forbid me anything!" She was fearful suddenly, of what she had done in agreeing to join with him. How much control did he really have over her? "It's as if you don't trust me . . ."

"It is d'Arcy I do not trust, and there it stands," Firewalker said tautly. "I must leave now. I will return as soon as I am able."

"Take your time," Hope cried. "And you might as well know because I won't lie to you—I'll continue seeing anyone I choose. You have no right to rule me just because you call yourself my husband!"

Firewalker nearly choked on his resentment. He had every right. He was a Lenape warrior and she was but a woman. His woman. But there would be time enough in the future to smooth out such things between them.

He forced himself to say more calmly than he felt, "Let us not part in anger on the first day of our joining. I will ask only that you be wary of the devil."

Mollified, Hope nodded. "That I can agree to. I will be wary."

"Promise me?"

"I promise."

Chapter 23

Stands Tall had told no one that he had a son. It was a thing he wished to savor in secret, recalling it again and again and filling his head with such plans and dreams he could scarcely sleep at night. His great regret was that he had not known of Firewalker sooner, and he resented with fresh fury that Walks Alone had not defied her father those many years past and joined with him. After leading him to believe she cared, she should have come to him. She should have given him many sons. But that part of his life was ended. Long ago he had ceased thinking of Walks Alone. Now all that mattered was Firewalker. It was long past time the brave knew he was the son of a Mengwe chieftain.

And so it was that when Firewalker departed on his next hunt, Stands Tall followed stealthily after him. Waiting patiently from afar for an auspicious moment in which to approach him, he mused on the long-time hatred between their two peoples. They had been blood enemies from the very beginning, and the Lenapes' were so powerful, the Mengwes were on the verge of extinction. But then the Mengwes had devised a clever plan to use the Lenapes' own great strength against them.

They had followed the principle that conflict was never ended by men. The one who held the tomahawk in one hand could never hold the peace belt in the other, so that only through the intervention of women were wars ended. Stands Tall smiled, thinking of how those fierce long-ago Lenapes had been convinced by wily Mengwes that the constant warfare between their two tribes and their allies would decimate the entire Indian nation. The Lenapes had been convinced further that only they themselves could prevent such a disaster, so that in one luckless hour at Albany, they had signed the treaty to lay down their arms.

From that day forward, the Lenni Lenapes, the terror of the woodlands, became mediators and peacekeepers. They were honor bound to treat fairly and to protect the very ones they once had hunted down like beasts of prey. They became women and peacekeepers, while the Mengwes and their Five Nation confederacy had grown all-powerful. Many winters had passed since that day, and the Lenapes had declared themselves free of their petticoats. But the Mengwes knew better: the devils were still women. And their two peoples still hated each other, but not as much as they hated their common enemy, the white man.

Stands Tall deemed it a shame that they could not let bygones be bygones and unite to drive the devils out of this land they shared. It was one of his keenest pleasures to harass the settlers in these parts and keep them fearful. The thought of Firewalker, his son and comrade, riding by his side through the night on such a mission filled him with warmth. It was a warmth he had not felt since he first laid eyes on the brave's mother. . . .

Firewalker's spirits were high as the sun began its descent toward the horizon, and his hunting party divided and began their search for game. The scouts had said there were deer nearby, and he had arrows aplenty, spare moccasins, and a good supply of corn and pemmican. And he had a wife waiting for him at home. By the Eternal, he had a wife. . . . He knew now that she had been right to defy him and be angry with him. He could not treat her as a child. Not such a woman as Hope.

Hope . . .

His heart sang at the very thought of her, but only for an instant. A man on a hunt could not allow himself the pleasure of being filled with song. Animals so loved music that they heard and were warned away by those sweet sounds, even when they were only in one's mind. And so he could not think of his wife. He would think only of making his kill as swiftly as possible so that he could return to her on the morrow.

Firewalker's moccasins made no sound, and his dark form blended into the gold brown shadows about him as he stole to a spot to windward and within sight of the river's edge. As the night insects chirped and hummed and mist rose from the water, he silently strung his bow, removed his quiver from his back, and placed them both close to hand. He leaned against the mottled trunk of a great sycamore to await the coming of a buck to drink.

As he waited, he thought of Hope again, and again his soul sang. He forced away the image of her beautiful face and instead allowed a parade of letters to march through his head. *A . . . B . . . C . . . D . . .* It had been one week since his first lesson and he knew them all. His fingers itched to take up a stick and write them in the earth, but he crossed his arms and ordered his hands to keep still. He must make no sound nor movement, and he must be ready.

He had not long to wait. The sky was darkening and the mist had thickened as a buck came out of the woods and moved through the tall grass to the river. It was large and strong and glossy, and Firewalker offered thanks for it. Such a fine animal would feed many of his people for many days. Without a sound he took up his bow, notched an arrow, sighted, and waited while the buck drank. Never would he shoot an animal until it was looking into his eyes and had a fair chance to flee.

The buck drank long, and then raised its head, listening suddenly. Seeing its great rack of antlers silhouetted against the deepening sky, Firewalker's throat tightened. In his many years of hunting, he had always hated the slaying of such a magnificent beast. But in his village, there were many mouths to feed and winter was coming on.

He called softly, "*Achto*, my brother . . ."

The buck turned its head, spied him, and an instant later was making a great leap away from him. But Firewalker's arrow was swifter, speeding into the deer's heart and dropping him on the spot. Firewalker had always thanked those creatures whose lives he took so that his people might live. He did so now as he removed his arrow from the buck's brave heart and closed its eyes.

He put his sadness behind him, for he had much to do yet that night. But first he would build a fire for warmth and to see by. He was coaxing a small blaze to brightness when he sensed that he was not alone. Rising quickly to his feet, knife drawn, he was surprised to see a Mengwe brave at the edge of the clearing. The man stood gazing at him, silent and weaponless, his right hand raised in peace.

Firewalker said low in his own tongue, akin to the Mengwe's, "These are Lenape hunting grounds, Mengwe. You are not welcome here."

"I have not come to hunt," Stands Tall answered quietly. He moved a bit closer. "I have come for talk with you." He was filled with admiration for this tall brave, having watched his honorable slaying of the deer. He wished more than ever that he had known Firewalker as his son these many years.

Seeing a strange glow in the eyes of the Mengwe, Firewalker felt a tug of uneasiness. That the brave was his blood enemy did not worry him. He did not fear him. It was that the man seemed so familiar. He tensed as he wondered how this could be. He knew no Mengwes. For longer than he could remember, longer than long, his people had been forbidden to deal with them or even speak with them. Their ancient treachery still stung; that trickery which had led to the Lenapes' loss of their manhood. What was worse, the devils had never admitted to using trickery, but had insisted they conquered the Lenapes fairly in battle. It was a lie so heinous it could never be forgiven.

Seeing the Mengwe's smile, Firewalker scowled at him. "I have neither the wish nor the time for talk with you." It was an act of open hostility for him even to be there on Lenape land. Did he not know that?

"You will be glad I came. . . ."

Firewalker grunted. "That I doubt. I have much work to do this night, and you are keeping me from it." His heart thudded harder. Who was this devil? He knew him for a certainty, but how, and from where? "Why would you wish talk with me?" he muttered, knowing it would go hard on him were he even seen with a Mengwe.

Stands Tall said softly, "Is it so strange that a father would wish to talk with his son?"

Son? Firewalker stared long at the brave in the misty dusk, and then threw back his head and gave a silent laugh. "*Matta!*" He spat the word, and then spat on the ground.

"It is so, Firewalker," said Stands Tall. "I am your father."

Firewalker's gaze remained inscrutable, but as the brave came closer, his heart crashed against his ribs. He saw now why the Mengwe looked so familiar—but it could not be. This thing could not be. But then the brave's face was touched by the flickering light of the small fire, and Firewalker saw more clearly the coppery eyes and straight dominant nose. He sucked in a breath as he looked into his own face—and saw his own doom.

It was some moments before he rasped, "Who are you?"

"I am Stands Tall. I have brought my people recently to the lands west of here."

"You are the sachem?"

"Kehella."

Firewalker was frozen. He had a thousand questions, but to ask them would show his interest and his fear. It had come on him so suddenly and powerfully, he wanted only to empty his stomach and run. Run from this devil, and from his people and never return. His people? He realized then that he no longer knew who his people were.

"You belong with me, my son," Stands Tall said gently. He had seen the other's wild eyes and quickened breathing. He was a buck about to flee. "You are Mengwe, Firewalker."

At the thought, Firewalker's icy blood heated with his outrage. He, a Mengwe? He who had hated them from the first hour he had come into this world. *Matta!* He was no Mengwe. He moved closer to the chieftain. From an arm's length, he saw the streaks of white in that long black hair. Stands Tall was an old man.

"I would know how this all came about, Stands Tall. How did my mother come to carry the seed of a Mengwe when she was joined with my father?"

Stands Tall's eyes glittered in the firelight. "I am your father."

"I ask again"—Firewalker stepped closer—"how did this remarkable thing come to be? You, the enemy—and my mother, wed to Diving Eagle, a man she loved deeply." He fingered the knife he still held.

Stands Tall said gruffly, "Put away your knife, my son. Is it not obvious how it came to be? We lay together, your beautiful mother and I." He studied the brave's face for some moments before adding, "I have never wanted another as I wanted her. We would have joined but for her father. He would not give her to me and she was a dutiful daughter."

Firewalker felt suffocated by the emotions swelling within him: rage, bitterness, confusion. And he was sick. Heart and soul he was sick, realizing that he was not and never had been who he thought he was, the son of Diving Eagle. And Walks Alone—how could she have betrayed such a man to lie with this snake and carry his seed within her? Himself. Better had he been born dead than be the child of such treachery.

But then his heart grew lighter. He knew his mother. For twenty-eight years she had loved and taught and protected him. He knew her better than he knew any other. Walks Alone was a woman of strength and one who hated the Mengwes with a passion surpassed by none. Why should he believe the words of this devil without giving her the chance to defend herself? He straightened, and looked down on the chieftain from his greater height.

"I would hear what my mother has to say about this, Mengwe. Her I trust; you, I do not." He knew as he spoke that he would cut short his hunt. He would stay the night, skin and mark any other kills he made, and return home at dawn. His talk with Walks Alone over this matter could not wait.

Stands Tall smiled and waved Firewalker's words aside. "We all know how women embellish tales. Who can believe them?"

"I can believe my mother. She is the *meteinuwak* of the Shenango Lenape. She speaks the truth."

"Her tongue was crooked when I knew her," muttered Stands Tall, remembering how she had kissed and enticed him under his blanket and then turned from him.

Firewalker's hatred blazed. "Go while you still can."

Stands Tall's own wrath had been simmering as they spoke. "I watched you slay the deer, and I see that you are a man of honor and bravery. Come to us, and walk the way of the warrior. Walk by my side. You are Mengwe. Why squander your finest years with those Lenape women?"

Women? Firewalker saw Stands Tall through a sea of red. Struggling not to use his knife on him, he heard a sound that was a growl from his own throat. Never in his lifetime had any dared utter to him that old insult about women. He wanted to slay him where he stood, even though it would mean war. But he knew he could not. He could not bring that horror down on his people, no matter how loathsome the insult. He attempted to return his knife to its sheath, but his shaking hands would not obey him. In his mind, he saw Stands Tall dying in a pool of his own treacherous blood, and saw Diving Eagle avenged. Sweat started out on his body, and he felt the warring of muscle against muscle, the warring of his thoughts. Kill the bastard. Kill him! By the Eternal, how could he not? He closed his eyes, felt the emptiness and the pain and fury.

Memedhakemo, help me. . . .

Into his mind came the beautiful smiling face of his wife. Hope. Firewalker clutched at the shining thought of her as a drowning man might clutch a log. He was mired so deeply in his shame and rage, he had forgotten he even had a wife to care for and to guard. He had lost half of himself, hearing of Diving Eagle, but with Hope, he would be whole again. He slid his knife into its sheath and squared his shoulders.

"I am Lenape," he said quietly.

"You are Mengwe!" The golden eyes of Stands Tall shone like those of a bird of prey. All of his old rage toward Walks Alone erupted. "You are my son. Your place is by my side."

"I am Lenape," Firewalker said again, low, "and if I see you again, be warned—I will kill you for the dishonor you did my father."

His father. Stands Tall blanched at the insult. So the young devil thought of Diving Eagle as his father still, even knowing the truth. It was good to know.

Perhaps it was better to have no son at all than one who preferred living with women instead of warriors. But he had wanted a son for too long to surrender such a one as Firewalker so easily. He would force him to his side if need be, and he knew exactly how to do it. The Hope-woman. For the return of such a succulent squaw as that, a man might do anything. With no further word, Stands Tall turned and walked into the mist.

War Cloud had slept poorly. When he rose from his bed before dawn, he saw that his wife, too, must have been restless for she was gone. With the child growing big inside her, she spent many nights walking about or sitting and dozing against the trunk of a tree. Outside the air smelled damp and sweet, and on the horizon was a faint pearl-pink glow. It was quiet. The birds were not yet talking nor had the women risen to kindle the banked fires and prepare the morning food. The thought of food made him queasy. He might never eat again. His belly had been small and hard as an acorn since his talk with d'Arcy two nights past.

Helldamnfire, what had he done? Walking to the river to drink, he thought how much he despised the bastard. And he despised the whiskey that had brought him to this state—never could he have done what he'd done without d'Arcy's whiskey to give him the courage—but most of all, he despised himself. What manner of devil was he? What kind of brother to stay home from the hunt so that he could plot and drink with that damned Frenchman?

As the village awakened and the women kindled the cook fires, he paced the riverbank and shook inside. Was the deed done yet? But of course it was. If d'Arcy had hired a Mengwe yesterday as planned, the brave would have slain the cattle last night. But perhaps, for some reason, d'Arcy had not yet gone to them, or he had failed to hire anyone. War Cloud could not imagine such a thing, but he so wanted for it to be true that his heart grew lighter thinking about it.

Kehella, it was possible. But very soon now he would know for sure. If the whites did not come with the rising of the sun, it meant they had found no slaughtered cattle. It meant d'Arcy could return to the Mengwes this day and withdraw the order before it could be acted upon. But even as he thought it, a band of whites came splashing across the Shenango and into village. They were shouting and they were armed, and War Cloud steeled himself knowing the worst had happened. He walked toward the long-houses where their mounts snorted and pawed at the earth.

"You, Injun!" It was an angry shout.

War Cloud stood taller. "I am War Cloud," he said with dignity. He saw that the women had retreated and were huddled together looking on. The men, emerging from the longhouses, had armed themselves and were approaching the settlers warily.

"I'm Jeb Green." The settler slid to the ground and waved two arrows at War Cloud. "You ever seen these afore, Injun?"

War Cloud forgot sometimes how much he hated these intruders, pale as the slugs that lived under rocks. Now it was a hot wave washing over him, hatred greater even than that which he felt for himself. He looked at the arrows in the white man's hands and clamped his jaws shut. After betraying his brother to this terrible extent, he would not betray him further.

"Cat's got 'is tongue," Jeb Green growled to his now-silent comrades. He turned next to the braves who had gathered and were staring at him. He shook the arrows at them. "You seen these afore, Injuns?"

War Cloud held his breath. There was not one among them who did not recognize the arrows of Firewalker, but no one spoke. "You have come to the wrong place, white man," he muttered.

"Like hell . . ."

War Cloud was shocked to see tears fill the man's pale eyes. It was yet another difference between whites and Indians. A brave would never stoop to weep over a stolen wife, let alone a dead cow. Such weakness disgusted him.

"We want Firewalker," Jeb Green snarled, "fer we figure these is his arrers." At that a chant began for Firewalker.

"He is not here," War Cloud raised his voice to be heard.

"Where is th' bastard? We want 'im."

"He is hunting."

"By God, he were huntin' sure enough."

Suddenly flintlocks were raised and shot discharged into the air. The women screamed and babies shrieked. Lenape arrows were notched into Lenape bows targeting the intruders.

"Blasted savages," Jeb Green muttered. "We uns'll never git th' truth from 'em—except it's said th' old chief's an honest un." He growled to War Cloud: "Where's yer chief, Injun? We want Thunderhead."

"I am here," said Thunderhead. "Please, put down your weapons." The Lenapes obeyed, parting for him as he made his slow dignified way through them with Walks Alone by his side. "What is the problem?"

Jeb Green thrust out the arrows. "D' these b'long ter anybody here?"

War Cloud prayed to his manitou that his uncle might speak for once with a forked tongue. He held his breath as Thunderhead took the arrows and examined them. Walks Alone gazed on them with shuttered eyes.

Thunderhead said quietly, "Why do you ask this?"

"B'cause I pulled 'em out o' th' backs o' m' two dead sons this morning', that's why, you damn' heathen bastards!" Jeb Green shook his fist at the massed braves. "An' don't yer try an' tell me this ain't th' work o' Firewalker! He's been seen afore up ter no good. Cattle was killed las' night, too, but my boys—my God, man, what kinda devil is he . . . ?" He shook his head, unable to speak further.

Another settler, a husky six-footer with his flintlock cocked, took over for him and said brusquely, "We uns have a right ter know, chief. Is them arrers Firewalker's?"

"Firewalker has killed no one."

"Is these his arrers?"

Thunderhead pulled air into his lungs and expelled it. "They are his. . . ."

"Then I think it's only right we have a look ter see if he's here."

"He is hunting."

"So it's said, but I think we oughter look. . . ."

War Cloud was like a pillar of stone. He could neither move nor speak, but a veil was lifting from his eyes and it left him numbed. D'Arcy had done this thing. D'Arcy. He was a viper, and he himself was a fool beyond belief. Everything was out of his control now, and far beyond anything he had ever planned. Because of his own accursed pride, he had wanted Firewalker to fall from the mountain where he had always reigned—but he did not want him to die. By the Eternal, he did not want his brother to die. And now d'Arcy, damn his black soul, had offered him up to these whites as a blood sacrifice.

The talk of the whites was of seizing Firewalker when he returned and taking him to Fort McIntosh, to the south, but War Cloud saw well that they meant to hang him without a trial. As their angry voices grew louder, and they began a search of the first longhouse, he slipped unnoticed into his own longhouse, fetched bridle and blanket, and then walked to the small fenced field where the horses were kept. Moments later, he was galloping toward the Lenapes' southern hunting grounds and plotting his course. He would warn Firewalker away. They had kin in many distant places and he could stay with any of them until this danger was over. And when he was safely on his way, War Cloud himself would go to the trading post of d'Arcy the trader, and he would scalp him.

Kehella.

Chapter 24

Hope had been uneasy ever since Firewalker left to hunt. She regretted deeply that she had made such a fuss about Jacques for she did not care if she never saw the man again. It was Firewalker's domination of her that made her hackles rise. But why on earth had she not just allowed the thing to pass? Just that once on that day of days when they had agreed to join? She knew how much he hated Jacques and how jealous he was, but, nay, she had to fuss. Damn. She had not used her head. . . .

Unable to sleep, she had risen early and gone out to sit in front of her wigwam to watch the sun rise. She was about to pound corn for her breakfast corn-cakes when she had noticed that War Cloud was up and about. She had watched thoughtfully as he walked down to the river, knelt, drank, and then began to pace. It was unusual. In the three weeks she had lived there, he had never once shown himself before mid-morning yet now he walked the riverbank at dawn. As she pondered it, he had angrily skipped a stone across the water and walked toward the village. At the same moment, a band of white men had galloped across the Shenango and into the center of the village, shattering its calm.

Hope had watched, stunned, as they bellowed and waved their muskets, and when War Cloud approached them, she had feared for his safety. Her fear had turned to terror when they began shouting for Firewalker and demanding that he be turned over to them. In God's name, what was happening? Moving to where the other women were huddled, she had found the wife of War Cloud.

"Why do they want Firewalker?" she'd gasped.

"I not know," Sings Low had said and caught her hand. "My sister, I sorrow. . . ."

She'd been shocked to see the small wooden frame strapped on the girl's back and the tiny babe swaddled in it. "Sings Low, you've—had your baby!" She was dumbfounded. She had thought she would be called upon to help. "When did it come?"

Sings Low had smiled and shrugged. "In the night."

Hope had wanted to look at the little thing and talk with the mother, but there was simply no time, and she was frantic with fear. "I'm so happy for you. We must talk later. . . ." Seeing that Flower had emerged from the longhouse, she had rushed to her. "What's happening? Why do they want Firewalker?"

Flower's black eyes had been snapping. "I will find out."

But as she had walked toward where her husband stood among the braves, shots rang out. She had shrieked and flown back to Hope as the Lenapes had raised their bows and leveled their arrows at the intruders. It was then that Thunderhead had arrived, and the terrible news was revealed. The whites had with them the bloody arrows of Firewalker, and it was said he had slain two of their people in the night. Two half-grown boys . . .

Hope was filled with a strange calm as she watched the men milling about angrily and the women weeping. Not for one instant did she believe that Firewalker had gone out under the cloak of darkness to slay anyone, let alone children. She simply did not believe it. She saw suddenly and clearly that someone, for some reason, wanted him in deep trouble. Someone had betrayed him. She could not imagine who, nor how they had done it, nor had she forgotten the oddness of War Cloud's early rising and his pacing the riverbank. She saw then that she could not remain there doing nothing. She had to get help.

She whispered in Flower's ear: "I'm leaving."

Flower clutched her hand. "Hope, he did not do it! Do not put him aside!" She stared, seeing her friend's smoking gray eyes and square-set jaw.

"I know he didn't. It's why I must go. I must tell my father and bring him here. He knows these men, and he'll make them see reason." Hope squeezed her hand. "Everything is going to be all right, I promise you. There's nothing to fear. . . ."

It was a promise she made to herself as she hastened toward her wigwam and fetched Beauty's bridle and blanket. And when she saw that a search of the longhouses was about to begin, she told herself again that there was nothing to fear. Let them search. By the time Firewalker returned from his hunt, the killer would have been found. Surely he would have been found. Surely. She dared not think about any other possibility, but the truth was, she was terrified. And as she bridled her mare and mounted, her heart was breaking, thinking of the slain children and their families.

To escape notice as she left, Hope held Beauty to a walk and took her north a bit before fording the Shenango. She then galloped full out toward the highlands and her father. But when she reached Twin Oaks, he was not there and his horse was gone.

"Father!" She cupped her hands to her mouth and shouted. She rang the bell, and shouted for him again—screamed for him. Nothing. She was so disappointed and furious, she burst into tears. Firewalker was going to be seized and he was going to be hanged! Oh, aye, she saw well what was going to happen, and all because her father was not here. He was probably pulling stumps out of someone's stupid field! Oh, God, God . . .

She put her hands to her wet face, tried to slow her breathing, and tried to think. In another moment she would be hysterical—a weeping hysterical female. She could not let it happen. She gulped in huge breaths, patted her cheeks, smacked them hard, finally and bit her lips and her tongue. She could not afford hysterics. She had to find her father. Mounting again, she galloped from field to field, shouting his name, and telling herself that Firewalker was hunting to the south and would not return this day. She willed him not to return . . . prayed for him not to return.

Realizing suddenly that she was near the Springer land, Hope's spirits rose. Maybeth and Luke would help! Maybe they even knew where her father was, except—oh, Lord, they probably were both in the fields and she would have to look for them. She urged Beauty toward the cabin at a full gallop, and was weak with relief to find Maybeth on the stoop knitting.

"Oh, Maybeth, thank God you're here!"

"Good mornin', love." Maybeth rose from her rocker. She was as heavy in her heart as she was in her belly, for she knew why Hope was there. She saw that she'd been weeping, and she watched with grave eyes as Hope slid to the ground and tied up at the rail. And what a picture she was—fringed doeskins, that bright beaded band on her long black hair, even Beauty's mane was adorned with feathers. "God love thee, Hope Caldwell, ye look like some Indian princess."

Hope's lips were too frozen to smile. "Thank you." She looked around. "Have you seen my father?" Did Maybeth know, she wondered, how lucky she was, having a respected husband who was safe in the fields and a sweet little babe on the way? She shivered.

"He's not been by," Maybeth answered, and

watched her friend sink to the step, head in her hands. She said gently, "Hope, I know."

Hope looked up, her gray eyes stricken. "You know they're looking for Firewalker?"

"Aye." Maybeth sat down beside her. "They was here. But, lovey, it's goin' t' be all right. I'm sure of it."

Hope shook her head. "I'm so afraid. . . ." Firewalker was going to die, she knew it. Her man, her darling husband was going to die. He was going to be caught and hanged and their life together would be over before it had ever begun.

"There, there, now, mebbe not. Luke went along wi' th' bunch o' them an' he has a cool head. He respec's yer paw, an' yer paw respec's Firewalker an' that's all my man needs t' know. Yer Firewalker's a good un like 'is Uncle Thunderhead. Luke won't let no harm come ter your man."

"I'm glad you believe in him," Hope murmured. "It—means a lot." But she could not stop the fine trembling that held her in its grip, for what could one lone man do against an angry mob? "He's so good, Maybeth. No one knows how good. He never killed those children, and he didn't do any of the things it's said he did. He's kind and gentle and sweet and caring a-and so handsome and—" She jumped up, looking about and hardly knowing what to do next. "I'm talking too much—this isn't helping me find Father. I have to find him." Realizing then that Maybeth had called Firewalker "your man," she patted her hand. "I was going to tell you when I checked on you this week. We're wed."

Maybeth nodded. "An' about time. I knowed you was a woman in love."

Hope had to smile. "I wish you had told me—I just found out myself not so long ago."

"I knowed. That day when ye said th' twins was in love wi' Firewalker, I seen quick enough who was in love. . . ."

"I guess I knew, too, but I was fighting it. For all

kinds of reasons." She died, thinking of all the precious time wasted.

"I seen that brave jist once," Maybeth said, "an' I'll never forgit th' sight. He was settin' tall on that big black mare o' his wi' jist a scrap o' loincloth on an' them gold eyes o' his all glittery. . . ." Her lips curved. "Lovey, my heart went that hard—why, if I hadn't o' been took areddy, I just might o' snapped 'im up myself. An' now you say he's sweet an' kind an' gentle an' caring to boot. Lordy, it sounds like he's a prince. A king."

"He is—and you're royalty yourself, my friend." Hope still felt frightened, but not as badly. There was hope for Firewalker yet if folk like Maybeth and Luke were on his side. And her father. She untied Beauty and mounted. "If you see my father before I do, please tell him to go to the village right away. I'm headed for Twin Oaks now to see if he's returned."

"Go wi' God, Hope, you and yer fine man."

Hope bit her lip to hold back the tears. "What would I do without you?" She gave Beauty a nudge, and then reined. "I almost forgot— how are you feeling? Is everything all right?"

"I'm dandy." Maybeth nodded her flaxen head and rested her hands on her now-large belly. "Luke's put 'is foot down. He'll not let me in the fields now."

"Good for him. I'll be back in a day or two to examine you." Hope blew her a kiss and was off.

The rising sun found Firewalker riding swiftly to the north. He had taken three deer altogether, he had gutted them, left his mark upon them, and would return later that day for them. Now his thoughts were of Walks Alone and Stands Tall. He would not have any peace until he heard from his mother's own lips the truth of the matter. He was a league south, his thoughts churning with bitterness when War Cloud came toward him at a gallop. Seeing his brother's white face, he feared the worst. Something had happened to Hope. Or to his mother or Flower.

Dreading the answer, he asked quietly, "What has happened?"

"My brother, you must not come home. White men are there awaiting you. They have two of your arrows and—" War Cloud felt such shame he bowed his head. He could not continue.

"My arrows?" Firewalker laughed in his relief. He could not imagine why any whites might have his arrows; he could think only that Hope still breathed, as did his mother and sister. Nothing else mattered.

"My brother"— War Cloud girded himself for his terrible task—"two young whites were slain in the night, and it is thought you did it." His breathing quickened imagining the blood gushing from the Frenchman's head. For a certainty, he would scalp him for his treachery. He had not scalped for a long time, but d'Arcy he would scalp this day.

Firewalker frowned as he fought to consider this new thing. For hours, his mind had been consumed by his mother and the Mengwe, Stands Tall, and just now he had thought some terrible fate had befallen Hope. He still trembled thinking of it. Now this—two slain with arrows said to be his. "I do not understand. . . ."

"It is foolishness," War Cloud muttered. "Everyone knows you have never bent your bow against children. But the intruders do not know this, and therefore you cannot return home. Not now. They will seize you."

He recalled with bitterness the day he had stolen the arrows and wrapped them and buried them in the earth. He had hoped that some day, in some way, they could be used to cause Firewalker to fall from the high esteem in which he was held. And so they had, he thought, shame burning through him. It would have been far better had they been lodged in his own heart.

"Turn back, my brother. Ride swiftly to our people in Kuskusky or Indian Town, or flee to our kin in Ohio. We will come for you when it is safe."

"*Matta*. I will not leave without my wife, nor can I leave without seeing our mother."

His wife? War Cloud smiled. "So you have claimed the Hope-woman?" He had never thought the news would give him such pleasure. He would deliver it to d'Arcy before he killed him.

"We have claimed each other," Firewalker answered.

War Cloud's black eyes searched over his brother's face. There was not another like him, nor would there ever be, and more than anyone else he knew, he loved him. Strange to say, he knew also now that he would die for him. The idea was such a strange one, considering his betrayal of him that it made War Cloud smile.

"So be it," he said. "I will bring her to you, and I will bring our mother." But when he returned not long after, he had only Walks Alone with him. He said low to Firewalker, "I did not see your wife about, and the whites have departed. I fear they watch us from afar, and may even be on their way here now. You should not remain much longer."

"I will not leave without Hope." Firewalker caught his brother's arm. "Could the whites have taken her?"

"I do not know." Seeing the approach of their mother, War Cloud added under his breath, "I will look for her further and return as soon as possible. But I pray you will be long gone."

As Walks Alone dismounted and moved toward Firewalker, she composed herself. Her face did not show the terror that was making her heart flutter like leaves in the wind, for she knew now that it was Firewalker who would die. Her beloved, her beautiful Firewalker. He would be taken by the intruders and hanged by the neck until he was dead. It did not matter whether it was now or later, for it was his destiny. In her eyes, he was dead already as he stood there gazing down on her.

"Greetings, my son."

Firewalker inclined his head. "My mother . . ."

His heart hardened as he thought of her lying in the arms of that Mengwe devil, giving him pleasure and betraying the one he had called father. He wanted to turn from her and never look on her again, but he knew he was thinking exactly what Stands Tall wished him to think. Now he would hear the tale from her own lips.

He said brusquely, "As I hunted last night, a Mengwe came to me. He called himself Stands Tall." Seeing her eyes widen, he continued, "He says he is my father. . . ."

Walks Alone wilted. She was unable to answer. As she looked at Firewalker, she wondered why the Creator would further burden one who was already so heavily burdened. He was perfect, this son of hers. He had done nothing but good all his days, yet he was going to die for a crime he did not commit, and now he had learned the thing she would have spared him forever. How could this be, and how could she bear the unfairness of it? How could she not rail against it?

"What else did Stands Tall say?" she asked dully.

"He said he never wanted another as he wanted you, and you would have joined with him but for your father." Seeing her eyes grow distant, he said stiffly, "Is this so, my mother?"

Walks Alone knew that her shameful secret must now see the light of day. She whispered, "It is so. I was but a young maid when we met at a great gathering, and I did not know he was Mengwe. I knew only that he was the comeliest brave I had ever seen. I kissed him under his blanket, and when I learned he was the enemy, I still could not resist him. But my father would not give me to him, and I would not disobey."

Firewalker said grimly, "But you lay with him."

Walks Alone's eyes glittered. "After my father forbade it? I did not know you thought so little of me, my son. When I saw him next, I was joined with Diving Eagle. Stands Tall demanded that I leave my husband and join him. Even had I not a child, I would have refused. I was with the man I loved more than any other."

Firewalker rasped, "Yet you did lie with him, for I am here."

Walks Alone lifted her chin and gave him a scathing gaze. "But did I lie with him willingly, my son?"

She had never forgotten her shock and terror nor the darkening sky and the smell of the river as he had come on her, silent as the wind yet strong as a bull in his rage and passion. Although it seemed her life had hung by the thinnest thread, she fought him until she could fight no more. And then he had taken her.

Firewalker listened, gazing intently, and it was as if a blindfold was torn from his eyes. By the Eternal, he should have known his mother had not given herself to that devil. Stands Tall had raped her. Firewalker's rage was great, but his shame was greater. He had wronged her as surely as Stands Tall had wronged her. He dropped to his knees, wrapped his arms about her legs, and lay his head against them.

"My mother . . ." His heart was so full he could not speak to beg her forgiveness. He felt her stroking, stroking his hair as she had when he was a boy.

Walks Alone bent and pressed her lips to her son's forehead. She would have given anything, done anything to spare him this. She raised him up and held him, just held him, knowing it could be for the last time.

"You are the son of Diving Eagle," she said quietly. "It was he who guided and shaped you and made you the man you are. Never doubt it." She gave him a small shake. "Do you hear?"

For one bright and shining moment, Firewalker remembered how it had been between him and his father when Diving Eagle still breathed. His light and his love touched him now, warming and protecting him, dazing him.

He murmured, "I hear, my mother."

Seeing that War Cloud had returned, he climbed to his feet, frowning, still dazed. "Where is Hope?" he asked.

"She was not there." War Cloud replied. "Flower says she went to her father to seek his help."

"Then I will go to her."

"I will go with you."

"*Matta!*" Walks Alone said sharply. "You will leave now, Firewalker, while you are still able." To have that woman by his side could only hasten his doom. She had seen many times that Hope Caldwell would be with the one who died.

"I will not leave without her, my mother," Firewalker said gently. "Hope is my wife now."

Walks Alone stared at the light in his eyes, and felt herself shrivel. It was the thing she had feared from the first moment she had seen the woman, and now it had happened. They were joined. Yet it puzzled her that War Cloud had expressed no interest in her nor had she seen the two brothers fighting over her—nor fighting openly over anything. She did not understand any of it. The Twelve had prophesied that Firewalker would be the next sachem, yet he was going to die. And even if he did not, he could not be chieftain and be wed to a white. Not in these times of such great hostility. It was strange and beyond her ability to comprehend; she felt old and tired. More than ever, she yearned to feel the arms of Diving Eagle around her. But the time for that had not yet come. Gazing up at Firewalker, she made her mouth smile.

"Very well, my son. If Hope is your wife, then you must go to her."

Jacques d'Arcy spurred his mount mercilessly as he raced toward Twin Oaks. The die was cast, and it was in his favor. His small trading post had just been overrun by an angry mob looking for Firewalker. It was said two boys had been slain by him last night.

In truth, he was shocked, for he had ordered that men and livestock be slain, not children—yet this had accomplished his purpose so much more beautifully how could he complain? Most assuredly, Firewalker's doom was sealed.

But now he worried about War Cloud. His mouth was parched, and he grew sweat soaked thinking of him. But why should he be fearful? He was in control. He had the devil exactly where he wanted him. The brave would give him anything in exchange for whiskey. Anything. Even his obedience. And when they met this night, and sat over the fire drinking, they could both be outraged by the terrible way in which the Mengwe devil had disobeyed their orders. It would be just one more instance of Mengwe treachery. And War Cloud would never know the truth of the matter, for he was forbidden by tribal law to go near the Mengwes or speak to them. And he would be glad of the catastrophe eventually, Jacques told himself, for it would end forever his worries that Firewalker would become chieftain. *Mon dieu,* it had been tricky, and he still had a rough stretch of water to go through, but he saw clear sailing ahead.

The men had said Hope fled the village soon after they themselves arrived. She had been followed on the chance that she was going to Firewalker, but it appeared she was headed for Twin Oaks. Jacques smiled. He felt in his bones that she would not return to Firewalker now. She would have finally come to her senses. Doubtless she was at the house weeping, and it was fitting that he be there to dry her tears. Galloping across the clearing, he could not help but smile. *Oui,* there she was, standing in the doorway just as he had expected, and as he dismounted, he saw that she had indeed been weeping.

When Hope had returned home, and her father still was not there, she was too worried to wait for him any longer. She wrote him a quick note and was about to leave when she heard hoofbeats. She flew to the door. Oh, Lord—Jacques d'Arcy. He was the last person in the world she wanted to see just now.

"Hope, I have just heard," Jacques murmured, his solemn face masking his true feelings. "I am so sorry." He knew well this was not the time to mention the treachery of savages, but he could not resist. "Savage blood will out, I fear. There is no hiding it."

Hope felt the blood rush to her face. She said stiffly, "My husband is innocent."

"Your husband?" He stared at her and felt his face turning red. He pulled in a breath, shook his head, and gave a scornful laugh. "*Sacre!* To think, I gave you the benefit of the doubt, and all the while you were wallowing in sin with that bastard." He watched as she silently closed and locked the door behind her, her whole bearing one of icy rage. His own fury was growing. "What a stupid little bitch you are. With me, you would have had an honorable name and respectability."

Hope spun, her eyes blazing. "I wonder!"

She was more certain than ever that Firewalker had been betrayed and that War Cloud was involved. And War Cloud and Jacques were friends . . . But she couldn't accuse him of anything without proof.

Jacques's eyes roved over her. "Woman, you disgust me. You disgust every decent man in the valley."

"I think you had best leave."

"Oh, I will leave, have no fear. And I leave you to the savages, for I have no doubt you will be the squaw of another of them after Firewalker hangs. No white man will have you." He was enjoying himself even though a fortune had just slipped through his fingers. "And it is clear to me now why the two of you were drawn together. Two murderers would have much in common." He smiled at the look of shock on her beautiful face. "*Mais oui, ma chère,* I know about Laura Thorpe." He untied his horse and mounted.

Hope's flesh crept as she saw the way his lips curled. He was relishing this. He was actually enjoying tormenting her. She gasped, "I was accused of a thing I never did."

Jacques smiled down at her. "I am sure you did not."

"Jacques!" Heart drumming, she watched him wheel his gelding about and spur it. She ran after him. "Jacques, please don't tell the others. . . ." but she knew now that was exactly what he would do. Perhaps he already had.

Jacques was halfway across the clearing when he felt the hair rise on his neck. Red Buck, the Mengwe he had hired, and another brave were riding hell-bent out of the woods toward him, their horses seeming to float in a silent canter. He wanted nothing more to do with the devils, and for a certainty, they were up to no good coming here. He jerked his horse's head about, and spurred him in the opposite direction. As he did, he heard Hope's frightened cry.

"Jacques, don't leave me! Oh, God, please don't leave me!"

He shouted back over his shoulder, "It seems you are going to be the squaw of a Mengwe, *ma chère.*" They were the last words he ever spoke.

Chapter 25

Hope shrieked as an arrow thudded into Jacques's back. As he fell from his horse, she ran back toward the cabin, remembering as she did that she had locked the door. Even if she managed to get inside, it would not deter them. Perhaps if she could reach Beauty . . . But a dark hand had already grasped her arm.

"Squaw come."

Seeing the brave's face and his greased scalp lock, Hope wilted. Oh, God, please—It was the same Mengwe brave who had used her own knife on her and then tried to rape her. She was terrified, but she resisted. She planted her heels and struck at him with her free hand.

"Damn you, let me go!"

"You will come," Red Buck growled.

"Nay!"

He scooped her up, threw her over his shoulder, and carried her to where Jacques's gelding stood quietly by its fallen master. He dumped her on her feet.

"Woman stay."

Seeing Jacques's crumpled form and the blood streaming from the wound in his back, Hope feared the worst. "Please, let me help him."

"*Matta*. Squaw no make noise." The Mengwe bent, roughly removed his arrow from the Frenchman's back, wiped it on the grass, and returned it to his quiver.

Hope's teeth began to chatter. She clenched her jaws. He would not see her terror and her grief at Jacques's terrible injury. Even though this was a man who had hurt her greatly, a man she had lost all respect for, she was still a healer and the sight of his cruel wound broke her heart. She knelt and attempted to find a pulse, but was yanked harshly to her feet. The Mengwe spun her about and began tying a blindfold about her eyes.

"Nay!" Infuriated, she tore it off and hurled it at him. Eyes glinting, he slapped her. She staggered back and fell to the ground, certain her jaw was broken.

As she climbed shakily to her feet, he growled: "Squaw come or I kill. No make big noise. You hear?"

Hope shivered. "I—I hear."

The fight had left her. Her mouth was filled with blood, and her jaw ached like fury, but she could move it. It was not broken. As for escape, she knew she could not flee from this man now. It would have to be later. Without protest, she allowed herself to be blindfolded and lifted onto Jacques's gelding. Her feet were roped together under the roan's barrel, and her hands were tied behind her. All the while, she was aware that another brave was nearby. She had seen the two riding across the clearing, but the other had neither spoken nor showed himself to her. Now the two men spoke low and briefly in their own tongue before they began their silent departure from Twin Oaks.

"I suspect your woman was followed when she left the village," War Cloud said, as he and Firewalker rode northward through the woods.

"*Kehella*. In their place, I would put a watch on her house and the whole highland area south of it. We will therefore not go the usual way. We must approach from the north."

"But if they are watching the house . . ."

Firewalker was not sure even in his own heart what he would do when he got to Twin Oaks. Perhaps he would use his whippoorwill call. Hope knew it; and if he whistled from the forest, she would come—but he would not endanger her. He muttered, "Let us wait and see."

Moments later, he knew he would not have that chance. The enemy had emerged from the forest, muskets raised, to block the trail ahead of them. Wheeling about, he saw they were also behind him. He was surrounded by a large band, and it was clear they meant to hang him, for they carried rope. He had not a chance of fighting back; he would be dropped reaching for his bow. He drew a deep breath. He was not afraid to die, but he did not want to leave this life yet. He had just found Hope. He felt a great sadness thinking how she would grieve for him, as would his mother and his sister.

"Don't try nothin', Injun," Jeb Green growled. "We got ye good. Jist come peaceful now."

War Cloud burned to slay them all. "My brother killed no one."

"Y'r brother killed my boys, an' iff'n ye don't hightail it out o' here pronto, we'll string ye up alongside 'im."

War Cloud shot a look of anguish at the companion of his youth. That this thing was happening because he had betrayed him was a knife in his heart. "My brother . . ."

Firewalker shook his head. He would not have his mother lose two sons over this. "Go," he ordered. "Now."

"*Matta.* I will not leave you. . . ." He felt Firewalker's eyes and his very will impelling him to continue on to Twin Oaks, but War Cloud's own eyes shuttered. He was staying. If they hanged his brother, they would not do it without white blood being spilled.

Firewalker sat tall, his hands calm on the reins. As he gazed at his enemies with implacable eyes, he knew that War Cloud must stay. His brother could not have lived with himself otherwise. And even if he had found Thomas Caldwell at the cabin with Hope and brought him here, it would be too late for the man to bring any reason to bear on this madness. And now he himself had little time to prepare his heart-soul for the Sky Journey ahead of him. He began his death song.

"Gawd, I hate that caterwallerin'," Jeb muttered, running a nervous hand through his hair. "Grab those reins, an' tie th' bastard's bloody hands ahind 'im, else he'll git away. Ain't nuthin' slipperier 'en one o' these damned heathen."

"Look f'r a good strong branch t' fasten this rope on ter," said another. He pointed. "There's a good un. U'll ye shinny up it, Jeb, or sh'd I?"

"Let Guy Johnson do it. He's fast. Shake a leg n' git up that there tree, Guy. This here devil's damned caterwallerin' gives me th' shivers. What they do that fer anyhow? Hey, you, Injun, stop yer howlin'. Save yer breath, yer gonna need it."

Amid the laughter that followed, a voice suddenly rang out: "Kill this man an' ye'll have a war on y'r hands."

"Good! Mebbe we uns c'n do some housecleanin'. We got muskets. Ye think them bows an' arrers o' theirs c'n outshoot muskets? Why'nt we jist houseclean? I'm f'r it. Who's f'r housecleanin'? This here's our land, after all. We bin give it fair an' square."

Amid the shouts of agreement, the same voice rang again: "Ye told Thunderhead we'd take 'im to Fort McIntosh f'r trial."

"Hell, man!" Jeb protested. "Ye know an' I know Fort McIntosh is too damn far t' take anyone t' f'r trial. There ain't no fort close enough."

"Ye shouldn't ha' said it then."

"Luke, f'r Godsake's, are ye f'r these bastards er f'r us?" Jeb scowled at the tall pleasant-faced young man with the neatly clipped blond hair and beard.

"I have me a wife an' a babe on th' way," Luke said. "I want peace. I don't want t' worry about iff'n I'll have m' hair on m' head when I wakes up i' th' mornin'. If we fight th' Lenapes, we don't jist fight Shenangos. They'll come fr'm all over, an' they're friends wi' th' Hurons an' Wyandots an' Senecas. Use what brains ye have, man, an' let's not be hasty about this."

"Hell an' damnation, Luke Springer, I don't take kind t' this talk."

"Man," Luke's voice turned gentle, "ye've had heartache enough f'r a lifetime, let's not bring on more. Let's go wi' justice. Let's do th' right thing. He'll get his iff'n he's guilty."

"Iff'n he's guilty!"

There was the sound of uncertainty in the sudden murmurings.

"Hell, Jeb, mebbe he's right."

"Damn me, Sam Goff, not you, too!"

Samuel Goff sucked his big teeth and shook his head. "Luke makes sense. We uns c'n handle these local Lenapes, but iff'n he's right an' all them others come in—man, we uns'll never sleep again. It's uneasy peace up here as 'tis." He did not want to add that he had three young ones of his own to consider, not with Jeb's just having lost two of his.

"Hell."

"Holy damn, Jeb, mebbe we oughter think some more. . . ."

Firewalker had ceased singing his song of death when the tall fair-haired man called Luke Springer first spoke. Now there was much confusion among the whites as they all talked loudly and at the same time. He met War Cloud's eyes and saw their brightness. He, too, thought this was hopeful. As Luke Springer walked past him, Firewalker heard his whispered words.

"I'm Hope's friend, an' I believe i' ye, man."

Firewalker said nothing, but a rush of astonishment and gratitude shot through him. His hatred for whites was such that he could not even completely trust or like Hope's father. But now this tall blue-eyed stranger had touched his heart and saved him from certain death. Luke Springer was his brother, and someday he would repay his debt to him. Moments later, his feelings toward Hope's father were to change forevermore as the healer himself rode into their midst on a lathered horse.

Tom shook his head pityingly as he looked on the scene. This was the same red-faced wild-eyed bunch who had offered Hope up to the vultures—except for Luke. He knew exactly why Luke was there, for Maybeth had told him.

Breathing hard, he looked each of them square in the eye before he said, "Am I keeping you from your fun, lads?" When none answered, he growled, "I hope you have rope enough for two, because if you hang this man, you might as well hang me beside him. I'll be doing some murdering of my own!"

"Hell, Doc, these is his arrers what killed my sons. Thunderhead hisself said it." Jeb Green held them out for Tom to see.

"They might be his arrows, but whose hand held the bow? That's the main thing."

"Iff'n he didn't do it, who did?" Jeb argued.

"Man, that's what a trial by jury is for," Tom shot back. "To discover who. You can't take the law into your own hands like this." He had feared what he might find when he finally caught up with these hot spurs, but it seemed Luke's good sense had prevailed, at least temporarily. His wish now was for the real slayer to be found before Firewalker could be taken south to Fort McIntosh. He made his voice sound hearty. "Well, now, let's get back to the village, and tell them what we've decided. This man has family. They'll be worried."

Jeb growled, "What's left o' my family's worried,

too—an' I don't recall makin' no decision other than th' one t' hang this bastard."

Tom met Luke's eyes. "You agree with that, Luke Springer?"

Luke shook his head. "Nay, man, I tole 'em we'd be in big trouble iffen we string 'im up. We'll be swamped wi' Injuns fr'm all over. There's three more here who agrees wi' me. Iffen he's guilty, he sh'd be hanged, o' course, but I ain't convinced he bent his bow agin childer."

Tom nodded. "I know he didn't bend his bow against children." He took Jeb Green's arm. "Jeb, I'm damned sorry about your sons, God knows I am, and God willing, the killer will be found."

Jeb looked mutinous. "He done it. Ever'body knows he near killed a man over t' Kittanning, an'—"

Tom barked, "If he killed your boys, he'll be punished. That's that. Now let's get a move on."

"Dammit, he hangs!" Jeb Green shouted.

Tom's heart nearly thundered out of his chest, but he sat taller in the saddle. "As I said, lads, if you hang Firewalker, find a rope for me, too. But I don't think your neighbors will take kindly to your stringing up their doctor." Finding himself beside Firewalker's mount, he leaned over and took the reins. "Let's go, son. You all right?"

"Aye."

"Good. Let's get a move on then. Luke"— he beckoned the good-looking young man near—"let's have you and your friends ride before and behind Firewalker for a bit of an escort." He gave Jeb a friendly smile. "As I said, man, if my friend here is guilty, he'll hang, I promise. In fact, I'll put the noose around his neck myself. But until then, let's just assume he's innocent."

War Cloud had moved on foot to his brother's side. "I will go to Twin Oaks now if it is still your wish."

Firewalker nodded. "Go. If Hope is there, bring her back with you. She will be worried."

"I am on my way."

War Cloud did not follow the roundabout path he and Firewalker had decided upon earlier. He approached the cabin openly from the south at a fast gallop, but halfway across the clearing his eyes narrowed. What was that lying on the ground near the barn? He slowed to a walk and as he drew closer, he saw that it was a man. A white. As he dismounted and cautiously neared the sprawled, still form, he sucked in a breath seeing who it was that lay there lifeless. By the Eternal. D'Arcy . . .

His head seemed to swell and throb with the rage that filled him. Helldamnfire, who had deprived him of the slaying of this devil? D'Arcy was his. Kneeling, he examined the moccasin prints in the dust and the ugly wound in the Frenchman's back. He saw that an arrow had made it, and a woman had stood there. So. Hope Caldwell had been taken by a Mengwe—who else—and on the trader's roan, for her own mount still stood before the cabin.

War Cloud's mouth twisted at the irony of it. There lay d'Arcy dead, with not even one pelt in it for him. And the woman was gone and in truth, it gladdened him. She had made his life miserable, and it was no more than she deserved. But because his heart had changed so suddenly toward Firewalker, her loss touched him also. She was his brother's woman. And while it was unseemly for a man to concern himself over a stolen wife, he knew that Firewalker would mourn her.

He leapt onto his horse and, like an angry whirlwind, swept across the highlands and down the hill toward home. In the village, he found a crowd, both Indian and white, milling. His anxious gaze passed over his uncle and mother and sister. And there was Caldwell—and Sings Low. His eyes widened seeing her shy smile and the baby strapped on her back. He masked his pleasure and gave her a crisp nod. She was a good squaw, and he would tell her so later. Spying Firewalker, he hastened to him. He saw that his brother's hands were still bound behind him.

Firewalker frowned, knowing instantly that something was wrong. "Where is Hope?"

War Cloud wasted no words. "The Mengwes have her."

Firewalker reeled. "*Matta* . . ."

"They have killed d'Arcy. We have not a moment to lose."

Suddenly Tom was there. He had seen Firewalker's ashen face. "What is it?" He grabbed his arm. "Is it Hope?"

Firewalker said thickly, "The Mengwe's have her. They have killed d'Arcy."

"My God . . ."

Now Firewalker's own fear was turning to rage. Hope could not be lost to him; he would not allow it. He would go after her and get her back. He would see her again and hold her again—but not if he stood there behaving as if she were dead already.

"Untie me," he growled. "I am going after her. She has not been gone long. We will get her back."

"I'm with you, lad," Tom said, and shouted hoarsely to the others: "The Mengwes have Hope. We're going after her. Firewalker will lead us." He drew his knife to slash the brave's bonds, but Jeb Green stepped between them.

"This devil ain't leadin' anyone anywhere, Doc. He's alive f'r one reason—t' stand trial f'r murder, an' we'll not have 'im slink off inter them woods so we'll not see hide nor hair o' him agin."

Only once before in his life had Tom felt such helpless fury. It had been in Pittsburgh when he'd confronted Charlton Thorpe over Hope. He shook his head. "You're a fool, Green."

"He stays."

"He's not your killer."

"He stays," Jeb muttered.

Firewalker turned abruptly to War Cloud. "There is no time to lose. You must go without me. Give the call to arms."

"I'll be goin' too," Luke Springer said, stepping forward. "So will a couple o' th' others."

"My brother, thank you." Firewalker's eyes met Luke's, and those of War Cloud and Thomas Caldwell. "Thank you. And now, it is my thought that we should approach the Mengwes in this way . . ."

As Walks Alone watched in silence, Firewalker gave his instructions to the three men, and the drum summoned the braves to ready their mounts and arm themselves. She was wrenched, knowing the torment of her younger son, but she did not plead with the whites for his freedom. The doom she had foreseen for him these many months was fast approaching, and she wanted him nowhere near Hope Caldwell and the lash of Stands Tall's fury. Here he would be safe, at least for a while longer. As for that woman, she prayed to the Great Manitou that Stands Tall would never give her back.

"We are ready," War Cloud declared when the braves were assembled. "We will get your woman for you, my brother." His black eyes dripped scorn upon the whites guarding Firewalker, and despite his loathing for himself, he felt the stirring of a pride he had not known for many winters. He raised a hand with a tomahawk in it. "We go!" He gave a whoop.

"Wait!"

Firewalker swallowed a groan of impatience as the old chief's voice rang out. "What is it, my uncle?"

"I must speak," Thunderhead said, coming to Firewalker's side. He was leaden in his heart and in his step. Shortly before the whites had returned with Firewalker captive, his sister had revealed to him her long-held secret. He was stunned by the brave's tragedy, and determined that another would not be heaped on top of it. Walks Alone had told him also of Firewalker's joining with Hope. He turned now to the white clutching Firewalker's arrows in his hand. "Jeb Green, no harm must come to my good friend, Caldwell the healer."

Jeb did not meet the chief's burning brown eyes. He muttered, "None o' us wants 'er harmed. We'll not stop yer goin' after her."

"Firewalker must go also. Only he can win her release."

Jeb kept his eyes firmly on the arrows. It was said this old fellow with his feather cape and scepter was a sachem. He wondered if sachems were kings. And the woman beside him, he supposed she was the medicine woman he'd heard about. He wondered if it meant she was a spell worker and if she could cast a spell on him. The thought made him shiver. Even so he said stubbornly, "I reckon War Cloud there kin git 'er loose jist as well."

Thunderhead shook his silver head. "Nay, my friend, he cannot. There is a special reason why none can win her freedom but Firewalker. You must allow him to go. I promise you, he will return. But to stay your fears, I give myself to you in his place. If for any reason he should not return, I am yours to do with what you will."

In the silence that followed, Jeb Green looked at the old man's face for the first time. He himself was not an educated man—he was only a farmer—but he knew a king when he saw a king. A man with eyes like that and a bearing like that; a man who'd make a gesture like that could only speak the truth. He gave a sigh of resignation and shook his head.

"Ye got 'im, man." He cut Firewalker's bonds.

Within moments, the Lenape war party and the small band of whites was thundering toward Ohio with Firewalker riding at its head. The remainder of the whites followed Thunderhead back to the royal wigwam. After he went inside and lay himself on his bed shelf, they settled themselves for a long wait.

* * *

As he rode westward, Firewalker could not push from his mind the terrible memory of Hope and the three Mengwe devils. It was burned there. His beautiful Hope pinned to the earth with those devils about to rape her. The thought made him shake, and had he been alone, he would have wept in his terror for her. He would have shouted to *memedhakemo* to watch over her. He would have demanded it—but he was not alone. He could not allow himself such weakness. It would also terrify her father. *Matta*, he must hold to the thought that Stands Tall had stolen her to control him, and would not harm her. And that they would get there in time. Looking over at War Cloud riding by his side, he felt a closeness to him that he had not felt for many winters. This day, for the first time in a long time, they were brothers. . . .

War Cloud's pride had vanished as their band thundered single file through the deep woods toward Ohio. With every hoofbeat, he sank more deeply into a mire of guilt and shame and dread. What had that devil d'Arcy told the Mengwes? Had he revealed that it was he, War Cloud, who had supplied the two arrows and plotted his own brother's downfall? Had he lied and told them that it was he who ordered the slayings? Even if the devils had killed on their own, it mattered little. He knew the Mengwes—if they had his name, they would blame him. He shivered, tasting the terror that filled him and feeling the doom that surrounded him.

This day it was all going to come out, and in truth, he was glad to be done with hiding. He had betrayed his brother, and he would have betrayed his people had he become chieftain. He had known exactly what the Frenchman expected of him. Lenape furs for a pittance. And he would have supplied them in exchange for all the whiskey he craved. Now he had nothing, neither scepter nor whiskey nor honor. It was just as well; it was what he deserved. He thought fleetingly, almost wistfully, that Sings Low cared for him. She had given him a child, and he had not even learned if it was a son. He hoped it was not. Thinking how ashamed the boy would be to have such a father, he yearned for the bright Land of Death where all was made right. He felt it beckoning. . . .

Hope rode in blackness, the blindfold shutting out all light from her eyes. She was certain they were headed west, for she had heard there was a Mengwe village there. She kept careful count of the streams they crossed, and she noted any uncommon odors that reached her nostrils, because when they reached their destination, she hoped to escape and make her way back home. Her other hope was that when Firewalker learned of her abduction, he would come for her. Unless he had been captured . . .

The thought sent her plunging into such black gloom, she dared not think it, not for an instant. Firewalker would come for her. With him all things were possible. He would come for her and everything would be all right. And until he came, or until she could flee, she would put on a brave, dignified face, no matter what happened to her. Her husband would be proud of her.

After what seemed an endless time, she heard shouting and drums beating, and her courage left her. They had arrived, and her fate, whatever it was to be, awaited her. As rough hands lifted her off the roan, she prayed that her terror would not show.

When her blindfold was removed, Hope stared in dismay at the throng of women and children swarming about her. They were all sizes and all ages, and they were laughing and shouting and pointing at her. Soon they began, none too gently, to stroke and explore her skin and hair. She tried to fend them off, but she soon saw that it was useless. They were insistent, and there were too many of them. Their babble was a din which beat at her ears, and their closeness and the stench of their bear grease and stinking breath overwhelmed her. The younger children struck at her and pulled her hair as she was driven deeper into the village, but she kept her head high and her eyes straight ahead. The taunting only stiffened her resolve not to show fear and to plot a way of escape as quickly as possible.

But when she was tethered by a bit of rope to a post, with her hands bound together, and when she saw that the large Mengwe lodges were not in an open village like the Lenapes, but were enclosed within a high stockade, her spirits sank. She might never leave this place or see Firewalker again. And she could not live without seeing him again—nor would she want to. . . .

She glared at a moon-faced woman who was cautiously edging closer to her. Hope saw in those sly almond-shaped eyes exactly what the squaw was thinking: she was wondering how best to torment and break her. Well, she would not be broken. She stood tall, pointed at the squaw with her tied hands, and hissed, *"Ni meteinuwak!"*

She slitted her eyes, and bared her teeth as she had seen Walks Alone do upon occasion when she shook the doll being. Let them think she was a medicine woman and a force to fear. Let them. As the woman drew back, uncertain, Hope saw a tall, familiar figure at a distance. She gasped. Firewalker? Oh, God, it was! She could hardly believe he had come for her this quickly, yet she should have known he would. There was nothing he could not do. But as he moved toward her, deep in talk with the brave at his side, she grew uneasy. Why did he walk so slowly, and why was his attention on the brave alone? When he finally stood before her, studying her, Hope understood.

This was not Firewalker. This man had threads of silver in his long black hair and his golden gaze held a cruelty that made the hair stand on her arms. Dear Lord, she did not know how it could be, but this man must be Firewalker's father. She knew instinctively that he was someone of importance, probably the chieftain, and as she stared at him in shocked disbelief, her heart pounding, he gave a sharp command. The brave tried to force open her mouth.

"Matta!" Hope cried and struck out at him with her bound hands. When she attempted to kick him, he caught her from behind and once more pried open her jaws. The sachem peered at her teeth and nodded in satisfaction. "Bastard!" she choked. Next his hands moved over her breasts, feeling their contours, squeezing them, seeming to weigh them. *"Matta!"* But her voice broke in terror.

The tall golden-eyes chieftain said nothing. His mouth lifted in a slight smile, and as he and the brave walked away, Hope sank to the earth and wept. She could no longer hold back her tears. If Firewalker did not come for her, she was going to spend the rest of her days in this horrible place as that man's squaw. She had seen it in his eyes.

Chapter 26

Firewalker was consumed by thoughts of his wife as he thundered through Mengwe country. Her beautiful face and sweet smile and her laughter like the low murmuring of the river . . . her hair like the blackness of night and her eyes dawn silver . . . and her skin . . . He tried to swallow the fullness in his throat remembering how soft and white her skin was, and how silken. He had loved stroking it, feeling and tasting and inhaling the scent of it. . . . And if something were to happen that he could never see nor touch nor hold her again—if she had been slain . . .

He recoiled as the thought filled him with a wild terror he had not known since his father was murdered. *Matta!* He dared not think it. Soon he and his men would be at the enemy village and he needed a clear head. He was going to learn what this was all about—whether it was a ploy of Stands Tall to get him there and win him over, or if one of his braves had seen her and stolen her for himself. Whichever, he needed his wits to deal with it, yet he grew increasingly tense, thinking of his coming confrontation with Stands Tall.

It pained him that all who saw the two of them would know they were father and son, for now his mother's shame would be revealed. He sorrowed for her. For himself, he was neither the first nor would he be the last to carry two bloods in his veins. What mattered was that, in his heart, he was Lenape, and in his heart, Diving Eagle would always be his true father. And what mattered just as much was that Hope be returned to him unharmed. Hope, Hope, Hope, Hope . . .

He found himself saying her name to the beating of the drums that had begun to sound. Mengwe drums. It meant their presence was known, and he wondered if the gates to the stockade would be open, or would they have to be stormed? His pulse quickened as the stockade came into sight and he saw the gates were open. It encouraged his belief that they were expected, that Stands Tall had stolen Hope as a means of getting him there and bargaining with him. The trick now would be to get her away from the devil without surrendering himself.

As they galloped toward the opening, he looked about at his men with a heart full of pride and gratitude: War Cloud, Glad Tidings, his two white brothers, Thomas Caldwell and Luke Springer, the rest of the men in his village, all of them friends and kinsman. Before their departure, he had warned them there must be no war cries and no shooting unless he commanded it. No matter what happened, no shooting. To Thomas Caldwell, he had given a special warning: no matter what he saw or heard, he was to remain quiet. Nothing must be done to further endanger Hope. Now they rode in grave-faced silence, bows and tomahawks at the ready.

The drumming ceased as they entered the stockade, and for an instant, Firewalker feared a trap. These were Mengwes, the ancient enemy. Had his people been lured inside to be fired upon? But his head told him this was not about war. This was about kinship. His blood father wanted a son to walk by his side in his old age.

Waiting impatiently for all of his men to arrive, he looked down on the startled faces of Mengwe braves, squaws, and children, and said sharply, "Get Stands Tall. I have come for talk with him."

Firewalker saw the chieftain in the distance. He already was walking toward them slowly and with great dignity, his sub-chieftain by his side. Firewalker dismounted and waited, War Cloud at his own side. He heard the murmur that swept his own ranks as Stands Tall drew near, and he saw that War Cloud stared, agape, at the tall sachem.

"My brother, what—is this?" War Cloud said low. He was shocked to the core. He had never thought to see that comely face and those golden eyes on anyone except Firewalker. Was witchcraft at work here?

"It is exactly as it seems," Firewalker muttered. "He is my father."

War Cloud felt the wind leave him. He croaked, "How can this be?"

"This devil took our mother by force. I learned it but two days ago."

War Cloud emitted a soft groan. He had never loathed himself as much as at that moment. He, who had always envied the very ground on which his brother walked, was of the purest blood, whereas Firewalker was half Mengwe. And because of his jealousy, he had ruined both their lives. He would never hold the scepter, and he had brought down shame and grief on his brother when he was already sinking under this horror. Mengwe blood—Firewalker carried Mengwe blood in his veins. He saw suddenly, as if a light shone on it, that it was Stands Tall who had gone rampaging over the countryside, burning fields and barns and stealing horses. And those who saw him thought they had seen Firewalker.

"My sorrow for you is great," he muttered. "My hands long to slay this bastard for you. . . ."

"*Matta*, my brother. If he is slain, we all die. Let me handle this." He turned to face his blood father, knowing that every eye, Mengwe and Lenape alike, was looking on with dread and fascination.

"Greetings, my son." Stands Tall spoke quietly.

Firewalker gave no return greeting. His eyes were wintry, yet for the space of a heartbeat he felt sadness and understanding for this man. If it were in him to give Stands Tall the son he craved, a son to walk by his side, he would; but it was a thing he could not do. He was Lenape.

He said gruffly, "I have come for my woman, Stands Tall."

Stands Tall nodded. "I thought you might. She is very beautiful, and I can see that she would give you much pleasure—but she is mine now." When Firewalker said nothing, but gazed at him with death in his eyes, the chieftain continued: "My two wives had grown fat and lazy and for years have produced only daughters. Perhaps this new wife of mine will give me the sons I crave."

The golden lion-eyes of the two men blazed as they studied one another. Firewalker knew that, by rights, Hope now belonged to Stands Tall. He knew also that there were not enough horses in his valley to buy her back. And if he spilled blood for her return, he would get back only her lifeless body. Stands Tall would slay her before he would give her up. Firewalker licked his dry lips. He must remain calm and reason with this devil, talk with him, try to barter for her. But in his heart, he knew it was a waste of time. Stands Tall was not going to yield, and neither would he. He was going to pillage this place and slay him, and in the doing of it, Hope would die. He drew a shuddering breath. *Matta*, he could not do it.

Firewalker gazed dully at his blood father, contemplating the fact that he was going to yield. There was no other way. He must abandon his own people and become the son of this enemy-father of his, for only then would Hope be his again. It was his only choice. But the thought of himself as a Mengwe warrior numbed him.

"My brother," War Cloud spoke in his ear. When

Firewalker made no move but stood like a log, he shook his arm. "They are bringing your woman!"

Firewalker came out of his daze to see Hope being led toward them by three squaws. His rage, coiled tightly within him, quivered as he spied the dirt and blood on her face, and saw that under the blanket she was naked. He told himself it did not mean she had been raped, but rather that she had run the gauntlet—a corridor between two lines of stick wielders bent on striking and tormenting their stripped prisoner.

For that act alone, Firewalker thought bitterly, Stands Tall deserved to die. He had allowed it solely to terrify and humiliate Hope, to give his people an excuse for revelry. Never would he have allowed his squaws to slay her even had she not been fleet as a doe and brave as a buck; she was needed, after all, to win back his son. Firewalker commanded himself not to dwell on the outrage now, for she breathed. He stayed his ever-tightening coil of fury, telling himself there was nothing more important than that: Hope still breathed. And she moved with such quiet dignity that his pride in her bounded.

Meeting her eyes, his own told her that soon he would hold her again . . . soon she would be safe . . . keep her courage burning bright.

His own courage faltered at what lay ahead, but his voice was strong as he said to Stands Tall, "I would buy her back from you."

Stands Tall nodded. "That is a possibility." He strode to Hope, roughly tore off her blanket, and threw it to the ground. He then drew her slender naked body within the circle of his arm and ran appraising hands over her. He fondled her breasts, and her belly and buttocks. "Our taste in women is very similar, my son. I think this one will give whichever of us owns her many fine braves."

Firewalker heard the growl that came from the throat of Thomas Caldwell, and saw War Cloud move to still him. The deadly coil within him wound tighter seeing Hope's terror. "You bastard."

Stands Tall smiled, thinking how like his own his son's molten eyes were. He said softly, "*Matta,* I am not the bastard, and I am quite willing that this squaw be yours again." He raised his voice. "You know what you must do. You are Mengwe, my son."

Firewalker watched in dread as Hope, like a pale slim doll in those cruel dark arms, tried to wrench herself free. His heart stood still. She must not . . . she did not know the danger. He shouted, "Hope, *matta!*"

But Stands Tall had seized her long hair, and tilting back her head, gave her a brutal blow that knocked her to the ground. As she crumpled and fell, Firewalker saw a large scarlet flower of blood blossom and swell on her temple, and saw clearly the cruel welts and bruises from the gauntlet run on her body, the streaks of blood on her soft buttocks. Within him the coil unwound, hissing free and loosing a war cry from his throat. He drew his knife and leapt for the heart of Stands Tall.

War Cloud had known from the moment the Mengwe fondled the woman what the outcome would be. He smelled battle. He doubted now if his own treachery would even be brought to light this day, but there was no time to savor the thought. As Firewalker gave a hoarse cry and drew his knife, War Cloud drew his. He would take the subchieftain. But catching the sudden glint of sun on a tomahawk as it sliced through the air, he gave a mighty leap to intercept it. Firewalker must not die yet. Not until he had slain the Mengwe bastard.

Firewalker heard Hope's scream at the same moment he was knocked heavily to one side by War Cloud. He spun, his fury at being thwarted turning to disbelief as he saw the brave fall, a hatchet buried deep in his ribs. *Matta!* Not his brother! He dropped to a crouch, knife in one hand, tomahawk in the other, waiting for the Mengwe onslaught, a war cry trembling in his throat, but no attack came. The Mengwes did not move, but looked on stonily.

Firewalker did not understand, nor did he have the time to try to understand. He knelt and gently turned War Cloud onto his back. He did not attempt to remove the tomahawk, so deeply sunk into bone and muscle, for he saw that War Cloud could not survive his terrible wound. He stroked his face and took his hand, and when his brown eyes opened, Firewalker saw Death waiting behind them.

"My brother . . ." War Cloud whispered.

"I am here," Firewalker replied, attempting to still his own soul which was raging for revenge. In the sudden quiet, he was surprised to see his men part and Walks Alone ride through their ranks. He understood now why no battle had erupted. It was clear that Stands Tall had seen her coming. But it was too late for War Cloud. Swept with bitterness and grief, he gripped his brother's hand. "Our mother is here."

War Cloud's dim eyes kindled as he discerned his mother's slight, still-youthful form in her doeskins. He smiled as she knelt and took his hands in hers. He knew that his great journey was nearing, and he felt strangely peaceful. Helldamnfire, at long last he had done a thing which pleased him. Because of him, Firewalker lived.

"I go, my mother . . ."

"My son, do not leave us!"

But Walks Alone saw that he must. He could not live. She gazed hungrily on his face and saw that the color was leaving it. She allowed no tears to come, but inside, she, too, was dying. Certain that Firewalker was about to be slain, she had followed the war party unseen to this enemy place. And all the way here, she had prayed, she had pleaded with the Creator that War Cloud would be taken instead. And it had happened. There he lay, dying, having saved his brother.

The heart of Walks Alone gaped open with her grief, and she was ashamed. She was so ashamed.

She had always thought that Firewalker was her best loved, but she knew now that it was not so. She loved them both equally. It was that she had resented this true son of Diving Eagle's being so unlike him. She had wanted him to be perfect as his father was perfect, and she had not understood that it was not his fault he was not. Now she knew better. She knew it was not in him to be so. Could anything, man or beast, be anything other than what it was? She lay her head on his blood-soaked chest and sent up a wail.

Raising her head afterwards, she saw Stands Tall's startled golden eyes upon her. And she saw Hope Caldwell, huddled on the ground at the chieftain's feet. She looked with scorn upon her nakedness and the blood streaming from her face. Because of that woman, her son lay dying and he had not even wanted her. It was Firewalker and Stands Tall who wanted her. She sent up a fresh wail at the unfairness of it, and wept into her hands.

Hope gazed forlornly at the three: War Cloud lying so still, Firewalker bent over him, Walks Alone weeping. It had all happened so fast, and she was so confused. She still did not understand what was happening or why, for the tongue was not her own, but with Firewalker there and her father and Luke, surely she would soon be freed. What mattered this moment was that War Cloud was dying, and she could not let him go without thanking him. As she struggled to her feet, the sky spun around her. She swayed.

"Woman stay!" It was a growl from the golden-eyed chieftain.

"I am a doctor," Hope murmured. "I am going to him." She was surprised that he did not knock her down again or prevent her from retrieving the blanket from the ground and carrying it to where War Cloud lay, his brother and mother kneeling over him. She dropped heavily to his side.

Firewalker's eyes widened seeing her there beside

him. He put a gentle hand to her forehead where the blood still flowed. "Are you all right?"

"Aye . . ."

By the Eternal, now that she was in his hands, they had a way out of this. He beckoned Thomas Caldwell and Luke Springer. "Take her. Keep her surrounded. We will be leaving soon."

"Nay, please," Hope said. "I want to be here."

"Great God almighty, girl," Tom growled, "put my shirt on then!" He quickly pulled it off over his head and helped her don it.

With her nakedness partially covered, Hope knelt beside War Cloud and lay her hand to his cold forehead. Meeting the damp, glittering eyes of Walks Alone, she whispered, "I'm so sorry."

"You killed him. . . ." Walks Alone rasped.

The words were so unexpected, Hope flinched. "I—don't understand. . . ."

Firewalker growled, "My mother, you will be silent."

Trembling under those burning eyes, and convinced that the woman would always hate her, Hope turned her attention to War Cloud. Seeing that he had little time left, she gently covered his icy body with her blanket and slipped his quiver under his head to raise it and ease his breathing. Her heart broke when he smiled at her.

She bent, her lips close to his ear, and said in Lenape, "*N'tschu*, thank you for his life. Thank you. . . ."

"I will—take no thanks." The blood whistled in War Cloud's lungs. He was realizing, despite the deepening shadows, that his work was not done. He had prevented Firewalker's death, but it was not enough. It was not enough. . . . "I would . . . speak. . . ." he gasped. Seeing that his mother and brother drew close and bent low to hear him, and feeling their hands on him, he was comforted. "My brother, I have . . . wronged you."

Strengthened by Firewalker's strong grip, War Cloud swallowed, licked his parched lips, and sucking in many bloody breaths, gasped, "D'Arcy hired the Mengwe for me. . . . Your arrows meant . . . to kill cattle, not boys. . . . I wanted you to fall, not . . . hang, but he . . . betrayed me as I . . . betrayed you. . . ." His eyes sought Hope. "Hope Caldwell, I . . . was not your friend nor . . . was d'Arcy. He was . . . a snake. . . ."

Seeing that his mother wept, War Cloud shook his head. "My mother, it . . . is better I go." He pressed Firewalker's fingers with his last bit of strength. "In all my days, my brother, only this I . . . have done right. . . . Only this dying . . . for you . . ." He closed his eyes, and his death song, when it came, was a whisper which ended nearly as soon as it began.

Walks Alone sat staring, uncomprehending, at her dead son. What he had just said was impossible. He had not done such a treacherous thing. He had not! Surely he had not . . . But she knew that he had. Nothing else could explain it as well. He had left this life, not because of Hope Caldwell as she had always thought, but because of a thing he himself had brought about.

Firewalker felt as if he had been stabbed in the back. War Cloud had done that to him? His brother? He was only too glad to thrust the horror from him. He would dwell on it later and try to understand it, but for now he must get his people away from this place. He closed his brother's eyes, removed the blanket from his body, and covered his wife's half-clad body with it. As he helped Hope to her feet, grateful that she was in his hands once more, he decided to ask later if she had been raped. If she had, his revenge would be swift and sure. For now, it was more important to get the women away from here safely. He ignored Stands Tall, although his father's scorching gaze burned through him, and he ignored his men's blood hunger. They craved revenge for War Cloud's slaying, but his own common sense had returned. He was not going to have his wife and his mother in the center of battle.

"Place my brother's body on his mount," he said gruffly to his men. "We are taking him home."

Stands Tall's voice rang out sharply: "I might have known you would have become a Lenape woman. Know that I would not have you as my son now if you crawled to me on your yellow belly. Go from my sight, but you will leave the white woman behind. She is mine."

Firewalker maintained his temper and his silence as he lifted Hope onto Nightwind. He would no more leave without her than he would stay behind himself. Perhaps they would die there together, but he prayed they would not. At his silent signal, his men readied their weapons. At his second signal, they would ride for the gate. He prayed the Mengwe devils did not want their blood shed as much as his men wanted to shed it. It was at that moment—he blinked, disbelieving—that he saw his mother standing before the chieftain. She was a small, brave figure in her doeskins, legs firmly planted, arms crossed, head held high.

Although she was deep in grief, Walks Alone's wits had not left her. She saw that Firewalker meant to force his departure, but he would not succeed. He did not know Stands Tall as she knew him. There was going to be carnage. Lenape honor craved it, and the Mengwes would respond eagerly. Even now they looked on hungrily, their weapons drawn. But Walks Alone was not going to lose another son to this devil, nor would she allow him to have Hope Caldwell. Hope belonged to Firewalker. And after the way she herself had treated the woman, she had many amends to make.

She said loudly, "Your ways have not changed, Stands Tall."

Stands Tall felt all of his old hunger stirring as he looked down on her tear-streaked face. He said for her ears alone, "You should have been mine. . . ."

Walks Alone lifted her voice for all to hear. "And because I refused to be yours, you saw fit to give me grief." She looked toward her son's body lying across his horse. "You continue to give me grief." Her voice broke.

"Woman, I gave you a strong son. You should have sent me word. He is Mengwe. He should have been raised Mengwe."

"He is Lenape."

"*Kehella.* He is now. You ruined him. He is fit for nothing but cooking and fetching water." He wanted to slay her.

"He is a man of honor, unlike your people. Had he slain you he would have offered himself to your kin to replace you." Walks Alone's eyes flashed her scorn. "A thing the killer of my son has yet to do, but then the Mengwes never were noted for their honor." Seeing his face darken, she knew that he raged. It was a dangerous game she was playing, but only because she was certain she would win. She watched as he spoke to his subchieftain, and waited, head high, her arms crossed, as the man stepped forward.

"Lady, I am Red Buck, and I will live with your people and provide for you in place of your son if you will have me."

Walks Alone looked at him with ice in her eyes. "I will not have you. I will choose another."

"Choose then," Stands Tall grated.

He was bewitched suddenly to see her damp eyes widen and soften as they had when she was a young maid and he had desired her beyond all reason—and did still. He wanted to slay her for rejecting him, but he wanted her in his bed as much as ever. By the Eternal, he could not think straight when she looked at him that way.

"You would never honor my choice," Walks Alone said softly. She held her breath.

"Woman, I will honor it! Choose before I change my mind."

Walks Alone sent no questing gaze over the Mengwe braves who stood looking on, but turned immediately and pointed to the woman astride

Firewalker's mare. "I choose her," she said, "I choose Hope Caldwell."

Stands Tall's face grew red as he realized how cleverly she had tricked him. Everyone had heard him say he would honor her choice. His blood boiled even as he felt a grudging admiration for her boldness and cleverness. What he would not give for such a one. In fact, he was tempted to keep both women, but he knew well it would start a war larger than any he wanted or could win. He was growing too old and too tired for such things. The silent runs in the night through the quiet countryside were far more to his liking. . . .

Seeing his great anger, Walks Alone feared for them all, but then she glimpsed a look in his eyes she remembered from long ago. It was admiration. She said quietly, "I will accept only the white woman, Stands Tall. None other."

Stands Tall knew that he had lost. He had always lost with this woman. And all along he had known that Firewalker would never be his. He breathed a deep breath, shook his head.

"Take her and go, Walks Alone. Go in peace."

Chapter 27

The sun was setting as they left Mengwe country and rode back toward the hills of Pennsylvania with War Cloud's body. Even with Firewalker's arms about her, Hope could not quell the trembling that held her in its grip. Remembering War Cloud's death, she feared she would never know a moment's peace again. But she told herself something wonderful had happened, too. She had heard, word for word from Firewalker, how cleverly Walks Alone had chosen her to replace him. Walks Alone who had hated her from the moment she had first laid eyes on her, had chosen her, and tricked her away from the Mengwe chieftain without more blood being shed.

It was a lovely warm spot of color in Hope's grim gray reflections of the day. But instead of the color, she kept seeing the gray in every horrible shade and shape: Jacques's cruelty and his abandoning her ... his death ... the gauntlet ... the tomahawk slicing into War Cloud's bones and muscles. She could not keep the memories from overpowering her, and when she shuddered, Firewalker's arms immediately tightened around her, and his deep voice was soothing in her ear.

"It is all right; you are safe with me now." But he could not halt the fine trembling within his own body. His thoughts tortured him: War Cloud's dying for him, War Cloud's treachery, his own earlier fears for Hope. He had never known such terror as when he feared she might have been slain. The thought still overwhelmed him: never to hold her soft warm body in his arms again, never to hear her low laughter or see her shining gray eyes or kiss her sweet mouth . . .

"I knew you would come for me," Hope murmured.

She had held fast to that thought when she was taken away; and when her clothing had been stripped off and she was forced to run between those two rows of shrieking, laughing savages with their clubs and sticks, she had promised herself he would come. And he had. And he'd nearly been killed. She felt cold, sick. What if War Cloud had not taken the death blow himself? What would she have done then? How could she survive without Firewalker? She lifted his hands holding the reins and pressed her lips to them, inhaling their wonderful scent of pine and leather and kissing them over and over, almost frantically.

"Oh, Firewalker . . ." She tilted back her head, touching her cheek to his.

"Hope, I love you. . . ."

"Wh-what?" His voice sounded so strange and strangled she was not even sure she had heard him correctly.

"My wife, I love you." Firewalker's arms tightened about her as he brushed his lips over her hair and temple, across her cheek and down the side of her throat. "I could not walk this earth without you. I love you."

Hope turned and was shocked to see the grim lines of his face and that it was stained with tears. She could hardly believe it. She *had* heard him: she had thought he'd said he loved her and he *had* said it. This man who could scarcely force the word past his lips earlier was now weeping with his love for her. It was what she had wanted to happen, and what she had promised herself she would hear someday, but she had never dreamed she would see him as stricken as this. As she stroked his cheek and turning, tenderly kissed his lips, she saw that he needed comforting more than she did.

She said, calmly, softly, "My husband, I'm here now. I'm safe. It's all right."

"I love you. . . ."

"And I love you. You are my sun and my moon. You are—the rainbow that arches over my head. . . ."

Despite his inner chaos, Firewalker was smiling as they reached the village. The little fox had grown more adept at the talk of his people than he was himself.

For the next three days, friends and kin came to the village from far and near to wail over the body of War Cloud. On the fourth morning, his corpse was carried into the deep woods far from the village, it was lowered into the ground to the wailing of the women, and, as was the custom, his personal belongings were given away. In the eleven days that followed, Hope wept at his grave morning and evening with the rest of the women, and her grieving was real. In the flash of a tomahawk, she had forgotten she ever disliked or feared War Cloud, and she forgave his treachery. He had given his life for Firewalker, and with his confession, had twice saved him.

Everyone in the valley now knew about the rampaging Mengwe chieftain who looked like Firewalker, and they knew about the stolen arrows, and that Firewalker was innocent of all wrongdoing. It was Stands Tall whom the authorities would deal with if that time ever came, not Firewalker. Her father and Luke Springer had seen to that. But as Hope began slowly to heal from the things that had happened on that terrible day, Firewalker himself remained inconsolable. For the eleven nights of the mourning period, she lay by his side in their wigwam and gave him what comfort and strength she had to give.

"I was not a good brother," he muttered. "If I were, War Cloud would not have hated me so."

"You were a good brother, and he didn't hate you, he loved you. He died for you."

"I knew he was troubled and not content—I should have tried harder to help him."

"You did help him. You tried to guide and protect him. . . ."

"But I did not try to understand him. His ways angered and disgusted me, and when we were boys, I tormented him. I gave him no mercy . . . which he dearly needed."

Such talk exasperated Hope. "If you had, he really would have hated you. Imagine Stargazer if he thought any gave him mercy . . ."

"I was proud that I won every race and every game," Firewalker argued bitterly. "I was too proud. It mattered nothing to me that I hurt him."

Hope asked gently, "Did you know even that you hurt him?"

Firewalker shook his head. "*Matta,* they were but games to me."

Always after they talked, they lay in each other's arms, warming, healing each other, and then making love quietly and without joy. For War Cloud's soul was nearby. It still walked the village and the flaming woodlands he had loved, and ate the food left at his grave for him. It was but biding time until the Twelfth Day, when it would set out on its twelve-year Sky Journey to the Twelfth Heaven.

Hope and Firewalker, walking arm in arm on that day through rustling leaves in the warm red-gold autumn dusk, saw a star falling. Hope cried, "Oh, Firewalker, look, there he goes. . . ."

It seemed to Hope the saddest thing in the world, for now that these twelve days of mourning were ending, it would be as if War Cloud had never existed. No one would ever speak of him again, and all of his belongings were gone. Not a trace of him was left—except Little Acorn, the beautiful boy babe he had left behind. Hope had been shocked when Flower told her that a widow must live by her own industry the first year of her bereavement. It was the custom that none were allowed to help her. It was a horrible, heartless custom as far as Hope was concerned.

"What will become of Sings Low?" she asked suddenly. "I worry about her."

Firewalker had felt a burden lifting as the star streaked westward into the sunset. Perhaps it *was* his brother leaving on his Sky Journey, but more likely it was a sign. Appearing on this Twelfth Day as it had, it told him that War Cloud was on his way home, and finally at peace. And it told him that perhaps he himself could find peace again. He tightened his arm about Hope's slender waist as he answered her question.

"Sings Low is still the wife of my brother. You must not fear for her, for he will not forsake her. This coming year, his spirit will watch over her, and I will bring her meat. . . ."

Hope frowned up at him. "Flower says it forbidden."

Firewalker's mouth tilted. "It is true there are those who fear their bow arms will wither and fail if a widow eats the game they provide."

Hope smiled. "But not the Great Hunter. His arm remains strong. . . ."

"Aye." As his gaze flickered over her pink face and dancing eyes, he knew that this night, for the first in a long time, they were going to make love as it should be made. "Sings Low will be provided for, and when this year ends, she will have a new husband to care for her and her babe. I promise you."

Hope slid her arms around her husband's waist and pressed the length of her body against his. Standing on tiptoe, she kissed his mouth, long and hungrily, and then found that he would not release his hold on her. She whispered, "Have I ever told you how much I love you?"

"A time or two." He held her closer still, and touched his hungry tongue to her lips and the dimples on either side of them.

"And have I ever told you"—shivers were rippling over her—"that you're the most wonderful, beautiful, brave, generous man I know?"

Firewalker chuckled. "And the wisest. I chose you."

Hope lay her head on his chest, loving the sound of his low laughter and the strong steady beating of his heart. "I would not have let you choose another. . . ."

Firewalker wondered how she would react to the news Walks Alone had given him that morning. It was a dark cloud hanging over his head suddenly. He stroked her hair, raised her small hand to his lips and kissed it.

Hope noticed instantly the change in his mood. "What is it?"

"Nothing that matters at this moment." He kissed her other hand, and mused that she knew him too well. He was ready to make love, but she had seen into his very thoughts. "It might not matter for a long time."

"If it matters at all, I want to know it."

He slid his arm around her waist and resumed walking. "It seems I could be the next sachem."

"My goodness . . ." She smiled, but the thought made her uneasy. When they had first met, War Cloud, the elder son of Thunderhead's sister, was destined to be the next chief. Since his death, she had given no thought to his successor. "Is it what you want?"

In truth, he did not want it. He had never craved to be chief, and his mother had stunned him, saying it had been prophesied by the Twelve. He shrugged. "I will accept it if my people want it. It will be voted upon when the time comes."

"I see. . . ." Jacques's last words were haunting her. He had threatened to tell everyone why she'd left

Pittsburgh, but then he'd been slain. Since then, she had decided she could not live under such a shadow. She would not let Firewalker hear such news from any lips but her own. But she so dreaded telling him that she had put if off.

"I see this does not please you," Firewalker said.

"I fear I could lose you. . . ."

"What foolish talk is this?"

"Your people might not want the wife of their chieftain to—to be the enemy. . . ." She hardly knew how or where to begin.

His tawny eyes moved over her, disbelieving. He shook his head. "The skill and beauty and bravery of my woman are exceeded only by her humility. You are Caldwell the healer, and Caldwell the teacher."

"Firewalker, there's something you must know. In Pittsburgh, I was respected at first, but in the end, I was Caldwell the quack, and Caldwell th-the murderess. It's why I came here with my father." Her heart was galloping. "I had to flee. I was forced to flee. . . ."

He asked gravely, "And were you a quack and a murderess?"

"Nay! It was a terrible misunderstanding."

He studied her worried face before he said quietly, "Doubtless you will have heard that I nearly slew a white."

"Aye. And doubtless it is as cruel a lie as—"

"It is not a lie," Firewalker answered gruffly. "The devil slew my father without cause and received no punishment from his own people. But for my kinsmen, I would have removed him from this earth. Because my mother feared for me, my tribe left our home in haste and came here. We, too, fled."

Hope went into his arms. "How strange the way our paths crossed . . ." Except for tragedy in both their lives, they never would have found each other.

"And now you are my wife." Firewalker lifted her and held her close against his thudding heart. Their lovemaking had been postponed long enough. "You will be the mother of my sons. . . ." Bending to kiss her, he encountered a pair of flashing gray eyes.

"Indeed. And what if I give you daughters? Will you put me aside?"

He gave an easy laugh and kissed the tip of her nose. "I will cherish all of our children, daughters and sons—but I will love none of them as I love you."

"Most wisely said, my husband." Hope offered her parted lips for him to kiss as he carried her back into the woods.

His fires hotly kindled, Firewalker placed her on the grass beneath the streaming canopy of a green-gold willow, and gently lay her back in it. He stretched out beside her, molding her yielding body to his, and exalting in the heat and the excitement that was crackling between them once again. Her small white hands caressed his bare skin and tangled themselves in his hair as his own hands slid beneath her shirt to gently squeeze the small taut peaks of her nipples between his fingers, and stroke her soft breasts. Contemplating the sight of them, pink-tipped satin, he moistened his lips and felt his shaft swell in anticipation—but he forced himself to take his time.

His golden eyes burning over her, Firewalker undressed her slowly, sensuously, first removing her moccasins, and then her leggings and shirt, all the while caressing, kissing, gently and hungrily licking each inch of silken white flesh as it was exposed, and lowering his head finally to the rounded beauty of her breasts. Her lips were parted and her breath was coming in small gasps as he touched his tongue to first one hard rosy nipple and then the other. When he took them in his mouth to gently bite and suck them, Hope arched against him. He heard her small gasp, and felt her tugging wildly at his breechclout. He gave a low husky laugh.

"It is true, I should remove it. . . ."

Hope was laughing, almost crying, as she watched

him strip it off in one swift movement, toss it into the grass, and then return to her, his eyes a-glitter.

"Oh, beloved . . ." Running eager hands over his nakedness, she pulled him close, closer and closer, and wrapped her legs about him. She was ravenous for him, and seeing his hot eyes, and feeling his hot mouth and hot hungry hands moving over her more and more urgently, she knew this night was going to be one of joy and passion. This night, War Cloud would be forgotten.

As Hope taught her class the following day, the first since War Cloud's death, she observed that Walks Alone drew near and stood watching her. After dismissing her pupils, Hope said politely, "Good morning, my mother-in-law. How may I help you?"

"I would talk with you privately," Walks Alone replied.

Leading the *meteinuwak* to her dwelling, Hope wondered what this was about. The woman had saved her from the Mengwes, aye, but she feared Walks Alone still despised her. "Please sit down." As she pondered whether to offer her food and drink, her mother-in-law settled herself on a mat before the small cook fire.

"Has my son told you of our talk yesterday morning?"

"*Kehella.*" Hope sat on a rush mat opposite her and lay several twigs on the fire. It flared brightly. "He says he is to be sachem." She marveled at the serenity on the woman's lovely face. If she herself had recently lost a son, she would be weeping still.

Walks Alone continued, "When the Twelve decreed that my elder son would not be our next chieftain, they prophesied then that it would be Firewalker. Did he tell you that?"

Hope stared at her. Prophesied? "He mentioned no prophecy."

"It is not that which I came to talk about," Walks Alone said softly. "It is about you and me."

A thrill of disbelief swept Hope as she discerned the warmth in Walks Alone's brown eyes. "I don't understand."

"I myself have only come to understand, for I have been blind. And I have been jealous and greedy beyond all belief."

"My mother, nay—" Hope bit her lip. She had overstepped. To call this woman of dignity her mother was surely to insult her. "I'm sorry, I—"

Walks Alone smiled. "You honor me. But now I would tell you what I came to say before this day grows any longer. Will you hear me?"

"Aye, please. . . ." Gazing admiringly at the *meteinuwak's* thick, carefully coiled hair and youthful form, Hope thought how lovely she was.

"It was in the month of the corn-growing," Walks Alone began, crossing her arms, "when I saw in a vision that one of my sons was to die."

"Oh, my mother . . ."

"I did not know which son, I did not know by whose hand he would perish, nor did I know when or why. I knew only that the doom of one was sealed and that a young woman with long black hair would be there when he died. I did not see her face then, but I saw it in many visions thereafter. I knew she was a white woman."

Horror crawled up Hope's spine. A young white woman with long black hair. She whispered, "You saw me?"

"*Kehella*. And I assumed, foolishly, that you were the reason for the coming tragedy. I assumed each of my sons wanted you, and that they would fight over you, and one would kill the other to have you. That night when I saw you for the first time, I—forgive me—I hated you. I hated you as much for being the Bringer of Death as I did for your being the Bringer of Life to my brother. I was jealous that you had saved Thunderhead when I could not. I prayed for you to leave and never come back, and I prayed for my sons never to see you again. I—prayed for Stands Tall to keep you. But the die was cast."

"Your vision of me—" Hope breathed, her thoughts fastened on it. "How can this be? You had never seen me before. . . ." It seemed strange and terrifying even.

"There are those among us who have an affinity for such things. We are trained."

"I'm—awed. I've never heard of anything like it before. And as for my coming here, please believe I never meant any harm."

"I know you did not," Walks Alone murmured, "and it shames me now that I ever thought it. I ask your forgiveness."

Hope could scarcely believe this was happening. She had dreamed about being friends with Walks Alone. "There is nothing to forgive," she declared. "Nothing. Let me thank you instead for raising a son who is the most perfect treasure on this earth. I thank you from the bottom of my heart for Firewalker. I—I love him so. . . ." She could only produce a strangled whisper.

With thoughtful eyes, Walks Alone studied her new daughter-in-law. She had been greatly impressed as, for the first time, she watched her teach. She recognized now, as long last, that Hope Caldwell was a woman of great inner strength as well as outer beauty. She would be a good companion for Firewalker, and she would give him many fine babes. And she would be the doctor she herself had never been. Walks Alone saw well that her own skills lay in the spiritual world of the medicine woman. As for Hope's teaching her son, she foresaw that his natural leadership and abilities would be magnified by it. When Thunderhead was gone, Firewalker would guide their people in ways his uncle never could.

Gazing into the flames, Walks Alone felt a great sense of peace. War Cloud was on his Sky Journey now and would one day be with his father. Soon she would be making her own journey to join them.

Thinking of seeing her beloved again, she was filled with quiet jubilation. She had never forgotten how it felt to lie close by the side of Diving Eagle with his strong arms about her.

Seeing the strange, veiled look in the eyes of the *meteinuwak*, Hope whispered, "May I get you food or drink?" When Walks Alone did not reply, but gazed upon her as if from a great distance, she asked, "My mother, is anything wrong?"

Walks Alone rose in one easy graceful movement. "*Matta*, my daughter. All is well." She smiled then. "All is well. . . ."

It was the beginning of the hunting month, and there was such an abundance of game in the valley that, for the first time since they had come there, the Lenapes had not moved to their winter camp in the north. As Firewalker tracked buck through the softly falling snow, he thought how fortunate it was, for Hope would not have accompanied him there. She would have stayed with her father, for she had made a promise to deliver the Springer child that was due, and her promise was as good as gold. He was considering that it must be very close to the woman's time when he heard his name shouted. He turned, scowling. What fool would come galloping so wildly and bawling his name when it was obvious he was there to hunt?

"Firewalker, thank thee, God . . ."

Seeing that it was his brother, Luke Springer, Firewalker's wrath vanished on the instant. "Has your woman's time come?" he called.

"Aye. She's been laborin' since late morn—five, six hours now—but she's took bad all of a sudden. Kin ye' fetch Hope for us, man?"

"Aye!" Even as he said it, Firewalker was headed back toward the village through the falling snow.

It was storming heavily as, bundled head to foot in furs, he and Hope cantered across the highlands toward the Springer cabin. They rode in silence for the wind carried away their words, and Firewalker again gave thanks to his manitou that he had not gone north but was there for her. He would not have her out in such weather with darkness falling with any but himself.

But he was uneasy at the thought of being present for the birth. This was a matter for women, not warriors, and he intended to wait in the barn until the babe came. Suddenly, a torch-bearing rider galloped toward them, wild eyed, white faced, hair and beard and cloak white with snow.

"Hurry, Hope—f'r God's sake, hurry!" Luke cried. "She be dyin', I fear."

Within moments, they had arrived at the cabin. As Hope jumped down from her mare and hastened across the snow-covered stoop, Firewalker called to her: "I will take our mounts to the barn." And there he would stay until she was ready to leave.

Hope turned, her eyes wide in the torchlight. "You'll hurry back, won't you?"

Firewalker saw with surprise that she was frightened. He had not known she feared so greatly for her friend and the babe. He nodded. "I will come back."

He took Luke's mount to the barn with their own, and after brushing the snow from their coats, and blanketing them, he plowed his way back to the cabin. He forced himself to open the door, and was stunned by the sight before him. By the Eternal . . . The woman lay half naked on a let-down bed, shadows dancing over the huge white mountain of her belly and her plump white legs parted wide. Her hands clutched the bedposts behind her head, and as she strained and grunted and strained, scarcely a whimper escaped her lips. When the terrible straining ceased, her pain-glazed blue eyes met his. A smile lit her face.

"'Evenin', Firewalker. . . ." It was a whisper as Maybeth sucked in great gulps of air. "Thank thee f'r . . . bringin' me . . . m' doctor. . . ."

Shocked beyond words, Firewalker finally replied

thickly, "Good evening, my friend. My wife would have been here even without me."

"I think thee's right, man."

In a daze, he saw that Hope had removed her outer garb and was bathing Maybeth's face, while Luke hovered anxiously and helplessly by his wife's side. And then the woman was straining again, gasping, sweat drenched, her huge effort contorting her pretty face and turning it beet red. He stared in horrified amazement. He knew well that women gave birth with much suffering, but he had never witnessed it. The women of his people slipped away, alone or with another, and returned quietly with their babes neat and clean and at their breasts or carried on their backs. Now, the full reality of the birthing of a child struck him. This female had been laboring for hours to force from a small opening in her body a full-sized babe. He swallowed. The room was stifling suddenly.

Sparing Firewalker a quick glance, and seeing him clutch the mantelpiece, Hope hid a smile. It never ceased to amaze her. No matter how strong and brave the man, he needed only to see a woman in childbirth to be turned to water. She felt a deep glow of excitement and contentment gazing over at him. This night she could tell him with certainty that they, too, were going to have a child. . . .

She returned her attention to Maybeth. She was doing beautifully, and not at all as Luke had led her to believe. In fact, all was going normally, and the little one should arrive within an hour or two. She wiped the sweat from Maybeth's face, stroked her arm, and spoke small endearments. In between the contractions, which were beginning to come closer and closer, the two chatted. And as the second hour wore on, Hope saw that she had judged correctly. The actual birthing drew near.

"Love, it's on its way," she crooned. "I see its little crown—and it's dark-haired like Luke. Just rest now, sweet . . . rest a little while and take some nice deep breaths. . . ."

She could not believe Maybeth's tremendous strength and stoicism. She had not uttered a sound louder than a whimper, but had bitten hard on a quilt and tossed her head from side to side. Hope was bursting with pride for her. Seeing another contraction coming, she stroked back the limp wet hair.

"Push again, honey, you're doing fine. It won't be long now, lovey, and I'm so proud of you. . . ." She pressed firmly on Maybeth's huge abdomen, felt movement, felt its rapid shrinking, and suddenly the babe slipped out and into her waiting hands. Half laughing, half weeping, Hope cried, "Oh, Maybeth, love, you have a boy! It's a beautiful little boy. . . ."

Firewalker, rooted to the hearth since their arrival, looked at the clock ticking on the mantelpiece. The woman had struggled for eight hours. They themselves had been there only a short time, two and a half hours, but it seemed like an eternity, and what he had just seen, he would never forget. The silently borne agony and bravery of that small woman, his brother Luke weeping and gathering her tired body into his arms and cradling her. It was a new and strange thing to him, and he saw that it was a right and good thing. He understood well the terrible fear and relief of his brother, and did not scorn the tears that streamed from Luke's eyes and down his bearded face.

But he brooded as he watched Hope clean the babe, cut and tie the cord, and then smack its tiny rump so that it squawled. He had wanted sons from her, and aye, daughters, too, but now, as the mother put the tiny crying bundle to her breast, he was filled with fear. How could he put Hope through such torture as he had just witnessed? Yet loving and desiring her as he did, how could he not . . . ?

Chapter 28

The new mother slept, content, her babe in her arms, while the men sat in the kitchen, eating and talking in low voices of crops and hunting. Hope had neatened the house—Maybeth would not be doing it for a while—and joined them. She smiled at Luke and patted his hand.

"Congratulations again. Your son is strong and healthy and beautiful, and Maybeth—well, Maybeth is wonderful. In every way. There's not another like her."

Luke grinned. "She's somethin' all right. B'fore she drifted off, she said she wants ye both f'r supper soon."

"Tell her we'll come. In fact, I'll tell her myself when I stop by tomorrow."

Luke frowned. "You're t' stay th' night, both o' ye. She changed th' bed, thinkin' y would. . ."

Firewalker had gone to the door and opened it as they talked. It was quiet outside, and the moon shone high and small and silver. "It has cleared," he said. "I thank you for the hospitality, my brother, but I must leave now. I hunt tomorrow." He looked at Hope. "Stay if you will."

"It's a thought. Maybeth mentioned it, but I'm just not sure . . ." She was too restless, too filled with the excitement of the birth and with her own news for Firewalker to be able to sleep in a strange bed. She went to his side and looked out at the night, her eyes widening. "How beautiful it is." It was a dreamland, a fairyland. White, still, the snow a diamond-glittered blanket, and the stars so clear and bright and close she could almost reach out and touch them. She took her husband's arm and smiled up at him. "I'll leave with you. I can't stay inside and sleep and miss all of this. Luke, crawl into that nice bed yourself. You need it more than I do."

But on their way home, Hope was concerned. Firewalker was so quiet. In fact, ever since their arrival at the cabin, he had been withdrawn. She was riding ahead, leading the way through the moon-sparkled woods, but now she slowed Beauty's pace and finally stopped. Firewalker drew abreast of her.

"What is it, my wife?"

"I was about to ask you that." She smiled, thinking how magnificent he was in his furs and with the moon turning his eyes to silvery gold. No one else in the world had eyes like that. Except Stands Tall . . . She thrust his image from her thoughts and said quietly, "You've not been yourself tonight. I hope you're not ill."

"*Matta*, I am not ill."

When he pulled back his hood, and Hope saw the gauntness of his face, she felt real concern. She dismounted, sliding down into the deep snow, and went to him. "What is it?"

Firewalker slid off Nightwind, and wordlessly opened his fur cloak. He pulled her inside and holding her tightly against him, folded it about her. He tilted up her face and kissed her mouth, gently at first and then more hungrily.

Hope responded eagerly, but her worry for him intruded. "Beloved, tell me, what is it?"

Standing in the snow, their bodies pressed close, he kissed her again and smoothed back her long hair from her moon-pale face. "I fear for you," he whispered.

She remembered suddenly the way he had looked

when he'd first seen Maybeth, the way he had gripped the mantelpiece. She was awash with guilt realizing that he must have been shattered by the whole experience. And to think she had been amused. She could kick herself. Why had she not realized that a Lenape brave never even saw a woman having her menses let alone having a child! Oh, the poor love . . . She slipped her arms around his waist under his coat and massaged the taut muscles of his back and shoulders. She asked gently, "Is it Maybeth?"

He was mortified by his weakness, but he would not lie about it. He muttered, "Aye, and my heart trembles that someday you must face that because of me."

Hope's heart soared. He was amazing. Just when she thought she could not possibly love him more than she did, he said a thing like that. She smiled up at him. "It is not so bad, really." She saw his panther eyes widen, their centers dilating with the fear he felt for her.

"Not so bad?" His growl reverberated throughout her body.

"Nay. A woman doesn't dwell on the pain once it's over. She forgets it." For if she did not, Hope thought wryly, no more babies would be born. Not ever . . . Suddenly he was clasping her shoulders so tightly she winced.

"By the Eternal, Hope, the woman could have died!" His head was filled with the horror of those hours and hours of sweating and grunting.

"But she did not die," Hope answered calmly. "She's fine and she has a wonderful new babe now, and all is well." She kissed his mouth again, and again, many small teasing kisses, but when his only answer was a scowl, she was warned. This was not the time to tell him her news or tell him that Maybeth's delivery had been a fairly easy one. She stroked his thick black hair from his brow and said quietly, "I fear for you, too, you know. I wasn't going to say so, but every time you go on a hunt, I die thinking of what might happen. But I know you can't stop hunting, nor can we stop living. Women cannot stop having babies. . . ."

Firewalker snugged her closer, his face buried in the fragrant cloud of her hair. He drew in a deep breath, and said finally, "You are right. It seems my woman is wiser and braver by far than I am myself." He began kissing her then, small hungry kisses covering her soft mouth, her cheeks and chin, her eyelids, the tip of her nose, her tongue. . . . They became devouring kisses that he could not stop. "My wife, I love you. . . ."

"And I love you," Hope returned, breathless.

And the night was glorious and he was holding her so tightly she could scarcely breathe and they were going to live and love each other and make love forever. And now he was growing so passionate, he was tickling her. She began to giggle. When his own deep laughter rang out, she knew she had to tell him. She could not hide it another moment.

"Firewalker—"

"You are beautiful, my wife." Firewalker kissed her again. "The moon and the stars are in your eyes, the night in your hair, the sun in your heart—"

"And your babe in my belly . . ." Her eyes dancing with excitement, Hope watched his slow blink of astonishment.

He asked hoarsely, "You are carrying my child?"

"Aye."

It filled him with such elation, he gave a wild whoop and swept her off her feet high into his arms. He gave her another kiss. He could not get enough of kissing her, his sweet soft woman. And then he realized—this was the very thing he had dreaded. He had planted a child within her.

Hope knew exactly what he was thinking. Cradling his face, she said gently, "Women have been bearing children forever. I don't fear it, I look forward to it. I want to give you a child. This is our baby." Seeing that he could not speak, but could only hold her, she whispered, "It will be all right. My father will be there to help, and your mother, and"—she slid her arms around his neck and clung to him—"and I am so happy and— Oh, Firewalker, thank you! Thank you for this child."

Standing in the silver-white night with his woman in his arms, Firewalker sensed the forest spirits beginning to stir around them. And then the earth and the moon and the night and the wind, spirit kin all, were speaking to him and trembling with his joy and telling him that all would be well. He touched his lips gently to Hope's.

"You have pleased me greatly, my wife."

Hope's gray eyes were filled with teasing moonbeams. "Even if I give you a daughter?"

"Even if you give me a daughter." But it was his son she carried. He willed it to be so.

Walks Alone was ready. She had been ready these seven long years. Her people were assured a strong ruler on that day when Thunderhead passed on, and now Diving Eagle waited for her. She had made her plans carefully, knowing it would not be easy to slip away, but finally the perfect time had arrived. It was snowing and the night was bitter. Most important of all, Firewalker and Hope were both away. She had been about to leave the longhouse for their wigwam, saying she wanted to mend a blanket there, when the interruptions began. It seemed a night for sickness as, one after the other, she was presented with stomachaches, earaches, sore throats, and headaches. She had told herself to be patient, she would never see these folk again, and so she was. She treated them with love and gentleness and left each of them with a silent blessing. It was long past sundown and snowing thickly when she looked about her for the last time and departed the longhouse, her mare's bridle hidden beneath her coat.

She blessed her son's wigwam as she rode past it,

regretting that Flower and Firewalker and Thunderhead would grieve for her, perhaps even Hope and Sings Low would shed a tear. And she would have loved the little ones that Hope and Flower would bear one day even as she loved Little Acorn, but she could not wait. Not when Diving Eagle himself waited for her. She smiled, for she could see him as clearly now as on that day when he left to hunt and had bade her good-bye. She saw him ahead of her in the moonlight, sometimes on the snowy path she followed, sometimes walking among the pines, but always turning, smiling, giving her that dear familiar wave of his and then beckoning, beckoning her on.

Oh, beloved, I am coming. . . .

She urged her mare to hasten through the deepening snow. She was grateful for it—the snow—for if any happened to notice she was gone too long, the tracks soon would be filled. She was grateful, too, for the bitterness of the night. Already her lungs ached, and she knew that her passing would be swift and with little pain, unlike his. . . .

She saw with tenderness that Diving Eagle was leading her to War Cloud's grave, and she wondered, had her elder son known she would be leaving soon and waited for her that they might make their Sky Journey together? She would know before long. After sheltering her mare under an overhang of rock, she returned to War Cloud's grave, a mound marked by the single pole that bore his totem. Gathering her bearskin close about her, Walks Alone lowered herself into the snow. It was deep and welcoming, but now she must put it and all else from her mind. Now she had the business of dying to do.

She positioned herself to face the east because it was there, in Kittanning, that her beloved had died, and because she wanted the morning sun to touch her face as it rose. She sat straight backed, crossing her legs and her arms, and musing that her own dying should not take long. Already her teeth were chattering, and it seemed colder than when she had left the village. It was good. She gazed about, hoping to see Diving Eagle again, but he was gone. Perhaps he had returned already to the Bright Land of Death to await her.

Walks Alone clutched tightly in one hand the only thing of his that she had, an arrowhead he had been making before he went off to die. All else had been given away at his funeral as was the custom. Now she pressed it to her lips, closed her eyes, and felt the snow, like moth wings, fluttering across her lids and lashes and gently patting her face and hair and lips. It tickled. She made to move, to lick it off, to rock back and forth a bit to warm herself for she was growing cold, but she caught herself. *Matta*. She was supposed to grow cold. She was there to die, and she would not stir her blood to warm it. She would sit there like a stone until she turned into one. And they would find her with a smile on her lips. . . .

As Firewalker and Hope came down off the highlands, their mounts carefully traversing the deep snow, Firewalker's thoughts galloped ahead of him. A child was coming. Was there no end to the joy that this woman might bring him? Imagining the telling of the news to his mother, he phrased and rephrased it, thinking of those ways in which it would give her the most surprise and pleasure. He chuckled. She would be pleased, his mother, for he had seen how she loved Little Acorn, his brother's son. And he had been heartened by her good spirits lately. He had not seen her eyes so bright for many winters. Not since Diving Eagle lived . . .

Firewalker caught his thoughts, preventing their drift backward toward his slain brother and father. *Matta*. Not tonight. It was never good to think of the dead, and especially not on this night when he had learned of the new life that was on its way. Seeing that the trail had widened, he slowed so that Hope could ride beside him. In silence, he extended his hand and took hers, gripping it hard as they neared that place where War Cloud lay in the ground. He was surprised to hear a sound, a familiar soft mournful cooing that he knew could not be there. Not in the dead of winter. He reined Nightwind and, holding his breath, listened. It came again.

"Do you hear it?" he whispered.

Hope looked at him, bewildered. "Hear what?"

Firewalker shook his head. Often only he himself saw and heard *memedhakemo*. With narrowed eyes, he gazed toward the grave mound and he felt his skin prickle. He sensed an unbelongingness there which he could not place. Something was strange.

"Firewalker, what is it?"

"Wait here," he ordered.

He rode slowly into the small clearing toward the object that did not belong there. It was snow covered and still, and it seemed, in the moonlight, to be a bush or boulder. He dismounted, his feet in their tall deerskin boots sinking into the deep snow. He approached, frowning, and bent low to get a better look, his warm breath clouding the icy air. He reached out a curious hand and touched the thing. He was surprised, for it was neither bush nor boulder. There was a familiar softness beneath the deep layer of snow. He knelt, stared, hissed in a breath. "My mother . . ."

Firewalker's hand shot out to brush the snow off that white pinched face, but then he hesitated. *Matta*. What right had he to interfere when this was her wish? No one had brought her here and sat her in the snow to die. It was she who had brought herself, and he had no doubt why. These many years she had mourned in secret for his father, and now they would be joined again. *Matta*, he could not interfere, much as he yearned to. He trembled with his yearning, and with his effort to remain still and not lift her up out of the snow and warm her and breathe life into her.

"Firewalker, what is it?" Hope called finally. She had been watching, puzzled and impatient, as he knelt and stared long and quietly at the object. When he did not answer, she gave Beauty her heels and trotted in. Quickly dismounting and kneeling beside him, she gasped to see it was Walks Alone sitting there, eyes closed and pale as death. She was shrouded in snow. Hope was horrified. What in the world was Firewalker's mother doing here, and how could such a terrible thing have happened?

"Is she alive?" Hope cried, pulling off her fur mittens. She was about to lay a hand to her mother-in-law's cheek when Firewalker's hand closed about her wrist.

"You must not." He rose and drew her up beside him.

Hope shot him a look of disbelief. "What do you mean, I must not?" Only then did a bell ring faintly. She asked, small voiced, "You mean she came here—to die?"

"*Kehella.*"

"But why?" Hope stared at him, appalled, her gaze going from his tortured face to that small, still white figure propped against the post. "Firewalker, we simply can't let this happen!"

"I do not want it to happen," Firewalker answered gruffly, "but my mother has chosen to die."

"She doesn't know of the baby!" Hope gripped his hands. "What if it would have made a difference?"

His heart lifted as he realized that she was right. It could well make the difference between his mother's wanting to live and wanting to die. And if after learning of the new babe, Walks Alone still wanted to make her Sky Journey, so be it. He would not interfere a second time. He knelt again and felt her face.

Hope, too, knelt, and put her hand to the *meteinuwak's* cheeks and forehead. The skin was still soft and held a trace of warmth. "It's not too late," she said. "With luck, we can save her, but we must work quickly!"

Walks Alone had been comfortable in her soft cocoon. When rough hands were suddenly laid on her and she was shaken and dragged from the warmth and light in which she was wrapped, she struggled weakly against it. She wanted only to sleep. She needed to sleep. There was an important reason for it, although she could not remember now what it was. She felt herself lifted up as an unpleasant sound beat against her ears. She shook her head. It was loud and insistent and she wanted only to get away from it, to return to her long slumber.

Firewalker patted her face, gently at first and then sharply and more urgently. "My mother, wake up. Mother!"

"We must warm her," Hope said. "Hold her against your body under your coat. I'll stand behind her."

Firewalker quickly removed his mother's snowy coat, bared his chest, and pressed Walks Alone against his warm skin. He then enfolded them both in the warmth of his own fur cloak. Hope did the same, embracing Walks Alone from behind. She was shocked to silence, thinking that the woman had gone there to die. What had happened to make her do such a thing? Was it grief over War Cloud? She lay a hand on her own belly and sighed, thinking of the child there and of how hard it would be to lose it, be it babe or grown.

"My mother . . ." Firewalker placed his mouth to his mother's face, breathing his hot breath onto her eyes and lips and nostrils. "Mother"—his voice broke—"come back to us." He was numb with the horror of the thing. Why had he not seen this coming—for it had not sprung full-blown into her mind. It was well planned. The bitter night, the heavily falling snow, himself and Hope gone perhaps for the entire night. But why? Was it the loss of War Cloud as well as that of Diving Eagle? He began to sway, the three of them moving from side to side in the cold, still, white night. By the Great Creator, he would not let her go. "Mother, you are to waken," he ordered her angrily.

Walks Alone was climbing through darkness to the top of a steep hill. She knew now that the sound pressing so insistently and annoyingly against her ears was a voice. The voice of Firewalker. And he was holding her close and rocking her . . . rocking . . . rocking. . . . But why? Or was it a dream? She had held and rocked him in such a way when he was a small thing. She had rocked all of her children. She smiled, for the thought gave her a hazy pleasure. She yearned to dream more of those younger happier days when her little ones were underfoot, always needing her for one thing or another—those days when Diving Eagle breathed. She remembered now; she had been on her way to meet Diving Eagle. . . .

"She is awakening," Firewalker muttered, feeling a first small glimmer of hope that she was not lost to them. "Mother, speak to us." She had been his strength and his guide for so long, he had not realized how small and fragile she was. His throat tightened. "Mother, you are going to wake up now. You are going to talk to us."

Walks Alone shook her head. Behind closed eyes, she saw clearly that Diving Eagle waited still in the distance. She whispered, "I—would go to my husband."

Her husband . . . Hope was wrenched. She could imagine Walks Alone's terrible emptiness, and meeting Firewalker's eyes, she saw the despair in them and the glitter of tears. "My mother"—she placed her lips to the *meteinuwak's* ear—"it is Hope. We need you. I need you."

Walks Alone did not reply. The way was long and dark and cold to the top of the hill where Diving Eagle stood, but she knew that it was warm there. He stood smiling in the light, beckoning her still.

"Mother, please." Hope felt a growing urgency. "Listen to me. You are going to have a new little one to teach and guide. Mother, do you hear? Firewalker and I are going to have a babe. Mother—?"

A babe? Walks Alone stayed her step on her steep

climb. She was almost too tired to continue, but she was also too cold and tired to return to those woods in the valley where she had begun her journey, but—a babe? A tiny new babe . . .

"Mother, Hope speaks the truth." Firewalker trembled, he felt such fear for her. They were losing her. They could not compete with Diving Eagle. He gave her shoulders a gentle shake and said firmly, "She needs you now, and our babe will need you. He will want his grandmother." Seeing a smile wisp brush those pale lips, Firewalker added, "Who else but you knows those little games and songs you taught us? Those of your mother's mother?"

"I—would stay," Walks Alone gasped finally. But she was so cold and her heart beat so slowly, she yearned for sleep once more. But now it frightened her.

"We must get her home," Firewalker said gruffly.

"It is too far," Hope cried. "We must make her walk. Keep her moving and pat her face. Oh, Mother, please, please open your eyes. Walk and talk. Please. . . ."

"I—will try. . . ."

Firewalker thought with a pang how much like Flower she looked suddenly. That frightened little Flower whom he had brought out of the burning woods so many years ago. His manitou had led them out—and had she not led him now to where Walks Alone had sat perishing? He saw suddenly and clearly that this would end well. He would allow himself to think no other way. He swiftly bundled Walks Alone's coat about her and slid his arm around her.

"Get on the other side of her, my wife. She is going to walk, and she is going to talk, and she is going to live." They began to walk around the small clearing, dragging Walks Alone between them. "Move your feet, my mother," Firewalker said sharply, "and stir your tongue." When Walks Alone emitted nothing but a sigh, he shook her. "Help me say our little song. 'I weave my blanket—' " He shook her again. "Complete the verse!" he growled. " 'I weave my blanket—' "

" 'Red . . .' " sighed Walks Alone.

" 'I weave my blanket—' " Another shake. "Say it!"

" 'Blue . . .' "

Firewalker met Hope's eyes over the *meteinuwak's* drooping head, and he smiled. " 'I weave my blanket all my—' "

" 'Life . . .' "

" 'Until I come—' "

A shuddering sigh. " 'To you. . . .' "

Around and around the clearing they trudged, wearing a track in the snow. The breathing of Walks Alone grew deeper and steadier, and she was moving her legs finally. Hope's jubilation mounted as Firewalker began the little song for the third time. He was singing it now: " 'I spread—' "

" 'My blanket red . . .' "

" 'I spread—' "

" 'My blanket blue, I spread my blankets for your bed,' " Walks Alone continued firmly. " 'We belong now to you.' "

Firewalker gazed down on her with shining eyes. "Well done, my mother. I think now we can go home."

Walks Alone nodded. "My mount is under the ledge. I tethered and blanketed her."

When Firewalker left to get the mare, Hope mused on how very thorough the *meteinuwak's* planning had been. She must have wanted very much to rejoin her mate, whereas Hope had never once realized that she even missed him.

She said gently, "I am glad you are here, my mother."

Walks Alone tried not to feel the emptiness where her heart was beating. "Tell me of the little one. When does it come?"

"The month of the roasting ear." At least, Hope suspected it would be early August or late July.

"It gladdens me."

"And us . . ."

Walks Alone did not hear her. She saw only vaguely that Firewalker was bringing her mare, for beyond him, in those white, silent, glittering woods, was a tall figure. Diving Eagle just stood there, not moving, and then he smiled at her and raised his hand. But he no longer beckoned her, he was bidding her good-bye. Holding her sorrow-joy close, Walks Alone watched and watched until she could not see him anymore. So. The time was not yet—but it was all right. She was needed still, and it would be nice to hold Little Acorn again and to have a new little one on the way. She looked one last time, but the woods were empty. She closed her eyes. Good night, beloved, and good-bye. . . .

Firewalker was leading the bright-eyed mare toward them, and Hope's heart soared at the sight of him. He was so tall and young and strong, and his long hair shone blue black in the moonlight. He was so beautiful, her breath caught and her heart fairly ached with her longing for him. He lifted Walks Alone onto the mare's back, and then in silence, held out his arms to Hope. In silence, she went into them, slipping under his great bearskin coat, sliding her arms around him waist, and pressing her body close to feel his strength and to warm herself at his flame.

Epilogue

Hope lay a hand on her belly and felt its brief almost-imperceptible hardening. Her first contraction had come during the night and now, seven hours later, they were still far apart. There was no need to do anything other than what she was doing, teaching her first class of the week. Moving about among her pupils gathered under the willows, youngsters under one tree and braves under another, Hope smiled down on them. And she smiled on Joshua, sleeping contentedly nearby. Who would have ever thought he'd fit in so well with these other dogs? And who would have ever thought so many of the Lenapes would want to learn and would stay with it so faithfully? Not she. She credited Firewalker, for they all wanted to be like him. Of course, he was her prize. He outshone them all, and after him, Stargazer, and then Flower. But Firewalker shone. In the ten months she had been teaching him, his marvelous memory had enabled him to fairly swallow three books whole.. He was reading and writing. . . .

As Hope's time had drawn near, Flower and Stargazer were doing most of the teaching. But it was Hope herself who told them what to do and who kept careful watch over the classes. Now as she finished examining the slates of the children, and was moving among the braves making corrections of their work, another twinge came. She stood quietly, feeling it, rejoicing in it, thinking, hoping that at this same time tomorrow her babe would be safely birthed.

She put the thought from her then, for this was class time. These folk needed her attention. Moving heavily to the small desk her father had made her when she first began teaching, Hope sat down. She made further corrections, answered questions, and gave the next day's assignments.

When everyone had left, she said quietly to Flower, "I think this is the day, my sister."

Flower stared at Hope's pink face and glowing eyes. "Your babe is coming?"

"Aye, it's on its way."

"I will tell my mother!"

"It's going to be hours yet."

"She will want to know. Oh, *n'tschu*, Firewalker is going to be so surprised when he returns—and so happy!"

Hope nodded and patted her belly. "I know. . . ." He and Glad Tidings were hunting, and she told herself it was all for the best—he would worry too much if he were here. But she thought wistfully of how Luke Springer had stayed by Maybeth's side comforting her the entire time. Nay, she'd not think it, nor was it fair to compare the two men, for Luke was not a Lenape brave.

"Is it time for Stargazer to fetch your father, do you think?" Flower asked.

Watching her nervously collecting books, papers, and quills and dropping them in her haste, Hope chuckled. She herself was feeling so extraordinarily peaceful, there seemed no urgency.

"Honey, calm down. I don't expect him to come and sit with me and hold my hand all day. This babe won't be here for quite a while, I promise you—but what I should do is tell him things have started."

"Stargazer has said he will go."

"I appreciate it." Hope was already writing a note.

"You can give him this, and tell him to leave it in the box by the door if my father isn't there. . . ."

Thomas Caldwell had not been there when Stargazer had arrived, but Hope was not concerned. It was early afternoon, and she was still in the first stages of labor. There was time aplenty. Having finally convinced Flower and Walks Alone that she was comfortable, she called Joshua, and then strolled lazily along the river path enjoying the sights and sounds of late July. Blossoms were everywhere—blue, white, gold, and lavender—and honeybees were vying with hummingbirds for their nectar. She spied raccoon tracks in the mud at the river's edge and saw corncobs scattered there, too. She laughed, seeing they had feasted. Hearing quacking, she gazed across the river and saw swimming in the shadows, safe from muskrats and hawks, a mother duck and eight babies. She melted. How sweet and downy and precious they were. And how beautiful this new land of hers was, and how glad she was to be here.

Her thoughts were filled with the memories of these past months she had lived among Firewalker's people. They had been the happiest days of her life. She even had had satisfaction from her own people in the form of gifts and apologies. It had amazed and touched her, but she had no desire to go back and live among them. Her own father understood and agreed that here in this small Lenape village on the Shenango, she had found everything that she ever wanted—a gentle husband and exciting lover, a wise mother, and a loving sister. Here she was a doctor and teacher, she had made many friends, both Indian and white, and she was about to become a mother. How could she be any more blessed and complete?

As she continued walking, enjoying, stopping from time to time to feel the building pressure, her mind overflowed with anticipation and excitement—but she was not without fears. She knew well the many things which could go wrong in birthing. But her father would take good care of her, and Walks Alone had helped deliver many babies. She gazed dreamily across the river as Firewalker came into her thoughts. As much as she'd denied it, she did want him with her. She wanted him in the worst kind of way, and she envied Maybeth with all her heart as she leaned against a willow and waited for a contraction to pass.

But the reality was that he was not here, he was not going to be here, and even if he were here, he certainly would not want to be with her. Birthing was woman's work. Hope knew she must accept all Lenape traditions as her own, even the ones she did not like. She drew a deep breath and, kneading her back, straightened. It seemed she was more tired than she had thought. It was time to lie down for a bit. She was walking back toward the village when she heard splashing behind her and heard Joshua's wild barking. She turned, her eyes widening as she saw Nightwind picking her way delicately through the shallows. On the mare's back was her husband.

Hope gave a glad cry. "Firewalker! Oh, Firewalker . . ." As she started toward him, another pain gripped her. Harder and longer and stronger than the others. She stopped, unable to walk, and clutched her abdomen. The severity of the contraction shocked her. It seemed she was entering the second stage of labor sooner than she thought she might. As she was pondering it, Firewalker came to her, lifted her into his arms, and kissed her, tenderly and hungrily. The hurt vanished in her joy, and as he carried her toward their wigwam, she stroked his face and hair. "I can't believe you're here. . . ."

"Where else would I be at such a time?"

"But how did you know?"

"I knew." He smiled, kissed her again. Someday he would tell her about *memedhakemo*. He saw his mother hurrying toward them with Flower.

"My son, we did not expect you. . . ." Walks Alone was glad he had come. It helped a woman to know her husband was somewhere close by instead of off in the woods when a babe was on its way. "My daughter"—she took Hope's hand—"we will take good care of you. Carry her to the hut, my son, and—"

"My mother, one moment." Firewalker said low to Hope, "Where would you be, my wife? In our own dwelling, or where the women give birth?"

"I—should do what the others do, of course." She had seen the small dreary hut where the women birthed, and while there was nothing wrong with it, it was not home. But she would never say so. She whispered, "I will go to the hut." She gasped as another pain gripped her. How quickly she was moving along, but instinct told her it was much too soon to bear down. She must try and hold back so as not to waste her energy and damage herself unnecessarily.

"My mother," Firewalker said with quiet authority, "my wife will have the child in our dwelling."

His words put a smile into Hope's heart. It spread to her lips when the *meteinuwak* replied, "It is good, my son. I approve."

Walks Alone sighed. She was seized with a sudden deep yearning for her slain son, War Cloud. She regretted deeply that she had not been able to prevent his jealousy of Firewalker, and for that, rightly or wrongly, she blamed herself. She would always blame herself. But these nine months she had been thinking and praying—if Firewalker's babe were a son as was War Cloud's, perhaps she would have a second chance to right the terrible wrong that had come between their fathers. Perhaps the two boys would not be merely cousins, they would be as brothers, and she herself would work to nurture the love between them. Little Acorn was a wonderful child. Already she saw the heart and the traits of Diving Eagle within the baby's body. And she knew well that any son born to Hope and Firewalker would be a loving one. *Kehella*, above all, she would have the two little ones love one another. But what was she doing, mulling such a thing at a time like this?

"Carry Hope to your wigwam," she directed Firewalker, "and then you may safely leave her in our hands." She turned to Flower. "Go and brew some tea, my daughter, the white baneberry leaves." To Hope, she said, "It will induce the milk flow, and I myself will brew other tea to quiet you."

As Firewalker carried her into their wigwam and gently lowered her onto the bed shelf, Hope felt her anxiety mounting. She did not want to be quiet. She wanted to be wide awake so she could push when the time came and have this mounting misery over with. Lord, she had had no idea. . . . She almost wept with relief when her eyes lit on her father's smiling face.

"Hello, girleen."

"Oh, Father, thank goodness . . ."

Tom bent, gave her a kiss, and shook Firewalker's hand. "Good to see you, son." He put down his bag. "Water broken yet, princess?" He lay a competent, businesslike hand on her belly.

"Nay." Hope's eyes flickered to Firewalker. She willed the sac not to break while he was there, for he would think she was dying for certain. She gave him a reassuring smile and reached up for his hand. "Thank you for being here, and for—for this." She looked about her at their wigwam that she had made into a home. "It's so much cozier. . . ."

Firewalker raised her hand to his lips, kissed it, and stroked back the damp black cloud of hair from her face. He kissed her forehead. "I love you."

"And I love you." She gripped his hand as a spasm caught her. She managed a bright smile. "You'll—want to go, I think." She stared as he shook his head. He lowered himself to the mat beside her bed shelf.

"I will not leave you," Firewalker said. When her beautiful eyes widened, glittering with a sudden sheen of tears, his heart nearly broke. She was so brave, his woman, and although he feared greatly for her, he would try to be at least as brave. He lay a protective hand on her abdomen. "I would be here to welcome our child when it comes."

When Walks Alone returned with the tea, she found a sight she had never witnessed in all of her days: a Lenape warrior tenderly bathing the face of his birthing woman and whispering words of comfort to her. Her hair fairly stood on end with the thrill that shot through her. Many changes would be taking place from now on, she mused, as she handed Hope's tea to her son.

"Have her drink," she ordered. "It will soothe her."

When Firewalker held the cup to Hope's lips, she gulped it down, more than ready to be soothed, and to sleep even, blissfully drugged, between contractions. Even the worst of the pain seemed blunted by the wondrous tea of Walks Alone.

Yet when the babe came, many hours later, she was fully alert and in a state of bliss to see the tiny, howling bundle being passed from her own proud father to the loving arms of Walks Alone and thence to the eager hands of her husband. For long moments, Firewalker held the child, gazing at it proudly, his eyes glowing, and then, smiling, he put it into Hope's arms.

"Meet your mother, my son."

Hope took her babe and, snuggling him close, touched her lips to the dark fuzz on his beautiful little round duckling head. Looking on the three whose eyes held such love for her, she murmured, "I'm going to cry. I'm sorry, I'm going to cry. It's just that—I'm so happy. . . ."

She wept softly and easily in sweet release, her tears dropping onto her son's little head as she kissed each of his tiny fingers. She whispered, "He's beautiful—and perfect. How perfect . . ."

"Like his mother." Firewalker still sat on the floor beside the bed, his arm across the two of them. He looked on them wonderingly, hardly daring to belive his good fortune.

Hope laughed through her tears. "*Matta.* Like his wonderful father . . ."

She saw that they had been left alone, the three of them, and she saw that those golden eyes that had looked on her with such leashed savagery not all that long ago now had tears in them. She smiled up at him. She had wondered earlier, how could she be more complete and more blessed? Now she knew.

Author's Note

At the time of the Revolutionary War, the Lenapes and the Wyandots occupied a large territory west of the Allegheny River and north of Pittsburgh. The Pennsylvania Legislature promised army volunteers donations of this land after the war. The Indians were not a party to the Treaty of Fort Stanwix in 1784 at which their title to the land was extinguished.

I have used the name Mengwe for the Iroquois as the Lenapes most commonly called them that. And since accounts vary as to when the last Lenapes left the Donation Lands, I have chosen to keep them in my own Shenango Valley for this tale.

If BELOVED INTRUDER has touched your heart as it did mine as I wrote it, please drop me a line at PO Box 905, Sharon, PA, 16146. Every letter helps me to do better.

JOAN VAN NUYS

Jamison pulled a
U.S. Army pen fr
kept his face impassive as he thought of questions that begged to be answered.

Why'd you leave me, Michele? What happened that made you run away?

Shoving them aside, he asked, "Did you see anything out of place, Miss Logan, before you noticed the body?"

"Miss Logan?" She narrowed her gaze. Evidently she didn't understand his decision to forgo first names.

No matter how alluring Michele might be, Jamison needed to remain professional but aloof and firmly grounded in the present.

"The room was dark...the smell of blood. I—I saw Yolanda," she said.

"What happened next?"

"Someone shoved me into the couch."

Jamison swallowed, knowing all too well what the killer could have done to Michele. "Can...can you describe the person?"

She shook her head. "He struck me from behind. I never saw him, *Agent Steele*."

Jamison almost smiled at her attempt to play hardball. Evidently she didn't realize he'd built a wall around his heart and added armor for protection.

COMMANDING JUSTICE

USA TODAY BESTSELLING AUTHOR

DEBBY GIUSTI

2 Thrilling Stories

The Colonel's Daughter and *The General's Secretary*

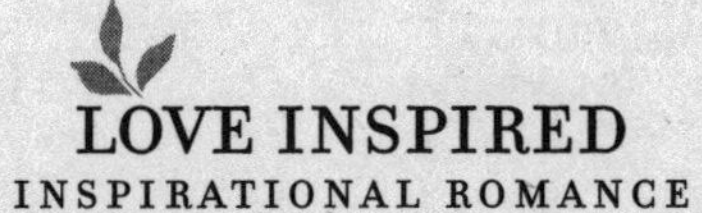

Recycling programs for this product may not exist in your area.

ISBN-13: 978-1-335-43062-5

Commanding Justice

The Colonel's Daughter
First published in 2012. This edition published in 2022.

The General's Secretary
First published in 2013. This edition published in 2022.

For questions and comments about the quality of this book, please contact us at CustomerService@Harlequin.com.

Love Inspired
22 Adelaide St. West, 41st Floor
Toronto, Ontario M5H 4E3, Canada
www.LoveInspired.com

Printed in U.S.A.

CONTENTS

Debby Giusti is an award-winning Christian author who met and married her military husband at Fort Knox, Kentucky. Together they traveled the world, raised three wonderful children and have now settled in Atlanta, Georgia, where Debby spins tales of mystery and suspense that touch the heart and soul. Visit Debby online at debbygiusti.com, blog with her at seekerville.blogspot.com and craftieladiesofromance.blogspot.com, and email her at Debby@DebbyGiusti.com.

Books by Debby Giusti

Love Inspired Suspense

Her Forgotten Amish Past
Dangerous Amish Inheritance
Amish Christmas Search
Hidden Amish Secrets
Smugglers in Amish Country

Amish Witness Protection

Amish Safe House

Amish Protectors

Amish Refuge
Undercover Amish
Amish Rescue
Amish Christmas Secrets

Visit the Author Profile page
at LoveInspired.com for more titles.

THE COLONEL'S DAUGHTER

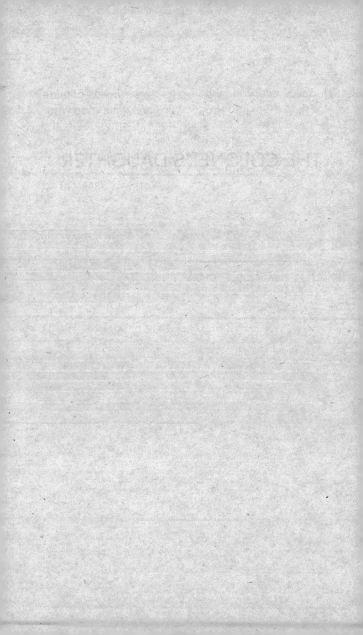

Therefore everyone who hears these words of mine and puts them into practice is like a wise man who built his house on the rock. The rain came down, the streams rose, and the winds blew and beat against that house; yet it did not fall, because it had its foundation on the rock.

—*Matthew* 7:24–25

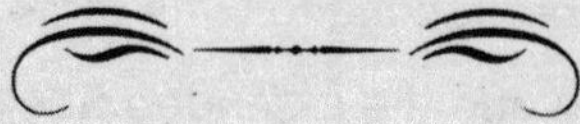

This book is dedicated to
the deployed members of our Armed Forces
and to the families who await their return.

To my husband, who has always been my hero.

To Liz, Joe, Mary, Eric, Katie, Anna, Robert,
William and John Anthony.

To the parishioners at Holy Trinity
who encourage me to write more stories.

To the Seekers and the extended Seekerville family
for your friendship and support.

To Anna Adams with gratitude
for our weekly meetings at Panera's.

To Emily Rodmell, my editor,
and Deidre Knight, my agent.

ONE

Angry storm clouds turned the evening sky over Fort Rickman, Georgia, as dark as the mood within the car. Michele Logan pulled her eyes from the road and glanced at her mother, sitting next to her in the passenger seat.

Roberta Logan, usually the poised colonel's wife, toyed with the collar of her blouse and gave voice to a subject that had weighed on Michele's heart for the past two years. "Despite what you think, dear, you haven't gotten over your brother's death."

Ever since she and her mother had left her parents' quarters en route to the potluck dinner, Roberta had insisted on talking about the accident that had claimed Lance's life. The topic added to Michele's anxiety, especially with the inclement August weather and the darkening night.

"Aren't you the one who insists life goes on, Mother?"

"And it does, dear, but that doesn't mean you've worked through your grief." Roberta turned her gaze toward the encroaching storm. "As I've told you before, you weren't to blame."

True enough that Michele wasn't to blame for the

crashed army helicopter, yet she still felt responsible for her brother's death. If she had visited that weekend, he never would have been on board the fateful flight.

"I don't like the looks of those clouds." Distracted by the storm, Roberta worried her fingers. "Maybe Yolanda should have canceled the potluck."

"And disappoint the wives in Dad's brigade? You said it's important for the women to come together socially when the men were deployed."

"But the weatherman mentioned another line of storms moving into Georgia." Her mother's voice grew increasingly concerned. "You should have stayed in Atlanta until the bad weather passed, dear."

"I told you I want to help with preparations for the brigade's return to Fort Rickman."

"Which won't be for another week. The real reason you came home early is to visit the cemetery tomorrow. It's been two years. You don't need to spend each anniversary crying at Lance's grave site."

"I'm not crying."

"But you will be tomorrow." Roberta shifted in the seat and sighed. "You never should have left post in the first place."

Although she wouldn't admit it, Michele sometimes wondered if moving to Atlanta ten months ago had been a mistake. She hadn't seen Jamison Steele in all that time, but she'd thought about him far too often. They had dated for almost a year, and she had believed he was everything she'd wanted in a guy. When an investigation turned deadly on post, she realized her mistake.

As if sensing her struggle, Roberta gazed knowingly at her daughter. "Your father and I would love to have you move back, dear. You could work from home."

"I…I can't."

Roberta rubbed her hand over Michele's shoulder. "Just think about it."

Moving back wasn't an option. Michele had made a new life for herself. One that didn't involve the military. She was happy in Atlanta, or so she kept telling herself.

Droplets of rain spattered against the windshield as Michele turned into the Buckner Housing Area. She activated the wipers and flipped the lights to high beam, exposing broken twigs and leaves that had fallen in the last downpour.

The street was long and narrow and led to a two-story home at the dead end of a cul-de-sac surrounded by a thick forest of hardwoods and tall pines. Michele pulled to the curb in front of the dark quarters.

Mrs. Logan eyed the house completely devoid of light. "Yolanda must have lost power in the storm." Thunder rumbled overhead, and fat raindrops pummeled the car.

"I'll get the casserole, Mother. You make a run for the door." Michele grabbed the ceramic dish from the backseat and raced behind her mother to the covered porch.

Roberta tapped twice with the brass knocker. When no one answered, she glanced questioningly at Michele and then pushed the door open.

"Yolanda, it's Roberta and Michele. We're early, but we wanted to help before the others arrive." Roberta stepped inside and motioned Michele to follow. A bolt of lightning sizzled across the sky. A second later, thunder shook the house.

An earthy smell wafted past Michele. She closed the door and looked left into the dining area. Flames from two large candles flickered over the linen tablecloth, highlighting the plates and silverware stacked on the sideboard.

"Yolanda, where are you?" Roberta walked toward the kitchen, her heels clipping over the hardwood floor.

Michele placed the casserole on the dining table before she returned to the foyer. At the opposite end of the hallway, her mother stopped short, hands on her hips.

"Yolanda?"

Roberta's raised voice and insistent call twisted more than a ripple of concern along Michele's spine. A sense of foreboding flooded over her as intense as any she had felt for her father in the twelve months of his deployment. With the silent quarters closing in around her, she was now equally worried about Yolanda.

A floorboard creaked in the living room. Michele turned toward the sound. The settling house, the wind howling down the chimney…or was someone there?

She crossed the hallway, drawn by a need to discover not only the source of the noise but also the mineral smell that increased in intensity the closer she got to the living room. Her neck tingled, but she ignored the warning and stepped toward the oversized couch and love seat that filled the center of the living area.

A small table and chair sat nestled in an alcove behind the love seat. Michele tried to make out the dark outline on the pale carpet.

"Yolanda?" From the kitchen, Roberta called one more time. Her voice was filled with question and a tremble that signified she, too, sensed something was wrong.

Michele's pulse quickened as her eyes adjusted to

the darkness. Newspapers lay scattered around an overturned lamp.

Her stomach tightened.

A roar filled her ears. She stepped around the couch and saw the woman lying in a pool of blood.

"No!" Michele's hand flew to her throat in the exact spot where Yolanda's neck had been cut.

A rustle sounded behind her. Before she could turn, a violent force lunged into her. She crashed against the back of the couch. Her ribs took the blow. Pain exploded along her side and mixed with air that whooshed from her lungs. She gasped, and for an instant saw only darkness.

Retreating footsteps sounded in the hallway.

Her mother screamed.

Michele fisted her hands and willed herself to remain conscious. A door slammed shut in the rear of the house.

Still gasping for air, she struggled to her feet and stumbled out of the living area, her only thought to find her mother and make sure she was alive.

Lightning turned the darkness bright for one terrifying second. Roberta lay slumped against the wall.

Dropping to her knees, Michele touched her mother's shoulder. "Mama?"

Roberta moaned. Her eyes blinked open.

Relief rushed over Michele along with a wave of nausea. She hung her head to stave off the passing sickness and dug in her pocket for her cell phone.

A face flashed through her mind. Without weighing the consequences, she punched Speed Dial for a number she should have deleted ten months ago.

He answered on the second ring.

"Criminal Investigation Division, Fort Rickman, Georgia. This is Special Agent Jamison Steele."

The memory of his warm embrace and tender kisses washed over her. For one sweet, illogical second, she felt safe.

"Hello?" He waited for a response.

"Jamison—"

A sharp intake of air. "Michele?"

"I need help." Rubbing her free hand over her forehead, she tried to focus. "I'm at Quarters 122. In the Buckner Housing Area. Contact the military police."

"What happened?"

"One of the wives... Her husband's in Afghanistan. He's in my father's brigade. She was hosting a potluck for the brigade wives. Someone broke in—"

Jamison issued a series of commands to a person in his office. "I'm on the way, Michele. The military police are being notified. I'll be there in three minutes. Are you hurt?"

"I...I'm okay. It's Yolanda Hughes."

Michele swallowed down the lump that filled her throat. "Yolanda's dead."

Heart in his throat, Jamison pulled to the curb and hit the ground running, weapon in one hand, Maglite in the other.

Stay calm. Ignoring the internal advice, his gut tightened when he stepped into the house and spied Michele on the floor with her arm around her mother.

For an instant, he was once again the man who loved Michele more than anything. Swallowing hard, Jamison shoved aside any lingering hope for a future together, a future that had died when she walked out of his life.

Raw fear flashed from her blue eyes and cut through his resolve to remain neutral. Ten months ago, her smile had lit up his world. Today Michele's face was as pale as death and furrowed with pain.

Head buried in her daughter's shoulder, Mrs. Logan cried softly. Michele nudged her gently. "Jamison's here, Mama."

The older woman glanced up, her eyes red and swollen. "Oh, Jamison. Yolanda… A man raced past me and out the back door. I…I tried to stop him."

"Did he hurt you?" His gaze fell on Michele. Tousled brown hair hung around her oval face.

"We're both a little bruised. Nothing serious. But Yolanda—" Unable to continue, Michele raised a trembling hand and pointed to the living area.

"Stay where you are," he cautioned, struggling to remain objective. "The ambulance is on its way."

A rank, coppery smell greeted Jamison as he entered the living room. He aimed his light over the blood that had soaked into the thick carpet, blackening the fibers.

His gut twisted at the tragic sight.

The victim was an African-American female. Probably mid- to late-thirties. Shoulder-length brown hair. Dark eyes wide open. The look of terror etched on her face.

A deep laceration had severed her carotid artery. Massive blood loss pooled under her upper torso.

Kneeling beside the woman, he felt for a pulse, yet knew full well life had been heinously snatched from Yolanda Hughes. Her wrist was supple and still warm. No rigor mortis. Not yet.

He tried the light switch, then played the Maglite over the living room. His gaze settled ever so briefly on the family photograph above the mantel. The deceased was smiling warmly, her hands on the shoulders of a man in uniform. Major's rank on his epaulets. Two children. A boy and girl.

The dread of finding the children dead roared through Jamison. He strode back to the hallway. "Mrs. Hughes had kids?"

Michele held up her hand, palm out. "They're at the Graysons'. Lieutenant Colonel Grayson is my father's executive officer. The two families are close. The Grayson kids invited Benjamin and Natalie to stay with them tonight."

Breathing out a sigh of relief, Jamison moved quickly into the kitchen and edged open the back door. He stepped outside and studied the darkness, knowing the killer was long gone.

Retracing his steps, Jamison headed toward the flickering candlelight and checked the dining area before he scurried up the stairs to the second floor. Sirens screamed in the distance.

Finding nothing out of place and no one upstairs, he returned to the main landing and ensured that Michele and her mother were all right before he opened the front door and stepped onto the porch. Three military police cars screeched to the curb. An ambulance followed close behind. Across the street, neighbors came out of their homes and stared with worried expressions at the activity.

Jamison directed the military police. "The victim's in the living room, first floor. Two children are spending the night with friends. Husband is deployed. Colonel Logan's wife and daughter are in the hallway and need medical attention. The electricity is down. Get some temporary lighting in there ASAP."

A military policeman began to cordon off the area with crime scene tape.

"Someone go door to door," Jamison ordered. "Question the neighbors. See if anyone saw anything suspicious."

"Roger that, sir." A stocky military policeman motioned for another MP to join him, and the twosome hustled to a nearby set of quarters.

The medics raced up the front steps. Jamison followed them inside. One man moved into the living area. The other two knelt beside Mrs. Logan and Michele.

Assured they were being adequately cared for, Jamison returned to the porch to oversee the bevy of activity. A young military policeman approached him.

"Sir, the power line to the house appears to have been severed. The on-post maintenance company has been notified. They're sending someone to fix the line."

"Dust for prints first."

"Roger that, sir."

"How long until he arrives?"

"They said he'd be here shortly."

"Did they give you an exact time?"

"No, sir."

A car pulled into the driveway. CID special agent Dawson Timmons—a tall blond with a thick neck—climbed onto the sidewalk. Favoring his right leg, he approached Jamison, who quickly filled him in.

"What do you need me to do?" Dawson asked.

"Take care of the crime scene. I want to question Mrs. Logan and her daughter and get them out of here as soon as possible. The victim was hosting a potluck for the brigade wives. The guests should be arriving soon. Talk to them individually to see if they have information pertinent to the case."

"How many ladies are we expecting?"

"Eighteen plates were stacked on a table in the dining room."

Dawson glanced at the unit insignia plaque on the front door. "First Brigade, Fifth Infantry Division should be home next week."

Jamison nodded. "Contact Lieutenant Colonel Grayson, the unit's executive officer, in Afghanistan. Tell him I need to talk to Colonel Logan. Once the other wives arrive, word about the murder will get out. I don't want Major Hughes to learn what happened to his wife via Twitter or Facebook."

As Dawson placed the call, Jamison reentered the house. Huge battery-operated floodlights illuminated the earlier darkened interior. The medics had moved Mrs. Logan and Michele to the kitchen, where the women sat at the small breakfast table.

Mrs. Logan sported a bandage on her forehead and stared up at one of the EMTs. "If my blood pressure is okay after all that, young man, I'm not going to the hospital. But I appreciate your advice and the excellent care you've provided tonight."

"I still think you and Miss Logan should have a doctor check you, ma'am."

Michele stood and stepped toward Jamison, her voice low when she spoke. "Mother insists she's okay, although I'd feel better if a doctor looked her over."

"Are you planning to take your own advice?" Frustrated by Michele's attempt to slip back into their old familiarity, Jamison realized his tone was sharp.

She stared at him for a long moment, then turned and walked back to her seat. "If Mother has any problems, we'll reconsider her decision."

She was closing herself off from him. Again. He shouldn't be surprised. Being with Michele drove home the point Jamison had known for months. The colonel's daughter wasn't for him. She had left him high and dry without as much as a so long, see you later. He thought he had healed, but tonight the memory festered like an open wound.

"Jamison, any clue who the murderer might be?" Mrs. Logan asked once the medics had cleared the room. Her face was blotched, but she seemed more in control than she had been earlier.

"No, ma'am. But I ordered a post lockdown on the way over here. No one goes on or off Fort Rickman until the military police search the garrison. Right now they're crisscrossing the post in an attempt to find the perpetrator."

"Curtis Hughes needs to be told."

"We're placing a call to your husband so he can personally notify Major Hughes."

Mrs. Logan nodded her approval. "I want to talk to Stanley after you do."

"Yes, ma'am."

Michele's cheeks had more color than when he'd first spotted her in the hallway, but her jaw was tight and her eyes guarded.

He pulled a small notebook and a U.S. government pen from his coat pocket and kept his face impassive as he thought of questions that begged to be answered. *Why'd you leave me, Michele? What happened that made you run away?*

Shoving them aside, he asked instead, "Did you see anything out of place, Miss Logan, before you noticed the body?"

"Miss Logan?" She narrowed her gaze and squared her shoulders in an attempt to cover the flash of confusion that clouded her face. Evidently, she didn't understand his decision to forgo first names.

No matter how alluring Michele might be, Jamison refused to expose his own inner conflict. He needed to remain professional and aloof, firmly grounded in the present.

Michele tugged at a wayward strand of hair and glanced down as if struggling to find the right words to express what had happened.

"I…I heard a noise and decided to investigate." She pulled in a deep breath. "A lamp…the room was dark… the smell of blood. Wh…when I stepped closer, I…I saw Yolanda."

"What happened next?"

"Someone shoved me into the couch."

Jamison tensed. His mouth went dry. He swallowed, knowing all too well what the killer could have done to Michele. "Can you describe the person?"

She shook her head. "He struck from behind. I never saw him."

Jamison turned to Mrs. Logan. "Did you see him, ma'am?"

"I'm afraid not. My eyes hadn't adjusted to the darkness, and everything happened so fast."

"Before entering the quarters, did either of you notice anyone outside? Or anything that seemed out of the ordinary?"

"Mother and I were talking as we drove up. I'm afraid we weren't being observant, *Agent* Steele."

Jamison almost smiled at her attempt to play hardball. Evidently, she didn't realize he'd built a wall around his heart and added armor for protection. Michele wouldn't hurt him again. He'd learned his lesson and had the scars to prove it.

"You're still working for that insurance company?" he asked.

"That's right. Patriotic Life."

"Doing risk management?"

"And working from home, if that's your next question." She crossed her legs and braced her spine, confrontation evident as she shifted positions.

The pulse in his neck throbbed. "Do you have a list of tonight's guests?"

"Mother does on her computer. I can print a copy for you."

"How many people, other than the eighteen women who were invited, may have known about the potluck?"

Michele glanced at her mother for help. "I'm not sure."

"Seventeen women and one man," Mrs. Logan corrected Jamison. "Major Shirley Yates is in charge of logistics for the brigade. Her husband, Greg, usually attends the events when we get together."

"Has he been to Mrs. Hughes's home previously?" Jamison asked.

Mrs. Logan nodded. "Yes, of course. Yolanda entertains often."

"Mr. Yates lives on post?"

"In Freemont. Greg has a son from a previous marriage, but I believe he's in college. No telling who else knew about the potluck. Yolanda probably shared the information with some of her neighbors. She scrapbooks with a group of women in her housing area. Those wives might have known."

"Had she mentioned anyone acting strangely in the neighborhood? Or had she reconnected with anyone from her past recently?"

"Not that I'm aware of."

"Is she on Facebook or Twitter?"

"Yolanda emailed her husband and kept up with the brigade news on our wives' loop. She never mentioned being on any social media sites."

"How about her marriage?" Jamison glanced at both women. "Were there problems?"

Michele forced a sad smile. "They seemed to be the perfect couple. Devoted to each other and to their children."

"Any other men in her life? An old friend?"

Mrs. Logan held up her hand. "You can stop that line of questioning, Jamison. Yolanda was a devoted wife. She adored her husband. I'll vouch for their love and their marriage."

"What about Greg Yates, the major's husband? Were he and Mrs. Hughes friendly?"

"Friends but that's all."

"And his marriage?"

Mrs. Logan dropped her gaze and thought for a moment before she spoke. "Deployments are tough, Jamison. There's been some talk, but only that."

"Meaning?"

"Meaning Shirley and Greg plan to separate once she returns home with the unit."

"How's Mr. Yates handling the situation?"

"In my opinion, he's in denial."

"And Major Yates?"

"Stanley's said she seems withdrawn."

Jamison made note of the information. "Major Yates asked for the separation?"

"Evidently Shirley told Greg she was leaving him. He suggested they go through a period of separation first." Mrs. Logan pursed her lips momentarily. "A few wives thought Shirley was interested in someone else."

"Someone in the brigade?"

"I don't know."

"Could she be involved with Major Hughes?"

Mrs. Logan's eyes widened in protest. "Absolutely not."

"Is there anything about Major Hughes that seems questionable, ma'am? As far as you know, does he get along with the other officers in the brigade? Is there anyone who might hold a grudge against him?"

"My husband has always given Curtis high praise. He went to Iraq with Stanley, when my husband commanded his battalion some years ago. Stanley was thrilled when Curtis was assigned to the First of the Fifth shortly before the brigade deployed to Afghanistan."

Jamison turned to Michele. "You've known Major and Mrs. Hughes since he worked for your father in the battalion?"

She nodded. "I used to babysit their kids. But if you think either Yolanda or her husband were involved in something that led to her death, you're wrong."

"I don't suspect anything at this point." Although he wanted to question Greg Yates. A spurned husband might retaliate against the man he perceived had stolen his wife. Even though Mrs. Logan vouched for Major Hughes's fidelity, things happened, especially during a deployment.

Jamison closed his notebook and tucked it into his sports coat pocket. "What about the children, ma'am? Does Major Hughes have family in the area?"

"No one close by. Yolanda and Curtis are both from Missouri. I'm sure Benjamin and Natalie can stay at Erica Grayson's house until relatives arrive."

Dawson entered the kitchen. He handed the phone to Jamison. "Lieutenant Colonel Grayson is on the line."

Jamison quickly explained the reason he had phoned. Grayson relayed the information to the commander. Colonel Logan knew Jamison from when he and Michele had dated, but there would be nothing personal about tonight's call.

The commander's voice was husky with emotion when he came on the line. "Was Roberta hurt? What about Michele?"

"They're okay, sir." As much as he hated giving Colonel Logan bad news, Jamison had to be forthright. Being deployed half a world away meant the colonel couldn't protect his wife and daughter. Jamison could relate. Once upon a time, he had wanted to be the man keeping Michele safe.

"The perpetrator was in the house when Mrs. Logan and Michele arrived on the scene. Both women were shoved to the floor, sir. The medics checked them out. At this point, I don't believe they're going to need further medical care."

"Thank God."

"My sentiments exactly, sir."

"How did it happen, Agent Steele? Aren't the military police patrolling the housing areas? I've got a brigade of soldiers over here fighting to ensure that our world remains safe. Their families need to be protected, yet a killer gets on post and attacks my S-3's wife."

"Sir, we'll use every resource available to apprehend the perpetrator and bring him to justice."

"I want more than that. I want your assurance no one else will be injured."

"That's our goal, sir."

The colonel let out a sigh. "I know you're not to blame, but it's hard to believe something like this could have occurred."

Jamison filled him in on the few remaining details he knew, although he didn't mention his concern about Greg Yates and his wife's rumored infidelity. That could wait until the CID had more information.

"How's Roberta taking it?" the colonel asked.

"As well as can be expected, sir. She wants to speak to you." Jamison glanced at Michele before handing the phone to Mrs. Logan.

"I'm fine, Stanley," she said immediately.

Jamison left the kitchen. Major Bret Hansen, the medical examiner, had arrived and was examining the body. The major looked up as Jamison entered the living room.

"Appears the perp used neuromuscular incapacitation to subdue her," Hansen said.

"A stun gun?"

"More than likely."

"That explains how he got in. Mrs. Hughes probably thought one of the wives had arrived early when she opened the door. The killer incapacitated her with the stun gun and was able to walk in without confrontation."

"I'll do the autopsy in the morning and let you know the results."

"Sounds good, sir."

Returning to the kitchen, Jamison caught Mrs. Logan's eye. She raised her hand as if ready to finish her conversation.

"Erica should be able to keep the children until Yolanda's sister arrives. Have Curtis call me when he feels like talking." Mrs. Logan nodded. "I love you, too, dear."

Handing the phone to Michele, she said, "Your father wants to speak to you."

Taking the cell from her mother, Michele walked to the corner of the kitchen to talk privately with her father.

Jamison helped Mrs. Logan to her feet.

"I'm sure Stan's telling our daughter to take me home and keep me there. The man has enough to do without being concerned about my safety."

"He loves you, ma'am."

She nodded. "I'm lucky, Jamison. God gave me a wonderful husband and a good daughter, although she has an independent streak that worries me at times."

"She knows what she wants."

Mrs. Logan cocked her head and stared up at Jamison. "I'm not so sure about that."

Hearing noise outside, Jamison headed to the front of the house. Opening the door, he saw three women standing on the sidewalk, their faces twisted in disbelief.

"Excuse me, Jamison. Those are some of the brigade wives." Mrs. Logan shoved past him onto the porch.

Pulling up the crime scene tape, she hurried toward the women.

Knowing her determination and desire to help the others, Jamison let her go. Any questions he still needed answered could wait.

Michele stepped onto the porch and handed him the phone. Her blue eyes had lost their brilliance, but they still had the power to draw him in just as they had done the first night they'd met at the club on post.

He turned from her, remembering the bitter taste of betrayal when Michele had left without explaining why. Usually he wasn't prone to hold a grudge, but in this case, he couldn't get past the sting of rejection. Maybe if she had told him what he had done wrong, Jamison might have been able to move on.

A beige van bearing the post maintenance company's logo pulled into the cul-de-sac. A tall, lanky fellow, mid-forties, eased to the pavement, toting a toolbox and a flashlight. "Someone called in an emergency request?"

One of the military policemen motioned for him to follow. "Right this way."

The tall guy smiled at Jamison. "Sir." His gaze took in Michele. "Evening, ma'am."

She nodded and, once again, wrapped her arms across her chest.

Extricating Mrs. Logan from the other brigade wives took longer than Jamison had expected. The women huddled around her like chicks surrounding a mother hen. She tried to assuage their fears, while Jamison cautioned them to remain vigilant until the killer was apprehended.

Michele knew most of the women and seemed as

much a part of the group as her mother. She had the makings of a good army wife. Not that she seemed interested in marrying into the military. Her hasty departure from Fort Rickman had been ample proof she wanted nothing to do with Jamison or the army.

When the questioning had been completed and all the wives had left the area, Jamison drove Michele and her mother back to their home. A military policeman followed in Jamison's car.

"We're increasing patrols, especially in the housing areas, Mrs. Logan. I don't want to alarm you, but as I told the other women, you need to be careful and cautious."

"We will be, Jamison."

"Did you hear from Greg Yates? I didn't see him tonight."

Mrs. Logan checked her phone. "He didn't call. Maybe the weather kept him away."

Maybe. Or maybe not.

After saying good-night, Mrs. Logan hurried inside, leaving Michele to linger on the front steps. Gazing down at the cement, she chewed her lower lip.

Finally, she glanced up. "Thanks for responding to my call for help."

Jamison gave her a halfhearted smile that revealed nothing. "It's my job."

"Right." She looked away but not fast enough to hide the frown that tightened her brow.

He glanced at the street where the military policeman had parked his car. Memories of other times they had said good-night on this very same porch flashed through his mind.

Pushing aside the thoughts, Jamison squared his

shoulders. “You had best get inside. Be sure to lock the door behind you.”

She let out a frustrated breath. “Can’t we, at least, go back to first names?”

“All right.” He waited to see if she had anything else to say.

Michele tapped her hand against the wrought-iron banister and stared into the darkness, the silence heavy between them.

Finally, she broke the standoff. “How many military policemen will be in the area, Jamison?”

Her need for reassurance touched a chord in his heart. “Enough to keep you safe.”

“I guess—” She raised her chin and regarded him with questioning eyes. “That’s all we have to discuss.”

“Michele—”

Before he could say anything else, she opened the front door. “Good night, Jamison.”

The door closed, and the lock clicked into place.

If only we could go back in time. The thought came unbidden. Jamison slammed his fist into the palm of his other hand to dispel the temptation.

He was finished with Michele. End of story. Going back would only cause more pain.

Jamison double-timed back to his car, slid behind the wheel and pulled onto the roadway. He needed to distance himself from the colonel’s daughter.

He had been hurt once.

Michele would never break his heart again.

TWO

Post security was imperative when a killer was on the loose. Jamison drove around Fort Rickman to ensure that the roadblocks were in place and the gates were well guarded. Heading back to his office, he realized, too late, that he had passed the turnoff to the CID headquarters and ended up in the area where the ranking officers lived.

The large brick quarters, built in the 1930s and '40s, circled a parade field where units marched and bands played in better times. Tonight the post was locked down and on high alert.

His headlights cut through the foggy darkness, revealing the two-lane street littered with fallen leaves and branches stripped from the trees during the earlier storms. Had the murderer chosen tonight because of the adverse weather conditions, or had something else triggered his assault?

At the onset of any investigation, Jamison felt like a man in a rowboat, paddling through uncharted waters in the middle of a black night, never knowing where his journey would end. The fog lifted momentarily, revealing the Logans' quarters.

Jamison almost smiled. He didn't need to check on Michele. Military police were patrolling the colonel's area. They were trained and competent, but for some reason, his radar had signaled the need to ensure that Michele was safe.

The front porch light was on and mixed with the glow from a lamp in the living room. Upstairs, a single bulb shone through a bathroom window. Slowing his speed, he studied the area around the house, looking for anything that could signal danger for the women inside. Extending his search, he checked the entire block before he returned to her street.

A military police patrol car approached from the opposite direction. Not wanting to explain why he was in the area, Jamison turned at the next intersection and headed back to CID headquarters.

Along the way, he tried to convince himself that he would have done the same thing no matter who had been a witness in the investigation. Deep down, he knew the truth. Michele had been the only reason for his late-night detour.

Once behind his desk, Jamison placed a call to the CID in Afghanistan and filled them in on what had happened at Fort Rickman. A special agent by the name of Warner took the information and assured Jamison he'd see what he could uncover about Major Shirley Yates. If she had previously had a romantic relationship or was currently having an affair, Warner would find out who was involved and contact Jamison with the information. He would also check out Major Hughes to ensure that the murder wasn't an act of revenge against the victim's husband.

For the rest of the night, Jamison pored over the

crime scene photos and information collected so far. By morning, his shoulders ached. He scooted his chair back and picked up a photo taken of the Hughes' kitchen and the door through which the killer had escaped.

In the corner of the same picture, the photographer had also captured Michele, standing by the table, arms wrapped across her chest. The look on her face provided a clear image of the turmoil she must have been experiencing internally. The shock of finding a murder victim was hard on anyone, especially so for a woman who ran from conflict. Michele might consider herself strong and determined, but Jamison knew better.

They had met a little over a year after the helicopter crash that had taken her brother's life. Michele worked with insurance actuary tables and knew the dangers those in the military faced, especially when deployed or training for combat. A job with the CID brought danger even closer to home, something she wasn't willing to face.

Ten months ago, Michele had run away from a relationship that would have required her to look deep within herself and determine whether she cared enough about Jamison to live with the constant threat a job in law enforcement entailed.

Since she had never told him why she had moved back to Atlanta, Jamison had been left with two possible conclusions. Michele had decided he wasn't worth the risk or she hadn't been able to determine what she wanted in life.

On occasion, she had mentioned her struggle with God. If she didn't feel loved by the Lord, chances were she didn't feel worthy of anyone's love, including Jamison's. Either way, she had run to Atlanta, where she thought she could live life on her own terms. Her own safe terms.

Love involved risk, and Michele wasn't ready to put her heart on the line. At least, that's the excuse Jamison had used to work through his own pain. He thought he had healed, but coming face-to-face with Michele made him realize he wasn't over her yet. For some reason—maybe lack of sleep or the horrific crime scene that had been captured in the photos on his desk—Jamison felt raw as if being near Michele had opened the old wound to his heart.

Tossing the picture of her back onto his desk, he looked up as Dawson entered the cubicle with two steaming mugs of coffee in hand.

"Otis perked a fresh pot," Dawson said in greeting.

"God bless him." Jamison reached for a mug and inhaled the rich aroma.

Dawson's gaze trailed over Jamison's desk and stopped at the photo of Michele. Inwardly, Jamison flinched, waiting for a jabbing comment about a pretty face and a former love.

Relieved when the other CID agent raised his gaze without commenting, Jamison asked, "What about the door-to-door search in the neighborhood? Anything turn up yet?"

"Only questions about the maintenance man who fixed the wiring at the Hughes quarters last night."

"The guy from Prime Maintenance?" Jamison took a swig of the hot brew. High-test, loaded with caffeine, just what he needed after a long night without sleep.

Dawson nodded. "A couple folks mentioned seeing his truck drive through the housing area earlier in the evening."

"Their main office isn't far from the Post Shopping Area. I'll stop by and talk to the supervisor." Jamison straightened the stack of photos on his desk and pulled out an eight-by-ten of Yolanda's dining room. He tapped his finger on the bouquet of cut flowers in the center of the table. "The crime scene team found a floral wrapper from the post flower shop in the victim's trash. I plan to question the florist, as well, after I shower and change. He may have seen something when he delivered the bouquet."

"Let me know what you find out."

"Will do." Jamison took another sip of his coffee. "Send one of our guys into Freemont to talk to Mr. Yates. We need to know why he never showed up at the potluck last night. And keep an extra detail of military police on the front gate. Every vehicle leaving and entering Fort Rickman needs to be searched. If the killer got away last night, we don't want him coming back on post and doing more harm."

"You worried he'll strike again?" Dawson asked.

"Aren't you?"

The other agent shrugged. "Maybe I'm being optimistic, but knife wounds are personal, which is what I keep thinking this crime was. The perp knew Yolanda Hughes. He wanted to kill her for some reason we need to determine. Maybe it involved a love triangle or maybe it was something else and she's his only intended victim. Once we learn his motive, we'll be able to track him down."

"And if he kills again before we find him?"

"Then I'll have to admit I was wrong." He stared at Jamison for a long moment. The memory of walking into the ambush ten months ago hung between them.

Jamison still felt responsible. "Look, Dawson—"

As much as he wanted to clear up what had happened, the words stuck in his throat. Instead of his own voice, he heard his father's taunts about his inability to do anything right. "Jamie-boy, you're a failure," replayed over and over in his mind. Not that anything his father said should have bearing on his life today.

Frustrated that the long-ago censure still affected him, Jamison let out a lungful of air and placed his cup on his desk. "After I shower at the gym, I'll talk to the maintenance company and the florist. Call me if anything new surfaces."

When he left the gym, Jamison planned to stop by the maintenance office, but just as last night, he ended up in front of Colonel Logan's quarters. A number of cars were parked at the curb. Jamison hustled up the steps and rang the bell. Mrs. Logan answered the door. Women's voices sounded from the living room.

"Morning, ma'am. I wanted to ensure that you and Michele had an uneventful night and are doing okay." He peered around her to the women inside, recognizing many of the wives who had gathered at the Hughes residence last night.

"We're fine, Jamison, but it's nice of you to stop by and inquire about our well-being. Michele's right here—"

Mrs. Logan stepped away from the door.

"Ah, ma'am—"

He didn't need to talk to Michele.

"Jamison?" Dressed in a pretty floral blouse and cotton slacks, Michele appeared in the doorway, looking like a summer garden.

Internally, he groaned. "I was just checking to see if you're all right."

"Yes, of course." Her lips smiled, but her eyes remained guarded. "The military police are patrolling our area and keeping us safe."

Her tone caused him to bristle. *Note to self, Michele doesn't need you in her life.*

"Sounds like you've got a full house."

"The wives wanted to be together. They're worried and grieving and ready for their husbands to return home." She stepped onto the porch and pulled the door closed behind her. "How's the investigation going?"

"We don't have much at this point. A few people to question. We're checking everyone coming on and off post and have enhanced security in all the housing areas."

"I noticed the military police driving by a number of times last night."

From the look on her face, Jamison wondered if she had seen his car. He cleared his throat, trying to ignore the smoothness of her cheeks and the way her hair gleamed in the morning light. "Any word on the Hughes children?"

"Their dad plans to talk to them tonight on Skype." Her voice softened and sadness tugged at the corners of her mouth.

Jamison's heart ached for the children. His own mother had died when he was young, and he knew how hard life could be for kids without a mom.

"I made chocolate chip cookies and took them over early this morning. Yolanda's sister is scheduled to arrive later today. She and the kids will stay in the VIP guest quarters until Major Hughes arrives home."

"Any idea about the burial?"

"They have a plot in Missouri. Once everyone is reunited, Major Hughes and the children will fly her body home. Mother and Dad will probably attend the funeral. I'm not sure what I should do."

Knowing Michele, she would probably run back to Atlanta. Just as she had done ten months ago.

He glanced at his watch, needing to distance himself from the colonel's daughter. "You have my number. Call if you need anything."

"Thank you, Jamison."

He hurried back to his car. Five minutes with Michele and suddenly his ordered life was anything but. His focus needed to center on the investigation and the supervisor at Prime Maintenance he planned to question, as well as the florist on post.

Pulling away from the Logan quarters, Jamison shook his head, frustrated with the swell of feelings that were bubbling up within him.

A woman murdered.

A killer on the loose.

A very personal complication he hadn't expected that tangled up his ability to be objective.

"Oh, Michele," he groaned aloud. "Why'd you have to come back to Fort Rickman now?"

Traffic was light as Michele drove across post. The gray sky and the weather forecaster's prediction that another round of turbulence would hit the area added to her unease.

Over the last few hours, Michele's mood had dropped as low as the barometer. She needed time away from her mother and the women who filled the Logan home.

Sweet as they were, their long faces and hushed tones as they spoke of what had happened forced her to confront the terrible tragedy she had stumbled upon last night.

Knowing two children had been left without a mother added to her struggle. Seeing their sweet faces earlier in the day had put an even heavier pall around her shoulders. Michele needed fresh air and time to process her emotions, but no matter how hard she tried to block the crime scene from her memory, the gruesome pictures of Yolanda's death continued to haunt her.

The expression on Jamison's face when he had come crashing into the house, gun in hand, mixed with the other still frames. Ten months ago, she had thought she loved him, but when an investigation almost claimed his life, she realized her mistake. Maybe in time, she'd find Mr. Right. At the moment, she was more concerned about her confrontation last night with Mr. Wrong. Seeing him again this morning had added more confusion to the day.

Despite his good qualities, Jamison wasn't the man for her. Everything inside her warned that a U.S. Army warrant officer, who was also a CID special agent, was off-limits and could end up being a deadly combination. Plus, her recent history with the military wasn't good.

In quick flashes, she thought of her brother's death, her father's injury soon after he arrived in Afghanistan and the shoot-out on post that could have left Jamison wounded. Or dead.

Dawson had taken the bullet meant for Jamison. In spite of the close call, Jamison continued to handle investigations that put him in danger, which further proved the CID agent wasn't for her.

So why had she called him yesterday? Jamison, of

all people. She'd reacted without thinking. Now she had to pay the price for seeing him again.

Last night, he had been cool, calm and totally in control, dressed in a starched white shirt, a silk tie and a sports coat expertly tailored to fit his broad shoulders and trim waist.

Instead of a military uniform, CID agents wore civilian clothes to ensure that rank didn't get in the way of their investigations. Maybe that's what had attracted her to Jamison the night they'd met at the military club on post. He had looked drop-dead gorgeous in his coat and tie when he extended his hand in greeting, along with a smile that instantly melted her heart.

Slipping her right hand into his and gazing into his deep-set brown eyes had made her world stop for one breathless moment. Something had clicked inside her, and she had been instantly smitten by the very special, special agent.

He'd been equally put together last night, although his eyes had been darker than she remembered. Probably because he had refused to hold her gaze, which bothered her more than she wanted to admit. This morning he'd seemed a bit on edge, although it was no wonder after what had happened.

Anyone who didn't know him wouldn't notice the tiny lines around his eyes or the fatigue that played over his features. Committed as he had always been to his job, he had probably slept little last night.

Heaving a sigh, she turned into the main shopping area on post and parked across from the floral shop. A bell tinkled over the door as she entered the air-conditioned interior and stepped toward the counter.

The florist, in his early forties and with a muscular build and military flattop, glanced up. "May I help you?"

"I called in an order last week for a bouquet of cut flowers."

"Name?"

"Logan. Michele Logan."

Recognition played over his angled face. "You're Colonel Logan's daughter."

"That's right."

"I served with your dad in Iraq when he was a battalion commander. Best commander I ever had."

Michele never tired of hearing good things about her father. Three years ago, after bringing his battalion of soldiers home from Iraq, her dad had been promoted to full colonel and selected for brigade command. Some said he was a shoo-in for general officer. Not that he allowed praise to impact the way he did his job.

Their family's only dark moment during that time had been Lance's death. A helicopter crash shortly after her brother had graduated from flight school and moved to his new military assignment at Fort Knox, Kentucky. A freak accident that never should have happened.

The hardest part was knowing she could have prevented the tragedy. Lance wouldn't have been flying if Michele had accepted his invitation to visit him that weekend. She had made the wrong decision, a decision that led to her brother's death.

Unable to work through her grief and her guilt, Michele had eventually buried her pain. Finding Yolanda yesterday had brought everything to the surface.

The florist stretched out his hand. "Name's Teddy Sutherland."

Michele returned the handshake, noting his firm grip and thick, stubby fingers. "Nice to meet you, sir."

"I've got your order. You said you wanted a container appropriate for your brother's grave site?"

"That's right." She momentarily averted her gaze, blinking back unexpected tears that flooded her eyes. Her emotions hovered close to the surface today.

Teddy flipped through a stack of order forms. "I remember hearing about the helicopter crash. Wasn't your brother the only one on board who died?"

She nodded, wondering yet again about the inequity of the accident. Not that she had wanted anyone else to lose a loved one in the crash. She just didn't understand why her brother had to die.

"About this time of year, as I recall?"

The florist's concern touched her. She nodded, her voice halting when she spoke. "It…it happened two years ago today."

"Tough on your mom, no doubt, especially after last night."

"You heard about the murder?"

"News travels fast on post. Wonder if they'll ever find the guy." He reached into the large walk-in refrigerator and pulled out a bouquet of red gladiolas and white mums arranged with miniature American flags and wrapped together with a blue ribbon.

Placing the flowers on the counter along with a plastic vase and a small attachment to anchor the arrangement into the ground, the florist glanced up, waiting for her reaction.

"They're beautiful, Mr. Sutherland."

"It's Teddy, please. Tell your mother I'm ordering flowers for the welcome-home ceremony."

"To give to the wives in the brigade?"

He nodded. "Mrs. Grayson, the executive officer's wife, asked me to help." He glanced down, somewhat embarrassed by his gesture. "The way I feel about your dad, it's the least I could do."

"I know my mother and the other wives will appreciate your generosity."

The bell over the door tinkled. Michele turned, expecting to see another customer. Her breath caught in her throat as Jamison entered the store.

She smiled, trying to override the tension that wrapped around her as tightly as the wire holding the floral bow in place. He nodded, then glanced away for a moment in an obvious attempt to cover his own unease.

Turning back to the flowers, Michele fiddled with the ribbon.

Jamison stepped closer and touched the plastic vase lying on the counter. "Two years ago, wasn't it, Michele?"

She hadn't expected him to remember. The empathy she heard in his voice caused her eyes to cloud again. Jamison had understood when no one else seemed interested in how a younger sister felt about the death of the brother she idolized. Even her parents hadn't wanted to talk about their son's future cut short.

Teddy swiped her credit card and ripped off the tape register receipt. Holding out the thin strip of paper, he handed Michele a pen. "I just need a signature to complete the transaction."

Relieved to focus on something other than the special agent, Michele hastily signed her name. Grabbing the flowers and vase, she turned to find Jamison standing much too close.

She dropped her gaze, trying to ignore his muscular shoulders and the manly scent of his aftershave. Instead her focus settled on his right hip, where—beneath the smooth line of his sports coat—he carried a SIG Sauer, loaded and ready to fire.

"Sorry." He stepped aside. His demeanor and voice, now devoid of inflection, reminded her that their involvement had ended months ago. Just as with Lance, she had no reason to think about what might have been.

Ironically, on her brother's last trip home, Lance had laughingly teased that only a military guy would make her happy. Michele had agreed, but his death had changed her mind. Now she just wanted to guard her future and her heart.

The bell tinkled as she pushed the door open and stepped into the Georgia humidity, grateful no one was standing close enough to see the confusion she couldn't hide and shouldn't be feeling. She'd left Jamison months ago. A good decision, or so she'd thought.

Slipping behind the wheel of her car, she glanced back at the florist shop. Would she have felt differently if her brother hadn't died?

Maybe then she wouldn't have been afraid of her feelings for the CID agent. But Lance *had* died and her father had been injured in Afghanistan, and then Dawson had taken a bullet meant for Jamison in a bloody shoot-out that had made her run scared.

Now Yolanda.

If only Michele could run away again, just as she had done ten months ago. She wanted to go back to the secure life she'd made for herself in Atlanta, but she couldn't leave her mother alone after the tragedy that had happened. The brigade would return sometime next week. Michele would wait until her father came home before she left Fort Rickman and the military.

By then, Jamison would have found the killer.

Her stomach tightened and a gasp escaped her lips as she realized that finding the killer would, once again, put Jamison in the line of fire.

Why did Michele continue to get under his skin?

Jamison clamped down on his jaw and pulled in a deep breath, needing to distance himself, at least emotionally, from the colonel's daughter and concentrate on the florist, who continued to stare at him.

"Can I help you, sir?" he asked a second time.

Glancing at the clerk's name tag, Jamison held up his CID identification. "I need information about any floral deliveries you've made in the last couple days, Mr. Sutherland."

The florist nodded. "You're here because of that murder on post."

A crime everyone seemed to have heard about by now. "What can you tell me?"

"Mrs. Hughes ordered a bouquet for yesterday afternoon." Sutherland flipped through his order forms. "Here it is. A bouquet of cut flowers, carnations and daisies, interspersed with a few yellow roses."

Glancing up at Jamison, he added, "Yellow roses are a popular homecoming flower. As you probably know, Major Hughes's unit is scheduled to return to Fort Rickman next week."

"Did Mrs. Hughes discuss her husband's return to post?"

The florist shook his head. "Not to me, but it's common knowledge. Plus, the local chamber of commerce keeps track of all the homecomings. Having the brigade back will be good for business."

Jamison pulled his notebook and pen from his pocket. "What time did you deliver the flowers to the Hughes residence?"

"I didn't. Mrs. Hughes stopped by the shop yesterday and placed the order before she went to the commissary. I had the table arrangement ready when she finished shopping."

"Did she say why she wanted flowers?"

"No, sir, but Mrs. Hughes bought flowers once a month or so. Usually for a wives' event. Sure is a shame."

"How'd you learn about her death?"

"One of her neighbors stopped in earlier today. She was pretty shook-up. Fact is everyone's upset."

"Do you recall the neighbor's name?"

"I can find it if you give me a minute." Once again, he sorted through the order forms. His face lit up as he pulled a paper from the pile and held it out to Jamison. "Ursula Barker bought an arrangement shortly after I opened this morning. She lives down the street from the Hugheses and shared that the whole neighborhood is worried. Course, I don't blame them with a killer on the loose. I'm worried, too. You guys have any idea who did it?"

"I'm not at liberty to say." A pat answer, but the truth was that the CID and military police had nothing concrete to go on so far.

The florist pursed his lips. "Guess I shouldn't have asked, but just like everyone else on post, I'm looking over my shoulder, if you know what I mean."

Jamison did know. No one wanted a murderer on the

loose. He continued to question the florist but learned nothing more that would have a bearing on the victim's death. After leaving the floral shop, Jamison called CID headquarters. He quickly filled Dawson in on his interview with the florist before he turned the discussion to his earlier stop at Prime Maintenance.

"I talked to the supervisor. The only maintenance man on duty last night was Danny Altman. He's prior military, worked in Atlanta and was questioned when his girlfriend died unexpectedly. Her death was ruled accidental." Jamison passed on Altman's Freemont address. "Find out more about the girlfriend."

"Roger that. I'll talk to Mr. Altman and see if he remembers anything pertinent concerning last night, as well." Dawson paused for a long moment. "I talked to McGrunner."

Both Dawson and Jamison thought highly of the young military policeman who had a good work ethic and the makings of a future CID special agent. He had been on patrol last night, and Jamison knew where Dawson was headed.

"Look, Dawson, I drove by Colonel Logan's quarters," Jamison admitted. "That's all."

"Military police were on patrol in the colonel's housing area. You didn't need to worry about Michele."

"The killer left two witnesses behind."

"Yes, but neither Michele nor her mother can identify him."

"He may not realize that. If I were a killer, I'd get rid of everyone involved." The muscles in Jamison's neck tensed as he thought about what could happen. "Did any of the neighbors hear sounds of a struggle?"

"Negative."

"I blame that on the storm. Most folks were probably hunkered down inside their quarters. Thunder and wind would have muffled any noise coming from the victim's quarters."

"Roger that," Dawson agreed. "And if the killer had used a stun gun, Mrs. Hughes would have quickly lost muscle control and couldn't have screamed for help."

What about Michele? The thought of her with the killer made Jamison clamp down on his jaw.

Thank God she and Mrs. Logan hadn't been hurt.

He pushed the cell closer to his ear. "Any word from the medical examiner?"

"Negative."

Seemed they were still batting zero. Although it might be a long shot, Jamison thought of another person who needed to be questioned. "The florist said a neighbor by the name of Ursula Barker told him about the victim's death. Have one of our people check with Ms. Barker and verify the florist's story."

"You think he's lying?"

"I just want to be sure."

Dawson was quiet for a long moment. "You're still stalled because of the last case we worked on together."

"I told you, I'm okay."

"You can trust your instincts, buddy. Whatever you think you did wrong—"

Jamison let out a blast of pent-up air. "Dawson."

"Seeing Michele yesterday…" The CID agent sighed. "I know how you felt about her."

"It's over, Dawson. End of discussion."

"Yeah, right."

"Don't forget Ursula Barker. Then get back to me."

Frustrated, Jamison disconnected and hustled to his

car. His mind relived visions of when Dawson had taken the hit meant for Jamison. Fast-forward to yesterday and what could have happened to Michele.

Climbing behind the wheel, he started the ignition and pulled out of the parking lot. At one time, his instincts had been good, but he and Dawson had walked into an ambush any rookie cop could have seen coming. Now he had to check and double-check his actions to keep from making another mistake.

Dark clouds billowed in the sky overhead, and a strong gust of wind tugged at his car. Gripping the steering wheel, Jamison eyed the rapidly worsening weather.

What had he missed last night? Mrs. Logan and Michele hadn't provided information that could identify the killer, but just as he'd told Dawson, if the perpetrator thought they could ID him, wouldn't he come after them?

Jamison called Dawson back. "Increase surveillance around Colonel Logan's quarters."

"Did something happen?"

"Not yet, but I want to make sure it doesn't."

Disconnecting, he increased his speed.

Michele was driving along narrow back roads with a storm rolling into the area. More threatening than the weather was the out-of-the-way location of the cemetery, where she would be alone and at risk. This time, he didn't need to double-check the facts.

Michele was vulnerable and unprotected.

Every instinct warned Jamison to hurry.

THREE

Michele drummed her hand on the steering wheel as she sat in the line of cars snaking their way through the Main Gate. Up ahead a military policeman worked with two civilian gate guards, checking the vehicles leaving post.

Across the median, a swarm of MPs searched the interior—as well as under the hood and in the trunk—of every car entering the garrison. Trucks were subject to more detailed scrutiny. With Fort Rickman on lockdown, law enforcement was ensuring that no one brought anything suspicious on or off post without their knowledge.

Though she was reassured by the thoroughness of the military police, Michele was frustrated by the delay. Her eyes turned upward, taking in the darkening sky and the wind that picked through the Spanish moss hanging from the stately oaks that lined the side of the road. If she didn't reach the cemetery soon, she could get caught in a downpour.

The whole post was on edge, and rightfully so. Anyone with a smattering of knowledge about army operations could easily learn the names of the deployed soldiers. A quick search of a Fort Rickman phone book would provide home addresses where family members would be easy targets.

Had Yolanda been a random victim? Or was she chosen because her husband was deployed and she was alone?

A number of times last night, Michele had heard cars driving by outside. Looking from her bedroom window, she'd seen a steady stream of military police sedans patrolling the area. The added protection should have made her feel more secure but only drove home the fact that a killer was on the loose. The only time she'd felt safe was when Jamison was with her. But his presence created its own set of problems.

Michele rubbed her hand over her stomach in an attempt to quell the nervous confusion eating at her. She needed to push thoughts of him aside and concentrate on getting to the cemetery before the next round of storms.

The line of traffic moved forward. Michele edged her car toward the gate and stopped in front of the guard. He glanced into the interior of her vehicle and then checked her trunk before he waved her on.

As she left the post, she passed three media vans parked in a clearing at the side of the road. Camera crews stood in a huddle, no doubt eager to broadcast the latest news about Yolanda's death.

Once she was on Freemont Road, Michele increased her speed and after a series of turns spied the front entrance to the cemetery up ahead. Putting on her signal, she turned onto the narrow road, full of twists and turns, that meandered through the sprawling grounds of gentle knolls and stands of trees.

Lance had loved the outdoors, and her parents had

chosen a secluded burial plot atop a small rise that provided a clear view of the surrounding grounds. Michele parked on the grass just short of the rise.

As a precaution and noting the recent drop in temperature, she grabbed a raincoat off the backseat and, with her purse and flowers in hand, trudged up the incline. The ground, still damp from last night's rain, cushioned her footfalls.

Over her right shoulder, she noticed a car parked near a cluster of monuments shaded by a giant oak tree. A man stood nearby. As she watched, he raised binoculars to his eyes and stared in her direction.

The hair on the back of her neck tingled. Unable to ignore the warning, she shivered, not from the wind that whipped around her but from her own nervousness. Lightning danced across the sky followed by the rumble of thunder.

Thankful for the waterproof slicker, Michele shrugged into the thick vinyl and pulled her hair free from the neck of the coat. She felt violated by the man's prying gaze and wrapped the coat across her chest as she hurried on to the crest of the hill.

Once there, she glanced back, relieved to see that the man with the binoculars had climbed into his car to leave the cemetery. Turning her thoughts to Lance, she approached the rear of his monument.

Instead of a small and simple military marker, her parents had chosen a larger memorial with Lance's picture etched into the front of the stone. As a template for his likeness, they had used a photograph Michele had taken at his graduation from flight school.

She and her parents had attended the ceremony at Fort Rucker, Alabama, and had been so proud of Lance, standing tall in his uniform in front of the American flag he loved. Three months later, his chopper crashed and exploded into a flaming inferno that took his life.

Stopped by the painful memory, Michele touched the cool granite. "Oh, Lance," she sighed, wishing she weren't alone with her grief. Her mother never came with her, never even wanted to, which Michele didn't understand.

She thought of Jamison. Would he have accepted her invitation if she had asked him? Probably not. He had a murder to solve.

From out of nowhere, the smell of blood wafted past her. Yolanda's bleeding body swam before her eyes. Michele bristled, annoyed with the tricks her mind was playing.

Struggling to shrug off the frightful memory, she rounded the monument and peered down, expecting to find her brother's likeness smiling up at her.

At first unable to comprehend what she was seeing, Michele leaned closer. Then, like an arrow to her heart, realization hit.

She gasped. The flowers dropped to the rain-dampened earth. Lightning ripped across the sky. Seconds later, thunder mixed with the roar of her pounding pulse.

Vandals had chiseled thick gashes into Lance's image, turning his handsome countenance into a macabre caricature. The marks cut into the stone exactly where the killer's knife had slashed Yolanda's flesh. A dark, viscous substance covered the mutilation and dripped like blood over his name and the date of his death.

Unable to look any longer at the defacement, Michele turned and ran away. Down the hill she fled, trying to distance herself from the desecration of her brother's grave. Fat raindrops pummeled her face and mixed with the tears cascading down her cheeks.

She skidded. Her feet slipped on the wet grass. Stumbling, she righted herself and hurried on. Michele reached the road on the opposite side of a sharp curve from where she had parked her car.

The sky opened up as if it, too, were weeping for the dead. She dug in her purse, searching for her keys, and raced around the bend, hardly able to see because of the tears flooding her eyes.

The sound of tires rolling over asphalt startled her. She glanced up. Her heart jammed in her throat.

A car loomed in front of her.

Black sedan, tinted windows. The chrome hood ornament was headed straight for her.

She lunged, trying to jump clear.

The fender and outer side panel swiped against her thigh and sent her flying like a rag doll. Hot streaks of pain ricocheted through her body. She fell to the ground, clutching her leg and gasping for breath.

Unable to cry for help, Michele lay in pouring rain enveloped by darkness.

Jamison's heart stopped as he pulled into the cemetery. In one terrifying flash, he saw it all play out.

Michele!

Accelerating, he raced forward, taking the turns at breakneck speed. *Please, God, let her be okay.*

Punching Speed Dial on his cell, he connected with the local police. "Hit-and-run at the Freemont Cemetery. Send an ambulance and police. *Now!*"

Fear clamped down on his gut. Would he get to her in time?

Halfway into the last curve, the tires lost traction. Jamison eased up on the accelerator and turned the wheel into the skid. Once the car had straightened, he put his foot on the gas and closed the distance to where she lay.

Leaping from his car, he charged across the rain-sloshed grass. His only thought was Michele.

Fingers of dread clawed at his throat. The rain eased as he dropped to his knees beside her.

"Michele, it's Jamison. Talk to me."

Water-drenched hair covered her face. He pushed away the wayward strands. Her skin was pale, too pale.

Please, God!

Long lashes moved ever so slightly, fanning her cheeks.

He touched her neck, feeling a steady pulse, and gasped with relief.

She jerked at his touch.

"It's okay, honey. An ambulance is on the way."

Sirens screamed in the distance.

"Open your eyes, Michele."

She groaned. Her lashes fluttered, revealing corn-flower-blue orbs clouded with confusion.

"You're going to be all right. There's nothing to worry about." As he tried to comfort her, Jamison worked his hands over her arms and lower legs, ensuring that none of her bones had been broken.

She flinched when he gently prodded her knee, probably where she had taken the greatest impact from the hit.

Anger surged through him at the maniac who had

done this to her and then had driven away, never checking to ensure that she was still alive. Jamison wanted to pound his fist into the wet earth at his own stupidity. He shouldn't have let her leave the floral shop alone.

"La…Lance's grave site." She tried to sit up.

He gently touched her shoulder. "Lie still until the EMTs arrive."

She grabbed his hand. "The m…monument was desecrated."

Sirens filled the air. Two Freemont police cars pulled into the cemetery and stopped close to where Michele lay. An ambulance turned onto the grounds. Overcome with relief, Jamison remained at her side as the officers neared.

The older of the two made the introductions. "Sir, I'm Officer Tim Simpson with the Freemont Police Department." Mid-forties, the guy had a buzz cut and thick brows that he raised as he pointed to the wiry, younger officer next to him. "This is Officer Bobby Jones."

Jamison flashed his identification, gave his own name and Michele's and quickly explained what he had witnessed.

"I saw Miss Logan when I pulled into the cemetery. She was hurrying around the curve in the road toward her car. The rain was falling hard, and she was trying to pull her cell phone or her keys from her handbag."

"M…my keys," she responded, her voice weak.

"The car appeared to accelerate just before it hit her," Jamison added.

She glanced at Simpson. "I…I didn't hear a motor."

"Can you give us a description of the vehicle, ma'am?"

"Black or dark blue with a silver hood ornament."

She shook her head. "I'm not sure about the make or model."

"Were you able to see the driver?" Jamison asked, still hovering over her.

"The windows were tinted. Earlier, a man…by the oak tree. He had binoculars."

"Military binoculars?"

"I'm not sure. I thought he'd left the cemetery by the front entrance." She wrinkled her brow. "It could have been the same car."

The cop looked at Jamison. "Did you get a visual, sir?"

"Not on the driver. I was too far away, and he left through the rear exit. The vehicle was a small, four-door sedan with tinted windows, as Miss Logan mentioned. Late model. Dark color. Could have been a hybrid."

Simpson pursed his lips. "Which would have been the reason she didn't hear the engine."

"Exactly."

The ambulance pulled alongside the police cars, and two EMTs quickly approached. "Sir, can you step back and give us some room?"

As much as Jamison didn't want to leave Michele's side, he had to let the medical team do their job.

He squeezed her hand. "I'll talk to the police while the EMTs ensure that you're okay."

Her grip tightened. "Lance's grave. Someone cut into his marker."

"I'm heading there now."

As the EMTs strapped Michele to a backboard, Jamison turned to Officer Jones. "Can you get the names off the headstones near the oak tree? The family members need to be questioned in case one of them was the man with binoculars."

"Good idea. I'll take care of it."

Jamison motioned to the older cop and then pointed up the incline. "Let's take a walk and check out the marker."

Having visited Lance's grave with Michele on occasion, Jamison led the way. His stomach soured at the sight of the damage done to the monument. What kind of vicious person would do such a hateful act?

Bending down, he studied the cuts in the granite and the spattered liquid. "Looks like blood, although it might not be human."

Simpson nodded. "A piece of raw steak could provide enough blood to cover the entire monument." He scratched off a sample and dropped it into a plastic evidence bag. "Whatever it is, I'll have it analyzed and let you know the results."

Jamison glanced back at where the EMTs were talking to Michele. A heavy weight settled on his shoulders.

The grave desecration was a vindictive act against the Logan family. Judging from the location of gash marks on Lance's etched likeness, the defacement appeared to be connected to the murder on post.

Jamison's heart lurched with a terrifying realization. The cold, hard truth sent chills along his spine. Just like with Dawson, Jamison hadn't put the pieces together fast enough to realize Michele would be an easy target at the cemetery. That mistake had almost cost Michele her life.

FOUR

As much as Michele didn't want to go to the hospital, she gave in at the insistence of the EMTs. Freemont had a modern facility with a good emergency room where she could be checked over by a physician.

"You're one lucky lady," the driver of the ambulance told her as the EMTs repacked their equipment and prepared to leave the cemetery.

Michele didn't feel lucky. Her thigh ached, and she must have pulled a muscle in her back when she landed on the rain-soaked grass. Nothing serious, she felt sure, but not what she wanted today, of all days.

Jamison stood away from the circle of first responders, cell phone jammed to his ear, as he relayed what had happened back to CID headquarters. She had warned him not to call her mother. Not yet, at least.

Roberta had enough to worry her without hearing her daughter was involved in a hit-and-run accident. Once the doctor at the hospital gave the all clear, Michele planned to call home with positive news that she was all right.

Disconnecting, Jamison approached the stretcher where she lay and touched her hand. His eyes were darker than usual, his brow drawn in what seemed like a continuous frown. Jamison had laughed so often when they were dating that she considered asking him to force a smile or, at least, relax the tension that tugged at his full lips.

She remembered how he used to tease her with his kisses. In the beginning, the warmth of his embrace and the sweet gentleness of his caresses had melted the cold interior of her heart, a heart that had frozen after Lance's death.

Jamison had been a good influence when they'd dated. His optimism had rubbed off on her. Without realizing it at the time, Michele had started to share his vision of how life was meant to be lived, in the present and with hope for the future.

After she left Fort Rickman, the light Jamison had brought into her life dimmed, leaving a noticeable void.

Jamison's love for life seemed to have diminished, as well. Could ten months have made such a significant difference in both of their lives?

Tragedy was transforming and not necessarily for the better. The shoot-out on post ten months ago could have been the catalyst that caused the change in Jamison. Or had something else been the reason?

Something or someone?

Unable to accept that she might be to blame for Jamison's newfound gloom, Michele fisted her hands.

Jamison leaned over the stretcher, his face so close she could feel his warm breath against her cheek. "What's wrong, Michele? Did you remember something?"

She remembered his kisses. "Did you tell Dawson not to call my mother?"

"I said you planned to notify her once you arrived at Freemont Hospital."

The EMT tapped Jamison's shoulder. "We're ready to transport."

He squeezed her hand and smiled, not only with his lips but also with his eyes. For a brief moment, his gaze bathed her in a warmth that took away the chilling fear that had blanketed her for too long.

"You'll be with me at the hospital?" she asked, needing assurance he wouldn't leave her.

"Ah, sir," the medic interrupted. "You can drive your own vehicle and meet us at the E.R."

Releasing her hand, Jamison took a step toward the surprised EMT and jammed his finger into the guy's chest.

"Let's get this straight. I'm riding in the ambulance with the patient."

The medic's eyes widened for a moment before he shrugged. "Whatever you say, sir."

True to his word, Jamison hovered close to her side not only during the drive to the hospital, but also while she waited in the exam room to see the doctor. Once the physician appeared, Jamison moved into the hallway. He stood guard outside her door while the doctor completed his assessment and ordered a battery of laboratory tests and X-rays.

"You can come back in here," Michele said to Jamison through the half-opened door after the doc had moved on to the next patient.

"Thanks, but I'll stay put." Jamison's stance, his pursed lips and the tight pull on his square jaw were outward signs he was in full bodyguard mode. Had something else happened that had put him on high alert?

Before she had time to ask, an aide appeared and pushed her to X-ray. Jamison followed close behind the stretcher. His focused gaze swept the corridor. Every few seconds, he turned to scan the hallway behind them.

Surely he was being overly cautious. Although after Yolanda's death and her own run-in with the driver at the cemetery, Michele was relieved to have someone watching her back, a very stoic someone who said little and kept his facial expressions to a minimum.

A friendly tech x-rayed her legs and spinal column, after which Michele returned to the exam room. Just as before, Jamison remained in the hallway, eyeing the flow of medical personnel and patients.

"Did something happen?" Michele finally asked, no longer able to keep her curiosity in check.

Jamison leaned into her room. "While you were with the doc, one of the nurses mentioned some strange dudes in the waiting area."

Michele rolled her eyes. "Are you always on duty?"

His lips twitched ever so slightly before he returned to his guard post.

She glanced at her watch. What was taking so long? A few minutes later, she checked the time again. And then again.

Everything moved slowly in the emergency room, which frustrated Michele. She had told her mother she planned to run a few errands when she left the house earlier in the day. By now, Roberta would be worried something had happened.

Closing her eyes, Michele tried to stave off the growing anxiety and opened them seconds later to find Jamison next to her, cell phone in hand. "Time to call home."

"How…how did you know what I was thinking?"

"You kept checking your watch."

Her mother sounded relieved when she heard Michele's voice. Choosing her words carefully, Michele relayed what had happened in an upbeat, breezy way.

Of course, Roberta instantly picked up on Michele's attempt to soft-pedal the news. Before she could completely reassure her mother, a lab tech appeared, needing one more vial of blood.

"Don't say anything to worry her," Michele mouthed as she passed the phone to Jamison and then fisted her hand for the blood draw. He retreated to the hallway and finished the conversation there.

"You were on the phone for a long time," Michele said once the tech returned to the lab and Jamison pocketed his phone. "You didn't make matters worse, did you?"

"Michele, please. Your mother can handle the truth."

Truth? She turned her gaze to the lime-green walls and the Norman Rockwell knockoff hanging over the stretcher.

Mildly annoyed with Jamison's reticence, Michele was more irritated at herself for causing the problem in the first place. With an ongoing investigation, the CID agent needed to be back at his office, and her mother needed to deal with the plans for the homecoming without having to worry about her daughter.

A nurse stuck her head through the door and smiled. "The lab needed to rerun a test. The results should be back shortly."

Shortly lapsed into thirty minutes of Michele trying to think of anything except Jamison standing guard in the hallway. Closing her eyes, she counted sheep but found the woolly animals even more stubborn than her CID bodyguard.

At some point, she must have dozed off. A noise from the hallway jerked her awake. Michele glanced up to find her mother standing in the doorway.

With three strides, Roberta closed the distance to where Michele lay and reached for her hand. "Jamison arranged for two nice military policemen to drive me here, and despite their assurances that you hadn't been hurt, I kept thinking of what could have been."

"I'm fine, Mother. As soon as the results come back from the laboratory, the doctor plans to release me."

"Which is what Jamison said." Roberta glanced back to where he stood in the hallway. "Why don't you come inside and wait with us, Jamison?"

Peering around her mother, Michele rolled her eyes to indicate how frustrated she was with Jamison's attempt to help. If he hadn't provided an escort to the hospital, her mother probably would have remained at home.

He ignored Michele's theatrics. "Thank you, Mrs. Logan. But I prefer the hallway."

Michele thought of another way to take him off guard duty. "Jamison arranged for my car and his to be brought to the hospital, Mother, so you can drive me home."

"Of course, dear." Roberta patted Michele's arm and then smiled at Jamison through the open doorway. "Don't let us hold you up, if you need to get back to post."

"It's not a problem, ma'am."

He returned her mother's smile, then grabbed the doorknob and fixed a steady gaze at Michele. "I'll be in the hallway until you're released from the E.R. Then I'm driving you home, Michele. Your mother can ride with us or drive back with one of the military policemen who brought her here. The other officer will follow us in your car."

With that, he closed the door, cutting off Michele's attempt to object. Irritated by his pronouncement of what would happen as well as the laboratory results that were taking much too long, Michele dropped her legs over the edge of the gurney, sat up and huffed.

"Jamison hasn't been in the best of moods since the ambulance brought me here."

"I'm sure he's just worried about you." Roberta patted Michele's arm. "I was worried, too, after you called. That's why I had to see for myself that you were okay."

"I'm fine, Mother." Even she was getting tired of the pat response she offered whenever anyone questioned her well-being.

Roberta raised her hand to her neck and fiddled with the collar of her blouse. "And Lance's gravestone? Jamison said someone had vandalized the marker."

"One of the police officers mentioned a group of local teens who have been getting out of hand." Michele didn't bring up a possible connection between what had happened at the cemetery and the murder on post.

"The police wanted to know the last time anyone had visited the grave site," she said instead. "I said no one in the family had been there recently."

Her mother studied the picture on the wall of a young boy in a Boy Scout uniform, standing proud while his mother pinned a medal on his chest.

"Is that right, Mother?" Michele pressed.

Seemingly lost in her own thoughts, Roberta hesitated before she looked at Michele. "What did you say, dear?"

"How long has it been since you visited Lance's grave?"

"Not long." Roberta's response came too quickly. She bit down on her lip and turned toward the door just as it opened.

The doctor stepped into the room, a medical file in hand. "The lab results look good, Ms. Logan, and the X-rays were fine. Nothing broken. Remember, ibuprofen as needed, and take it easy for the next couple days. The muscle relaxers should help your back. Call if anything changes."

A nurse handed Michele her final paperwork and an aide pushed a wheelchair into the room as soon as the doctor had left. Once outside, Michele waited while Jamison retrieved his car.

"You have to be more careful, dear," her mother chattered at her side, her hand, once again, tugging nervously at her collar. "When I think what could have happened…"

"But it didn't. Besides, Jamison arrived immediately after the accident. He called the police and EMTs."

"And if he hadn't followed you to the cemetery, you could still be lying by the side of the road."

Although Michele knew her mother was right, she wouldn't waste time worrying about could-have-beens. Right now she wanted to go home and take a hot shower and change into something other than her rain-damp clothing.

Jamison pulled his sports car up to the curb. A military policeman parked behind him, and a second MP angled Michele's car into the lineup.

Roberta waved a greeting to the young man at the wheel of the second car before she turned back to Michele. "You ride with Jamison, and I'll go with the nice military policeman who brought me."

"Are you sure, Mother?"

Roberta nodded a bit too enthusiastically. "Of course, dear. Besides, you and Jamison probably have a lot to talk over."

Michele's mind was too fuzzy to override her mother. She had a headache and her left leg ached.

Jamison opened the passenger door and helped Michele out of the wheelchair. Wobbly as she was, she appreciated his strong arms supporting her. She inhaled the scent of him and, for an instant, rested her head against his shoulder, comforted by his closeness.

"Easy does it." His voice was filled with warmth as he gently ushered her forward.

Fighting off the desire to remain wrapped in his embrace, Michele slid onto the leather seat, feeling an instant weariness. She waited for Jamison to round the car and climb behind the wheel.

"I could have driven my own car back to post." Although she attempted to sound strong, the faint tremble in her voice spoke volumes about how she really felt.

"Not after that blow you took. You need to take it easy. The EMTs agreed, as I recall."

She nodded. "They did say something to that effect." The doctor had done so, as well, which she didn't mention. "I appreciate your help, Jamison, and hate tying up your day. I shouldn't have been so careless."

He put the car into gear and pulled onto the main road, heading back to Fort Rickman. "Stop blaming yourself for everything that happens, Michele. I never should have allowed you to drive to the cemetery alone. As soon as I realized your safety could be at risk, I raced to catch up to you." His eyes were filled with regret as he turned to look at her. "You weren't at fault, Michele. I was."

"I'm just glad you got there when you did."

He reached out and briefly squeezed her hand. "Have you remembered anything else about the driver?"

She shook her head. "Everything happened so quickly. All I could think about was getting out of the way."

"Thank God, you weren't seriously hurt."

The muscles in her neck tightened. "I'm not sure God had anything to do with it."

She turned toward the window. When they had dated, Michele's heart had softened to the message Jamison had shared about a loving God who wanted the best for His children. Jamison's enthusiasm and commitment to Christ had made her rethink what had happened to her brother and the reasons she had retreated from the Lord. She knew there was a higher power who gave life. Her problem was the seemingly fickle way in which He took that life away.

Oil and water didn't mix. Jamison was a believer and deserved someone who shared his faith. Not a woman who rejected anything to do with God.

"It's still about Lance, isn't it, Michele?"

Jamison deserved answers that she didn't know how to put into words. Michele worried her fingers and tried to pull the random thoughts pinging through her mind into some type of order.

"It's…it's not just Lance," she finally admitted. "Other things have happened."

"Like?"

What could she tell him? Like her father being wounded shortly after he had arrived in Afghanistan. Her mother had prayed for his safety, but God hadn't listened, just as He hadn't listened two years ago when Michele had asked God to keep Lance safe.

Fast-forward to when Michele's resolve had started to soften, and she had tentatively asked the Lord to watch over the CID agent she was beginning to care about in a very special way. Not long after that, her worst fears had been realized when the shooting on post almost claimed Jamison's life.

Suddenly chilled, Michele ran her hands over her arms.

"Cold?"

Without waiting for her reply, Jamison turned on the heat. She was grateful for his response to her unspoken need. Her body temperature had plummeted since she had gotten into the car.

"Why don't you close your eyes and relax?" Jamison suggested. Relieved she wouldn't have to answer any more questions, she settled back in the seat.

Her eyes grew heavy, probably from the muscle relaxer the doctor had given her. She drifted in and out of sleep, hearing snippets of a conversation Jamison had on his cell.

"She's okay, Dawson. We're headed back to post now. Tell Chief Wilson I'll brief him back at the office, once I ensure Mrs. Logan and Michele are safe at home."

Feeling the car decelerate, she blinked her eyes open, surprised they were already at her parents' quarters.

Both military policemen parked behind Jamison. Roberta met them on the sidewalk, her cell phone in hand.

"Your father just called with good news. He pulled a few strings and got the general's approval to move up the brigade's return. If everything goes as planned, they should arrive Friday morning."

Michele attempted to smile. "That's wonderful news."

"Major Hughes will be on board the first plane." Roberta glanced at Jamison. "Stanley wants him escorted off the aircraft ahead of the other soldiers so he can be reunited with his children in a private area."

"I'll ensure that's taken care of, ma'am."

Supporting Michele's arm, he helped her from the car and guided her toward the house. "Security needs to be tightened for the homecoming ceremony, Mrs. Logan. It might be wise to schedule a briefing for the family members this evening. Although it's short notice, I can reserve the auditorium on post."

Roberta nodded. "The wives were already planning to get together tomorrow to make goody bags for the soldiers who don't have families. The barracks need to be swept out and dusted for the guys, the beds made, that type of thing. I planned to send a reminder email to the wives later this afternoon. Information about the briefing will be easy enough to add."

"I'd like to review some safety measures they can take around their homes, as well as the security we'll put in place at the airfield."

"Of course."

Michele and Jamison followed Roberta inside. A few of the wives had remained at the house and were still in the living room. They looked up as Michele excused herself to change clothes. She stopped on the stairway to hear her mother share the good news about the unit's return. The women seemed visibly relieved.

Michele felt just the opposite.

Bad news came in threes.

Yolanda had been murdered.

Lance's gravestone had been desecrated, and Michele had been wounded in a hit-and-run accident.

What worried her now was her father's safety during his last hours in Afghanistan.

Michele rubbed her hands over her arms to stave off the chilling anxiety that swelled up within her and filled her with dread. Until tomorrow morning when her father's plane took off, Michele would be waiting to learn if tragedy would strike again.

FIVE

Jamison stared after Michele as she climbed the stairs to the second floor of her parents' quarters, inhaling the scent of her perfume that still swirled around him. She had gone through so much today and seemed exhausted on the way home. Suggesting she rest in the car had provided the short-term reprieve she had needed.

Wanting to ensure that she was okay before he returned to CID headquarters, Jamison stepped into the kitchen and made a series of phone calls to reserve the post auditorium for the briefing that evening and line up the military police to patrol the area. His last call was to the Fort Rickman airfield to alert them about the returning flights on Friday and the need for secure arrangements for the reunion ceremony. The doorbell rang just as he disconnected.

Roberta greeted Chief Agent in Charge Wilson, a tall and muscular African-American who was the head of Fort Rickman's CID.

"Good to see you, Mrs. Logan, although I'm sorry about the circumstances." The chief pointed to Dawson who followed him into the foyer. "You know Special Agent Timmons."

"Yes, of course. We met earlier." She smiled as Jamison joined them. "Agent Steele has been a great help both last night and today."

"Sir." Jamison nodded to his boss, then acknowledged Dawson. "Miss Logan just returned home from the hospital. Other than being tired and bruised, she seems okay."

Wilson turned to Mrs. Logan. "A relief to all of us, ma'am."

The few ladies who remained in the living room stood, gathered their purses and walked into the foyer, nodding to the CID agents on their way to the door. "Roberta, we need to be going."

Mrs. Logan escorted them outside to say goodbye. While she was gone, Jamison filled his boss and Dawson in on the brigade's new flight schedule. He also informed them of the wives' briefing that evening and the requests he had made for security from the military police.

The chief pursed his lips. "After what happened at the cemetery, I want round-the-clock protection for Mrs. Logan and her daughter."

Jamison was one step ahead of the chief. "I have two men stationed outside, sir, and two additional military police will be here shortly to provide increased surveillance."

"Excellent."

"The Freemont police are compiling names of people in town who may have visited the cemetery today," Jamison continued. "I want to question anyone who might have seen the black car that hit Miss Logan."

Wilson's eyes narrowed ever so slightly. "Agent Timmons can work with the Freemont police. You need to focus on Colonel Logan's family."

Jamison held out his hand. "Sir, I'm more than able to ensure their safety and handle the investigation."

"I'm not insinuating you can't, but Agent Timmons will be the lead investigator on this one. In addition to keeping the colonel's wife and daughter safe, I want you to coordinate security for the brigade's return."

Jamison swallowed his frustration. Although the shift was subtle, his relationship with the chief had changed after the shooting ten months ago, and not in a positive way. Being taken from the lead on this case drove home the point that Wilson wasn't pleased with his performance.

The front door opened, and Mrs. Logan stepped back inside. "Can I offer you gentlemen a cup of coffee?"

The chief shook his head. "Not for me, ma'am, but I would like to talk to you for a few minutes about Mrs. Hughes."

"Certainly." Mrs. Logan pointed to the living room. "We'll be more comfortable in here." Dawson and the chief quickly settled into two Queen Anne chairs across from the couch where she sat.

Unable to move forward, Jamison remained in the hallway, hearing his manipulative father's voice taunt him from the past. *"You'll always be a failure, Jamie-boy."*

Turning at the sound of footsteps, he watched Michele descend the stairs, bringing with her more of the sweet floral scent he had noticed earlier. Her hair was damp, and she had evidently showered before donning a flowing skirt and a silk top that hugged her slender body. She smiled, and the voice from his childhood disappeared.

"You look lovely," Jamison said, feeling a swell of emotion in his chest.

Before she could reply, the doorbell rang.

He glanced out the window. A beige van bearing the florist's shop logo was parked on the street. The florist stood on the steps, a bouquet of flowers in hand.

Surprise flickered from his eyes when Jamison opened the door. "Hey, sir. Long time no see. I've got a delivery."

"Miss Logan was in your shop earlier today, Mr. Sutherland. You could have saved yourself a trip."

Embarrassment tugged at his lips. "Actually, the order came in after she left. After you left, too, sir. And the flowers are for *Mrs*. Logan. Is she home?"

Gently nudging Jamison to the side, Michele reached for the bouquet. The arrangement included yellow roses and white mums with baby's breath and a few other varieties Jamison couldn't name. "They're beautiful. I'll give them to my mother."

Mrs. Logan excused herself from the living room. "Why, isn't that bouquet exquisite? Who are they from, dear?"

Michele opened the card. Her expression clouded ever so slightly as she read the card. "Dad sent them."

Mrs. Logan either didn't notice the change in Michele or refused to respond. Instead, she turned her gaze to the florist. "Thank you, Teddy."

"The pleasure is all mine, ma'am. Be sure to let me know when Colonel Logan plans to return to Fort Rickman so I can place the order for the welcome-home ceremony."

"If everything goes as scheduled, the unit should arrive on post Friday morning."

"I'll contact my wholesaler about the delivery." With a brief nod, he walked back to his truck. Jamison waited until the florist's van was out of sight before he closed the door.

Michele had taken the flowers into the kitchen. From where Jamison stood, he could see the colorful bouquet lying on the kitchen table. Sometimes he felt as if he were stumbling around in the dark without night vision goggles when it came to Michele. After she had run away to Atlanta, he had phoned her a number of times, but the calls always went to her voice mail. Finding out where she lived had been easy enough. The hard part had been trying to stay away from her.

One night when he had allowed his emotions to get the better of him, Jamison had driven to Atlanta and parked outside her apartment, trying to decide what to say when he knocked on her door. Just before he'd climbed from his car, Michele had stepped outside on someone else's arm.

Driving back to Fort Rickman that lonely night, he'd vowed to wipe her memory from his mind. The problem was he hadn't been able to remove Michele from his heart.

In hindsight, he should have sent flowers to woo her back or bouquets while they were dating to convince Michele that, despite the danger of his job, what they had was special.

No matter how he tried to rationalize her actions, he still felt betrayed. He had loved her once. Seeing Michele today, lying injured on the side of the road, had made him realize how much.

* * *

Michele leaned against the counter in the kitchen and stared at the flowers, feeling the lump that had instantly formed in her throat when she'd read her father's card.

Footsteps sounded behind her. She turned to find Jamison staring at her as if he could see the need written on her heart.

"What's wrong?" he asked, concern softening his gaze.

"Nothing." She wrapped her arms defiantly across her chest. "As I keep telling everyone, I'm fine."

Instantly she regretted the sharpness in her tone.

He bristled. Of course, he would.

If only he would join the other agents in the living room so she could have a moment to pull herself together.

He stepped toward her.

Needing a distraction, she grabbed scissors from a drawer and reached for the bouquet. With quick decisive motions, she plucked a flower from the bunch and snipped off the lower end of the stem.

Jamison moved closer. "Was it something I said?"

"Of course not." Pulling in a deep breath, she tried to untangle the confusion she felt. "It…it was my mother."

Michele reached for a second flower. "She didn't mention why Dad sent the bouquet. He knew today would be hard on her."

"Because of Lance?"

Michele nodded. "She doesn't talk about my brother, although for some reason she did last night. I don't think she goes to the cemetery or leaves flowers at his grave. It's as if…"

Still aware of the medication's effect on her, Michele

tried to gather her thoughts. "It's as if she doesn't want to deal with his death."

"Maybe that's her way of running away."

Michele glanced up at Jamison, knowing there was more to his statement than just her mother's response to losing a child. For a long moment, what was unspoken hung in the silence between them.

"We all handle grief in different ways," she finally said, reaching for a glass vase and another flower.

He watched her work and then wrinkled his face as if he had never seen anyone arrange flowers. "You cut off the ends of the stems?"

She ran water into the vase. "The blooms last longer when the old ends are trimmed away."

"Like a gardener prunes a bush or vine?"

She smiled. "You weren't a country boy, were you?"

"Hardly." He choked out a rueful laugh, brief and bitter. "More of a drifter. My dad and I moved often, usually in the middle of the night when he was running from the law."

Something he hadn't revealed to her when they were dating. "I take it your father wasn't the best of role models."

"That's an understatement." Jamison tapped his fingers on the counter as if to diffuse the nervous energy that came over him along with the memory of the past.

"Yet you're a good man."

He stopped tapping. She saw conflict in his eyes.

"So, who helped you growing up?" she asked, hoping to deflect the intensity of his gaze.

Jamison rolled his shoulders, perhaps to ease the tension she could see in his neck and splayed hands. "I threw the discus in high school. My coach encouraged me to go into the army. A chaplain when I was in basic training filled in more of the blanks. He taught me about working hard and doing my best."

Michele heard the admiration he had for both men in his voice and saw the stress lift ever so slightly from Jamison's physical bearing. The memory also brought a smile to his lips.

"The chaplain made his point to a bunch of green recruits by explaining how we needed to whittle away at the deadwood of the softer life we had lived before we came into the military. After a ten-mile road march, his message started to have meaning. By the time I graduated as the top trainee, I had taken his words to heart."

"Top trainee." Michele raised her brow. "That's impressive."

Jamison shoved off the praise with a shake of his head. "My drill sergeant takes all the credit, as well as the chaplain."

"Because he encouraged you to succeed?"

Jamison nodded, then paused for a moment as if thinking back to those beginning days in basic training. "In retrospect, he was probably talking about pruning, although he never used the word. He said changing was painful, but we would be stronger in the end."

Michele reached for another flower. Her fingers touched the fragile petals of the bloodred rose. "Losing someone I loved changed me—but it hasn't made me stronger."

He stepped closer. Too close. She could smell his aftershave, a masculine scent that reminded her of sea breezes. She couldn't help but think back to the nights she'd kissed Jamison on her doorstep and then come inside with the smell of him clinging to her hair. Those nights, she had fallen into bed, hugging her pillow and reliving his lips on hers.

As much as she wanted to change the subject, she couldn't. "Is Lance's death supposed to make me stronger?"

"Michele." He closed the gap between them.

She squared her shoulders, determined to remain in control. "What about Yolanda?"

"We live in the world, Michele. Evil exists. Bad people who do bad things exist, no matter how much we want to pretend they don't. We can't control what they do—only how we respond."

A roar filled her ears. She wrapped her arms across her chest and stepped back again, wanting to distance herself from Jamison and his hollow rhetoric.

Yolanda shouldn't have died, and Michele shouldn't have made a bad decision that resulted in her brother being on board the helicopter that fateful day. A decision everyone in her family refused to talk about.

As if in a dream, the memory from ten months ago of Jamison's blood-smeared white shirt returned unbidden. Dawson had been hit, but when she'd gotten the call about the shoot-out on post, Michele thought Jamison had been the one not expected to live.

She turned away, no longer able to look at Jamison, and fled into the hallway. Tears burned her eyes. Her hand grabbed the banister.

"Is something wrong, dear?" Her mother's voice came from the living room. "Michele?"

She didn't answer. She couldn't reply or she would break down on the stairway. At the landing, she turned into the first bedroom. Her room. Closing the door, she slipped the lock into place.

Lance's picture smiled at her from the dresser. She opened the top drawer and saw the Bible he had given her. A book she hadn't read since his death.

Her gaze fell on a small framed verse she'd received as a child. *All things work together for good to those who love God.*

After everything that had happened, she couldn't trust the Lord. Not now. Not ever.

A small wooden box nestled next to the Bible. Her fingers touched the wood, unwilling to open the lid. She pushed the drawer shut and fell onto her bed.

She clenched her eyes closed, hoping to block out the moment. Instead, her mind filled with the horrible vision of Yolanda's body.

"No." Michele shook her head and groaned.

Lance's funeral. The cloying smell of flowers surrounded his casket.

The minister's voice sounded in her ears. "The Lord giveth life and the Lord taketh away life."

Once again, she saw Jamison's blood-smeared white shirt, only this time he was dead.

"Why, Lord?" she cried. "Why do You always take the ones I love?"

SIX

Cell phone in one hand, Jamison gripped the steering wheel with the other as he talked to Dawson. "I'm on my way to the auditorium. Mrs. Logan and Michele should be along shortly in their own vehicle. Stiles will remain at the quarters while McGrunner follows the ladies. I told him to stick like glue to both of them."

"Mac's a good man."

"Who understands the importance of protecting the colonel's wife." Jamison's tightened his grip on the steering wheel. Just so long as Mac would keep Michele safe, as well.

"Were all the spouses notified about the briefing?" Dawson asked.

"Affirmative. Mrs. Logan sent out an email to the Family Readiness Groups earlier today. All the spouses should have received the information. Everyone has been waiting for word of the brigade's redeployment, so the briefing wasn't a total surprise, despite the short notice. Those who don't have internet access were contacted by phone."

"You checked the auditorium?"

"The building's clean. I've got men patrolling the

parking lot and surrounding area. They'll remain on-site until everyone leaves the premises."

Dawson blew out a breath. "You're expecting the killer to show up tonight?"

"It's a possibility. Having that many people, mainly women, amassed in one area is a perfect opportunity for a psychopath to wreak havoc on Fort Rickman."

"Yet there's no indication he's on post."

"That doesn't mean he's not. I plan to stress that point when I brief the families tonight. I'll also discuss the welcome-home ceremony as well as the security issues at the airfield."

"I'll be glad when the brigade returns to post. Soldiers home from a war zone are a formidable protective force."

"Even then, we can't let down our guard until the killer is apprehended."

"We'll find him."

Jamison wasn't as confident. "What's happening with the press?"

"The commanding general is asking the media to go through the Public Affairs Office. They issued a statement, and so far everyone's been compliant."

"No one tied the run-in at the cemetery to the murder?"

"Not that I've heard so far. I contacted the Freemont police. They're still tracking down the names of townspeople who have relatives buried near the oak tree."

"Simpson was the officer at the cemetery today. He seemed competent."

"Freemont P.D. verified the blood on the gravestone was bovine, not human."

"Exactly as Simpson suspected." Jamison made a

mental note to call the Freemont cop. "Did you discuss the autopsy with Major Hansen?"

"The doc seems to be as busy as we are. He finally returned my call. What he found was consistent with the victim's wounds. The autopsy revealed nothing we didn't already know."

"What about the Prime Maintenance man?"

"Danny Altman? Evidently he took a couple days' leave."

"Convenient." Jamison focused his gaze on the road ahead. "Any word from Special Agent Warner in Afghanistan?"

"Negative. You want me to call him?"

"I'll handle it."

"Listen, buddy—" Dawson hesitated. "I was as surprised as you were today when the chief gave me the lead on this case. You know I wouldn't go behind your back or ask for you to be taken off the investigation."

Jamison didn't want to rehash a decision the chief had already made. "Wilson's in charge. He did what he thought was right."

"It's not how it looks."

"He believes in you, Dawson. Let's leave it at that."

"But—"

"No buts. Just keep me informed," Jamison said before he disconnected.

Dawson was a good agent. A few months junior by date of rank to Jamison, but Dawson had excellent instincts and was a bulldog when it came to tracking down evidence. Plus, he could handle the pressure of both the chief and the commanding general demanding an arrest. As much as Jamison hated being removed from the investigation, finding the killer and putting him behind bars was the goal, no matter who took the lead.

Turning into the parking lot, Jamison flicked his gaze over the large freestanding auditorium. Military police stood guard at the doors, ready to check the identification cards of all who sought entry. Each MP had a list of spouses' names, which had been pulled from the master roster at the brigade. Anyone seeking entrance other than family members would be questioned. Purses and totes would be searched, and every precaution would be taken to ensure the safety of all those attending the briefing.

Leaving his car at the far side of the auditorium, Jamison double-timed toward the building. Once he confirmed that the proper security measures were being implemented, he stepped back outside and eyed the stream of cars heading into the parking lot.

Car doors slammed as women exited their vehicles and walked toward the large central structure. Despite the news of the unit's impending arrival, the women's eyes were solemn and their faces strained with worry—no doubt, because of Yolanda's death.

A light blue sedan turned into the lot. Michele sat behind the wheel, her mother next to her in the passenger seat. A military police cruiser followed close behind. As Michele parked, the cruiser pulled over to the curb where Jamison stood.

Corporal McGrunner, a tall Midwest farm boy with a lanky body and a ready smile, rolled down his window and saluted. "Both Mrs. Logan and her daughter are present and accounted for, sir."

"Anything happen at the Logan quarters after I left?"

Mac shook his head. "Negative. Except Mrs. Logan offered us sweet tea and chocolate chip cookies."

"I won't ask whether you succumbed to her Southern hospitability."

The MP's eyes twinkled. "Mrs. Logan can be insistent."

Jamison had to smile. "Remain outside, Mac. Keep watch. After the briefing, we'll escort the ladies back to their quarters."

"Yes, sir."

Jamison adjusted his tie as he hustled across the parking lot. He approached the sedan and held the door open for Mrs. Logan.

"Ma'am."

"Evening, Jamison."

Michele dropped the keys into her handbag. She stepped onto the asphalt and turned to close her door.

Their eyes met for an instant, causing a muscle in Jamison's jaw to twitch. "Evening, Michele."

"Jamison."

She wore a pretty dress that hugged her waist and flowed around her knees. A gentle breeze pulled at her hair. She arranged the wayward strains back into place and heaved a sigh that reminded him of her struggle earlier this afternoon.

"How's the leg?" he asked.

"Not as sore."

"And the muscle in your back?"

"Better."

A car turned into the lot and drove toward them. Jamison placed his hand on Michele's arm, warning her of the approaching vehicle.

Moved by her closeness, he tried to ignore the swell

in his chest and guided her forward once the car passed. "Did you get some sleep?"

She nodded, her eyes on the pavement.

Evidently, she didn't want to talk.

He turned to Mrs. Logan. "Ma'am, as you probably know, the chaplain's been on temporary duty in South Carolina. He returned to post this afternoon and will be available if any of the women want to schedule an appointment. He also mentioned a prayer service tomorrow for the unit's safe return."

"You and the chaplain have thought of everything, Jamison."

"What are you planning to tell the ladies tonight?" Michele asked, raising her gaze.

Pointing Michele toward the auditorium, he tried to concentrate on what she had asked instead of her smooth skin and silky hair and the vulnerability he felt emanating from her whenever he got close.

"Basic safety with emphasis on being cautious. And I'll encourage those gathered to call us if they're concerned about anything. We've increased the number of phone lines coming into CID headquarters. Plus, we've set up a neighborhood watch program in each housing area. Luckily, some of the units aren't deployed, so we've got military personnel organized on foot patrols."

Michele raised her brow. "What about the women who live off post?"

"We haven't forgotten them," he said with a flicker of a smile. "The Freemont police have the names and addresses of all the military families in the surrounding area. They're organizing neighborhood watch programs, just as we are at Fort Rickman."

Mrs. Logan patted Jamison's arm. "I certainly appreciate all you're doing."

"It's my job, ma'am."

"Yes, but you go above and beyond." Her attention turned to a minivan that had just parked.

"Excuse me for a minute." Always the thoughtful colonel's wife, Mrs. Logan stepped toward the three wives who climbed from the van and greeted each of them with a warm embrace.

Jamison guided Michele across the street. His hand touched the small of her back, and her hair blew against his shoulder. For an instant, he had a sense of the world's being in right order.

Then he glanced at the military police standing at the entrance to the auditorium. With a killer on the loose, nothing was right tonight.

Tugging the free-flowing strains of her honey-brown hair behind her ear, Michele drew in a shallow breath. "I need to apologize about the way I acted earlier. The muscle relaxer made me tired and emotional."

He flicked his free hand, trying to dispel her concern. "Michele, it's okay. You've been through so much. No need to apologize for anything."

"I wasn't myself, Jamison. You know I'm usually levelheaded."

Levelheaded? Michele was beautiful in so many ways and stronger than even she realized, but while she tried to make good decisions—levelheaded decisions—she saw life through a prism that twisted reality.

"You've had two shocks in the last twenty-four hours that have taken a toll on you," he offered, knowing she was waiting for his response. "The hit-and-run accident today was stressful enough without what happened last night. Everyone reacts differently, and you need time to rest and heal. You probably should have stayed home this evening."

She shook her head. "I needed to be here for my mother. She seems in control on the outside, but she's struggling inside. Yolanda's death, compounded by the anniversary of Lance's crash. It's a lot to carry."

Michele was able to recognize her mother's struggle but not her own. The last rays of the setting sun shadowed her flushed cheeks and expressive brows raised in question as if she wanted him to agree.

When he didn't respond, she continued, her voice low so only he could hear. "Even though Mother rarely talks about Lance, I know she's still grieving."

Michele was, as well. Jamison held his tongue, hoping she would make the transition to her own internal struggle. Exposing her pain would be healing, but as he waited for her response, he sensed she needed prodding.

"What about you, Michele? Are you still grieving?"

She stopped her forward progression and seemed to try to mask her own confusion by straightening her spine and raising her jaw. Although determination flashed from her eyes, he could read through her false bravado.

When they had dated, Michele had given him only a glimpse of what she held within. Now that they'd been thrown together again, he could see that her grief was still so raw.

Wanting to console her, he said, "You were lucky."

She titled her head and looked defiantly into his eyes. "In what way?"

"From what you've said, Lance was a great brother. You had a close relationship. The pain you feel is because you loved him. Some people don't grow up surrounded by love."

Jamison thought of his own childhood and his wayward father who didn't know anything about raising a child. "I can only imagine the blessings you experienced growing up. The affirmation alone—"

He had already said too much. She was starting to shut him out. Jamison had to stop, but he couldn't resist making one more attempt to pull down the wall she had built around her fragile heart.

"Some people—" He hesitated, needing to choose his words. "Some people don't know how to love. Treasure the close relationship you and your brother had, but don't allow it to keep you from living life in the present." Jamison struggled every day to keep his past from poisoning his happiness. He hated to see Michele suffering the same way.

In truth, his father had been a dysfunctional narcissist, who had taken everything from his young son and given him nothing in return. Nothing except condemnation.

"You're a failure, a good for nothin'."

Michele had grown up with strong role models who practiced loving, giving relationships. She would never be able to understand a man who thought the world owed him everything and who resented his son's drive and determination.

Only through the grace of God had Jamison been able to hold on to the truth. He didn't want a handout or a leg up, nor did he want to live on the dole like his old man. His refusal to compromise on that had destroyed any chance of a working relationship between him and his father, but it had allowed him to build new relationships that he treasured. Relationships with his colleagues. His friends. And God.

Jamison had worked hard to distance himself from his father and his past. The military had been a good influencer, and the chaplain who had taught him about the Lord had given him a firm foundation on which to stand.

But now the military community that had given him so much was in danger. That was why he had to push forward and right the wrongs and protect the innocent and catch the bad guys so no one else would get hurt. Jamison had to succeed. If not, he would turn into the person his father wanted him to be. A failure just like his old man.

Jamison caught up to Michele as she neared the security checkpoint at the entrance to the auditorium. Had they made any progress tonight? The fact was, he had revealed more than he needed to, which made him wonder about his own internal struggle. As usual, Michele had been more reticent.

She gave her name and handed her driver's license to the military policeman, who checked her off the roster. Jamison escorted her to a seat near the stage.

The woman next to her had rosy cheeks and expressive blue-green eyes and evidently knew Michele because they embraced in a long hug and talked about the last time they had been together.

"It must have been the battalion's homecoming," the rosy-cheeked woman said. "What was it, three years ago when the guys came back from Iraq?"

"Then you moved on to a new assignment. I didn't know Paul had been transferred back to post."

"He was reassigned to Fort Rickman five months

ago," the woman explained. "Paul left for Afghanistan after we moved into quarters." Her smile waned. "I...I'm sorry about your brother. His death must have been hard on all of you."

Michele nodded and then glanced up at Jamison. "Have you met Special Agent Steele?"

"Alice Rossi." She extended her hand. "I'm Sergeant Paul Rossi's wife."

"Nice to meet you, ma'am."

Knowing Michele was in good company, Jamison excused himself and joined Mrs. Logan on the stage.

The seats in the auditorium quickly filled, and a buzz of conversation carried across the hall as the audience chatted among themselves.

Chaplain Grant, a tall lieutenant colonel with a long face and a sincere smile, joined them on the stage.

Jamison accepted his outstretched hand. "Thanks for being here, sir."

"Terrible what happened last night, Agent Steele."

"Yes, sir."

The chaplain stepped to where Mrs. Logan was sitting in a folding chair. They talked about the prayer service scheduled the next day while Jamison scanned the crowd. His gaze came to rest on Michele, who continued to chat with Mrs. Rossi.

An unwelcome yearning filled Jamison that set him back to where he had been ten months ago. He had tried to convince himself that he had moved on with his life, but after being with Michele for these last twenty-four hours, he had to face facts. He still cared for the colonel's daughter.

At that moment, she turned and raised her eyes to meet his. Jamison's chest constricted. He needed to remember that everything had changed when Michele walked away from him.

No matter what he read in her gaze, Michele Logan didn't want anything to do with a military guy and especially a CID agent. Bottom line, she didn't want anything to do with Jamison.

Michele had trouble sitting through the briefing in the auditorium, mainly because Jamison was onstage. Seeing him dressed in his crisp white shirt and dark suit brought back memories of when they had dated.

Concern and compassion for the family members warmed his expression as he answered their questions and offered suggestions to keep everyone safe. He gave out his phone number, asking to be called if anyone had a problem or felt the least threat of danger.

"He certainly is a fine man," one of the wives said to a woman sitting behind Michele.

She had to agree. Jamison was a good man with a big heart and a willingness to help others. He believed in doing what was right and worked hard to keep military personnel and family members safe from anyone out to do them harm.

Michele had recognized his dedication and commitment when they had first met, although at that point in their relationship, she hadn't realized the danger he faced each and every day. The shoot-out ten months ago had brought that reality front and center and sent her running scared.

If Jamison worked in another profession, one that didn't require him to risk his life, she never would have left Fort Rickman.

After the few comments Jamison had made at her

house today, she better understood his commitment to the military. His childhood had been difficult, and the army had provided stability and security and a feeling of being part of a team that was making a difference. It would be hard to let that go and move into the civilian world, no matter how much she wanted him to do exactly that.

On the stage, Jamison stood beside her mother, who continued to address the gathering. "The major portion of the unit is scheduled to leave Afghanistan tomorrow," Roberta said to those assembled. "If everything goes as planned, the planes should land at the airfield on post Friday morning. I'd ask you to please notify any of the spouses who aren't here tonight. Some of the families have been staying with relatives in other parts of the country and will be returning to Fort Rickman soon. We've activated the calling trees, and the rear detachment is trying to contact everyone not in the area, but you can help by spreading the word."

She glanced out at the audience and smiled. "Because this is such a difficult time, Chaplain Grant will be having a special prayer service at the Main Post Chapel tomorrow, at 11:00 a.m. We'll be asking the Lord to bring the brigade safely home and to protect us so we can all be reunited with our deployed loved ones."

Glancing down at her notes, she continued. "At 1:00 p.m. tomorrow, we'll meet at the brigade to get the barracks ready for the soldiers. We could use everyone's help. Also, we need baked goods and candy for the welcome-home goody bags each soldier will have waiting for him or her in the barracks." She smiled. "The work will keep us occupied while we await the brigade's return."

Motioning toward Jamison, she added, "Don't hesitate to call Special Agent Steele if you have any questions or concerns."

After a round of applause, the family members exited the auditorium. The night was hot and humid when Michele stepped outside. Her mother followed a few minutes later, surrounded by a group of women eager to discuss the brigade's new arrival date.

Alice Rossi had stopped to talk to some of the wives inside before she caught up with Michele. "It was good seeing you tonight."

"Don't you want to say hello to Mother?"

Alice glanced at the women gathered around Roberta. "She's busy, and I need to get home. Thank her for all she's done to help the wives while the brigade has been deployed. I'm sure she encouraged your dad to bring the unit back a few days early. After what happened to Mrs. Hughes, knowing the men will be home has been a big morale boost."

"Do you have to rush off?"

Alice's expressive eyes twinkled. "Paul said he'd call. It's our wedding anniversary, and I want to be home when he phones."

Michele smiled at the good news, which didn't seem to come often enough these days. "How many years?"

"Fifteen. Seems like only yesterday I was a new army wife. I wasn't sure where we'd go, but I wanted to be with Paul, no matter where the army sent him."

Michele thought of her own struggle. "Did...did you ever worry about his safety?"

Alice laughed. "Of course, but we made a pact early on in our marriage never to leave the house without a kiss and a prayer to keep us safe until we could be reunited. Trusting God helped me put aside any undue worry."

Michele held her tongue. Hadn't she prayed for her brother's safety?

"You'll be at the welcome-home ceremony?" Alice asked.

Michele nodded. "Yes, of course."

The wife squeezed her hand. "I'll see you there."

Watching Alice scurry to her car, Michele marveled at the lightness in her step, wishing she, too, could be free of the weight that seemed to always drag her down. No matter how much she longed to live in the moment and not worry about what tomorrow might bring, Michele couldn't change who she was and the way she reacted to fear.

Jamison was right. A lot had happened in a short amount of time. Hopefully, once her father was safe on U.S. soil, her outlook would improve.

Glancing over her shoulder, she peered into the auditorium where Jamison stood, still surrounded by women. Even from this distance, she could see how focused he was on those who needed more information or had questions. His broad shoulders seemed strong enough to bear the concerns and fears of all the wives.

Michele trusted Jamison, but she couldn't trust her heart to a man who placed himself in danger.

One of the wives hurried from the auditorium and edged close to Michele. She held a tote bag in her left hand. "I found this on the floor where Alice Rossi was sitting. She was in a hurry to get home and must have left it behind."

Michele pointed to the car disappearing in the distance. "Alice just drove away."

The woman rummaged in the bag. "Her cell phone's here, so we can't call her. I've got to pick up my kids at the babysitter's or I'd drop it off at her house."

Overhearing the conversation, Roberta excused herself from the group of ladies and reached for the bag. "You need to get your children. Michele and I can take the tote to Alice." Relieved, the woman hugged Roberta before she raced to her car.

Michele glanced back at Jamison still answering questions in the auditorium. Her mother followed her gaze.

"Looks like he'll be tied up for quite a while." Roberta pointed to Corporal McGrunner, standing nearby on the curb. "I'll see if Mac can escort us home."

"Jamison wanted to follow us, Mother."

"I know, dear, but you said Alice is expecting Paul to call. If so, she'll need her cell phone."

"I had the feeling he was calling on their home landline."

"Either way, she'll want her bag. I'll talk to Jamison and Mac while you get the car."

By the time Michele pulled up to the curb, Mac had climbed into the military police sedan. Roberta opened the passenger door and slipped into the seat next to her daughter.

"I sent one of the wives back inside to tell Jamison. Mac's in his car and ready to follow us."

Michele raised her brow. "Are you sure what we're doing is okay with Jamison?"

"Yes, dear."

Roberta gave Michele directions to Alice's house, but she continued to worry. Pulling out her cell, she hit Speed Dial. "I'm phoning Jamison."

The call went to voice mail. Michele left a message, explaining why she and her mother hadn't waited for him.

As they left the parking lot, Michele glanced in her rearview mirror at the stream of cars behind them. "Mac appears to be caught in a traffic jam."

Roberta glanced over her shoulder at the bottleneck. "We should go ahead. I want to get home as soon as possible. I'm sure Mac will be along shortly."

"I'd feel better if we wait."

"You know how hard it is for the guys to place a call from Afghanistan. I don't want Alice to come back to the auditorium for her tote and miss the call." Roberta nudged her daughter. "Go on. Drive. I've got Jamison's cell number programmed on my phone. I'll call him if we run into a problem."

Roberta's voice sounded tired. The day had been long for both of them. There was no reason for Michele to make more of the situation than was needed. The detour to Alice's house wouldn't take long, and they would probably arrive at her parents' quarters before Jamison realized they had left the area.

Roberta pointed to the upcoming intersection. "Turn left at the light. Alice lives in the Harding Housing area at the southern edge of post."

Once the housing area came into view, Michele noticed headlights in her rearview mirror and smiled. "Looks like Mac caught up with us."

Roberta glanced back. "That's good, dear."

Michele felt a sense of relief. Although she had complied with her mother's wishes, she hadn't been able to shake the sense they were making a mistake.

Jamison had been so insistent about their need for

protection. Usually, he was overly cautious. This time she agreed with him, yet the briefing had gone well, and none of the wives had mentioned any concerns at their own homes. Many of the women sitting around her had talked about Yolanda's death being a random killing, which had probably been the case.

Michele was tired and her leg ached. Just like her mother, she wanted to get home. Turning into the housing area, she glanced again at the vehicle following behind them. Her optimism plummeted when the car continued straight ahead on the main road.

Roberta pointed to the next intersection. "Turn right. Alice lives at the end of that road."

Michele reached for her cell. "I'm calling Jamison again. Something happened to Mac. Did you explain we were making a stop before heading home?"

Roberta tilted her head and hesitated. "He said he'd follow us."

Michele hit Speed Dial and sighed when she was, once again, connected to voice mail.

"Mother and I are making a quick stop in the Harding Housing area," she said into the phone. "Mac got tied up leaving the auditorium parking lot. We'll be delayed arriving home. Don't worry, we're fine." Breathing a bit more easily, she returned her cell to her pocket.

"Jamison is probably still talking to the ladies," Roberta said. "We'll be pulling into our driveway before he ever gets your message."

"Maybe so, but I don't want him to worry."

Roberta raised her brow. "I didn't know you were so concerned about Jamison."

"He's in charge of our security, Mother. I've caused him enough problems already."

"I don't think you're a problem, dear."

Before Michele could question the meaning behind her mother's last comment, Alice's house appeared at the end of the street. Pulling the sedan over to the curb, Michele glanced at the small quarters. The lights were on inside, although the blinds were drawn and the front stoop was dark.

Michele grabbed the tote and stepped onto the pavement. "Stay in the car, Mother. I'll be right back."

Roberta's cell phone rang. "Maybe that's Jamison."

She read the name on the screen. "It's Erica Grayson." She waved to Michele. "Go on, dear, while I find out if Yolanda's sister arrived."

Michele slammed the car door and hurried along the sidewalk to the house. As she neared the porch, she heard a telephone ring inside the quarters. Paul was calling on their landline.

Knocking lightly, Michele eased the front door open. "Alice? You forgot your tote bag at the auditorium. I'll leave it in the dining room."

Stepping inside, Michele placed the bag on the table. The phone rang again.

"Alice?"

Why didn't she answer the expected call?

A hallway led into the darkened kitchen. The phone rang a third time.

Michele's heart pounded a warning.

A shuffling noise sounded behind her.

She turned.

A man, wearing a black face mask, lunged from the shadows. He held a stun gun in his hand, aimed at her arm.

Ice-cold panic froze her for half a heartbeat before he released the charge.

Fire exploded through her body.

Her muscles convulsed and her limbs writhed in spastic movements she couldn't control.

His maniacal laughter filled the house and sent even more involuntary tremors to twist her spine.

She fell to the floor, tried to scream and heard only the deep guttural groan that came from her drooling mouth.

He grabbed her shoulder and flipped her over. The black ski mask leaned into her line of vision.

Michele tried to backpedal along the floor, but her legs wouldn't respond.

A knife. Razor sharp.

She gasped.

Unable to move, Michele could only think of Jamison, who tried so hard to protect her.

This time, he would be too late.

SEVEN

After the last woman thanked him for his help, Jamison hurried from the auditorium and searched the near-empty parking lot, frowning when he was unable to find Michele or her mother.

Anxiety threaded through his veins and headed straight for his heart. Surely he was overreacting. Corporal McGrunner had probably escorted the women home.

Jamison pulled out his cell phone. Three voice mails. The first was from Michele. "We have to stop by Alice Rossi's house on the way home. Mac's following us, so you needn't worry."

Jamison couldn't calm the alarm clanging through his head. He tapped into the second message. Corporal McGrunner's voice. All Jamison could hear was the worry in the soldier's usually calm baritone.

"Sir, I was following Mrs. Logan and her daughter back to their quarters. A traffic jam formed as I was getting out of the parking area and onto the main road. I…ah… Well, sir, they drove on. As soon as I could get free, I headed along the route we used earlier, but I can't locate them. I'm at their quarters now, and Stiles is the only one here. What should I do, sir? Where should I look?"

Jamison's gut tightened. Shoving aside his need to punch a hole in the brick wall of the auditorium, he raced to his car and hit the prompt for the third call.

Michele's voice. Maybe everything was all right after all. When he listened to the voice mail he felt anything but relieved.

"Mac got tied up leaving the auditorium parking lot. We'll be delayed arriving home. Don't worry, we're fine."

Don't worry! As if he could do anything but worry. The two women had gone off alone. Exactly what Jamison had told them not to do. Slipping behind the wheel, he dialed Michele. Before the call went through, his phone buzzed.

Mrs. Logan's name appeared on the screen. Mother and daughter were probably back at their quarters, but Jamison couldn't hide his frustration as he raised the phone to his ear. "Where are you, ma'am? Corporal McGrunner lost you. Tell me you're all right."

"Oh, Jamison…something's happened…Michele…"

A sickening feeling swept over him, making his head swim and his ears ring. He backed out of the parking space and stomped on the accelerator, leaving a black line on the roadway.

"Where are you, ma'am?"

"Alice Rossi's place in the Harding Housing area. Quarters Thirty-seven."

"Is Michele with you?"

"That's the problem. She went inside to return Alice's tote bag. She…" Mrs. Logan gasped. "She never came out. I pounded on the door and tried to get in, but—"

"Michele's inside?"

"I saw a man through the sidelight window. He ran from the room when he heard me knock but he's still in the house." Roberta's voice broke.

"Get back in your car. Lock the doors and drive to the military police headquarters. I'll have McGrunner meet you there."

Once again, Jamison had failed to keep Michele safe.

Disconnecting from the colonel's wife before she could respond, he hit Speed Dial for Dawson and relayed the address Mrs. Logan had given him. "We need every military police officer in that area. The perpetrator is holed up inside with Michele. Use caution approaching the house. Have Otis contact McGrunner. Mrs. Logan's on her way to the military police headquarters. Have Mac meet her there."

"Roger that."

Jamison shoved his cell phone into his pocket and gripped the steering wheel with both hands. He increased his speed and drove like a madman toward the housing area.

Please, Lord, keep her safe. Just because I couldn't protect her doesn't mean You won't.

If anything happened to Michele, Jamison would never stop blaming himself. For the first time, he began to understand Michele's hesitancy to embrace the Lord. In her mind, God hadn't saved her brother, so she refused to turn to Him in her need. The difference was that Jamison knew if he didn't put his trust in the Lord, everything he believed in would be a lie.

The drive across post took too long. Jamison's heart

threatened to explode as he screeched to the curb, jumped from his car and raced toward the Logans' vehicle still parked on the street. Mrs. Logan sat huddled in the passenger seat.

"Get out of here." He waved her on. "Now. Corporal McGrunner is on his way to MP headquarters. You'll be safe with him. I'll take care of Michele."

She cracked the window, her eyes filled with fear, and pointed to the thicket behind the quarters. "I…I just saw a man run into the woods."

Jamison flicked his gaze into the tall stand of trees. "Drive away, ma'am."

She shook her head. Tears welled up in her eyes. "Michele has the keys. Besides, I…I won't leave my daughter."

"Then get down and stay put."

She slumped lower in the seat. Her muffled sobs cut through Jamison's resolve.

He darted up the front steps and crouched at the side of the door. Glancing through the sidelight, he saw nothing, heard nothing except his own heart thumping in his chest.

The fingers of his right hand tightened on his weapon. He reached for the brass knob with his left and groaned silently when it failed to turn.

Needing to get inside as soon as possible, he took a running leap and lunged, throwing his body against the door. Once. Twice.

The lock sprang, and the door flew open.

Weapon raised and finger on the trigger, he entered the house, his eyes searching the darkness.

A moan brought bile to his gut. He followed the

sound into the dining room and dropped to the floor when he saw Michele.

Blood spattered the front of her blouse.

He touched her neck.

She blinked her eyes open. "Al…Alice?"

"What happened?"

"My muscles…spasms…I tried to fight, but…I couldn't move…."

"Did you see him?"

She nodded. "He…he was wearing a black ski mask…. He had a knife."

Jamison pushed back her hair, searching for the source of the blood, relieved to find none. At the same time he raised his cell and called Dawson.

"Send an ambulance. I've got Michele. The guy ran. Set up roadblocks. Have foot patrols search the housing area. Lock down Fort Rickman."

"Alice?" she asked again when he disconnected.

"I'll find her."

Michele tried to sit up. Jamison put his hand on her shoulder. "Stay where you are."

He headed for the kitchen and adjoining breakfast area. The woman Michele had introduced him to at the auditorium lay on the floor beside the table. Her blue-green eyes had been full of life earlier. Now they were covered with a deadly haze.

He stooped and felt for a pulse. Faint, but she was still alive. "Hang on, ma'am. An ambulance is on the way."

Her neck had been cut, but the artery was still intact.

She was lucky, or would be if she lived.

He heard a noise and turned.

Michele was standing in the doorway. She gasped

and ran to kneel beside the wounded woman. "Oh, Alice."

Jamison checked the rest of the house. Glass from a small window next to the back door had shattered onto the floor. Easy enough for the perpetrator to stick his hand through the window and turn the lock, which must have been the mode of entry.

Jamison retraced his steps to the kitchen. He found Michele holding Alice's hand and reassuring her with a calming voice. "Hold on, honey. You're going to be okay."

Glancing up, Michele shook her head.

"The ambulance is on the way," he offered for support.

"Will it get here in time?"

Before he could respond, the house phone rang.

They both stared at where it sat on the kitchen counter.

"It's her wedding anniversary." Michele's voice was no more than a whisper. "Her husband said he'd call."

If Sergeant Rossi was on the line, Jamison would have to tell him about his wife. He glanced once again at Michele, her lips tight, her eyes wide.

Pulling his handkerchief from his pocket, Jamison wrapped it around the receiver and raised the phone to his ear.

"I used a stun gun." A muffled male voice. No hint of a Southern drawl.

Jamison needed to keep him talking. "How'd you get inside the house?"

"You're smart enough to figure that out."

"You attacked Yolanda and now Mrs. Rossi. Why?"

"I thought you were good at what you do."

"You've got a grudge against the military."

Laughter.

Jamison's fisted his free hand, wanting to reach through the phone and yank the killer by the throat.

The laughter halted abruptly. "I love the military, but not everyone acts heroically."

"Is killing an innocent woman heroic?"

A growl sounded in Jamison's ear. "I defended my country. I went to war and came home, but—"

"But what?"

"It was too late."

"Too late for what? Were you hurt?"

"I died." The line disconnected.

"Wait—" Jamison tapped in the digits to retrieve the caller's number.

Using his own cell, he phoned CID headquarters. Corporal Raynard Otis answered.

"The killer called the Rossi quarters." He relayed the home phone digits and the incoming number. "See if you can find where the call originated."

"I'm on it, sir."

"What'd the killer say?" Michele asked when Jamison hung up.

"That he was a soldier who was redeployed home from the war too late."

Sirens wailed toward the house. Jamison started toward the front door, but stopped when the phone rang again. Just as before, he used his handkerchief and raised the phone to his ear, expecting to hear the killer's voice once more.

"Happy anniversary to the most beautiful woman in the whole world. I'm coming home, baby. Won't be long and you'll be in my arms."

Jamison's mouth went dry.

"Alice?"

"Sergeant Rossi, this is CID Special Agent Jamison Steele. I have bad news."

Michele clutched Alice's hand and watched Jamison's face as he explained what had happened to her husband over the phone. All too vividly, Michele remembered the call from her parents when Lance's chopper crashed.

The scream of sirens stopped out front, and the house filled with military police. EMTs hastened to help Alice. Michele moved away to give them room to work.

Jamison hung up with Sergeant Rossi as Dawson walked toward him. The two men lowered their voices. Jamison was a few inches taller than Dawson and leaner. His neck was taut, his gaze intense as they conversed.

They turned in unison and looked at Michele. Still overcome with fatigue, she stared back, unable to mask her fear. Another woman had been injured—almost killed—and the attacker had come after her.

Dawson approached her. "Jamison told me you saw the attacker."

"Yes, but I can't tell you what he looked like. He wore a ski mask and surgical gloves on his hands, like a doctor. His eyes were dark. Maybe brown, but I'm not sure."

"Any other features you recall? Height? Build?"

"Everything was a blur."

"Take your time," Dawson said.

She glanced from the lead agent to Jamison. His jaw was set and his eyes were dark. Ten months ago, Jamison's eyes sparkled, and his easy smile used to make her insides quiver. Right now the raw look on his face had her quivering again. Both of them knew she was lucky to be alive.

Michele and her mother never should have left the auditorium without Jamison. But then another thought struck Michele full force. If Jamison had escorted them, he would have confronted the killer. Knowing what could have happened to Jamison mixed with the memory of the knife and the spasms that had rocked her body.

"He was medium height," she finally said. "Well built. Like Jamison."

"Caucasian?" Dawson asked.

"Yes." She thought again of the knife and saw his hands holding the sharp blade. This time, she saw the knife at Jamison's throat.

Jamison stepped closer."Is there anything you can tell us about the knife, Michele?"

She closed her eyes and rubbed her hands over her forehead, forcing her mind to focus on Jamison's question instead of the image of the sharp blade and Jamison's exposed flesh.

"Metal handle?" he asked.

She nodded.

"Serrated blade or smooth?"

"Smooth. Sharp." She pursed her lips and shook her head. "The killer put it against my—" She touched her neck. "He stopped when someone pounded on the door."

Jamison nodded. "Your mother was worried about you. When she couldn't get in the house, she called me."

He leaned close to Michele as if he were trying to support her with his presence. She wished the others would go away so she could step into his arms. At the moment, with her insides still shaky and the memory of what had happened all too real, she wanted to be surrounded by his strength.

Looking into his eyes, a flash of connection passed between them, and she knew in that instant that Jamison understood.

"The effects of the stun gun will pass, Michele," he said, his voice soothing her fears. "The fatigue is due to your muscles convulsing and the lactic acid buildup."

"I…I'm the lucky one." She turned her gaze to the EMTs. They lifted Alice onto a gurney, ready to take her to the ambulance.

A medic approached Michele. "Ma'am, I'd like to check your vitals and see how you're doing."

"I…I'm okay."

"Yes, ma'am. But it's a good idea to let us make sure your stats coincide with how you feel."

Jamison's hand rubbed against her arm. "Dawson and I will be outside."

"My mother?"

"An MP is with her," Dawson said. "I'll tell him she can come in now."

Michele nodded. She didn't want Jamison to leave her. As she watched him walk away, she felt empty, drained, unable to think of anything except the urge to call him back to her.

Had she made a mistake by leaving him ten months ago? As much as she wished everything was different, she knew there was no way she could change what had happened. She had left Jamison for a good reason, or so it had seemed at the time. Now she wasn't sure of anything.

* * *

Once the signal was given, the military policeman allowed Mrs. Logan into the house. "Michele's in the kitchen," Jamison said as she rushed past him.

The two agents stepped outside. "How'd Michele end up with the killer?" Dawson asked.

Jamison explained about the tote bag and Michele and her mother trying to be Good Samaritans.

"Was he waiting for Mrs. Rossi to return home from the briefing? Or was he going through the house for some other reason, and she surprised him?"

"Nothing was disturbed, Dawson. He was there for one reason and one reason only. He targeted Yolanda Hughes and Alice Rossi. We need to find a tie between those two women. From what Michele said, he would have killed her if Mrs. Logan hadn't pounded on the front door and scared him off."

Jamison thought of the cemetery. Surely it was too much of a stretch to think the killer on post was the same person as the hit-and-run driver. Another thought chilled him. Could two attackers be targeting the same group of women?

Dawson's cell rang. He raised it to his ear and nodded. "Keep searching." When he disconnected, he turned worried eyes to Jamison. "We set up roadblocks as soon as you called. Teams are canvassing the surrounding area on foot. No sign yet of anyone suspect."

Jamison pointed to the area behind the house. "The woods lead to the vast training area. If he headed that direction, he could be anywhere."

Dawson's gaze narrowed. "Plus, he could exit the post from one of the back roads. If what he said to you on the phone is true, he's prior military. Anyone previously stationed at Fort Rickman would know the post as well as the outlining ranges and training areas."

"He loves the military, but claims he died when he came home."

"Maybe he was injured," Dawson suggested.

"Or watched a comrade die."

"Or something happened when he came home."

"A wife left him perhaps? A family member died?" Jamison stared into the night. All around him, the crime scene team scurried to capture evidence.

"The husbands of the two victims currently serve in Colonel Logan's brigade, but they don't work together." Dawson mentioned what they both knew.

Jamison rubbed at his jaw. "But they served together under Logan when he took his battalion to Iraq. The unit came home three years ago. If that's the common thread, what would trigger the killer to strike now?"

"A relative in the battalion could have died in combat. If the killer identified with the deceased, he might start to believe he himself had served."

Jamison slapped Dawson on the back. "Which is why we need that list of names from the cemetery in Freemont. I'll give Simpson another call."

Pulling out his phone, Jamison tapped in the digits for the Freemont P.D. Simpson wasn't on duty. Neither was the other police officer, Bobby Jones, who had accompanied Simpson to the cemetery.

A third cop claimed Simpson had made some progress in tracking down the family members and would return Jamison's call in the morning. He hung up less than satisfied and turned back to Dawson.

"You better contact the cemetery director first thing tomorrow. See if he can provide the information we need. Also, find out if anyone in the brigade has been killed during this deployment. A grieving father, a brother, even the son of a deceased soldier might want to cause problems for Colonel Logan when he brings his unit back this time."

Dawson nodded. "I'll check it out."

"Keep exerting pressure. We need a breakthrough on this case."

Again Dawson shrugged and flicked an embarrassed gaze at Jamison. "I told you, buddy. I didn't ask to take over the lead."

Jamison held up his hand. "Let's just get it done."

The blond agent shook his head. "Yeah, but the killer has struck twice. Add what happened at the cemetery and we've got three incidents. As far as finding the killer goes, we're batting zero."

Jamison stared into the darkness. His stomach roiled as he thought of what the killer had planned to do. The two of them were on opposite sides. The perpetrator wanted Michele dead. Jamison, if he did nothing else, had to ensure that Michele stayed alive.

Ten months ago, she had made it perfectly clear she didn't want Jamison in her life, but he would sacrifice everything to ensure that she had a life to live.

Even if it meant she'd leave him once again.

EIGHT

Michele huddled in the passenger's seat next to Jamison. Her mother sat directly behind her in the rear, lost in her own thoughts.

The three of them had followed the ambulance to the Fort Rickman Hospital and remained in the waiting room as Alice had been rushed into surgery. She'd come through that ordeal and was now in intensive care, monitored by a roomful of machines and a bevy of nurses and doctors who had insisted they go home. The medical staff promised to call at any change in her condition. Whether Alice would be strong enough to pull through was the question.

Physically drained, Michele knew her mother and Jamison had to be equally fatigued. On the ride home, they all seemed lost in their own worlds. Michele kept thinking about Alice and her husband and the prayer they must have said for his safety when he left for Afghanistan. It was doubtful either of them thought Alice would be the one critically injured and fighting for her life.

Overcome with the irony, Michele sighed.

Jamison turned to gaze at her, his face bathed in

the half-light from the dash. Although her heart was heavy, she appreciated the concern she saw in his bittersweet smile.

"I'm glad the E.R. doc checked you out." He reached over the consol to take her hand.

She appreciated the warmth of his touch. "Two hospital visits in one day isn't a habit I want to continue."

He nodded. "I agree."

Turning her gaze toward the window, she thought of the killer still on the loose. What kind of man would attack so vengefully? Yolanda and Alice were wonderful women. Why had they been victims of such heinous attacks?

As much as she wanted to forget what had happened, the memory of the killer kept circling through her mind. She had looked into his eyes and had seen evil. Jamison had talked about bad people in the world. She was beginning to think he had sugarcoated the reality of whom they were up against.

Always considerate of her needs, Jamison helped her from the car when they arrived at her parents' home. The effects of the stun gun had been short-lived, but Michele gladly accepted his steadying arm and the attention he showered over her.

Once inside their quarters, Roberta made a pot of coffee, which she served to Jamison and Michele at the dining room table. Despite the mug she held, Michele still felt cold and longed, once again, for Jamison's hand to cover hers with warmth.

She stared at him from across the table. He had a string of questions for her mother, and from the intensity of his gaze, Michele realized he had slipped back into military CID mode.

"Can you recall anyone in the past that might have had a grudge against your husband, Mrs. Logan?"

She shook her head slowly. "No one who made his or her grievances known. I'm sure some of the soldiers were disgruntled from time to time if Stanley canceled their leave or kept their battalion in the field for an extended period of time. But if you're talking about anything significant, then I'd have to say no."

Michele wondered if he was getting too far off track. "Do you really think a person would attack women on post to get back at my father?"

Jamison sighed as if he, too, regretted the need to probe into brigade affairs. "We have to consider any situation that would make someone strike out, Michele."

Well aware that he was the expert in such matters, Michele held back from saying anything else and sipped her coffee.

Turning back to Roberta, Jamison continued, "Did any soldiers lose their lives under your husband's command?"

"A sergeant in his battalion died in Iraq. Stanley flew home with the body. Both of us attended the funeral."

"He was from the local area?"

Roberta nodded. "He had graduated from Freemont High School and had been the captain of the football team. Everyone loved him. His mom had died of cancer two years earlier, and he was an only child. It broke my heart to see his father grieving. I'll never forget him standing at the cemetery by the grave site."

"The Freemont Cemetery where your son is buried?"

Roberta nodded. "That's right."

"Do you recall the soldier's name?"

"How could I forget? Sergeant Brandon Carmichael. His father was so proud of him."

"What about this current rotation, ma'am?"

"The Lord's been good to us, Jamison. No loss of life."

Michele placed her mug on the table and rubbed her fingers over her arms. "Don't be too hasty, Mother. The brigade hasn't left Afghanistan yet."

Roberta patted Michele's hand. "Your dad's going to make it home."

Michele stood and stepped away from the table. "You were equally sure Lance would be okay."

Her mother's expression clouded. "You've got to stop blaming yourself."

"I'm not blaming anyone except the army."

"Accidents happen, Michele." Although Jamison's eyes were filled with concern, his voice was matter-of-fact, as if death was an acceptable part of military life.

She bristled and turned to gaze out the window into the night.

Her mother stepped toward her. "You still feel responsible for what happened to Lance."

"Do I?" She quirked her head at the woman she loved but didn't always understand. "How would you know, Mother? We never talk about him."

Roberta held out her hands. "What can I say that would change your mind?"

"You can tell me I made a mistake. Lance wouldn't have been in the helicopter if I had visited him."

"But you made the right decision, dear."

The phone rang. Roberta hesitated as if questioning whether she should answer. Checking the caller ID, she turned apologetic eyes toward her daughter. "It's Erica

Grayson. She probably has information about Yolanda's funeral. I should take the call."

"Of course," Michele said, her energy drained.

Roberta stepped into the living area, phone in hand.

Michele grabbed her mug and headed for the kitchen, hoping a second cup of coffee would help clear her head.

Jamison followed. "You want to talk?"

"You don't need to get involved with our family problems."

"Whatever you need is what I want, Michele."

She would have laughed except she knew why she had left him and how much she had missed him over the last ten months. "I'll pretend I didn't hear that last statement."

He stepped closer, seemingly oblivious of the real root of the problem between them. "You may not want my input, but your mother's right. You haven't worked through your brother's death."

Anger rose within her. She pointed a finger back at herself. "It's not my problem, Jamison. It's my mother's problem and your problem. I keep telling everyone I'm fine, but no one believes me."

The sound of her mother's voice came from the living room. Roberta Logan—a woman who would have done anything for her daughter—was talking on the phone to one of the brigade wives who needed support. Michele had needed her mother's support when her brother died, but Roberta had gone back to helping with all the wives' activities and hadn't been able to reach out to her only remaining child.

Michele didn't want to talk about what had happened, yet the words spilled from her mouth as if they had a will of their own. "Remember when that last big storm hit the coast of Georgia?"

Jamison nodded. "Wasn't it about two years ago?"

"That's right. Homes were destroyed. People needed food and water. My insurance company wanted to provide hands-on help as well as aid with the insurance claims. We filled a number of trucks with nonperishable items, water, blankets."

Jamison's open gaze encouraged her to go on.

"Days before the storm, Lance had invited me to visit him for a long weekend. I planned to drive to Fort Knox, his new duty station. Then my boss asked for volunteers to help with the coastal relief, so I canceled my plans to be with Lance."

Truth was, she had chosen to help the storm victims because she was beginning to buy into the gospel message about helping others, which Lance always said was the Christian thing to do.

"If I hadn't chosen to help those people, Lance would have been on leave instead of in the helicopter that terrible day."

Jamison reached for her. "You're not to blame."

She jerked away from his touch. "How would you know? You put yourself in danger after my father left for Afghanistan. You knew I was worried because of the Afghani strikes we kept hearing about on the news and the attack he had already been involved in, yet you walked into that ambush on post. Did you think by praying to God you could put yourself in the line of fire and not suffer the consequences?"

His face clouded. "Oh, Michele, I…"

"You what, Jamison? You weren't thinking about the danger, were you? You probably had your Bible in one hand and your gun in the other and thought nothing could harm you."

He shook his head. "I made a mistake."

"A mistake? Do you know what that did to me when I heard about the shoot-out? I raced to the hospital and saw the stretcher being wheeled into the E.R. I learned later that Dawson had taken the hit, but at the time, I thought you were the one not expected to live."

"I'm sorry, Michele."

"Sorry isn't what I want for my life. I thought we were good together and wanted something long-term. I saw us growing old with kids and grandkids." She laughed ruefully, but tears stung her eyes. "The day of the ambush brought home the truth I'd been ignoring. With you, my future would be at a cemetery with the honor guard folding your flag and the commander presenting it to me with the thanks of a grateful nation."

She pointed into the dining room where Lance's flag sat on the buffet. "That's all we have left of my brother's memory. He doesn't have the luxury of falling in love and marrying a nice girl who will bear his children. All we have is a flag."

Jamison reached for her, but she shook her head. She didn't want his touch. She wanted him to admit he could see the truth.

"A flag doesn't bring comfort or grandchildren for my parents. Lance was a believer, Jamison. And so are you, but you can't count on God. The only one you can count on is yourself."

"Oh, Michele, you've got it all wrong."

She shook her head, not wanting to hear anything he had to say. "God doesn't want good things for His children. He wields His might with a fickle hand. Maybe

He likes to see His children in pain so they turn to Him. That's what I would have if we were together. Pain and grief and a flag to remember what could have been. That's not enough."

She had to leave. She couldn't stand the look of disbelief on his face or the pity in his eyes. She wanted his love but without the military, without the constant danger and the chance she could lose him when she least expected. She had received one phone call that had broken her heart when Lance's helicopter crashed. A second phone call had informed her of the shoot-out on post.

She couldn't take a third call telling her Jamison had walked into danger again and would never be coming home.

Michele couldn't bear losing him. Better to guard her heart than to have it break again.

Jamison left the Logan home with Michele's words ricocheting through his mind. *"You made a mistake. You put yourself in danger. You walked into that ambush."*

Once he had ensured that the military police guards were in place and her neighborhood was being patrolled, Jamison drove back to CID headquarters.

Michele was right. He had failed tens months ago. He couldn't fail again. The stakes were too high.

"You'll never succeed." His father's voice rumbled through his head.

Jamison had to prove his dad wrong, but more important was the knowledge that if anything happened to Michele, Jamison would never be able to forgive himself.

She couldn't reconcile herself to what had happened to her brother. The anger and accusation in Michele's voice were outward signs of her long-term internal struggle. Would she ever be able to forgive herself?

Without a change of heart, she would never accept Jamison again. She had loved him once and had said as much tonight, but a terrible realization clamped down on Jamison's gut.

Sometimes love wasn't enough.

NINE

Tree frogs and cicadas sounded in the night. Jamison stood at the curb close to his car and eyed the brick facade of the Logan quarters. The light from the front porch spilled onto the walkway and the shrubbery that edged the house. Inside, a few lamps were on in the living room. Upstairs, where Michele slept, the house was dark.

He'd worked for hours on the investigation until his head ached and the muscles in his neck screamed for relief. Getting into his car, Jamison had driven back to check on Michele because he could find no rest until he knew she was safe.

The memory of her words stabbed at his heart. If only she could turn her problems over to the Lord and allow Him into her life. Ten months ago, she had gone to church with Jamison, and both of them had talked about wanting to put God first. Everything had changed after the shoot-out. When she'd run from Jamison, she'd run from her faith, as well.

Comfort her in her time of need, Lord. As the prayer left his mouth, one of the military policemen assigned to guard Mrs. Logan and her daughter walked around the corner of the house.

Jamison met him halfway. "How's it look in the rear?"

"Quiet, sir. Rogers and Yeoman are patrolling the woods to ensure that no one is lurking nearby. So far so good." He glanced at the house. "We need to find that guy and make sure he never strikes again."

Jamison agreed.

As the military policeman returned to his post, headlights cut through the darkness. Dawson's car pulled over to the curb. The special agent's limp seemed more pronounced when he exited his vehicle and walked along the sidewalk, the night air, no doubt, adding to his stiffness.

Jamison should have been the one injured instead of Dawson. The injury would have been easier to bear than being reminded of his own mistake each time he saw his friend.

When the wounded agent was coming out of surgery, Jamison had tried to express how he felt. Regrettably, he had choked on the words, and Dawson had never mentioned Jamison's attempt to ask forgiveness.

"We did some checking on the maintenance man," Dawson offered as he neared. "Danny Altman worked in Atlanta for a couple years after he got out of the army and only recently moved to the Fort Rickman area."

"Did you contact his old company?"

Dawson nodded. "He was a good worker, but with the downturn in the economy, the Atlanta firm had to cut back. They laid off a number of employees. He was one of them."

"What about the girlfriend's death?"

"Evidently, she was abusing prescription drugs and died of an overdose. The Atlanta P.D. interrogated the boyfriend, but he turned out to be clean."

"That doesn't mean he didn't have anything to do with the crimes on post."

Dawson shrugged. Even in the half-light from the streetlight, Jamison could see the question in the other man's eyes. "I didn't have any reason to hold him, but we'll keep our eyes on him and see what happens. If he's guilty, he won't like us getting in the middle of his life."

"I'd feel better if we restricted him from post."

"The man needs work."

"As long as that's all he's doing." Jamison didn't want Danny Altman anywhere near Michele.

He glanced up at her bedroom window, and his neck burned when he realized Dawson had followed his gaze.

"How is she?" Dawson asked.

"Struggling with a lot of things."

"Being the first at a crime scene can play with a person's mind. Double that by two and anyone would have problems."

"Mrs. Hughes's death brought back memories of her brother. Michele blames herself. That's hard to handle."

Dawson looked away and studied the sky. "Guilt's a funny thing. Once you take it on, it's almost impossible to release." He turned back to Jamison. "Asking forgiveness after the fact isn't always enough."

Jamison felt the weight he carried increase. Dawson was right. Guilt had a tight hold. Like a man-of-war that wraps tentacles around its victim, guilt's grasp has the same deadly sting.

"Look, Dawson—"

The sound of the front door opening made Jamison

turn toward the brick quarters. Michele stood just inside the threshold.

Dawson patted Jamison's shoulder. "Looks like Michele wants to talk. I'm heading home for some shuteye. Call me if anything comes up."

"Will do." Jamison stepped from the shadows and onto the sidewalk leading to the Logans' front stoop. Michele wore jeans and a print top that reminded him of sunshine and flowers.

As much as Jamison needed to think of Michele as a witness in an investigation, the emotions welling up within him were anything but professional. The late hour, the almost full moon, the sounds of the peaceful night and a beautiful woman waiting for him at the front door added to the anticipation teasing through his gut.

He hastened up the stairs, staring into her eyes. "Everything okay inside?"

She looked tired with puffy cheeks as if she had spent the better part of the night crying. His heart went out to her, wishing she would step outside so he could wrap her in his arms.

The only thing that kept him from reaching for her was the detail of soldiers pulling surveillance. Jamison would never allow them to see the way he really felt about the colonel's daughter.

Glancing past Michele, he saw Mrs. Logan in the dining room. She was arranging a pot of coffee and a plate of cookies on the table.

Michele hesitated a moment before she spoke. "I…I said too much earlier."

"It's okay. I wanted to know how you felt." He rubbed his finger across her cheek. "I'll always want to know."

She stepped onto the porch and wrapped her arms

around her waist. A gentle breeze ruffled her hair and wafted a swirl of her sweet-smelling perfume to tempt him.

"Chilly?" he asked, wanting any excuse to touch her shoulder and pull her closer.

"The breeze feels good. The house seemed stuffy. Mother tries to conserve energy and turns the air conditioner thermostat down at night."

"I thought both of you were sound asleep."

She shook her head, her eyes filled with sadness. "Mother and Erica Grayson have been calling back and forth, discussing ways to help Yolanda's husband and his children."

"Mrs. Hughes's sister-in-law arrived today."

"That's right. She's trying to arrange a leave of absence from her job so she can stay indefinitely. The family will move temporarily into the furnished quarters reserved for visiting VIPs. The commanding general said he'll authorize anything they need."

Jamison nodded. "A crew is cleaning their old quarters, although I'm not sure if Major Hughes will want to move his family back in."

"Curtis can decide that after the funeral. He plans to have a memorial service at the Main Post Chapel when he and the children return from Missouri."

"Your mother talked to him?"

"After he broke the news to the children on Skype. He wanted to see their sweet faces and measure their reactions. The Graysons and his sister-in-law were sitting with the children when he told them. He said they needed to be strong and that they'd be together as soon as he got home."

Her voice hitched, and she blinked back tears.

"Yolanda had miscarried a few years back. He said their mama was with their little brother now."

Jamison's throat thickened. "The whole family must be devastated, but it's got to be so hard on the children."

"Erica said they were brave kids and told their dad to be careful and stay safe. She doesn't think they understand everything at this point. They're in shock, in another home. When they disconnected, they told her they didn't want their dad to worry about them."

"Good kids, huh?"

"Army brats are usually pretty resilient. Moving from place to place, always having to make new friends, they get used to new areas, even foreign countries. But this is tough."

Michele glanced momentarily into the night. "Can you imagine how often the children will wonder if they could have done something to have changed the events that day? If they hadn't gone to the Graysons' and had stayed home to help their mom that night, or if their dad hadn't been deployed or in the military? All those questions will run through their heads."

"Michele, that's what you've done with your brother's death. You keep thinking 'what if.' What if you hadn't helped with the relief effort? What if you had visited Lance that weekend? Talk to your mother. You've got to share your feelings with her before you can heal."

A tear ran down Michele's cheek. She pushed open the door.

He reached for her. "Don't run away."

"I'm not running. Not this time. But it's late, and I'm tired. You need sleep and so do I."

Before he could respond, Michele entered the house and raced up the stairs.

Mrs. Logan peered outside and saw him standing there, unable to speak, his throat still thick from the thought of the Hughes children and the window Michele had opened to reveal her own inner turmoil.

"I've perked a pot of coffee and put out cookies. Help yourself, Jamison, and have the other men get something, as well."

He held up his hand. "Nothing for me, ma'am, but I'll tell the men."

Backing down the steps, he glanced up at Michele's window. The light from the hallway shone into her room. She had pulled back the curtain and stood, looking down at him, never realizing Jamison could see her outlined against the faint glow from the hallway.

She was grieving for Yolanda but also for her brother. And Jamison? He was still grieving for Michele.

TEN

Michele woke the next morning with a dull headache and the sniffles. She felt achy and sore as if she'd battled some unseen foe all night. Truth was, she had slept little and had been barraged with images of Yolanda's and Alice's battered bodies.

Jamison's face had traveled through her thoughts, as well. His smile of old had been replaced with a perpetual look of determination that revealed his own personal struggle to find the killer. In endless waves of terror, the knife, the blood, the carnage had all visited her in the night.

Wiping her hand over her face, she pulled herself from the bed and padded toward the window. Low cloud cover hid the sun and cast the day in a dirty gray that felt as heavy as her spirits.

Once upon a time, she had been strong and self-reliant. Now she doubted her own ability, her resolve and even her desire to do the right thing. Everything inside her was mixed together in a chaos that got darker with every turn.

She peered around the curtain at the yard below. Two military policemen stood on the sidewalk. Even without checking, she knew two more would be guarding the house in the rear.

Straining to glance down the street, she failed to see Jamison's car. He must have left sometime in the night. No reason for him to stay round the clock. He needed rest and time off. Surely he had a life outside of work. Maybe even a new girlfriend, although the thought of him with another woman soured her stomach and turned the gray day even darker.

Coffee would clear her mind. Michele headed to the kitchen and was soon pouring the first cup from the pot she brewed. The rich aroma filled the kitchen and stamped normalcy on the new day.

Except nothing was normal about this Thursday.

"Morning, honey." Her mother stepped into the breakfast area and pulled a cup from the cupboard. "Coffee smells good."

"I didn't hear you come down the stairs."

"That's because I was in the living room. I couldn't sleep and got up at the first light of dawn. I've been reading my devotionals and writing in my journal. Somehow it's helped."

Michele took another long sip from her cup. There was no reason to upset her mother by sharing her own thoughts on God.

"I walked by your door a number of times." Her mother raised her brow. "You were tossing and turning most of the night."

Michele tried to smile. Her mother had an innate ability to sense whether her daughter had had a good night's sleep. "I couldn't seem to get comfortable. The last time I looked at the clock, it was 4:00 a.m. I must have dozed off by the time you came downstairs. I kept thinking about Alice. Any news on her condition?"

"Only that she's still in ICU and critical." Roberta poured coffee into her cup. "Your father called this morning. The planes are on the tarmac. He'll let me know once they board."

Michele thought of his smile and twinkling eyes and wanted him home safely. Then she thought of Jamison, and her cheeks burned.

"Something wrong, dear? You look a little flushed." Her mother touched her forehead with the back of her hand. "Do you have a fever?"

"It's probably the coffee."

"I'm going to shower. Chaplain Grant scheduled the prayer service for 11:00 a.m."

Michele refilled her cup and followed her mother upstairs. When she heard the shower running, she opened the drawer on her dresser. Her eyes fell on the Bible Lance had given her. She touched the leather cover and sighed.

As much as she wanted to stay home this morning, she didn't want to have to answer her mother's probing questions. Michele had never shared her change of heart concerning faith, a faith her parents had hoped to instill in both their children.

The lessons had found a home in Lance. If he hadn't been snatched away so young, they might also have taken hold in Michele. As it was, she couldn't trust a God who disregarded the well-being of His children.

Her own internal struggle continued as she walked into the Main Post Chapel and took her seat in the pew next to her mother. At least they were sitting by the aisle. If she needed to excuse herself from the service, she could do so without disrupting anyone.

Glancing around, Michele saw many of the brigade wives and family members. The choir leader stood and invited the congregation to do likewise. He led them in a poignant hymn that called upon the Lord to come to the aid of His people in their need.

As much as Michele wanted to sing, the words stuck in her throat. Her mother didn't seem to notice, nor did she see how Michele worried her fingers and had to hold herself in check not to run from the assembly when the chaplain stepped to the pulpit.

Her head pounded even more as she tried to ignore his words about God's loving providence. Everything inside her cried out against the hypocrisy of the teaching. She started to rise, but someone slipped into the pew next to her, blocking her escape.

Frustrated, she closed her eyes and sat back, silently counting to ten before she glanced at the newcomer.

Jamison.

Her heart accelerated.

He crooked a smile and leaned close. "Thanks for saving me a seat."

She clasped her hands together in an attempt to appear in control, all the while wanting to race out of the church and away from a God she didn't trust and a man who made her think back to when life was good.

Her mother glanced around Michele and smiled. "Morning, Jamison."

"Nice to see you, ma'am," he whispered.

"Any news on Alice?"

"Her condition hasn't changed."

"What are you doing here?" Michele said out of the

side of her mouth, once her mother turned her attention back to the service. Michele kept her voice low so only Jamison could hear.

"Giving honor to God."

"I mean, why are you sitting next to me?"

"I'm protecting you."

She crossed her legs and wrapped her arms over her chest, trying to tune out the chaplain's message.

Instead she was tuning in Jamison and the aftershave he wore and the dark sports coat and gray slacks and blue tie that made his ruddy complexion even more appealing. He might be clean shaven and showered, but the creases at the corners of his eyes confirmed he hadn't taken her advice about getting sleep.

Michele kept her guard up. The last time she'd been in church with Jamison had been shortly before he and Dawson had walked into the cross fire. More than a year earlier, Lance had died after she had begun to test the gospel message. Every time she got close to God, He raised the price of faith.

She needed to block out the chaplain's words. If she began to believe again, someone else might be taken from her. Michele looked at Jamison, knowing he was the likely target.

Jamison settled into the pew and enjoyed Michele's closeness. Her immediate reaction had been to bristle when he sat down. Before long, she'd relaxed and even smiled at him as they'd joined in singing one of the hymns.

The service concluded too quickly in his opinion, and once outside, his cell vibrated. He checked caller ID. Dawson.

"I've gotta go," he said to Michele.

She looked disappointed. A good sign.

"You'll be at the barracks later today?" he asked.

She nodded.

"Corporal McGrunner will be your escort."

"He followed us here."

"Good. He'll follow you home, too." With a nod to Mrs. Logan, he left Michele and headed to his car, opening his cell phone on the way.

"Yeah, Dawson, what's up?"

"The chief called a briefing."

"What time?"

"As soon as you can get here."

"Anything new I should know about?" Jamison asked as he settled behind the wheel and pulled out of the church parking lot.

"Only that the commanding general wants the killer in custody, and he's putting pressure to bear on the chief, who will, no doubt, pass the pressure on to us."

"That's the way the army works."

"Unfortunately. I got in touch with the cemetery director. Sergeant Brandon Carmichael's grave site is located near the central oak tree."

"Bingo. Tell me his daddy drives a black car with tinted windows and I'll be happy."

"A white SUV. I sent a couple of our men to talk to Mr. Carmichael. He's out of town. The new Mrs. Carmichael was cooperative. According to her, Carmichael left Freemont last Sunday on a weeklong fishing trip with some of his old pals. He wasn't in town yesterday, so he didn't visit the cemetery. In fact, he rarely goes to his son's grave site. She says it's too painful."

Mrs. Logan could probably relate.

"What about Greg Yates?" Jamison asked.

"He showed up with his son in tow. The kid's nineteen and flew into Atlanta on Tuesday night."

"Where's he usually live?"

"With his mother in Texas. Yates said he got a surprise call from his son the afternoon of the potluck and had to hustle to Atlanta before the plane landed, only the storms rolled in. Flights were delayed, and once the son finally arrived, it was late. They got a motel room and took in a Braves game the next day."

"And they drove back to Freemont last night."

"Roger that."

"Did you ask him about the possible divorce?"

"He blames it on lack of communication, and hopes his wife will consider counseling. Yates said he'll do anything to save his marriage."

Jamison glanced at his watch. "Tell the chief I'm on the way."

Nothing new came out of the very lengthy meeting with Wilson except the reminder of the need to wrap up the investigation as soon as possible. Finding Mrs. Hughes's killer was key, not that the chief needed to tell anyone. The entire CID and military police force were committed to finding the perpetrator and bringing him to justice. After the briefing, Jamison completed a few additional tasks that needed his attention and that Wilson had requested.

By the time he left CID headquarters, the day was well spent. He had wanted to be with Michele earlier, but what he wanted had to take a backseat to the job that needed to get done. At least McGrunner was with her, keeping watch, ensuring that she and Mrs. Logan were safe.

Jamison drove to the brigade headquarters. Double-timing inside, he flashed his CID identification to a staff sergeant standing near the door. "Mrs. Logan and some of the wives are working in the area."

"Yes, sir." The sergeant pointed through a nearby window to a building one block south of the headquarters. "You can see their cars from here."

With a nod of thanks, Jamison hustled outside and moved his own vehicle to the front of the barracks the sergeant had indicated. Getting out of his car, he spied Corporal McGrunner carrying a large potted plant.

The military policeman shifted the greenery to his left hand and saluted with his right. "Sir, Mrs. Logan and her daughter are on the third floor in the Day Room. The florist donated plants, and the ladies are making welcome-home bags for all the soldiers."

"Any sign of trouble?"

"No, sir. Except Mrs. Logan needed help bringing in the plants."

"Isn't the florist around?"

"He's upstairs arranging some of the flowers."

"Flowers in the Day Room?"

McGrunner nodded. "He donated potted plants and a few cut arrangements. Mrs. Logan says he's been extremely generous."

Jamison harrumphed. He doubted the male soldiers cared about flowers, but the few female soldiers in the unit would probably appreciate the florist's generosity.

Memo to self. If he ever fell in love again, he'd send flowers. Lots of flowers on a regular basis.

Jamison headed for the stairwell and hurried upstairs. On the third floor, he turned right and followed the sound of voices.

Approaching an open door, he glanced inside. Michele stood at the foot of a single bed, straightening the end of the blanket.

"Need some help?"

She looked up, startled.

"Sorry to frighten you." The room smelled like lemon furniture polish. He noticed a man standing near the corner, holding a dust cloth. Dressed in civilian clothes, he was tall with a muscular build. Mid-forties.

"Have you met Greg Yates?" Michele asked. "His wife is in the brigade."

"Special Agent Steele." Jamison extended his hand, which Yates shook with a firm grasp.

Michele stepped toward the door. "Mother's in the Day Room, if you need to talk to her. I'm headed that way."

Jamison followed Michele into the hallway. She glanced at him over her shoulder. "You had a phone call after the service this morning. Did something happen?"

"Information came in on Carmichael."

"The soldier who was killed in Iraq?"

"That's right. Do you have any idea how old the man at the cemetery might have been?"

"He was too far away to tell.

"Gray hair? Stooped shoulders? Perhaps a hesitation in his gait?"

"He appeared strong and healthy."

After making the bed in a second room, Jamison and Michele headed to the Day Room, where Greg had joined a group of wives, stuffing individually wrapped baked goods into plastic bags.

Mrs. Logan had a wide smile on her face. "We could use your help, Jamison." She pointed to the florist.

"Teddy's donated some lovely plants that need to be brought into the building, if you can lend a hand."

Teddy waved from the desk where he was adding American flags and red, white and blue bows to three large floral arrangements.

McGrunner entered the Day Room. He placed the plant he carried on the table where Teddy worked and smiled. "Follow me, sir."

Jamison turned to the major's husband. "You want to lend a hand, Mr. Yates?"

The guy shook his head. "No can do. Bad back."

Yet he appeared bulked up as if he pumped iron on a regular schedule.

Shrugging out of his sports coat, Jamison hung it over the back of a chair and followed McGrunner down the stairs. On the first floor, he grabbed a cart from a utility closet. Unloading the remaining plants onto the cart, they pushed them toward the inside stairwell and, from there, carried them up the stairs.

Michele wasn't in the Day Room when he returned. "Where's your daughter?" Jamison asked Mrs. Logan.

"She and Teddy took a couple of flower arrangements to one of the other floors."

Leaving McGrunner to bring up the rest of the plants, Jamison went in search of Michele.

The overhead lights were out at the rear of the building, sending shadows to darken the hallway. Turning a corner, he spied Teddy walking toward him.

"Where's Miss Logan?"

"Giving directions to a soda distributor named Perkins. He couldn't find the soft drink machines."

Jamison hadn't seen any distributor's truck parked out front.

"Where'd they go?"

"Downstairs." Teddy pointed over his shoulder. "End of the hall, then left. The machines are directly below, on the second floor."

The muscles in Jamison's shoulders tightened as he raced to the end of the hallway. Taking the steps two at a time, he called Michele's name and pushed through the fire door into the unlit second floor. "Michele?"

Silence.

Then a gasp. A scuffling sound followed.

"Michele?" He turned the corner, ready to confront anyone or anything doing her harm.

She stood in a narrow room surrounded by soda dispensing machines. Hand at her throat, she stared at a man crouched on his hands and knees in the corner.

"Step toward me, Michele."

She looked surprised. "What?"

"Step away from the man. Now."

"I'm okay. Really. It was a mouse."

Jamison frowned. "What?"

Michele pointed to where the man was peering under one of the vending machines. "I was showing Mr. Perkins the soft drink machines when a mouse ran across the floor."

"Looks like he's disappeared." Perkins stood. "You'd better report it. Someone needs to set a trap and catch the critter."

He glanced at the SIG Sauer on Jamison's hip. "Then again, you could shoot him."

The guy wore navy chinos and a polo shirt. Solid build, probably weighed somewhere between two-ten and two-twenty. Pudgy hands, well callused.

Jamison zeroed in on the scratch marks around his wrists and lower arms.

"Michele, go back to the Day Room."

"What?"

Why did she always have to question him when he was trying to keep her safe?

"Go upstairs to the third floor and rejoin the other women."

She narrowed her gaze. "I don't understand."

"Michele, please—" He jerked his head toward the door. "Upstairs. Now. Rejoin the other ladies."

Finally, she did as he had asked. Jamison was relieved when her footfalls sounded going up the stairs.

"I'm Special Agent Steele, CID." Jamison flashed his identification. "I'd like to see the paperwork authorizing you to be on post."

Perkins rolled his eyes. "You've got to be kidding."

"No, sir. I need your authorization."

Despite his attitude, the distributor pulled the papers from his pocket.

Pete Perkins. Freemont address.

"You want to tell me what you're doing here, Mr. Perkins?"

He spread his hands and took a step toward Jamison.

"Stay where you are, sir."

The guy stopped, brows raised. "Look, I don't want to cause any problem."

"Where's your truck?"

"Out back. I came in through the rear door."

"Aren't you supposed to wear a uniform shirt with your company's logo?"

"I'm not on the clock. I work for my brother-in-law

and was helping him out. The machines need to be filled before the brigade returns."

"How'd you get those scratches on your arm?"

The guy furrowed his brow. "What are you talking about?"

"Two women were attacked on post."

His eyes widened. "You think I was involved?"

"You can explain everything at CID headquarters."

"That's ridiculous."

"Is it? Then I suggest you explain about the scratches."

The guy fisted his hands and shoved out his chest. "Who do you think you are?"

"As I mentioned earlier, I'm a special agent with the CID, and I'm hauling you into CID headquarters unless you explain why you're so agitated about answering a few questions."

The guy cursed.

Jamison pointed to the hallway. "After you, Mr. Perkins."

As they walked from the building into the late afternoon, Corporal McGrunner approached Jamison. "Problem, sir?"

"Take Mr. Perkins back to headquarters. I'll contact Special Agent Timmons and let him know you're bringing him in for questioning.

"Roger that, sir."

Perkins, grumbling under his breath, climbed into the rear of the military police sedan. As McGrunner pulled away from the barracks, Perkins stared at Jamison out the rear window.

Sensing someone behind him, Jamison turned and

saw Michele standing in the doorway of the barracks. The florist stood beside her, along with Mrs. Logan.

"We're finished," Michele said as they stepped outside. She glanced at the military police sedan heading away from the building. "Corporal McGrunner drove us here, but he seems to be busy. Any chance you could give us a ride home?"

"Of course."

Their fingers brushed together as she handed Jamison his jacket. "You left this in the Day Room."

Her touch threw him off-kilter. He didn't need to stare into her questioning blue eyes to know she thought he'd overreacted upstairs.

Maybe he had. But Mr. Perkins had balked at answering a few questions. With a killer on the loose, anything and anyone suspect had to be questioned. The CID needed to know if Perkins had something to hide.

The florist waved as he ambled toward his truck. "See you folks tomorrow at the airport."

Michele waved back. "Thanks, Teddy."

Jamison shrugged into his jacket. "After I drive you home, I want to ensure that there's enough security around your quarters before I head to the hospital to check on Mrs. Rossi."

He held open the passenger and rear doors. Mrs. Logan climbed into the backseat, leaving the front for Michele. Jamison strengthened his resolve to remain unaffected by the colonel's daughter, knowing after the investigation was over, he wouldn't see Michele again.

ELEVEN

Michele glanced over her shoulder to where her mother sat in the rear seat of Jamison's car. "Check your cell, Mother. Dad may have phoned."

"I just did, dear. No messages and no new calls."

Michele sighed. "I thought the brigade would have been on board the plane by now."

"Your father will do everything in his power to let us know when they're ready to take off."

"Do you think something happened?" Michele couldn't help expressing the concern that bubbled up inside her.

"I'm sure he's fine." Jamison's voice was filled with understanding. "Hurry up and wait is the army way of life."

"My dad uses that same phrase, but its hard being the one at home who's watching the clock."

"The word I got was that everything was on schedule." He pulled out his cell. "I'll call the rear detachment."

"Roger that," he said at the conclusion of the rather terse conversation with the duty officer.

Jamison turned to Michele. "Good news. The planes

are airborne. They had an hour delay in boarding, but they're on their way home."

Michele looked back at her mother. "Why didn't Dad let us know?"

"Your father has a lot to take care of, dear. He probably ran out of time before takeoff. I'm sure he'll phone when they land to refuel."

"He's as anxious as you are to get the brigade back to Fort Rickman," Jamison offered along with a warm smile.

He was right. As a brigade commander, her father would put his soldiers' needs first. They'd been deployed for a year and were eager to get back to their families. The fact that two wives in the unit had been brutally attacked would make them even more anxious to be reunited with their loved ones.

In a way, Michele felt guilty for enjoying the comforts of home when so many gave up so much in order to serve their country. Recently, she had lived with a constant dread that something would happen to her dad. As she waited for news of his departure, her concerns had grown even more pronounced. She should be feeling relief, knowing he was airborne, but Michele still worried and needed something to occupy her thoughts and her time.

She turned to Jamison. "I'd like to go to the hospital with you when you check on Alice." Michele glanced over her shoulder. "You'll be all right while I'm gone, won't you, Mother?"

"Of course." Roberta shifted in her seat. "Jamison, how long will you keep the guard stationed outside Alice's hospital room? Corporal McGrunner said someone is with her at all times."

"Until we capture the killer. If he learns Mrs. Rossi is alive, he may try to finish the job. I want to make sure we find him before he does more harm."

He glanced at Michele. "You need to be especially careful. Tell the military police assigned to guard your house when you're leaving. Don't go any place without letting me know, either."

She wrapped her arms around her waist. "You're starting to scare me."

"I'm trying to ensure that you don't do something foolish."

"Like drive away from McGrunner when he's tied up in a traffic jam?"

Jamison nodded. "Exactly."

"In my own defense, if I had waited any longer, I wouldn't have gotten to Alice in time."

"And if your mother hadn't pounded on the door, we wouldn't be having this conversation." Jamison's voice was chillingly cold and devoid of inflection.

If he was trying to upset Michele, he was succeeding. She hadn't felt afraid for herself after Yolanda's death. She'd been more concerned about the other wives. But coming face-to-face with the killer and knowing he might finish the job he'd started sent pinpricks of fear tingling along her spine.

"I'll make sure I stay close to my military police guards until you find the killer."

Jamison glanced in the rearview mirror. "That goes for you, too, Mrs. Logan. Watch yourself at all times. Check before you open the door. Don't take walks alone or visit one of the wives without an MP escort."

"Michele and I will follow the rules, Jamison. But

I worry about the wives who aren't getting the VIP treatment."

"I understand your concern, ma'am. As I told you earlier, we've increased law enforcement's presence on post and are patrolling the housing areas. The neighborhood watch programs are working. If anyone spots something suspicious in the housing areas, they're calling CID headquarters or the military police. We've been able to apprehend a number of people who haven't had a good reason to be on Fort Rickman."

"But you don't have a suspect."

"Not yet, but with the number of tips coming in, we're optimistic about finding the killer soon."

"That would certainly be an answered prayer," Mrs. Logan said with a sigh.

"Yes, ma'am."

Once again, Michele felt Jamison's gaze. She shifted away from him and looked out the window. Too many thoughts circled through her head, thoughts of her father and his men already in the air and the families counting down the hours and minutes until they would be reunited.

She thought of Alice's husband frantic to be at his wife's bedside and Major Hughes, who needed to reunite with his children. Knowing Yolanda wouldn't be at the airfield to greet him put an even darker reality on the rapidly descending twilight outside the car.

Everything Jamison had said was true. Michele needed to be careful, but so did the other women on post. No matter what the CID and military police hoped would happen in the upcoming hours, everyone knew the killer could strike again.

Jamison would keep her safe, but a question kept circling through her mind that was more troubling than any concerns about her own well-being.

Who would protect Jamison?

Silence filled the car as Jamison turned into the Logans' housing area. In the rear seat, Mrs. Logan seemed in her own world. She was probably thinking of the planeload of men flying back to Fort Rickman and the commander she was eager to have home.

If body language meant anything, Michele had distanced herself from Jamison and was wrapped in her own struggle, which he wouldn't attempt to understand. Hopefully, her outlook would improve when Colonel Logan was safe at home. Key word: safe.

Jamison mentally ticked off the plans he had put in place for the homecoming reunion at the airfield. Security would be as tight as a steel drum. The family members would wait in the terminal where military police and CID could protect them. The chaplain would be standing by to take Major Hughes to his children. Another escort would transport Sergeant Rossi to the hospital, where he could be reunited with his wife.

Dawson was encouraged by the recent influx of phone tips, and Jamison had passed on that optimism to Mrs. Logan when she had asked about the investigation. The truth was the killer was still on the loose.

As much as Perkins's attitude concerned Jamison, the soda distributor probably wasn't involved. Hauling him into the CID headquarters was a precautionary measure, which would also help to adjust his outlook. Anyone coming onto Fort Rickman needed to realize the military followed a strict set of rules that everyone, even civilians, needed to follow.

Once again, he glanced at Michele, who still found the outside world more intriguing than what went on inside the car. If only he could read her mind. Fact was, he wasn't sure of anything concerning Michele right now. Ten months ago, he had thought they were good together.

His mistake. A big mistake that had cost him dearly.

Luckily, he was wiser and stronger now.

When the killer was brought to justice, Michele would return to Atlanta, and Jamison would move on with his life. The thought should provide welcome relief. Instead all Jamison could think of was the sense of emptiness he would feel when Michele left him again.

TWELVE

The hospital smelled like a mix of cleaning products and rubbing alcohol as Michele stepped into the elevator ahead of Jamison. He pushed the button, then placed his hand on her back and nudged her forward when the door opened on the third floor.

Any other time, she might have balked at his attempt to guide her toward the Intensive Care Unit. This evening, she found the warmth of his hand splayed across her back reassuring.

Not that she was ready to open the door they had closed months ago. Correction. The door *she* had closed. Jamison hadn't run after her, but he had phoned her several times, although she had never answered his calls.

Fear had kept her from talking to him, fear of hearing his voice and knowing how quickly she might run back to Fort Rickman. She couldn't endure life always wondering if the man she loved would be coming home at night.

Walking next to Jamison at this moment brought another thought to mind: the heady possibility of what their future could be if only he would leave the army and law enforcement.

Of course, she knew that would be asking more than he was willing to give. The military and his job defined who he was. Better to maintain their current status quo than to try to mend a relationship that could never be fixed.

Entering the ICU, she and Jamison approached the nurses' desk. He held out his identification to the receptionist who pointed out Alice's room.

"Mrs. Rossi's condition has improved ever so slightly, but she's not strong enough to answer questions."

Jamison nodded. "I just need to talk to the military policeman guarding her."

The MP sat outside Alice's door. He had a ruddy complexion, auburn hair and green eyes that reflected the warm smile covering his face. The name tag on his uniform read Riley.

"Sir." He stood as they neared and nodded to Jamison before he looked at Michele. "Ma'am."

"How's everything going, Corporal?" Jamison asked.

"Fine, sir. The nurses are on top of things. I overheard them saying Mrs. Rossi is somewhat better."

"Anyone other than the nurses trying to gain access to her room?"

"A couple folks from the lab were here earlier to draw blood. A guy from respiratory therapy gave her a breathing treatment. No one else has been around."

As the two men talked, Michele slipped into the small ICU room. Alice's face looked pasty white against the bleached cotton bedding. Her neck was bandaged and her eyes were closed and lined with deep, dark circles. Her chest rose and fell under the sheet as oxygen entered her lungs through a nasal cannula.

Michele stepped closer. For half a heartbeat, she considered offering a prayer for the sweet lady who needed to survive, and for her husband, flying home from the war zone. Sergeant Rossi had survived enemy attacks and scud missiles that blasted through their forward operating base without being harmed. Hard to believe his wife had been the one injured during his deployment.

Hearing footsteps, Michele turned as Jamison entered the room and stopped at the foot of the bed. His face revealed his own concern as to whether Alice would survive her injuries.

Before Michele could consider what she was asking, the words tumbled from her mouth. "Will…will you say a prayer?"

Although her voice had only been a whisper, Jamison raised his gaze, his eyes locking on hers. She had the sense that he could see into the depths of her being. Maybe he understood her fear of losing another person about whom she cared.

Jamison raised his brow. "Is that something you want me to do?"

Glancing down at the unresponsive patient, Michele nodded. "I think it's what Alice would want."

Jamison's voice was husky when he finally spoke. "Father, we ask for protection and healing for Mrs. Rossi. See the love in her heart and the future You have planned for her. Let all things work together for her good."

"Amen," Michele whispered.

Overcome with sadness, she walked back into the hallway, needing to distance herself from the machines keeping Alice alive and from the prayer she had asked Jamison to say. What had caused her to seek God's mercy when the doctors and nurses and all the advances of medical science were working together to save Alice's life?

Michele knew better than to rely on the Lord or His healing love. She wanted to hear about Alice's improved test results, like her oxygen level and white blood cell count. Drugs and doctors and hospital personnel would bring Alice through, not Jamison's prayer.

"Michele, wait," he called after her.

She pointed to the water fountain in the alcove. "I'm getting a drink." Her throat burned and her mouth was as dry as cardboard. A heavy weight sat on her chest, and hot tears stung her eyes. If she gave in to her emotions, she would break down and cry, and she had shed too many tears already.

Resolved to maintain her control, she glanced back at Jamison. He was saying something to the military guard.

A phone rang at the nurses' desk. The ICU clerk answered the call and motioned to a male aide.

"Mrs. Rossi's doctor ordered a scan. Take her down on the back elevator. The MP needs to go with you."

A lump formed in Michele's throat. Seeing Alice brought back the terror she had felt last night.

Michele's knees went weak, and air rushed from her lungs. The memory of the explosive pain from the stun gun returned and made her muscles spasm as if it were happening again. She saw the killer hovering over her, the knife in his hand.

Unable to face the images that ran through her mind, Michele raced along the hallway.

Jamison called her name, but she couldn't turn back.

Just as before, Michele needed to leave Fort Rickman and everything that had happened. Then she realized leaving the post would mean she had to leave Jamison, as well.

Jamison found Michele near the elevator, arms wrapped protectively around her waist. Tears swam in her eyes, and her head rested against the cool tile wall.

"What's happening to me?"

He rubbed his hand over her shoulder. "You've been through a lot, Michele."

"I want to be strong, but I keep seeing the killer. What he did to Yolanda and then Alice. I'll never get those images out of my mind."

She bit her lip. "You probably think I need to see a shrink."

"What you need is a good night's sleep. You look exhausted."

"I could say the same about you."

He wrapped his arm around her and pulled her close. "You were attacked and almost run over. Plus, you've lost a friend and don't know if another one will survive. That's a lot to carry." She smelled fresh like flowers and was just as soft as he remembered.

Holding Michele brought back memories he had tried to forget, like the sense of completeness that swept over him whenever she was in his arms. Running away from him had been a mistake, but he couldn't tell her that, especially now. If there was any hope for them in the future, she had to come to that conclusion on her own. All he could do was keep her safe until she realized that love sometimes was hard, but always worth the effort.

Feeling the tension in her shoulders, he rubbed his hand along her back. "Your dad's on his way home.

Once he arrives, you can be a family again. Everything will be better then."

She edged back and looked up into his eyes. "You… you don't understand. Without Lance, we'll never be a family."

Would she ever get over her brother's death?

"Oh, honey." He pulled her closer. "Life is filled with joy and pain. We have to accept both."

"But my father—"

"He'll be home tomorrow. All you have to do is get through the night."

She sniffed. "But…"

He shook his head. "No buts. I'll be close by if you need me."

A heavy weight settled on Jamison's heart as he thought of what could be between them and the reality of what they had instead.

No matter how much he wanted to reconcile with the past, Jamison and Michele stood on opposite sides of a huge divide that seemed impossible to traverse. His love hadn't been enough for her to stay with him ten months ago. He doubted much had changed, except for his own desire to have her back in his life.

He ushered her toward the elevator and past a number of people on the first floor as they made their way toward the hospital's main entrance.

Always concerned about Michele's safety, Jamison scanned the lobby. A few people were milling around the main information desk, probably requesting room numbers for patients they planned to visit.

His gaze swept to the double glass doors that opened into the emergency room. A woman sat in the E.R. waiting area, head in her hands. A man huddled close by, rubbing her back. Other folks waited to be seen. A hospital security guard stood by the receptionist's desk, arms crossed over his chest. Behind the tall counter, a young clerk chatted with someone on the phone.

Everything looked normal. Nothing to worry about.

The tension in Jamison's neck began to subside. He pulled in a deep breath, but before he could exhale, the public address system screeched to life.

"Code Silver. Third floor. ICU. Code Silver."

Jamison's gut turned to ice. Code Silver meant an active shooter was in the hospital.

He grabbed Michele's arm and herded her into the E.R. waiting room, flashing his identification at the security guard.

"Lock down all the doors to the E.R.," he told the clerk. "Don't let anyone in or out until you hear from me. Call the military police. Ensure that they know about the code, and get backup."

He motioned for Michele and the patients in the waiting room to hide behind the tall, wraparound counter. "Stay down. You'll be protected by the desk. An accomplice might be outside. Don't leave the E.R."

Fear flashed from Michele's eyes. "It's Alice, isn't it?"

"I don't know, honey, but don't move until an all clear comes over the PA system." He tapped the security guard's shoulder. "Come with me."

The two raced into the lobby. Jamison glanced back to ensure that the clerk had closed and locked the doors behind them.

Ignoring the elevator, Jamison opted for the stairs and climbed at breakneck speed, pulling his weapon as he raced toward the danger. The guard followed, but his steps were labored, and he was gasping for air by the third floor.

Weapon at the ready, Jamison opened the door and stepped into pandemonium.

In one sweep, he saw it all.

His throat thickened. Alice lay sprawled across the transport gurney with a gunshot wound to her side. Corporal Riley was on the floor, unconscious and surrounded by a growing pool of blood.

A doctor reached for the portable defibrillator on the floor next to the guard. A nurse cut open his uniform.

"Clear." The doc lowered the paddles onto the MP's sunken chest.

Additional medical personnel raced forward.

"Get her to the O.R. stat!" someone shouted. Hands pushed Alice toward a second elevator.

Jamison raised his voice over the chaos. "Which way did the shooter go?"

Someone pointed to an exit at the end of the hall. "Back stairway. Two security guards ran after him. The guy's wearing a black ski mask."

Jamison raced forward, shoved on the door to the stairwell and flew down the steps. At the bottom landing, he pressed through the first-floor exit and rushed into the humid night. Two security men stood under a streetlight in the rear parking area. One raised a handheld radio to his ear.

Hearing Jamison approach, the other guard turned and shook his head. "He got away."

Jamison pulled out his cell to notify the CID. Anger and frustration boiled up within him. He wanted to scream with rage. The killer had struck again. Alice was alive but only barely, and Jamison had no idea if she or Riley would survive the new injuries.

Jamison had been close. Yet not close enough.

He thought of Michele holed up in the E.R. At least she was safe.

The killer had a gun and was on the run. One thing was certain. He would strike again.

Jamison had to ensure that Michele wasn't the next person he planned to kill.

THIRTEEN

Michele hunkered down behind the counter in the emergency room, fearful of what was happening upstairs in the ICU. Sirens sounded in the distance and grew steadily louder, crescendoing in a deafening scream as a caravan of squad cars screeched to the curb outside. Flashing lights spilled through the windows, bathing the E.R. in a strobelike effect that made her dizzy and even more afraid for Jamison's safety.

Military police swarmed into the lobby and ran for the stairwell. Peering over the top of the desk, Michele saw Dawson Timmons race past.

"We'll be all right," she said, trying to calm the patients gathered around her.

"The shooter must be that serial killer on post," a man said.

Next to him, a woman cried softly. "He'll find us," she said, her voice edged with fear.

"The CID and military police have everything under control." At least, that's what Michele wanted to believe.

The woman sniffed. "How can you be so sure?"

Michele shoved a box of tissues into her hands. "I

know the special agents working on this case. They've had a lot of leads. The killer will be apprehended."

A second woman stood up. "I need to get home to my husband. He'll be worried."

Michele gently touched her arm. "Wait until the all clear. A few more minutes won't make a difference." The woman hesitated and then sat back down.

Michele breathed a sigh of relief. One problem averted, although she understood the woman's concern about her loved one. Michele's mother was home. Hopefully, she was occupied with homecoming plans and wouldn't hear about the attack at the hospital.

The clerk, in her early twenties with long hair and a tiny nose ring, leaned toward Michele, her voice low. "Does your boyfriend work for the police?"

Boyfriend? Michele had to smile. Once upon a time, Jamison had been even more than that to her. "He's a CID agent on post. Criminal Investigation Division."

The girl looked confused.

"You didn't grow up in the military?" Michele asked.

"My dad runs the Laundromat in town."

A civilian who didn't know about the army. "CID agents handle felony crimes against military personnel and their family members."

"So he's working on the murder case?"

"That's right." Although if Michele had heard Jamison's boss correctly, Chief Wilson had put Dawson in charge of the investigation. Jamison's job was to keep her and her mother safe.

Tough duty, especially when Michele had been so careless at the cemetery yesterday. If she had kept her head up and her eyes wide open, she would have gotten off the road at the first sign of the approaching car.

She also would have waited for Jamison before driving to Alice's house last night, although as she'd told him earlier, arriving any later could have proven fatal to her friend.

Michele rubbed her hands over her brow and rested the back of her head against the counter. No matter how much she wanted to be optimistic, she was worried about Jamison.

The clerk pulled her legs to her chest and placed her chin on her knees, eyes closed. The other people sat with their own thoughts. Michele checked her watch, wishing she'd hear something about what was happening on the third floor.

"Tell him thanks."

Michele glanced at the clerk. "Pardon?"

"Thank your boyfriend for me. He tried to protect all of us." Her thin lips twitched into a soulful smile. "You're probably used to all the good he does, but I don't know guys like that." She chewed on her lip. "Your boyfriend's a hero. A superhero."

Michele closed her eyes. The young clerk had Jamison pegged. He was a man who always reacted in the face of any danger. Superheroes survived in spite of insurmountable odds because of their special powers, but Jamison survived because he was good at what he did and because he cared enough to try. Michele hadn't recognized what this young girl had noticed immediately. Jamison was a very special agent.

Voices sounded in the lobby. Glancing over the counter, she saw Jamison talking to Dawson. Relief swept over her. At least tonight's danger had passed.

A car engine sounded outside. She glanced out the window on the way to open the doors, planning to throw her arms around Jamison. But when he stood in front of her, all she could see was his face, twisted in pain, and the smear of blood across his once-white shirt.

"What happened?" she asked, fearing the worst.

"It's Alice."

Michele's hand flew to her throat.

"She's in surgery." Jamison hesitated. "They…they don't expect her to live."

Michele wanted to be a superhero like Jamison, but too much had happened. Tears clouded her eyes, and her knees went weak. She felt herself falling, but instead of crashing to the floor, she fell into Jamison's strong arms.

"It's going to be okay, honey," he soothed, rubbing his hands over her back.

Even superheroes sometimes lied, if the truth was too hard to accept, and the truth about Alice was more than Michele could bear.

Lance.

Yolanda.

Now Alice.

Michele's father was flying home from a war zone, and a killer was stalking his next victim.

Who would he come after next?

Terror seized her.

Superhero or not, Jamison would always be in the line of fire.

As worried as Jamison was about Michele's physical safety, he was even more concerned about her emotional well-being. Leaving Dawson to wrap up things at the hospital, Jamison tucked her into the passenger seat of his car and glanced into the night sky.

Please, Lord, Michele has been through so much. Comfort her the way I wish I could and keep her safe.

He needed to take Michele home before something happened to her or to his heart. As far as she was concerned, they weren't good together. She had made that perfectly clear ten months ago, but tonight he didn't care about what had been, he cared about the present moment. At the moment, he wanted to wrap Michele in his arms and never let her go.

FOURTEEN

Even with Jamison at her side, Michele felt drained as she climbed the stairs to her front porch. He had spent much of the ride home on the phone with Dawson. Alice and the nice military policeman assigned to guard her were both in surgery. The doctors didn't offer much hope for either patient.

Jamison talked to the security detail at her parents' quarters and then followed her onto the porch. Rummaging in her handbag, she found her house key and dropped it into his outstretched hand. Always the gentleman, he unlocked the door, stepped aside for her to enter and then followed her into the foyer.

Michele had expected to hear chatter from the wives' group and was surprised to find the house empty except for her mother, who stepped from the living room.

"Hello, dear." She lowered her cheek toward Michele and accepted a kiss, then greeted Jamison with a welcoming smile.

"How's Alice?"

"She..." The words stuck in Michele's throat. Jamison took over, for which she was grateful, and brought her mother up to date on what had happened.

Hearing the news, Roberta put her head in her hands and moaned. "Oh, dear God, when will it end?"

"Not until the killer's apprehended." Jamison stated what they all knew to be true. If only the arrest would come about without additional loss of life or injury.

"There's been too much suffering." Roberta reached for the sturdy oak banister as if needing support. Her eyes reflected pain and struggle and many of the feelings that had bombarded Michele over the last two days.

Tonight, the tiny lines around Roberta's eyes seemed more pronounced. Her skin appeared less vibrant, and her shoulders drooped. Michele had always considered her mother young for her age, but the years and the circumstances appeared to be taking their toll.

Michele forced a smile. "Dad will be home in the morning. Everything will be better then."

Roberta glanced into the dining room.

Michele followed her gaze to the bouquet of flowers her father had been thoughtful enough to send. "The arrangement looks nice on the table, Mother."

Roberta nodded a bit too enthusiastically, all the while blinking back tears that swarmed her eyes.

"Are you all right?" Always the rock, her mother usually seemed unflappable. Tonight she appeared as broken as Michele had felt earlier.

"I'm fine." Which was what Michele had said so many times recently.

Studying her mother's drawn face, Michele saw beneath the capable army wife facade to a woman who tried to appear stronger than she was. Roberta squared her shoulders, but the expression she wore revealed her fragile interior.

"What's wrong, Mother?"

"There's something I need to tell you, dear."

As if sensing the importance of the moment, Jamison cleared his throat. "If you don't mind, ma'am, I'll step into the kitchen and call CID headquarters."

Once he left, Roberta squeezed Michele's hand. "Some things have been troubling both of us that need to be brought to light."

Michele wasn't sure where her mother was headed.

"I rarely talk about Lance, and I know that upsets you. The truth is his death left a hole in my heart that's been hard to fill. Your father dealt with his own grief by throwing himself into his work. When I tried to talk to him about what I was feeling, he told me to be strong."

She pointed to the table. "That bouquet is his first attempt to let me know he understands what I've been going through these last two years."

Regret swept over Michele. She had been so wrong about her mother. "I…I thought you didn't want to talk about Lance."

"I wanted to, but I couldn't. Even looking at old photos or visiting the cemetery with you was more than I could handle. I forced myself to go on for you and for your father. You were traveling a lot for the insurance company and seemed fairly self-sufficient. Dad had his work. Most of all, I didn't want to be a burden."

"Which you could never be, Mother."

A door had cracked open, but Michele still hesitated. Some doors needed to remain closed.

Her mother raised her hand to her throat and fingered the collar of her blouse. "I know you feel responsible for Lance's death, but you made the right decision to help with the storm relief."

Bitter denial welled up within Michele. "But if I

hadn't gone to the coast, Lance would have been on leave, showing me around his new post. He wouldn't have volunteered to take that mission."

"Your brother loved the military, and he loved to fly. Going up that day was his decision, Michele. You were *not* to blame."

"But—"

"We'll never know why God called Lance home, yet we have to trust he's with the Lord. Scripture tells us with God everything works together for good."

Michele still couldn't trust the Lord, but seeing her mother's pain and hearing the sincerity in her voice allowed Michele to finally accept the truth. Her mother didn't blame her for Lance's death, which lifted a weight she had carried for too long.

Roberta opened her arms, and Michele stepped into her mother's welcoming embrace, overwhelmed with a sense of homecoming. Tears filled her eyes, but they were joyful tears that washed away the struggle she'd had with her mother. Roberta's tears seemed equally cathartic, and mother and daughter cried freely.

Hearing the commotion, Jamison raced into the foyer. The look on his face said he had misinterpreted their reconciliation as something more threatening. "Are you all right?"

"We're fine," they both said in unison, which caused them to laugh and wipe their eyes and feel the strong mother-daughter bond that had been absent for too long.

Michele's heart nearly burst with love for her mother. An equally strong feeling swept over her as she smiled at Jamison, who had given them the privacy they needed to heal.

"I'm starving," Michele admitted, a bit light-headed but in a good way.

"I've got leftovers in the fridge." Roberta motioned Jamison toward the kitchen. "I know you must be hungry, too. Let's have something to eat."

Michele raised her hand to her neck, knowing she and her mother could now talk freely about her brother. "You go ahead. I'll join you in a minute."

Running upstairs, she opened her dresser drawer and removed the lid from the wooden box she kept near her Bible. Her eyes rested on the delicate silver cross Lance had given her. On the same chain, Michele had placed a silver heart charm that had been a gift from Jamison shortly after they'd started dating. He'd called the silver dangles her Cross My Heart necklace, a necklace she had taken off the day she left Fort Rickman.

Michele was beginning to believe she had been wrong to leave Jamison. Surely things would be different once he understood her fears about his safety.

Almost giddy, she started to laugh, then quickly sobered, thinking of Alice, fighting for her life, and the brigade flying home through the night.

Hearing Jamison's voice from the kitchen, Michele clasped the necklace around her neck. Jamison was a hero, just as the clerk at the hospital had said, but a killer was still on the loose, and anything could happen. Once again, she needed to guard her heart. Only this time, Michele wasn't sure if she could.

FIFTEEN

Jamison looked up as Michele entered the kitchen. His breath caught in his throat at her freshness and beauty. Not only had the exhaustion disappeared from her eyes, but her smile was bright and lit up the room and his weary spirit. From across the kitchen, he could feel the draw of her magnetism and would have pulled Michele into his arms if her mother hadn't been standing nearby.

While Michele had been upstairs, he had changed into a fresh white shirt he kept in his car. Mrs. Logan had arranged a baked ham and a number of salads on the table, along with a loaf of sliced French bread.

As she prepared the food, Jamison had called the hospital. Alice remained in surgery. The MP had been moved into the recovery room but was still in serious condition.

"Help yourself." Mrs. Logan pulled plates from the cabinet and placed them on the table. "Coffee or cola?"

"Coffee sounds great." Jamison accepted a steaming mug and waited until Michele had her food before he made a ham sandwich and heaped the salads on his plate.

Once they had all settled into chairs around the

kitchen table, Michele nudged his arm. "Would you offer thanks?"

Taken aback by the request, he was equally surprised to see the Cross My Heart necklace around her neck. Michele's talk with her mother seemed to have healed not only their relationship but also Michele's attitude toward the Lord. Overcome with relief, he wanted to cheer, but with both women waiting for the blessing, he rationalized giving thanks was a better way to handle his exuberance.

Following dinner, Michele refilled his mug and poured coffee for herself and her mother. "Any news from Dad?"

Mrs. Logan shook her head. "His plane will probably refuel twice during the flight. I'm sure he'll call, if he has the opportunity." She eyed Jamison over the top of her mug. "What about the security plan for the airport tomorrow?"

"Everything's in place, ma'am. We'll have the area well guarded. Only those who have a connection with the brigade will be allowed access."

"What time will you get there in the morning?"

He shrugged. "Hard to say. I've got to check on a few things at the airfield tonight, and I'll probably return well before sunrise. Tell the wives they can come as early as they want."

"My guess, Greg Yates will be the first to arrive. He's in charge of the decorating committee. Welcome-home signs need to be hung as soon as possible."

"That won't be a problem. There's a scaffold he can use, and I'll be around to help."

"Chief Wilson called me earlier today." Mrs. Logan sipped her coffee. "He said the families will remain in the terminal and watch the planes touch down on live video."

"That's for your security, ma'am. We don't want any civilians on the tarmac. We'll announce the landing and then program a large clock on the wall to count down the minutes until the unit marches into the secure area."

Michele wrapped her hands around the mug. "Will the general give a welcoming speech?"

Jamison smiled. "He assured me he'll be brief. Your mother will be on the dais with him."

Mrs. Logan laughed. "But I won't be speaking. I agree with the general. The shorter we can keep the formal portion of the ceremony, the better. All the soldiers want is to be reunited with their families."

"You're right about that, ma'am." His gaze turned to Michele. She smiled from across the table, igniting a spark within him.

As if understanding their desire to be alone, Mrs. Logan pushed back her chair. "You two stay put as long as you like, but I need some rest."

Jamison stood as she left the room. Once Mrs. Logan had climbed the stairs, he rounded the table to where Michele sat. Touching her hand, he pulled her to her feet and gently turned her around to face the window.

The curtains were open to the night sky. He pointed to the full moon that shone through the darkness.

"I'm taking that as a good sign," he said, slipping his arms around her waist.

She relaxed against his chest. "You always said moonlight was special."

He dipped his head and rubbed his cheek against hers. "With you in my arms, everything is special."

She turned, her smile warming him. Her blue eyes

sparkled like the stars. Michele's lips opened ever so slightly, and suddenly all he could think about was the sweetness of her kisses. Lowering his mouth, he captured hers, and the whole world turned bright for one electrifying minute.

The sensation sent shock waves through his body. For the first time in almost a year, Jamison knew he wasn't a failure. Nothing could stop him with Michele at his side. He would always be the victor because winning Michele was the best prize of all.

He pulled her closer, feeling her feminine softness and inhaling her heady perfume. Wanting to take in every detail of her, he opened his eyes, but instead of Michele he saw the darkness outside and realized, for one terrifying second, everything he thought was good could all be a lie.

The killer was still on the loose and would strike again. Another shoot-out might send Michele running back to Atlanta. If she left him a second time, Jamison didn't know if he could survive.

Michele luxuriated in Jamison's arms, intoxicated with the strength of his embrace and the intensity of his kiss. Being together again proved everything would be all right. Her dad would get home safely. Alice and the military policeman would pull through. She and Jamison would take up where they had left off ten months ago.

With a throaty groan, Jamison pulled away from her and adjusted his tie. Feeling at a loss without his arms around her, Michele turned to follow Jamison's gaze, troubled by his apparent rejection. A military policeman came into view in the yard outside the window.

Jamison hadn't wanted the men guarding the Logan home to see them together. Her initial confusion turned to appreciation for her chivalrous hero. Jamison had a strong sense of propriety and put her honor before his own desire.

"Did he notice us?" she asked.

"We're safe." Jamison's lips twitched in an adorable way that made her want to kiss him again. "It's Stiles, and he's making his rounds. I checked earlier. No one was there when I pulled you close."

She sighed contentedly, enjoying his nearness and the familiar way they had stepped back in time. "If we're going to be on display, perhaps it's time to do the dishes."

Jamison raised his brow teasingly.

She poked him in the ribs. "Consider it payment for your dinner."

"And well worth the meal, but didn't I hear something about cookies?"

She laughed. "I told you I baked for the Hughes children. Leftovers are in the jar by the stove." Pointing him in the right direction, she watched as he slipped off his jacket and hung it over the chair.

He grabbed two cookies and then turned back to her. She laughed again as he shoved one in his mouth and winked good-naturedly as if in appreciation of both her and her baking.

Lost in the moment, Michele thought only of Jamison and the future they could have together. Then she looked down and saw the gun on his hip.

Her levity deflated, knowing the complications that still stood between them. If only Jamison would leave the military and law enforcement and move into another line of work.

"Did you…" She ran water in the sink, grateful for something to focus on instead of his questioning gaze. "Did you always want to be a special agent?"

He let out a breath and dropped the cookie on the counter. His eyes searched hers as if trying to determine the underlying meaning to her question.

"I told you my mother died when I was young and that my dad raised me."

She nodded. "You mentioned he didn't know how to parent."

Jamison shrugged. A wry smile tugged at his lips. "I was sugarcoating the reality of our relationship. My father thought the world owed him everything. If he didn't get what he wanted, he took it."

She turned off the water and reached for a paper towel. "I…I don't understand."

"He was a thief, Michele. We lived on the run, hiding out in fleabag motels, sometimes in whatever car he was able to steal."

"What about the police?"

"They had bigger crimes to handle in most cases. Plus, my dad could sense when the cops were closing in. He'd wake me in the middle of the night so we could hightail out of town."

"How did you attend school?"

"Sometimes he'd take a job, and we'd stay in one place long enough for me to get ahead in my studies. Luckily, learning came easily. When we moved on, he'd tuck my textbooks in the car with me, and I'd work on my own."

Michele felt for the little boy who always had to run

away from life. Her own childhood had been filled with stability and love. "But you mentioned throwing the discus in high school."

He nodded. "I needed to complete my senior year in order to get a college scholarship. My dad had a job at the plant in town at that time. The foreman complained he wasn't pulling his fair share of the weight. Dad got mad, picked a fight and came home bloodied and beaten."

Her hand rose to her throat.

"My father was determined to teach the guy a lesson. He had gasoline in the trunk of his car and expected me to go back to the factory with him later that night."

She was afraid to hear what happened.

"I told him I wouldn't do it. We argued." Jamison's face twisted as if he were seeing his father again. "He took off in his car like a madman. I raced after him."

Michele moaned, anticipating the outcome.

"I ran for ten blocks across town to where he worked. By the time I got there, he had already poured gasoline on lumber that was piled against the corner of the building."

Jamison drew his hand to his chest. "The acrid smell filled my lungs. Dad had a lighter and screamed for me to stay away from him. He said he hated me and who I had become. I tried to reason with him, but he kept saying I was a failure and would never succeed in life."

Michele wished she could wipe away the pain she saw on Jamison's face.

"I stopped in the middle of the street, not knowing whether to rush him and try to pull him away or to just keep talking." He shook his head. "I made the wrong decision that night."

"Oh, Jamison."

"He struck the match. There must have been gasoline on his hands. It had spilled onto his clothes."

Closing the distance between them, Michele wanted to pull him close, but Jamison needed to keep talking.

"I tried to get to him in time." His voice was husky with emotion.

"You did the right thing. You weren't to blame."

Jamison shook his head. "I never wanted to be like him. When I was a kid, he forced me to steal so we could eat. Produce from a farmers' market. Bread from a bakery. Meat from a mom-and-pop grocery store. I knew it was wrong, but I wanted to earn his love."

"You were only a child."

"The army was my way out. Talking to the chaplain, hearing about Jesus's love allowed me to ask forgiveness and put all that behind me. Until ten months ago, when I thought I could talk a gunman down, that he'd listen to reason, just as I thought my father would the night he died in the fire."

Michele remembered all too clearly that deadly day on post.

"I rushed forward to save the shooter because that's what I should have done for my dad. But I made a mistake that almost killed Dawson. I was thinking like a kid, instead of a special agent."

"Oh, Jamison, the reason I left ten months ago was that I couldn't love a man who always put himself in danger. You can leave the military. There are other jobs that don't require you to carry a gun."

He shook his head. "I'm not a guy who runs away like my father did. I have to stay and work through my problems. That's the only way I can live with myself."

She took a step back. "But you said you made a mistake."

He nodded. "That's right."

"Don't you see?" Tears stung her eyes. "I understand what you're going through because I made a mistake that cost my brother his life."

Jamison's face softened and his voice was low when he finally spoke. "The difference between us, Michele, is that I've forgiven myself."

Which was something she could never do.

Frantic to hold on to to their fragile relationship, she reached for him. "If you care about me, you'll walk away from the military so we can be together."

His eyes narrowed. "You sound like my father. He put me between his love and what I knew in my heart was right. I won't run away. That's not who I am. The military taught me to be a better man than my father."

Why couldn't Jamison understand? "You can be that better man with me."

He shook his head. "You don't know what you're asking."

A sword pierced her heart, and she gasped at the pain. They were worlds apart. He was the kid who still had to prove himself to his father, and she was the sister who couldn't forgive herself for her brother's death. Neither of them would give up the past to forge a new future together.

A lump formed in her throat. Jamison gazed into her eyes, and she saw that he, too, realized the terrible divide that hung between them, a divide too broad and too deep to cross.

Only she didn't know how she could ever say good-bye to the man she loved. If only something would change his heart.

The phone rang. The shrill tone cut through that divide, bringing them back to the moment, to the reality that one woman had died and two other lives hung in the balance.

Michele reached for the phone. She turned toward the window and glanced outside. The moon had disappeared behind the clouds.

"Colonel Logan's quarters, Michele speaking." She reverted to the greeting she had used growing up when her home was happy and life was good.

"I can see you."

Michele's heart exploded in her chest.

"I'm coming after you, Michele."

The blood drained from her head. She felt lightheaded and nauseated.

"You'll be the next to die."

"Michele?" Jamison's voice. Insistent. Demanding. "It's him, isn't it?"

She couldn't respond. All she could do was stare into the darkness where the killer waited.

Jamison followed her gaze. "He's out there."

Drawing his gun, he pulled open the back door and raced into the night.

The killer's maniacal laughter filled the phone. "Before I kill you, I'll kill Steele."

Jamison ran across the backyard. He was that kid, long ago, running to save his father, only tonight he was trying to save her.

"Jamison!" she screamed, racing through the doorway. This time, Dawson and the military police weren't going to take the hit. This time, Jamison would be the one to die.

The night was hot and humid and filled with sounds that intensified the fear hammering at her heart.

"Jamison!" she screamed again.

A bullet whizzed past her, striking the brick wall just a fraction of an inch from her head.

The sound of a second shot cut through the night.

Dazed, she took a step back. Jamison screamed her name. Before she could react, his arms were around her, pulling her to the ground.

A third round exploded.

Jamison gasped. Wet warmth ran down Michele's back. The coppery smell returned, overpowering her.

Without turning to see the blood, Michele knew the terrible truth. Jamison had been hit.

SIXTEEN

"I'm all right," Jamison insisted as the medic finished the triage. The ambulance sat parked in the middle of Michele's backyard surrounded by crime scene experts searching for clues.

Fort Rickman was on lockdown. Military police were canvassing the area, going door to door, and checking every nook and cranny where a man could hide.

"You're one lucky guy," Dawson said, leaning over the stretcher where Jamison lay.

"It's a flesh wound."

"You need stitches."

"The medic bandaged me up, Dawson. I'm fine."

"You're headstrong and not thinking straight. You never should have run into the night."

"Michele told you?"

"She's angry, Jamison, and fed up with you. She's holed up in the house, refusing to see anyone."

"I'll talk to her."

Dawson shook his head. "I wouldn't tonight. Give her time. The medics prescribed a sleeping pill. From what Mrs. Logan said, she hasn't slept the last two nights."

Jamison knew she was exhausted.

"Not that any of us have slept." Dawson stated the obvious. "Look, Jamison, you should have called for backup. McGrunner and Stiles were on the sidewalk in front of the house."

"By the time I contacted them, the killer would have been long gone."

"And you wouldn't have taken a hit."

"It's minor."

"You're one stubborn fool." Dawson's cell rang. He stepped away to take the call.

Mrs. Logan came out of her quarters and walked straight to where Jamison lay.

"How's Michele?" he asked as she neared.

"She's resting. I suggest you wait until tomorrow to talk to her."

"Are you sure, ma'am?"

Mrs. Logan nodded. "Tomorrow will be soon enough."

So much would happen in the morning. Once her father was home, Michele would be free to head back to Atlanta.

"Stanley called," Mrs. Logan continued. "His plane had landed to refuel so he and Michele had a chance to talk. Hearing her father's voice helped. She promised me she'd try to sleep."

Mrs. Logan's gaze was warm as she looked down at Jamison. "You saved her life. I can never thank you enough for being such a hero. If…if you hadn't pushed her to the ground…" She shook her head. "I would have lost my daughter as well as my son."

"I'm not a hero, ma'am."

"Maybe you don't think so, but I do. I'll see you in

the morning at the airfield." Turning, she retraced her steps and entered her house.

Dawson neared, smiling. "Good news. We've got him."

Jamison felt a surge of relief. "Who? Where? How?"

"A sergeant, trying to leave post. The front gate security guards found a gun in his glove compartment. A 9 millimeter. The bullets in the chamber matched the caliber of slugs we dug out of the brick wall."

"Had the gun been recently fired?"

"Roger that. Plus, he had gunpowder residue on his hands. His name's Kenneth Cramer. Claimed he was out on one of the training ranges doing an impromptu target practice. He's part of the First of the Fifth's rear detachment. Seems he wanted to deploy to Afghanistan with the brigade, but he had a medical profile at the time. Guess who made the decision to keep him at Fort Rickman?"

"Major Hughes?"

"Bingo. Now that the unit's coming home, he decided to take his anger out on the major by killing his wife."

Jamison saw a hole in the theory. Namely, why had he come after Alice Rossi? "Is there a connection between Cramer and Sergeant Rossi?"

"We'll find one." Dawson rubbed his hand over his tired face. "It's over, Jamison. We can all breathe a sigh of relief."

"Do me a favor. Keep the guards posted on the Logan home."

"There's no reason, buddy."

"Maybe not, but it would make me feel better."

Dawson shrugged. "Okay. Until morning."

"The chief won't want the information about apprehending the killer to go public until ballistics confirms the bullets were fired from Sergeant Cramer's gun."

"Of course. But I'm sure we've got our man."

Jamison wasn't convinced.

Dawson started to walk away, then turned to look back at Jamison. "One more thing. You don't always have to be the hero."

Jamison glanced at the brick quarters. Mrs. Logan had thanked him for saving Michele, yet he'd been reckless to run from the house into the killer's path.

No matter what Mrs. Logan thought, she was wrong. He hadn't saved Michele. He had placed her in danger. Jamison had been a fool instead of a hero. If he hadn't run from the house, Michele never would have followed him.

"Failure...a disappointment... You'll never succeed, Jamie-boy." The words tumbled through Jamison's mind.

Time was running out. He had to ensure that the plans for the airfield were in place. Dawson might think the killer had been apprehended, but in his gut, Jamison didn't feel it was over yet.

He'd been wrong before, and he had questioned his own ability too many times since Dawson had been wounded. Tonight, he couldn't shake the overwhelming sense that the case wasn't closed. Jamison would wait until the ballistics came back before he'd sigh with relief.

The wound on his side throbbed, but Jamison refused to take the painkiller the medic offered. He didn't want anything to hamper his ability to think clearly. He had a lot to figure out, about the killer, about Michele and what the future would hold.

Right now he needed to finish the job he'd been given. He would protect the women at the airfield and the soldiers coming home from Afghanistan. More than anything, he wanted the homecoming to be a time of joy and not sorrow. Then he thought of Major Hughes and Sergeant Rossi and knew some pain lasted a lifetime.

Michele would go back to Atlanta, and Jamison would ask for a change of assignment. He needed to get away from Fort Rickman and everything that reminded him of Michele. She didn't want him in her life, and he didn't blame her. He had made a terrible mistake. A mistake that had almost cost Michele her life.

Michele heard the ambulance drive away. The voices in the backyard quieted as, one after another, the military police cars pulled from the curb and headed back to their headquarters.

She stared at the sleeping pill the medic had given her, still on her nightstand. She couldn't and wouldn't take it no matter how much she wanted to sleep. Her father was on a plane coming back to the States. If something happened en route, she wanted to be able to accept the news and deal with it without some type of crutch to take away the pain.

Plus, she needed to be strong for her mother, although tonight—after Jamison had been hit—her mother had been the tower of strength.

Michele had run away from Jamison once more. This time, she had fled into her house instead of all the way to Atlanta. She couldn't face him again. If she did, she'd see the blood and his torn shirt and the bullet that ripped open the flesh on his side.

Once the ambulance had arrived and the medics assured her the wound wasn't life threatening, she had raced into the house overcome with nausea so strong she could hardly hold up her head.

Everything she feared would happen had come true. Jamison had charged into danger, and he'd been wounded. If the killer's aim had been better or if Jamison hadn't pushed her to the floor, he could—*would*—be dead.

The thought brought a sour taste to her mouth as bile bubbled up from her stomach. She rubbed her hands over her abdomen, trying to calm the chaos of fear that swirled within her.

She had tried to warn Jamison, to call him back, to tell him to stay inside with her. He'd ignored her warning and turned his back on caution and common sense. If she needed a sign that she had done the right thing ten months ago, she had one today. The message was as loud as the gunshots that rang through the night.

A door slammed and footsteps signaled her mother was downstairs. Water ran. At this hour, Roberta was probably brewing a cup of herbal tea before she climbed the stairs and went to bed.

A chill slid down Michele's spine. As much as she'd like a warm mug to hold in her hands and hot liquid to temper the frigid cold that washed over her, she couldn't face her mother now.

Roberta liked Jamison. She always had. Without saying as much, Michele knew her mother wondered how her daughter could have left such a good man. Roberta didn't understand Michele's fear that Jamison would walk into danger and be shot, just as had happened tonight.

Her worst nightmare had come true.

She heard a familiar voice outside and stepped toward the window. Pulling back the curtain ever so slightly she saw Jamison and McGrunner deep in conversation.

Farther away, she noticed additional military police patrolling the area around her house. Nothing seemed to have changed, even though she had overheard some of the men talking about the captured killer.

Her mother's footfalls sounded coming up the stairs. She knocked softly on the closed door. "Michele, honey, can I get you anything?"

She stared into the night, unable to answer. Hopefully, her mother would think the pill had worked and she was sound asleep.

McGrunner saluted and walked away. Jamison glanced up at her window. Even at this distance and in the darkness, Michele knew he saw her, and that caused her heart to break.

She loved him more than he would ever know, but she couldn't keep looking over her shoulder wondering when the next gunman would strike. Michele wanted Jamison, but she wanted him alive. She'd rather leave him behind than have her worst fears come true.

SEVENTEEN

Jamison spent most of the night coordinating security between flight personnel at the airfield, the military police and the Criminal Investigation Division. Once everything was in place, he reviewed the operation, checking to ensure that he hadn't missed some seemingly insignificant item that could become a stumbling block during the actual event.

When dealing with the safety of a brigade of soldiers as well as the families who loved them, every detail had to be checked and doubled-checked.

Even though Sergeant Kenneth Cramer was in custody, Jamison didn't have a sense of closure on the case. He used to be able to trust his instincts. Now he was never sure if the signals he was receiving were accurate. Hopefully, with time, his old confidence would return, but the memory of his mistakes still haunted him, especially when lives were at risk.

Corporal Otis arrived at CID headquarters shortly before 0500 hours. He brewed a fresh pot of coffee and poured Jamison the first cup. "Here you go, sir. Strong and black."

Jamison accepted the mug with a nod of gratitude.

The hot brew burned going down, but the effect gave him the burst of energy he needed.

"How are you feeling, sir?" the corporal asked.

"Like I should shower and shave."

"And the wound?"

"A little sore, but not really a problem." In truth, his side ached, although not enough to slow him down.

Otis returned to the main office. Jamison continued to work, not only because of the importance of the mission but also to keep his mind focused on anything except Michele. If he paused for even a moment, images of her from last night tangled through his mind.

He glanced up as Otis reappeared, carrying two donuts and a banana. "I scrounged up breakfast."

Jamison laughed. "You raided someone's stash of snacks."

The corporal laughed. "Sir, I plead the Fifth." He placed the contraband on Jamison's desk. "The chief's secretary told me to help myself anytime I was hungry."

"I'll spring for donuts next week." Jamison took a large bite out of the glazed pastry, enjoying the impromptu meal. After eating, he downed his coffee and stretched back in his chair. "So, tell me, Otis, have you ever been a fool for love?"

His light mocha face twisted into a wide grin. "More times than I'd like to admit."

Tapping a pen against his desk, Jamison hesitated before he asked, "Did you send flowers?"

The soldier nodded his head. "Matter of fact, I use the florist on post any time I want to tell a lady how special she is. Best way I know to get on a woman's good side. Does the trick just like that." He snapped his fingers, which caused Jamison to smile and wonder whether he needed to call the florist this morning and order a bouquet for Michele.

"Little secret I learned at a young age, sir, if you're interested."

Jamison nodded.

"The ladies like roses. Red, yellow, white. The color doesn't matter, but I can attest to the return such an investment might bring on your behalf."

Otis chuckled and headed back to his own desk.

The corporal's wit brought a burst of fresh air into the stuffy office. Feeling encouraged, Jamison closed the files, nodded to Otis as he left the CID headquarters and drove to the gym. Thirty minutes later, Jamison had showered and shaved and donned a fresh white shirt before he headed to the airfield.

His optimism deflated as he drove across post. Flowers wouldn't change the situation with Michele. Jamison had been a fool to get close to her again. Holding her in his arms had wiped away the ten months they had been apart. The pain he felt at the moment was as real and as raw as when she had initially left him.

All his efforts to move forward without her had been foiled last night in her kitchen. He'd told her the moonlight was special, but he'd been wrong. The moon had lulled him into believing he had a chance.

She had seemed so willing to fold into his embrace. Her perfume was hypnotic, her eyes enticing. Touching her was like touching life itself. She was everything to him, but he couldn't walk away from who he was and what he did no matter how much he loved her.

Arriving at the airfield, he quickly ensured that everyone knew their jobs and were ready to execute them flawlessly. Word had spread that the killer was in custody, and a sense of euphoria settled over the military police and CID personnel on duty. Jamison cautioned them not to be lulled into believing the danger had passed. Ballistics needed to confirm the rounds fired at Michele's house matched those from the firearm found in the suspect's vehicle. Until then, Jamison wanted everyone to be vigilant and act as if the killer was still on the loose.

Jamison went person to person, ensuring all the security personnel realized the complexity of keeping the brigade safe and the necessity to be on high alert until the last soldier had left the airfield.

The three planes transporting the soldiers were scheduled to land at approximately 1100 hours. The estimated time of arrival had been released to the Family Readiness Groups, and people had already started to trickle in to the terminal.

Even now a sense of excitement permeated the air. Many groups on post had set up tables to support the families as they waited. The Red Cross provided first-aid stations. The Army Community Services carried in cases of bottled water they chilled on ice and handed out as needed. Morale Support personnel distributed small American flags that children waved as they played near their mothers.

Some of the families dressed alike in T-shirts bearing their hero soldier's picture. Others had buttons that read Proud Army Wife or I love my soldier husband. A few of the women wore stiletto heels and fancy dresses eager to welcome their returning loved ones with more than a kiss.

The army band warmed up their instruments in a corner of the large arena, adding to the growing excitement. Jamison knew the crowd would swell when the doors opened and the men and women in uniform marched into the terminal. He tasked two military policemen to rope off a central area large enough for the unit to stand in formation during the general's welcome.

Following the speeches, the dividers would be dropped, and a huge lovefest would ensue as families and soldiers united. Tears of joy would mix with laughter. Proud parents with beaming faces would embrace their returning sons and daughters. Babies born during the deployment would gaze with blank stares at the soldier dads they had never seen before, while older children squealed with delight and reached for parents who had been out of their lives for too long. Wives would scramble to find their husbands in the throng, and men would open their arms to the person they had dreamed of holding tight for the last twelve months. All of that would play out later today at the homecoming and would be the best part of the celebration.

The worst would be when Major Hughes and Sergeant Rossi were escorted off the plane ahead of the others. Military sedans would be waiting on the tarmac. The chaplain would be part of the transport detail. One van would drive the newly widowed major to the VIP quarters on post, where he would reunite with his children and sister-in-law. Alice's husband would be taken directly to the hospital. Although her condition had improved slightly, the homecoming would be bittersweet for both men.

The news media had requested to be on-site to film the welcome-home ceremony. Returning soldiers sold airtime, and the TV stations wanted to capture the event for the nightly news. Owing to the need for security,

Jamison had recommended they remain off post. Chief Agent in Charge Wilson and the commanding general had agreed with his assessment.

The sound of raised voices came from a side entrance to the terminal. Jamison hustled toward the commotion. A vendor wearing a shirt with the Freemont Sandwich Shoppe logo was growing increasingly antagonistic toward an MP guarding the door.

"Look, I've got cases of sandwiches we plan to sell today," the bulky civilian complained. "Why do all of them have to be searched?"

The MP stood his ground. "Sir, we need to check everything that passes through these doors."

"Is there a problem?" Jamison asked as he approached, flashing his identification. He glanced at the vendor's name tag. Rick Stallings.

Jamison's presence had a calming effect, but the vendor continued to state his case. "Here's the thing, sir. I've got cases of sandwiches we've been authorized to sell today. They're wrapped and crated." Stallings pointed to the MP. "This guy tells me he needs to check everything.

"Every case," the MP explained. "Not every sandwich. If you'll give us a little cooperation, we'll have you through the checkpoint so you can set up your concession table."

The vendor hesitated, then sighed. His body language shifted from confrontation to acceptance.

Still concerned by the outburst, Jamison took the guard aside. "Do a thorough search of Mr. Stallings and his merchandise."

"I'll take care of it, sir."

Pulling the complainer out of line, a guard frisked

him, while two other military policemen checked the cases of sandwiches. When the search was completed, the ranking MP nodded to Jamison. "He's good to go, sir."

Stepping away from the security checkpoint, Jamison raised the handheld radio that connected him to the security detail. He cautioned law enforcement to keep their eyes on the people working in the concession area as well as the family members.

Once Stallings had moved on, one of the guards sidled over to Jamison. "That guy's a problem waiting to happen, sir. Makes me grateful for the ones who cooperate." He pointed over his shoulder. "The florist was the complete opposite. He insisted I check him out when he arrived with his flowers."

Jamison turned to see Teddy Sutherland surrounded by a number of plastic buckets that held long-stem yellow roses.

"Had to cost him a pretty penny, sir, for all those flowers," the guard continued. "He wanted to do something special. Said he owed Colonel Logan. That's the type of guy who understands the military."

As much as Michele loved flowers, Jamison hoped Teddy would have a few roses left over, in case she showed signs of changing her mind. A bouquet of flowers might help to soften her heart toward Jamison and the military.

A number of wives he had seen at Mrs. Logan's quarters and at the brigade barracks yesterday arrived with homemade posters in hand, all welcoming the soldiers back to Fort Rickman.

Greg Yates followed them through security, carting a large oilcloth sign, professionally designed. Jamison had the scaffolding positioned so the tarp could be hung near the giant wall clock, as the military spouse requested.

"Do you need some help?" he yelled up to Yates, who seemed to be having trouble attaching the last corner of the sign.

The guy climbed down and shook his head. "For the life of me, I can't seem to get the grommet over the hook. It's probably fatigue. I drove my son to the airport last night." He tugged at the collar of his shirt with frustration. Noting his shaking hand, Jamison raised his brow. "Is anything else bothering you?"

Yates shrugged. "I haven't seen my wife since R & R. That was five and a half months ago. A lot can happen in that length of time."

Jamison knew how relationships could change.

"How 'bout I give you a hand?" Jamison took off his jacket and handed it to Yates, who scurried to the nearby concession area and tossed the sports coat over the back of a folding chair.

Jamison knew he had made a mistake when he climbed to the top of the scaffold. Not only did his side ache, but he felt moisture seep from under the bandage. Hopefully, not blood.

Grabbing the edge of the sign, he adjusted the hook and the grommet fell into place. He called down to Yates, "How's it look?"

"A little higher."

Jamison adjusted the tarp and waited for Yates's approval. A wide smile and a thumbs-up confirmed the sign was in place.

Climbing down, Jamison spied Rick Stallings sitting in one of the folding chairs next to his sports coat. The guy had a sandwich wrapper on his lap and was shoving what looked like a ham and cheese on rye into his mouth. Just so he didn't spray mustard.

By the time Jamison retrieved his jacket, Stallings had returned to the concession area and was hard at work.

The florist stood near the front door, handing flowers to the ladies who entered. The expressions on their faces confirmed their appreciation. Teddy seemed almost jovial. The somber mood that had gripped the post had lifted now that the brigade was coming home.

Jamison glanced at his watch. It was only 6:45 a.m., but a crowd was starting to form already. Everyone wanted to stake out an area close to the center of the terminal in order to have a good view when the unit marched forward. Being with other families enhanced the excitement as they waited for the planes to land.

He radioed the timekeeper in charge of the clock. "Do we have a definite arrival time for the brigade?"

"Yes, sir. Eleven-oh-five."

"Let's begin the countdown at eight hundred hours."

"Roger that, sir."

Lowering the radio, Jamison surveyed the terminal. Nothing should go wrong, but he knew that anything could happen. Like last night when he'd had his arms around Michele and had started to imagine what the future could hold. Just that fast, everything had changed.

He glanced once again at the giant clock. Mrs. Logan was scheduled to arrive between nine and ten o'clock. Michele would probably arrive with her. Hopefully, he'd have time to talk to her before the planes landed. As much as he longed to spend the rest of his life with Michele, he couldn't compromise who he was. If she needed to change him, then she had never loved him in the first place.

No matter how much he hoped it wasn't true, Michele would probably leave Fort Rickman and return to Atlanta. He would try to carry on as best he could, but the thought of living life without Michele left a hole in his heart, a hole he doubted he would ever be able to fill.

Michele woke at 7:00 a.m., feeling like bread dough that had been kneaded too long. The muscle in her back still ached, and the bruise on her thigh looked like green marble with a swirl of yellow.

She glanced at the sleeping pill still on her dresser. As much as she had wanted to rest, she was glad she had skipped the medication. Padding downstairs, she perked coffee and took a steaming mug upstairs while she changed into navy slacks and a red, white and blue silk top. She attached an American flag pin to her collar.

The Cross My Heart necklace lay on her dresser near the Bible she had pulled out of her drawer last night. When sleep had eluded her, she'd found comfort in the familiar scripture passages she had loved in her youth.

Michele reached for the necklace, not because of the heart charm Jamison had given her, but because of the cross that had been a gift from Lance. Her father's plane would land in a few hours, and their small family would be together again. Wanting something that represented her brother, she hooked the chain around her neck.

Before heading downstairs, Michele peered into her parents' bedroom. "Can I bring you some coffee?" she asked her mother.

"Not now, dear. I woke up with a headache and want to stay in bed a bit longer."

Probably because of the stress Roberta had been under.

Downstairs, Michele entered the kitchen, thinking of last night and everything Jamison had told her about his childhood. The story of his past had been painful to recount. No doubt, living that life had been even more difficult.

Wrapping her arms around her waist, Michele stared out the window. Sunshine streamed into the kitchen and held the promise of what the new day would bring.

More than anything, she wanted to hold Jamison and feel his arms around her. If the gap between them wasn't so large, there might be hope for them. Then she sighed, realizing she was being foolish. Hope had disappeared last night.

A knock sounded on the front door. Peering through the window, she saw McGrunner standing on the front steps.

Opening the door, she smiled. "Morning, Corporal."

"Ma'am." He glanced down at the cell phone in his hand. "I received a text message from Special Agent Steele. He wants you to meet him at the airfield as soon as possible to discuss how the day's events will unfold. He mentioned needing help arranging some of the banners and flags."

"I thought a committee was decorating the terminal."

McGrunner shrugged. "All I know, ma'am, is that Agent Steele said he didn't want to disrupt your mother this early."

"Are you supposed to follow me to the airfield?"

"No, ma'am. A suspect's in custody, and Agent Timmons pulled the guard detail from your quarters as of this morning. Agent Steele directed me to escort your mother to the airfield, and I plan to do what he requested."

"Yes, of course." Already, she missed Jamison's protective closeness.

McGrunner glanced once again at the phone in his hand. "Agent Steele said traffic might be backed up on post with everyone heading to physical training. He suggested you take the back road that weaves through the training area. No one will be using that route at this time of the morning, and you won't be hung up with any delays."

Mrs. Logan was sleeping by the time Michele went back upstairs. Not wanting to disturb her mother's slumber, Michele wrote a note and explained the reason she had gone ahead to the airfield.

Waving to McGrunner as she left the quarters, Michele slipped behind the wheel of her car and headed toward the training area. After making a number of turns, she realized Jamison had been right. No one was on the road in that remote part of the post.

The weather report on the radio called for clear skies and sunshine, a welcome relief after the storms and overcast skies. Her father would be home within a few hours, and she wouldn't have to worry about his safety any longer.

Plus, Jamison had asked to see her, which she took as a good sign. Maybe he had changed his mind about the military or was ready to make a compromise that could keep them together. A surge of elation she hadn't expected flowed through her. Knowing she would see him soon opened a door deep within her, a door she had thought would never open again.

Up ahead, the narrow road curved to the right. She

eased up on the accelerator. Halfway through the curve, she jammed on the brakes. Her car screeched to a stop, almost hitting a beige van stalled across the roadway. The side panel on the truck read Prime Maintenance.

An accident? A deer could have run in front of the van. She pulled her cell phone from her purse to call the military police, then decided to see if anyone was hurt first. Michele opened the door and stepped onto the pavement.

She approached the vehicle and put her hands against the driver's window to peer inside. The front seat was vacant. Michele tried to see into the rear of the truck, then startled as a twig snapped behind her.

A warning flashed through her mind.

Footsteps sounded on the pavement.

She pivoted and raised her hand protectively as a man wearing a ski mask jammed a stun gun against her arm.

Pain ricocheted through her body. Her muscles convulsed. Unable to maintain her balance, she fell to the pavement. Her forehead cracked against the asphalt.

Inwardly, she screamed, yet only a guttural groan issued from her mouth. Fear clamped down on her spastic spine.

All she could see were the military boots of the man standing over her. His laughter mixed with her panic and caused her heart to pound at breakneck speed. Even if she survived her body's contortions, she would never survive him.

"I've got you now, Michele," he said with a sneer. "You're going to die."

EIGHTEEN

Michele moaned. Lulled by the motion of the moving vehicle, she longed to remain in the semiunconscious darkness. If she opened her eyes, the terror of what had happened would be real.

Her head throbbed, and her muscles screamed in protest. She lay next to the side of the van with her cheek pressed against the metal flooring, and her hands tied behind her back. She tried to turn over, but her feet were bound, as well.

A blanket covered her, and although the van was air-conditioned, sweat dampened her neck and under her arms. The stale smell of the thick wool sickened her. A wide strip of tape covered her mouth. If she got sick, she would gag on her own bile. Asphyxiation wasn't the way she wanted to die.

Michele thought of Jamison and longed for the strength of his arms and the protection only he could provide. She had run away from him last night after telling him she didn't want him in her life.

Another mistake.

She had made too many.

Michele had lost Jamison. She was about to lose something else today.

Her life.

Mrs. Logan arrived at the terminal shortly after 9:00 a.m., dressed in a navy suit with white blouse and a patriotic-print scarf tied around her neck. From where Jamison stood at the far end of the terminal, he was struck by how much Michele resembled her mother with her big eyes and high cheekbones.

To her credit, Mrs. Logan still had a youthful vitality. Confident Michele would be beautiful at each stage of life, Jamison wanted to be the man at her side, but he feared that dream would never come true. Not after last night.

Always the dedicated First Lady of the brigade, Mrs. Logan talked to the wives and children who gathered close to the security rope. Everyone carried cameras and signs and American flags they had received as they entered the terminal. A number of the wives held the yellow roses Teddy had distributed.

The clock on the wall ticked off the time.

Seeing Jamison, Mrs. Logan waved and walked toward him.

He met her halfway. "Morning, ma'am. Everything's ready."

She looked around the terminal and smiled. "You've done an excellent job, Jamison."

"A lot of folks wanted to get involved." He glanced at the concession area. "As you can see, we've got food and drinks for the families as they wait. A magician will entertain the children at 0945. Once his act is over, we'll show cartoons on the giant wall screen until the planes fly into Georgia airspace. At that point, we'll broadcast a map pinpointing the flight progress."

"And the families will be able to watch the planes land?"

"Yes, ma'am. Via a live video feed that will stream onto the big screen."

"Wonderful." Once again, she glanced around the terminal, but when she looked back at him, her brow was creased. "Have you seen Michele?"

"As far as I know, she hasn't arrived yet."

"That's impossible." Mrs. Logan's hand touched her collar. "She left the house some time ago."

A drum pounded in Jamison's temple. "Could she have gone back to Atlanta?"

"Absolutely not. Michele wanted to be here when Stanley's plane landed. She left me a note saying she was driving to the terminal to meet you. Corporal McGrunner said you had contacted him about needing Michele's help."

Jamison's heart thumped a warning as he called the corporal on his cell. "Where are you?"

"Directly outside the terminal, sir."

"You told Mrs. Logan I called you this morning?"

"Not a phone call, sir. You sent a text message."

Jamison hit the text icon on his phone. Filled with dread, he read the message he was supposed to have written. Someone had accessed the cell phone he kept in his coat pocket.

Greg Yates had taken his jacket when Jamison was on the scaffold. Turning his gaze to the concession area, he searched for Rick Stallings, who had eaten a sandwich seated right next to Jamison's jacket when he was adjusting the tarp. Would either man have been able to retrieve the cell and send the text?

Mrs. Logan grabbed his hand. "What's happened, Jamison?"

Before he could answer, his cell phone rang. He glanced at Dawson's name highlighted on the caller ID.

"We've got a huge problem," Jamison said as he raised the cell to his ear.

"You can say that again, buddy. Ballistics called. The initial exam of the bullets shows a disparity in the markings. Although nothing is definite yet, it looks like Sergeant Kenneth Cramer may have been telling the truth."

Jamison's heart jammed in his throat as more pieces of the puzzle fell into place. The killer was on the loose, and he had Michele.

NINETEEN

Michele woke with a start. For an instant, she forgot about the killer and his van and the smelly blanket that covered her.

Then her memory returned full force. Tears stung her eyes, but she couldn't cry. She had to remain alert and ready for any opportunity to get away from him, whoever he was. All she knew was that he had killed before, and he would kill again.

The sound of his voice filled the van and made her skin crawl. He was ranting about her father, Major Hughes and Sergeant Rossi. She couldn't make out everything he said over the hum of the van's motor, but she heard enough to know he was delusional. As she listened, she began to understand why he had killed Yolanda and tried to end Alice Rossi's life as well as her own.

Michele tugged at the restraints on her hands and legs until her flesh was raw. She tried to roll over, hoping to free herself from the blanket. Her leg struck against something that toppled onto the floor of the van. The crash of metal upon metal made her heart pound even harder.

He stopped his tirade.

Michele lay still, barely breathing. If not for the blanket, she would be able to see what he was doing and read the expression on his face. As it was, she was surrounded by darkness.

The van slowed. He pulled off the road and braked to a stop. Waves of nausea rolled over her. She needed to be strong, but she wasn't. She was scared to death.

Her heart raced, and her pulse pounded in her ear.

The driver's door opened and then slammed, sending a volley of aftershocks exploding through her head. Footfalls sounded on the pavement as he rounded the van.

She tried to scream, but the duct tape muffled her cries for help. Her throat burned, and her mouth was as dry as sandpaper. She jerked her head from side to side, struggling against the putrid blanket.

Oh, God, help me!

If he opened the rear doors, she might be able to kick him or hurl herself onto the roadway. Surely someone driving by would see her. Then she listened and heard nothing except his footsteps and her pounding heart.

A rear door opened. He grabbed her ankles and yanked her along the rough metal bed of the van that scraped her cheek. She thrashed her feet, needing to free her legs from his hold.

He continued to spit hateful words about her father and his former battalion and how everyone would pay. He talked about cutting into Lance's gravestone and other things that didn't make sense, but nothing made sense about a man who killed.

Then he laughed. The sound sent another round of shock waves through her body. She tried to backpedal.

His fingers gripped her upper arm. Michele expected to crash onto the pavement at any second.

What she hadn't expected was the stun gun. The violent shock caused her back to arch. Repeated spasms racked her muscles. Her legs and arms writhed and convulsed and twisted in tandem as the restraints held. Pain radiated throughout her body and sapped the little strength she had left.

Her head exploded. She saw bursts of white lightning and then, when she couldn't endure anything more, she slipped away into darkness.

Jamison jammed his cell phone closer to his ear. "I'm leaving the terminal to search for Michele," he told Dawson after filling him in on the text message.

"Stay where you are until I get to the airport. I'm headed there now."

Disconnecting, Jamison pocketed his phone, feeling as if he'd been beaten to a pulp with a steel beam. Just as in his youth, everything was spiraling out of control, and he couldn't react fast enough, or think decisively enough or have the vision he needed to get into the killer's point of view. Where was Michele?

As a CID agent who had handled numerous investigations, Jamison knew what could happen, what might already have happened. The realization sent waves of terror through him that chilled him to the core.

His eyes turned to where Rick Stallings was working at the concession stand. Not far away, Greg Yates sipped coffee and glanced at the giant clock on the wall.

Jamison barked a number of orders into the security radio. Responding immediately, four military guards removed the two men, without incident, from the central area of the terminal and sequestered each of them in separate office rooms located toward the rear of the large complex.

Although Jamison needed to question the men, he had to inform Mrs. Logan about the current situation. When he turned to face her, he realized she was well aware of what had happened. Her eyes reflected his own fears, sending another jab of pain deep to his gut.

Looking suddenly older than her years, she took his hand and held it tight. "You'll find her, Jamison. You have to."

He wished he shared her confidence. "Yes, ma'am."

She shook her head, perhaps sensing his own faltering optimism. "I don't want the wives to know what has happened. The spouses and family members have worried enough and need this time to welcome their husbands home."

He had to object. "Ma'am, our first priority is to find Michele."

"That's what I want, as well, Jamison. But the brigade needs a homecoming. Nothing should be canceled unless it specifically impacts my daughter's safety."

At some point, Mrs. Logan needed to put her family's well-being before the brigade's. "Ma'am, there's a lounge located near the Red Cross first-aid station, if you'd like someplace to wait."

He radioed one of the female soldiers in the military police detail to escort the colonel's wife to the lounge and remain with her at all times.

Jamison admired Mrs. Logan's grit, but he didn't want his hands tied when it came to finding Michele. If he had to halt the welcome-home celebration, he would. He would do anything to save Michele.

But right now he needed to move forward. Fast.

Hastening toward the rear of the terminal, he entered the first office.

"Where is she?" Jamison demanded, leaning across the conference table where Stallings sat. Given any sign of provocation, Jamison would throw him against the wall and pound the truth out of him.

The vendor's eyes widened, antagonism evident as he bristled. "What are you talking about?"

"I'm talking about a missing woman. And that's on top of one woman murdered, another in critical condition and a military policeman who may have to get a medical discharge because of you."

"You've got the wrong guy."

"Where were you this morning?"

"At the sandwich shop in Freemont. You can call my boss. We worked most of the night, preparing the food for today."

"What time did you arrive on post?"

"Uh—" Stallings hesitated.

"Trying to do the math and make it all work out in your favor? Your information was captured electronically when you showed your identification to the guard at the Main Gate. Won't take long to retrieve the time."

"Traffic was backed up getting on post. I'm not sure when I actually passed through security."

Jamison changed gears. "Do you like to text?"

Surprised by the question, Stallings pushed back in his chair. Jamison leaned in closer, knowing he was emotional and apt to do something he would later regret, but he needed information.

The door to the office opened. Corporal Otis motioned to Jamison. "Sir."

"What?" Jamison demanded in the hallway, his anger on a short fuse.

"Special Agent Warner, from Afghanistan, called CID headquarters asking to speak to you, sir. He said it involved our case."

Jamison glanced at the nearby office where Greg Yates waited. Maybe everything was about to break.

Punching Speed Dial on his cell, Jamison was relieved when Warner answered. "Major Shirley Yates appears to be squeaky clean. No involvements on this side of the world."

"There were rumors of infidelity."

"Rumors that got out of hand."

"Are you sure there wasn't some truth behind them?"

"Not that we could uncover. She was mentoring a captain, prior enlisted. The guy had run into a little problem with his report of survey. He had signed for equipment that he couldn't account for when the brigade was getting ready to redeploy home. The captain was about her age. They spent time together and tongues wagged. You know how that is. Everyone jumps to the wrong conclusion."

Which was exactly what Jamison had done concerning the major's husband. Glancing at the room where Rick Stallings waited, he realized he might have been wrong about both men.

Jamison blew out a lungful of air. Right now all he wanted to do was pound his fist into the wall until it was bloodied. Somehow he needed to feel the pain he feared Michele was experiencing. "Please, God, no."

"Jamison?"

He turned to find Dawson approaching him from the central terminal. "I've got military police canvassing the colonel's housing area. Fort Rickman's under lockdown. The only people who are being allowed on post are active duty personnel and then only after a thorough search of their vehicles and person."

"I'm more concerned about anyone leaving the garrison."

"No one's allowed off at this point."

"What about the training area?"

"The military police have been along the back roads from the Logan home to the airfield. No one has spotted her yet. Now they're searching the ranges, one at a time."

Which would take hours.

Jamison quickly filled Dawson in on Stallings and Yates. "I can't stay, Dawson. I've got to find Michele."

As he raced out of the terminal, Jamison looked up at the bright sky. "God, I need your help today, more than I've ever needed anything."

He couldn't rely on his own ability. He had made too many mistakes. He had to rely on the Lord so that this time his mistakes didn't end in tragedy. If Jamison lost Michele, he lost everything, maybe even his soul.

TWENTY

Michele knew she was alone because of the silence. No running motor, no air-conditioning, no jumbled ramblings from a delusional killer. All she heard was her heart pounding. Then voices in the distance.

If only she could attract someone's attention. She raised her legs and kicked the wall of the van over and over again, until her muscles ached, and her energy was sapped.

The blanket, wrapped around her face, constricted her breathing. In the closed vehicle and with the hot August day, the temperature had risen too fast. Frantic, Michele fought against the thick wool blanket around her face and felt instant elation when a portion of the covering slipped aside. Like a crazed woman, she inhaled the stale, hot air.

Sweat beaded on her upper lip and dampened her neck. The temperature rose even higher. How long could a person survive in an enclosed vehicle? She didn't want an answer and wished she hadn't even thought of the question.

If You're a loving God, I'm begging You to help me. I've made so many mistakes. Forgive me, Father.

Michele had been wrong about Jamison. He was a wonderful man, and she wasn't worthy of his love. If only she could tell him, but it was too late.

If Alice didn't pull through, three women would have died because of a maniac who wanted revenge. God had nothing to do with him and everything to do with Jamison and the other good people in law enforcement who put their lives on the line to help others.

Instead of running away from Jamison, Michele should have been running into his arms.

Jamison drove like a madman, backtracking through the training area along the deserted road Michele must have traveled earlier. He had to find her.

Flicking his gaze right and then left, he hoped to catch sight of her, of her car, of something the military police had missed that would provide a clue to her disappearance. The only thing he knew was the killer had taken her. But where?

Jamison wouldn't allow his mind to imagine what had been done to her. *Please, God, keep Michele safe.*

He shouldn't have left her alone last night. He should have checked on her this morning. He wished he had told her he loved her and needed her and would do anything to be with her.

Right now the thought of a quiet civilian existence sounded perfect, a life where Michele would be safe. If anything happened to her, he'd never be able to forgive himself.

He was a trained special agent. How could he have let a killer get to Michele?

"You're a failure. You'll never succeed."

His father's words played over in his mind. But his

dad's wasn't the only voice he heard. Jamison was berating himself, as well.

"Think! Think!" he screamed to no one except the tall Georgia pine trees that edged the training area. "Where could she be?"

The road curved up ahead. Jamison lifted his foot from the accelerator. Before he completed the curve, sunlight reflected off something in the woods. He stomped on the brake.

Leaping from his car, he raced across the narrow asphalt roadway and pressed through the dense wooded area that opened into a clearing where he found Michele's car. The ground was still damp from the storms two nights ago, and thick, red Georgia clay caked her tires.

He searched the area, looking for signs of a struggle. The only thing he found was a muddy boot print.

Jamison fisted his hands with rage. The killer had ambushed her. Maybe he had flagged her down, pretending to be hurt. Then he'd tried to hide her car in the woods, but the wheels had stuck in the mud.

He called Dawson. "I found Michele's vehicle hidden in the woods just east of the live-fire training range. I want it gone over from top to bottom. We need fingerprints that can lead us to the killer. There's a boot print located approximately five feet from the hood of the car, size 11 or 12."

"I'll send a team to check out the vehicle. Right now I'm headed out to the tarmac. The brigade's due to land ahead of schedule." Dawson paused for a long moment. "Look, buddy, I'm to blame on this one, and I owe you an apology."

"For what?"

"For being so confident Sergeant Cramer was the killer. You told me to wait until the ballistics report came back. I was too pigheaded to listen. You were right last night. You were also right ten months ago."

"What are you talking about, Dawson? I was the one who suggested we confront the shooter."

"After I insisted we close in. You wanted to wait until backup was in place."

"You've got it wrong."

"No way, Jamison. I've relived what happened a million times. I got us into it at the beginning."

"The chief's well aware of who was at fault."

"That's why he assigned you to handle the security at the airfield. He knew we'd all work together to track down the killer. He wanted his best and brightest to ensure the safety of the entire brigade."

Jamison didn't have time to process what Dawson had told him. He needed to keep looking for Michele.

Disconnecting, Jamison turned back to his car. Glancing down, he spied something he had missed earlier.

Michele's Cross My Heart necklace. The clasp had broken, and the necklace must have fallen to the ground. He had visions of the killer roughhousing her. The images sent ice-cold terror through his veins.

"Please, God." He reached for the necklace. "I've got to find Michele."

His cell rang. "This is Steele."

Dawson's voice. "The chief wants you back at the terminal. Now."

"I need to keep searching."

"He wants to make sure the homecoming goes off without a glitch."

Jamison knew the real reason. Chief Wilson didn't want a special agent who was emotionally involved with the case to do something that would reflect badly on the CID.

"You're a failure...a disappointment."

Jamison wanted to ignore the chief. Michele was more important than any order from a superior.

Before he gave breath to the words, Jamison saw something else on the pavement. Something that didn't make sense in the middle of the training area.

Stooping, he picked it up and examined it in the sunlight. A long shot, one he didn't want to discuss with Dawson. Only one way to find out if it would lead him to Michele.

"Tell Chief Wilson I'm heading back to the terminal."

TWENTY-ONE

Jamison raced into the terminal, grabbed the military guards at the doors and ordered them to sweep the area. As they took off in opposite directions, he circled through the swarm of people, needing to connect what he had found on the back road with someone here in the building.

The band stood ready in the far corner. Video played over the large overhead screen. The live feed showed the soldiers disembarking from the three planes parked on the tarmac. Cheers erupted when families recognized their loved ones. The excitement was palpable and then grew even more so as the soldiers made their way toward the terminal.

On the opposite side of the arena, one person stood out from the crowd. Jamison raised the radio and gave specific orders to the security patrols.

The guy pushed through the throng and headed for a rear door. Seeing families reunited would be too painful for a prior military guy who felt as if he had "died" when he was redeployed home.

Jamison raced forward, shouting more orders into the radio. His gut tightened as he realized the back door wasn't being guarded. "Rear door security, return to your position. Return to your position."

Following him outside, Jamison spied the van at the edge of the overflow parking area, away from any other vehicles. The guy had opened the driver's door and was climbing inside.

Expecting to hear the sound of backup behind him, Jamison looked down at the radio. He groaned inwardly seeing the flashing red light. Low battery. He tossed the useless device and didn't have time to pull out his cell.

"Wait up," Jamison called, hand on his hip as he neared the van.

The guy had slipped behind the wheel and closed the driver's door. He smiled through the open window as if he didn't have a care in the world. "How's it goin', sir?"

"You tell me."

"No problem, except I've got a delivery to make across post."

"A delivery of flowers for some lucky army wife, waiting for her husband to return home?"

Teddy Sutherland dropped the smile and raised the 9 mm Beretta he held in his hand.

Before Jamison could draw his own weapon, a round exploded into his left shoulder, throwing him back against the van. He grabbed for the sign on the side of the delivery truck to keep his balance. The metal strip bearing the floral logo ripped free and dropped to the pavement, exposing another interchangeable magnetic sign underneath: Prime Maintenance.

Once again, Teddy leaned out the window and took another shot at Jamison. The second round missed him by a breath.

The engine roared to life. The van lurched forward.

Jamison pulled open the door and grabbed the florist. The wheel turned, and the van rammed into the light pole that twisted on impact.

Jamison yanked him to the asphalt and pulled his own weapon. "Where is she? Where's Michele?"

"You'll never find her."

Jamison wanted to crash his fist into the sneer covering the florist's twisted face.

Footsteps pounded pavement. McGrunner came running.

"Cuff him," Jamison ordered. "And call Dawson. Tell him we've got the killer."

Jamison raced to the rear of the van. He pulled open the door and shoved aside cardboard cartons containing roses that had wilted in the heat. The smell of decaying flowers hung in the hot air.

A wool army blanket. He lifted the corner.

Relief swept over him.

Michele.

But when he looked closer, he saw her flushed face and her labored breathing.

He'd found her—but was he too late?

Michele jerked as the tape was ripped from her mouth. She blinked her eyes open and saw Jamison.

Screaming for water, he cut through the ropes that bound her hands and legs. "You're going to be okay, honey."

She reached for him. "Oh…Ja…Jamison."

He grabbed the water bottle McGrunner shoved into his hand and held it up to Michele's lips. She drank gratefully. Wetting his handkerchief, he wiped her face with the cooling cloth.

“Teddy—” She had to tell Jamison everything the florist had said as he drove along the back roads. “He… he kept talking about my dad and what happened in the past. Teddy worked for Yolanda’s and Alice’s husbands when my father had his battalion.”

“In Iraq?” Jamison asked.

Michele nodded. “He…he asked to come home early. His wife…was running around.”

“They refused his request.” Jamison filled in the blanks.

“My…my father did, as well. Teddy’s wife ran off with the boyfriend. No one was there to meet him when the unit redeployed home. Then he—” Michele choked on the words. “He found her and killed her.”

“And came back to Fort Rickman. But why did he open a floral shop?”

“The store had been his wife’s dream.”

Jamison nodded as if he could see how it all unfolded. “Once he found both men were serving in the same brigade, he decided to kill their wives.”

“And my mother. Then I got in the way.”

She shook her head. “He…he said, when the men marched into the terminal, everyone would suffer. He called it a patriotic homecoming…like…like fireworks on the Fourth of July.”

“‘Fireworks’? That was the word he used?”

She nodded, but Jamison was already out of the van. “McGrunner will take care of you,” he yelled, looking back one last time.

She reached for him, but Jamison was running toward the terminal. Running into danger, just as he’d done last night.

“Oh, God,” Michele cried. “Don’t let him die.”

TWENTY-TWO

The band played a patriotic march. Throngs of people swelled forward toward the cordoned off area. Cameras were poised to take pictures of the soldiers that would soon march into the terminal.

Seconds ticked off the giant clock.

Not enough time.

"We've got a bomb!" Jamison screamed into the radio he had grabbed from McGrunner as he ran into the terminal. "Clear the area. Stop the brigade."

"Sir, you're breaking up," the message came back. "Repeat all after—"

Static. Squelch.

Jamison shouted the orders again and again.

The large clock on the wall continued its countdown.

Ten…nine…eight…

His heart pounded. His throat went dry.

"Fan through the crowd." He motioned to the military police gathered around him. "Herd the people out of the building."

The giant double doors opened.

The brigade stood in formation ready to march forward on command. A sea of American flags fluttered. Screams of joy erupted from the crowd around him.

Jamison's gaze turned to the dais.

The general stood at the microphone. Mrs. Logan was next to him. Her eyes were on Jamison, begging for information.

He nodded, and the relief on her face told him she understood her daughter was safe. What she didn't know was that she and everyone else in the terminal were in danger.

Jamison had to find the bomb before it detonated, before the terminal exploded, before more people died.

Glancing down, he spied something under the platform where Mrs. Logan and the general stood. Something the same color as the flower petal he had found on the pavement in the training area.

All around him throngs of people strained to see their returning loved ones. *Please, Lord.*

He pushed through the crowd, weaving his way forward, surrounded by the groundswell of excitement and the thump of the band's rousing military march pounding in his ears.

Seven…six…

Nearing the platform, he focused on the bucket containing yellow roses. His fingers closed around the handle. He pulled the container forward and peered down into the water, seeing a bundle of wires wrapped in plastic and taped to the bottom of the container.

Five…

The wall clock counted down the seconds.

Bucket in hand, he raced toward the side exit behind the dais.

Four…

Needing to clear the building, he willed his legs to move faster.

Three…

He pushed on the door. Drums pounded out a cadence. The cheering reached a fever pitch as the soldiers began to march into the central area.

No time.

The tarmac lay before him.

Two…

Pulling in an even breath, he started to wind like a coiled spring, just as he had done throwing the discus in high school. Shoulders balanced. Weight even. He circled, building momentum.

One…

Release.

The bucket left his hand.

The band played. Men marched. The crowd cheered.

The bomb flew through the air and exploded over the tarmac.

Jamison gasped for air and clutched his side. He turned, needing to go back inside, not sure he could find the strength.

"Oh, Jamison." Michele's voice. She wasn't running away, she was running toward him.

"You saved my life. You saved everyone's life. I…I…"

He held up his hand to stop her. The last thing he needed was false hope.

"It's my job, Michele. It's what I do. I love you more than anything, more than life itself, but I have to be true to who I am. That's the only way I can look myself in the eye each day. I've got to make a contribution in this life, and I'm making a difference in the military."

She stopped, her arms still outstretched. She had been through so much today. Her face was scraped and smudged with dirt, but the look he saw in her eyes filled him with encouragement.

"Oh, Jamison, I was thinking only of my own needs before and not what we could be together. You built your life on a firm foundation of God and military and knew what was right and what was wrong. It took me longer to find out what's important. 'God first' is what Lance always told me. I understand that now. God first and the man I love second. I know it's the same for you—that you need to follow God's path for your life, regardless of whether or not I approve."

She stepped closer, her arms inviting him. "The man I love is you, Jamison. I want to keep on loving you forever."

He stepped into her sweet embrace.

Those in the terminal were oblivious to what had happened as cheers of joy and patriotic strains from the band mixed with the revelry of the soldiers who had been gone so long and were once again in the arms of their loved ones.

On the tarmac, Jamison lowered his lips to Michele's, knowing the negative voice from his past had been silenced. He was a new man, a better man, a triumphant man because, in spite of all the mistakes he had made in life, Michele had come back to him.

"Welcome home," he whispered as he kissed her again and again and again.

EPILOGUE

Michele was giddy with excitement.

"What time is Jamison picking you up, dear?" her mother called from the kitchen.

"Six-fifteen."

Her father came down the steps, looking a bit more rested after two weeks of block leave. He had lost weight in Afghanistan and his hair had grayed, but his smile was as wide as ever and his eyes were beginning to twinkle again. The war and the stress of command had taken its toll on him, just as his deployment had been hard on the family he had left behind.

Stepping into the hallway, Roberta stared up at her husband and smiled. "Did you have a good nap, dear?"

"You're making me feel like an old man, Roberta."

She laughed playfully, and Michele realized there was nothing old about either of them or the love they had for each other.

"Erica Grayson called," Roberta informed him. "Curtis, Yolanda's sister and the children are having dinner with the Graysons tonight. Spur-of-the-moment, but she asked if we wanted to join them."

Her father nodded. “Whatever you want to do is fine with me.”

“I told her yes.”

Stan laughed and winked at Michele. “Then it’s already decided. Maybe we can run by the hospital first. Paul Rossi’s spending all his time with Alice. They’re hoping she’ll be released in a day or two.”

“That’s wonderful news.” Michele checked her makeup in the hall mirror. “I baked cookies. Why don’t you take some to the hospital? The Hughes children might like some, too.”

“Where are you and Jamison going tonight?” her father asked, watching as she refreshed her lipstick.

“He’s taking me to dinner at the club, but he’s been a bit secretive.” Michele knew her cheeks were flushed with excitement. She felt like a high school girl on her way to the prom.

Moving to stand next to her husband, Roberta smiled as if she, too, had a secret.

Michele glanced at her mother. “Do you know anything about what Jamison has planned?”

“Why, no, dear.”

“I don’t believe you, Mother.” Michele laughed, feeling even giddier as the doorbell rang.

“I’ll get it.” Stanley opened the door and extended his hand to Jamison. “Good to see you, son. Michele said you two are going to the club tonight.”

“Yes, sir.” Jamison accepted the colonel’s handshake and stepped inside.

Dressed in a dark suit and a red tie, he looked better than any prom date, and Michele had to remind herself to breathe. His white shirt was starched and as bright as the smile that lit up his face when he saw her standing in the hallway.

"You look beautiful," he said, sounding somewhat breathless himself.

"Thank you." She stepped into his arms and kissed his cheek. "And you look handsome in your new suit."

"What time are your reservations?" Roberta asked.

"Six-thirty, ma'am."

"We'd better be going." Michele reached for her purse. "Mother and Dad are having dinner with Curtis Hughes and his sister-in-law and children this evening."

"How are the children?"

"Adjusting. Curtis is optimistic about the future. I heard the MP who was injured has improved, as well."

"Yes, ma'am. He should make a full recovery."

"What about you, Jamison? Did you see the doctor?"

"The wound's almost healed."

Roberta smiled. "I'm so glad."

Stanley held the door open. "We don't want to hold the kids up, Roberta."

Michele laughed as she hugged her mother and dad. Accepting Jamison's outstretched hand, she walked with him to his car. The ride to the club took less than ten minutes. When they stepped into the foyer, Michele turned toward the main dining room.

Jamison caught her arm and pointed her in the opposite direction. "Our reservations are for the Lincoln Room."

"Really?" The room, decorated in dark mahogany, was a favorite of hers and usually reserved for small, private functions.

Jamison placed his hand on her back and guided

her through the outer reception area. "I wanted to do something special."

Opening the door to the private room, Jamison bowed with a flourish and invited her into the dignified parlor. In front of the mammoth fireplace, a round table, draped in a linen cloth, was set for two with fine china and silver and lit candles.

Instead of a blazing fire this summer day, the hearth contained a huge bouquet of flowers more gorgeous than Michele had ever seen. Carnations and gladiolas and lilies and baby's breath and daisies mixed with roses—red and white and coral—into an exquisite arrangement that made her want to cry as well as laugh with joy.

"Flowers are important to a woman," Jamison stated matter-of-factly. He raised his brow and kissed her lips. "Which I learned almost too late."

He wrapped his arm around her waist and ushered her toward the table, where he reached for a rectangular box and placed it in her hand.

Her heart pounded, and her mouth went dry. She couldn't talk, even if she had known what to say. So many emotions mixed through her, all good.

"Open it," he prodded, his eyes twinkling.

She lifted the top and smiled, seeing the Cross My Heart necklace.

"I found it in the training area near a yellow rose petal that led me back to you." Jamison's voice was suddenly husky, no doubt with his remembering all they had been through. "I replaced the chain with something more sturdy."

"It's beautiful, Jamison." The new chain would last a lifetime.

"Before we sit down, there's something else I want to show you."

She waited as he dug in his pocket. Her heart fluttered like a butterfly, searching for a place to land. The look on his face was full of expectation and added to the tingle of excitement that teased her neck and sent delicious waves of energy scurrying along her spine.

Time stood still as he pulled forth a small box. His strong fingers reached for the object, hidden inside, that he held up for her to see. A beautiful solitaire diamond ring. The radiant stone sparkled in the candlelight and reflected the love she saw in his eyes.

"Michele, I'm asking you to be my wife. It won't always be candlelight and roses, but if you'll have me as your husband, I promise to honor you and cherish you and love you all the days of my life."

Her eyes burned and a lump formed in her throat. "Oh, Jamison." She couldn't talk for a long moment as she looked at him, seeing the good man, the honorable man, the righteous man he had always been. She had just needed to look beyond her fear to see the possibility of a future together.

Extending her left hand, she smiled as he slipped the ring on her finger. "I would be honored to be your wife," she said, gazing into his eyes. "I promise to love you and cherish you and go wherever you go for the rest of my life."

She stepped into his arms, feeling his strength and his gentleness at the same time. They had a lot to learn about each other, but God would give them time, a lifetime together.

Jamison had taught her to live in the present and be grateful for every blessing the Lord provided. Life was a mix of joy and sorrow. Theirs would be no different, but she no longer had to fear God or the future.

"I belong in your arms," she sighed as he lowered his lips to hers. Jamison kissed her as if he never wanted to let her go, and she knew what they had together was more perfect than any diamond or flower or the fine china or anything else the world might offer in comparison. They had chosen the better portion, the love that would last a lifetime and carry them into eternity. Which is how long she wanted to stay wrapped in his arms.

"How long is eternity?" she asked.

"Not long enough." And then he kissed her again and again and again.

* * * * *

THE GENERAL'S SECRETARY

Cast your cares on the Lord and He will sustain you;
He will never let the righteous be shaken.

—*Psalm* 55:22

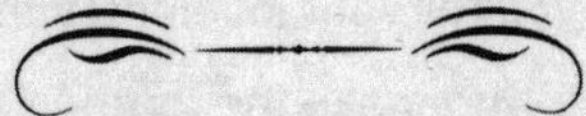

This story is dedicated to
our brave men and women in uniform.
May the Lord protect them from harm.

To my wonderful husband and beautiful family.
Thank you for your love and support.

To the Seekers who make the journey so much fun.

To my critique partner Anna Adams.

To Emily Rodmell, my editor,
and Deidre Knight, my agent.
Thank you!

ONE

Lillie Beaumont gasped for air and fought her way through the dream that came too often. Her heart pounded a warning as she blinked open her eyes, allowing the dark outline of her bedroom to sweep into focus. She lifted her head off the pillow and anticipated the distant thunder before the sound reached her ears.

Low. Rumbling. Menacing, like cannon fire at nearby Fort Rickman, Georgia.

Weeding her fingers through the sheets, she grasped for anything that would calm her spinning stomach and racing pulse.

Another rumble, this time closer.

Then another and another in rapid succession, each encroaching on her space, her air, her life.

The thunder escalated, its cadence steady like the giant footfalls of an evil predator, stalking an unsuspecting prey. Only Lillie wasn't oblivious to its approach. She knew the storm, felt it in her inner being, breathed it into her soul where she battled the terror and torment of a thousand deaths.

Another volley. Her airway constricted. She touched

her throat, yearning to be free of the stranglehold of fear that wrapped around her neck.

Don't cower. Face your phobia. The words of reason echoed in her head.

"Something happened before she came to us," her foster parents had told concerned friends after taking Lillie into their home when she was a child. "Our little girl is terrified of storms."

She wanted to laugh at the understatement. Instead, tears trickled from the corners of her eyes.

The musky scent of wet earth and damp air seeped through the partially open window and filled her nostrils, like the cloying odor of that night so long ago. Eyes wide, she stared into the darkness, anticipating the next bright burst of lightning.

A blast of thunder rocked her world, hurling her from the bed. She ran, as she always did, her footfalls echoing on the hardwood floor. No matter how much she longed to ignore the gathering storm, she had no control over the memories that made her relive the terror of that night so long ago.

In her mind's eye, she was once again four years old.

"Mama," young Lillie had cried, longing to be swooped into her mother's outstretched arms.

Instead, *he* had opened the bedroom door.

"Go back to bed, child."

The door had closed, leaving Lillie alone in the hallway, huddled in a ball, shivering with fear, tears streaking her face and trembling body.

Another round of thunder, followed by a kaleidoscope of light that blinded her eyes and made the past fade and the present come back into focus.

Finding the corner, the twenty-nine-year-old Lillie

crouched, knees to her chest, heart on a marathon race as thunder continued to bellow. Rain pummeled her copper roof, the incessant pings reminding her of the gossip of the townspeople after her mother's remains had been found fifteen years ago.

Murdered. Sealed in a steel drum. Buried beneath the earth.

"Mama," she whimpered, trying to be strong enough to fight off the memories.

Outside, the storm raged as if good and evil battled for her soul, only she was too weak, too crazed, to fight off the attacks.

A pounding.

Close, persistent. *Rap, rap, rap.*

"Lillie?"

Someone called her name.

"Lillie, open the door."

"Mama?"

She ran to the front of the house, undid the lock and flung open the door. Frigid rain stung her face, soaking her pajamas and mixing with her tears.

"Help me, Lillie."

A man she knew only from newspaper photos stood before her. Mid-fifties, with gray, rumpled hair and weather-worn skin stretched across a bruised and bloodied face. Doleful eyes, swollen, suffering, seemingly entreated her to forget the past and think only of his need. "They…they found me…beat me."

His hand stretched to hers. A small metal key dropped into her palm.

"I uncovered information. The…the answers I've been looking for," he said.

She took a step back.

"I never—" He shook his head. "Your mother—"

A shot rang out.

He gasped, his face awash with pain. "Free us..." He reached for her. "Free us from the past."

Slipping through her fingers, he collapsed onto the rain-drenched step. She screamed, seeing not only her own bloodied hands but also the battered body of her mother's killer.

The phone call dragged Dawson Timmons from a dead sleep. Flipping on the bedside lamp, he rubbed his hand over his face and raised the receiver. "Special Agent Timmons."

"Sorry to wake you, sir." Corporal Raynard Otis from the Criminal Investigation Division.

"What's the problem, Ray?"

"Agent Steele is on duty tonight, sir, but he's tied up, handling a possible overdose, and we're short-staffed since Agents Patterson and McQueen were transferred."

With the recent reduction in force, the whole army was short-staffed. "I'm aware of the situation, Ray. Plus, the chief's on leave until Monday."

"Yes, sir. That's why Agent Steele asked that I contact you." The corporal's voice was strained. "The Freemont police just notified us about a shooting."

"Military personnel?"

"Negative, sir. But the location has bearing."

"Fort Rickman?"

"No, sir. Freemont."

"What's the tie-in?"

"The house where the shooting took place belongs to the general's secretary."

Dawson groaned inwardly, dropped his feet to the

floor and stood. "General Cameron's secretary? The commanding general?"

"Yes, sir. The deceased pounded on the secretary's door in the middle of the storm. She answered the knock just before the victim was shot."

"A drive-by shooting?"

"I'm not sure, sir."

"We're talking about Lillie Beaumont?"

"Affirmative."

"Was she hurt?"

"Negative, sir."

"The victim..." Dawson swallowed, hoping to keep his voice level and free of inflection. "Do you have a positive ID?"

"Granger Ford. The guy was serving time for the murder of Ms. Beaumont's mother. Fifteen years ago he was tried and found guilty. His case was recently reviewed, and new DNA testing exonerated him. Ten days have passed since he got out of prison in Atlanta. Now he's dead."

Dawson hung his head. Ringing filled his ears. His stomach soured, and for an instant, his world went dark. Granger had called him three nights ago. Not that Dawson had expected or wanted the phone call from his past.

"Shall I notify the staff duty officer at post headquarters?" Ray asked.

"Let headquarters know, and call General Cameron's aide as well. Tell him I'll check out the situation and report back to the general when I return to post."

Dawson would tell the commanding general what the Freemont police had determined about the shooting and Lillie Beaumont's involvement in the case. He wouldn't reveal the truth about Granger Ford and the child he had fathered thirty-one years ago. A little boy raised by an unwed mother who had hardened her son's heart to his drifter dad.

Dawson could forgive his mother's bitterness, but he never forgave his father's rejection. Now, with his death, the truth would come out. The last thing Dawson wanted was for the military to know his father was a murderer.

The storm had subsided by the time Dawson climbed behind the wheel of his Camry. Twigs and leaves cluttered the roadway as he left post and headed to the far side of Freemont, where Lillie lived. Turning his headlights to high beam, he pressed down on the accelerator and reached for his cell phone.

"I'm on my way into town," Dawson said when Jamison Steele answered. Working together, the two agents had formed a strong friendship. Trust ran deep, and just days earlier Dawson had told Jamison about his past and the father he had never met.

"Otis said you agreed to handle the shooting." Jamison let out a breath. "Look, I'm sorry about what happened and that you have to be the one to handle the case."

"It's not like Granger and I had a relationship. The last thing he wanted was a kid. My mother said he hightailed it out of town as soon as she told him she was pregnant. I never met him."

"Still, it puts you in a difficult spot. I'll explain the situation to Chief Wilson when he gets back to work on Monday."

Dawson pursed his lips. "No need. I can fight my own battles. Besides, tonight should be fairly straightforward. I'll ensure the Freemont cops handle the case appropriately. Once I share the information with General Cameron concerning his secretary, I'll file my report and move on to the next case."

"It's Friday, Dawson. I'm hoping the weekend is crime-free."

"Which might be wishful thinking."

Jamison hesitated. "Have…have you told anyone else about your dad?"

"I didn't see the need." Dawson stared into the roadway ahead. "Of course, his death changes everything."

"We'll talk at the office."

"Roger that."

Dawson disconnected and shook his head with frustration. Granger had made a huge mistake visiting the daughter of the woman he was supposed to have murdered. From what Dawson had pieced together about his wayward father, Granger's life had been as littered as the pavement with a series of wrong places, wrong times. Exactly what tonight felt like—a wrong turn that could end up detouring Dawson off the straight course he had chosen for his career in the army.

When he saw the secretary's house in the distance, his gut tightened. Police lights flashed from the driveway. The crime-scene crew hovered around the front porch, where a man's body lay spotlighted in the rain. Maybe this homicide wouldn't be as cut-and-dried as he had first imagined.

Pulling to a stop, Dawson sucked in a deep breath before he stepped into the wet night. His left leg ached. More than a year had passed since he'd taken a bullet, but the pain remained and grew more insistent with the cold weather.

He rubbed his hands together and grabbed the keys from the ignition, his mouth dry. Steeling himself against any unwanted rush of emotion, he approached the crime-scene tape and held up his identification to the closest cop.

"CID, from Fort Rickman. Who's in charge?"

The guy pointed to the house. "Head through the kitchen. Sergeant Ron Pritchard's inside with Ms. Beaumont."

"Is she a suspect?"

The cop shrugged. "All I know is that we found her huddled in the hallway, crying like a baby."

Dawson hesitated for a moment and then glanced down at the victim's twisted body. Regret washed over him. This wasn't the way life should end. Granger had been shot in the back, probably with a forty-five caliber hollow point from the appearance of the wound.

In stark contrast to the grisly death scene, beds of yellow pansies edged the small front stoop. Ignoring the flowers, Dawson circled the house, picking his way through the wet grass. The back porch, trimmed in white latticework, was graced with more winter blooms that danced in the wind, oblivious to the crime that had recently been committed.

Stepping into the kitchen, he opened his navy windbreaker and wiped his shoes on the small entry rug. The smell of the wet outdoors followed him inside and mixed with the homey scent of pumpkin and spice. A large melon-colored candle sat on the counter near a bouquet of yellow mums and a plaque that read, *God bless this home and all those who enter.*

The irony wasn't lost on Dawson, yet surely death hadn't been Granger's just reward. The estranged son might have argued the point before the phone call, before Granger had asked forgiveness. Something Dawson hadn't been able to give. Now he wasn't sure how he felt. A little numb, a bit confused, even angry. Long ago, he had realized it was better not to feel anything than to feel too much.

Entering the living area, he signaled to the officer in charge, held up his badge and nodded as the local cop continued to question the woman huddled on the couch.

Lillie's life had been inexplicably intertwined with Dawson's, although he doubted she was aware her mother's killer had a son. They'd never been introduced, but Dawson had seen her on post. It was hard not to notice the tall and slender secretary. Usually she was stylishly dressed and perfectly coiffed. Tonight wild, honey-brown tresses fell across the collar of what appeared to be flannel pajamas. Even from where he stood, Dawson noticed the blood spatters on the thick fabric.

She turned, hearing him behind her.

He hadn't expected her eyes to be so green or so lucid. She wore her pain in the knit of her brow, in the downward tug on her full lips, in the tear-streaked eyes whose sadness wrapped around his heart. His breath hitched, and time stood still for one long moment.

Pritchard asked another question. She turned back to the lead cop, leaving Dawson dangling. He straightened his neck, trying to work his way back to reality.

Long ago, Dawson had learned to weigh everything, never to take a chance. He put his faith in what he could do and affect and impact, not on emotions that left him hanging in thin air.

"The middle of a stormy night." Pritchard restated

the last question. "Yet you opened your door when Mr. Ford knocked?"

"I…ah…" She searched for an answer.

"Do you always open your door to strangers, Ms. Beaumont?" Pritchard pressed.

She shook her head. "Of course not, but—"

Once again, she glanced at Dawson, as if asking him to clear the confusion written on her oval face.

"Had you been asleep?" Dawson knew better than to prompt a witness, yet the question sprang from his lips before he could weigh the consequences.

She nodded, her brow raised and lips upturned for the briefest of moments. "I was dreaming. The knock sounded. Before I realized what I was doing, I was staring at him through the open doorway."

Pritchard cleared his throat and jotted her answer in a notebook. After recording the statement, he glared at Dawson. "I'm finished questioning Ms. Beaumont. If there's anything you want to ask her, go right ahead. I'll be outside."

Dawson read between the lines. Pritchard didn't want his interrogation compromised by a newcomer from post. A subtle reprimand, perhaps? Not that Dawson would be intimidated by a small-town cop.

As Pritchard left through the kitchen, Dawson took a seat on the chair next to Lillie and held up his identification.

"Special Agent Dawson Timmons, ma'am. I'm with the Criminal Investigation Division at Fort Rickman. The Freemont Police Department is handling the murder investigation, but the CID was called in because you work on post. I'm here as a liaison between the local police and the military."

"Does…does General Cameron know what happened?" Lillie asked.

"He's being notified."

"I don't want anything to—"

"To jeopardize your job? I don't see how that could happen. Unless your position as the general's secretary has a bearing on this crime."

"No, no." She held up her hand. "This has nothing to do with General Cameron."

"What does it involve, Ms. Beaumont?" He leaned closer. "May I call you Lillie?"

She nodded. "You're not from around here?"

"Georgia born and raised, but my home's in Cotton Grove, close to the Florida border."

She swallowed, the tendons in her graceful neck tight. "I don't know where to start."

"How 'bout at the beginning."

She tucked a strand of hair behind her ear. "I was born in Atlanta and moved to Freemont with my mother when I was a baby. We lived in a remote area, not far from the highway."

Dawson pulled a notebook and pen from his pocket.

"My…my mother disappeared when I was four." Lillie's voice was weak. She cleared her throat. "Most folks thought she had abandoned me and returned to Atlanta with a man." She shrugged. "Her lover. Sugar daddy. Whatever you want to call him."

"Granger Ford?"

"No. The man she was seeing at the time."

"How can you be sure it wasn't Granger?"

"There was a storm the night she disappeared. The thunder awakened me. I was frightened and ran to my mother's bedroom."

Dawson's could envision young Lillie, green eyes wide with fear, golden-brown hair tumbling around her sweet face, scurrying down a darkened hallway.

"The door opened and he…he told me to go back to bed."

"Who was he, Lillie? Do you know his name?"

She shook her head. "But the memory of that night still haunts me, especially when it storms."

"Can you still see his face?"

"Enough to know it wasn't the man who died on my doorstep tonight."

Dawson did the math. "It's been twenty-five years. Appearances change."

She straightened her shoulders. "I know what I saw. The man that night was someone else."

Dawson made a notation on his tablet. "Who raised you after your mother disappeared?"

"Sarah and Walter McKinney took me in. They were an older couple and didn't have children of their own."

"Good people?"

She nodded. The gloom lifted for an instant, revealing her love for her foster parents.

"They wanted to adopt me, but I…" Once again, her eyes sought his. "Maybe it was foolish, but I kept thinking my mother would come back for me."

A nail to Dawson's heart. Did all kids give wayward parents the benefit of the doubt? Must go with the territory. Children wanted to be loved. Hope provided comfort during the dark times. When hope gave out, the reality of life had to be accepted, although some people never made the transition and spent a lifetime looking for the love they never received as a child.

"But your mother didn't come back," Dawson prompted.

Lillie licked her lips as if gathering courage to continue. "When I was fourteen, the river flooded. Not long afterwards, a steel drum was found close to the water, on Fort Rickman property."

Dawson knew about the raging waters that had washed the drum downriver. Dental records confirmed the decomposed body found within was Irene Beaumont, who had gone missing ten years earlier.

"The last time you saw your mother was that stormy night?" He repeated what he already knew to gauge her response.

"That's correct. The night she disappeared."

"You were four years old?"

She nodded.

"Ten years later, your mother's remains were uncovered in a steel drum."

"And found along the river, although I've never visited the actual site. Someday..." Her voice was wistful. "Someday I hope to be strong enough to do just that."

Dawson made another notation on his tablet. "At the time of her disappearance, the townspeople thought your mother had run off to Atlanta with her boyfriend."

"That's...that's what I thought too."

"Finding her remains must have changed local opinions."

"The folks in town started to realize my mother had probably been killed the night she disappeared."

"What did you think, Lillie?"

"I didn't know what to believe."

Dawson heard the confusion in her voice. "What happened next?"

She hesitated before she spoke. "Granger Ford worked for Nelson Construction at the time. The police were investigating the employees and found a picture of my mother under his mattress in the motel where he was staying. They accused him of murder. He was found guilty and sent to jail."

Dawson tapped his pencil against his notepad. "Did you testify at the trial?"

"Supposedly, the case was open and shut. They didn't need to place me on the stand."

Hearing Lillie's response ignited a fire deep within Dawson's belly. From what he had read about the trial, the prosecution had deemed the case open and shut because Granger was a drifter who worked construction when he needed money. Personnel records at Nelson Construction verified the laborer had been on the payroll at the time of Irene Beaumont's disappearance and again when the steel drum, bearing the Nelson Construction name and logo, had been found.

"Do you know anything about the case?" Pritchard stood in the doorway to the kitchen. Dawson hadn't heard him come back inside.

"I did an internet search before I got here." Dawson pocketed his notebook. "Easy enough to access news stories about Granger's release from prison. The article included information about Irene Beaumont's murder."

"The article probably didn't mention that they found the T-shirt she must have been wearing in the drum along with her decomposed body." Pritchard sniffed, unaware of the pained expression on Lillie's face. "Two blood types were identified on the fabric. A-positive, which was Irene Beaumont's blood type, and B-negative. That matched Granger Ford's type."

Anger welled up within Dawson. He had read the transcript of the trial and knew Granger had denied, under oath, ever seeing the bloodied T-shirt or having known the victim.

Dawson made sure his voice was even, his gaze level, before he spoke again. "Yet Mr. Ford was recently released from prison?"

The cocky cop nodded. "Law students from the University of Georgia got wind of the case. They probably hoped to make a name for themselves."

"And the outcome?" Dawson knew too well what the determination had been.

Pritchard pursed his lips. "Something about the blood type being incorrect."

Granger's blood had proved to be a rare "Du"-positive, which would appear negative on an initial rapid-slide test. More definitive blood typing had not been run prior to his trial, and the jury found Granger guilty because of a bloodied T-shirt and an inaccurate blood type. In addition, DNA testing had not been done, and as Lillie had mentioned, a photo of the deceased had been found under the mattress in Granger's motel room, which anyone on the housekeeping or janitorial staffs could have accessed.

"An open-and-shut case, eh?" Dawson couldn't resist the barb that went over Pritchard's head.

"Recent DNA testing verified the B-negative blood on the T-shirt wasn't Granger's. He was released from prison ten days ago, but we're not sure when he arrived in Freemont."

At least seventy-two hours earlier, judging from the phone call Dawson had received when Granger got to town. He kept the information to himself. Pritchard could do his own investigation.

A second cop opened the back door. "Sarge, we're ready to transport the body." Pritchard followed him outside.

Once they were alone, Dawson turned back to Lillie. "What did Granger say when you opened the door tonight?"

"That someone had found him and beat him. I heard the shot. He fell forward." She stared at her hands. "I…I tried to catch him."

"Did he mention who had found him or did he say anything about your mother?"

She shook her head, but something about her expression told Dawson the secretary knew more than she had revealed.

"Do you think Granger killed your mother?"

She chewed her lip. "I…I don't know."

"Don't know or won't say?"

She hesitated.

"Did Granger contact you after he was released from prison?"

"He called me and wanted to meet. I refused. He said he had information about my mother's death."

"Yet you turned him down?"

"Part of me didn't believe him. The other part wanted to keep the past locked away."

She lowered her gaze and picked at her sleeve.

"There's something else, isn't there?" Dawson asked.

"I know it sounds crazy after a man has died, but…" She pulled in a nervous breath. "I'm worried about what this will do to military and civilian relations in the local area."

"Meaning?"

"You've heard about the new Fort Rickman Museum scheduled to be built on post?"

Dawson narrowed his gaze, trying to make the connection. With construction ready to commence, the huge, multistoried structure promised to be state of the art, with an extensive collection of historical memorabilia and artifacts. In addition, a grand ballroom, auditorium and banquet facilities would attract large-scale events and needed revenue to this part of Georgia.

"I know the museum will be a boon to the local economy," Dawson said, "but I don't see how one man's death could adversely affect the project."

"Funding is the problem." She sighed. "Which sounds so inconsequential compared to the taking of a human life."

"But—"

"That's why I didn't want to meet Granger when he called a few days ago. I knew if anything about my mother's death was brought to light, the construction project could be affected."

Dawson rubbed his hand over his jaw and let out a frustrated breath. "I still don't get the tie-in."

"You're not from around here so you probably don't know Karl Nelson."

"Only by name. Didn't the stolen barrel your mother's body was found in belong to his company?"

"That's right. Nelson Construction Company was the low bid on the museum. Mr. Nelson has been more than generous keeping the projected costs at a minimum."

"He also owns a number of businesses in town?"

"And is known for his charitable contributions. Over the years, he and his father before him have done a lot for the local area. Mr. Nelson has also donated heavily to the museum building fund and has been working with General Cameron to attract more donors. They're hosting a special ceremony on Wednesday to secure the remaining pledges."

Dawson was aware of the event. "The CID, along with the military police on post, will be providing security for the high-profile guests."

Lillie nodded. "General Cameron wants everything to go without a glitch. Mr. Nelson personally assured the donors that Freemont and Fort Rickman are exemplary communities that will showcase the best in Georgia living and draw new businesses and attractions to this part of the state."

"You're afraid the murder investigation could cause the donors to change their minds?"

She nodded slowly, as if struggling to find the words to express her feelings. When she finally spoke, she splayed her hands. "I work in General Cameron's office and am the contact person for those attending the ceremony. A pending murder investigation that involves the company, especially since Granger was killed on my property, could shed the wrong kind of light on Freemont and the project, maybe even on General Cameron. Especially if information leaks out about my mother's murder."

After everything that had happened, Lillie wasn't thinking rationally, but Dawson understood her concern. The museum project had been the talk of the post for months and everyone was eager for construction to commence. Small-town gossip could get out of hand, and with an abundance of charities needing funding, negative publicity could sway donors into changing their minds about supporting the building project.

Before Dawson could offer her reassurance, Pritchard stepped back inside.

"We're ready to wrap things up." He glanced at Lillie. "The front step is sealed off. Some of my men will return in the morning to go over the crime scene again. Use the kitchen entrance until I give you the all clear, and stay in the area in case we have more questions."

"I'm not planning to leave town."

Dawson stood and pulled two business cards from his pocket. He gave one to Pritchard. "The CID office phone number and my personal cell are under my name."

Retrieving the pen from his pocket, Dawson jotted down an additional number on the back of the card he handed Lillie. "I live in the bachelor officers' quarters on post. The handwritten digits are for the direct line to my apartment at the BOQ."

A uniformed cop approached Pritchard. "We found some numbers scratched on a scrap of paper tucked in the victim's jacket."

Pressure pushed on Dawson's chest as Pritchard read from the paper. "Nine-seven-one-four."

Lillie stared at Dawson's business card and silently mouthed the last four digits of his BOQ phone number. Nine-seven-one-four. The same numbers found in Granger's jacket.

She glanced up at Dawson. Her forehead furrowed.

Oblivious to her questioning gaze, Pritchard pulled out his cell. "Might be a portion of a phone number. I'll add the local prefix and see what we get."

Pritchard tapped in the digits and then shook his head as he disconnected. "The number's not in service."

Dawson needed to leave the little house in the woods before the Freemont cop tried the unique prefix for Fort Rickman phone lines.

He turned to Lillie, who continued to stare at him. "Don't hesitate to call me, ma'am, if you think of anything else that might have bearing on this case."

One of her finely arched brows rose ever so slightly. "Shall I use your cell phone or your BOQ number?"

The muscle in Dawson's neck twitched. "My cell."

Lillie knew he was withholding information from Pritchard. Just as she was.

Maybe they could trade secrets.

TWO

The CID agent climbed into his car as Pritchard and his men prepared to leave the area. Instead of returning to Fort Rickman, Dawson turned right out of the driveway and sped along the rain-washed road that headed north toward the interstate. Rounding a bend, he passed under a train trestle and spied the lights from the Hi-Way Motel in the distance.

The triangle of red, green and blue neon pointed toward the one-story brick building that offered small rooms at a modest rate for those who couldn't afford the larger chain motels closer to Freemont. *Vacancy,* the sign flashed, begging for business.

Pulling into the drive, Dawson cut his lights and circled to the rear of the complex. He parked under an oak tree away from the handful of cars in the back lot.

Grabbing a pair of latex gloves from his console, Dawson hustled toward the last room on the far end of the building, the room where his father had said he was staying when he called three days ago. Dawson slipped his hands into the gloves and tried the knob, relieved when it turned.

His eyes adjusted to the darkness. The bed was rumpled, pillows and comforter strewn over the nearby throw rug. Two dresser drawers hung open. An unzipped duffel bag sat on the floor next to a small desk and overturned lamp.

Either a scuffle had ensued or someone had ransacked the room. Maybe both.

Using his cell phone for light, Dawson checked the duffel, finding only underwear and socks. He opened the remaining dresser drawers. Empty except for a hardcover Bible. Standard toilet articles in the bathroom. Two shirts and a pair of jeans hung in the closet.

A car pulled to a stop outside. Footsteps approached on the walkway that edged the rooms. Dawson's pulse kicked up a notch, realizing, too late, he had failed to flip the latch.

Rap, rap, rap.

He glanced at the bathroom that offered no place to hide. The closet hung open. Small, dark, confining. Exactly where he didn't want to go.

A key scratched against the lock. The knob turned.

Sweat pooled around his neck. He didn't have a choice and slipped into the closet's confining darkness. His heart skittered in his chest. He left the door ajar and peered through the crack.

Someone stepped into the room.

Five-seven and slender with shoulder-length hair and big eyes that took in the room with one glance.

Lillie?

The last place Lillie wanted to be was Granger Ford's motel room, but she had thought the key would unlock the door and lead to information about her mother's death.

Three nights ago, Granger had phoned and asked her to meet him here. In hindsight and despite her concern about the museum project, she should have accepted his invitation.

He'd claimed to have answers, which she took to mean information about what had happened on that stormy night so long ago. Obviously, from the disarray, someone had searched the motel room, looking for the information that must have played into Granger's death.

Lillie pulled in a deep breath to calm her runaway pulse. As her eyes adjusted to the darkness, she stepped toward the duffel bag. After rifling through the contents, she opened the dresser drawers. Her fingers rested briefly on the Gideon Bible. *Lord, let me find the truth.*

Granger claimed he had never known her mother and had had nothing to do with her death. Not that Lillie was sure she believed him. Easy enough to beg forgiveness after the fact.

"Go back to bed, child."

Yet Granger's voice wasn't the one she heard in her dreams. Nor was his face the one that returned to haunt her with each passing storm.

Knowing it was only a matter of time before the Freemont police or the muscular CID agent from Fort Rickman found where Granger had been staying, she tugged on the closet door.

A man stood shadowed in the recesses.

Her heart exploded in her chest. She screamed.

Turning to flee, her foot caught on the leg of the bed. She lost her balance.

"Lillie."

Hands reached for her, easing the fall. He took the brunt of the blow as they both crashed to the floor.

She kicked, heard him groan and kicked again.

He pinned her down, the weight of his legs impeding her movement. "I won't hurt you."

She screamed again.

He covered her mouth with his hand. His breath warmed her cheek.

"Lillie, stop." His voice was low, insistent.

She bit his hand.

"Augh," he groaned. "Listen."

Sirens sounded in the distance.

"The police are coming. You don't want them to find you here."

Reason tangled through her fear as she recognized Dawson's voice.

"I'm going to let you go. Leave the room. Take the back road out of the motel. Meet me at the truck stop one exit north on the highway. We need to talk." His hand eased up ever so slightly. "Do you understand?"

She nodded.

He drew away from her and stood.

Scampering to her feet, Lillie raced for the door and threw it open. Light filtered into the darkness. She turned, seeing the special agent bend down and pick up something from the rug.

Dawson Timmons was a fool to think she would meet him anywhere except at military police headquarters on post.

"You dropped something." The key dangled from his hand.

The sirens screamed in the distance. Not much time to get away.

"Meet me at the truck stop," he said again. "We can share information."

The police would never understand how she had known about the motel room and why she had been there with the CID agent. Leaving the parking lot, she headed out the back way.

On the phone, Granger had said he'd been framed. At the time, she hadn't wanted his excuses to buy her sympathy. Now she wasn't sure about anything or anyone, especially the special agent who seemed to be one step ahead of her.

General Cameron had spoken highly of the Criminal Investigation Division on post. A number of big cases had been solved over the past few years because of their hard work. That's why she had felt comfortable sharing her story tonight with the special agent.

Now she wondered if she could trust him. How had he known about the motel room? Could he have been one of the people Granger claimed had framed him? If so, Dawson was the last person Lillie should meet. Yet, he now had the key that might unlock information about her mother's disappearance.

Lillie needed to be smart and careful, which meant having something to hold over Dawson's head if things got ugly. Grabbing her phone, she dialed her private line at work that hooked into the voice mail she checked each morning as soon as she arrived at her desk.

If something happened to her, General Cameron's aide would eventually review the messages. "This is Lillie Beaumont," she said once the call transferred to voice mail.

She glanced at the clock on her dash. "It's four-thirty a.m. I'm on my way to the truck stop at the exit north of town to meet CID Special Agent Dawson Timmons concerning Granger Ford's death. If something should happen to me, question Agent Timmons."

Years earlier her mother had disappeared on a stormy night. She glanced at the leaves and branches strewn across the road. Meeting Dawson could put her own life in danger.

A shiver slipped down her spine. Lillie had to ensure that she wouldn't disappear on this stormy night like her mother.

THREE

Dawson parked on the far side of the truck stop where his car wouldn't be seen from the interstate. Quickly pulling out the wax kit he kept in his glove compartment, he made a mold of Lillie's key. Later, if need be, he could make a duplicate.

Leaving his car, he rounded to the front of the one-story stucco building and glanced at the few cars driving along the highway, their lights cutting through the darkness. The rain had stopped, but a wind blew from the west. He rubbed his bare hands together as he approached the all-night diner and peered through the large windows. Standing behind the counter, a waitress poured coffee for two husky guys in parkas.

Dawson wiped his feet on the doormat, frustrated by the damp cold that gnawed at the old gunshot wound to his leg. He thought of the investigation that had left him injured, hating the ever-present limp and accompanying pain.

Stepping inside, Dawson unsnapped his windbreaker and nodded to the waitress, who raised a pot of coffee. He held up two fingers and pointed to the booth where

Lillie sat. She watched him approach the table and slide into the seat across from her.

"Thanks for meeting me," he said, adding a smile to counter her frosty glare.

"You have something that belongs to me," she said in lieu of a greeting.

The waitress approached with two mugs she quickly filled. "You folks want breakfast?"

"Coffee's fine." Lillie dumped a packet of sweetener and a significant amount of cream into her mug.

"Two eggs over easy, hash browns, sausage and biscuits." Dawson eyed Lillie. "You like grits?"

"Of course, but—"

"Make that two orders with grits."

The waitress scurried back to the kitchen.

Lillie raised her brow. "I don't need breakfast."

"Maybe not, but it's been a long night." He glanced at the men at the nearby counter and lowered his voice. "I'm glad you decided to meet me."

She wrapped her fingers around the chunky mug. "Did I have a choice?"

"You could have gone home."

"I need my key."

She held out her hand, palm up, which he ignored.

"You tried the key at the motel," Dawson said, "thinking it would open the door. Evidently Granger didn't tell you what it unlocked when he called you."

She tilted her head and braced her shoulders before she leaned across the table, her voice low. "When did he call nine-seven-one-four, the number on your business card?"

Touché. Ms. Beaumont had a mind and wasn't afraid to use it. He stretched back in the booth. "You've developed a bit of an attitude since you left your house, Lillie. What happened?"

"I realized you may be more of a problem than an asset."

"Which means?"

"I thought I could trust you."

He shrugged. "I'm working for Uncle Sam. I'm trustworthy."

"Really, Dawson?" She raised a brow and stared at him across the table.

He almost smiled at the cute way her nose turned up and the handful of freckles that dotted her cheeks, neither of which he had noticed earlier. "Let's make a trade. Okay? You go first."

She shook her head. "I've already told you everything."

"Why did Granger pick tonight to stop by your house?"

"He was on the run. As I mentioned, someone found him and beat him."

"But why?"

"Because he was trying to uncover the truth about what happened to my mother." Lillie glanced at the waitress then back at Dawson. "I overheard the prosecuting attorney talking to my foster parents before Granger's trial began. The lawyer was worried the evidence wouldn't be enough to find him guilty. Everyone wanted to pin the crime on someone. Granger was the logical choice."

Dawson's muscles tensed. "Do you know that for sure?"

She leaned in closer. "All I know is someone wanted

my mother dead, only I never knew who. At the time, it was easier to believe Granger was guilty."

"And now?"

"Now I want everything to go back to the way it was before Granger knocked on my door." She sighed. "Only there's no going back."

"Why would someone want to kill your mother?"

"I thought it was because of me. That I had done something wrong."

"Which doesn't make sense, Lillie."

"Not to an adult, but children always believe they're at fault when something bad happens."

Dawson thought of his own childhood. For too long, he had blamed himself for his absentee father.

Lillie pointed a slender finger at him. "Now it's your turn, Mr. CID Agent. How are you involved?"

"I'm representing the military in the investigation."

"There's something you're not telling me."

She was right, but Dawson wasn't ready to reveal anything else.

His cell rang. He pulled the mobile phone from his pocket. "Timmons."

"Pritchard here. Thought you might be interested in the latest."

"Hold on a second." Dawson glanced at Lillie. "I need to take this call."

Without waiting for her response, he slid from the booth and hustled outside. The chilly night air swirled around him. He pushed the phone to his ear. "Go ahead."

"The victim rented a room at the Hi-Way Motel. We're there now."

"Did you find anything that has bearing on his death?" Dawson asked.

"A photo cut from the local newspaper of a guy named Billy Everett was hidden in the motel Bible."

The one place Dawson hadn't looked.

"Everett got into trouble a few years back," the cop continued. "The news photo was taken when we hauled him in for questioning. We didn't have enough evidence and eventually had to release him."

"Had he been arrested before?"

"For possession. Did some time. Claimed he had cleaned up his life, but the guy's got problems. Not too smart, and years of abusing drugs haven't helped."

"So why would Granger have his picture?"

"Your guess is as good as mine."

"Do me a favor," Dawson said. "Fax me a copy of the photo."

"Will do."

"Any indication Everett was involved in tonight's shooting?"

"A lamp was overturned, and the bedding was disheveled. Looks like there could have been a scuffle."

Or someone was looking for something, such as a key, which Dawson didn't mention. He raked his hands across his face, needing the coffee he hadn't had a chance to drink.

"If they had argued—" Dawson went along with Pritchard's theory "—why would Granger go to Lillie's house?"

"The guilty always return to the scene of the crime. Irene Beaumont's house burned down years ago, but her daughter was still in town. If Granger killed Irene, he might want her daughter to know about his release from prison."

"Lillie was only four years old when her mother disappeared."

"She heard a man's voice that night," Pritchard said. "Irene Beaumont had a Fulton County license plate on her car when she arrived in Freemont. Initially, folks thought she had gone back to Atlanta with her lover. No mention of a husband. Most people presumed she had never married."

"And left her child home alone?"

"No one said she was the best of mothers."

Small towns were all alike. Similar talk had lived on in Cotton Grove. Hard for a kid who heard what people said behind his mother's back.

Pritchard sniffed. "Of course, all that changed when they found her body."

"Did the motel manager know anything about what happened today?" Dawson asked.

"He saw a guy who matched Everett's description. Red hair and a scar on his right cheek. Hard to miss. Highway Patrol's on the lookout for him. I'll keep you posted."

Dawson disconnected and pocketed his phone as he returned to the booth.

"That was the police, wasn't it?" Lillie wrapped her arms defensively across her chest. "Did they find anything at the motel?"

"A photograph of a guy named Billy Everett was tucked in the Bible. Red hair. Scar on his right cheek. Do you know him?"

She shook her head.

"Pritchard thought there had been a scuffle."

Lillie shrugged. "Granger's face was bloodied, but I got the impression someone had searched the room."

She thought for a moment. Her face clouded. "You were there when I arrived."

Dawson pointed a finger back at his own chest. "You think I messed up the place?"

"You didn't tell Pritchard about the motel room." She held his gaze. "Granger had your BOQ phone number in his pocket. You didn't reveal that either."

"And you failed to mention the key."

"Which belongs to me." Once again, she held out her hand.

Disregarding her request, Dawson stared into her pretty eyes. "Granger knew he had been set up. The case was open and shut, as you mentioned, only because they had a fall guy, a transient construction worker who came to town when he needed money. A guy who didn't have resources to defend himself."

"The court appointed an attorney."

Dawson laughed ruefully. "A lawyer who should have retired years earlier. You probably didn't follow the local news when you were a kid. Not long after the trial, the lawyer was diagnosed with dementia and was placed in a nursing home where he died a bit too soon thereafter."

"If you grew up in Cotton Grove, why were you interested in a murder that took place in Freemont?"

Her question caught Dawson off guard. He looked down at his mug, weighing his response. "I planned on making the army a career. My local library carried the Freemont papers as well as information about Fort Rickman."

Lillie shook her head. "My mother's death had nothing to do with the military. What aren't you telling me?"

He ignored her question. "I still don't understand

why Granger would return to Freemont and jeopardize his new-found freedom?"

"He wanted to clear his name, to make good on the past. At least that's what he told me over the phone. He said he'd made mistakes. He'd abandoned someone and wanted to make it up to him."

A muscle in Dawson's neck twitched. "Him?"

"His son."

Inwardly, Dawson groaned. "A son was never mentioned in the news reports. Maybe Granger was lying to get on your good side."

"It's possible." Her bravado faltered. She rubbed her forehead. "Actually, I don't know what to believe. I boxed up all the memories of long ago, hoping I could hide the past. Granger's death forces everything out into the open."

Maybe Lillie understood how he felt growing up as the kid without a dad. Dawson had put the snippets of gossip together. Some people never forgot the drifter who had left his mother pregnant. No name on his birth certificate meant legally Dawson didn't have a father. It didn't mean he didn't know who his father was.

Just as Lillie had indicated, Granger's death forced everything into the open. It was time for the truth.

"You said Granger mentioned having a son." Dawson let out a lungful of pent-up air. "He was talking about me. Granger Ford was my dad."

Her eyes narrowed. "Why didn't you say so earlier?"

"Because I buried the past just like you did."

"I don't believe you." She grabbed her purse and slid from the booth.

He stood and reached for her wrist. "Don't leave, Lillie."

She jerked free of his hold. "You used me to get information."

"I did no such thing." He dug in his pocket and pulled out a twenty-dollar bill. Throwing it on the table, he turned to find the two truckers glaring at him.

The waitress came around the counter. "Is there a problem?"

"The lady's not feeling well."

Dawson hurried after Lillie, but when he stepped outside, all he could see were the taillights of her Honda Civic racing away in the distance.

Climbing behind the wheel of his own car, Dawson pulled out of the lot and backtracked along the winding road. The temperature had warmed somewhat, and a thick fog rose from the wet earth, clouding his view of the roadway.

Lillie said the past had found her. It had found Dawson as well, but the past wasn't the issue. The present was the problem. For a father who never claimed him as his son, Granger's death was liable to change Dawson's life forever—and not for the better.

Lillie drove too fast along the narrow road, wanting to get away from Dawson Timmons. If not for the key, which he still had, she never would have stopped at the diner.

He had hidden the truth from the Freemont police and from her, pretending he had her best interest at heart. All the while, he was gathering information about his father.

She didn't understand anything, including her mixed feelings about the determined CID agent whose eyes were rimmed with sorrow. On one hand, she didn't want to reveal anything to him, then she found herself opening up and saying more than she should.

Coming around the bend, she slowed her speed. Headlights approached, faster than the limit allowed on the twisted back road. She pulled her Honda to the right, hoping to give the speeding vehicle more room.

The glare blinded her for an instant. When her vision cleared, she saw an SUV had crossed the line and was headed straight for her.

Her heart stopped.

She turned the wheel and swerved off the road, narrowly missing a head-on collision.

Her car hit the shoulder and skidded in the wet grass. She lifted her foot from the accelerator and pumped the brakes. Keeping the wheels in line took all her strength.

The engine died, and the Honda rolled to a stop. Heart in her throat, she gasped for air and glanced in her rearview mirror.

A tingle of ice ran down her spine. The SUV that had almost run her off the road had turned around and was racing toward her.

Lord, protect me.

She turned the key in the ignition, relieved when the engine purred back to life, but when she accelerated, the wheels dug into the rain-soft earth. The tires spun over and over again.

"Oh, God, please."

In a flash of motion, the large sport-utility vehicle passed by and then braked to a stop just ahead of where she was stuck in the mud.

A door slammed.

A figure cut through the fog.

Opening her door, she sprang into the wet night and started to run.

Footsteps sounded behind her.

Her heart thumped a warning.

She pushed forward.

Another set of headlights cut through the darkness.

The man behind her swore. He skidded to a halt and ran back to his car.

She flailed her arms, needing to flag down the approaching motorist. The vehicle stopped and someone stepped onto the pavement. A big, burly blond.

Lillie might have made a mistake.

The man who ran her off the road was someone to fear, but the man walking toward her might be as well. How could she trust a man whose father had killed her mother long ago?

FOUR

Dawson saw Lillie spotlighted in the headlights. Fear strained her face. She glanced quickly over her shoulder at the fleeing man and then back at Dawson. She hesitated, as if unsure whether to approach him.

"Lillie." He softened his voice and opened his arms to reassure her. "I'm not a threat. You're safe with me."

Her eyes filled with confusion. Then, as if the fog had lifted, she stepped into his embrace.

Her trembling body molded to him. He drew her closer, touched by her need. As strong as she tried to appear, beneath the facade was a woman who longed to trust someone. Hopefully, to trust him.

Her head nestled into his shoulder. Tears streamed from her eyes as if an emotional dam had given way. Dawson drew her to himself, a desire to keep her safe surging within him. The warmth of her closeness and the silky softness of her hair sent confusing signals to his heart.

He had never experienced anything like this dealing with other investigations. Usually he remained uninvolved and in control, but at the moment, his professional side was playing Russian roulette with his emotions.

His eyes watched the light-colored SUV—maybe an Expedition or Suburban—drive off, wheels screeching in the night as the taillights were enveloped by the fog. The license plate was obscured, but he saw a reflective army decal on the rear bumper. As fast as the maniac was driving, Dawson wouldn't be able to catch up to him, so he kept his arms around Lillie.

"Shhhhh," he soothed, smelling the heady scent of her perfume, a floral mix that made him think of springtime and sunshine—so the opposite of the dark night and heavy fog that surrounded them now. "You're safe. I won't let anyone hurt you."

Except someone wanted to do her harm. Someone who had gunned down Granger because of what he had uncovered. The killer probably thought the ex-con had passed information on to Lillie, information the killer—or killers—didn't want revealed.

Anger bubbled up within Dawson. He wanted to slam his fist into the gut of anyone who tried to hurt Lillie. He had to keep her safe, not just because she worked on post and had a very important boss, but because his own father had put her in danger.

She pulled back and turned her puffy but pretty face toward him. "I...I'm sorry. Usually I'm not this emotional."

"Fear has a way of changing everything, Lillie." He wanted to reassure her. "You were scared. Once the danger passes, the natural response is to release emotion. Tears can be cathartic."

She tried to smile as she wiped her eyes.

He dug his right hand in his back pocket and pulled out a handkerchief, which he held out to her.

"Thanks." She patted the cloth against her cheeks and sniffed again as she attempted to laugh. "I feel silly."

"Don't." He put his hands on her shoulders and turned her toward her car. "Let's see if we can get you back on the road. Tell me exactly what happened."

"The SUV came around the curve too fast. I swerved to avoid a collision."

"The same guy who chased after you?"

She nodded. "When he made a U-turn, I knew he was coming for me. If…if you hadn't stopped…"

She didn't need to finish the sentence. Both of them realized how vulnerable she had been on the back road in the early-morning hours with the heavy veil of fog closing in around her.

"Did you see his face?"

She shook her head. "All I could think about was getting away."

Dawson hadn't recognized the man or his vehicle and would be hard-pressed to provide a description other than a large SUV, either white or beige. He hadn't been able to read the license plate, and the only thing he had seen was the decal.

Keeping his arm around Lillie, he guided her to a safe spot just a short distance from her Honda. Sliding behind the wheel, Dawson started the ignition and eased down on the accelerator, giving the engine enough gas to move the car forward and free of the trough the wheels had dug earlier.

After steering onto the blacktop, he put the gear in

Park and opened the door. "Looks like you're good to go. What time do you have to be at your office?"

"Eight o'clock, but I'm usually there by seven-thirty." She glanced at her watch. "I need to change before I head to post."

"I'll follow you."

"I hate to hold you up."

"Not a problem."

"Thank you." She attempted to smile.

"I won't let you out of my sight."

The drive to her house was uneventful, and soon both cars were parked in her driveway. Ignoring the front entrance, still draped with crime-scene tape, they walked around the house and entered through the kitchen.

Lillie made a pot of coffee, which Dawson sipped as he looked around her living area. The house was nicely furnished with a contemporary couch and love seat and a mix of antique wooden pieces, including an oak sideboard and carved bookshelves.

The inlaid wood and the fine lines of the detailed ornamentation verified the pieces were works of art, which Dawson admired. Ironic that, since Lillie didn't have a family history of her own, she decorated with treasures from someone else's past.

Side tables topped with marble—exquisite rock that added beauty to the room—sat on each side of the couch. A few knickknacks were scattered about, and two framed photographs rested atop the mantel. One showed a beautiful woman with a small child in her arms.

Glancing closer, Dawson recognized Lillie's sweet face and curly honey-brown hair. The other picture was of an older couple. An adolescent Lillie stood with her arms around both of them. Probably the McKinneys, the foster parents with the big hearts and willingness to open their home to a small child who had no one.

Dawson instantly knew he liked both of them. His gaze returned to the other photo. Although the picture had faded, he could see the resemblance between Lillie and the woman holding her, no doubt Irene Beaumont.

Had his father killed her? Dawson's gut tightened. Turning away from the mantel, he headed for the kitchen and refilled his mug.

Outside, the fog had lifted, and as he sipped the coffee, the sun colored the horizon.

"I need to apologize for my actions at the diner."

Dawson turned at the sound of Lillie's voice. She had combed her hair and changed into a stylish dress that hugged her curves and made his breath jam in his throat.

"I…I was only thinking of myself and my job and what's happening at Fort Rickman." Her pretty eyes were filled with compassion. "Your father died this morning. I'm…I'm sorry."

He placed his mug in the sink. "I never knew him. Never talked to him until he called a few nights ago. He…he wanted to meet."

Dawson pulled in a breath. "My father had rejected me all my life, so I rejected him. Only now—" He shrugged, unable to find the words to express the way he felt.

She took a step closer. "Granger wanted to make it up to you. He didn't want his son to be ashamed of him."

Since the trial, Dawson had blocked his father out of his life. He hadn't talked about him or acknowledged him or allowed him into his heart. It was easier to deny him than to accept who his father had been—a convict, a criminal, a killer.

"I went into law enforcement to right the wrongs my father had committed. Now I find out he may not have been the man I thought he was. That's hard to get my mind around."

Dawson glanced out the window, wondering what the new day would bring. If he had made a mistake about his father, maybe there were other things he needed to reconsider, but he couldn't share his feelings with Lillie. Not now. Not when they were involved in a murder investigation. Even if the victim was his dad.

As Lillie watched the confusion play over Dawson's face, the memories from her own childhood bubbled up within her. "After my mother disappeared, I cried myself to sleep night after night. More than anything, I wanted a normal life, someone to love me, to tuck me in when I went to bed and help me get dressed in the morning."

She pulled in a fragile breath. "I was fortunate the McKinneys took me in. They were patient and loving, but at four years old, I wanted my own mother to wrap me in her arms."

With a rueful smile, she added, "Sometimes I think I never stopped mourning her loss, and as much as I wanted to block out everything that had happened, I feared the McKinneys would be taken from me as well."

Understanding mellowed Dawson's gaze and made her question why she told him things she had never told anyone else. She reached for her purse, trying to shield herself from what she saw in Dawson's eyes.

"I can't be late for work."

He grabbed her hand. "Lillie."

She stopped and looked up, her breath stalled by his closeness.

"I'm sorry," he said.

She tried to smile. "Life can be a tough place for kids, but I…I shouldn't have mentioned my own problems, Dawson. You have enough of your own."

"You don't have to hide anything from me." His voice was gentle, like the morning mist.

As much as she wanted to believe him, she had spent her whole life covering up the pain of being a child left behind. She couldn't admit the way she really felt to anyone. Especially not to a man whose crystal-blue eyes could see into her heart.

She dug her keys out of her purse and tilted her head, trying to lighten her tone and her expression. "I don't want to keep General Cameron waiting."

Dawson nodded and followed her outside. "You lead. I'll take up the rear."

"Once we get to post, I'll be fine."

He opened her car door. "I'll follow you to your office."

She climbed behind the wheel. He closed the door and gazed through the car window. "Lock your doors," he mouthed.

So like a cop, but she complied with his request, feeling oddly relieved that someone was concerned about her well-being. Dawson was probably just doing his job. No reason for her to jump to any other conclusion, which she continued to tell herself as they entered Fort Rickman and drove toward post headquarters.

Lillie parked close to the building and met up with him on the sidewalk. "Thank you."

His hand touched her back. “I’ll follow you inside.”

Her cheeks flushed as they hurried along the walkway and climbed the steps. Dawson held the door for her, and her heels clicked along the tile floor.

She stopped in front of the elevator.

“Let’s take the stairs,” he suggested.

The elevator door opened and she stepped inside. “This will be faster.”

He hesitated before joining her. As the door closed, Lillie could tell something was wrong. Dawson’s face paled. He licked his lips and clenched his fist until the doors opened on the second floor.

She stepped onto the landing. “I take it you don’t like elevators.”

“Actually, the problem is confined spaces.”

“I’ll try to remember that.” She pointed him toward the general’s suite, located at the far end of the hallway.

Dawson studied the long corridor, probably assessing her safety. Leaving him to do his job, she entered the office and nodded to the general’s aide.

“Morning, Mark.”

Medium height with broad shoulders and a military haircut, Captain Mark Banks stood near her desk, holding a phone to his ear. Hopefully he hadn’t retrieved the message concerning Dawson.

“I was worried, Lillie.” He held her gaze longer than necessary.

As much as the aide wanted to be part of her life, Lillie had rejected his advances. She didn’t need a relationship with someone with whom she shared an office or worked with on a daily basis.

“The CID called.” His brow creased with concern. “They said you were involved in a shooting.”

Dawson had evidently completed his hallway security check because, at that moment, he entered the outer office and glanced from Lillie to the general's aide.

Mark squared his shoulders. "You're from the CID?"

"That's right. Special Agent Dawson Timmons." He flashed his identification.

"Lillie's not in trouble, is she?" the aide asked.

"Of course not." She let out a frustrated sigh. Suddenly her life had gotten complicated. "A man was shot. He died. No one knows why he chose my front porch."

As if doubting her overly simplistic explanation, the aide puffed out his chest. "Surely Mr. Timmons has some idea of what happened."

Ignoring the aide's sarcasm, Dawson nodded. "We're working with the Freemont police. At this point, nothing significant has come to light."

Lillie had hoped coming to work today would ease her anxiety. Standing between two men playing a game of one-upmanship made her wish she had called in sick.

The best way to rectify the situation was to send Dawson on his way. "Thank you, Agent Timmons, for all your help. I'll be fine from now on."

He glanced at his watch. "I want to update General Cameron on what happened. I'll stick around until he arrives."

Mark raised his brow. "I thought you didn't have additional information?"

What was it about men? They were always in competition.

Edging away from Mark, she rounded her desk and dropped her purse in the bottom drawer. "The general's tied up this morning, Dawson, but I can pencil you in later."

At that moment, the outer door opened and General Cameron stepped into the office. Mark and Dawson came to attention.

Lillie smiled. "Good morning, sir."

In his early fifties with a square face and receding hairline, the general nodded to the two men and then softened his stern expression as he turned to Lillie. "The staff duty officer called me at home and told me there had been a shooting at your house. You're all right?"

"I was never in danger, besides..." She extended her hand toward Dawson. "Special Agent Timmons arrived shortly after the shooting. He followed me to post to ensure I arrived safely."

The general extended his hand. "Thank you for helping Lillie."

Dawson accepted the handshake. "The Freemont police are handling the investigation, sir. I'll be working with them."

"Any leads?"

"Not at this time."

"Keep me abreast of the situation."

"Will do, sir."

The general nodded to his aide. "Morning, Mark." He then headed through another door that led to his inner office suite.

Lillie pulled out her desk chair. Before she sat down, the outer door opened again, and Karl Nelson hustled into the office. Forty-something and slightly out of breath, the head of Nelson Construction smacked of small-town wealth in his hand-tailored suit, starched white shirt and red tie.

"I'm early for my appointment with the general, Lillie." Five-ten and wearing twenty extra pounds, Karl approached her desk. "I heard about the shooting. Are you all right?"

"I'm fine, Mr. Nelson, but I wish I could say the same for Granger Ford."

Karl harrumphed. "The man was a murderer. He never should have been released from prison. In my opinion, he received his due."

Dawson flinched. "I beg to differ, sir."

Lillie's stomach tightened. If only Dawson could shrug off the comment and not let the contractor get under his skin.

"What's that?" Karl turned, as if only now realizing the CID agent was in the room.

"Granger Ford was recently released from prison, Mr. Nelson, because of new DNA testing that proved the trial was a mockery of justice."

So much for hoping everyone would get along. Glancing from Dawson to Nelson, Lillie felt like a drop of water on a hot iron.

Dawson pointed his finger at the contractor. "People in this town stood by and allowed an innocent man to go to jail."

Nelson's eyes narrowed. Before he could respond, the door to the inner office suite opened.

General Cameron stood in the doorway, his hand outstretched. "Glad you stopped by early, Karl. We'll have more time to go over the plans for the new museum."

The construction company owner shrugged off his displeasure with Dawson, returned the handshake and followed the general into his inner office.

Once the door closed behind them, Lillie looked at Dawson, willing him to understand she needed to get to work. "You'd better go."

Digging in his pocket, he pulled out Granger's key and dropped it into her hand. "I'll stop by later this afternoon and follow you home after work."

Before she could object, he was gone, leaving her stomach in knots and her nerves stretched thin. She glanced through the window as he hurried along the sidewalk to his car.

Handsome though he was, Lillie needed to realize the special agent was trouble, and right now, she had more than enough to last a lifetime.

FIVE

Leaving post headquarters, Dawson glanced up at the second-story corner suite. In deference to the general, he should have kept his comment about Granger to himself, but he had bristled when the construction tycoon claimed the ex-con had deserved to die.

Dawson had blurted out his objection not just because Granger had been his dad, but because false rhetoric, like idle gossip, could be deadly. Dawson had experienced it firsthand with the hateful words spread around Cotton Grove when he was growing up.

Just like Lillie, Dawson had closed the door to his past. In fact, he had slammed it shut and walked away. Only now Granger's death had cracked it open again.

As he walked past Lillie's car, he thought again of the pretty secretary. High cheekbones. Expressive brows. Emerald eyes that seemed to look beneath the surface and see into the parts of him he closed off from the world. Could she look deep enough to uncover the real person behind the badge?

Did she see a man who wanted to know the truth about his father? Or a man who still harbored ill feelings toward the one person he had needed most when he was growing up?

Sliding behind the wheel of his Camry, Dawson shook his head ever so slightly. As a kid, instead of listening to his mother's constant bashing of his absentee dad, Dawson had created an imaginary bigger-than-life hero.

That false bubble had burst when Granger was convicted of murder. From then on, Dawson had become his own man and no longer held on to the flawed belief that his father loved him. Like folks said, love was overrated. At least that's what Dawson told himself.

Now, with the emotional upheaval rumbling through his gut since he had gotten the call about the shooting, he wasn't sure of how he felt about Granger, and while Lillie was in a completely different class, he didn't know how he felt about her either.

Dawson tried to refocus his attention on the investigation. Instead he kept seeing Lillie, dressed in blood-spattered pajamas and tugging nervously at her silky locks.

Once he arrived at CID headquarters, he poured two cups of coffee and headed for Jamison's office. He needed to brief him on what had happened at the secretary's home and then explain a rather complicated situation that could have bearing on his future.

The sergeant who had recruited Dawson into the military had insisted army entrance forms mirror each recruit's legal birth certificate. If Dawson's mother had failed to provide his father's name, then as far as the sergeant was concerned, Dawson's military paperwork needed to duplicate that same lack of information, even if Dawson had been willing to provide a name.

All of which Dawson would explain to the chief on Monday. Since Jamison was in charge during Wilson's absence, he needed to be brought up to date as well.

"Thanks for taking the call this morning," Jamison said when Dawson handed him the cup of coffee.

"Not a problem."

Jamison took a long slug of the hot brew before asking, "How's the secretary?"

"Back at work."

Raising his brow, Jamison asked, "You okay?"

Dawson nodded. "I'm fine. Just need to get a few things off my chest."

"You've got my attention."

Dawson quickly filled Jamison in on the shooting and the man who had run Lillie off the road. "Her safety's an issue, but she's more concerned about the new Fort Rickman Museum and whether negative publicity about the shooting could impact donations."

"A lot of high rollers will be on post Wednesday along with their checkbooks."

"That's the problem. You've heard of Karl Nelson?"

"As in Nelson Construction Company? He's a local hero. Evidently his father did a lot to foster relations between Fort Rickman and the local community. Once he passed on, Karl took over. Nelson money has put Freemont on the map."

Dawson nodded. "I had a little run-in with Karl this morning."

"Oh?"

"He made a negative comment about Granger." Dawson shrugged. "I set him straight."

The corners of Jamison's mouth twitched. "I'm sure

you were respectful and handled the situation with great diplomacy."

"I wanted to jab my finger in his pudgy midriff and tell him to drop and give me fifty push-ups."

Jamison chuckled. "He's probably harmless, but my advice would be to temper your remarks when you're in the general's office."

"Roger that." Dawson downed the rest of his coffee and threw the paper cup in the trash.

"There's something else we need to discuss." He pulled in a deep breath and then explained the tight-rope he was walking by investigating a case in which he had a personal interest.

Jamison pursed his lips once Dawson had finished speaking. "I'm not sure what the old man will say on Monday. Wilson likes everything done by the book, but he knows we're down two agents. I was tied up with another case, and anything involving the general's secretary, in my opinion, could become high profile. When the call came in, we needed someone from post to represent the military. You were the only agent available."

Dawson nodded. "Which sounds well and good today, but the chief might see it in a totally different light come Monday."

"I'll take the heat."

Dawson held up his hand. "I don't want you involved, Jamison. This rests on my shoulders."

"But I was the one who assigned you to the case. We'll let the Freemont police handle the investigation while you ensure Ms. Beaumont's safety. If Wilson wants to make a change come Monday, so be it, but until then your job is to keep her safe."

"I want to be up front about everything," Dawson said.

"Which you have been."

"There's one other thing. My father's name was not on my birth certificate. If my relationship to the victim becomes public knowledge, I don't want anyone to think I tried to falsify military records."

"We'll handle that problem when we need to. For right now, focus on security for the general's secretary."

Dawson let out a frustrated breath as he left Jamison's office. He was treading in treacherous waters, especially where Lillie Beaumont was concerned. Keeping her safe meant keeping her under surveillance. Not a difficult task on the surface, but one that could force him to ignore the emotional pull she had on his heart.

Maybe the delay would work to Dawson's advantage. Over the weekend, more facts could come to light. He was probably being overly optimistic, but anything could develop in the next forty-eight hours.

All he had to do was keep Lillie safe until then, but when he returned to her office later that afternoon, the only person he found was the general's aide.

On more than one occasion, Dawson had seen the rather egotistic captain at the club, throwing his weight around and demanding faster service because of his connections with the general. Evidently, the aide didn't realize he had silver bars on his shoulders instead of stars.

"When did Lillie leave?" Dawson asked as he spied her empty desk.

The aide checked his watch. "Probably twenty minutes ago."

"Did she say where she was going?"

"Only that she needed to check on a few things that may have played into the murder."

Dawson's gut tightened. Someone had run Lillie off the road this morning and placed her life in danger. The last thing she needed was to snoop around in a homicide investigation.

To his credit, the captain's face showed the concern he must not have realized earlier. "I…I thought she was meeting you."

"What did she say, exactly?"

"Something about unlocking the answers to what had happened."

Dawson never should have given her the key. More than likely Granger wouldn't have had access to the facilities on post, which Lillie would have realized. She must have driven back to town.

Dawson wasn't sure what he would find in Freemont, but one thing was certain. He had to find Lillie before trouble found her.

Lillie needed to discover what Granger's key unlocked. Confident Dawson planned to follow her home after work, she wanted to distance herself from the CID agent with whom she had already shared too much. She didn't want anyone getting too close, which he seemed to do whenever they were together.

Case in point, she had ended up in his arms this morning. Lulled by his warmth, she had felt secure in his protective embrace. Even the masculine scent of his aftershave played havoc with her normal control. No matter how she reacted emotionally to the CID agent, she didn't need him. She didn't need anyone.

Earlier, she had planned to take a long lunch break

to investigate on her own, but with only a few workdays until the big donors would be on post, the last-minute details for the kickoff event for the Fort Rickman Museum required attention.

Lillie had produced a program for the ceremony, which General Cameron needed to review before the end of the workday. She had stayed at her desk throughout the lunch hour to ensure the task was completed on time. She had also contacted the various organizations on post taking part in the special event and asked for a confirmation of the number of people participating.

When she had finally cleared her desk, Lillie bid Captain Banks a hasty goodbye and briefly explained her reason for leaving early. An incoming call captured his attention and allowed her to get away without having to share additional information.

Once in her car, she pulled Granger's key from her pocket. What would it unlock, and what secrets would be revealed about the past? Torn between learning the truth and keeping the past hidden, Lillie jammed it back in her pocket.

Lillie had learned at a young age to protect her heart and had vowed to never allow herself to be vulnerable again. Granger's death forced her to rethink the past, something she hadn't wanted to do.

This morning, she had watched Dawson through her office window as he hustled to his car. *Penny for your thoughts.* The old adage had come to mind when he stopped on the sidewalk and glanced up at the window where she stood.

Surely with the tinted panes he hadn't noticed her staring down at him. Nor had he realized the way her heart tightened in her chest. Before she allowed herself to explore the reason for the internal reaction, she had returned to her desk, intent on focusing on her work instead of the CID agent.

Except here she was hours later, drifting back to his blue eye and blond hair and strong arms that had comforted her this morning.

She shook her head, sending the thought of his strength fleeing, and concentrated instead on the twisting road she needed to follow into town.

Freemont had grown recently with the influx of military to the area. The south side, closest to post, had rapidly spread into an assortment of fly-by-night businesses that catered to soldiers. Used-car dealerships, pawnshops and bars now populated the outskirts of the Georgia town.

A bowling alley and pool hall complex appeared ahead, housed in a prefabricated warehouse that took up most of the block. She found a parking space on the street and, remembering Dawson's warning earlier, locked her doors before she hurried along the sidewalk toward Southside Lanes.

The neon lights inside the building beckoned a welcome that couldn't cover the smell of stale beer and dirty socks. Bowling balls crashed against the lineup of pins, filling the air with the *ding-ding-ding* of the scoreboards. The clerk, mid-thirty-something and as many pounds overweight, stood behind the counter and talked to two guys, who from their buzz haircuts were obviously military.

Lillie stepped into the women's locker room, lifted by a sense of euphoria when she spied a row of lockers along one wall. She tried the key in the various locks, but none opened.

Realizing Granger wouldn't have used the women's locker room, she retraced her steps to the main bowling area. The two military guys had selected their balls and were warming up on a distant lane. The clerk had left the counter unmanned, and the only other patrons were focused on the scoreboard and their games.

Walking quickly, Lillie eased through the open doorway into the men's area and tried the key in the nearby lockers, discouraged when they also failed to open.

Footsteps sounded behind her. Lillie tensed. Her heart hammered in her chest.

"Hey, lady," a deep voice bellowed. "What are you doing?"

Her hands shaking, she dropped the key in her pocket. "I, ah…I thought this was the ladies' room."

Lowering her head, Lillie brushed past the indignant bowler and hurried toward the door, only to walk into the wide body of the clerk.

He grabbed her arm and glared down at her. "What were you doing?"

She tried to wrench free of his grasp. "I…I thought this was the ladies' room."

The other man followed her out. "She was fooling around with the lockers."

The clerk's hold tightened on her arm. "Maybe we should call the cops."

Things were going from bad to worse. "No, please, I was here last week, and I thought I'd left my hairbrush in the locker I used. For some reason, I got mixed up and went in the men's area."

"Open your purse," the clerk demanded.

"What?"

"You heard me. We've had things stolen out of the lockers recently. What did you take?"

Lillie stared indignantly back at the clerk, attempting to appear defiant rather than afraid. Her job. Her reputation. So much was at stake.

"I told you what happened," she insisted.

"And I told you to open your purse."

The man gripped her arm even more tightly, and he pushed her forward toward a small office. "That's it, lady. Maybe you'll be more responsive when you talk to the police."

"Is there a problem?"

Relief buckled her knees as Lillie recognized the voice and turned to see Dawson holding up his CID identification and leveling an intense gaze at the clerk.

"Someone's stealing from our customers. We found this woman in the men's locker room. She refuses to open her purse so I can see if she's taken anything."

"I'm sure there's been a mix-up." Dawson's calm voice appeared to ease the tension in the clerk's stance. "Release her arm, and she'll open her purse." Dawson raised his brow at Lillie.

"Of course I will," she said quickly, relieved when the clerk dropped his hand.

Lillie followed Dawson's suggestion and removed her wallet and a package of tissues so the clerk could view the few items that remained in her handbag.

"As I told you," Lillie said, feeling confident again with Dawson at her side, "I walked into the wrong locker room. My mind was somewhere else."

The clerk didn't seem totally satisfied with her explanation and, once again, Dawson came to her aid.

"A perfectly logical mistake." He smiled at the clerk.

"I'll ensure the lady finds her way out. Call Fort Rickman CID if you ever have trouble with military personnel here at the bowling alley."

He slipped his card into the clerk's open hand. "We work closely with the local police. In fact, I was with Sergeant Pritchard this morning. You probably know him."

"Sure." The clerk nodded. "He bowls on Tuesday nights."

Dawson withdrew a twenty-dollar bill from his pocket and offered it to the clerk. "Tell Pritchard the first game's on me. You keep the change."

The man's face brightened. "Will do." He glanced at Lillie. "Sorry for the confusion, ma'am."

"And I apologize for the mix-up."

Dawson took her arm and hurried her toward the door.

"What were you doing?" he asked, his easy demeanor a thing of the past as soon as they stepped outside.

"I told you. I got confused."

"You were checking lockers in the men's room, Lillie. That wasn't smart. When I left this morning, I said I'd be back after work. Why didn't you wait for me?"

"I don't need a bodyguard."

Dawson's eyes focused on a guy slumped behind the wheel of a Chevrolet Suburban parked across the street. She followed his gaze and felt a chill sweep over her.

"A bodyguard is exactly what you need." Dawson continued to stare at the Suburban as the driver started his engine and drove out of sight.

"Was that the same car as this morning?" Lillie asked.

"The only thing I saw was an army sticker on the back bumper."

She shivered. "Just like the car that ran me off the road."

"Which is why you shouldn't be here."

"I need to find out what the key unlocks."

"That's my job, Lillie. Your job is to stay safe."

She shook her head. "I'm going to keep searching."

"You're doing no such thing."

She put her hands on her hips. "You can't tell me what to do. Besides, I don't appreciate being followed."

"I drove into town and saw your car. Easy enough to know you were inside. The bowling alley is on the road from post."

"But you were looking for me."

He shrugged. "I wanted to ensure you didn't get into trouble."

Which had happened when the man at the bowling alley grabbed her arm.

Dawson raised his brow and stared down at her, making her skin tingle. "The way I see it, Lillie, you need to do two things. Number one: go home. Number two: don't get involved."

"Those both entail getting me out of the picture, and that's not happening. There's an option you haven't mentioned."

"What's that?"

"We work together." She shrugged. "If not, we'll say goodbye here."

"You're being headstrong and foolish."

She straightened her spine and leveled him with a confrontational glare. "People have said many things about me, but I won't give up or give in. A man died this morning before he could tell me something about my mother. I have to find out what he wanted me to know."

"You're putting your life in danger."

She nodded. "If so, then I do need a bodyguard." Before she could stop herself, she quirked her brow. "You seem to be volunteering for the job."

Dawson was as determined as she was and had left her no choice but to suggest they team up. Hopefully, she wouldn't regret making the offer.

Then looking into Dawson's blue eyes, which sparkled with an audacity that matched her own eyes, she realized the CID agent kept showing up when she was most in need. Surely it was only a coincidence. She shouldn't worry, but Dawson's father was an ex-con. Maybe the handsome CID agent had secrets of his own. Secrets involving her mother's death and what had happened long ago or secrets about what had caused a man to be murdered on her front porch this morning.

Either way, Dawson was the last person she should be working with yet, at the present moment, she had nowhere else to turn. She needed answers that perhaps only he could provide.

SIX

Dawson kept Lillie's Honda in sight as he followed her across town to a small gym that smelled like floor mats and sweat. A few lockers stood against the wall in the common area. Lillie tried the key but with no success, and before anyone noticed them milling about, Dawson escorted her back to her car.

"The main workout center is on the other side of town." He opened her car door. "Follow me. If there's a problem, flash your lights."

The scent of her perfume wafted past him and made him want to step closer and breathe more deeply. Her dark lashes fluttered over her cheeks, and her lips parted ever so slightly as if she wanted to say something. Maybe that she appreciated his help.

All too quickly, the moment passed. She slid behind the wheel and nodded for him to close the door.

Dawson would let her pretend to be Miss Independent, but he'd seen behind her strong facade this morning when she sat huddled on the couch in her living room.

Traffic in town was light, and Lillie followed close behind him as they headed to the newer facility. Parking next to the gym, he noticed the Fort Rickman stickers on a number of the cars in the lot.

"Must be a popular place," Dawson said as Lillie joined him on the sidewalk.

"You're not a member?"

He smiled. "I use the gym on post."

When they stepped inside, Dawson was impressed by the rows of treadmills and elliptical machines, the rack of weights and other bodybuilding equipment available to the members. Maybe the state-of-the-art facility was worth the hefty membership and monthly fees.

The locker rooms were on opposite ends of the central workout area. A number of men looked up as Lillie headed toward the ladies' room. Dawson kept watch to ensure no one bothered her.

He didn't have long to wait and was relieved when she reappeared. Lillie shook her head and dropped the key into his hand. "Only a few of the lockers were in use. No luck with the key."

Dawson found the same thing in the men's changing area. The entire trip seemed a waste of time until they headed for the parking lot and spied Captain Mark Banks digging in the backseat of his BMW. Standing next to the general's aide was a big, burly guy with a shaved head and massive biceps.

Mark pulled out a workout bag and slammed the door before he noticed Dawson and Lillie. He swaggered toward them, smiling. "You two don't look like you're dressed for working out."

"Just wanted to check out the equipment." Dawson flicked his gaze over the expensive Beemer. "Seems like a top-of-the-line facility."

"Tom Reynolds runs the place." Mark pointed his

thumb to his beefy friend, probably early forties, and introduced Dawson and Lillie. "Tom keeps the equipment running like clockwork. Ten times better than what we have on post."

Dawson extended his hand. The beef had a killer grip.

"Good to meet you." Tom flicked his gaze to Lillie. "Ma'am."

"Do you also manage the smaller gym on the other side of town?" she asked.

Tom shook his head. "That's a private operation. Karl Nelson brought in this franchise. I've been the manager for the last five years."

"Invite Tom to post to advise our gym director on how to upgrade," Dawson told the aide.

Mark nodded. "Remind me on Monday, Lillie. I'll run it by General Cameron."

The look on his face confirmed what Dawson already knew. The general's aide was interested in Lillie. She probably hadn't noticed.

Tom Reynolds dug in his pocket and pulled out two small cards. "Here're a couple free passes good for a week of workouts. See if you like what we've got to offer."

"Will do. Thanks."

"You two stay safe." Mark smiled at Lillie as both men headed toward the front entrance.

Dawson pointed her toward their cars. "Something about that guy bothers me."

She shrugged off his comment. "Mark's nice enough, although he sometimes thinks he's the man in charge instead of General Cameron."

Maybe Dawson didn't have to worry about Lillie,

after all. As pretty as she was, working in the same office with the general's secretary could take a man off track, which is what Dawson needed to ensure didn't happen to him.

"Where to next?" he asked.

"There's a bus station downtown."

"You lead the way this time."

They parked on a side street in the older section of Freemont. A number of buildings sat abandoned, and the few businesses still in operation looked as if they were hanging on by a thread.

The sun sat low in the sky, casting long shadows over the abandoned storefronts and sagging facades badly in need of repair. His eyes searched the area for anything that spelled danger.

"Stay by my side." His right hand flexed closer to his hip, aware of the weight of his weapon. He didn't want anything to happen, but he was prepared in case something did occur. "Maybe you should have remained in the car."

"You've been watching too much television, Dawson. This is Freemont, Georgia." Then, as if realizing her error, she raised her hand to her throat. "I almost said nothing happens in this small town."

He touched her elbow. "You don't have to do this if it's too difficult."

"Yes, I do."

The bus station had a musty smell, as if rising water from the nearby river had at some point flooded the aged structure. Fluorescent lights cast the terminal in an artificial glow that made Lillie's face look paler than usual. Wide-eyed, she glanced at the row of lockers on the back wall.

A clerk, wearing a cardigan sweater and bow tie, stood behind the counter. Two men were slumped in chairs, chins on their chests. Threadbare jackets and well-worn shoes screamed "down on their luck." A woman with platinum hair and too-bright lipstick sat with her arm around a little boy, not more than eight or nine, who fiddled with a small electronic device he held in his hands. She gazed at Lillie and Dawson with tired eyes and then checked her watch. A fourth patron sat on a far bench, his face obscured by the newspaper he was reading.

The clerk raised his brow, but before he said anything, a bus braked to a stop at the side of the building. The driver stepped through the double glass doors. "Got any passengers for me, Harry?"

The clerk nodded in his direction before announcing, "The six p.m. bus to Atlanta is now ready to board."

Taking up his post at the door, he prepared to collect the tickets as the four adults and one child slowly gathered their belongings and lumbered forward.

Dawson motioned Lillie toward the lockers where, once again, she tried the key. Glancing over his shoulder, Dawson watched the blonde woman hug the little boy, who was apparently traveling on his own. The clerk waited as she gave the boy final instructions to sit behind the driver and to call Mama when he arrived at his destination.

Turning back, Dawson pointed to a locker on the bottom row. "Try that one."

Lillie inserted the key. The lock clicked open. She glanced up at Dawson and smiled.

Both of them bent down and stared into the compartment, big enough for a suitcase. Dawson's elation plummeted, seeing the empty space.

"Only bus patrons are allowed to use the lockers."

Dawson bristled at the sound of the clerk's voice. He didn't want to show his CID identification and raise the clerk's suspicions or have him call the local authorities. Some of the good old boys on the force didn't cotton to sharing information with the military. Pritchard had seemed guarded this morning, and although Dawson planned to notify the police if they found anything, he wanted the CID to have the first look at evidence they uncovered.

The man moved closer.

Lillie closed the locker and stood. She handed the key to the clerk. "My uncle bused in from Atlanta last week. He has a memory problem. We're worried it might be the start of Alzheimer's. He was sure he had left something in the locker, but it was empty."

The clerk's frown faded. "I understand completely. We're just glad your uncle used our bus service. Anything I can do for you, just let me know."

"You've been most helpful." Lillie placed her hand on Dawson's arm and turned her sweet face toward him. "Well, dear, we need to get home for dinner."

Dawson steered Lillie toward the door. The sun had set, and darkness covered the area by the time they stepped into the chilly night air. Neither of them spoke until they neared their cars.

"I'm sorry we didn't find anything," he said, patting her soft hand.

She smiled before she opened her fist. Even in the half-light from the lone streetlight, he could see the small flash drive.

"Good job," he wanted to say, but when he looked up he saw an SUV with tinted windows parked in an abandoned lot across the street.

"Get in your car, Lillie. Lock your doors and drive back to post headquarters. I'll question the guy in the car and keep him here. As soon as I'm satisfied he's not a threat, I'll follow you to post."

She started to hesitate.

"Now."

Dawson kept his eyes trained on the Suburban as he crossed the street, relieved when Lillie's headlights disappeared from sight. Before he could get close enough to the parked vehicle, the engine purred to life, tires screeched and the SUV raced away in the opposite direction from post.

Dawson had made a mistake thinking he could detain the driver, but at least the SUV was headed away from Lillie. Once again, he saw the military decal on the rear bumper. Only this time he saw the license plate as well.

Raising his cell, he hit speed dial for CID headquarters. Corporal Otis answered. Dawson relayed the number. "Find out who owns the vehicle."

"Roger that, sir."

"And get back to me ASAP."

Darkness settled in around Lillie's car as she headed along the winding road that led to Fort Rickman. Overhead, tree limbs swayed in the night. The temperature had dropped. She turned up the heater and adjusted the vent, but even with the warm air blowing over her, she still felt cold.

Glancing at the rearview mirror, she saw approaching headlights. Her heart pounded, and her throat went dry, remembering the light-colored Suburban. The same man who had come after her earlier today could be barreling down on her once again.

She pushed on the accelerator, determined to stay well ahead of the vehicle. It had big, boxy headlights elevated well off the ground that marked it as an SUV.

Lillie glanced at her cell phone in the passenger seat, wondering whether to call Dawson and tell him she needed help.

Another, more frightening, thought circled through her mind. Dawson kept talking about Lillie being in danger. What if the man who had killed Granger had come after his son?

A queasy feeling settled in the pit of her stomach. She pulled her left hand from the wheel and rubbed it over her abdomen, hoping to quell the upset.

Her heart lurched again when she saw the lights nearing even as she increased her speed.

She pressed down on the accelerator, willing her car to go faster. At any moment, she expected to feel the huge sports vehicle crash into her rear fender and send her swerving off the road.

Her hands gripped the wheel.

A cry escaped her lips.

Her phone rang, but she ignored the sound and focused totally on the road.

An intersection loomed ahead. She had no choice but to keep moving forward.

"Please, God." She prayed no one would be approaching from the other direction.

The trill of her phone continued to fill the car. The

reflection from the headlights blinded her. Her heart exploded in her chest.

She charged through the intersection, expecting to be hit either from the rear or by some unknown driver approaching on the side road.

In the blink of an eye, the SUV was gone.

A rush of nausea swept over her. Her head pounded with delayed tension, and tears of relief and confusion clouded her vision. She blinked them back, trying to determine what had happened.

Before she could put the pieces together, she saw another set of headlights not far behind her. Once again her cell rang.

She pushed the phone to her ear.

"Lillie?" Dawson's voice. "I'm right behind you. You're safe. Ease up on the gas and pull to the side of the road."

"But—"

"You're okay, Lillie. The Suburban turned at the intersection."

Still unsure of what had happened, Lillie decelerated and angled off the road. She kept the engine running and her foot poised on the accelerator until she saw Dawson step from his car.

"I lost the guy in town," he said as she stumbled onto the pavement. "He was headed north, away from post. Evidently he circled around and caught up to you."

Dawson stood in the glare of the headlights, big and protecting. Once again, he had saved her.

She felt dizzy with the rush of emotions. Suddenly she didn't know whether to cry or laugh so she did both, causing Dawson's eyes to widen and his arms to reach for her.

Lillie's knees weakened, and for one glorious moment, she fell into his outstretched arms. Her heart beat against his and the fear left her, replaced with another feeling that caused her to be equally as emotional. Tears overflowed her eyes and cascaded down her cheeks, tears of gratitude that Dawson had arrived in time.

She'd been alone for so long and had never thought she needed or wanted anyone else in her life. At this moment, she realized her desire to go through life alone might have been a mistake.

SEVEN

Dawson didn't want Lillie to leave his arms, but they were on a lonely stretch of back road and exposed both to the dropping temperature and to anyone who might be watching and waiting in the night.

"Let's get back to Fort Rickman." He looked into her tearstained face. "You'll be safe on post."

He had given her his handkerchief earlier. Now he wiped her tears with his fingertips, wanting to touch her cheeks and trail his hands through her hair.

Holding himself in check, he gave her an encouraging hug before he walked her to her car. "Can you drive?"

She nodded and sniffed and tried to smile at him with that determined expression she used to cover her own insecurity.

"I'll follow close behind you. I don't think he'll come back tonight."

"If it hadn't been for you—"

"The Suburban turned off the road and raced away, Lillie. That's what you need to keep in mind. Besides, I never should have let you leave the bus station alone."

"No, Dawson. I…I owe you my—"

"You don't owe me anything. Now get behind the wheel, and we'll meet up at your office. My cell phone will be on."

She nodded and tried to appear strong, but Dawson was worried. Lillie had to be exhausted and in shock from the string of incidents that had happened, one after the other.

He planned to call Pritchard in the morning and fill him in, but first he needed to see what was on the flash drive—information Granger's killer or killers didn't want brought to light?

Dawson followed Lillie while he flicked his gaze back and forth, searching the surrounding area. Thankfully, they only passed a few cars along the way. He sighed with relief when both he and Lillie passed through the main gate and headed toward her office.

Once parked, they walked along the sidewalk and up the stairs together. Dawson's attention was on the darkness and anyone who might be hiding in the shadows. Although it was doubtful the elusive Suburban had gained access to post, Dawson wouldn't let down his guard.

Lillie had a master key to the main door. The staff duty noncommissioned officer, Howard Murphy—a sergeant with a square face and serious eyes—met them in the hallway. Lillie introduced Dawson and made an excuse about needing to catch up on some work, which the NCO seemed to accept, before she led Dawson upstairs to the general's suite.

Once there, she shrugged out of her coat and hung it on a rack. "I could make coffee."

He nodded. "That's probably a good idea."

The smell of the rich roasted beans filled the office

as he took off his coat and loosened his tie. Even without caffeine, he knew he would spend another sleepless night. At least until he was sure Lillie was safe. Maybe then he'd be able to relax.

"Cream or sugar?"

"Neither, thanks."

She poured the coffee and handed him a mug. He took a long swig of the hot brew and watched as she stirred sweetener and two packets of creamer into her own cup. Since they had entered post headquarters, Lillie had seemed more composed, as if she had stepped back into the role of the very competent administrative assistant to the commanding general.

Whether she was totally in control or showing her emotions, Dawson wasn't sure which side of Lillie he liked better. Certainly he didn't want fear to be the reason she allowed him to see behind her tough facade, but if truth be told, he was drawn to the woman who exposed her feelings. As much as he tried to focus on the investigation, he would never forget the way she felt in his arms.

Dawson couldn't think about that. Not now. Not when she was looking at him and waiting for him to tell her what they should do next.

He motioned her toward her computer. "Let's see what's on that flash drive."

Lillie sat in her desk chair and slipped the small memory device into the USB port. She opened the file that popped up.

Dawson leaned over her shoulder. He drew closer, inhaling her perfume and enjoying the feel of his arm against hers.

As he watched, Granger's face appeared on the

screen. Dawson had only seen photographs of his father while he was still alive. Now he stared at the angular jaw, gray hair and wrinkled face, hardened by the elements from years of working construction.

The ex-convict's eyes were guarded and cautious. He glanced over his shoulder as if to ensure he was alone.

"My name is Granger Ford. I've uncovered information about a number of crimes that occurred twenty-five years ago. Hopefully, what I've found will eventually lead to Irene Beaumont's killer. I loaded the information into a jump drive and hid it in the locker at the bus depot. If you're watching this, you found the memory device. More information needs to be uncovered so Irene's killer can be arrested and brought to justice."

Granger's deep voice sounded from the speakers. The same voice Dawson had heard over the phone just a few nights earlier—a voice and a request to meet, both of which Dawson had rejected.

A weight hung heavily over his shoulders. He knew he had made a terrible error. Granger had wanted to share information with his son. If Dawson had put his personal feelings aside, his father might still be alive. Instead Granger had turned to Lillie for help, hoping she would continue the search for Irene Beaumont's killer.

Now, leaning close to her, Dawson knew he couldn't let his personal struggle with his father cloud his ability to be an effective agent. He also had to ensure his desire to protect Lillie didn't get in the way of uncovering the truth. Somehow her mother's death played into his father's murder.

Right now, Dawson needed answers, yet the lives both he and Lillie had created for themselves could be destroyed in the process. If the investigation uncovered too many secrets from the past, she could lose her job on post. Similarly, Dawson's chance for promotion might end once the truth about his father came to light. The stakes were high, and they needed to move forward carefully.

Would either of them be hurt as the truth was revealed? Only time would tell. And right now, Dawson and Lillie were running out of time.

Lillie stared at the computer screen, seeing the man who had pounded on her door less than twenty-four hours earlier. Sitting at her desk with Dawson hanging over her shoulder caused her neck to tingle with a mix of apprehension and attraction. Although tired, she was also on edge and anxious to hear what the video would reveal.

Granger seemed equally anxious and glanced repeatedly to where a cheap reproduction of an oil painting hung askew over a double bed.

Lillie recognized the bedspread. "He's at the Hi-Way Motel."

Dawson nodded. "You're right." His breath fanned her cheek. She forced herself to concentrate on the monitor.

"Someone knows I'm getting close to learning what happened to Irene Beaumont," Granger said on the screen. "If I'm killed, I hope whoever has these files will continue to investigate on their own."

With a drawl, Granger laid out the backstory. Slowly, methodically, he talked about the jobs he had picked up working construction in various towns around the South, including the times he had been employed by Nelson Construction.

"On-site, the guys were tight-lipped," he said from the video. "After work, with a few beers under their belts, they talked. Property theft was a fact of life. Everyone knew the steel drum had been stolen. Probably from Nelson's company."

Lillie pulled in a sharp breath when he mentioned a woman's body found near the river.

"Irene Beaumont had left Freemont years earlier and had abandoned her little girl," Granger continued. "Although I kept my opinions to myself, I felt the woman had been wrongly judged by the entire town."

Lillie scooted her chair back as if to distance herself from Granger's statements, but the video continued to play.

"At the time, I wondered why the police hadn't made more of an effort to find Ms. Beaumont instead of writing her off as a bad mother who wanted nothing to do with her daughter."

Granger sucked air through his thin lips. "I had been working for a few weeks on a short-term project with Nelson Construction when she initially went missing, but I moved on to another area of the state after that job ended. When I returned to Freemont ten years later, I never suspected the police would come after me."

Dawson leaned in closer.

"At the time, I was staying at the Hi-Way Motel. They ransacked my room and found Mrs. Beaumont's picture stuffed under the mattress."

Lillie turned from the monitor.

Dawson touched her arm. "We can stop the video if it's too difficult to watch."

She shook her head and slipped from her chair. Wrapping her arms across her chest, she walked to the window and stared out into the night, wanting to clear her mind.

Dawson approached her. She could see his reflection in the window. Eyes wide, brow raised, he lifted his hand to her shoulder. The tenderness of his touch eased her internal struggle. She swallowed down the lump of confusion and regret that had threatened to suffocate her only moments earlier.

"I'm being foolish, Dawson. We need to know what's on the video. All of it."

"I can watch and tell you what Granger said."

She shook her head. "No, she was my mother. I need to hear everything."

"Maybe tomorrow, Lillie."

She turned to face him, never expecting his concern to be such a powerful draw. She wanted to move even closer and rest her head on his shoulder and allow his arms to encircle her.

Granger's voice drawled on from the computer, but her focus was on Dawson's eyes and the depth of his own struggle that reached out to her like a lifeline.

"We're in this together, Lillie," he said. She wanted to believe Dawson, but right now she wasn't sure of anything, especially when it involved a CID agent whose father had been accused of murdering her mom.

Dawson might be grieving, but he was still a cop. Would he remain an ally or would he turn on her and close her out just as the voice from her mother's bedroom—a voice she would never forget—had done that night so long ago?

She glanced at the monitor. "Granger's still talking." Dawson hesitated a long moment before he stepped aside.

Lillie pulled in a determined breath. Returning to her desk, she slipped back into her chair, but she kept her eyes on the computer screen instead of the CID special agent next to her. They might be in this together, but they were coming from opposite directions.

Dawson was looking for clues and evidence and bits and pieces of two murders that were joined over time. Lillie felt like a bystander, watching a drama unfold that was pulling her into the action when all she wanted was to return to the safe and solitary life she had known.

Before Granger had knocked on her door.

Before the bullet had taken his life.

Before Dawson had stepped into her controlled existence with his broad shoulders and blue eyes that saw more than she wanted to reveal.

If she went back to the way life had been, she would be alone again. Dawson wouldn't be there, and at the moment, she wasn't ready to lose him. Someday, in the not too distant future, their paths would part. No telling how she would feel when they said goodbye.

All she knew was at this moment she needed someone at her side. Someone willing to walk with her into the darkness and discover the truth—no matter how twisted it would be—about her past.

At this moment, she needed Dawson.

Dawson watched the video as Granger explained about his trial and the defense attorney who'd seemed less interested in what his client had to say and more interested in copping a plea. To his credit, Granger had refused to plead, knowing nothing could be gained by admitting guilt when he was innocent.

Easy enough to read the writing on the wall, Granger

mused on the tape, his face drawn. "The prosecution needed someone to pin the murder on, and I had a bull's-eye painted on my back."

When the video stopped, Dawson turned to Lillie, concerned about her well-being. "It's getting late. Why don't you take a break?"

"We have two more files to open, but a cool drink of water sounds good. There's a small refrigerator near the conference room."

Dawson followed her down the hall and paused beside a table on which a model of the new Fort Rickman Museum was displayed. The three-story structure was surrounded by large cement flowerpots and shade trees. A path headed toward the nearby river where benches provided picnic areas for visitors to enjoy after touring the facility.

He whistled under his breath. "The layout's pretty impressive."

"Karl Nelson used an Atlanta architect who's well thought of in the South." Lillie reached into the refrigerator.

"Maybe I should have cut him a little slack this morning."

She smiled. "He and his father have done a lot of good. Burl Nelson's memory is revered because of the work he did to ensure Fort Rickman remained open when many posts were forced to close. Without the military, Freemont would go back to being a sleepy little farm town."

Lillie handed a bottle of water to Dawson. "Karl has funded a lot of businesses in town and helped a number of folks. After my mother's body was found, he stopped by my foster parents' house, visibly upset that the steel drum had been from his own construction company, even though everyone knew it had been stolen. My foster parents were good people, but they didn't have anything extra. Karl insisted on paying my tuition and books at a small college not far from Freemont."

No doubt about it, Dawson had misjudged the construction mogul.

"When it came time to find a job," she continued, "he made a few phone calls. I had to go through the application process, but I was eventually offered a position on post."

"And worked your way up to the top."

She shrugged. "It's a respected job with good benefits, which I want to keep."

Dawson understood the deeper meaning to her statement. Lillie didn't want anything about Granger's death and the investigation to tarnish her standing with the general or the civil service administration that had hired her. He glanced down at the museum model, knowing she didn't want anything to affect the building project either.

Water bottles in hand, they returned to her desk. The next file they opened was a text document that contained three women's names.

"Somehow the women must tie in with what Granger found." Dawson wished he had more information.

Lillie opened the last file.

Granger's face reappeared. "With long hours to kill in prison, guys talk, sometimes more than they should."

Dawson's inner radar told him to pay attention. He leaned closer to the screen.

"A guy named Leonard Simpson told me his dad owned a bar in Atlanta. Some college kid got drunk one night over the Martin Luther King weekend and talked about three prostitutes his brother had killed."

Lillie's eyes widened. Her hand flew to her mouth.

"The women in the previous file," Dawson said, making the connection.

"The college kid claimed their bodies would never be found," Granger said on the video.

Dawson's gut tightened.

"They would never be found," the ex-con repeated. "Because the three women had been placed in steel drums and buried underground."

EIGHT

Dawson and Lillie searched the internet to find more information about the three women listed on Granger's flash drive, but without success. Lillie was unable to hide her fatigue. Dawson encouraged her to relax on the couch and close her eyes.

Glancing up from the computer, he was relieved when she finally fell asleep. Rising from the desk chair, he reached for a throw that lay on the opposite end of the couch. Opening the plush velour, he covered her arms and legs and smiled as she cuddled into the warmth of the blanket.

Hopefully she'd get some much-needed rest. Returning to the computer, he accessed his own email and opened the attachment from Pritchard that contained the picture of Billy Everett. After printing the photo, he logged in to the archives of the Atlanta newspaper and searched for information about the women. Eventually, he located three short fillers on their disappearances, noting the dates the women had last been seen were in consecutive years, all in January.

Wondering if the dates were significant, Dawson plugged them into the search engine. The answer popped onto the screen. The dates coincided with the Martin Luther King Jr. holiday in each of the three years.

What Dawson needed now was something that tied the Atlanta women to Irene Beaumont. The muscles in his neck tensed as he read story after story. He flexed his shoulders and, once again, glanced at Lillie, relieved she was able to rest. Morning would come soon enough. Hopefully by then Dawson would know where to turn next.

Refocusing on the archives, he eventually found a short piece buried in the Metro section. The article made note of the three Atlanta women who had disappeared in different years, but each over the Martin Luther King holiday. Jessica Baxter, the reporter who penned the story, dubbed the three women the "MLK Missing Women."

Because the women were prostitutes, the journalist claimed their disappearances had seemingly gone unnoticed. Homicides were commonplace in Atlanta. Dawson knew the reality of police investigation in a big city and the large number of crimes that went unsolved.

Stepping into the hallway so as not to wake Lillie, he called the Atlanta prison to ensure Leonard Simpson, the convict Granger had mentioned, was still behind bars. Once confirmed, Dawson made arrangements to interrogate Simpson the following day.

His next call was to CID headquarters to check on the Suburban's license plate, which turned out to have been stolen. Whoever was after Lillie knew enough to cover his tracks. Eventually, the guy who had come after Lillie would make a mistake.

Dawson's third call was to the Atlanta police department. After all these years, he doubted anyone would remember the three women who had gone missing, but as the saying went, nothing ventured, nothing gained.

The police sergeant who answered his inquiry seemed less than willing to search through the files of missing women. He sighed over the phone when Dawson pressed the issue. "Do you know how many missing-persons cases are reported in Atlanta each year?"

Dawson got the message. He thanked the sergeant for his time and, on a hunch, called the Atlanta newspaper. The night-shift reporter who answered was more accommodating than the cop, but what he told Dawson was equally frustrating. Jessica Baxter had retired from the paper five years earlier.

Dawson was batting zero. "Any chance you could contact Ms. Baxter? Tell her the Criminal Investigation Division at Fort Rickman is interested in information about the MLK Missing Women." He provided his name and cell number, but feared the message would never be relayed and would prove to be another dead end.

Discouraged, Dawson returned to Lillie's office and stared out the window, wondering what the new day would bring. Hopefully, Leonard Simpson would confirm the story Granger had provided. A lot of years had passed, and the trail of the missing women could be not only cold, but completely obscured by time.

While Lillie slept, Dawson retrieved his gym bag and a change of clothes he kept in his car and used the shower facilities outside the duty NCO's office. Dawson accepted a box of doughnuts from Sergeant Murphy.

Returning to Lillie's office, Dawson perked a fresh pot of coffee. As he drank the first cup, he couldn't keep his eyes off Lillie's sweet face. Her beauty was more than surface. Over the past twenty-four hours, he had seen glimpses of the inner strength and courage that made him admire not only her beauty but also her resolve to learn more about her past. Yet that determination could also get her in trouble if she charged into areas that were outside her realm of expertise. For her own safety, Lillie needed to leave the investigation to him.

As first light of dawn warmed the distant sky, Dawson touched her shoulder. Her eyes flew open.

"You fell asleep." He smiled at the mix of emotions that played over her face, first confusion, then recognition, then embarrassment as she pushed aside the throw and pulled herself up to a sitting position.

She raked her fingers through her hair in an attempt to adjust the wayward strands into a semblance of order. The beguiling locks invited his touch. He stepped back to ensure he didn't succumb to the temptation.

"You should have awakened me earlier," she said. "I closed my eyes for a moment, never expecting to sleep all night."

"You were exhausted." He handed her a filled mug. "See how you like my coffee."

She took a sip and smiled. "Perfect."

Dawson pointed to the box of doughnuts. "Sergeant Murphy stopped by the bakery this morning and brought back breakfast."

"Did he ask what we were working on all night?"

"I told him you were on a deadline for a project the general wanted."

She raised her brow. "Stretching the truth?"

"Isn't the general interested in getting to the bottom of Granger's murder?"

"Yes, of course."

"Well, so are we."

Lillie tilted her head. "You changed clothes?"

He nodded. "And showered downstairs."

"Were you on the internet the rest of the night?"

He shrugged. "I closed my eyes for a few minutes."

"I think you're stretching the truth just as you did with Sergeant Murphy." Lillie glanced at her computer. "Did you find anything new?"

"The significance of the mid-January disappearances. Each of the three Atlanta women disappeared over the Martin Luther King holiday."

Lillie's eyes grew wide. "The kid who claimed his brother buried women in steel drums talked to the bar owner over the MLK weekend."

"That's right." Dawson handed her Jessica Baxter's article. "I also found this."

Lillie quickly read the piece. "Call the newspaper and talk to the reporter. She might have more information."

Dawson almost smiled at her enthusiasm. "I already did. Unfortunately, Ms. Baxter retired from journalism a number of years ago. The guy I talked to said he'd pass on my message, but I'm not holding my breath."

He handed Lillie the picture of Billy Everett. "Does he look familiar?"

She shook her head. "Growing up, I didn't know many people in Freemont. My foster parents lived in the country. After my mother's body was unearthed, I was homeschooled."

"What about the missing Atlanta women? Anything familiar about their names?"

"Nothing comes to mind. Do you think their disappearances have bearing on my mother's death?"

"Granger made note of their names, so he must have thought there was a connection. I plan to drive to Atlanta today and talk to the convict."

"Leonard Simpson, the man Granger knew?"

"That's right. I want to hear the story from his own lips and then track down his father. Hopefully he might be able to provide more information."

"Which could lead to my mother's killer?"

"You said you were born in Atlanta, Lillie. Maybe the killer knew her there and followed her to Freemont."

Her face clouded. "Are you sure you're not making too much of a leap between what happened to my mother and the three women who disappeared in Atlanta?"

"What else do we have to go on?"

She placed the mug on the table and rubbed her hands over her arms. "How's Billy Everett play into the picture?"

Dawson shrugged. "The motel clerk saw him hanging around town. Granger was looking for information about your mother's murder. He could have contacted Everett."

Lillie nodded. "And Everett could have told the killer that Granger was snooping around."

"It's hard to know what's relevant, but the important thing right now is to keep you safe. You need some place to stay while I'm out of town. Do you have a girlfriend you could visit?"

She shook her head.

"What about your foster parents?"

"They live in the country and are getting on in years. I don't want them brought into the situation."

"They love you, Lillie."

"And I love them, which is exactly why I want them kept out of this. Besides, I'm going with you to Atlanta."

"No way."

"I'm as involved as you are, Dawson, maybe more so."

"A prison's not the place for a woman."

"Then I'll wait outside in the car."

"You're staying in Freemont."

"I'll follow you to Atlanta. You can't stop me."

Working on her own, Lillie could get into a lot of trouble, especially with someone on the loose who wanted to do her harm.

Keeping Lillie close was the only way Dawson knew to keep her safe, and the most important job was doing just that.

Sitting next to Dawson in the passenger seat, Lillie realized she might have made a mistake to insist on going with him to Atlanta. He hadn't wanted her to tag along, but she wanted access to the information he might not otherwise share with her. She seemed to be the only one insisting they were in this investigation together. Dawson was always encouraging her to stay safe while he put the pieces of the puzzle together.

Leaving Freemont, they had stopped at her house so she could change out of her slept-in clothes from yesterday. Once on the highway, Dawson remained silent, as if focusing on something other than the headstrong woman sitting next to him.

Lillie watched the mile markers tick off their progress. By midmorning, they had accessed the connector into the heart of the downtown area and, after a series of turns, pulled into the parking lot at the state prison.

Looking through the car window, Lillie sucked in a shaky breath, feeling intimidated by the huge stone structure. Entering the building seemed even more threatening.

After Dawson signed them in, two prison guards escorted them through a maze of security checks. Sliding steel doors opened, allowing them access into a series of protective barriers, and then clanged shut behind them as they headed deeper and deeper into the interior of the confinement facility.

Lillie's neck tingled with apprehension. She glanced at Dawson, who must have been aware of her unease. He placed his hand on the small of her back and drew her ever so slightly closer as their footfalls echoed down the long, tiled corridor.

Finally seated at an interrogation table, they watched as Leonard Simpson, in his late forties with a receding hairline and pasty complexion, was ushered into the room.

After introducing himself and explaining he was on official CID business, Dawson asked the convict a number of questions about how he had known Granger Ford and the various topics they had talked about while incarcerated.

Eventually Dawson wove his way to the reason for their visit. "Granger said your father owned a bar in Atlanta and mentioned a bizarre story that involved three Atlanta women and steel drums."

A spark of interest flashed from the convict's eyes. "The drunken college kid who spilled his guts one night about the three prostitutes."

Leonard shook his head as if even he couldn't believe the kid's stupidity. "Everyone thinks a guy that goes to college is supersmart. That's what Granger thought. Always talking about his own kid who got a degree through the military."

A muscle in Dawson's jaw twitched.

"I got tired of hearing about what a good kid he was and how proud Granger was of him." Simpson glanced at Lillie. "You know what I mean?"

"What...what else did he say about his son?" Lillie asked.

"Granger's former girlfriend didn't let him contact his son. Some kind of deal they made. It ate at him. Probably why Granger talked about the kid so much. Especially after he got involved with the Christian prison ministry." Leonard sniffed and eyed Lillie. "You know how people are after they get religion. They want everyone to know about the mistakes they've made. How they need to do something good to make it up to the person they hurt."

Lillie glanced at Dawson. She could see the tension in his neck and the way his fingers gripped the edge of the table.

"How had Granger hurt his son?" she asked.

"Not being there for the kid. Granger said the Lord had forgiven him, but he needed to beg forgiveness from his son as well." Simpson flicked dust off the table and stretched back in the chair. "Fact was, Granger believed what the chaplain told him about God's love and mercy. When his case was overturned, Granger was sure God had given him a second chance. Said he was going to find the real killer so his son would know the truth."

Dawson let out a ragged breath and then leaned across the table. "Let's go back to the college kid in the bar. What did he tell your father that night?"

"That his brother killed three hookers and buried them in steel drums." Simpson pursed his lips. "Upset my dad real bad. He didn't know what to do."

Dawson continued the questioning until, seemingly satisfied with the information, he finally asked, "Did your father ever see the college kid again?"

"You'd have to ask him."

"Which is exactly what I plan to do."

Leonard provided his parents' address before the prison guard prepared to escort him back to his cell.

The convict sniffed, his eyes on Lillie. "If…if you see my parents, tell them I'm okay."

"Maybe you should consider talking to the chaplain," she offered. "The lessons Granger learned about love and mercy are for all God's children."

Simpson narrowed his gaze. "Just tell my mama to keep praying for me."

Dawson remained silent as they left the prison grounds. Lillie knew he was probably thinking about his father. He needed time to process what he had heard, especially about Granger being proud of Dawson.

"I could use a cup of coffee," he finally admitted as they headed through the downtown section of Atlanta.

She spied a colorful awning in the distance. "There's a coffee shop in the upcoming block on the right."

They parked on the street. Once inside, Dawson pointed her toward a table by the window while he stood in line to place their order.

Lillie glanced at the stream of traffic outside, noting a number of light-colored SUVs with tinted windows. Although she should have felt safe, she couldn't shake the anxiety that had wrapped around her ever since entering the prison.

A few Saturday shoppers walked along the sidewalk, carrying purchases in plastic bags. None of them seemed the least bit threatening, yet Lillie couldn't overcome the feeling that someone was watching her.

She drummed her fingers on the table and tried to think of something—anything—except three Atlanta women who had been murdered long ago.

A car horn blew. She looked up in time to see a white SUV swerve away from the curb and into the flow of traffic. Her heart lurched when she noticed the army decal on the rear bumper, exactly where the decal had been on the sport-utility vehicle that ran her off the road.

Her neck tingled. She flicked her gaze back to where Dawson stood waiting in the long line.

A man bumped into her table as he walked past. She couldn't see his face, but she did see the backpack strapped over his shoulders and his unkempt red hair. Billy Everett's picture came to mind.

Before she could get Dawson's attention, the guy had left the coffee shop and disappeared into a throng of people passing by. Surely the redhead hadn't followed them to Atlanta.

Once again, she looked at the street where three teenage boys huddled together on the sidewalk. One of them, a muscular kid with baggy pants that hung from his hips, pointed to her through the window. His friends raised their eyes, their smiles guarded.

The big kid led the others into the shop. Lillie grabbed her purse. Tension pounded across her forehead that felt as if it would explode. She stumbled out of the chair, relieved to find Dawson walking toward her.

"What's wrong?" he asked, as if sensing her distress.

She nodded toward the boys. The teenager with the

baggy pants said something to the guy behind him as he sidled down the aisle. Nearing her table, the kid stopped short.

His eyes focused first on Dawson and then on the weapon visible on his hip. The teen pursed his lips and shrugged, then pointed the other two boys to a large table in the back of the shop, where three teenage girls waved. Dawson stared at them until they took their seats and huddled together, laughing.

Taking Lillie's arm, he ushered her toward the front of the shop and grabbed their coffees on the way outside.

She breathed in the cool winter air, feeling suddenly foolish. "I…I kept thinking someone was watching me."

"From all appearances, the three boys were meeting their girlfriends for coffee."

He was right, of course. "I'm a little paranoid."

"More than a little, but you have every right to be apprehensive, which confirms you should have stayed in Freemont."

She straightened her shoulders. "Then I would have been worried about you."

Dawson's lips twitched as he opened the car door for her. She slipped into the passenger seat and let out the breath she had been holding. His aftershave lingered in the car. Her insides turned to jelly, not because of the masculine scent, but because of everything that had happened.

Despite what she had told Dawson, she wanted to run back to Freemont and the security of her home, but after the tragedy that had played out yesterday morning, her home was no longer a safe haven.

Dawson started the ignition and pulled into the

stream of traffic. She stared at his strong hands gripping the wheel and knew her life had changed forever.

For better or for worse?

Definitely for the worse.

Dawson couldn't stop thinking about the prison interview. Leonard Simpson had confirmed Granger's story, but he had also mentioned the chaplain who preached words of love and forgiveness. Without prompting from Dawson, the convict had also shared Granger's belief that his prayers had led the University of Georgia law students to review his case and seek to right a wrong.

After a number of years on the job, most CID agents had a sixth sense about those who chose to walk on the path of darkness, and Dawson's gut feelings usually proved to be right. This time, he couldn't come to terms with his father's newfound faith, yet Leonard seemed convinced of Granger's transformation.

How could someone who turned his back on his own child find solace in the arms of a just God? As far as Dawson was concerned, Granger's change of heart was just a convict trying to come to grips with his past. Right now, Dawson needed to keep his eyes open and focused on the case.

He turned his attention back to Lillie. "Leonard Simpson verified everything Granger said on the video."

"Do you believe the story about the college kid and the murdered women?"

"Guys like to brag. Having a tale to tell, like the bar incident, gives a convict status. That's why we're going to visit his dad."

Dawson's phone rang. He raised the cell to his ear. "Timmons."

"My name's Jessica Baxter. You contacted the newspaper last night and said you wanted to talk about the MLK Missing Women."

Dawson flicked his gaze to Lillie. "The reporter," he mouthed before pushing the phone closer against his ear.

"I'm with the Criminal Investigation Division at Fort Rickman, Georgia," he told the woman. "We're investigating a homicide that occurred approximately twenty-five years ago in Freemont. I'm trying to determine if that murder is related to the three women who went missing in Atlanta."

"What do you want to know?" the journalist asked.

"How did you determine the disappearances of the women were related?"

"The girls lived in the Techwood Drive area of Atlanta."

"The projects near the Georgia Tech campus?"

"That's right. The area was torn down just before the 1996 Summer Olympics."

"Surely more than three women have disappeared in the city. Did you have other evidence to link them in addition to where they lived?"

"Printed T-shirts were left in their cars."

The journalist had Dawson's full attention. "Go on."

"The shirts were custom-made, similar to what college kids wear for special-event weekends. These particular shirts were to commemorate the MLK weekend."

"Did the police determine where they had been purchased?"

"Unfortunately, no. The cops came up empty-handed."

"And no additional women went missing?"

"That's right."

"What about your gut, Ms. Baxter?"

"How's that?" she asked.

"What's your gut tell you about the missing women?"

"They were murdered, and a serial killer was on the loose for those three years. I never could determine what stopped him from killing again."

She paused for a moment before adding, "I always thought the killer was trying to leave a message or a clue or a warning, perhaps."

"What kind of warning?"

"Who knows? I'm just telling you what I thought back then. The women disappeared more than twenty-five years ago. Their bodies have never been found, and the killer could be still on the loose. You might be the right man to bring him to justice."

"I'll let you know if I find him."

"I'll be praying for your safety and your success."

NINE

Dawson drove along the winding two-lane that wove through an older residential area in the suburbs of Atlanta. Lillie checked the street addresses, searching for the house where Leonard Simpson's parents lived. The community had been beautiful at one time, but the homes had aged, and many had fallen into disrepair.

On the way, they had passed a number of vacant strip malls and closed gas stations, providing further evidence of the neighborhood's decline with the passage of time.

Lillie pointed to a faded number painted on the curb. "Two-forty. The next house on this side of the street should be two-forty-two."

Dawson pulled into the driveway and helped Lillie from the car. His gaze focused on the one-story ranch with a small, screened side porch and two large oak trees that would provide shade in the summer.

Together they walked along a cracked sidewalk toward the small front porch. A handmade sign had been taped over the doorbell. *Bell Broken. Knock.*

Following the instructions, Dawson rapped twice. Footsteps sounded inside the house.

A lock turned, and the door opened a crack. Eyes stared at them over a chain lock still in place.

"Mrs. Simpson?" He held up his identification. "I'm Special Agent Dawson Timmons, from the Criminal Investigation Division at Fort Rickman."

The elderly woman read his ID then searched his face as if ensuring he matched his picture.

"Is this about Leonard?" she asked.

Dawson nodded. "We saw him earlier today and wanted to confirm information he provided."

The guardedness in her expression lifted. "You talked to my boy?"

"Yes, ma'am. He looked healthy, ma'am."

"And sends his love," Lillie added before she introduced herself.

"Just a minute." Mrs. Simpson closed the door. The guard chain rattled before she opened the door, this time wide. "Why don't you folks come in and tell me about Leonard."

"Thank you, ma'am." Dawson waited until Lillie stepped across the threshold before he followed her inside. The living room was neat and clean.

"Sit down, please." Mrs. Simpson pointed them towards the couch. "I could perk a pot of coffee."

Dawson held up his hand. "Thank you, ma'am, but that won't be necessary."

"Perhaps some sweet tea?" she offered.

"A glass of tea would be very nice," Lillie said before Dawson could decline the offer.

The old woman's face twisted into a smile. "I baked cookies this morning. They'll taste good with the cool drink."

"Harriet?" a male voice called from the rear of the house.

"Yes, dear." She hesitated, waiting for a reply. When none came, she glanced at her guests. "That's my husband, Charles. He stays in bed most days, but he loves when people visit."

She motioned them toward a narrow hallway. "Follow me. You can chat with him while I get the tea and cookies."

Dawson nodded optimistically at Lillie.

"Charles, these are some nice army folks who know Leonard," Mrs. Simpson said as they entered the bedroom.

The elderly man sat propped up against a pile of pillows with a heavy crocheted afghan thrown over the bedding, giving another layer of warmth to his fragile body.

His wife introduced them and then asked Dawson to open two folding aluminum chairs.

"It's good to meet you, sir." Dawson arranged a chair at the foot of the bed and invited Lillie to sit.

"These people talked to Leonard today, dear."

Recognition played over Charles's face.

Harriet excused herself and headed for the kitchen while Dawson settled into the second chair, which he positioned closer to the infirmed man's bedside.

"Your son looked fit, Mr. Simpson. He's doing well."

"Leonard..." The old man drew out the name. "He's a good boy."

His eyes glistened with pride for a son who had killed a convenience-store clerk in an armed-robbery attempt. Perhaps age or dementia had obscured Mr. Simpson's memory of his son's felony offense.

"Sir, I'm with law enforcement at Fort Rickman, two hours south of Atlanta. I'm investigating a murder that occurred in nearby Freemont, Georgia, which may have ties to a young man you spoke with at your bar years ago. Leonard said one of your customers talked about three possible homicides. Do you remember that conversation, sir?"

The old man closed his eyes. Dawson feared he had drifted to sleep.

"Do you recall a customer who talked about burying women in steel drums?" Lillie asked from the foot of the bed.

The tired eyes blinked open. He lifted his shoulders ever so slightly off the pillow, attempting to see her more clearly.

She stood, walked to the opposite side of his bed and patted his hand. "I'm sure your customers sometimes told you more than you wanted to hear?"

He nodded, his gnarled fingers picking at the afghan.

"The young man's story about killing women troubled Charles," his wife said as she stepped back into the room, no doubt having overheard the conversation from the hallway. She carried a tray with four glasses of tea and a plate of sugar cookies.

Placing the tray on a small table in the corner of the room, she handed Lillie and Dawson their drinks and offered them cookies, which they both accepted.

"Thank you, ma'am." Dawson bit into the rich shortbread. "Delicious."

Harriet beamed as she stuck a straw in Charles's glass and held it to his lips. The old man drank greedily and nodded with appreciation when she returned the half-empty glass to the bed stand.

"I told Charles he couldn't take everything to heart, but the story affected me as well." Harriet patted her chest. "The boy said his brother had killed three women. Charles notified the police, hoping they could track down the boy and the victims."

"The Atlanta police?" Dawson asked.

The older woman nodded. "They said a lot of kids tell stories when they're under the influence, but Charles felt there was some truth to this young man's tale."

Dawson leaned closer to the bed. "Do you remember what he looked like, sir?"

The older man rubbed his chin and stared into space.

Harriet helped him out. "Remember, dear, you said he reminded you of our boy."

"Brown hair, brown eyes, medium build?" Dawson ticked off the convict's description and stared down at the old man.

When Charles failed to respond, Harriet nudged his arm. "You remember, don't you, dear?"

"College boy," he said at last.

"How do you know he was in college?" Dawson asked. "Did he mention the name of his school?"

Mr. Simpson pointed a shaky hand to his own chest. "His shirt."

"Did it say something about the MLK holiday?"

"G—"

"UGA?" The University of Georgia campus was in Athens, about an hour drive from Atlanta.

Charles closed his eyes for a long moment. "G…T."

"Georgia Tech? Did you ever see the guy again?"

The old man shook his head.

"What did he tell you, sir?" Dawson needed to ensure Leonard's details were accurate.

"His...his brother killed three women. Buried them in steel drums."

"Do you remember the year?"

A frown played across Charles's drawn face.

Harriet helped him out. "Leonard went to jail that spring, Charles. It's been twenty-five years."

She turned to look at Dawson with serious eyes. "I've been praying for our son ever since, and for those women as well." Wringing her hands, she added, "I've been praying for the killer too. That he'll tell the police where he buried the bodies. Think what those families have endured by not being able to come to closure about their children's disappearances."

Dawson continued to question Charles, but neither he nor Harriet could recall anything else about the young man that night.

After thanking the couple for their hospitality and help, Dawson and Lillie headed back to his car. Before he backed out of the drive, the Simpsons' door flew open. Harriet flagged them down from the porch.

Lowering his window, Dawson called to her. "Is something wrong, ma'am?"

"It's Charles. He remembered the boy in the bar."

A plane flew overhead, and the sound drowned out her voice. "What's that, ma'am?"

She cupped her hands around her mouth. "The boy from Georgia Tech..."

Dawson waited until a car drove past the house.

"Could you repeat what you just said?"

She walked down the steps and stood on the sidewalk. "Charles remembered something else about the boy from Georgia Tech." She pointed to her head. "The boy had red hair."

* * *

"Is Billy Everett the redhead?" Lillie asked as Dawson pulled out of the driveway.

"From what Pritchard mentioned, it seems unlikely he went to Georgia Tech."

"But the college kid said his brother committed the crimes."

"Then we need to find out if Billy Everett has a brother with red hair who attended school in Atlanta."

Lillie stared out the window as they left the Simpsons' neighborhood, lost in her own thoughts. Dawson seemed focused on the road, and they rode in silence for a period of time, until the freeway appeared in the distance.

He glanced at his watch. "It's late in the day, and we haven't eaten. Let's get some food before we head back to Freemont."

"There's a diner about thirty miles south of the city that's known for fast service and home cooking," she suggested.

"Sounds good."

Snippets of information kept floating through Lillie's mind. "Maybe if we go over what we know so far, something might fall into place."

Dawson smiled. "You're thinking like a cop. Go ahead."

She held up her finger. "First of all, we're looking for a Georgia Tech college student with red hair?"

Dawson nodded. "That's right, and if what he said in the bar was true, his brother killed three women. Any idea how many kids from Freemont High get accepted to Tech each year?"

She shrugged. "Not many. The school has stiff entrance requirements. Standardized test scores have to be high, and good grades are a must."

"I'll call the high school on Monday and see if the guidance counselor can give me a list of anyone who attended Tech twenty-five to thirty years ago. Hopefully, the records will still be on file."

"Excuse my pessimism, but it's not much to go on, Dawson."

"Sometimes the smallest scrap of information can be the missing link that pulls an entire case together."

"What if the Georgia Tech student and his brother weren't from Freemont?" Lillie asked. "Suppose they were from Atlanta or knew my mother when she lived in the city."

Dawson nodded. "The killer could have found out where she was living and come after her in Freemont."

Instead of finding clarity, Lillie was more confused than ever. "If he killed my mother in Freemont, why had he killed the women in Atlanta first?"

"When were you born?" he asked.

"October twentieth." She provided the year.

"The first woman listed on the flash drive disappeared three months after your birth."

"What does that prove?"

Dawson shook his head and let out a deep breath. "Nothing. But let's go the other direction."

"You mean nine months before I was born?"

He nodded. "That's right. Nine months earlier would be the month in which you were conceived."

Lillie did the math. "That would have been January."

"As in the MLK weekend." Dawson's face was serious as he turned to her. "I think we may have uncovered a connection."

"I'm not following you?"

"Your mother's pregnancy may have upset the killer." Dawson shrugged. "I'm not sure of the reason, but he could have been angry or jealous so he strikes out at other women for three years, always over the MLK weekend."

"To get back at my mother?"

"Maybe. His rage could also have been directed toward your father."

"So he kills three women, then finally comes after my mother." Lillie let out a deep breath. "Which means she died because of me."

Dawson shook his head. "You didn't do anything wrong. He was upset about your mother's pregnancy, not at you."

The diner came into view. "Let's get something to eat. We can pick up where we left off after dinner."

Although Lillie was hungry, she didn't know if food would help unravel the threads of the past that were tied together in a huge knot. Would she ever know what happened so long ago?

She glanced at Dawson as he pulled into the restaurant parking lot. Before Granger died, he had asked her to free them from the past. Would the truth set them free or handicap them even more?

TEN

Full from dinner, Lillie felt her eyes grow heavy on the drive back to Freemont. Dawson had ordered the meat loaf with fresh green beans and mashed potatoes, and she had followed suit. The meal was delicious. Then he had ordered apple pie à la mode and insisted she indulge as well.

At the cozy roadside restaurant, they'd talked about everything except the investigation. His hand had touched hers twice when they reached for the saltshaker at the same time.

Lillie had to admit she enjoyed being with Dawson. He was committed to his job, and like the other army guys she knew, he loved his country and felt privileged to be able to serve. He also liked small towns and Southern cooking and sweet tea, which he had gulped down along with two refills.

The waitress had told them to come back soon, and Dawson said they would. Not that his comment meant anything, but the thought of returning to the city with him, perhaps to tour the aquarium—which they both wanted to see—and stopping again at the quaint restaurant on the way home made her smile.

"What's so funny?" he said, pulling his eyes from the road.

The sun had set, and his face was shadowed by the lights from the dash, causing more than a tingle of interest to meander lazily along her skin.

She shook her head. "Just thinking about the nice dinner. Thank you."

"Thank you for suggesting the restaurant. We'll have to do it again."

Another wave of energy, only this time it did more than meander. She sat up in the seat, knowing her thoughts were getting way ahead of where their relationship was going.

Note to self. Dawson is investigating his father's death, not taking me home from a date.

For some reason, she preferred thinking about the date and found her eyes growing heavy once again.

"I'm not good company." She laughed.

"You don't have to worry, Lillie. Go ahead and close your eyes."

He was right. She didn't have to worry with Dawson. For so long, she'd been on her own. The McKinneys had been there for her growing up, but her foster parents had tried to keep her insulated from the town gossips with homeschooling and living on the farm. Lillie had never felt a part of anything, not even the country church community that had welcomed her with open arms.

The problem wasn't with the congregation or the McKinneys. It was with her. She always kept up her guard so she wouldn't be hurt again. She'd even kept up her guard with God.

Tonight she didn't want to think about anything that had to do with the past. She wanted to think about eating mashed potatoes and gravy and meat loaf with a man whose eyes made her think of bright sunshine and blue skies.

Lillie's cheeks burned when she realized she had drifted to sleep and had been dreaming about Dawson.

He took her hand in his own and rubbed his fingers over hers, which made her flesh feel alive and brought delightful tingles to her neck.

Their exit appeared in the distance. Dawson squeezed her fingers before he released her hand to make the turn. Once off the exit ramp, he steered the car along the back road that led past the Hi-Way Motel.

They were back to where they had been yesterday morning. He was the cop, and Lillie was a witness in the investigation.

What had she been thinking? As soon as the investigation was over, Dawson would be working on something else, and maybe in the future he'd be reassigned to another military post far away from Fort Rickman and Freemont.

She pulled her hand through her hair, chastising herself for being so foolish. She wasn't made to share life with a man. Especially a good man like Dawson.

She had her job, her house and a future working at Fort Rickman. She didn't need anything else. But when she looked at Dawson again, she realized she was deluding herself. A happily ever after was what every girl dreamed of having in her life. Although not every dream came true.

Surely, Lillie was asking too much.

Dawson had a hard time keeping his eyes on the road with Lillie sitting next to him. He flicked his gaze toward her when she wasn't looking and studied the fullness of her lips. It made him want to pull to the side of the road and take her in his arms. Which, of course, he didn't do, nor would he while the investigation was still in progress.

Besides, Lillie wasn't interested in him except for the help he could provide in finding out about her mother's death, which she had mentioned more than once. Although during dinner she had seemed to relax and enjoy herself. When she laughed, his own mood lightened as if they were connected and nothing could pull them apart. Foolish of him to think that way.

She had drifted off to sleep, and he hadn't been able to stop himself from reaching for her hand. At the time, it seemed such a natural response after their day together.

Passing the Hi-Way Motel brought back memories of yesterday morning. Granger had hidden Billy Everett's picture in a spot where Dawson had failed to look. Now it appeared the redhead might be involved.

The train trestle appeared overhead. Dawson squinted into the darkness, trying to see what was hanging from the bridge.

He lifted his foot off the accelerator. Blood rushed to his neck. Adrenaline, mixed with a chilling fear, turned his veins to ice.

A boulder, large, gray, deadly, dropped from overhead.

He swerved. The huge rock crashed against the edge of his right fender with a loud *whack*.

Feeling the car lurch, Lillie gasped. Her hand reached protectively for the dashboard.

Dawson pulled to the curb. Throwing open the door,

he stepped into the night, his eyes searching the bridge for any sign of the person or persons who had hurled the giant boulder.

Seeing nothing except the pine trees that bordered the road, he rounded the car and studied the deep dent in his front fender.

Lillie watched him through the window, her eyes wide. Dawson's stomach sickened, realizing if he hadn't swerved, the rock would have shattered the windshield and crashed into Lillie.

He turned away, unable to look at her, because all he could see was her bloodied body and the terrible what-could-have-been consequences of the falling rock.

The car door opened. She stepped onto the pavement and stared up at the now-empty trestle. "It wasn't an accident, was it?"

He swallowed down the bile that had filled his throat. "Rocks don't drop from the sky or from train trestles."

Pulling his phone from his pocket, Dawson tapped in a series of digits. "I'm calling Pritchard. The entire area needs to be searched."

To his credit, the police officer promised to be there within a few minutes. Dawson didn't want Lillie to wait in the open for the cruiser, not when she was a target. He slipped his arm over her shoulders, as if his closeness would offer protection.

"You need to get in the car," he said. "Hunker down in the seat. I'll stay out here until Pritchard arrives."

"You're worried someone's still in the area?"

"He's probably long gone by now." Dawson smiled, trying to make light of the situation yet knowing full well that Lillie saw beyond his attempt to soft-pedal the deadly seriousness of what had happened. "I just want to keep you safe."

He squeezed her shoulder and opened the door. She hesitated before slipping onto the leather seat, then hit the lock and smiled weakly when he gave her a thumbs-up through the window.

With determined steps, Dawson walked to the rear of his Camry and felt under the fender. A siren sounded, approaching from town. He brushed off his hands as the police sedan pulled to the side of the road. Pritchard stepped onto the pavement.

A second car braked to a stop. Pritchard instructed the two officers who emerged from the cruiser to climb the rise and look for anything that might indicate a person had been on the trestle.

Once they hustled off, the lead cop approached Dawson. Still sitting in the front seat, Lillie glanced at Pritchard over her shoulder.

"Evening, ma'am," he said through the window.

Turning back to Dawson, he raised his brow. "You folks out for a nighttime drive?"

"We were coming back from Atlanta."

"Something happening in the city I should know about?"

Dawson didn't want to divulge anything. At least not yet. If and when he pulled the pieces of this very strange case together in some type of order, maybe then he'd be more forthcoming.

"We went out for dinner."

"Long way for a meal." Pritchard stared at Dawson with dark eyes. "Ms. Beaumont is a witness in a murder investigation. Seems strange you'd ask her out on a date."

"It wasn't a date."

Lillie stepped from the car and joined the men.

"How was Atlanta, ma'am?"

Dawson kept his gaze fixed on the trestle. Pritchard was fishing, trying to get Lillie to divulge the real reason they had been in the city.

She wrapped her arms around her waist. "Getting away from Freemont for the day was good for both of us."

"Sir," one of the officers called down to Pritchard. "We found a gum wrapper."

"Bag it." Pritchard glanced at Dawson. "Although a gum wrapper doesn't prove anyone was lying in wait."

Dawson tensed. "The boulder couldn't have dropped on its own."

Frustrated with the small-town cop who seemed to have his own agenda, Dawson stooped down and felt under the fender of his car.

"Looking for something?" Pritchard asked.

"A hunch. That's all." Dawson's fingers touched something small and metallic. He yanked the attachment free and stood to examine the device in the light from the police cruiser.

"What is it?" Lillie asked.

Dawson turned it over in his hand. "A magnetic GPS tracking device."

She raised her brow. "They followed us from Atlanta."

Pritchard stepped closer. "Someone thought you were doing more than enjoying a good meal."

Dawson didn't respond to the cop. He was looking at Lillie. No wonder the killer had been able to pinpoint their whereabouts and the exact moment when they drove under the trestle.

The rock had missed the windshield, but only barely. Dawson had to make sure from now on nothing hurt Lillie. Not an out-of-control SUV or a hurled boulder or a killer who seemed to have her in his sights.

Lillie waited in the Camry while Pritchard and the two other officers returned to their squad cars. Worry strained Dawson's face when he slid into the seat next to her.

He gave her a tepid smile that did nothing to lift her spirits. No matter where they turned, the killer—or killers—seemed one step ahead of them.

"I gave Pritchard the tracking device." Dawson started the engine and pulled onto the roadway. "He'll try to determine who purchased it and where."

"I don't see how they'll be able to find the buyer. In fact, I doubt we'll ever know who's behind all this."

Dawson held out his hand. She placed hers in his, buoyed by the warmth of his touch.

"Finding the GPS system was a plus for our side. No doubt they hoped to keep track of our movements for days."

"How long has it been attached to your car?"

"Probably not more than a few hours. We were inside the prison for quite a while. The parking lot was accessible to anyone who happened by." He squeezed her hand. "The important thing is that you're safe."

"And tired. I'll be glad to get home."

"With everything that's happened, I don't want you to stay in your house tonight. You can get a room on post in the Lodge."

She sighed. "I know you're thinking of my own well-being, but I want to go home."

"You want everything to go back to how it was just a few days ago."

Dawson was right. That was exactly what she wanted.

"What about your foster parents?" he asked. "You said they live in the country. The killer or killers might not look for you there."

"Or they might and then my foster parents would be placed in danger. Besides, I don't want them to know what happened. They rarely leave their farm, so I'm sure they haven't heard about Granger's death yet."

"Hasn't the story run in the local papers?"

"The Sunday edition went to press a few days ago. The next issue won't be out until Wednesday."

"Your parents deserve to know what happened, Lillie. Call them and ask if you can stay until Monday morning. By then, this might be behind us."

"I think you're being overly optimistic."

"Please, Lillie, if you won't do it for yourself, then do it for me. I don't want anything to happen to you."

Dawson's concern touched her deeply, and an unexpected lump formed in her throat. He sounded sincere, but she was a witness in his father's murder investigation, which was probably the reason he was worried about her safety.

No matter what he had meant by the comment, she knew complying with his request was the wisest and safest thing to do.

"Drive me home, Dawson. I need to pack a few items, no matter where I stay tonight."

He smiled. "Now you're being smart."

Lillie didn't feel smart. She felt trapped in the middle

of a huge maze. Glancing at Dawson, she wondered if he felt the same way.

Once his father's murder was solved, he would move on to the next case. Where would that leave Lillie? At home in her little house with only the memory of the CID agent who had made her feel safe.

ELEVEN

Dawson was relieved when Lillie agreed to spend the rest of the weekend with her foster family, although she insisted he also spend the night there.

"They have a guest room," she told him. "And my mother's a great cook."

The thought of another home-cooked meal was tempting. An even stronger draw was getting to know the folks who had taken Lillie in as a child. They had to be good people.

The cop side of him hoped they might provide additional information about her mother's death and Granger's trial. He also hoped Lillie would let down her guard and share some of her own struggle with him.

Dawson pulled into the driveway of her own small, secluded home. The crime-scene tape had been removed from the front porch, but they still entered her house through the kitchen, as if the spot where Granger had died was consecrated ground upon which neither of them wanted to tread.

Once inside, Lillie headed to her room, while Dawson lounged on the couch. He closed his eyes and felt the tension that had built up over the past two days ease.

A nice place to call home. Surprised by the thought that came unbidden, he stood, realizing he had become much too comfortable. Lillie appeared soon thereafter with an overnight bag in hand, which he took from her and carried to his car.

Driving through Freemont, Dawson kept watch in his rearview mirror to ensure they weren't being followed. As an added precaution, he made a series of turns and checked for any sign of a white SUV. Once he was certain they were on their own, he followed Lillie's promptings and eventually headed west into the rural farmland.

Lillie directed him along a number of back roads. Hopefully, the rather difficult-to-find location of the McKinney farm would keep trouble at bay, or at least prevent anyone who wasn't familiar with the area from finding her.

"My mother will like you," Lillie said when Freemont was far behind them.

"What about your dad?"

"He'll want to know what you do and why you're with his daughter. Mom will be more direct. She'll think we're dating. If the conversation turns to weddings, just play dumb."

He laughed. "She thinks it's time for her daughter to find a husband?"

Lillie smiled. "In her day, women married young. She's afraid I'll be a spinster for life."

Dawson turned his gaze to Lillie's long legs and slender body and tried not to chuckle at her foster mother's concern for her daughter's future. The only reason Lillie wasn't taken was because she hadn't found the right guy.

At least, he hoped she didn't have someone waiting in the wings. Or stationed at another army post.

Shoving the thought aside, he said, "So what happens if they ask about my intentions for their daughter?"

Lillie glanced at him, her lips smiling and her cheeks pink with embarrassment. "If they go that far, I'll step in and rescue you. They mean well, but they can both be overly exuberant."

"You're lucky, Lillie."

She raised her brow and stared back at him. "You mean because they took me in?"

"Because they love you."

She bit her lip. "Sometimes I think I didn't appreciate them enough growing up." She was quiet for a long moment and then asked, "How's your relationship with your mom?"

He weighed his answer. "It's hard to explain. She always tried to justify the mistakes she made in life."

Lillie shifted in her seat. He could feel her gaze. "You weren't a mistake, Dawson."

"My mother claimed falling in love with Granger was the problem. She expended too much effort trying to convince herself she didn't love him and that he wasn't worthy of her love."

"How did that affect you?"

"If my father wasn't worthy, I figured I wasn't either. I kept hoping my dad would come back to Cotton Grove and take me away with him."

Lillie arched a brow. "Did he ever return?"

"Only once. One of my friends saw him with my mom. I was in school at the time. I thought he'd pull me out of class, but he didn't."

"From what Leonard Simpson said, your mom didn't want Granger in your life."

Dawson swallowed, hoping to end a conversation that was headed where he didn't want to go.

"Did you ever ask her about your dad?" Lillie pressed.

"I learned early on not to bring up his name."

"Where's your mom now?"

"Still in Cotton Grove. She works for a local grocery chain."

"But you don't talk to her?"

He shrugged. "I call her at Christmas and holidays."

Dawson kept his gaze on the road, and they rode in silence until Lillie indicated the next turn and then pointed to a small farmhouse that sat on a rise in the distance. Floodlights illuminated the two-story white structure and a portion of the long driveway and expansive front yard.

Two wooden rockers sat on the porch.

Dawson parked next to the house and helped Lillie from the car, wondering how the welcome home would play out. "Maybe you should have called your parents."

"I did when I was packing," Lillie said. "They're expecting us."

Dawson should have felt relieved. He grabbed Lillie's overnight bag and headed for the front door, concerned he had made a mistake by agreeing to stay the night.

The door opened before they climbed onto the porch and a short woman with a round face, welcoming grin and arms held wide stepped from the house. "Hello, darlin'. Daddy and I were just saying we thought you should be arriving any minute."

After Lillie hugged her mother, she moved aside and

motioned Dawson forward. Without waiting for an introduction, Mrs. McKinney wrapped him in a bear hug that made him smile.

A man, probably in his early seventies, with gray hair and a sun-dried face, came onto the porch. His arms were extended equally as wide as his wife's had been.

"How's my little girl?" he said, embracing Lillie. "Now that you've got that good job on post, we don't see you enough, honey."

Lillie kissed his cheek. "You and Mother can always come to visit me in Freemont."

"You know we're homebodies." Her father stretched out his hand. "Who's this young man?"

Lillie smiled at Dawson, who returned the older man's handshake. "Dawson Timmons, sir. It's a pleasure to meet you."

"Thanks for bringing Lillie home to us. Come in out of the cold." Her father took Lillie's bag and motioned both of them inside.

Mrs. McKinney patted Dawson's arm. "Lillie said you had dinner in Atlanta, but I hope you saved room for dessert. I baked a chocolate cake earlier today."

He looked at Lillie for help.

"Dawson would love some cake, Mother." Lillie winked at him.

"How about you, dear? Surely you can eat a little piece. There's ice cream too."

"Just some cake, Mother. Half a slice."

"Where's your bag?" her father asked Dawson before he closed the door.

"In the car, sir. I'll get it later."

The house was comfortable and inviting, and Dawson instantly felt at ease with the McKinneys' warm welcome. The women headed for the kitchen while Dawson stopped in the living room to admire the assortment of firearms displayed in an antique gun rack. Hanging on the wall next to the weapons were framed awards, evidence that Lillie's father was an accomplished marksman.

"That's quite a collection of guns and awards, sir."

"My daddy always said a man needs to be able to protect his land and his family."

"Yes, sir."

"Who wants coffee?" Mrs. McKinney called from the kitchen.

"Be right there, Sarah." Mr. McKinney pursed his lips as he turned his full attention to Dawson. "You're not a stranger to guns."

"No, sir."

"What are you packing tonight?"

"A Glock, sir. I'm with the Criminal Investigation Division stationed at Fort Rickman."

The older man nodded. "The Glock's a good weapon."

"Yes, sir." Dawson pulled in a breath. "There's something I'd like to discuss with you, sir. Mrs. McKinney needs to know as well."

"Let's have some cake. Then we can talk." Without commenting further, Mr. McKinney headed for the kitchen.

Standing at the counter, Mrs. McKinney cut the cake and arranged the slices on four plates. "There's a potluck lunch after church tomorrow. Everyone will enjoy meeting Dawson."

The smell of fresh-perked coffee filled the kitchen.

Dawson tried to catch Lillie's gaze. "I doubt I'll be able to stay for church, ma'am."

"Do you attend services in the city?"

"The city?" he asked.

"Freemont." Lillie helped him out.

After taking the cake plates from her mother, Lillie placed them on the table. "Dawson lives at Fort Rickman, Mother. I'm sure he goes to church there."

"How nice." Mrs. McKinney smiled broadly.

He didn't have the heart to tell the charming woman that his relationship with God was presently on hold.

"We'd love having you join us tomorrow, if you can spare the time."

Dawson was outnumbered. He could confront armed criminals without flinching, but he had trouble worming his way out of attending church with the McKinneys.

As he bit into the cake and allowed the rich chocolate to melt in his mouth, he smiled at the warm family dynamic. Mrs. McKinney and her husband were committed to one another, and Lillie, whether she realized it or not, was the center of their world.

Bringing up a topic such as her biological mother's murder seemed out of place at this moment. Lillie was right. He needed to bide his time.

After the dishes were washed and put away, Dawson knew he needed to broach the subject Lillie continued to ignore. He glanced at her over the top of his coffee cup.

She shrugged and then sighed. "Mother and Dad, there was an incident outside my house yesterday morning. A…a man was shot."

"Oh, good Lord in heaven." Mrs. McKinney patted

her chest. Eyes wide, she plopped down onto one of the kitchen chairs and stared at Lillie. "Who was it, dear?"

"Granger Ford, Mama."

Her father threw an angry glance at Dawson. "Isn't he still in prison?"

Dawson cleared his throat. "The court reviewed his case, sir. DNA testing overturned the validity of the previous evidence. He was released from prison two weeks ago."

"Who killed him?" Mr. McKinney's gaze remained fixed on Dawson.

"We're trying to track down those who were involved, sir."

Dawson and Lillie quickly gave her parents an overview of what had happened. Neither of them mentioned the driver of the SUV who had run Lillie off the road. Nor did they discuss their day trip to Atlanta or that Granger Ford was Dawson's father. Some things were better left unsaid.

"I felt Lillie shouldn't stay alone in her house and suggested she come here for the weekend," Dawson finally concluded.

Mrs. McKinney reached for Lillie's hand. "I never liked you living by yourself."

"Mama, it's just for the weekend. Dawson feels a suspect may be in custody by Monday."

Her father didn't look optimistic, and her mother shook her head and tsked.

Dawson turned to Mr. McKinney. "The thing is, sir, I knew you would be able to keep Lillie safe. I feel even more confident after seeing your marksmanship awards and gun collection."

Her father nodded, as if somewhat placated by Dawson's acknowledgment of his ability. "If Granger didn't kill Irene Beaumont, then who did?"

"I don't know, sir. That's what the Freemont police are trying to uncover."

"But you're working on the case?" her father asked.

"I've been assigned to protect your daughter. I was hoping you and I could work together over the weekend."

Later when the McKinneys had gone to bed and Lillie was in her room, Dawson went outside to get the gym bag he carried in the car.

He glanced around the expansive front yard and surrounding fields and was stirred by a desire to work the earth. Mr. McKinney had turned off the floodlights, and the sky seemed alive with the glittering stars.

The door to the house opened, and Lillie stepped onto the porch. She waited until he had his bag in hand and then met him on the stairs.

"I told you my mother would want to feed you."

"They're good people, Lillie." He placed his gear on the top step.

She nodded. "I know they are. They gave me a life, and I'll always be grateful."

"But?" He heard the hesitation in her voice.

"I always worry they'll be taken away from me. Just as my mother was."

"Which is why you didn't want to come here."

"And why I didn't want them to know what had happened. I keep thinking if I don't talk about something, it might not be true." She tapped her foot against the bottom porch railing. "As I mentioned, growing up I thought my mother had abandoned me. That's tough on a kid. Then when her body was found—"

She looked into the night and shrugged. "Somehow I couldn't get past all those years of thinking she had left me. I closed her out of my life, and I never let her back in."

He reached for her hand and ran his fingers through hers. "You've got to forgive yourself. You were young and had gone through a terrible experience."

"I thought if I had been a better daughter or if I hadn't been afraid of storms, my mother would have loved me. Every time another storm hit, I was overcome with fright and thought my actions continued to keep her away. Before long, I convinced myself that I didn't want her back in my life."

He glanced up at the house. "Did you tell them how you felt?"

She shook her head. "I kept everything boxed up inside me. They had done so much. I couldn't let them know how I really felt."

"You could talk to them now."

She shook her head. "It's my problem. I'll deal with it."

"You don't have to always be so strong." He stepped closer to her and touched her hair, which was what he had wanted to do since yesterday morning.

Her eyes searched his, and her lips opened ever so slightly. The earth stood still for one long moment. He drank in her beauty and longed to pull her into his arms.

Almost without thinking, he reached for her. She shifted closer, and then, as if both of them had been waiting for this moment, he lowered his lips to hers.

Her mouth was soft and warm and welcoming, and every fiber of his being wanted to keep kissing her forever. Although his eyes were closed, he was sure fireworks illuminated the night sky. He could almost see bursts of color as his heart exploded in his chest. All he could think of was holding her tight for the rest of his life.

She pulled back too quickly. He wanted to kiss her again, but seeing her brow crease and the downturn of her mouth, he dropped his hands to his sides. Instantly, he felt a sense of detachment and a stab of confusion as she stepped back and wrapped her hands around her arms.

"I need to go back inside."

He nodded. She was probably upset that he had kissed her. Without further explanation, she climbed the steps and entered the house.

Dawson didn't follow her. He couldn't. He needed time in the cold night air to steady his pounding heart. His leg throbbed, which he hadn't noticed when Lillie was in his arms.

A car drove along the road. Dawson watched it slowly disappear into the distance. Lillie would be safe here, especially with Mr. McKinney's desire to protect his family.

What he had always wanted most in life was a loving home where he could be accepted. Tonight he'd had a taste of how good that life could be, but this was Lillie's home, not his.

When he stepped back into the house, he found her father waiting for him. "Lillie went to bed."

Dawson knew there was more the man wanted to say. "Yes, sir."

Mr. McKinney pointed to the kitchen. "I put on a pot of decaf. We need to talk."

Dawson followed Mr. McKinney into the kitchen.

He was back to being the special agent. Lillie was a witness to a murder who needed to be protected, even though he wanted her to be so much more in his life. Right now, the investigation took precedence, and Lillie's safety was his paramount concern. Her father probably felt the same way.

But what about Dawson?

Whenever he was with Lillie, he knew he had to guard his heart. She could be his downfall.

Lillie got up early and followed the smell of eggs and bacon to the kitchen. Her father sat at the table, reading the Sunday paper and sipping from a steaming mug of coffee.

Her mother stood at the stove. "Can I fix you breakfast, darlin'?"

Lillie headed for the coffeepot. "Maybe when Dawson gets up."

"He's been outside for a couple hours." Her father's voice came from behind his paper. "Said he wanted to see the place. I took him down to the barn and the livestock pen. Filled him in on how a farm this size operates."

Lillie walked to the window and stared into the backyard, where Dawson was spreading hay for the livestock. "You put him to work?"

"Men like to stay busy, Lillie. Being outside in the fresh air is good for him. Besides, he wanted to help."

"He certainly is a nice young man," her mother said. The upturn in her tone told Lillie about the plans the older woman was already making.

"We're friends, Mother, which I told you over the phone when I called last night."

"Of course, dear. Your father and I are best friends."

Lillie smiled, knowing some battles couldn't be won.

Glancing out the window again, she watched Dawson add feed to the troughs. Then he stamped his feet on the frosty earth and brushed off his hands. "Looks like he's coming inside for breakfast."

"Grab a mug from the cupboard, Lillie, and pour him a fresh cup of coffee."

The back door opened, blowing in a gust of cold morning air as Dawson stepped inside, rosy cheeked and eyes twinkling as he looked at her. "Morning, sleepyhead."

His lazy voice and ruddy complexion, made even more pronounced by the brisk winter air, stirred something deep inside her. *Watch yourself,* a voice warned as a delicious tingle rolled over her body.

"Ready for some coffee?" she asked, trying to come back down to earth.

He held up his hands. "Let me wash up first."

Placing the filled mug on the table, Lillie took the plate her mother had fixed for Dawson and set it next to the coffee, along with silverware and a cloth napkin.

"How about you, dear?" her mother asked.

"I'll just have some fruit." Lillie reached for a banana and pear and placed them on a small plate.

Before she could get back to the table, Dawson had returned to the kitchen, filling the air with the clean scent of soap and the outdoors.

A girl could get used to that combination, she thought as she dropped into the chair he held.

His good manners weren't lost on her father, who always held the door for her mother. He stared at Dawson over the top of the paper and pursed his lips in approval before Dawson found his seat.

Lillie bowed her head as she silently gave thanks, noting Dawson followed her lead and hesitated before he picked up his fork.

"Delicious, Mrs. McKinney," he said after swallowing a rather hefty portion of eggs and grits.

"You worked up an appetite helping Walter."

"I enjoy working with my hands."

Once again, her father eyed Lillie over the paper. "There's an article in the Community Doings section about that new museum at Fort Rickman. The article said Karl Nelson's company won the bid."

"Nelson Construction has done a lot for the people in this town," her mother added as she joined them at the table with her own plate. "Although he's nothing like his father. Burl was a kind and patient man."

Her father folded the paper and raised his brow. "Burl had to have patience to stay with that wife of his."

Mrs. McKinney jabbed her husband's arm. "Now, Walter, no reason to repeat stories. At least Karl takes after his daddy."

"The community is invited to the opening ceremony," Lillie said. "I could get you special seats. You'd enjoy the speeches. The Fort Rickman Army Band will play."

"Why, dear, it sounds lovely, but your father and I rarely get to town. You spend the day with Dawson."

"I'll be working the event," he said.

Mrs. McKinney's eyes widened. "You're not expecting anything dangerous to happen, are you, Dawson?"

"No, ma'am. Just normal security issues." He glanced at Lillie for encouragement.

She smiled, feeling her cheeks warm and knowing the direction of the conversation needed to change. "Dawson's from Cotton Grove, Mama."

"A Georgia boy." Mrs. McKinney couldn't hide the pleasure in her voice. "How nice. Won't you have some banana bread?"

"Thank you, ma'am." Dawson took two large slices before asking, "You folks ever know a local guy named Billy Everett? He attended Freemont High. Red hair. He's got a scar on his cheek."

Mrs. McKinney placed her fork on her plate. "Of course I remember Billy. His family was poor. He was the baby."

"Not the brightest kid around," her father added.

"Billy dropped out of school," Mrs. McKinney continued. "I heard he got into trouble with drugs and did some time in prison." Mrs. McKinney shook her head. "Such a shame."

"Prison does terrible things to a man." Mr. McKinney reached for his coffee and took a long swig of the hot brew. "I don't believe in rehabilitation. Doing time just makes a bad man even worse."

Lillie had never heard her father be so vindictive. "Some folks find God in prison," she said, hoping to turn the conversation in a more positive direction.

"I'm just glad we never had anyone in our family who ended up behind bars. It'd be a black mark for sure."

He folded the paper. "Now if you'll excuse me, I need to get ready for church."

Lillie looked at Dawson and the set of his jaw as he dropped the remainder of the banana bread onto his plate and pushed away from the table.

"Breakfast was delicious, Mrs. McKinney. I need to get back to Fort Rickman."

"Won't you join us for church?"

"Not today, ma'am."

"I'll get my things," Lillie said.

He looked at her, his gaze steady. "You stay here. I'll pick you up tomorrow morning."

"Dinner's at six," Mrs. McKinney said.

"Ma'am, you don't need me underfoot."

"Nonsense. I'm frying chicken. Easy enough to put another plate on the table. We'll expect you at six o'clock."

"Thank you, ma'am."

Lillie followed him to the door, wishing she could say something to soothe the rough moment that had to have hurt Dawson. "My father wasn't thinking."

"He said what he believes, Lillie. And he's right. Most cons return to a life of crime shortly after getting out of prison."

"Your dad was exonerated of any wrongdoing, Dawson."

"He was in prison for fifteen years. Things happen to a man behind bars."

Lillie reached for his hand. "On the phone, Granger told me he had made his peace with the Lord."

"Yeah? Too bad he never made peace with his son."

"He tried, Dawson."

"Maybe, but by then it was too late."

TWELVE

When Dawson arrived back at his BOQ, he was still stewing about Mr. McKinney's comment concerning ex-cons. Lillie's dad had no idea Dawson's father had been incarcerated, and although his comment troubled Dawson, her father had the right to his own opinion on such matters. Besides, Dawson knew the statistics fell in line with what the older man had mentioned.

Law-enforcement personnel were well aware that more than four in ten offenders returned to prison within three years of being released. Recidivism was a national problem and one with no easy solution.

The previous night, after Lillie had gone to bed, Mr. McKinney had talked openly about Irene Beaumont's death and his concern for his daughter. The McKinneys had taken her in as a terrorized four-year-old. When her mother's body had been unearthed, the middle-school-aged Lillie had suffered a setback, and both parents worried about her emotional health.

The prosecutor had talked to Lillie's foster father about Granger's trial. Mr. McKinney had been forthcoming with Dawson concerning his own fear that Granger's guilt had been too quickly decided.

At the time, the McKinneys had been focused on Lillie. They wanted to ensure their daughter didn't experience another setback or more pain than what she had already suffered. In an effort to insulate her from the wagging tongues in town, Mrs. McKinney had decided to homeschool Lillie. In hindsight, they wondered if they had protected her too much.

All in the name of love.

Love was a word Dawson rarely used. Never in conjunction with his mother or his missing father. Hearing it associated with Lillie's name gave him pause. Surely, the way he felt about the pretty secretary wasn't love. Or was it? He thought of her kiss and the way she had molded into his embrace.

As much as he enjoyed kissing her, he didn't like the turmoil of emotion that welled up within him today. Plus, Lillie had pulled away from him last night, so she must be equally confused.

More than anything, she needed closure, which Dawson hoped would come when all the facts about her mother's death were brought to light.

Dawson hadn't told Mr. McKinney about his own personal involvement in the case. Eventually, the two men who cared about Lillie would have another heart-to-heart talk. Although after learning the truth, Mr. McKinney might not want to ever see Dawson again.

His phone rang. He grabbed the cell off the kitchen counter and smiled when he saw Lillie's name on the caller ID.

"I'm sorry about what my father said this morning," she said in greeting.

"It's okay, Lillie."

"He's really a good man, who thinks the best of people. That's why I'm not sure where that comment came from."

"He's worried about you. We shared a pot of decaf last night after you went to bed."

"Oh? Then maybe fatigue was playing into the mix this morning."

Dawson laughed, although when he thought of the cozy farmhouse and her loving parents, he had a pang of regret. Lillie would soon be going to church with her parents. He wanted to be sitting next to her in the pew.

"Something's troubling you," Lillie said as if she could sense his mood. "It's more than my father's comment. You haven't been yourself since you visited the prison yesterday."

"I'm okay."

"I'm sure seeing where Granger had been incarcerated made everything real."

"It was real before, Lillie."

"But you hadn't experienced it firsthand."

He leaned against the counter in the kitchen. "I've been in jails before."

"You came face-to-face with who he was, or who you thought he was, and it hit you. Hard. Then my father's comment this morning drove home the point even more so."

She was right, although he wasn't ready to admit the way his gut had twisted when the door to the cell block closed behind them. Stepping into the prison where his father had lived for fifteen years had affected him, and not in a good way.

"As you told Karl Nelson," Lillie continued, "your father's trial was a sham. He wasn't guilty."

"All we know is that the blood on the shirt wasn't

his, Lillie. That's different than being completely exonerated."

"But if Granger had been guilty, he wouldn't have come back to Freemont."

"Perpetrators often return to the scene of their crime."

She let out a frustrated sigh. "Granger was searching for information and was murdered because of what he uncovered."

Dawson nodded. "You're right."

"Of course I am. You and I saw the videos. We heard his voice and watched as he looked over his shoulder, fearful that the killer was after him."

"We don't know who was after him," Dawson corrected her. "Granger could have made enemies in prison who sought him out once he was released. Cons have friends on the outside who do their bidding. The only thing we do know for sure is that my father was released from prison, and someone came after him. Besides, Lillie, I was more upset about the prison per se, not that my father had been held there."

"I don't understand."

"The four walls seemed to crowd me in."

"You told me you didn't like confined spaces."

He wanted to change the subject, but Lillie refused to let it drop.

She pulled in a sharp breath. "Did…did something happen? Your mother—"

Sensing her concern, he held up his hand as if she could see his nonverbal gesture. "Nothing like that. No abuse. No locked closets with me inside, if that's what you're thinking."

As much as he didn't want to tell her, Lillie deserved

to know. "I worked summer construction jobs during high school."

"Following in your father's footsteps."

Intuitively he knew she was right, but he couldn't admit the truth. "I worked construction because it provided good money. Not because of Granger Ford."

"Are you sure?"

"Of course I'm sure." He pulled away from the counter and stepped toward the window. The sun was hidden from view by a line of clouds. "I was on the job late, finishing a ditch. Must have been seven or eight feet deep and just wide enough for the main sewer pipe. The earth started to crumble. Before I could get out, the sides collapsed, trapping me under a huge mound of dirt."

The memory of being buried alive swept over him again. He was surrounded by the cloying scent of the Georgia clay that blocked the daylight and sucked air from his lungs.

He shuddered, trying to shake off the memory.

Don't look back, an interior voice warned.

Sweat dampened his neck.

Lillie's voice came to him like a warm touch on a cold day. "You survived, Dawson."

"Yeah." He laughed ruefully. "Thanks to the men who dug me out."

"Did your dad know what happened?"

"Of course not."

She sighed. "Ironic that neither of us knew our fathers."

"But it doesn't seem to bother you."

"I never knew my birth father. My foster father was a good man. He filled the empty role."

"What about your foster mother?"

"I…I always held something back, which was probably a self-protective measure, because I didn't want to be hurt again."

Lillie's voice was almost devoid of emotion. He imagined the firm set of her jaw and her braced shoulders. She had her own painful memories from the past, maybe more than she was willing to admit.

Silence filled the line until she finally spoke again. "I…I found something when I was online this morning. It probably doesn't have any bearing on this case, but you said sometimes the smallest item can be important."

"That's right."

"I searched for missing women in the surrounding small towns. I only looked at the month of January."

"What'd you find?"

"Valerie Taylor went missing ten years ago and was last seen on Saturday of the MLK weekend that year. Roseanne Manning disappeared the same weekend."

"Lots of women go missing, Lillie."

"Roseanne was from Millsville, Georgia, which isn't far from Freemont."

"And Valerie?"

"She lived in Culpepper."

Dawson pursed his lips. "Interesting."

"But probably doesn't mean anything."

He glanced at his watch. "Don't you have to get ready for church?"

Lillie laughed. "Sounds like you're trying to get rid of me."

"I'll call you later."

After they hung up, Dawson kept thinking about Lillie's foster family. Being with her parents had made him realize the hole in his own heart and the desire he'd always had to live the kind of life she had known.

Both he and Lillie approached relationships with caution, as if they lived under a yellow stoplight. Most folks rode through life on green, going full steam ahead and never glancing over their shoulders. In comparison, Lillie and Dawson weighed where they were going in relation to where they had been.

He envisioned her sitting in the pew at church and then at the potluck lunch after the service. In his mind's eye, he saw a line of farm boys, bulked up from baling hay, falling over themselves to refill her sweet tea or bring her another slice of Mrs. McKinney's chocolate cake.

Dawson let out a ragged breath. He was being irrational, but no matter how much he tried to focus on other things, he kept thinking about her emerald eyes and full lips, lips he had kissed last night and wanted to kiss again.

He changed into his running clothes and hit the trails around Fort Rickman. The fresh air cleared his mind and pushed aside the crazy thoughts about the country suitors. As soon as he was back at his apartment, he showered and changed and headed through the main gate and back to Lillie's house.

He had good reason to return, he kept telling himself, even as he stood on her porch and saw the surprised look on her face when she opened the front door.

"I decided to visit the town of Millsville, where Roseanne Manning was last seen before she disappeared. I wondered if you felt like taking a drive."

"I'll get my purse and tell my mother we'll be back later."

With Lillie sitting next to him, Dawson's mood lightened. "How was the potluck?" he asked, as if he hadn't been thinking about it nonstop.

"I ate too much." She laughed. "And ran into a lot of folks I hadn't seen in a while."

"Some of the local farmers?"

She nodded. "Mainly I talked to my mother's friends. The folks my age have moved away from the area."

"Probably a few single guys hanging around." As much as he didn't want to seem needy, the words sprang from his mouth.

"No one of interest."

"Really?"

"Of course Jermaine Daniels was there. We had cake and ice cream together."

Dawson's optimism plummeted. "Nice guy?"

"One of the best." Her lips twitched and her eyes twinkled with the laughter she tried to contain.

"What's so funny?" He felt as if he'd missed the punch line of a joke.

"Jermaine is ten years old and the cutest kid in the area." She poked Dawson in the ribs.

He grabbed her hand and laughed. "Okay, so I was thinking about all the men hovering around your table."

"You sound jealous."

"Of course not." But when he looked at her, he knew he was easy to read. "You're right. I was jealous."

"Jermaine's the only one you need to worry about, and I think you can handle a ten-year-old."

He continued to smile, enjoying her playful banter and the sun that peeked out from behind the clouds.

Their Sunday drive ended when they pulled into

Millsville, a sleepy crossroads that appeared to be in hibernation.

The only cars were those parked on the grass around the AME church, where a cluster of men stood talking. The women gathered to the side, dressed in their Sunday finest, including large-brimmed hats in deep russets and reds that accentuated their dark skin.

Dawson helped Lillie from the car. "You talk to the ladies, and I'll see what the gentlemen remember."

The men were friendly and grateful someone was looking into the case of the missing eighteen-year-old. "Roseanne was an attractive child with a wandering spirit. She claimed Atlanta was where she was meant to live."

"Do folks think she left town on her own?"

One of the men shook his head and tsked. "We don't know. Most think something happened to her. Something bad. Her mama died of a broken heart not long after the child disappeared. She never had a daddy, at least not one that stayed around."

Dawson felt his own gut tighten. He could relate.

"When was Roseanne last seen?"

"Martin Luther King Day, ten years ago. She was hanging around some red-haired man from a neighboring town."

The lazy Sunday turned sour. "Anyone recall the guy's name, or do you remember what he looked like? Anything that would make him stand out from the crowd?"

"His hair," one man said, causing the others to nod in agreement. "And the scar on his right cheek."

"What about Valerie Taylor, from Culpepper, south of here. Does her name sound familiar?"

An older man rubbed his jaw and nodded. "Matter a fact, Val and Roseanne were friends. The girls did everything together."

Lillie and Dawson met up at the car. Her eyes were wide as she climbed inside. "I've got something."

Dawson waved goodbye to the church folks before he pulled onto the roadway. "Okay, what?"

"Roseanne had been seeing a boy from Freemont."

"Red hair?" Dawson asked.

Lillie pointed to her own face. "He had a scar on his right cheek and his name was Everett."

"What's that tell you?"

"Billy Everett may be our killer."

"Guess who Roseanne's good friend was?"

Lillie dropped her jaw. "Valerie Taylor?"

"You got that right."

Heading back to the McKinney farm, Dawson felt a weight lift from his shoulders. Billy Everett seemed to be in the middle of this case no matter where they turned. Finally something was paying off. Plus, Dawson planned to clear the air completely with the McKinneys and tell them who his father really was.

A car Lillie didn't recognize was parked in the driveway when Dawson pulled to a stop in front of the farmhouse. He followed her inside and helped her with her coat, which she hung in the hall closet.

Motioning him forward, she headed through the living room with Dawson close behind. "Mother? Dad?"

"We're in the kitchen, dear." Her mother's voice.

As Dawson entered the airy room, a man sitting with Walter and Sarah shoved his chair back from the table.

"Nice to see you again, Agent Timmons." Sergeant Ron Pritchard rose to his feet. "I was talking to the

McKinneys about what's been happening in Freemont. Seems you didn't tell them everything about the murder case."

Lillie took a step forward. "Officer Pritchard, please."

Mr. McKinney stared at Dawson. "Granger Ford caused Lillie enough pain. I don't want her to be hurt again."

"Sir, I can explain everything." Dawson turned to Pritchard. "Why did you come here?"

"I wanted to know if Granger had contacted them." Pritchard smiled at Lillie's parents. "Nice talking to you folks. I'll see myself out."

Dawson opened the front door for the cop and followed him onto the porch. "You've got bad timing."

Pritchard raised his brow. "At least I tell the truth."

"What's that supposed to mean?"

"You weren't forthright, Agent Timmons. Why didn't you tell me Granger Ford was your father? We contacted the prison to see if he had any family. He had listed you as his next of kin."

Pritchard walked toward his car, then, pausing to glance at Dawson, he nodded. "Have a nice day."

Dawson turned to go back into the house. Mr. McKinney stood in the doorway, his eyes narrowed, his mouth pulled into a tight line.

"Maybe you should leave now, young man."

"Sir, I need to ensure Lillie's all right."

"I can take care of my daughter. You head back to Fort Rickman and don't come around here again."

"Sir—"

The door closed and the lock slid into place.

Dawson stood on the porch for a long moment before he hustled back to his car. Mr. McKinney was right. Lillie didn't need an ex-con's son in her life. Especially an ex-con who might have killed her biological mother. How could he and Lillie have a future together when their pasts revolved around a murder?

Now a killer was on the loose.

Although Dawson was committed to keeping Lillie safe, her father—with his arsenal of guns and his awards for marksmanship—would have to protect her tonight.

THIRTEEN

"I'm sorry, Dawson."

Lillie sat next to him as he drove her back to Fort Rickman the next morning. He had called last night and arranged to pick her up bright and early.

"My father reacted without thinking," she said. "He's a good man but extremely protective. Plus, he's worried about me."

She tugged at a wayward strand of hair. "Which is exactly why I didn't want either my mother or father to know about Granger's death."

Dawson tightened his grip on the steering wheel. "In my opinion, Pritchard is a jerk."

"He questioned them about my birth mother's death and the trial. He also wanted to know how they heard about me after my mother disappeared."

"What did they tell him?"

"One of the men from church mentioned a child in need. My mother was a retired schoolteacher. It didn't take long before they were awarded custody."

"Do you know anything about when you first arrived at their house?"

"Only that I didn't talk for a number of weeks.

When I finally did speak, I refused to mention my birth mother. They soon realized I had blacked out everything, except the memory of that night in the storm."

"What about the man's voice?"

"They heard me screaming from my bedroom one night and found me huddled in the corner. I told them not to let the man close the door."

"Your mother's house burned to the ground?"

She nodded. "Not long after she disappeared."

"Was anything salvaged?"

"Only a few trinkets my foster mother boxed up for me." Lillie gazed out the window and settled back in the seat.

Dawson seemed equally lost in his own thoughts until he pulled to a stop in the driveway of her Freemont home. "I'll wait out here while you change for work." He reached for his cell. "Pack a bag for a couple nights. I'll make a reservation for you at the Lodge."

"I'd really like to stay in my own home."

"I know, but we've talked about this before. Your safety comes first."

Lillie smiled and the day brightened. "Actually, I'm grateful you're concerned about me."

While she was inside, he called the Lodge and reserved two rooms—one for Lillie, and one for himself across the hall so he could keep watch over her room throughout the night.

She reappeared, carrying her bag. Dawson met her on the sidewalk and helped her into his car, placing her case behind her seat.

By the time they arrived at Fort Rickman, traffic jammed the entrance to post. Soldiers who lived off post were heading to their early-morning physical training, and the long line of cars snaked slowly through the main gate checkpoints.

"Join me for lunch?" Dawson asked when he parked in front of post headquarters.

"I usually work at my desk through the noon hour, but I could make an exception today."

"What about dinner instead?" he asked. "I'll cook. Although don't expect anything too elaborate. I'm a meat and potatoes type of guy."

"I'll like whatever you serve. Plus I'm willing to help."

She hustled toward the front of the headquarters and turned to wave at him before going inside.

He headed back to his BOQ to shower and change. What would happen today was important and could alter the future of his military career. If Pritchard had uncovered Dawson's relationship to Granger Ford, the CID would be able to as well.

Better to be proactive and let the chief know right away, just as Dawson had wanted to do on Friday. The last thing he needed was for Wilson to hear the news from someone else.

Entering CID headquarters, Dawson nodded to Corporal Otis, who manned the front desk. "How's it going, Ray?"

"Ah, sir, the chief wants to see you in his office."

"Now?"

"He said as soon as you arrive."

The look on the corporal's face wasn't encouraging. "Anything I should know?"

"You know what I know, sir."

Dawson headed for the chief's office. He rapped

three times and opened the door when he heard Wilson's command to enter.

"Morning, Chief." He nodded to Wilson before he noticed the commanding general, sitting in a chair to the right of Wilson's desk. "Sir."

"Come in, Agent Timmons." Wilson motioned him forward. "General Cameron and I have some questions about Granger Ford's death in relation to Lillie Beaumont."

Dawson quickly filled both the chief and the commanding general in on the investigation and the information Granger had saved on the flash drive. He told them about Leonard Simpson and his parents and about the college boy in the bar as well as the three Atlanta women and two younger girls who had gone missing over various MLK weekends.

"I know it sounds somewhat complicated, sirs, but I feel confident the person who killed Granger Ford also killed Lillie's mother. Right now, a man named Billy Everett is of interest. The Freemont police are looking for him."

"You've kept Sergeant Pritchard apprised of what you've found?" Wilson asked.

Dawson swallowed. "Not everything, sir."

"Oh?"

"I wanted to check out the information on the flash drive first."

"Which you did Friday night."

"Yes, sir."

"Then you and Ms. Beaumont drove to Atlanta on Saturday to confirm what Granger had revealed on the video."

Dawson nodded. "Yes, sir."

"And you saw Pritchard that evening as you returned to Freemont, yet you were still less than forthright about what you had uncovered."

"Sergeant Pritchard did not indicate he wanted to share information at that time, sir."

Wilson raised his brow. "Perhaps because you had the flash drive."

"Roger that, sir."

"What did Special Agent Jamison Steele tell you on Friday morning about the investigation?"

"Excuse me?"

Wilson splayed his hands on his desk. "Agent Steele told you to protect Ms. Beaumont and leave the investigation to the Freemont police."

A muscle in Dawson's neck twitched. "Ah, yes, sir. That's correct."

"Yet you proceeded with the investigation."

"I was confirming information I had received, sir."

"What is your relationship to Granger Ford?"

"Sir, he—" Dawson let out a ragged breath. "Anecdotally, I believe he is my father."

"Anecdotally?"

"Yes, sir. His name is not on my birth certificate, but my mother claims he was my father. He was never in my life. In fact, I first talked to him over the phone only a few days before his death, and I never met him face-to-face."

Wilson nodded. "I spoke briefly with Agent Steele this morning. He said you were concerned about your military paperwork because of that very issue."

"That's correct, sir, but I want to assure you Agent Steele did not know about the flash drive or my trip to Atlanta."

Wilson sat back in his chair and tapped his pencil on his desk. "Why didn't you inform Agent Steele?"

"We're severely understaffed, and he was tied up on other cases. I didn't want to pull him away from his own investigations."

Wilson nodded, then turned to the commanding general. "Sir, is there anything you would like to ask Agent Timmons?"

"Ms. Beaumont expressed her concern that the investigation could adversely affect the funding drive for the new museum on post," the general said.

"Yes, sir. She expressed those same concerns to me as well."

"Have you uncovered anything that would paint Fort Rickman in a negative light or anything that would tarnish the military's stellar reputation in south Georgia?"

"No, sir."

"You will continue to ensure Ms. Beaumont's safety?"

"That has my highest priority, General Cameron."

"Excellent."

Chief Wilson raked his hand over his jaw and eyed Dawson before saying, "I expect a full report on my desk by Wednesday afternoon. Share the information you've uncovered with Sergeant Pritchard. He's in charge of this investigation."

"Yes, sir."

"I'll talk to the Judge Advocate General's Corps on post and ask them to review your military file. I don't have to tell you, Dawson, if JAG determines you falsified military records, it could mean the end of your career."

"I understand, sir."

Dawson left the chief's office with a heavy weight on his chest, knowing his time in the CID could be coming to an end. He had told the general that Lillie was top priority, which she was, but finding her mother's killer was the best way Dawson knew to keep her safe. Once the killer was brought to justice, Lillie would be able to return to her own home and the life she had lived before Granger's death. Where would Dawson fit into the mix?

Hopefully not fighting his own court battles about fraudulent military records. Ironic that he could be found guilty just as his father had been. Dawson had never thought Granger Ford's misfortune with the law would rub off on him.

Lillie looked up as Karl Nelson entered the general's suite, briefcase in hand. "Good morning, sir."

"How are you, Lillie?"

"Fine, sir, but I'm afraid General Cameron hasn't arrived yet this morning."

The aide glanced up from his computer. "The general's at CID headquarters."

Which Mark hadn't mentioned earlier. Concern tugged at Lillie. What was General Cameron doing with the CID? Surely it didn't have anything to do with Dawson.

"I'll wait until the general arrives." The construction contractor took a seat on the couch, the same couch Lillie had slept on two nights ago. She noted the afghan needed to be folded and walked over to readjust the throw.

"May I get you some coffee, Mr. Nelson?"

He held open his hand. "Two cups in the morning is max for me, Lillie, so I'll have to say no. Any chance

I could spread out the plans for the museum before the general arrives? I want him to see the updated design that just came back from the architect."

"There's a table in the conference room."

Karl followed her along the back hallway and stopped in front of the museum model. "Beautiful, isn't it?" His full face beamed with pride.

"Yes, sir. It will be a wonderful facility for both the military and civilian communities."

"General Cameron and I plan to name one of the rooms after my dad. He worked diligently throughout his lifetime to help the military."

"That would be a perfect tribute to your father's memory."

Karl smiled. "Thank you for saying so. I'm not sure if folks understand my need to perpetuate his good name."

"Maybe they've never lost a loved one who worked so hard to make the world a better place."

"I appreciate that, Lillie. You're probably right."

When General Cameron returned to headquarters, Lillie directed him into the conference area, where he shook hands with Karl.

Wanting to find out why the general had been at CID headquarters, she slipped back to her desk and called Dawson's cell phone. When he failed to answer, she left a message. Pinpricks of anxiety rumbled along her spine. She shouldn't be worried, but she was.

Pritchard couldn't be trusted to keep the information about Dawson's dad to himself. The CID had probably been notified.

Hopefully the disclosure wouldn't adversely affect Dawson's career. His father had been released from prison because of an inaccurate blood test. Many folks would probably wonder if he should have remained behind bars, just as Karl Nelson had mentioned the day of the shooting.

By the time the contractor and the general finished their meeting, Lillie still hadn't heard from Dawson.

The general escorted the civilian into the outer office. "The sooner you can get the construction completed, Karl, the better."

"My feelings exactly, General. Now that the donations are starting to pour in, I'm feeling even more optimistic. If everything goes according to plan, the museum should be ready to occupy by summer. Just so you know, I've restricted access to the site for safety reasons and instructed my crew to start working on the foundation as soon as possible. As much rain as we've had recently, I want to take advantage of every good day."

"I agree. The ceremony on Wednesday is to build enthusiasm for the project and garner more funding. We'll hold an even bigger celebration when the building is completed."

The general turned to Lillie. "Have we gotten many RSVPs back yet?"

"Yes, sir. More than forty guests will be in the special seating area. Bleachers will be available for folks from town and the surrounding area."

Karl nodded his approval, then winked at Lillie before he turned back to the general. "I hope Lillie and Mark will be able to attend."

The general smiled. "Everyone in headquarters will be there."

After shaking hands, the general returned to his office. Before the construction company owner opened the outer door, he hesitated. "I'm happy you're working here, Lillie, and doing so well for yourself. I never knew your mother, but I always regretted that Nelson Construction equipment played a role in her death."

Lillie appreciated the older man's words. "At least her body was recovered." She paused, thinking of the names on the flash drive. "I fear there might be other women who have suffered the same demise, yet they'll never be found and their families will always wonder what happened to them."

Karl nodded, his face drawn. "There's so much sorrow in the world these days. Even within families. Sometimes the person we know best can cause us the most pain. Human nature is hard to understand. I was fortunate. My dad was a great man. He lived a life of virtue, the way I try to live mine." Karl pursed his full lips. "Big shoes to fill. I'm just glad the museum will be a lasting reminder of the man he really was."

Lillie wished she could remember her own mother in such a positive way. Just as Karl had said, those closest to a person often caused the most pain. Growing up, Lillie had thought she had done something wrong that had made her mother abandon her.

Although she hadn't told Dawson, Lillie had never looked in the box of her mother's mementos that had been saved from the fire. Secretly, she feared it would contain proof her mother hadn't loved her.

By noon, Lillie knew what she had to do. She told Mark she'd be back later and headed for her car. In the parking lot, she met up with the bodybuilder manager from the Freemont gym.

Tom Reynolds greeted her with a warm smile. "Mark's taking me to the post fitness center to work on a reciprocal membership for military personnel with our facility in town."

"Good for you, Tom."

He shrugged off the praise. "Actually, Karl Nelson came up with the idea. He's always trying to help the army guys and gals."

"Karl was here earlier but didn't mention anything about the gym agreement."

"Probably because he's so focused on the new museum."

"He did say donations have been pouring in, which makes all of us happy."

"You'll be at the ceremony Wednesday?" Tom asked.

"I wouldn't miss it."

Once off post, Lillie grabbed her cell phone and left a message for Dawson.

"I can't meet you for lunch. There's something at my house I need to get, which shouldn't take long. Don't worry. I'll be fine."

As she drove through Freemont, dark clouds appeared overhead. She needed to hurry so she could get back to headquarters before the rain started to fall.

Pulling into her driveway, she felt a sense of relief, as if everything had been blown out of proportion. No one had followed her. She could make a quick stop and be back on post within the hour.

She entered through the front door, wanting to return to her normal life, and shoved thoughts of what had happened aside. Walking purposefully through her living room, she continued on into the hallway where she had huddled on stormy nights, just as that little girl had so long ago. A little girl who'd grown up thinking she had done something wrong.

Lillie now knew she could face the truth about the past. She was a stronger woman. She believed in God's mercy and knew He was always with her and would ensure she wouldn't be harmed no matter what she found.

After opening her bedroom closet, she pushed aside the shoe boxes stacked on the shelf filled with off-season shoes, sandals and strappy pumps she wore on warmer days. Stretching on tiptoe, she touched the wooden box in the back of the closet.

Swallowing down a lump of apprehension, she dusted off the top with her hand and placed the box on the edge of her bed. Lillie drew in a fortifying breath before she lifted the lid. Her heart warmed when she looked inside.

The box contained a few pieces of jewelry, not the fake costume jewelry that Lillie usually wore, but what appeared to be expensive items. She held up a strand of fine pearls, perfectly matched and brilliant in color, along with a gold bracelet and matching necklace.

On the underside of the bracelet, she noticed "14K" etched in the precious metal. Both gold pieces were weighty and would cost a small fortune in today's economy.

A tiny gift card was tucked under the jewelry. She opened the note and rubbed her finger across the swirl of ink. The script was bold and the letters perfectly formed.

"To my precious Irene. I am forever yours."

Had the note and the jewelry been gifts from the man Lillie heard in her dreams?

Returning to the box, she pulled out a brooch in the shape of an American flag, set with red, white and blue rhinestones. Another gift, perhaps?

Toward the bottom was a piece of construction paper she unfolded. A child's drawing. Someone had written along the top, *My adorable Lillie is such an artist,* and the date, just a few days before her mother disappeared.

Hot tears swarmed Lillie's eyes. Unable to control her emotions, she lowered her head to her hands and cried for the mother's love she had lost too early. For a life cut short. For her own mistake in thinking her mother had purposely left her alone on that stormy night so long ago.

The tears were cathartic. Maybe now she would be able to reach out to her foster mother without fear of being left again.

Lillie clutched the brooch and held it to her heart. Her mother's body had been found along the river, not far from the museum construction site. Wearing the brooch to the military ceremony on Wednesday would be a fitting and patriotic tribute to honor her mother, whom Lillie had closed out of her heart for too long.

She dabbed tissues to her eyes and blew her nose. Then, grabbing the note and drawing to show Dawson, she stuck both papers in her purse. As she started to stand, she noticed a man's cuff link, partially broken, wedged in the bottom of the wooden container.

Lillie held it up, trying to determine the initials set in gold. The first letter was almost completely missing, but the second looked like the letter *T. GT,* perhaps, for Georgia Tech?

A bolt of lightning brightened the day. Thunder cracked, so strong it took her breath away. Her heart stopped for a long moment. She closed the box and jammed it in her closet.

Her stomach roiled. An odor wafted past her and

mixed with the earthy, musky scent of the approaching rain.

Fear threaded through her veins.

She couldn't hide from the storm or from the smell of smoke. Lightning must have struck her house.

"Fire," she wanted to scream.

Another crash of thunder.

Unable to move forward, she huddled on the floor. As on that night so long ago, she saw the door to her mother's room and heard the man's voice closing her out.

"No!" she screamed.

"Lillie." Dawson's voice sounded above the thunder. He wrapped her in his arms and guided her outside.

A portion of her garage was scorched. A pile of smoldering pine straw had been pushed away from the structure.

Glancing up, she saw that someone had written terrible slurs and disparaging names with spray paint across the side of her garage. Why hadn't she noticed them earlier when she had parked in the driveway?

Lillie looked at Dawson, not understanding what had happened. "The lightning hit the house?"

He shook his head. "It wasn't lightning. Someone used gasoline. I must have scared him off before the fire took hold. The water hose was close by."

Suddenly things weren't making sense. "How…how did you know…?"

"You left a message on my phone."

She glanced at her own cell. "But you didn't return my call."

"I was driving as fast as I could, Lillie. Why did you come back here? I told you to be careful."

Lillie pulled something from her pocket. Opening her hand, she looked down at the broken cuff link with the letters she had thought were *GT* for Georgia Tech. In the light of day, she realized the second letter could be an *F*.

Dawson had arrived just as the fire had started. Or had he started the fire to convince her she was in danger?

"I'll call the police and let them know what happened," she said, digging in her purse for her cell.

He shook his head, his eyes dark. "The fire's out. We need to get back to post, where you'll be safe. I'll call Pritchard on the way."

A feeling of dread swept over her. Her ears rang a warning as she glanced down at the cuff link.

GF. Granger Ford.

He wasn't her mother's lover. Lillie knew that without a shadow of a doubt. But he could have been her killer.

Dawson was his father's son. Karl Nelson's words returned to haunt her. *"Often the people we know best are the people who cause us the most pain."*

Lillie had thought she could trust the CID agent, but she was wrong. Dawson had started the fire to prove his point about her need for safety.

Since Granger was dead, if someone came after Lillie, people would think the killer was still on the loose.

Which is exactly what Lillie had thought.

Now she wasn't sure who was trying to do her harm—a killer from the past, or a CID agent who seemed intent on clearing his father's tarnished name?

Dawson followed Lillie back to post and knew she was upset about more than just the storm. She hadn't told him why she had gone back to her house, but he wasn't blind and had noticed the patriotic brooch she had pinned to her jacket.

The pin looked old and valuable. Maybe it had belonged to Mrs. McKinney. Or Lillie could have bought it for herself. Then again, maybe an old boyfriend had given it to her as a gift. Dawson rubbed his right hand over his chin, trying not to envision Lillie with someone else.

Surely there had been a line of men who wanted to court the pretty secretary, especially with all the single soldiers stationed on an army post. Had there been a very special person in her past? Maybe someone still in the military? Deployed? Returning soon?

The more he considered the options, the more confused he became. He hadn't seen photographs of a guy displayed in her home or on her desk at work. But with digital photography, most folks kept their pictures on their computers. While she was asleep the other night, he could have opened her photo file.

Then he'd know.

Although in reality, he didn't want to know about any guys, and he would never intrude upon her privacy. What he was interested in was her safety and getting to the bottom of this investigation. Then both of them would go their separate ways. The thought of not seeing Lillie sent another wave of frustration that tightened his shoulders into a knot.

Dawson reached for his cell and called the Freemont police. Once Sergeant Pritchard was on the line, Dawson filled him in on the fire and the graffiti written on Lillie's garage.

"I'm escorting Ms. Beaumont back to post." Dawson glanced at his watch. "I'll meet you at her house in thirty minutes. We need to talk."

By the time he pulled into the post headquarters parking lot, she was already on the sidewalk headed toward the building.

"Lillie?" he called after her.

She glanced over her shoulder.

"Are we still on for dinner tonight?"

"I can't, Dawson. I have too much work to do."

"You've got a room at the Lodge," he reminded her, knowing how vulnerable she'd be if she returned to her house.

"I'll stay at the Lodge, but I won't be available for dinner." With that very definite rejection, she hurried up the steps and into the building.

Dawson jammed a fist into his hand. How had things changed so quickly between them?

He thought back to what had happened earlier. She'd been frightened by the thunder and had readily accepted his open arms as he'd helped her outside. Was she upset because he hadn't called her on the way? A niggling voice that he couldn't explain had insisted he needed to hurry. He hadn't even thought about phoning her.

His mistake.

A mistake that seemed to have made a difference with Lillie. With so many things stacked between them, no wonder she wanted to call a halt to spending time together.

Her dad had probably talked to her yesterday. He was worried about her safety and rightfully so. Dawson was as well.

Only Dawson wasn't the one she needed to fear. He

glanced at the cars driving by the headquarters building. Someone was out there, waiting for Lillie.

Even if she didn't want his help, he would do everything to ensure she remained safe. Hopefully the case would break soon so Lillie could go on with her life.

He didn't want to say goodbye to Lillie. Not tomorrow or the next day or the day after that. Maybe not ever.

FOURTEEN

Sergeant Pritchard and two of his officers were searching the area around Lillie's garage when Dawson parked in her driveway. Pulling in a deep breath, he stepped onto the pavement.

After instructing his men to keep searching, Pritchard brushed off his hands and approached Dawson. "Looks like the killer may have returned to the scene of the crime."

"Lillie was inside at the time. I arrived just as the pine straw started to ignite. He must have run off into the woods."

"Did you see anyone?"

Dawson shook his head. "I barely had time to grab the water hose and douse the flames."

"Had Ms. Beaumont heard anything?"

"Thunder rumbled overhead, which probably drowned out any noise he might have made."

The cop held up two fingers. "The killer dropped the boulder on your car Saturday night and tried to burn her house today. Anything else I should know about?"

Dawson explained about the key Granger had given

Lillie, and the SUV that had tried to run her off the road and then followed her in Freemont.

"We found a flash drive that had information Granger had uncovered, along with two videos he made shortly before his death. He wanted to get the information into the right hands in case something happened to him."

Pritchard narrowed his eyes. "You didn't think I should know about the information?"

"I wanted to ensure it was accurate. That's why we went to Atlanta on Saturday." Dawson explained about meeting with Leonard Simpson and his parents.

The cop scratched his head. "Seems a stretch to think three prostitutes in Atlanta could tie in with Irene Beaumont's death."

"Which is exactly why I wanted to ensure the information was accurate before I handed it off to you."

Pritchard seemed to accept the explanation. "You still should have told me about your relationship to Granger Ford."

"You're right, but at the time I wasn't ready to accept the fact myself. I'd closed him out of my life for so long and couldn't find the gumption to acknowledge he was my father."

Pritchard looked into the distance and let out a ragged breath. "I don't condone what you did, but I understand. Fact is, I never got along with my old man. He was a mean buzzard who hurt a lot of people, including my mother. If I found him dead on someone's doorstep, I'd walk over his body and never look down. No way would I claim he was kin."

Dawson appreciated the cop's candor. It was hard to admit bad blood in a family, especially when the family member was your dad. He continued to fill Pritchard in on what he had uncovered as well as the two local women who had been seen with Billy Everett. "His name keeps popping up."

"I'll send out another BOLO for law enforcement in Georgia and the surrounding states to be on the lookout for Everett."

"Sounds good. As soon as I get back to my office, I'll email the flash drive files to you."

The two men shook hands before Dawson climbed into his car and drove back to post. He and Pritchard had ironed out their differences, and Dawson felt sure they would be able to work together in the future.

Once at his desk, he sent Pritchard the files and then placed a call to the guidance counselor at the local high school.

"She's tied up with testing this afternoon," her secretary said.

"Would you have her call me when she's free?" Dawson asked. "I'm interested in Freemont High graduates who attended Georgia Tech twenty-five to thirty years ago."

"Records that old might be difficult to access." The secretary stated the obvious.

"Please, just pass on the request."

He left his name and phone number. Hopefully the counselor would return his call later in the day.

Wanting to update the chief, Dawson tapped on Wilson's door.

"Enter."

"Sir, I met with Sergeant Pritchard and brought him up to date. He sent out a BOLO on Billy Everett, who, at the present time, is our only suspect. The Freemont police will keep us posted if anything new develops."

"Sounds good."

Dawson hesitated before finally asking, "Sir, have you heard anything from JAG?"

"Not yet. I'll let you know when I do."

"Yes, sir."

Dawson wasn't encouraged when he left the chief's office. Everything seemed to be moving at a snail's pace, and he was hanging in thin air when it came to Lillie and what the JAG Corps would determine. Dawson wanted the case resolved as soon as possible. Then he'd try to figure out his future, knowing without Lillie, the future looked anything but bright.

Lillie hurried into her office, determined to review the files on Granger's flash drive. Dawson had been with her when she'd watched the video the first time. Feigning concern, the solicitous CID agent had even suggested she *not* watch the tape, which made her wonder if there was something Dawson hadn't wanted her to see.

Thinking back to that night, Lillie remembered her own internal struggle and how often she'd turned away from the screen unable to go on. What had she missed?

She opened the bottom drawer on her desk where she had placed the flash drive, but the memory device wasn't there. She searched through all the drawers. A cold suspicion took hold that Dawson had taken the flash drive without telling her.

Lillie reached for her phone and tapped in his number.

"Timmons."

His voice made her heart hitch, but she pushed aside the feeling. She had to be careful. Things weren't always as they seemed and right now she couldn't trust anyone. Especially not Dawson.

"I wanted to relook at the files on the flash drive we viewed the other night, but I couldn't find it in my desk. Did you take it?"

"You put it in the bottom drawer."

Which was the first place she had looked.

"Are you sure you don't have the flash drive?" she asked again.

"Lillie, I don't know what happened today, but I'm not the bad guy. You can believe me when I tell you something. I don't have the flash drive. However, I did forward the files to my computer. I can email you a copy if that would help."

"Have you deleted anything?"

"Lillie, where's this coming from? Did your father tell you to not trust me?"

Her father had cautioned her to be careful, but he'd also said he liked Dawson. His main concern was for her own peace of mind. Eventually, he had told her to trust her instincts, which she was trying to do.

"Just send me the files, Dawson."

As she hung up, Mark entered the office. He stopped, noting the papers and other items scattered over the top of her usually neat desk.

"What's wrong?"

She waved her hand in the air, hoping to make light of the situation. "I can't find a flash drive. I thought it was in my desk. Have you seen one lying around? It's small, eight gigs, encased in blue enamel."

He shook his head. "But I'll let you know if I find it."

"Was anyone hanging around the office this morning?"

"Tom Reynolds stopped by. He wanted to talk to me about the gym on post."

"Did he touch anything on my desk?"

"Of course not." Mark pursed his lips. "I came in late Saturday morning and found Sergeant Howard Murphy looking out the window. He was the staff duty NCO and thought he saw the general's car in the parking lot."

"General Cameron was out of town for the weekend, Mark. You knew his schedule, so why were you here?"

The aide glanced down. "I got behind last week and wanted to catch up on some paperwork. The NCO said you and the CID agent had stayed at the office Friday night."

"Dawson didn't think it was safe for me to return home. I've got a room at the Lodge for the next two days. He assures me I'll be safer on post."

Mark nodded. "He's probably right. I'll be working late tonight. Call me if you have a problem. The Lodge isn't far. I could get there in no time."

Lillie appreciated his offer. The cocky aide seemed to have come back down to earth. She felt better knowing he would be close at hand.

When she checked into her room at the Lodge later that afternoon, Lillie knew she had a long night ahead of her. The last time she had opened Granger's files, Dawson had been at her side, offering support. Only now she couldn't depend on him, and just like when she was growing up, the only one she could depend on was herself.

FIFTEEN

Dawson wanted to knock on the door to Lillie's room at the Lodge and demand to know what was bothering her. She had given him more than the cold shoulder earlier. In fact, he'd call it an arctic freeze. But bottom line, she didn't want him around right now, so whether he liked it or not, he needed to give her space.

The room he had reserved for Lillie was at the end of a long hallway on the second floor, away from the central stairway and other guests who might be going to and from their rooms. Dawson holed up across the hall with the door to his room cracked open so he could keep tabs on any activity in the hallway.

Earlier he had alerted the military police to keep the area secure outside, and he was reasonably certain the night would be uneventful, at least from a safety angle. The only problem was he knew Lillie was right across the hall.

Dawson ordered a pizza in hopes of wooing her out of her room with food. Forty-five minutes later, he glanced out the window and saw the delivery car pull up in front of the building.

Footsteps sounded. Grabbing cash from his wallet,

he stepped into the hallway only to find the general's aide standing in front of Lillie's door.

The captain's brow furrowed. "What are you doing here, Timmons?"

Lillie's door opened. She appeared surprised to see Mark, which gave Dawson a moment of relief, but when she glanced at Dawson, her surprise turned to confusion.

"Evening, Lillie," he said, hoping to deflect the question he saw in her eyes.

"I found the flash drive." Mark ignored Dawson and dropped the small memory stick into her outstretched hand.

"Thanks. Where was it?"

"Stuck in the corner of your inbox. I saw it when I was searching for the plans for the museum."

The delivery guy hustled toward Dawson with a pizza in hand, making an awkward moment even more complicated. Dawson paid the driver, who quickly scurried back to his car as if even he sensed the growing tension.

Unwilling to let the general's aide have the last word, Dawson forced a smile. "Hungry? I've got more pizza than I can eat."

Lillie glanced from Dawson to Mark and then back to Dawson again. He continued to hold the outstretched box of pizza, feeling like a third wheel. His hope was that the aide would get the hint and leave, although from the way Mark puffed out his chest and sidled closer to her room, Dawson could end up being the odd man out.

"I've already eaten." Lillie's emphatic statement shattered his hopes for the night. The aide seemed equally deflated.

"Now, gentlemen, if you'll both excuse me, I need to get back to work." Confidently in control, Lillie turned on her heel and retreated into her room. The door shut with a definite slam, followed by the clink of the dead bolt falling into place. Evidently she really did want to be alone.

Mark harrumphed and appeared somewhat exasperated with her abrupt departure. He stared at the door for a long moment before he looked over his shoulder at Dawson. "Enjoy your dinner."

Once the aide had left the building, Dawson placed a portion of the pizza on a paper plate and walked across the hall. He tapped on Lillie's door.

She opened it ever so slightly. "Yes?"

"Just in case you get hungry later." He shoved the plate into her hands. "I'm staying across the hall. My cell will be on all night. Call me if you want to talk."

The rather bewildered look on her face made him smile. He reached for a loose strand of her hair and tucked it neatly behind her ear. "I won't bother you. Cross my heart."

Just as she had done earlier, he turned about-face and walked back to his room. After closing the door, he peered through the peephole.

Lillie stood staring down at the pizza. Then, as if her stomach had gotten the best of her, she reached for a slice and took a big bite. Even with the distortion of the peephole, he could still recognize the look of pleasure on her face as she licked her lips. Score one for the CID, Dawson thought as she returned to her room.

Maybe tomorrow she'd be more willing to talk to him. At least that's what he hoped. Tonight he'd stand guard and ensure she was safe.

Dawson wanted her to need him, but not only for protection. He was beginning to realize he wanted Lillie to need him in an entirely different way as well.

Try as she might, Lillie couldn't find anything on the flash drive that she hadn't seen with Dawson just a few nights ago. Nor did she find anything that indicated Granger Ford was confused or had falsified information, especially since Mr. Simpson had confirmed the story about the college boy in the bar.

Poring over the information, Lillie stayed up too late and hit Snooze when the alarm went off in the morning. Rushing to get to work, she didn't have time to knock on Dawson's door and thank him for the pizza. Before she pulled into the post headquarters parking lot, she saw him in her rearview mirror.

She appreciated his watchfulness and hadn't felt personally threatened in the night. Although she had thought too much about the three women from Atlanta who had gone missing and Granger Ford's death and the two local women who may have been MLK victims as well.

Her mother had been a victim, and for so long Lillie had refused to open that door. Better to feel abandoned than to come face-to-face with a heinous act of violence against someone she loved.

Seeing the contents of the box yesterday made her realize how much she had loved her mother. Lillie was beginning to realize her mother had loved her in return. Hopefully time would heal some of the wounds she had lived with for so long.

Once at her desk, the time passed quickly as she worked on reports General Cameron needed updated.

Mark was equally busy and somewhat aloof this morning, although she was grateful he didn't talk about last night.

As much as Lillie tried to keep her mind on office matters, she kept thinking of Dawson and the way her ear had tingled when he'd touched her hair. She also thought about his kiss outside her parents' house and how her heart had almost stopped, which had scared her so much she had run back inside.

For so long she had guarded her feelings and walled herself off from people who got too close. Dawson had somehow broken through the barriers she had placed around her heart. She was vulnerable and had reacted irrationally yesterday at her house, when the storm had thrown her over the edge.

In hindsight, she knew Dawson hadn't started the fire or spray-painted the terrible words on her garage. He would never do anything to harm her. She needed to apologize to him and ask his forgiveness.

Dawson was a wonderful man who worked overtime to keep her safe. He deserved something better than a woman who needed to make her own peace with the past.

Hopefully, when the investigation was over, he would still be around. She couldn't imagine how she would feel if Dawson wasn't in her life.

Dawson tried to tie up the loose strings on the investigation once he got to work the next day. So many things still needed his attention.

The high-school guidance counselor called him back with information about the local students who had attended Georgia Tech around the time of Lillie's mother's death.

"Four girls were accepted to Tech during the years you mentioned to my secretary. Three of them graduated. One girl dropped out to get married. Only two male students were accepted. One enlisted in the military after his freshman year. The other boy moved to Nevada following graduation."

"And those were the only students?"

"That's right. I'll email their names and current addresses, if we have them on file."

"I appreciate your help."

"No problem. This is my last year before retirement. Not many folks need information that goes back to my beginning days in education." She chuckled, then paused.

"I just pulled up another file. A third male student was accepted to Tech. He didn't know if he'd have enough funding. Student loans eventually came through for him, and he received a sizable scholarship from a donor in town. The student was Bobby Webber."

Dawson jotted down the name.

"Bobby was a smart young man. We were all glad he was able to attend Georgia Tech. The family was poor. Three boys with three different fathers. Bobby was the oldest and excelled academically. The youngest boy was a slow learner. You'd never think they were from the same family except for their hair, which they inherited from their mother."

Dawson sat up. "What about their hair?"

"All three boys were carrottops. Bright red. Stood out in a crowd, if you know what I mean."

"What was the youngest boy's name?"

"Billy," she said. "Billy Everett."

SIXTEEN

True to her word, the guidance counselor emailed the names of the former Georgia Tech students. Bobby Webber's current Colorado address was on the list.

Dawson punched in a long-distance number and waited until he heard Special Agent Kelly McQueen Thibodeaux's answer. "This is a voice from your past," he teased.

"How are you, Dawson?" Kelly was one of the best shots in the entire CID, maybe the army. She had married a captain from Fort Rickman, and they had both been transferred to Fort Carson, not far from where Bobby Webber now lived.

"I could use your help, Kelly."

"Shoot."

He told her about the investigation and gave her a brief rundown on what he needed. "Find out anything you can about Bobby Webber, especially whether he could have been the drunken college kid shooting off his mouth."

"I'll team up with a friend on the local police force and see what we can find."

As soon as he disconnected, Dawson got a message that Chief Wilson wanted to see him in his office.

"Yes, sir?"

"Pritchard just called. Florida State Highway Patrol apprehended Billy Everett in the Jacksonville area. He was hitching a ride on the interstate."

Finally the case seemed to be coming together. "Did they question him, sir?"

"They're holding him until someone from here can escort him back to Georgia. Pritchard is sending one of his men and asked if you could go along."

"The only problem is Ms. Beaumont's security. She's got a room at the Lodge so she doesn't have to return to her own residence in town."

"I'll authorize the military police to keep the facility under surveillance. You should be back on post tonight."

Much as Dawson didn't want to leave Lillie, he appreciated the chance to be the first to question Everett. He also wanted to ensure nothing happened during transport that would allow the suspect to escape. Especially after learning his brother had gone to Georgia Tech.

As Dawson left Fort Rickman to meet the local police officer escort, he considered calling Lillie and telling her he would be away from post for the remainder of the day. Chief Wilson had assured him the military police would keep the Lodge under surveillance, and Dawson was certain she would be safe while he was gone.

She hadn't wanted to see him last night. No reason for him to think she would have changed her mind. He decided to call her when he got back to post. Maybe she would join him for dinner at his BOQ.

Lillie had taken the pizza bait last night. Tonight he

would tempt her with rib-eye steaks, baked potatoes and cheesecake from the commissary.

Although he would probably need more than a good meal to soften her heart. Lillie believed in the Lord. If only God would help her resolve her past. Maybe the Lord would help Dawson as well, yet he had been away from his faith for so long. Dawson wasn't sure the Lord—or Lillie—would want anything to do with him again.

Lillie and Mark worked without a break until noon, when he picked up burgers at the Post Exchange food concession. Tom Reynolds stopped by to go over plans for the military gym membership. Seeing how busy they were dealing with last-minute details for the museum building project kickoff, he offered to return later in the week.

General Cameron called Lillie into his office in the afternoon. "I got a phone call from Chief Wilson. Looks like they have a suspect in custody in Jacksonville."

"Florida?"

"Actually, he's from Freemont." The general glanced down at the note he had made. "The suspect's name is Billy Everett. Special Agent Timmons is bringing him back to Georgia."

Lillie was relieved Billy was in custody and proud of Dawson for his role in the investigation. "Thank you for letting me know, sir."

"It's been a long time coming, but you'll soon have closure on all of this."

By six o'clock, Lillie was worn out and ready to leave the office. Mark had left ahead of her with his workout bag in hand, headed for the gym. She decided to call Dawson, hoping he might be back in the area by now.

As much as Lillie wanted to go home, she had the room at the Lodge for one more night. Dawson would probably be tired from his long day, and he might want to get together for dinner. Nothing fancy, but Lillie wanted to hear what had happened and if he had learned anything new from Everett.

Her call to Dawson went to voice mail. She decided not to leave a message. There was so much for her to explain, plus she needed to apologize for acting like a spoiled child instead of a rational adult.

Once back at the Lodge, Lillie changed into jeans and a sweater, knowing she needed fresh air after being cooped up in the office all day. She knocked on Dawson's door, and when he didn't answer, she called his cell again. Either he was out of range or had turned off his phone.

Lillie knew a walk would do her good. She had a lot to think about concerning her mother's death and everything that would be brought into the open now that Everett was in custody. Plus, she was ready to see where her mother's remains had been uncovered.

"Oh, Lord, help me understand what happened. Maybe then I'll be able to put it all behind me and move on with my life."

She thought of Dawson, and of the future they might have together. Or was she being too optimistic?

A nature trail ran along the river. She headed north, enjoying the sunshine and the moderate temperature for January.

After seeing her mother's items in the box, Lillie wondered if Everett had broken in to steal her jewelry.

Maybe her death had nothing to do with the murders in Atlanta or with the man who'd claimed to murder women and bury them in steel drums.

Lillie shivered as a cloud blocked the sun. The wind picked up over the water and whipped her hair around her face. She should have worn a heavier jacket. What had she been thinking? She was dressed for April instead of January.

In the distance, she heard the sound of earthmoving vehicles and realized she had walked almost to the site of the new museum. If she cut through the tall trees and bramble near the water's edge she would be able to see the construction area.

Wrapping her arms around her body, she tried to ward off the drop in temperature and the chilling reminder that her mother's body had been unearthed nearby.

Although she should turn around, Lillie kept moving forward, drawn to where the steel drum had been found. Just like everything else, she had closed off this part of her life and had never ventured to the water's edge.

For so long, she had wanted nothing to do with her mother. The thought of her own stubbornness wrapped around her and brought tears to her eyes. What kind of a daughter would exclude the memory of the woman who had given her life?

Tears fell as Lillie continued forward. The narrow pavement disappeared and led to a dirt path.

Time to go back to the Lodge.

She wiped her eyes and noticed a vehicle parked in the thickly wooded area.

A man stood nearby.

Her heart pounded a warning as her gaze cleared.

The vehicle was a white Suburban, tinted windows, with an army decal on the bumper.

Fear clamped down on Lillie's chest. Her hand flew to her mouth. A twig snapped underfoot.

He startled at the sound.

From the look in his eyes, she knew he hadn't expected anyone to find him.

"What an odd coincidence, Lillie. I had planned to come after you tonight."

She ran. Behind her, the sound of his footfalls sent waves of terror to tangle along her spine.

She willed her legs to move faster. The overgrowth snagged her sweater. Branches grabbed her arms.

Where was the paved path she had walked on earlier? Her foot caught on a root. She stumbled, righted herself and ran on.

His footsteps grew louder.

She pushed forward, hearing him pull air into his lungs. He was so close.

His hand grabbed her shoulder and sent her hurtling to the ground. She screamed, climbed to her knees and tried to scurry away.

"You can't run from me now, Lillie."

She screamed again as his hands wrapped around her neck, blocking the air from her lungs.

All she could think about was Dawson, who she had turned her back on yesterday. He had wanted to keep her safe, but she'd rejected him. Now Dawson would never be able to find her, and just like her mother, Lillie's body would someday be recovered by the water's edge.

SEVENTEEN

Traffic snarled along Interstate 10, delaying Dawson and the local Freemont cop. They arrived in Jacksonville at 5:00 p.m., during peak end-of-the-workday traffic and wall-to-wall gridlock. By the time they walked into the police headquarters where Everett was being held, both men were out of sorts and knew they had to face more traffic on the return trip to Georgia.

Everett refused to answer any questions en route, and Dawson eventually let him sulk until they arrived back in Freemont.

Pritchard arrived at police headquarters, and both he and Dawson questioned the redhead repeatedly. The only information they learned was that Everett had done yard work for Lillie's mother.

"What about the photo of Irene Beaumont?" Dawson asked. "How did it get under the mattress in Granger's motel room?"

Everett crouched in his chair like a tortoise trying to hide within his shell. "Somebody put it there, but it wasn't me."

The redhead had also done yard work for the prosecutor and had overheard him talking on the phone about setting Granger up to take the rap. Again, Everett failed to provide the caller's name.

"The cops found a newspaper photo of you in Granger's room. Had he contacted you?"

"He tracked me down when he got out of prison. All I could tell him was the prosecutor set him up. Then Granger got shot, and I hitched a ride out of town."

"What about Roseanne and Valerie? Were you dating Roseanne? Did you kill her?"

Everett shook his head, his eyes wide. "No. You've got that all wrong. Roseanne hated small towns. She wanted to get a job in Atlanta. I told her how to thumb a ride and find a place to stay when she got to the city."

"Because you visited your brother when he was in college there?"

"Yeah, that's right."

Dawson leaned across the table and got in the punk's face. "Is your brother Bobby a killer?"

"Ah, man, you're crazy. Bobby wouldn't hurt anyone."

"How can you be so sure?"

"Because he tried to help me even when I didn't want his help."

Dawson looked at the skinny guy with greasy hair and a week's growth of beard, and knew he was telling the truth about his brother. Dawson wasn't sure he could trust Everett about anything else.

It was late by the time Dawson returned to the Lodge. He saw two military police officers on patrol when he pulled into the parking lot and felt assured they had kept the area under surveillance throughout the evening.

Climbing the stairs, he hoped Lillie would be awake and hear him. When her door remained closed, Dawson knew he needed to get some sleep. He would see her tomorrow, if not before the museum ceremony then immediately after the luncheon for the VIPs at the club.

Hopefully everything would smooth out between them, but tonight, more than anything, Dawson wanted to wrap his arms around her and pull her close. She might not need him, but he needed her in his life. He had been alone for too long, and he was beginning to think he wanted her close for a long, long time to come.

Lillie groaned. Her head ached as if a giant sledgehammer had crashed into her skull. Her mouth tasted like bile, and she gagged. Trying to raise her hands, she realized they were bound. Her legs were as well.

Her eyes flew open. She was lying on a pile of rags in the corner of a garage. Tools hung from a pegboard overhead. Hunting trophies decorated the walls, along with a shellacked wooden paddle.

She squinted, hoping to decipher the letters—Greek letters—painted on the shiny wood. ΓΤ. Gamma Tau.

The words on the shirt Mr. Simpson had seen the boy in the bar wearing hadn't been Georgia Tech, but rather the name of a fraternity at nearby Georgia Southwestern, where she had gone to school.

Lillie peered at the only escape route—a small door on the far side of the garage that hung ajar, drawing in cold air.

Please, God.

She couldn't think about the dropping temperature outside or how long she would have to hide in the bushes waiting for someone to find her. Staying here meant certain death, and more than anything, she wanted to live.

Dawson's face swam into view. She had so much to

tell him about the good man he was and how he had been the only person to ever break down the wall she had built around her heart.

She hadn't wanted to let anyone in, until Dawson. Now she wanted him more than anything. If only he could find her. He probably thought she wasn't interested in seeing him again. She wanted to cry out at her own stupidity and self-centeredness.

Instead she tucked her chin to her chest and threw her left shoulder over her right, then flopped from her stomach to her back and continued to roll. Her shoulders and hips ached as they pounded against the cement floor, but she ignored the pain and forced herself to roll forward toward the partially opened door.

Footsteps.

Her heart exploded in her chest. She had to escape.

With a last push, she wiggled closer and cupped her chin around the bottom edge of the open door. Before she could inch it open, a force shoved the heavy oak, slamming the door into her neck.

She gasped. Pain radiated through her jaw.

He kicked her.

She screamed.

"What do you think you're doing?"

Instinctively, she curled into a fetal position, trying to protect herself. She saw the mud-covered boots as he struck her again and again. More frightening than his blows was the steel drum he rolled into the garage, identical to the one her mother had been buried in so many years ago.

Like mother, like daughter. Lillie would die tonight just as her mother had, buried alive where no one would ever find her.

EIGHTEEN

Before Dawson fell asleep that night, his cell rang. He checked caller ID and pushed the phone to his ear. "Hey, Kelly. Didn't take you long."

"I got one of my friends from the local police department to join me. We paid Mr. Webber a visit. The guy's squeaky clean. Runs a company that provides jobs for special-needs adults. He's also heavily involved in local charitable causes."

"Sounds like Burl Nelson from Freemont."

"Who?"

"Never mind."

"Mr. Webber says he's never touched alcohol, even in his youth. His pastor vouched for him. My gut feeling is he's telling the truth. I'd say you've got the wrong guy if you think he's involved in anything suspect."

"Thanks, I owe you. How's Phil?"

"Handsome as ever."

"You two ever plan to come back to Georgia?"

"Depends on Uncle Sam. Tell everyone in CID headquarters I said hello. Colorado is golden. Come visit sometime."

Dawson hung up feeling somewhat let down. Grateful though he was for Kelly's help, he had hoped Bobby Webber would turn out to be the missing link. The guidance counselor had mentioned another brother. He'd have Pritchard check it out.

At least Billy Everett was in custody, and something was bound to break soon. Everything pointed to wrapping up the case in the next day or so. Dawson should feel optimistic, but when the investigation concluded, he and Lillie would go their separate ways, which wasn't what he wanted.

He thought again of Kelly and Phil Thibodeaux and their happily-ever-after marriage. Was that what he wanted for his life? Or was he acting like a crazy fool for thinking an ex-con's son could find a woman who loved him despite his father and his past?

"Sweet Lillie, come to Mama. Your daddy's here."

She turned and saw her father, the man who traveled, or so Mama said. He laughed and so did Mama. Scooping Lillie into her arms, her mother kissed her cheek.

"A storm's coming, Irene. Put the child to bed." His voice.

"It's early, dear."

"But I don't have long tonight. Do as I say so we'll have enough time together."

"I want to stay with you, Mama."

"Hush, darling. We'll be together in the morning."

Only no one was there when the storm passed.

"Lillie?" Another voice broke into her memories. This one in present day and close to her ear. Stale breath, rough hands.

"You can't get away from me this time."

He shoved her into the drum. She fought and kicked

and screamed, but he was too strong for her. His fist crashed into her chest. Everything swirled around her.

With a loud *clang,* the lid crashed down into place. Lillie cringed with each horrific jolt as he pounded it shut. Darkness surrounded her.

She gasped for air.

How long before she'd die?

Too long.

Oh, Dawson, where are you?

NINETEEN

Ever so quietly, Dawson eased the door to his room closed the next morning as he left the Lodge so as not to disturb Lillie, sleeping across the hall. She would have to be up soon enough to get ready for work.

Even though he wasn't fully convinced Billy Everett was the killer, Dawson still felt confident Lillie was safe on post. The military police were on alert and checking each vehicle that passed through the main gate.

Not that something couldn't happen on federal property, yet chances were good Granger's murderer was a civilian from off post who wouldn't venture onto the military garrison.

Chief Agent in Charge Wilson had assigned CID personnel and military police to cover the ceremony at the museum this morning. With the number of wealthy businessmen and politicians in attendance, as well as the Freemont mayor and local officials, General Cameron wanted to ensure the VIPs could enjoy the ceremony in total safety.

Arriving on-site early, Dawson met up with Jamison near the raised special seating area. Both of them eyed the sky and the dark clouds in the distance.

"Looks like the weather might be a problem." Dawson stated what they both knew to be true.

"The general debated moving the ceremony to the auditorium on post."

"Which would have been a good idea."

Jamison nodded. "In hindsight. Although Karl Nelson asked to keep it out here. He wanted his construction crew to be able to hear the general's praise for what they are about to accomplish."

"I'd hate to see the weather bring everything to a halt, especially after all the preparations that have gone into today." Dawson thought of the hours Lillie had spent on the project. "Still, it's the general's call. Any idea what time the old man is expected to arrive?"

"Before long." Jamison checked his watch. "The ceremony is scheduled to start at oh-nine-hundred hours. My guess, he'll be here in the next few minutes."

By the time Lillie arrived at the construction site, Dawson would need to focus on the special guests. He wouldn't be able to talk to her until after the official program had concluded, and then only in passing. Following the ceremony, he had to proceed to the club and provide security at the luncheon.

With a few minutes to kill before the VIP vans arrived, Dawson jabbed Jamison's arm. "You'll never guess who I talked to last night?"

"Kelly Thibodeaux."

Dawson tried to hide his surprise. "Did she call you?"

Jamison laughed. "Only to ask if something was going on between you and the general's secretary."

"What?"

Jamison shrugged. "You know women have a sixth

sense about matchmaking. Kelly heard something in your voice when you mentioned Lillie's name."

"I was merely bringing Kelly up to date on the case."

Jamison raised his brow and stared at Dawson. "So was she right?"

"About what?"

"Oh, come on, Dawson, stop playing games. I'm talking about you and the general's secretary. My mother-in-law thinks Lillie's charming."

Jamison's wife was the daughter of one of the colonels on post. "How is Michele?"

"She's fine, but you're changing the subject." Jamison chuckled as he turned to study the construction area. "I heard you brought Billy Everett back from Florida. What's he have to say?"

"Only that he doesn't know who killed Lillie's mom or Granger Ford."

Jamison sniffed and then glanced back at Dawson. "I'm sorry about all this, Dawson. I told Wilson I was to blame for you taking the case in the first place."

Dawson held up his hand. "We've been over this before, Jamison. The problem's mine. I told him you were only doing your job."

"Maybe, but I still feel responsible." He patted Dawson's back and then walked off to check the VIP area.

Glancing at the dark clouds, Dawson thought about his father, who had been absent from his life. Growing up, he believed his mother had been the problem and not his dad.

Eventually, he'd realized his mother had done her best under difficult circumstances. Life wasn't fair, and some people managed better than others. Dawson had worked hard to ensure her woe-is-me way of looking at life didn't rub off on him.

No wonder he had created an imaginary father whom he tried to emulate. Lillie was right. Dawson had worked construction as a teen because of his dad.

Until the accident.

He should have known trying to follow in his father's footsteps could be his undoing.

The army had offered him another way out and a chance to make a success of his life, to do something right and make a difference. If only the JAG would find him innocent of any wrongdoing.

He glanced at his watch, wanting to call Lillie and hear her voice. No doubt she was still at post headquarters, working on last-minute details the general needed prior to the ceremony. Dawson couldn't interfere. Not now.

A handful of folks from town had already arrived and started to find their seats in the reviewing stands. The bus, transporting the Fort Rickman Army Band, pulled into the parking lot. The director studied the sky as if he too was worried about the storm.

What a shame to have everything come to a halt before the ceremony had even started. Although the weather should never be ignored. Dawson thought back to the day he'd been digging the ditch. No one had realized rain the night before had weakened the ground until the sides of the ditch collapsed in on Dawson.

He shook off the memory and turned his gaze to the pit in the middle of the construction site, where pylons and a crisscross of rebar established the layout of the building's basement foundation. A front-end loader and two dump trucks sat parked nearby.

Glancing over his shoulder, Dawson spied the caravan of vehicles, carrying the visiting dignitaries, pull into the makeshift parking area behind the bleachers. The VIPs disembarked, chatting among themselves as they made their way to the reviewing stand.

As people gathered in the stands, the band took up its position on the field and, after a brief warm-up, began to play military march music. The visitors kept time by tapping their feet or clapping their hands. The crowd seemed ready to enjoy the celebration. All was going well except for the approaching storm and General Cameron's absence.

Dawson checked his watch once again before glancing at the surrounding bleachers to ensure Lillie had not yet arrived.

In the distance, he spied the car carrying the commanding general. A flag with two red stars fluttered from the front bumper.

All eyes were on the sedan when it pulled to a stop at the side of the VIP area. The general's aide rode in the front passenger seat. Mark exited the vehicle and rounded to the far side to assist General Cameron with the door he had already opened.

Karl Nelson parked behind the general. He stepped from his car and shook hands with two men standing nearby. The general and Nelson exchanged greetings and chatted with a number of people as they walked through the growing crowd of onlookers. The general climbed the platform to where the distinguished guests were seated on folding chairs. Karl waved to the local townspeople in the bleachers before he joined Cameron.

Dawson expected to see Lillie's car. She would probably be wearing the attractive and very appropriate brooch that would draw the attention of many of the women in the crowd.

The post adjutant walked to the microphone and welcomed the dignitaries and local guests to the morning ceremony. He invited the visitors to stand as the band played the national anthem.

Dawson pulled his hand to his forehead in salute along with those in uniform. The women and civilians covered their hearts with their right hands. Many of the invited guests sang along with the words they knew so well.

At the conclusion of the anthem, Dawson scanned the crowd, but he still couldn't find Lillie. The chaplain stepped forward and prayed for God's protection for the construction crews working on the project and for good weather to see the museum completed in a timely manner.

Although heartfelt, his prayer seemed a bit late in coming as the sky continued to darken and the wind gathered strength. Many of the folks in the bleachers hustled to their cars in anticipation of the approaching storm.

The adjutant returned to the microphone and introduced the commanding general. Cameron leaned down to talk privately with Karl. The general pointed to the storm clouds. Karl waved his hand, his negative response easy enough to read.

A number of the dignitaries whispered among themselves, their faces drawn and eyes wide as they too studied the sky.

Dawson recognized a state representative from the local area. He helped his wife slip into her raincoat and then escorted her off the platform. General Cameron turned and watched them hurry toward the waiting vans.

A bolt of lightning cut across the horizon. A clap of thunder followed almost immediately.

Without glancing at his prepared speech, the general leaned into the microphone. "Ladies and gentlemen, the weather seems to be working against us today. For the safety of all, please return to the vans or your private vehicles. We will have to cancel the ceremony planned for this morning and move to the Fort Rickman Club. I'll join you there shortly."

Another bolt of lightning and the accompanying crack of thunder punctuated the general's remarks and hurried the people away from the metal stands. Before most folks reached their cars, the sky opened, and fat drops of rain pummeled the earth.

More concerned than ever, Dawson sought out the general's aide. "Where's Lillie?"

"She never showed up at work today. I thought she was with you."

Icicles of fear punctured Dawson's heart. "Didn't she call to say what had happened?"

Mark steeled his eyes. "I doubt she'd tell me much of anything after she spent the night with you."

Dawson wanted to grab the guy by the lapels and beat some manners into his affected grin.

"She didn't spend the night with me. Why would you think that? There's nothing going on between us. Besides, Lillie's not even sure she wants to talk to me at this point."

The aide raised his brow. "You're serious, aren't you? You really don't know where she is?"

"I wouldn't joke about Lillie's safety."

"I'm heading back to the club with General Cameron. I'll let you know if she arrives."

"Contact post headquarters. Maybe she's at the office by now."

"Will do. I'll get back to you as soon as I hear anything."

Dawson reached for his phone and speed-dialed Lillie's cell. His stomach tightened when an automated voice stated the number was not in service.

Standing in the midst of the mass of people running to their cars to get out of the rain, Dawson felt his heart drop lower than the cloud cover.

Where was Lillie? He had left post yesterday to apprehend Everett and hadn't seen her since.

Jamison helped the VIPs board the vans. Dawson hustled to his side. "Lillie never showed up for work today. I'm going to check the Lodge. If she's not there, I'll drive to her house in Freemont in case she went home. Cover for me at the club. I'll get there when I've located Lillie and know she's okay."

"Don't worry. We can handle it. I'll be praying you find her."

A lump formed in Dawson's throat. He wanted to thank Jamison, but he didn't know what to say in response to his offer to pray.

Looking back on the construction site, Dawson saw the giant earthmoving equipment standing idle at the edge of the deep pit. All around him, people were running for cover.

Without anyplace else to turn, he followed Jamison's lead. *"Lord, help me find Lillie."*

Then he climbed in his car and headed to the Lodge.

In Dawson's heart of hearts, he knew there was only

one reason why Lillie wasn't at the ceremony today. Someone had her. Someone who wanted to do her harm.

Dawson stamped down on the accelerator, knowing he had to find Lillie before it was too late.

TWENTY

Lillie's eyes blinked open. Darkness surrounded her along with agonizing pain and bone-chilling cold. Her spine was twisted, her head crushed against metal, her legs bent up.

Earlier her hands had been tied behind her back. Now she moved her fingers, surprised they responded and equally surprised by the rush of fear that swept over her at the sound of distant thunder.

Nausea overcame her. She swallowed back the swell of bile, refusing to think of the storm or the smell of wet earth that filled her nostrils and clogged her throat.

A boom of thunder startled her. She jerked. Her cheek scraped the rough metal drum. The top of her head jammed against the lid.

Pushing her feet off the bottom of the container, she pressed her weight upward, hoping to force the lid open.

A thunderous crash shook the earth and sent waves of terror sweeping through her.

She thought once again of that night long ago when she had run on four-year-old feet along the hallway. "Mama," she had cried over and over again until the door opened. She had heard the man's voice just before the door closed again. No one had saved her that night, just as no one could save her now.

"No," she screamed as another wave of thunder bellowed overhead.

En route, Dawson called the Lodge and told the manager to meet him on the second floor with the master key.

Screeching to a stop in front of the entrance, he climbed the stairs two at a time, took the key from the manager's hand and ran along the hallway to Lillie's room.

He pounded on the door. "Lillie, open up."

Without waiting for an answer, Dawson shoved the key in the lock and raced into the room.

His heart stopped.

Her purse and cell phone were on the small writing desk. Her laptop was open. He clicked it back to life and checked the history. The last time she had been online was yesterday afternoon.

Leaving the small sitting area, he hurried into the adjoining bedroom, noting the neatly made bed and the outfit she had worn yesterday hanging in the closet. A blue suit, upon which she had already pinned the patriotic brooch, hung nearby.

No one could have gotten to her at the Lodge. Dawson had kept his own door open and watched the hallway from the couch where he had spent the night.

Lillie hadn't slept in the bed. Someone must have taken her earlier in the day, before Dawson returned from Florida.

Leaving the Lodge, he called Pritchard and filled

him in. The cop promised to check her Freemont home and get back to Dawson.

The aide still hadn't called. Dawson drove to post headquarters, but when he entered the general's suite, it too was empty.

He called the military police and alerted them, but he didn't know where to tell them to look.

Her folks? He called the McKinneys' number and grimaced when Lillie's foster dad answered the phone.

"Sir, this is Special Agent Timmons."

"Oh, Dawson, I was planning to call you. I wanted to apologize for my actions Sunday afternoon. I was worried about my daughter and acted like a stupid fool, which is what Lillie called me."

The tension in Dawson's neck eased. "So Lillie's there with you?" He couldn't explain how she had gotten to their house since her car was parked at the Lodge, but Dawson wouldn't worry about that now. Just so she was safe.

"Lillie was right," Mr. McKinney continued. "I was a fool. You're a good man, Dawson, and Lillie cares for you a lot."

As much as he wanted to discuss the last statement with Mr. McKinney, Dawson had to ensure Lillie was all right. "Sir—"

"I hope you'll accept my apology. Lillie told me your father had been wrongly accused. A terrible travesty and then to have his death follow so soon after you two had just reconnected."

"Thank you, sir. I hate to cut you off, but could I speak to Lillie?"

"She's not here. I'm sure she's at work. You haven't seen her?"

"I'll keep looking, sir."

"She's all right, isn't she?"

"Right now I'm not sure of anything, sir. Just pray I can find her."

TWENTY-ONE

Dawson didn't know where to turn. Every place he looked for Lillie was a dead end. He wanted to scream to the heavens and beg the Lord to help him. But why would God listen to him now?

The few times Dawson had attended services when he was a new recruit, the chaplain had talked about a compassionate and merciful God.

If the Almighty truly was merciful, wouldn't He care about Lillie's well-being?

Think of her need, Lord, and not my own selfishness.

Dawson retraced the route he had taken earlier, not sure where he would end up. The first wave of the storm had passed with a downpour of rain and accompanying lightning.

Lillie feared storms. Wherever she was, she was frightened. Dawson was frightened too. Not for himself, but for the beautiful woman whose life had been somehow entwined with his since childhood.

Yet it had taken Granger's death to bring them together.

Oh, God, please, Dawson begged again. *Help me find her.*

Lillie had closed her mother out of her life and had only recently realized her mistake. If she wanted to be close to her mother again, where would she go?

A heaviness slipped over Dawson's shoulders.

The night they met, Lillie had said she hoped someday to be strong enough to visit the spot where the steel drum and Irene's decomposed body had been found. It wasn't far from the main road. Dawson put on his turn signal as he approached the turnoff. The narrow side road wove through a forest of hardwoods that hugged the river's bank.

Dawson took the turn too fast. The rear tires hydroplaned on the wet pavement. He eased up on the gas until the car straightened and then increased his speed. The wind whipped whitecaps on the churning water to his right, now muddied by the rain and runoff.

When the pavement finally ended, Dawson got out of his car and glanced out over the river, knowing Lillie wouldn't have done anything foolish.

He refused to allow such nonsense to fill his head. Instead, he turned to stare at the underbrush. The sounds of the forest surrounded him along with another sound that floated through the air.

The whine of a diesel engine. Not military, but some type of a construction vehicle. Surely Nelson hadn't allowed his men to work when another storm was moving into the area. As if to prove his point, a streak of lightning punctuated the sky.

Dawson cut through the bramble and emerged in the clearing. In the distance stood the now-empty bleachers and reviewing stand. The bunting that had covered the VIP area hung limp from the rain.

Scanning the cordoned-off worksite, Dawson saw a

front-end loader move across a cleared stretch of land. The guy at the controls was a fool to be out in the elements with the threat of lightning overhead.

Even from where he stood, Dawson could see the tops of the steel pylons that, once buried, would provide a strong foundation for the new building. As he watched, the loader dumped a bucket of dirt into the gaping hole. The side of the pit crumbled under the vehicle's weight.

The memory of the collapsed earth sent fear roiling through Dawson's gut. The guy on the track didn't realize how easily the side of the pit could collapse, sending him and his vehicle crashing down the embankment.

"Stop," Dawson yelled. His words caught in the wind. He waved his arms and started to jog across the expansive clearing.

The temperature had dropped, and his leg ached. Each step sent pain down his calf. Despite his awkward gait, he pressed on.

Where was Karl Nelson? Probably eating lunch with the bigwigs, never realizing what was happening on the construction site. Not knowing Nelson's number, he phoned Mark's cell. The call went to voice mail.

"This is Dawson Timmons, CID. I know you're with the VIPs. Tell Karl Nelson to get over to the construction site before one of his men gets electrocuted in the storm."

Drizzling rain started to fall. Dawson squinted through the mist. The man at the switches was big and built. To add to his stupidity, he was working the machinery without a hard hat. The guy paused for a moment to wipe his hand across his bald head. He glanced up, for the first time, seeing Dawson.

"Get away from the worksite. Take shelter from the storm." Surely the guy would stop once Dawson had his attention, but instead of stopping, the man threw the vehicle into Reverse.

Dawson's phone vibrated in his hand. Raising it to his ear, he expected to hear the aide's voice. Instead Kelly McQueen Thibodeaux's words tumbled one after another.

"I failed to mention that Bobby Webber talked about his middle brother, Tommy. He graduated from Georgia Southwestern."

"Kelly, it's a bad time."

"Wait, Dawson. Here's the thing. Tommy's fraternity—Gamma Tau—went to Atlanta each year to party over the MLK weekend."

The pieces Dawson had been struggling to connect suddenly came together. Tommy was the missing brother and the missing link in the two murders.

He pushed the cell closer to his ear. "Call CID headquarters at Fort Rickman. Tell them I'm at the museum construction site and need backup. Now."

Disconnecting, Dawson unholstered his weapon.

"Stop," he screamed over the whine of the engine and the *clink-clank* of the treads.

Working the two control levers, the guy scooped up another bucketful of earth and drove straight for the pit.

As the loader neared, Dawson recognized the muscle-bound man at the controls.

Tom Reynolds, the manager of the Freemont gym, was Billy Everett's brother.

Lightning flashed overhead, yet the bodybuilder continued to push forward, seemingly intent on filling in the foundation.

Dawson glanced down. His heart lurched. A buzzing sounded in his ears. His gut tightened as realization hit him full force.

A steel drum lay at the bottom of the pit, half-buried by dirt. One more dumped load, and the drum would be completely covered.

Dawson had to get there first.

He knew what he'd find when he opened the drum.

Dead or alive, Dawson knew he'd find Lillie.

Dawson fired two rounds.

One hit Tom's leg. He fired back, grazing Dawson's arm.

The Glock slipped through Dawson's fingers and dropped into the dirt far below.

Half sliding, half falling, he slipped and skidded and tumbled down the pit until he reached the steel drum.

His hands clawed at the dirt. He had to free Lillie.

Dawson tugged on the lid. It failed to open.

Frantically, he searched for something—anything—to use as a wedge. Spying a piece of rebar, he raced forward.

The wet Georgia clay clung to his shoes and sucked him down like quicksand. He tripped and then righted himself.

Grabbing the twisted metal, he retraced his steps.

The earth rumbled overhead.

The grinding sound of the diesel engine was deafening. Dawson couldn't hear, couldn't think, all he knew was that he needed to open the drum.

"Oh, Lillie."

Using the rebar, he pried at the lid. The lip gave way ever so slightly, and the edge started to pull free.

Metal scraped against metal.

He looked up just as the bucket tilted and a wall of dirt crashed down upon him. Dawson inhaled the cloying earth and thrashed at the free fall of debris.

Blinded by the dirt, he flailed his arms. His lungs burned like fire.

God, please.

The engine died. In its place, he heard laughter.

Wiping his sleeve over his eyes, Dawson glanced up. The muscular bodybuilder stood on the edge of the pit. Blood darkened his pant leg.

"You're a fool, Dawson. One more bucketful of soil, and they'll never find you or the steel drum."

"You..." Dawson gasped for air. "You killed three prostitutes in Atlanta."

The beef shook his head. "My brother killed them."

"Billy?"

"He's too dumb."

And Bobby was too smart.

"You got drunk and told your story to a bar owner in Atlanta." Dawson needed answers. "He said you were wearing a college T-shirt. Only it didn't say Georgia Tech. It said Gamma Tau, your fraternity."

Tom stopped laughing. "Maybe you're smarter than I thought."

"You mentioned your brother." Dawson realized his own mistake. "Not a biological sibling, but your fraternity brother."

A smirk spread across Tom's full face. "The cops, the town, no one suspected who the murderer was."

"What about Granger Ford?"

"I had to kill him. He was getting too close to the truth."

"And you ran Lillie off the road."

"Only to scare her, but she kept digging for information."

With a groan, Tom hoisted himself back into the cab of the front loader and settled onto the padded seat.

The engine roared to life.

Dawson groped for his weapon, his fingers burrowing through the mud. Relief rushed over him when his hand touched the cool metal.

He raised the Glock.

Tom came into view.

Dawson squeezed the trigger and fired.

TWENTY-TWO

Dawson swept away the dirt that covered the drum. He clutched the rebar and pried off the lid. His heart hitched when he looked inside.

Lillie lay folded upon herself like a rag doll.

"Oh, honey." Grabbing her shoulders, he gently lifted her free.

Please, Lord, let her be alive.

Feeling for the artery in her neck, he was rewarded with a faint pulse and gasped with relief.

She was still alive.

His euphoria was short-lived, washed away when the loader rumbled back to life.

Glancing up, he expected to see Tom.

Instead, he saw the bucket suspended overhead. With a screech of metal, the load dropped. Dawson hunched over Lillie to protect her from the deluge of rock and soil and bramble.

The machine reversed and disappeared from sight. Dawson had to get Lillie out of the pit. Wrapping his arm around her waist, he dragged her up the fresh mound of dirt.

His feet slipped. He struggled to move forward.

Holding her close with one hand, he used the other to grab at the roots and debris tangled in the earth. They had to be clear of the pit before the next load of soil rained down upon them.

Dawson willed himself to keep moving, finding footholds that propelled him forward. His fingers locked on anything that would support his weight and Lillie's.

The sound of the diesel engine grew louder.

Finding a small ledge of packed earth, he tucked her behind him. The undercarriage of the loader appeared overhead. Dawson strained to see who was at the controls while his fingers curled around his weapon.

Karl Nelson leaned over the edge. Eyes bulging, hair disheveled and matted with mud.

"She has to die," he screamed over the drone of the engine.

Anger welled up within Dawson. "You killed her mother."

"I didn't have a choice."

Karl's face reddened with rage. "My father wanted to divorce my mother and marry his lover. I couldn't let that happen. He built Nelson Construction Company for me." He jammed a finger against his chest. "Why would I share my inheritance with his bastard child? My father did everything for everyone else, but he ignored me when I told him to get rid of Irene."

"They met in Atlanta, didn't they, Karl?" Dawson moved protectively in front of Lillie. "You saw them together over the MLK weekend."

"Their love child was born nine months later. For three years, I went to Atlanta to drown my sorrows. Each time my anger made me kill."

"Then you came after Irene. There was a storm that night."

Karl sneered. "I went to her house. She thought my father was at the door. When I told him later, his weak heart couldn't take the shock."

The construction boss disappeared from sight.

The idling engine throttled up, the sound deafening. The loader moved closer to the edge. The bucket rose overhead.

The cab came into view. Dawson raised his weapon and fired.

Karl grabbed the arm in the front loader.

The loader shifted. One track sank into the wet and weakened soil. The side buckled with the weight.

The edge gave way, and the huge machine rolled, releasing Karl's body. He fell headfirst against the steel pylon. The front loader teetered for a long moment and then, with a loud groan, crashed down on top of him.

Clawing his way up the last few feet, Dawson lifted Lillie free of the pit. He laid her on the ground, hearing the sirens in the distance.

Help was on the way.

Too late for Karl. But would they be in time to save Lillie?

TWENTY-THREE

Dawson stood outside the ICU, looking into Lillie's room. Pale as death, she lay unmoving on the bed. Wires hooked her to machines that monitored her heart rate and oxygen level. Dawson's only medical training was battlefield emergency triage, but even he knew the odds weren't good that Lillie would survive.

At the construction site, the EMTs had worked feverishly to stabilize her so she could survive the short ride to the hospital.

Because of his grazed arm and the amount of dirt he had inhaled, they transported Dawson in the same ambulance with Lillie. Being that close as they worked to keep her alive had almost been his undoing.

The sirens had screamed, clearing traffic and causing Dawson's heart to lodge in his throat, where it had remained ever since.

The phone call to her parents had been worse than walking into a minefield in Iraq. To their credit, the McKinneys hadn't blamed him. In fact they'd thanked him for saving her life.

Only her life still hung in the balance.

General Cameron and his aide had arrived almost

as soon as the ambulance had pulled up at the hospital. Both men were shaken when they saw Lillie's seemingly lifeless body wheeled into the E.R.

The general had talked to a number of the medical personnel, trying to find out more information, but no one knew what would happen in the next few hours.

To their credit and even without the commanding general's promptings, the medical personnel worked quickly to transport her to the ICU where Dawson now stood.

He heard footsteps in the hallway and turned to see Jamison. His buddy's face reflected the fear that ate at Dawson's gut. If anything happened to Lillie, he wouldn't survive. At least not emotionally. He might go through the motions, but under the surface, he'd be a broken man, unable to move forward.

"I came as soon as I could." Jamison grabbed his shoulders in an embrace that revealed the depth of their friendship and his own concern for Lillie. "What's the prognosis?"

Dawson choked on the words. "Her…her chances aren't good. Being out all night in the cold. Lack of oxygen. Her lungs are filled with fluid. She's spiking a fever that they can't bring down. Right now, the pneumonia is her biggest problem. She's on a ventilator that's pushing oxygen into her lungs, but they're also worried about her kidney function."

An ICU nurse scooted past them and entered Lillie's room. She hung a new bag of antibiotics and adjusted the mechanical pump to ensure the proper flow of medication into Lillie's bloodstream.

Leaving the room, she smiled weakly at Dawson. "Agent Timmons, there's nothing you can do right now.

We won't know anything until the antibiotics start to work. I'll call you if her condition changes."

"I don't want to leave her side."

Jamison squeezed his shoulder. "I brought the change of clothes you keep in the office and your Dopp kit. Why don't you find a shower and clean up, otherwise the janitorial service will have to work overtime."

Dawson looked down at the red clay that caked his shoes. His white shirt was stained with blood, and he didn't need a mirror to know dirt matted his hair and probably covered his face as well.

"There's a shower you can use at the end of the hall," the nurse offered, her eyes encouraging. "Packages of fresh toiletries and towels are on the shelf."

"When Lillie comes to, she won't want to see all that dirt," Jamison added, which convinced Dawson to follow his friend's advice. He didn't want anything to remind Lillie of what she had just endured.

The hot shower eased his sore muscles, but it did little for his outlook. He scrubbed the light flesh wound on his arm that he'd refused to let the medics treat. Later there would be time for him. Right now he was worried about Lillie. He'd never felt so helpless, and he knew her recovery rested solely in the hands of the medical team.

The nurse caught up to him in the hallway and covered his skinned flesh with antibiotic ointment and a thick four-by-four bandage. "Have one of the docs look at it tomorrow."

He found Jamison in the ICU waiting room. "The McKinneys arrived a few minutes ago. They saw Lillie and are in the chapel now."

"I...I should talk to them. The nurse said she'd call my cell if there's any change in Lillie's condition."

"How 'bout we get your shoulder treated first."

"It's already been taken care of."

The two special agents walked silently along the hospital corridors until they came to double doors and a sign that read *Peace be to you.* Jamison stood back so Dawson could enter.

A large bronze mosaic hung on the wall behind the wooden altar. A giant sun with streaming rays of light was depicted in tiny tiles pieced together into a tranquil scene of a country field and meandering brook. Dawson thought of Mr. McKinney's farm and the quiet farmland where Lillie had grown up.

"Oh, Dawson."

He turned to see Mrs. McKinney. Her face was wrapped in worry, but she opened her arms and pulled him close. Touched by the affection he sensed in her embrace, his eyes stung, and he bit down on his cheek to keep his emotions in check.

"We heard what you did to save our Lillie." She pulled back to look into his eyes. "How can we ever thank you?"

Unable to speak, he shook his head. Why would they thank him when Lillie was still in danger of losing her life?

Mr. McKinney stepped forward.

Dawson deserved everything the distraught father was about to say. Only Dawson wanted to apologize first. "Sir, I—"

The older man reached for Dawson's hand and then pulled him close. "Sarah and I have been thanking God that you found our daughter. Jamison told us what happened. In twenty-five years, no one has been able to learn the truth about Irene Beaumont's death until you got involved. I'm proud of you, son."

Once again, Dawson couldn't speak. He didn't deserve anyone's thanks or praise. He hadn't done anything that the other agents wouldn't have done.

"We've been praying for Lillie." Mrs. McKinney touched his hand. "Come sit with us, Dawson. There's power in prayer, and we want the Lord to know how much Lillie means to us." She squeezed his hand. "To all of us."

"Yes, ma'am."

Ushered forward, Dawson sat between Mrs. McKinney and Jamison. Lillie's father was on the opposite side of his wife.

Totally out of his comfort zone, Dawson didn't know what to expect or what to do. Hopefully, he wouldn't have to express his thoughts out loud.

Within a few minutes, he realized each of the people gathered in the chapel was offering up private prayers to the Lord.

Mrs. McKinney closed her eyes and nodded a few times as if she could hear God's voice. Her husband wrapped his arms around his broad chest and stared at the floor, lost in his own world. Jamison reached for a Bible from a nearby table and turned to scripture for comfort.

Dawson stared at the mosaic and realized he had asked the Lord to help him find Lillie, but he hadn't thanked Him for doing just that.

Dropping his head into his hands, he struggled to clear his thoughts. *You...You had my back today, Lord, and Lillie's. Thank You doesn't seem to be enough to say, especially since I have more to ask of You. Heal her, Lord. Lillie doesn't deserve to die.*

Once again his eyes stung, but this time he knew he wasn't alone. In addition to the prayerful people sitting next to him, Dawson could feel the rays of God's love, just like the rays of the sun from the mosaic, flowing down around him.

Sensing the Lord's presence buoyed his spirits and gave him hope that Lillie would survive, but as the hours passed and her condition continued to fail, Dawson wondered if the feeling of peace that had flowed over him in the chapel had been his imagination instead of anything real.

The McKinneys believed in the power of prayer, but Dawson had turned his back on the Almighty for too long. Now when he most needed God in his life, Dawson couldn't trust anything, not even the Lord.

Eventually, the small group returned to the ICU waiting room. Jamison brought up sandwiches from the hospital cafeteria, although Dawson hadn't been able to eat.

Chief Wilson stopped by to check on Lillie's condition. He and Dawson stepped into the hallway to talk privately.

"The Freemont police got a search warrant for Karl Nelson's home. They found pictures of the three women from Atlanta along with a few shots of Irene Beaumont. The women were jammed into the drums, just like the photo found under Granger's mattress."

Dawson shook his head at the construction tycoon's depravity. "Evidently Mr. Nelson wanted to document his kills."

Wilson nodded. "I wonder if he showed his father the

photos to prove what he had done. Medical records indicate Burl Nelson died of a heart attack not long after Irene's body was found."

"Karl didn't want to share his inheritance with his father's illegitimate child."

"Ironic that what he killed to prevent will eventually come true," Wilson said. "Karl never married and didn't have any heirs, so the Nelson Construction Company and all of its assets will go to Lillie. Plus, he owned the workout facility in Freemont Tom Reynolds ran. Not that money is important at a time like this."

"No, sir. The only thing that's important is Lillie's return to health."

"We're digging up the construction area, hoping to find the bodies of those three women from Atlanta. Once we do their families will have closure. That's because of your hard work." Wilson patted Dawson's back. "You did an outstanding job."

"Thank you, sir."

"There's one more thing."

"Yes, sir."

"I pulled your file and ran a check on your birth certificate, which verified the absence of your father's name on the official document."

"Yes, sir. That's what I told you and General Cameron."

Wilson nodded. "The JAG office confirmed you were within your legal authority to withhold his name on your recruitment papers since paternity had not been established at the time you entered the military. I'm sorry I had to follow up on that, Dawson, but I wanted to ensure this would never be a problem for you again."

"Does that mean Granger Ford's name will not be added to my record?"

"That's correct. Unless you request an official change to your file."

"I'll give that some thought."

"I told General Cameron the issue had been resolved. I also told him you are an excellent special agent and an asset to the division."

"Thank you, sir."

After the chief left, the nurse approached Dawson in the hallway. "We're going to see if Lillie can breathe on her own, if you want to tell her parents."

Dawson passed on the information. Mr. and Mrs. McKinney joined hands and prayed while Dawson stood nearby. The nurse's expression was downcast when she came back thirty minutes later. "She still needs the ventilator. The doctor wants to wait until later this evening before he tries again."

Dawson had never realized how hard waiting in the hospital could be. Every hour the McKinneys were allowed to see their daughter for a few minutes, but Lillie remained unresponsive. Mrs. McKinney always returned with tears in her eyes and cried softly in the corner while Mr. McKinney circled her with his arms and tried to comfort her with words of encouragement.

After their five o'clock visit, they went to the cafeteria, but only after Dawson promised to contact them if there was any change.

He paced the room, feeling the walls closing in around him. Since the construction accident, he had never liked confining spaces, but today his struggle was Lillie's fight to survive. He stopped in front of the large bank of windows and gazed at the gathering twilight outside. A gray pall that rivaled the weight of his own despair hung over the horizon.

Ready to turn away, he stopped as a patch of blue sky broke through the cloud cover, and rays of sunlight showered down upon the earth. Was God giving him a sign?

Granger had made his peace with the Lord and Dawson wanted to do the same, but there was one person with whom he needed to reconcile.

He raised his cell phone and plugged in a number. His mother's voice sounded tired when she answered.

After exchanging awkward pleasantries, Dawson got to the reason for his call. "When I was a little guy, you taught me to pray. Somewhere along the way we both stopped doing just that. I need your prayers today, Mom, for someone special. Her name is Lillie Beaumont."

As the hours ticked by, Dawson tried to convince the McKinneys to go home for the night, but they wanted to be close to Lillie. He couldn't blame them, since he felt the same way.

Eventually, they fell asleep on two reclining chairs in the waiting room. Unable to relax, Dawson wandered the hallways and ended up at Lillie's room.

His heart lurched and fear chilled his soul when he saw the medical staff gathered at her bedside.

"She's breathing on her own," one of the nurses said as she left the room. "You can talk to her if you'd like. I doubt she'll respond, but she may be able to hear you."

Once the room cleared, Dawson approached Lillie's bedside. Using care not to disturb the tubes and wires, he took her hand in his.

"Lillie, it's Dawson. The nurse said I could talk to

you, only I don't know where to start." He paused to decide what to tell her first.

"I can't hide how I feel about you any longer. You're the most wonderful woman in the world, and I…well, I love you and I want to be with you for the rest of my life." He smiled. "Actually even longer than that."

He rubbed her hand. "So you need to pull through and open your beautiful eyes."

She moaned.

Encouraged, he leaned closer. "Open your eyes, honey. Please, for me."

Her lashes quivered.

Oh, God, let her wake up.

A muscle in her neck twitched.

"Lillie, come on. You can do it."

She blinked. Slowly, her eyes opened. They were just as he remembered and as emerald-green as the fields around her father's house.

"Daw…son." She whispered his name.

"It's me, honey. I'm right here."

"You…you…saved…me."

"I'll never let anything get between us again. At least for as long as you want me around."

She nodded.

"Does that mean you *do* want me around?" he teased.

Her lips trembled and a tear ran down her cheek, causing his gut to tighten. The last thing he wanted was to make her cry.

"Look, honey. I'm probably saying too much—"

Weak as she was, her fingers squeezed his hand. "For…ever."

He bent down closer. "Did you say forever?"

She nodded ever so slightly. "Love you…forever."

Dawson's heart nearly exploded. Not from fear or worry, but from the realization that God had listened to his prayer. Lillie would pull through, he felt sure, and despite everything that had happened, they would have a future together.

Although he'd never known his father, Granger had in a very strange way brought them together. Despite their pasts, Lillie and Dawson could move beyond the pain and rejection of their childhoods because they had each other. More importantly, they had a God who was on their side and a love that would only grow stronger with time.

He touched her cheek, feeling the softness of her skin. Seeing a faint tinge of pink gave him hope that her pallor would soon improve.

"My timing's never been good." He smiled, feeling suddenly unsure of himself.

Then he looked into her eyes and any hesitation left him. "I said it when you were asleep, but just in case you didn't hear me, I need to say it again."

Her face filled with expectation.

"I love you, Lillie, and I want to spend the rest of my life trying to make you happy."

Then, in spite of the wires and machines, he lowered his lips and gently kissed her sweet mouth.

She sighed when he pulled back.

"I…love…you," she whispered before her eyes closed and she fell back to sleep.

EPILOGUE

The May sun warmed Dawson's back as he dug in the soil and planted another rosebush.

"You look like a farmer," Lillie teased. Kneeling nearby, she spread mulch around a group of flowering hydrangeas, their blooms as blue as the sky overhead.

Task completed, she sat back and studied the three-story museum that would be open within the week. "The weather should be perfect for the dedication."

Dawson left his shovel in the dirt and scooted next to Lillie, wondering if he'd ever tire of seeing the sunlight in her hair.

"Chief Wilson gave me the day off for the ceremony. He said I need to be sitting next to the woman who made this all possible."

Lillie smiled. "The plans had already been finalized. All I needed to do was ensure Nelson Construction completed the project on time."

"And under budget. You're a savvy businessman just like your father was."

She raised her brow playfully. "That would be *businesswoman,* Agent Timmons."

He laughed. "Yes, ma'am."

Wistfulness washed over her pretty face as she looked toward the nearby river. A path of dogwoods edged the stone walk that led to a picnic area near the water's edge.

"I dreamed about him last night," she said. "He and my mother were laughing. Then he reached for me and raised me into the air while I giggled and begged to go higher."

"I'm glad the good memories are returning. Have you told your mom?"

Lillie nodded. "She said her prayer has always been for me to know how much my biological mother and father loved me."

"The McKinneys are good people."

"And the best parents I could ever have."

"Did you contact the families of the three missing Atlanta women?"

"They all seemed touched by the college scholarships and the trees in each girl's memory. I told them they were planted near Irene's Garden."

Dawson looked at the etched plaque to Lillie's mother erected in the middle of the flowering bushes and rows of blooming plants. "It's a perfect memorial to her memory."

Lillie nudged his arm. "Plus it lets you play in the dirt. Dad said you're a farmer at heart. He also told me you were looking at land not far from their place."

"I wanted to surprise you. A hundred acres are for sale."

She studied him with pensive eyes. "You've decided to get out of the military?"

He shrugged. "I keep feeling a need to work the soil."

"Maybe you could go into landscaping," she teased, making him laugh.

"You have your construction company," he reminded her. "And your gym."

She held up her hand. "I'm putting both of them up for sale."

"Are you sure?"

"It's not what I want, Dawson."

He leaned in, his gaze intent on the fullness of her lips and the curve of her smile. "What do you want, Lillie?"

"I thought we discussed that when I was in the hospital."

"You needed time to heal, emotionally and physically."

She scooted closer. "I'm all better now."

"But this isn't the best time. I was thinking of a candlelight dinner and a roaring fire."

"It's too warm to build a fire." She looked around. "Besides, a farmer's wife likes fresh air and sunshine."

He tickled her chin. "You know what you want, don't you, Ms. Beaumont?"

"You do too, soon-to-be Farmer Timmons."

"What I want—" he reached for her "—is for you to be my wife."

Without saying yes, she wrapped her arms around his neck and molded into his embrace. All around them, flowers danced in the breeze from the river.

"We'll get married at the main post chapel," Lillie said. "And hold the reception in the ballroom at the museum."

He kissed her cheek and then her neck as she discussed plans for their wedding, while he enjoyed the softness of her skin and the fragrant scent of her perfume.

Dawson wouldn't mention that he had seen the wedding magazines at her parents' farmhouse or that Mr. McKinney had already clued him in on how women always got what they wanted.

After all, marrying Lillie was what Dawson wanted more than anything. He had given her time to heal and experience life without always looking over her shoulder.

Dawson had needed time to heal his relationship with his mother and grow in his faith. Both he and Lillie were stronger now and ready to start their new life together.

Tonight, after they had a candlelight dinner, he would slip a ring on her finger and formally ask her to be his wife. But he already knew the answer. Their lives had been entwined, seemingly forever.

The storms of the past were over, and the future would be filled with sunshine and babies. Strong boys to help him on the farm and emerald-eyed girls who would steal his heart, just as Lillie had done the first time he saw her.

She continued to chatter, but then she stopped and smiled at him, her eyes making him think of lush green farmland and the home they would build on their new acreage.

Then thoughts of everything else left him and all he could think about was Lillie. Her lips on his, her arms holding him tight, the way their hearts beat in sync. They kissed and kissed and kissed again, while the sun warmed them and the gentle breezes wrapped them in a loving embrace.

* * * * *

LISTEN UP!!
N THE
IN FIVE MINUTES!! IF YOU'RE LATE, IT'S PORK BUN PUNISHMENT FOR YOU!!
AND IF YOU SQUEAL, IT'S THE PORK ROAST PUNISHMENT!!
GYAH HA HA HA HA!
I—
HFF!
HFF!
HARU...
HFF!
I...!!
DOSA (WHUMP)
NNGH...
UGH...
—BOY...
AH!

AH......
YOU'RE ...?
—DON'T YOU WANT TO GO FURTHER, BOY?
DON'T YOU WANT TO "ACCELERATE"?

CHAPTER
#01

PIKON (DING)
You have one new e-mail.
BIKU (SHUDDER)
KUI
KUI (JAB)
NIYA
NIYA (LEER)
CLICK CLICK
SO (SWF)
KUI
CHIRA (PEEK)
...IT'S FROM ARAYA. ...I JUST KNOW IT.

PI (BEEP)

Play sound file.

>>> pig-order/////

HEY, HEY, PIGGY ARITAAA!!

TODAY'S ORDER! C'MON!!

TWO YAKISOBA BUNS!! ONE CREAM MELON BUN AND THREE STRAWBERRY YOGURTS!!

BRING THEM TO THE ROOF WITHIN FIVE MINUTES AFTER LUNCH STARTS!!

ドーッ
DON (WHAM)
OH! MY BAD!
LET'S GO!
FOR REAL!?
AH HA HA...

GUUUUU (GRUMBLE)

......

I'M SO HUNGRY...

HARUYUKI, I CHARGED ¥500 TO YOU FOR LUNCH MONEY.

'KAY. I'M GOING TO SCHOOL NOW.

THE MONEY ENDS UP GETTING USED ON THEM...

SORRY, MOM...

—HOW LONG AM I GONNA KEEP GOING LIKE THIS?
GU (CLENCH)

I'VE SAVED ALL THE MESSAGES FROM ARAYA...
IF I JUST HAND THEM OVER TO THE SCHOOL AS EVIDENCE, THEN—!!
SU (SHF)

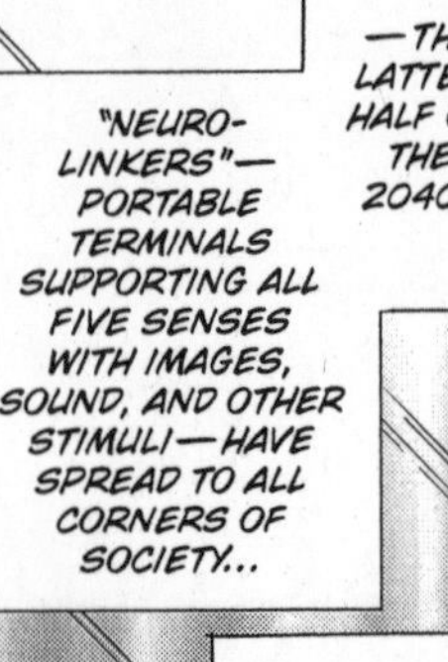
AND IF YOU SQUEAL, IT'S THE PORK ROAST PUNISHMENT!
BIKU (SHUDDER)
—I CAN'T DO IT!!!
—THE LATTER HALF OF THE 2040s
"NEURO-LINKERS"—PORTABLE TERMINALS SUPPORTING ALL FIVE SENSES WITH IMAGES, SOUND, AND OTHER STIMULI—HAVE SPREAD TO ALL CORNERS OF SOCIETY...
...AND HALF OF EVERYONE'S DAILY LIVES TAKES PLACE ON VIRTUAL NETWORKS.
BUT IN THE END, EVERY HUMAN BEING IS STILL JUST AN EXISTENCE BOUND BY THE CHAINS OF A "FLESH AND BLOOD" BODY.

IF HE HITS ME, IT'LL HURT.

AND CRYING 'COS IT HURTS IS SO PATHETIC I COULD DIE—

THAT'S WHY I...
ドスッ
DOSU (THUMP)
ぐー!!
GUUU (GROWL)
ギシッ
GISHI (CREAK)

ぼそ
BOSO (WHISPER)
DIRECT LINK.
I THROW IT AWAY— THE REAL ME.

KIIN
(SKREEE)
"FULL
DIVE"

POU (GLOW)
ポワー…
PIPI (BEEP)
ピピッ
—Umesato Junior High School. You are now logged into the school's local network.
THIS WAY... I DON'T FEEL HUNGRY.
NADE (PAT)
なで なで
NADE
EVEN IF I CAN ONLY SPEND MY LUNCH HOUR HERE...
TA (DASH)
...IT MAKES IT A LITTLE BETTER AT LEAST...

TA (TAK)
TA
TA
THAT'S...

SHE'S SOMEONE YOU HARDLY EVER SEE.
SECOND-YEAR STUDENT AND VICE PRESIDENT OF THE STUDENT COUNCIL—
KURO-YUKI-HIME, A.K.A. SNOW BLACK.

SHE BASICALLY RECREATED HER REAL-LIFE BEAUTIFUL SELF.
AN EXQUISITE, GORGEOUS, ORIGINAL AVATAR.

OOH, I DIDN'T KNOW YOU HAD SUCH A FANCY AVATAR?
GIMME!!
BUT IT TOOK ME DAYS TO MAKE THIS...!!
SHUT UP!! USE THIS, YOU LITTLE PORKER!! IT'S MORE YOUR STYLE!!
GYAH HA HA HA!
......

EVEN MY VIRTUAL SELF...

DA (DASH)

...IS...

LOGIN : Haruyuki Arita
HISCORE
LV 149 2467328 PTS
PI (BEEP)
PI
PI
PI
IT'S NOT POPULAR, SO THE AREA'S DESERTED.
THIS IS THE PLACE FOR ME.
THE "VIRTUAL SQUASH GAME"...
KACHA (CHAK)
START
PON (DING)
FREAKIN' REALITY!
WHO NEEDS IT ANYWAY...!!?
PAKON (THWACK)
DAMMIT... REALITY!
FU (FWSH)

KA (PLRK)
KA
DAMMIIIIT...
I HAVE TO...
PAKON (THWACK)
...ACCELERATE!!
PI (BEEP)
LV 87
SPEED UP
I HAVE TO...
...GO FASTER!! FASTER!!
PAKON
PAKON
PAKON

LV 146
>>> SPEED UP
HI SCORE
SO THAT...
...I CAN BREAK THROUGH...
...EVERY WALL IN THE VIRTUAL WORLD AND EVEN THE REAL WORLD...
...AND GO SOMEWHERE NO ONE ELSE CAN—!
THAT FAST!!
HYUN (WHIZ)
BIKU (JOLT)
AHHHHH—!!

SO THIS IS WHERE YOU LOCKED YOURSELF UP!!
CHI—
CHIYU...
HONESTLY, HARU! YOU DISAPPEAR EVERY LUNCH!
I'VE BEEN LOOKING ALL OVER FOR YOU!
I MEAN, YOU'RE PLAYING ALL BY YOURSELF, AND IT'S THIS LAME...
...HUH?
WHAT THE...!?
RANKING
LEVEL SCORE
1ST 152 2635924 PTS
2ND 149 2467328 PTS
3RD 148 2449783 PTS
4TH 146 2314334 PTS
5TH 145 2309603 PTS
LEVEL 152? AND A SCORE OF 2,635,924!?
DOKI (BADUM)
ドキッ
YEAH ......
HARU, YOU'RE AMAZING! I CAN'T BELIEVE YOU GOT SUCH A HIGH SCORE!!
DOKI
ドキ
DOKI
ドキ

—ARE YOU...
...A TOTAL IDIOT!?
......
WHAT ARE YOU EVEN DOING... SKIPPING LUNCH FOR THIS!?
LOG OUT RIGHT NOW!!
...I DON'T WANT TO.

PI (BEEP)
RETRY
THERE'S STILL HALF AN HOUR LEFT OF LUNCH.
YOU GO.
KACHIN (SNAP)

—OKAY, FINE!!
IF YOU'RE GONNA BE LIKE THAT...
...I'LL JUST HAVE TO USE FORCE!!
BOSO (WHISPER)
...GO AHEAD IF YOU CAN.

MUSSU (IRK)
BLEEEEEEH!
"LINK OUT"!!
HYUN (FWOOSH)
—I GUESS SHE WENT BACK OVER TO THE REAL SIDE...
GAN (WHAM)
!!?
! WARNING
Forced logout

HA (GASP)
CHI—
CHIYU...
H-HOW DID YOU GET IN HERE!!?
THIS IS THE BOYS' BATHROOM, Y'KNOW !?
SURU
SURU (WRIGGLE)
YOU GOT A PROBLEM WITH THIS?
AND I LOCKED THE DOOR! HOW DID YOU—!?
HYOI (SPROING)
GYO (GAPE)
...OHH, SO THAT'S HOW YOU GOT IN.

C'MON, COME OUT ALREADY, HARU.
...FIIINE.
OH, GOOD. THERE'S NO ONE IN THE HALL.
CAN'T BE SEEN IN A PLACE LIKE THIS...!
ANYWAY, CHIYU...
HOW'D YOU KNOW I WAS HERE?
......
I WAS ON THE ROOF BEFORE TOO...
SO I FOLLOWED YOU.
...YOU SAW?
......
I... I WON'T BUTT IN ABOUT THEM ANYMORE.
IF THAT'S WHAT YOU WANT, HARU ...
BUT!
YOU SHOULD EAT LUNCH AT LEAST!!
はっ
PA (SNATCH)
HERE! I MADE ONE FOR YOU!!

NO WAAAY! TAKKUN EATS THE SCHOOL LUNCH.

SEE? HERE, SANDWICHES.

PLEASE STOP... PLEASE, I'M BEGGING YOU TO STOP!!

BASHI (WHAP)
NO, THANKS ...!!
BECHA (SPLAT)
HA (GASP)
AH...
HARU...

I...
I...

I'M THE WORST ...!

SEE YOU!

CHIYU ...
I WONDER IF SHE WENT HOME ALREADY ...

ぼそ BOSO (WHISPER)

...... FULL...

...DIVE......

You are now logged into...

...the school's local network.

Virtual ... Game

TOBO TOBO

CHIKA (BLINK)

CHIKA

WHAT ...!?

BA (WHIP)

LEVEL... 166!?

BEST RANKING

	LEVEL	SCORE
1ST	166	3749182 PTS
2ND	152	2635924 PTS
3RD	149	2467328 PTS

THAT'S MORE THAN TEN LEVELS HIGHER THAN ME FROM BEFORE ...!!

LEVEL 166 152 14

WHO THE HECK COULD GET SUCH A CRAZY SCORE...!?

KUROYUKIHIME—!!
—SO YOU'RE THE ONE WHO...
...GOT THAT RIDICULOUS SCORE OVER LUNCH?

TSU (SSP)

BIKU (JUMP)

HUH?

DON'T YOU WANT TO GO FURTHER, BOY?

DON'T YOU WANT TO "ACCELERATE"?

HMM...?

UH... UWAH.
GASA (RUSTLE)
SHE'S REALLY HERE...
I-I REALLY DON'T HAVE THE TIME TO BE DOING THIS...
YAKISOBA BUNS AND CREAM MELON BUNS AGAIN TODAY! GOT IT!!?
I DON'T, BUT...

—I DON'T, BUT...
IF YOU DO...
...COME TO THE LOUNGE AT LUNCH TOMORROW.
......
—DAMMIT!
GU (CLENCH)
HERE I GO!!
HISO (PSST)
Hey... That tie.
HISO
Isn't he a first-year?
HISO
HISO
Doesn't he know that first-years aren't allowed in the lounge?
HISO
HISO
No way... It's second term already. How could he not know...?
HISO

MOJI (FIDGET)
もじ…
OH...
DID YOU NEED SOME-THING?
Err... Um...
もご もご
MOGO MOGO (MUMBLE)
ぱっ
PA (BEAM)
—WELL, BOY!
YOU CAME!!
ぱたんっ
PATAN (SHUT)
I'M THE SOME-THING.
SORRY, WOULD YOU MIND FINDING ANOTHER SEAT?
O-OH, SURE ...
ガタッ
GATA (KLATTER)
じろ じろ じろ
JIRO (STARE) JIRO JIRO

SFX: GOSO (DIG)

SU (SWF)

HUH?

ZAWA (MURMUR)

!!?

KACHI (CHIK)

"DIRECT WIRED TRANS-MIS-SION."
CON-NECTING NEURO-LINKERS WITH A DIRECT CABLE.
CALLED "DIRECTING" FOR SHORT, THIS INTERFACE...
...BASICALLY HAS NO SECURITY, UNLIKE THE USUAL WIRELESS TRANSMIS-SION.
WARNING !
Wired Connection
Connected...
Wired Connection
KACHI (CHIK)
Now then ...
Sorry for asking you to go out of your way to come here.
THIS IS WHY DIRECTING IS RESERVED FOR PEOPLE BOUND BY A STRONG SENSE OF TRUST.
PARENTS, SIBLINGS, AND—
Haruyuki Arita-kun.
Can you neurospeak?
LOVERS.
Y...
Yes...!!
TOKUN
TOKUN (BADUM)

Uh... Umm... What exactly is this... about?

Hm?

Some kind of... um... elaborate prank or ...?

......

Do you ...

...want to change your world?

!?

Right now, I'm...

...sending an application to your Neuro-linker.

If you accept it...

...the world you have known till now will be completely and utterly destroyed...

...and then rebuilt into something of which you can't even conceive—

MY WORLD...

...DESTROYED!?

TSUI (FWP)

WHAT THE...? NO WAY... NO CAN DO!!

I CAN'T POSSIBLY LAUNCH AN UNKNOWN APP...

...FROM SOMEONE I BARELY KNOW...!!

......

I MEAN, IF IT'S A VIRUS, WHO KNOWS HOW MUCH SERIOUS DAMAGE IT COULD DO...?

DAMAGE... BREAK THE WORLD.

...THE REAL WORLD...

PI
Yes
MY... REALITY...
......
Download started...
—JUST WHAT I WAS HOPING FOR...
AS LONG AS THIS WORLD...
...BREAKS.
Download started... ...100%
Complete
PI

THE

OH... A SCROLLING MESSAGE...

LET'S SEE... "WELCOME..."

WORLD !!

GOO
(WHOOOM)
!!?
WELCOME TO
ACCELERATED
"...TO THE ACCELERATED WORLD"?

PAKU (GAPE)
PAKU
Uh...
Umm...
This Brain Burst program. What exactly is it...?
So...
...you've managed to install it safely.
Well, I was certain you had the aptitude for it.
—Apti-tude?
Mm. The aptitude.
Brain Burst can't even be installed in people who...
...don't possess high-level cerebral nerve reaction speed.
For instance... the sort of speed required to get an absurdly high score in a virtual game.
OH......

If you didn't have the aptitude, you wouldn't have even been able to see the phantom flames or the logo.
—Still, I must say...
The old me hesitated for two minutes about accepting the program.
I'd even worked out a whole speech to persuade you...
It seems I was just wasting my time.
TSUI (FWIP)
...your quick decision surprised me.
What!? Oh... No, well...
KAAAA (BLUSH)
BA (WHAP)
Er... A-anyway, nothing seems especially different now that I've installed it!
What is this progr—
WHY, YOU!!
BIKU (JUMP)
SO THIS IS WHERE YOU ARE, YOU TWERP!!!

BA (WHAP)
HEY, PI... ARITAAA !!
WHO SAID YOU COULD SKIP OUT ON YOUR ORDERS !!!?
A......
ARAYA ......!?

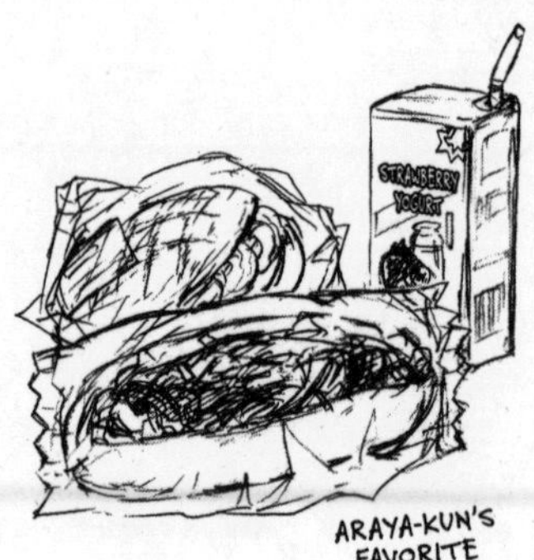
STRAWBERRY YOGURT
ARAYA-KUN'S FAVORITE LUNCH

CHAPTER
#02
ARITA! YOU...!!
YOU GOT A JOB TO DO...!!
ZA (SQUEEZE)
A...
ARAYA ....!!
GATA (TREMBLE)
GATA

ZUKA (STALK)
ズカ
ZUKA
ズカ

STOP... JUST STOP NOW...!!

BURU (SHAKE)
BURU
HM?

IRA (ARGH)
YOU...
YOU MAKING FUN OF ME!?
AH...!! NO, IT'S—!!

YOU'RE ARAYA-KUN...
!!
...YES?

I HEARD ABOUT YOU FROM ARITA.

—THAT YOU MIGHT HAVE BEEN...
...SENT TO JUNIOR HIGH SCHOOL FROM THE ZOO.
!!?!?
BU (FWSH)
WH—
WH—
GA (SLAP)
YOU ARE SO DEAD, PIIIIIIIIG!!
AH!
THAT'S IT!!
HE'S GONNA HIT ME—!!

NOW!! SHOUT IT!!
"BURST LINK"!!
B...
PAK!!!! (CRACK)
"BURST LINK"!!

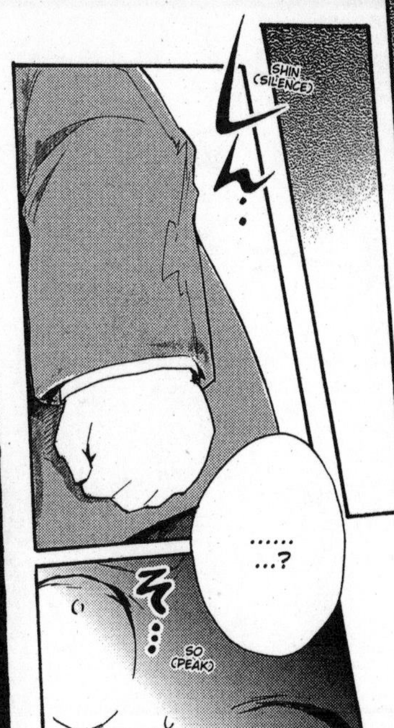

SHIN (SILENCE)
......
...?
SO (PEAK)
BA (GAH)
AAAAAAAH!!
ZUZAZA (SCRAMBLE)
AH!
HUH?
BA (GAH)
HUH...
HUH!?

HUUUUUU-UUH...!!?
TIME—HAS STOPPED!!?
EVERY-THING'S...
...COLORED BLUE.
KYORO (WHIRL)
きょろ
AH!
KUROYUKIHIME-SENPAI...!!

DA (DASH)
WH-WHAT IS GOING ON HERE!?
FULL DIVE!? OR...
...AN OUT-OF-BODY EXPERIENCE!?
HA-HA... NEITHER.
RIGHT NOW, WE ARE OPERATING IN THE BRAIN BURST PROGRAM.
WE'RE "ACCELERATED."
A...
ACCELER-ATED...!?
EXACTLY.
KA (KLAK)
KA
EVERYTHING AROUND US LOOKS LIKE IT HAS STOPPED, BUT IN FACT, IT HASN'T.
OUR CONSCIOUSNESSES ARE MOVING AT EXTREMELY HIGH SPEEDS.
KA

SU (SHF)
PITA (TAP)
THIS FIST...
IT IS MOVING VERY SLOWLY, CRAWLING FORWARD.
LIKE THE HOUR HAND OF A CLOCK...

IF WE WAITED LIKE THIS, AT SOME POINT...
...IT WOULD SINK SLOWLY INTO YOUR CHEEK.
Y-YOU'RE KIDDING!!

A-ANYWAY, THIS ISN'T AN OUT-OF-BODY EXPERIENCE.
IT'S ACTUALLY ALL HAPPENING IN OUR HEADS... IS THAT IT?
YOU LEARN FAST. THAT'S EXACTLY IT.
BUT... THAT'S CRAZY.
IF YOU'RE SAYING THAT JUST OUR THINKING AND OUR IMPRES-SIONS ARE ACCELERATED...
...THEN THERE'S NO WAY I SHOULD BE ABLE TO MOVE AROUND OUTSIDE MY BODY AND SEE MY OWN BACK...

...OR EVEN STAND HERE AND HAVE A CONVERSATION WITH YOU...!!
MM.
THAT'S A VERY NATURAL CONCERN.
SU...
HARUYUKI-KUN.
GO AHEAD AND TAKE A LOOK UNDER THE TABLE.
TON (THUK)
?
O-OKAY...
HYOI (POP)
HUH!?
WHAT THE—!?
IT'S NOT THE WOOD OF THE DESK OR ANYTHING...
IT'S LIKE IT'S A... POLYGON?
HA.
EXACTLY.

THIS BLUE WORLD IS THE REAL WORLD IN REAL TIME, BUT...
...IT'S NOT WHAT YOU WOULD SEE DIRECTLY WITH YOUR EYES.
IT'S A 3-D IMAGE RECONSTRUCTED FROM IMAGES CAPTURED BY SEVERAL SOCIAL CAMERAS IN THE LOUNGE...
...AND OUR BRAINS ARE SEEING IT THROUGH OUR NEUROLINKERS.
WHICH IS WHY THERE IS NO POINT IN TRYING TO LOOK UP THE SKIRT OF THAT GIRL THERE.
R-RIGHT.
MOJI (FIDGET)
JITO (STARE)
AH!
...DON'T LOOK AT MY LEGS.
THEY'RE IN VIEW OF THE CAMERAS.
DOKI (BADUM)
I-I WON'T!

S-SO THEN...
...THIS IS A 3-D VERSION OF THE REAL WORLD IN REAL TIME.
USING OUR AVATARS, WE'RE LOOKING AROUND US AND TALKING VIA THE DIRECT CONNECTION, RIGHT?
RIGHT. THAT'S EXACTLY IT.
OKAY... I GET THE BASIC LOGIC OF IT...
—BUT.
WHAT I REALLY WANT TO KNOW IS...
...WHAT EXACTLY IS...
..."ACCELERATED"?
I'VE NEVER HEARD OF NEUROLINKERS EQUIPPED...
...WITH A FUNCTION THAT STOPS TIME LIKE THIS...!!
—HMM.

HARUYUKI-KUN.
DO YOU KNOW THE PRINCIPLE BEHIND THE OPERATION OF THE NEURO-LINKER?
SO (PAT)

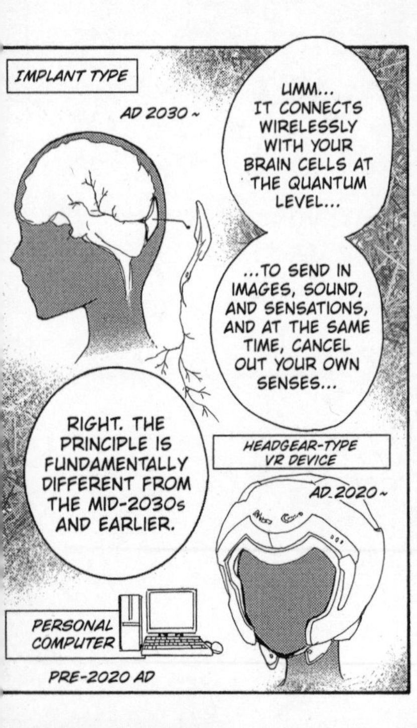

IMPLANT TYPE
AD 2030 ~
UMM... IT CONNECTS WIRELESSLY WITH YOUR BRAIN CELLS AT THE QUANTUM LEVEL...
...TO SEND IN IMAGES, SOUND, AND SENSATIONS, AND AT THE SAME TIME, CANCEL OUT YOUR OWN SENSES...
RIGHT. THE PRINCIPLE IS FUNDAMENTALLY DIFFERENT FROM THE MID-2030s AND EARLIER.
HEADGEAR-TYPE VR DEVICE
AD 2020 ~
PERSONAL COMPUTER
PRE-2020 AD

A QUANTUM CONNECTION IS NOT A PHYSIOLOGICAL MECHANISM.

THUS, YOU DON'T HAVE THE BURDEN ON THE BRAIN CELLS, AND YOU GET THIS UNEXPECTED EXCESS...

...OR SO A CERTAIN PERSON OUT THERE REALIZED.

NEUROLINKER

AD 2040 ~

GOKURI (GULP)

WH...

WHAT DO YOU MEAN... EXCESS?

YOU PROBABLY KNOW WHAT THEY CALLED THE BASIC OPERATING FREQUENCY OF THE COMPUTERS.
THE... BASE CLOCK?
YES...YOU OVERCLOCKED THE SIGNAL, WHICH CARVED UP TIME...
...LIKE A PENDULUM ON THE MOTHERBOARD TO RUN THE CPU.
—AND HUMAN BRAINS WORK THE SAME WAY.
WHAT!?
N-NO WAY!!
WHERE IS THIS PENDULUM INSIDE US THEN!?
HA-HA...
GYU (SQUEEZE)
ぎゅっ
TON (PAT)
HERE.
DOKIN (THUMP)
どきんっ
WH...
WHAT ARE YOU DOING!?
RIGHT NOW, YOUR CLOCK IS A LITTLE FASTER.
—YOU PROBABLY GET IT ALREADY.
KAAAAA (GAAH)
かあああああ

IT'S YOUR HEART!!
YOUR HEART'S NOT MERELY A PUMP SENDING OUT BLOOD.
THE BEATING OF YOUR HEART MAKES IT THE BASIC DEVICE DETERMINING THE DRIVING SPEED OF YOUR THOUGHTS.
MY...
...HEART?
DOKUN (THUMP)
FOR INSTANCE, WHEN YOU TRY TO STOP YOUR BODY...
...YOUR HEARTBEAT WILL SPEED UP DEPENDING ON THE SITUATION.
LIKE A RACE CAR DRIVER.
THIS IS BECAUSE...
...YOU NEED TO "ACCEL-ERATE"...
...YOUR THOUGHTS— YOUR AWARENESS OF THE SITUATION, YOUR JUDGMENT.

OR.
LIKE A PAIR OF LOVERS TOUCHING EACH OTHER...
..."YOU "ACCELERATE" TO MORE DEEPLY EXPERIENCE EACH MINUTE, EACH SECOND...
TON (POKE)
WITH EACH BEAT OF YOUR HEART...
...THE QUANTUM PULSE SIGNAL GENERATED IS SENT BACK TO YOUR CENTRAL NERVOUS SYSTEM...
...DRIVING YOUR BRAIN— THAT IS, YOUR THOUGHTS.
TSU (DRAG)
TSU
TSU
PITA (TAP)
SO.
WHAT DO YOU THINK HAPPENS WHEN...
...THE NEUROLINKER AROUND YOUR NECK CAPTURES THAT SIGNAL... AND OVERCLOCKS YOU?
......!!
YOUR...
YOUR THOUGHTS ARE "ACCELERATED"...!?
EXACTLY.
THE NEURO-LINKER...
...LETS YOU DO THAT.

RIGHT NOW, IN THIS EXACT MOMENT...
...OUR NEUROLINKERS ARE AMPLIFYING THE CLOCK GENERATED BY A SINGLE HEARTBEAT...
...AND SENDING IT TO OUR BRAINS.
IN FACT, IT'S DOING SO...
...AT A RATE OF MORE THAN A THOUSAND-FOLD!!
A... THOUSAND-FOLD...
ONE SECOND OF REALITY IS A THOUSAND SECONDS... IN OTHER WORDS...
...YOU'RE EXPERIENCING SIXTEEN MINUTES AND FORTY SECONDS...
I GOT CAUGHT UP IN EXPLAINING THINGS, AND I FORGOT...
...THAT YOU'RE ABOUT TO BE SENT FLYING.
AAH!?
GAN (GAUGH)
IT'S CLOSER THAN BEFORE!?
OH!
OH! SORRY.
I-IF I JUST MOVE IT HERE NOW...!!
BA (GAH)
JITA JITA (SQUIRM)
UNFORTUNATELY, YOU CAN'T. IN A CERTAIN SENSE, IT'S NOT REAL.

SO... THEN.
...HOW LONG DOES THIS "ACCELERATION" LAST?
IN THEORY, FOREVER.
BUT DUE TO THE LIMITS OF THE BRAIN BURST PROGRAM...
...THE LONGEST IS THIRTY FELT MINUTES...
...OR ONE-POINT-EIGHT REAL SECONDS.
...IN...
...ABOUT TWO...
...SEC-ONDS...?
BACOOOON!
H...
HE'S GOING TO HIT ME, ISN'T HE!?
HA-HA! DON'T WORRY.
YOU CAN STOP THE ACCELERATED STATE WHEN YOU WANT TO.
AH!
TH- THEN...
...I CAN AVOID THIS PUNCH WHEN I GO BACK TO REALITY...?
YEAH, IT'S SIMPLE.
THIS WAY OF USING ACCELERATION IS THE EASIEST TO UNDERSTAND.
I GUESS... UP TO NOW, I'VE BEEN SO SCARED, I HAVEN'T EVEN BEEN ABLE TO LOOK AT ARAYA'S FIST.
BUT IF I MOVE TO THE LEFT BY JUST FIFTEEN CENTIMETERS, I CAN AVOID THIS PUNCH...

—
BUT.
DON'T AVOID IT.
WHAT...!?
I-I DON'T WANT TO GET HIT!
IT'S GOING TO HURT...!!
—I'M ASKING YOU...
HURT WHAT?
??
WHAT DO YOU MEAN, "WHAT"?
...WHETHER IT'S GOING TO HURT...
...YOUR BODY OR YOUR MIND......
......
......!!!

ONE IS, OF COURSE ...
...THAT YOU HAVE JUST MEEKLY ACCEPTED HIS BEHAVIOR.
AND THE OTHER IS...
...THAT ARAYA HAS CLEVERLY STAGED THE SCENES OF HIS VIOLENCE AND EXTORTION...
...BEYOND THE VIEW OF THE SOCIAL CAMERAS...

UNFORTUNATELY, THERE ARE SOME STUDENTS LIKE HIM EVEN AMONG THE HIGHER GRADES.
WARNING
inside cameraview
THEY HAVE THEIR OWN NETWORK ...
...AND APPARENTLY, ILLEGAL APPS THAT WARN THEM OF THE FIELD OF VIEW OF THE SOCIAL CAMERAS ARE QUITE POPULAR WITH THEM.
THAT LOT WOULD NEVER GIVE THEMSELVES AWAY IN FRONT OF THE CAMERAS.
HE WOULD HAVE TO KNOW THAT— HE WOULD'VE BEEN ON GUARD UNTIL NOW.

AT MY EARLIER PROVOCATION, HE HAS FORGOTTEN HIMSELF...
...AND IS ACTING OUT IN VIOLENCE HERE IN THIS LOUNGE WITH ALL THESE CAMERAS.
BUT...
...HE IS STILL A CHILD, AFTER ALL.

THIS IS YOUR CHANCE ...
...HARU-YUKI-KUN.
UNDER-STAND?

IT WOULD BE EASY TO DODGE THIS PUNCH.

BUT IF YOU DO, ARAYA WILL COME TO HIS SENSES ...

...AND RUN OFF.

YOUR OPPORTUNITY TO PUNISH HIM WILL ONCE AGAIN RECEDE EVER FURTHER FROM VIEW...

....

...UM.

IF I MANAGED TO MASTER BRAIN BURST...
...WOULD I BE ABLE TO BEAT HIM IN A FIGHT?
YOU PROBABLY COULD.
SU (SSP)
YOU'RE ALREADY A "BURST LINKER"...
...WHICH MEANS YOU HAVE A POWER GREATLY EXCEEDING THAT OF THE UNACCEL-ERATED.
IF...
...YOU WERE SO INCLINED...
......
......
IS THERE SOME REASON I WOULDN'T BE?
GYU (CLENCH)
ぎゅっ

IS THERE ANY REASON I WOULDN'T—?

I'LL GET HIT...

...LIKE A GOOD BOY.

......
......

NO.

I WON'T DO IT.

I WON'T ...

...GET THE CHANCE AGAIN, AFTER ALL...

HA...

A WISE CHOICE.

ONCE THE ACCELERATION RUNS OUT, YOU LEAP BACK TO THE RIGHT WITH EVERYTHING YOU'VE GOT.
DON'T FORGET TO TURN YOUR HEAD TO THE RIGHT AS HIS FIST HITS YOU.
T-TO THE RIGHT...
...OH!!

I-I CAN'T!!
IF I JUMP FROM HERE TO THERE, I'LL END UP SLAMMING INTO YOU.
IT'S NOT A PROBLEM. THIS WAY IS MORE EFFECTIVE.
DON'T WORRY, I'LL MAKE SURE TO DODGE. I WON'T GET HURT.

ARE YOU READY?
Y-YES...
NOW I'M GOING TO TEACH YOU THE COMMAND TO RELEASE THE ACCELERATION.

BE STRONG—
"BURST OUT"!!

GYUN (VWOON)
BU (WHRR)
"BURST OUT"!!
BAKII (CRACK)
I CAN TASTE BLOOD.
MY MOUTH IS CUT, I GUESS.
BUT IT DOESN'T HURT ALL THAT MUCH.
SENPAI... PLEASE...

...MAKE SURE TO GET OUT OF THE WAY—!!
GATA (KLATTER)
GATSUN (THUD)
UNH...
SEN...P—
HA (GASP)

TSUU (FOO)
AH...
AAAAH...!!
BA (AH)
Don't move!!
B-but you're bleeding...!!
Don't worry. It's just a little cut.
I told you, aim to maximize the effect.
A—
After this, you'll never have to...
...deal with Araya again.

AAAAAAAAAAAAAAH...!!

HURRY! CALL AN AMBULANCE!!

GO GET A TEACHER!!

SIGN: HEALTH ROO

Oops... I forgot to tell you.
Do not take off your Neurolinker before you come to school tomorrow.
And you can't make a global connection.
Got it? Under no circum-stances.
WHAT WAS THAT SUPPOSED TO MEAN......?
PROMISE—

キーンコーン
KON (DONG)
KIN (DING)
カタン
KATAN (KLAK)
ピピッ
PIPI- (BEEP)
You are about to leave the school local net area.
Do you want to connect to the global net?
Yes
No/Disconnect
ピッ
PI
No/Discon
You have been disconnected.
...HARU.
DOKI (BADUM)
ドキッ
BA (GAH)
ばっ
CHI...
CHIYU...

R-RIGHT. I HAVE TO APOLOGIZE FOR YESTERDAY.
UH... UM... YESTER-DAY, I—
HARU.
I HEARD ABOUT...WHAT HAPPENED AT LUNCH.
HUH? LUNCH?
I HEARD HE HIT YOU AND YOU SERIOUSLY WENT FLYING!
ARE YOU HURT? ARE YOU OKAY?

I DEFINITELY CAN'T TELL HER I WAS THE ONE WHO SENT ME FLYING...
Y-YEAH, I'M OKAY.
I JUST GOT CUT A BIT. I'M NOT HURT ANYWHERE ELSE.
...YOU'RE NOT?
OH, GOOD.
JIRO (STARE)

A-ANYWAY...
...IT'S GOOD TO WALK HOME TOGETHER... SOMETIMES.
KURU (WHIRL)

HUH? OH...
すた すた
SUTA (KLAK)
SUTA
SOMETIMES? WE HAVEN'T DONE THAT ONCE SINCE WE STARTED JUNIOR HIGH.
BUT... RIGHT. I DO HAVE TO APOLOGIZE.
Y...
YEAH...
タタタ
TA (DASH)
TA
TA
スタ
SUTA
スタ
SUTA

てく
TEKU (TAK)
てく
TEKU
てく
TEKU
......

I HAVE TO SAY SOME-THING...
HEY.
KURU
くる
I HEARD YOU WERE DIRECTING WITH KUROYUKIHIME-SAN...
...IN EIGHTH GRADE. FOR REAL......?
HUH!?
WH- WHAT—

...YEAH.
WELL.
......
OH... HUH!?
???
SUTA
スタ
SUTA
SUTA
スタ

HEEEEY!!
A- ANYWAY, ABOUT... ABOUT YESTER-DAY...
SUTA (KLAK)
SUTA
WHY?
HUH? IS CHIYU MAD?
IT WASN'T ANYTHING SPECIAL.
IT WAS... I JUST COPIED AN APP FROM HER.
HARU!!
CHII-CHAN!!
BUN (WAVE)
OH...... TAKKUN.
WHAT A COINCI-DENCE.
YOU HEADED HOME NOW?
TATA (TAK)
HEY, HARU! IT'S BEEN AGES!
GASHI (WHAM)
HEY, TAKU!!
HAS IT BEEN THAT LONG?
TAKU'S AN OLD FRIEND OF ME AND CHIYU. WE ALL LIVE IN THE SAME APARTMENT BUILDING.
TEKU (TAK)
TEKU
I HAVEN'T SEEN YOU IN TWO WEEKS ALREADY IN MEAT-SPACE.
YOU NEVER COME TO THE CONDO EVENTS.
LIKE I'D SHOW UP AT A SPORTS MEET.
SHE WAS IN SUCH A BAD MOOD, AND YET...
WELL, IT MAKES SENSE.
I MEAN, SHE DID JUST RUN INTO HER BOYFRIEND.

THAT REMINDS ME, TAKU.
I SAW THE VIDEOS OF THE CITY TOURNAMENT ON THE NET THE OTHER DAY.
YOU'RE AMAZING, ONLY SEVENTH GRADE AND ALREADY WINNING.
TAKU WAS GOOD AT SCHOOL AND SPORTS AND MANAGED TO GET INTO A FAMOUS K-12 SCHOOL SEPARATE FROM US.
NAH, I WAS JUST LUCKY.
THE GUYS WHO WOULD'VE GIVEN ME TROUBLE GOT KNOCKED OUT IN THE PRELIMS.

AND THEN THERE WAS CHII-CHAN HERE COMING TO CHEER ME ON.
WHAT? ME!?
BECAUSE OF THAT, I'VE MANAGED TO KEEP TAKU FROM SEEING ME AS A TARGET FOR BULLIES.

SFX: TSUN (NUDGE) TSUN

I ASKED CHIYU...
...TO NEVER, EVER TELL TAKU ABOUT THE BULLYING.
SHE EVEN TOLD ME SHE WOULDN'T GIVE ME LUNCH IF I LOST.
OH, COME ON!! I'M NOT LISTENING TO YOU ANYMORE!
A HA HA HA HA HA!

SO THAT'S IT!
THAT'S WHAT ALL THAT SCREAMING ABOUT THE FINAL MATCH WAS ABOUT.
IF HE KNEW ABOUT THE BULLYING...

...WE WOULDN'T BE ABLE TO KEEP BEING FRIENDS LIKE THIS.
—THAT'S WHAT IT FELT LIKE......
WELL, YOU KNOW.
HA HA HA!

—IT'S BETTER THIS WAY.
MY CHOICE TWO YEARS AGO WASN'T A MISTAKE.
AFTER ALL, THE THREE OF US CAN TALK LIKE THIS NOW JUST LIKE ALWAYS.
I DON'T WANT TO RUIN THIS RELATIONSHIP.
HA HA HA!
DON'T SAY THAT!
BUT HEY, HARU.

YOU HAD IT YESTERDAY, DIDN'T YOU?
THE CHII-CHAN LUNCH SPECIAL?
BIKU (JUMP)
GYO (GULP)

WH-WH-WHAT SHOULD I DO?
SHOULD I APOLOGIZE NOW? OR MAYBE MAIL HER LATER...!?
FUI (FWP)

HOW...

...DID TAKU KNOW THAT?

CHIYU MADE THOSE SANDWICHES...

...BECAUSE SHE KNEW THEY WERE...

...STEALING MY LUNCH MONEY.

DID SHE...

...ACTUALLY...

...TELL TAKU...?

HARU...? WHAT'S WRONG?

SO HE KNEW.
CHIYU TALKED TO HIM.
ABOUT ME...
...BEING BULLIED.
SOME-THING THE MATTER?
かあっ
KAA (GAH)
HEY, HA—
ばしっ
BASHI (SHOVE)
ダッ
DA (DASH)
S-SORRY!!
THERE'S THIS SHOW I WANT TO WATCH!!
I'M GONNA RUN AHEAD! SEE YOU, TAKU!!
HUH?

H-HEY!
TA (TAK) TA TA TA TA
HARU...!!
AFTER I LEFT...
...THEY PROBABLY TALKED ABOUT ME AGAIN.
ABOUT HOW THEY CAN HELP ME...
JUST WHEN...
...ARAYA IS FINALLY OUT OF THE PICTURE.
HE KNEW ABOUT IT ALL ALONG.
AAAAAAAAAAH...!!
THE ONE PERSON I MOST WANTED TO KEEP IT FROM—

OW!! OW...!!

PLEASE! STOP IT...!!

バシャッ

BASHA (SPLASH)

ドカッ

DOKA (WHUMP)

GYA-HA-HA-HA-HA!

ゲラゲラ

GERA (GUFFAW)

GERA

ゲラゲラ

GERA

AH...

TAKU... CHIYU...!!

STOP...!!

DON'T LOOK AT ME WITH PITY LIKE THAT!!

I HATE THIS...

ENOUGH.

I HATE IT HERE.

A SINGLE BIRD...
...SOARING LIGHTLY.
I...
...WANT TO BE UP THERE TOO.
HIGHER. FARTHER.
TO THE OTHER SIDE.
I WANT TO FLY.
—IS THAT...

IS THAT YOUR WISH?

CRAP! I'M GONNA BE LATE...!!
KACHA (KACHAK)
I'M LEAVING FOR SCHOOL, MOM.
HOLD ON...I'LL CHARGE YOU SOME LUNCH MONEY.
......HMM?
HARUYUKI, YOUR LINKER'S DISCON-NECTED.
OH!

KUI (JAB)
PI (BEEP)
Neurolinker activated.
OKAY.
Credit charge: ¥500
PIKON (DING)
I'M LEAVING THEN.
Connected to the global net.

TA (TAK)
TA
TA
PIKII (CRRRACK)
!!?

BIKI (KRRK)
BIKI
BIKI
WHA...!!?
OOOO (RRRRRR)

WHAT THE—!?
"ACCELERATION"!?
WHY? ALL BY ITSELF—!?
AH!
...HUH!?
WHA...
WHAT IS THIS...

GOO (ROAR)
!!!
HERE COMES A NEW CHALLENGER!
GOOOO
WHA...... ......!!
KYORO (WHIRL)
WH...
WHAT THE HELL...!?
...THE CENTURY END STAGE! IT'S BEEN FOREVER.
DOURURU (VRR-VRR)
LUCKYYYY...!!

AND AS A SPECIAL BONUS...
...MY OPPONENT IS A SHINY NEWB.
SUPER LUCKYYYY!!!
DO
DO
DO
DO (VRR)
DO
DOURURUN (VRR-VRRRRR)

CHAPTER
#03

OOO
(RRR)
PI
(BEEP)
1800
KYORO
(WHIRL)
PI
PI
WH...
WHAT IS
THIS...!!
PI
1796

THE WORLD OF BRAIN BURST...!?

THAT'S... I...

BUT I DIDN'T GIVE THE BURST LINK COMMAND!?

WHY ALL OF A SUDDEN...!?

A...

AND THIS...

SERI-OUSLY...

BA (GAH)
SOME-ONE'S THERE!!

HISO (WHISPER)
SILVER CROW... I DON'T KNOW THAT NAME.
HISO
...TOO, BUT HE LOOKS LIKE THE JUMPY TYPE.

HISO
MAYBE A NEWBIE?
THAT CON-VERSATION.
THEY'RE NOT NPCs... LOGGED-IN USERS?
HISO
BUT HE'S METALLIC.
THAT'S GOTTA MEAN SOMETHING.

1538

Ash Roll

Silver Crow

PI (BEEP)

THIS... IS THIS THE BRAIN BURST APP SCREEN?

THE LEFT... IS ME? SO WHOSE NAME IS ON THE RIGHT?

Ash Roller

NO... WAIT. THIS LAYOUT.

I KNOW THIS CONFIGURATION, I TOTALLY KNOW IT...!!

BOOOON (VRRRRRRN)
ブォォォン
DOURURURU (VRR-VRRR)
ドゥルルル…
THE CENTURY END STAGE! IT'S BEEN FOREVER.
LUCKYYYY!
DO (VRR)
DO
BIKU (SHUDDER)
ビクッ
WHAT IS THAT!?
!!
DO
DO
DO
DO
HUH... AH...
Ash Roller
DO

DO
AND AS A SPECIAL BONUS...
...MY OPPONENT IS A SHINY NEWB.
THIS IS BAD!!
WH-WHOAAAA...
THIS... THIS IS...
DORURUN
WHOA!?
SUPER LUCKYYYY!!
DA (DASH)
THIS IS A FIGHT STAGE!!
BARI (VRRK)
HYA-HA-HA-HA-HA-HA-HA!!
BARI
BARI
BARI
WHOA! AAAH!
BARI
BURORORORORORO (VRRRRRRRRRRRN)
THAAAAT'S IT! RUN! RUUUUN!!
THIS... I CAN'T...

BUON
(KRRRRM)
THERE'S NO WAY I CAN WIN—!!!
DOKYA
(SKKRAK)
—
PFT!

HA-HA-HA!
So.
You're already being hunted?
...It's not funny.
I thought I was going to die...
That's because you broke your promise to me, boy.
WAI (CHATTER)
WAI
I mean, I know it's my fault for accidentally connecting to the global net, but—
KACHA (CHIK)
I suppose it's saved me the trouble of having to explain it all.
The truth about the Brain Burst program... It's just—

It's just...

...a fighting game.

I mean, think about what you could do with...

...this amazing acceleration technology!

Re-creating the world as in stages... And you go with a fighter!?

The genre was already obsolete thirty years ago!!

Hmm... I think you need to phrase it slightly differently.

We Burst Linkers are not accelerating to play fighting games.

Instead, we fight so that we can continue to be accelerated.

Wh-what do you mean?

I should probably explain the rest to you in the field.

Accelerate now and the two of us will fight.

Huh? Now!?

GU (NGH)

I'm not saying we're going to fight for real. We'll just let the time run out and end in a draw.
O-okay...
All right. Let's go.

BASHIIII
(CRRRACK)
BURST LINK!!
HMM... A TWILIGHT STAGE?
YOU PULLED A RARE ONE.
UH—
UH-HUH.

1766
Black Lotus
"BLACK LOTUS"...
THE PROPERTIES OF THIS STAGE ARE...
...BURNS WELL, COLLAPSES SOON, AND UNEXPECTEDLY DARK.

IT'S PERFECT FOR HER.
......UH-HUH.
A BEAUTIFUL NAME.
BLACK LOTUS-SAN.

KATSU (KLAK)
KATSU
THAT'S YOUR DUEL AVATAR, HMM?
"SILVER CROW"... GOOD NAME.

WAAH...!!
DOKI (BADUM)
HMM... GOOD COLOR.
SU (SSP)

I LIKE THE FORM TOO.
なで
NADE (STROKE)
DOKI (BADUM)
!?
KAAAA (GAAAAH)
S...
SO SOFT...!!
TOKUN (THUMP)
TH- THANKS...
THIS IS A REAL VIRTUAL REALITY...!!
NOT LIMITED BY ANY ETHICAL CODE LIKE THE SCHOOL LOCAL NET.
IT'S... COMPLETELY ...!!
TOKUN
I THINK IT'S KIND OF WIMPY, BUT...
TOKUN

...I CAN'T REDO IT, RIGHT?
I WANT SOMETHING COOLER—
IMPOSSIBLE.
THE DESIGN IS BY...
...THE BRAIN BURST PROGRAM AND YOU YOURSELF.
LAST NIGHT...
...YOU HAD A VERY LONG, SCARY DREAM, DIDN'T YOU?
!!
I-I DID...
THE PROGRAM...
...WAS ACCESSING YOUR DEEP PSYCHE.
BRAIN BURST CARVES UP AND FILTERS YOUR DESIRES AND FEARS AND OBSESSIONS...
...AND CREATES YOUR DUEL AVATAR.
MY PSYCHE...
MY FEARS AND DESIRES...

GAN (SHOCK)
ガーン
WHAT!? THEN...
...I WISHED FOR THIS WEAK, SMOOTH BODY?
ALTHOUGH I DO THINK IT'D BE BETTER IF I LOST A LITTLE WEIGHT...
WHAT THE PROGRAM READS IS NOT YOUR IDEAL IMAGE...
...BUT YOUR FEELINGS OF INFERIORITY.
YOU COULD'VE ENDED UP WITH THAT PINK PIG, YOU KNOW.
WHAT!? P-PLEASE DON'T SAY THAT.
ALTHOUGH I LIKE THAT PIG.
I DON'T LIKE IT.
SO... THEN...
DOES THAT MEAN...
...BRAIN BURST ALSO MADE YOUR AVATAR?
THAT'S THE IMAGE OF YOUR INFERIORITY COMPLEX?
BUT IT'S SO BEAUTIFUL...
...NO, I...

THIS IS... ONE I PUT TOGETHER MYSELF WITH AN EDITOR.
FOR MY OWN REASONS, I'VE SEALED OFF MY DUEL AVATAR.
SU (SHF)
SEALED?
UNFORTU-NATELY, MY DUEL AVATAR IS UGLY.
THE EPITOME OF HIDEOUS.
KUROYUKIHIME-SENPAI......?
ALTHOUGH THAT'S NOT THE REASON I'VE SEALED IT OFF...I'LL TELL YOU WHY SOMEDAY.
WHEN THE TIME COMES.
......

ANYWAY, ENOUGH ABOUT ME.
THIS MORNING, YOU WERE THRUST INTO A FIGHT...
...AND YOU WERE THOROUGHLY DEFEATED...... CORRECT?
UH...
PRETTY MUCH. HE CRUSHED ME.
YOU LOSE
DO YOU REMEMBER THE RESULTS SCREEN WHEN IT WAS OVER?
UH, UM...
IT SAID... BURST POINTS, I THINK? THAT WENT FROM NINETY-NINE TO EIGHTY-NINE.
BURST POINT
99
89
MM!! IT'S GOOD YOU REMEMBERED.
すとん
SUTON (STAMP)
THAT'S IT.
BURST POINTS!!

ACCELERATE ONE TIME...
...LOSE ONE POINT.
PUT SIMPLY, BURST POINTS ARE THE NUMBER OF TIMES WE CAN ACCELERATE.
WHAT!?
THOSE ARE THE VERY THINGS...
...THAT SEND US INTO THIS MERCILESS BATTLEFIELD!!
KATSUN (CRACK)
S-SO HOW DO YOU CHARGE THEM!?
ARE WE CHARGED REAL MONEY?
NO, WE'RE NOT.

THE WAY TO GAIN POINTS...

...IS TO WIN IN MATCHES.

FOR A SAME-LEVEL BATTLE, THE WINNER GETS TEN POINTS, THE LOSER LOSES TEN.

LIKE YOU DID THIS MORNING.

THEN...

IF YOU CAN'T WIN AND YOUR POINTS DROP TO ZERO...?

IT'S SIMPLE.

YOU LOSE...

...BRAIN BURST AND ACCELERATION FOREVER.

!!

LOSE BRAIN BURST...

KATSU (KLAK)

ACCELERATION IS EXTREMELY POWERFUL...

IT GOES WITHOUT SAYING THAT WE WIN IN FIGHTS...
...WE GET EXCELLENT RESULTS ON TESTS AND IN SPORTS.
IF THAT HAPPENS ...
WINNING BIG AT GAMBLING IS ALSO POSSIBLE.
...THEN I'LL ALSO LOSE...

...THIS CONNECTION TO KUROYUKI-HIME...
ONCE WE'VE TASTED THIS FORBIDDEN NECTAR...
...WE HAVE NO CHOICE BUT TO KEEP ACCELERATING FOREVER.
WE HAVE NO CHOICE BUT TO KEEP FIGHTING FOREVER...

—NOW THEN.
WHAT ARE YOU GOING TO DO, HARUYUKI-KUN?
?
AT THIS POINT, YOU CAN STILL GO BACK.
TO A WORLD WITHOUT ACCELER-ATION OR FIGHTING.
YOU WON'T SEE THAT BULLY ARAYA AGAIN.
...... I...
I...

I DON'T WANT...
...TO BE AWAY FROM YOU—
I-I...
I STILL HAVE TO REPAY YOU...!!
...OH?
YOU GAVE ME BRAIN BURST...
...AND PULLED ME OUT OF THAT HELL...
THERE MUST BE SOMETHING YOU WANT ME TO DO.
SOME OBJECTIVE THAT WAS WORTH TAKING THE TIME TO...
...CHECK MY SQUASH GAME SCORE AND STUFF...
HMM... AN ACCURATE INFERENCE.

I...I'M ACTUALLY NOT A SOMEONE WHO GETS TO TALK TO YOU LIKE THIS.
I'M A BLOB, A CRYBABY...
I...
GU (CLENCH)
I GET JEALOUS OF THE...
...ONLY TWO FRIENDS I HAVE. I RUN AWAY AT THE DROP OF A HAT.
I REALLY AM... I'M THE WORST.

I CAN'T STOP TALKING...!!
EVEN SO...
...YOU, THE GIRL EVERYONE LOVES...
... REACHED OUT TO ME...
...AND I KNOW IT'S JUST BECAUSE I WAS KINDA GOOD AT THAT GAME.
BUT I-I WOULDN'T EVEN, I MEAN...
SERIOUSLY, WHAT AM I SAYING HERE!?

SO...SO... THAT'S WHY I...

...WANT TO LIVE UP TO YOUR EXPECTATIONS.

I WANT TO REPAY...

...THE MERCY YOU SHOWED ME.

I WON'T UNINSTALL BRAIN BURST.

I'LL FIGHT...
...AS A BURST LINKER...!!
WHA...
WHAT THE— I SHOULD'VE ...
FURU (TREMBLE)
ふるふる
FURU
ふる
FURU
KAAAAA (GAAAH)
かあぁぁ
ああ
...JUST SAID THAT LAST PART!!
ALL THAT MAKES IT SOUND LIKE MR. SELF-CONSCIOUS HERE GOT THE WRONG IDEA ABOUT THINGS. AAAAAAH...!!
FURU
ふる
FURURU
ふるる
FURURU
ふるる
BOSO (WHISPER)
ボソッ
—
....CY?

AH!
MERCY?
DON'T USE WORDS LIKE THAT...!!
YOU'RE THE ONE ...
...CREATING A DISTANCE.
DO THESE TWO VIRTUAL METERS...
...FEEL THAT FAR TO YOU?
SU (SSP)
SENPAI ......

I'M SORRY.
THEY DO...
...YOU SAVED ME.
I DON'T NEED ANYTHING ELSE.
......
SU (SSP)
...IS THAT SO...
......
I GRATEFULLY ACCEPT YOUR AID.
IT IS TRUE THAT I HAVE A TROUBLING PROBLEM.
I'D LIKE YOUR ASSISTANCE IN RESOLVING THE MATTER.
KATSU (KLAK)
OF COURSE... WHAT DO YOU NEED?

FIRST OF ALL ...
...I NEED YOU TO LEARN HOW DUELS WORK.
KATSU
YOU WERE CRUSHED IN YOUR FIRST FIGHT.
BUT IT'S NOT BECAUSE YOUR OPPONENT WAS STRONGER.
YOU SIMPLY DIDN'T KNOW HOW TO FIGHT.
THUS, THE NEXT LECTURE WILL BE A HANDS-ON LESSON.
KATSU
HUH...? WHAT ARE WE GOING TO DO?
KURU (WHIRL)
OBVIOUSLY ...
...WE'RE GOING TO GO...
...AND GET YOUR TEN POINTS BACK.

NOW, THEN!!
LET'S EAT, ARITA-KUN.
BEFORE IT GETS COLD ON US.
GUUUU (GRRRR)
PI (BEEP)
O-OKAY!

HMM...
TO BE BLUNT...
KACHA (CHAK)
I TOLD HIM I LIKED HIM...
...AND HE BLEW ME OFF.
!?
WHAAAAAT!!?
DA
DA
DA
DA
DA (DASH)

KIN (DING)
KON (DONG)
SENPAI... WHAT WERE YOU THINKING!?
DOTA (STOMP)
DOTA
EVERYONE'S GOING TO PICK ON ME NOW!! THEY WILL TOTALLY BE PICKING ON ME!!
IT WAS A PROUD DECLARATION.
TEKU (TAK)
TEKU
I DIDN'T GO SO FAR AS TO TELL THE TRUTH, DID I?
AND I DON'T THINK YOU WERE AS DISPLEASED AS YOU'D HAVE ME BELIEVE.
KUI (SWIPE)
PIKON (DING)
?
You have received an image file
PA (AGH)
AUUUUGH!
WHEN DID YOU TAKE THIS CAMERA SCREEN-SHOT!?
I MEAN, HOW DID YOU DO IT!?
HA-HA-HA, IT'S A SECRET.

SASA (FWWSH)

AH...

JIRO (STARE)

JIRO

IT'S GETTING TO BE THAT TIME.
ONCE YOU PASS THROUGH THE SCHOOL GATES, YOU'LL BE CONNECTED GLOBALLY.
WHICH MEANS THAT ANY BURST LINKERS IN SUGINAMI AREA NUMBER THREE...
...WILL BE ABLE TO FORCE YOU TO FIGHT.
SO...
BEFORE SOMEONE JUMPS YOU, ACCELERATE.
FIND ASH ROLLER IN THE MATCHING LIST...
...AND CHALLENGE HIM FIRST ...!!
DON'T MAKE THAT FACE.
IF YOU JUST FIGHT WITH THE STRATEGY I OUTLINED BEFORE, YOU WON'T LOSE.
O-OKAY...

THIS IS YOUR REAL DEBUT BATTLE...
...SILVER CROW.
—GOOD LUCK.
BASH!!!!! (CRRRRACK)
OOOO (RRRRR)

OOOO
(RRRRR)
BUROOO
(VRRRRN)
THERE HE IS...!!

AFTER GOING OVER THE INFORMATION YOU GAVE ME...
...I'VE DETERMINED THAT ASH ROLLER HAS TWO SIGNIFICANT WEAK POINTS.
JISO (SKRTCH)
....
BUROROROROROR
THE FIRST IS THAT...
...HE MAKES A GREAT DEAL OF NOISE.
NOW!!
BURORO
THE ONLY CLUE TO THE OPPONENT'S POSITION...
...IS THE GUIDE CURSOR SHOWING THE DIRECTION.
PIPI (BEEP)
BURORORO
BUT THAT ENGINE NOISE TELLS ME WHERE HE IS...!!
BEFORE HE NOTICES ME HERE...
...I HAVE TO STRIKE FIRST!!
BA (LEAP)

AAAAAAH!
BURORORO (VRRRN)
HUH!?
GO (KRK)
OHWAAA...!!

BUWA (SKRRRK)
BAKYAAAA (SKREEECH)
DOSA (THUD)
BA (JERK)
YES!!

TA
(TAK)
TA
TA
BUSU
(CRACKLE)
BUSU

TA
TA
TA

HIS SECOND WEAK POINT...
KAN
KAN
(CLANG)
KAN
THE MAJORITY OF HIS AVATAR'S POTENTIAL IS TIED UP IN THE BIKE.

YOU... YOU BRAT!!
BA
(JERK)
KAN
KAN
KAN
PUSU
(PSSH)
PUSU

THE RIDER'S BATTLE POWER SHOULD BE ESSENTIALLY ZERO.
AFTER DAMAGING HIM IN YOUR INITIAL ATTACK...
...MOVE TO THE ROOF OF A BUILDING HIS BIKE CAN'T CLIMB.

1216
Silver Crow
RIGHT NOW, ASH ROLLER HAS...
HFF!
...CLEARLY TAKEN MORE DAMAGE...
HFF!
HFF!

NOW THAT HE'S TAKEN MORE DAMAGE THAN ME, I CAN JUST...
...RETREAT TO HIGH GROUND AND WAIT FOR TIME TO RUN OUT TO WIN.
THAT'S THE STRATEGY KUROYUKIHIME-SENPAI CAME UP WITH...!!
HUF
HUF
BOSO (WHISPER)
WOW, HE CAN PLAY, AFTER ALL.
BOSO
TOTALLY DIFFERENT FROM THIS MORNING, HUH? WONDER WHO HIS "GUARDIAN" IS.
KYORO (WHIRL)
KYORO
I'LL BE IN THE GALLERY TOO.
ALTHOUGH I WON'T BE ABLE TO HELP YOU.
THE GALLERY...
SHE'S... KUROYUKIHIME-SENPAI'S PROBABLY HERE TOO......
DURUN (VRRRRN)
HMM?
HYOI (POP)

!?
よいしょっ
HUP!
TON (THUD)
WH...
WHAT IS HE DOING!?
YOU REALLY THINK YOU'RE SOMETHING, HUH, BALDY!!
I'LL MAKE YOU DANCE TO THE SOUND OF MY V-TWIN!!
GAKI (SKREE)
BUOOO (KRRRM)
GA (KRR)
GA
GA
GA
GA
GA

BUO
OON (RRRN)
DO (VRR)
WHOAAAA...!!
DO
DO
DO
AFTER I BEAT YOU THIS MORNING ...
...I WENT UP TO LEVEL TWO.

DO (VRR)
AND I WAS HAVING SUUUUUCH TROUBLE DECIDING ON MY LEVEL-UP BONUS, YOU KNOW?
DO
DO
DO
IN THE END, I WENT WITH THE ABILITY TO DRIVE UP WALLS, GET IT?
AND DAMN, I WAS SO RIGHT!
NIYA (GRIN)
BISHI (CRACK)
AND YOU...
...ARE HELLA UNLUCKY-YYYYYY!!
IS...
IS THIS FOR REAL...!!?

PIRORIIIN
(DADADADING)
ぴろーん♪
FOOOOOOOO!!
ASH ROLLER
LEVELED UP!

HE CLIMBED THE WALL ...
HOW IS THAT EVEN POSSIBLE!?
DO (VRR)
DO
CHAPTER
#04
NII (GRIND)
DO
HEH-HEH...
SCARED OF MY SUUUUUUPER-COOOOOOL NEW POWER, HUH?
DO
IF YOU HAVE TO FIGHT ASH ROLLER ON HIS BIKE FACE-TO-FACE...
...I'M SORRY TO SAY YOUR CHANCES OF WINNING ARE QUITE SMALL.
TH...
THIS......

BECAUSE—
SPECIAL ATTACK?
MM.
GO AHEAD AND OPEN YOUR BATTLE HISTORY.

DUEL AVATARS HAVE A VARIETY OF ATTRIBUTES AND FIGHTING STYLES.
BUT THE OVERARCHING PRINCIPLE IS THAT THE GENERAL POTENTIAL AT THE SAME LEVEL IS EQUAL.

Battle History
Crow
VS
Ash Roller
Level.1
PI (BEEP)
PIPI
YOU WERE CRUSHED IN YOUR FIRST FIGHT.
BUT IT'S NOT BECAUSE YOUR OPPONENT WAS STRONGER.
YOU SIMPLY DIDN'T KNOW HOW TO FIGHT.

...HE WAS LEVEL ONE TOO.
BUT HE WAS SO STRONG ...!!

S-SO THEN... I MUST HAVE A STRONG SPECIAL ATTACK!?
MM. LET'S TAKE A LOOK.
YOU CAN CHECK IT IN YOUR STATUS.
DOKI (BADUM)
DOKI
PI

ピッ
PI
Punch
Normal attack
ピッ
PI
Kick
Normal attack
ピッ
PI
Special attack
Head Butt
Charge
Attack
....
ヒョイ
HYOI (POP)
SO?
...UM.
WHAT IS IT?
NORMAL ATTACKS PUNCH AND KICK... AND ALL I HAVE FOR SPECIAL ATTACK IS JUST A HEAD BUTT.
....
......
OH?

SH-SHE'S SHOCKED ...!!
N-NO, IT'S FINE. I MEAN, I EXPECTED THIS...!!
YOU TAKE ONE LOOK AT THIS AVATAR AND IT'S LEARLY NO GOOD. 'M SORRY I CAN'T LIVE UP TO YOUR EXPECTATIONS. YOU CAN KIND OF LEAVE ME BE. JUST THINK OF ME AS A—
YOU... IDIOT!!
BIKU (SHUDDER)
SIGH...
...I WON'T TELL YOU HOW TO LIVE YOUR LIFE.
AS JUNIOR HIGH STUDENTS, WE'RE ON THE SAME LEVEL.
HOWEVER... WHEN IT COMES TO BRAIN BURST, I HAVE OVER SIX YEARS MORE EXPERIENCE THAN YOU.
WERE YOU NOT LISTENING ...?
...WHEN I TOLD YOU THAT ALL THE DUEL AVATARS HAVE EQUAL POTENTIAL?
OH...
B-BUT...
I ACTUALLY JUST HAVE THREE ATTACKS—
IN WHICH CASE...
...YOU MOST CERTAINLY HAVE SOME STRENGTH SOME-WHERE...
...TO COMPEN-SATE!!

IT WAS YOU WHO GAVE BIRTH TO THIS DUEL AVATAR.
IF YOU DON'T BELIEVE IN IT, THEN WHAT DOES THAT SAY?
......
THAT THE PERSON WHO IS LEAST...
...ABLE TO BELIEVE IN ME... IS ME.
BUT...
I'M SORRY... I BELIEVE ...
MAYBE NOT IN MYSELF... BUT AT LEAST IN WHAT YOU SAY.
—HON- ESTLY...
IT SEEMS YOU NEED TO LEARN SOMETHING ELSE BEFORE HOW TO FIGHT.
STRENGTH IS... IT'S BY NO MEANS SIMPLY A WORD INDICATING VICTORY.
I SPENT A FAIR BIT OF TIME LEARNING THIS. AND...
BY THE TIME I LEARNED THE LESSON...
...IT WAS ALREADY TOO LATE.
BURORORORO (VRRRRN)
HEY! HEY! HEEEEEEEEEY!!
AH!

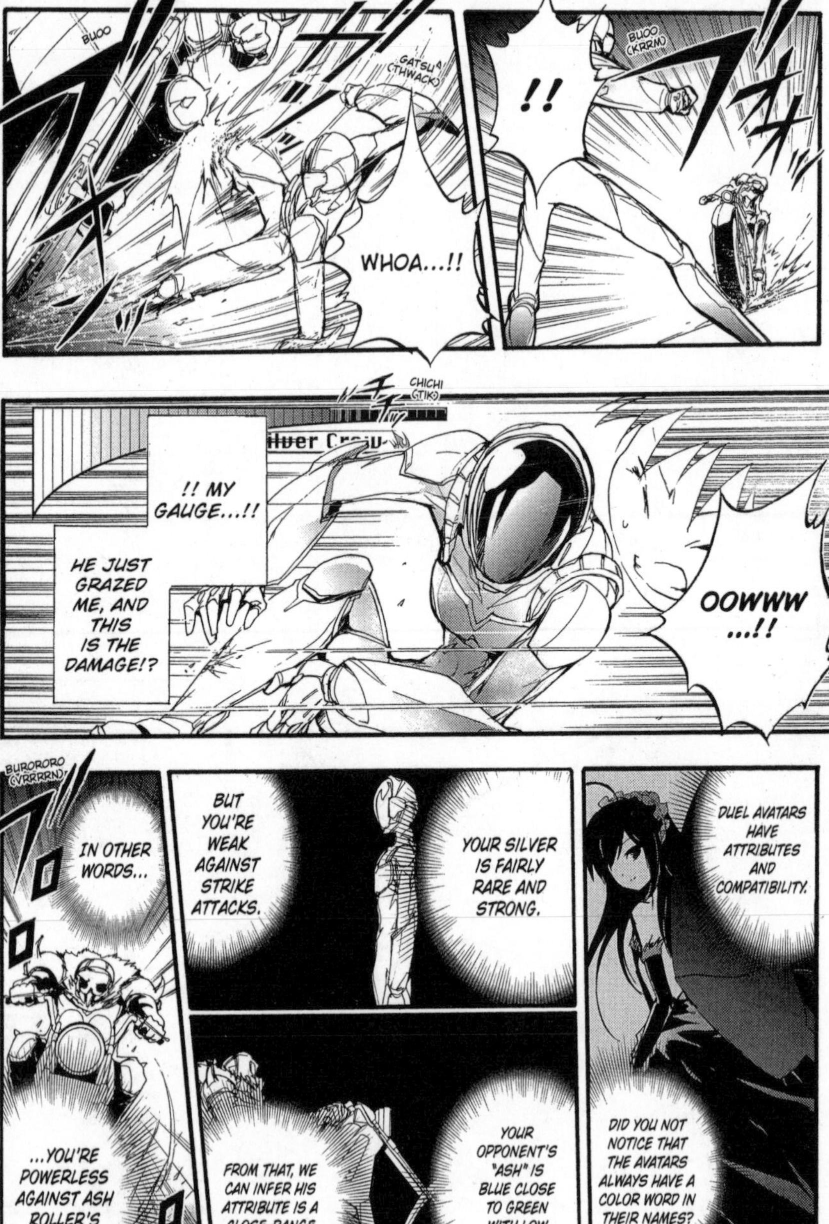

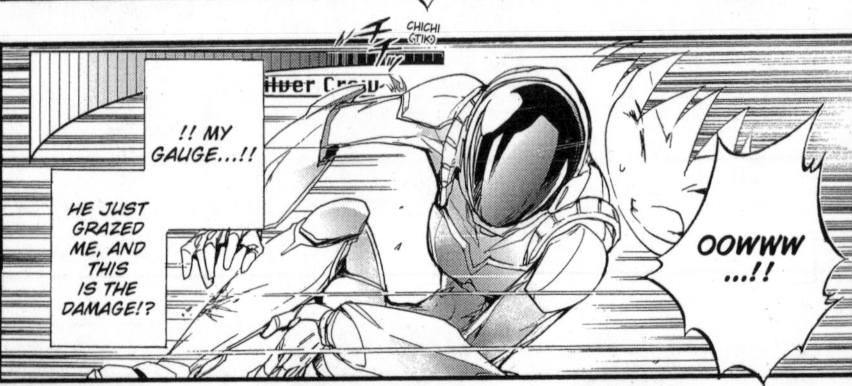

CHICHI (TIK)
OOWWW ...!!
!! MY GAUGE...!!
HE JUST GRAZED ME, AND THIS IS THE DAMAGE!?

DUEL AVATARS HAVE ATTRIBUTES AND COMPATIBILITY.

DID YOU NOT NOTICE THAT THE AVATARS ALWAYS HAVE A COLOR WORD IN THEIR NAMES?

YOUR SILVER IS FAIRLY RARE AND STRONG.

BUT YOU'RE WEAK AGAINST STRIKE ATTACKS.

YOUR OPPONENT'S "ASH" IS BLUE CLOSE TO GREEN WITH LOW SATURATION.

FROM THAT, WE CAN INFER HIS ATTRIBUTE IS A CLOSE-RANGE STRIKE TYPE.

BURORORO (VRRRRN)

IN OTHER WORDS...

...YOU'RE POWERLESS AGAINST ASH ROLLER'S ATTACK.

SO THERE'S JUST ONE RESPONSE IN THE EVENT YOU END UP IN A FACE-TO-FACE BATTLE.
BUOOO
BURORORO
HA-HA-HA-HA! NO FIGHT LEFT IN YOU?
RUN FOR YOUR LIFE.
SO THAT'S WHAT SHE SAID!!
WELL, THEN, ALLOW ME!!
DAM-MIT...
THERE... THERE HAS TO BE SOME-THING...
AH!
GU (CLENCH)
MY SPECIAL ATTACK!!
EVEN IF IT'S JUST CALLED A HEAD BUTT...
...IT MIGHT HAVE THE POWER TO CRUSH ROCKS OR SOME-THING!!
KIIII (SKREE)
ZAWA (CHATTER)
—RIGHT!!
BUN (FWSH)
—YOU CAN DO THIS!!

GATSU (THWACK)

SUKA (SHHRK)

!?

BAKI (SNAP)

NGAH!

GERA (GUFFAW)
GERA
GERA
GIGGLE
—TOO BAD.
LOOKS LIKE THIS IS THE END.
KAA (GAH)
!!

DAMMIT ...!!
I KNEW MY CHARACTER WAS TOO WEAK!!
I MEAN, A SPECIAL ATTACK THAT'S JUST SOME HEAD BUTT THAT DOESN'T EVEN HIT THE TARGET!
GIRI (SKREEK)

THIS KEEPS UP...
THIS KEEPS UP, I'M DONE FOR ...!!

HIRA (FLUTTER)
AH...
KUROYUKIHIME-SENPAI...?
GU (NGH)
NO... YOU CAN'T GIVE UP.
HM ......?
IF I LOSE ...
... THEN I'LL STRUGGLE AND FIGHT.
I'LL MAKE IT UGLY. —IF I CAN'T DO THAT MUCH...
GU
THEN...
...I CAN'T EVEN BE HER PAWN!!
THINK ...
GOSHI (CLENCH)
I HAVE TO THINK.

DORURU
DORUN (VRRRR)
OVER-WHELMING DETAIL...
...AND REALITY.
GYUN (HYOO)
...THAT BIKE ISN'T JUST A BUNCH OF POLYGONS.
HEY! HEY! WHAT'S UP? COME OOOOON!!
SO IN THE CASE OF THIS BRAIN BURST...
DORURURU
THERE HAS TO BE A WEAK POINT IN THIS METICULOUS REPRODUCTION!!
NOISY.
STINKS LIKE GAS.
THE BIKE'S FEATURES—
WHAT IF IT RAN OUT OF GAS?
A HOLE IN THE TANK—NO, I CAN'T PULL THAT OFF.
ISN'T THERE ANYTHING ELSE? ANYTHING...
AH!
BARURURU (KRRRRR)
GOT IT. THAT'S IT!!
YEEEEAH! HA-HA-HA-HA! DANCE! DANCE FOR MEEEEE!!
THE MAIN FEATURE OF AN INTERNAL COMBUSTION ENGINE BIKE...AND ITS WEAK POINT!!
SU (SHF)

NOW!!
HUP!!
GA (GRAB)
ZUDON (WHUMP)
!?
AH...
BURORORO (VRRR)
WHOA!
BACHI (KREE)
BACHI
BACHI
OW! OUCH, OUCH, OUCH, OUCH!
OW, OW, OW, OW, OW—!!
BURORORO
HA-HA-HA-HA! YOU DON'T LET GO SOON, YOU'RE GONNA BE AT ZERO IN NO TIME!!
ZA (KRK)
ZA
ZA
ZA
ZA

!!
ZA (KRK)
ZA
ZA
BURORON (VVRRRN)
FOR THE TURN... HE'S SLOWING DOWN!!
GU (YANK)
NOW!!
AAAAAAH...!!
DAN (BAM)
STOOOO-OOOPID!!
AS IF A LITTLE BUG LIKE YOU COULD STOP MY AMAZING MONSTER BI—

GYUOOON
(HEEEEEN)

GISHI
(CREAK)

HFF!

HFF!

!!

WHA—

WHAT?
NO
WAY!!

HE'S......
......

HFF!

THIS
IS...

...YOUR
BIKE'S WEAK
POINT, ASH
ROLLER...!!

HFF!

HE'S
LIFTING
IT UP!?

HFF!

THE WAY MOTORCYCLES WERE STRUCTURED IN THE PREVIOUS ERA...
...THEY WERE DRIVEN BY A CHAIN CONNECTING THE ENGINE TO JUST THE REAR WHEEL.

WHICH IS WHY IF I HOLD IT UP OFF THE GROUND LIKE THIS, THEN YOU CAN'T MOVE.
GYU (HEEN)
GYU
GYU
IN WHICH CASE... YOU CAN'T DODGE MY HEAD BUTT!!
Y-YOU ...!!

YOU BRAAAAT!!
スカッ
SUKA (SHRRK)
DROP IT, STUPID!!
JITA
JITA (PANIC)
JITA
JITA
じたじた
じたじた
—NAH.
GI (SKREE)
BIRI (CHRRN)
GISHI (SKREEK)

IF YOU'RE REALLY STUCK...
...TRY MAKING YOUR FRONT WHEEL TURN...!!!
Do you ... to disconnect?
Yes
PIPI (BEEP)
You have been disconnected from the global network.
SIIIIIGH...
SUU (SSSP)

YOU DID IT, SILVER CROW!!
PON (PAT)
DOKI (BADUM)
!!
TO BE HONEST, I THOUGHT YOU WERE DONE FOR!!
I-I THOUGHT I WAS DONE FOR TOO.
DON'T BE MODEST. THAT WAS AN AMAZING WIN!!
TERE (BLUSH)
TERE
I HADN'T GIVEN ANY THOUGHT TO THE INTERNAL STRUCTURE OF ASH ROLLER'S BIKE AT ALL.
THAT WAS PROBABLY THE FIRST TIME THAT WEAK POINT HAD BEEN ATTACKED, THANKS TO THAT QUICK THINKING OF YOUR AVATAR.
IN ANY CASE...YOU CERTAINLY DID GET YOUR POINTS BACK.
I GOT MORE THAN THAT.
TWENTY POINTS WERE ADDED TO MY TOTAL...HE WAS AT LEVEL TWO.

PFT!
BASHI
BASHI (WHAP)
HA-HA-HA! HE WAS? SO THAT'S WHY HE COULD RIDE UP LIKE THAT!!
I-IT'S NOT FUNNY!
OW, OW, OW!
HEE-HEE-HEE, NO, I'M SORRY.
BUT, WELL, THAT DID ALLOW YOU TO WIN IN AN INTERESTING, COOL WAY, DIDN'T IT?
THE GALLERY WAS ALL PRETTY WORKED UP TOO.
UH... UH-HUH.
YOUR MOVEMENTS WERE LOOKING BETTER AND BETTER.
AT THIS RATE, YOU'LL SOON BE READY FOR A MORE ORTHODOX OPPONENT.
KYORO (WHIRL)
...BUT. WHAT ARE WE STANDING HERE TALKING FOR?
!?
O-OH, RIGHT!!
WE'RE STILL RIGHT IN FRONT OF THE GATES!!
WHEN DID ALL THESE PEOPLE SHOW UP...!?
—!!?

SA (SLUMP)
SH- SHE'S MAD ...!!
ABOUT ME RUNNING AWAY YESTER-DAY?
TSUKA (KLAK)
BUT... THAT WAS BECAUSE SHE WENT AND TOLD TAKU.
IT'S NOT MY FAULT... IT'S NOT MY—
TSUKA
WHAT SHOULD WE DO? THERE'S THAT CAFÉ OVER—
CHI...
CHIYU...!!
PITA (STOP)
—HMM ...?
...YOU—
—WHAT DO YOU...
...WANT WITH HARU ...?

THE REASON HARU GOT INTO THAT FIGHT YESTERDAY WAS BECAUSE OF YOUR MEDDLING, WASN'T IT?

AND YET HERE YOU ARE AGAIN, MAKING A SPECTACLE OF HIM LIKE THIS.

WHAT DO YOU WANT? IS THIS FUN FOR YOU?

EEEP. WHAT IS THIS? WHAT IS GOING ON?

H-HEY, CHIYU—

SHUT UP, HARU!!

BIKU (SHUDDER)

HMM...

I DON'T QUITE UNDER-STAND...

ARE YOU SAYING THAT I AM PLAYING AROUND, THAT I AM...

...DOING SOMETHING ARITA-KUN IS NOT HAPPY WITH?

AREN'T YOU?

HARU HATES THIS KIND OF THING...
...STANDING OUT SO MUCH, BEING STARED AT.
CAN'T YOU SEE HE'S CLEARLY UNCOMFORT-ABLE?

HMM, I SEE. IT'S TRUE THAT...
...I MAY HAVE PLACED ARITA-KUN IN A SITUATION NOT ENTIRELY TO HIS LIKING.
HOWEVER, I BELIEVE THAT CHOOSING OR NOT CHOOSING IS UP TO HIM.
I WONDER IF YOU HAVE ANY RIGHT TO BE SAYING ANYTHING HERE?
I DO!
I'VE BEEN FRIENDS WITH HARU LONGER THAN ANYONE AT THIS SCHOOL.
MY...
FRIENDS, HMM? ...IN THAT CASE...
NIYA (GRIN)
...I RANK SOMEWHAT HIGHER.

YOU MAY HAVE HEARD THE RUMORS.
SU (SHF)
I CONFESSED MY CRUSH TO HIM...
...AND I'M CURRENTLY WAITING FOR A REPLY.
WE WERE JUST ABOUT TO GO ON A SHORT DATE.
SHIN (SILENCE)
GAAAAH.
I CAN'T, CAN'T, THIS IS THE END OF THE WORLD NO CHOICE BUT TO CHANGE SCHOOLS TOMORROW!!
DARA (DRIP)
だら
DARA
だら
GAKU (SHAKE)
GAKU
WHAT'S WRONG?
ALMOST WINTER AND YET.... YOU'RE A STRANGE ONE.
だら
DARA
だら
DARA
FUKI (WIPE)
FUKI
ふき
ふき

きゅ

KYU (GRIP)

—NOW THEN.

FARE-WELL.

MISS FRIEND.

......

IF I STOP COMING TO SCHOOL, IT'S ALL YOUR FAULT!

NOW, NOW, YOU DIDN'T LOOK ENTIRELY DISPLEASED, YOU KNOW.

—AND...

PITA (STOP)

I'M A LITTLE CONCERNED... OR RATHER...

...THERE'S SOMETHING I'D LIKE TO CONFIRM.

?

HUH? CONCERNED? YOU MEAN, ABOUT CHIYU?

UM... BEFORE, DID YOU SAY YOU ALREADY KNEW CHIYU'S NAME?

I DID.

I'VE BEEN PAYING ATTENTION TO HER FOR DIFFERENT REASONS THAN I HAVE BEEN YOU.

WH-WHAT DO YOU MEAN?

...I CAN'T EXPLAIN IT IN JUST A FEW WORDS.

IT'S DIRECTLY CONNECTED TO WHY I INVITED YOU TO THE ACCELERATED WORLD...

UIIN (CEEEN)

ANYWAY, LET'S DISCUSS IT AT LENGTH OVER TEA.

IT'S MY TREAT.

KACHA (CHIK)
Now, then.
Let me congratulate you on your victory once again, Haruyuki-kun.
Oh... Uh...
Thank you.
WHOA...
CHIRA (GLANCE)
THIS IS ALMOST LIKE...
CHUU (SLURP)
...LIKE A REAL DATE...
I-it's because of all your advice.
No... It was your own resourceful-ness.
If you keep it up, you'll be Level Two in no time.
You might even make it up to Three before the end of the year.
I can't even imagine being able to fight dozens of battles that fierce...
Mm. In fact, the road is difficult.
Level Four is the first wall. Level Five or Six is essentially impossible in solo play.
KARAN (KLINK)
Nearly everyone at Level Seven and Eight is a commander of an enormous group.
—Group?
Like the guilds or teams you often see in online games.

We call them "Legions" ......
The current accelerated world...
...is ruled by six enormous Legions.
And commanding these...
...are the only six Burst Linkers who have reached Level Nine.
Named Blue, Red, Yellow, Green, Purple, and White—

They are the Six Kings of Pure Color!

...Zero... people...
Yes.
Level Ten is untrodden territory.
In the seven years since the release of this game... Mm.

The sole reason is... the severity of the dictated rules.
...Do you mean you have to win an incredible amount of fights?
Like a few thou-sand?
No, just five times is sufficient.

However, for this purpose...
...you may only fight another Level Nine Linker ...

And if you lose once in such a battle...
...you lose all your points and...
LOSE
...Brain Burst is forcefully uninstalled...

YOU LOSE ALL YOUR POINTS IN ONE BATTLE...
—Haru-yuki-kun.
Do you know why Brain Burst, which makes possible the marvelous phenomenon of accelerated thought...
...has developed simply as a game for children like us?

Requirements? Like being good at games or something?

Nothing as ambiguous as that.

SU (SHF)

The most serious requirement...

...is having "continuously worn a quantum connection Neurolinker terminal from shortly after birth."

It is because of...

...how strict the requirements are for Brain Burst aptitude.

APTITUDE

The first-generation Neurolinkers went on the market...

...fifteen years ago. Which means...

...the oldest are a mere fifteen years old; i.e., there are no adult Burst Linkers.

In summer two years ago, the young kings all reached Level Nine at very nearly the same time.
A system message then informed them of the brutal way to reach Level Ten.
Did they, as a result, plunge into bloody dispute?
—No.
Because they are children, they will try to protect this privilege at all costs.
And because they are children, they share the same sweet fantasies.

WHAT THE KINGS CHOSE WAS...

...ETERNAL...

...ENDLESS...

...STAGNATION.

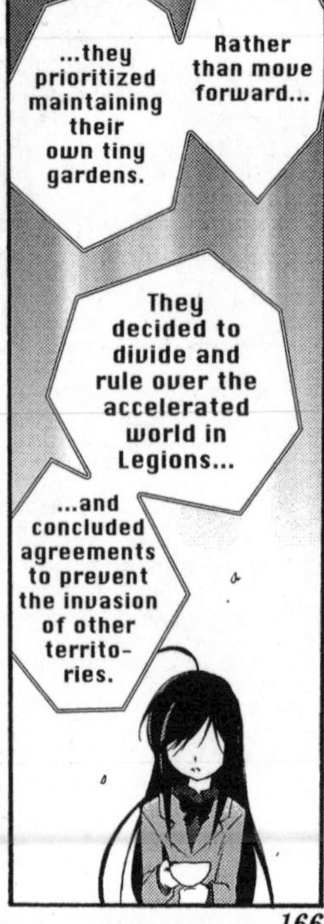

Rather than move forward...
...they prioritized maintaining their own tiny gardens.
They decided to divide and rule over the accelerated world in Legions...
...and concluded agreements to prevent the invasion of other territories.

...It's a total farce.
This, even though we had hunted...
...countless Linkers to reach Level Nine...
......
So you're saying... your objective is...
...to challenge these Six Kings of Pure Color?
No, I already did that.
Wha...!?
The six kings...
They used to be the Seven Kings.
Seven boys and girls, who although rivals...
...were bound by strong ties.
—Until the Black King betrayed them.

The Black King, Black Lotus, was the only one who spoke out against peace.

...and insisted we should throw ourselves into fighting, wagering our accumulated points.

I threw away friendship, ties, respect...

And when they refused to listen...

...I dyed the roundtable of our meeting... with fresh blood.

GOKURI (GULP)

Wh-what did you do...?

BLACK—KING!?

I-It couldn't be...!!

Yes.

It was me...!!

—I CUT HIS HEAD OFF!

The last night the seven kings met in one building...
...Although of course, we have never met in the real world.
Burst Linkers must do their utmost to hide their real names and faces.
GIVEN THAT THE GAME IS ABOUT STEALING POINTS FROM EACH OTHER...
...I GUESS THAT'S TO AVOID THREATS OR ATTACKS IN THE REAL WORLD...?

The meeting that night took place in Battle Royale mode...
...connecting all of us as fighters in the same field.
The Red King caught me off guard...
...preaching friend-shipand insisting we stop fighting.
So I...

A perfect critical hit...
He instantly lost the health in his gauge...
...and all his points...
— finally losing Brain Burst itself.
After that...all hell broke loose.
Purple, who had been in love with Red, screamed and wept; Blue went crazy with rage...
...and they all began to try and kill me, no honor, no respect.
I knew it was my first and last chance, you see...
HEH HEH...
I struggled desperately to take the other five heads.
I was so...... reckless.

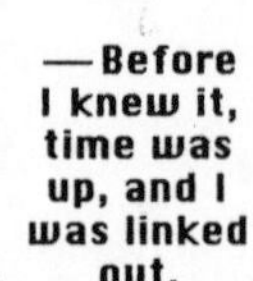

The ability to make rational judgments went out the window.
Stirred up by madness, I fought...
...and although I couldn't take another king...
...I was also not defeated.
—Before I knew it, time was up, and I was linked out.

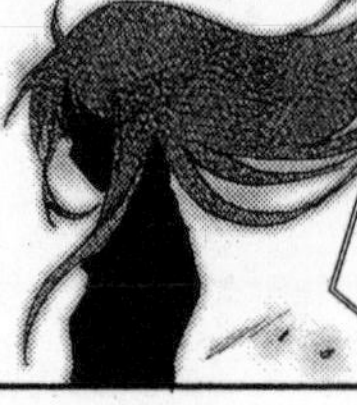

In the two years since ...
...I've focused on running and hiding. Right now...
...I am the biggest traitor in the accelerated world.
I have the largest bounty on my head.
—And I am the worst coward...

—Why...

...would you...?

Because I put it...
...far above friendship, above honor...
—Becoming Level Ten...
...above everything.

The system message also told us this.
That Burst Linkers reaching Level Ten would have the chance to meet the program creator...
...and would be told the true meaning behind the existence of Brain Burst, as well as its goal...
I...I want to know.
Whatever it takes, I have to know.
GU (CLASP)
Accelerating your thinking, you can get money, grades, fame...
Is this really the meaning behind our duels? Is this the compensation we seek, the limit we can reach...?
Isn't... Isn't there something beyond this...?
AAH.
Outside this... shell called a human being...
...isn't there... something more...
...I GET IT.
A LITTLE... HONESTLY, JUST A TINY BIT...

LIKE BEING ON THE GROUND WHERE IT'S HARD TO HOLD ON...
...LOOKING UP AT THE DISTANT SKY.
THAT KIND OF BURNING DESIRE—
...So?
Are you shocked?
Or maybe you hate me, Haruyuki-kun.
Perhaps I'll sacrifice even you at some point for my objective.
It's fine if you want to quit helping me.
....
Er ...

In any game...
...if there are people who want to forget about seeing the ending...
...and just roam around the map right before the end forever...
...then they're obviously idiots.
If there are any higher levels...
...it's only natural...
...to try for them.
—That's what I think.

I mean ...
...that's why Brain Burst exists.
It's waiting for someone to get there, right?

—Pft...
AHA... HA-HA-HA!
—How did this happen?
You're already more of a Burst Linker than I am.
I get it... Only natural to aim for it... That's where we are, is it...?
I-it's nothing to laugh at!
CHU (SLRP)
A-any-way.
That's why I'll keep helping you.
Thank you...
I mean, I want to get there one day too...
...to Level Ten.
—Haru-yuki-kun.
-SO (SSP)
!!
WH-WHOA ...!!

I'm so glad from the bottom of my heart that I chose you.
N-no, it's— Anyway.
...To get to the main part of it... please tell me why you invited me to the accelerated world.
Right.
The introductory bit ended up going long.

As I told you...
...I managed to survive these last two years, yes?
That doesn't mean that I've won against the kings or assassins they've dispatched.
These two years...
...I haven't once connected my Neurolinker to the global net.
WHEN I WATCHED BEFORE, THAT WAS THROUGH THE SCHOOL NET.
Guh... A-are you serious!?
Very serious.
With an old cell terminal, you can still view sites and read your mail.
PACHIN (SNAP)
But...

...there is one local net I must connect with daily...
O-oh. Umesato Junior High's.
H-huh !?
So, so, w-wait a minute. You can't mean...!!
I do mean.

HERE COMES
HALLENGER!
A N
Two months ago...
...the very day summer vacation ended...
...I was challenged to a duel through the school local net.
—By someone at Umesato, just like us.
Back then, I had changed ...
...my duel avatar to a dummy spectator avatar.
There's a function like that?
AVATAR MODE CHANGE
DUEL
DUMMY
Because my duel avatar would be too conspicuous.
However... when I think about it now, I was extremely careless.
At that time, I used my avatar for the local school net as my dummy.
What... ......!?
Your school net avatar... That black swallow-tail!?
Your enemy saw it!?
Your enemy who's in the school net...!?

...Then that's...
Yes...
A Burst Linker's greatest taboo: outed in the real world.
Immediately after...
...I was afraid of real attacks by assassins sent by the Six Kings.
But— There were none.
What ...?
There haven't been any.
Not one.
This is all I can think... My enemy intends to monopolize ...
...my points.
Whoever discovered me...
...wants to corner me and take every single one of my points...
...without telling the Legion they belong to.
Since then I've been attacked over a dozen times by one opponent.
I've managed to get away with draws so far...
Corner you...?
In the toilet. While I'm changing. In the shower ...
There are plenty of moments where I'm emotionally defenseless at school.
If someone targeted these and challenged me to a fight, I certainly wouldn't be able to respond at the top of my game.
In...
...the shower...
MON (FRET)
もん
もん
MON

......
JITO (STARE)
OH! ...NO, SO, UH!
S-SO THIS GUY'S SERIOUSLY GREEDY THEN!
B-but thanks to that, the fact that you've been able to get draws is the silver lining, I guess...
Well, better than an attack in the real world, anyway.
But that being said, I can't beat him down with all my strength.
My enemy might end up thinking it's impossible on his own and give up, and then sell my real world info to a king.
R-right...
You can't run... You can't even get back at him.
You have no way out.
There's only one way to break free...
I find out their real identity.
Right... If you both know who the other is...
...you'd be forced into a truce to protect your own identities ...!!
Exactly. That would put a stop to my enemy's move-ments.
!! Hold on a minute...
That's fairly simple, right?

Like at morning assembly or something, when all the students are together...
...you just challenge whoever it is to a fight on the school net.
It's a rule that students have to be connected to the school net.
So it's not like they could hide from a Brain Burst match challenge.
You can figure out their class and student number from where they appear...!!

Oh... Aren't you something?
It took me a full day to come up with that idea.
Oh... You've already tried that?

I have. —And the person wasn't there.
What ...!?
Oh... Maybe they were out that day?
Naturally, I checked the attendance later.
Not only that... Even immediately after being attacked, they were not on the list.
MATCHING LIST
Given the situation, they should have to be on the school net, and yet...
EMPTY
It's hard to believe, but they can block duels...
...by some means or other.
C-could they actually do that?
......
If they could, they'd have to be a super-hacker...
...so much so that they could change the Brain Burst program itself... Or someone with some connection with the program creator...

SHIN (SILENCE)
......

So then... you made me a Burst Linker so that...
...I could help you find out the true identity of your enemy, right?
Hmm... Well, that's about it, yes.

To be honest, I've obtained a fair bit of information already.
First, my enemy's name... "Cyan Pile."
Level Four.
Cyan Pile...
LEVEL FOUR... THAT'S PRETTY STRONG.

Blue: Short-range direct attack

Red: Long-range direct attack

Yellow: Intermediate attacks

BLUE

GREEN

Intermediate colors such as purple/green/orange have characteristics straddling two color types. Colors with lower saturation have characteristic attacks.

Metallic colors excel in defens abi

Affiliation is a fairly pure close-range blue.

I've seen this Linker punch right through the thin walls of the stage several times.

Conversely, they don't seem to have any flying equipment.

And... This is at best a guess, but...
That hurried style, that's the sign of a Burst Linker afraid of losing acceleration.
...whoever it is is on the verge of running out of points.

HYA HA HA—!!
People with points to spare try to have more fun with the matches as fights.
Like that Ash Roller you fought.
Oh—
He was definitely having a seriously great time......

Okay... Is that all you know?
No.
I have one other important source of information.
—The guide cursor.
Huh? That blue arrow that shows up during a duel?
Exactly.
It points in the direction of your enemy from the moment the duel starts.
So even if I can't see the exact moment when Cyan Pile appears...
...as long as I remember the direction the cursor is pointing when the fight starts...
...the real body of my enemy must be somewhere along that straight line...... That's the idea.
AH!
Oh... Oh!!
That's right!!
The stages are the real-world landscape as is.
So you can at least see what direction in the school Cyan Pile is hiding in!!
Exactly.
VUN (FWWZ)
—I have a file here.

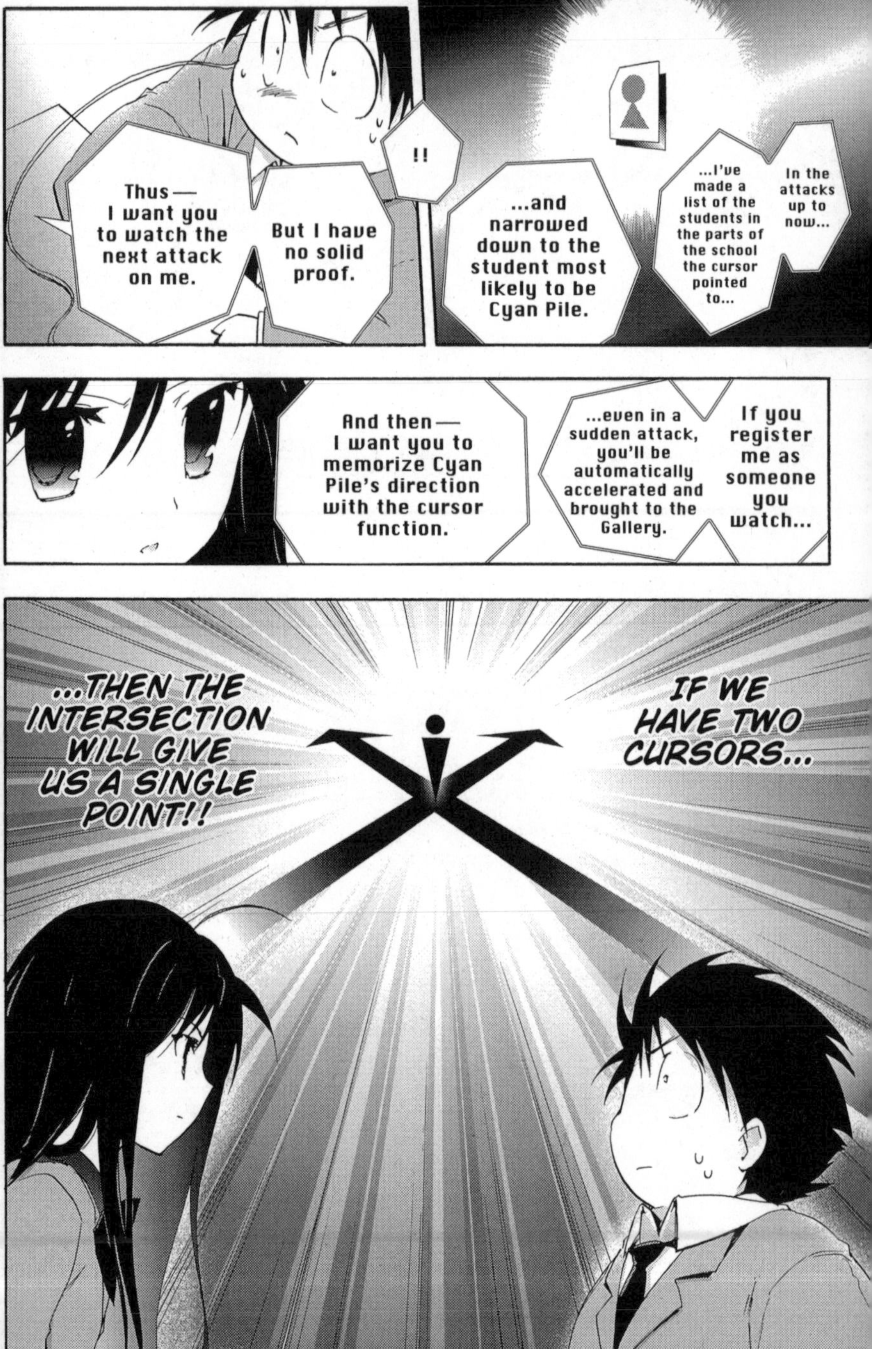

In the attacks up to now...
...I've made a list of the students in the parts of the school the cursor pointed to...
...and narrowed down to the student most likely to be Cyan Pile.
!!
But I have no solid proof.
Thus— I want you to watch the next attack on me.
If you register me as someone you watch...
...even in a sudden attack, you'll be automatically accelerated and brought to the Gallery.
And then— I want you to memorize Cyan Pile's direction with the cursor function.
IF WE HAVE TWO CURSORS...
...THEN THE INTERSECTION WILL GIVE US A SINGLE POINT!!

And then if this student is in that place ...
...I can settle this once and for all.
The real identity of Cyan Pile.
SU (SSP)

Via direct cable connection
Send
Cancel
PITA (TAP)

......
?
What's wrong? Hurry up and send the file...

......
... Listen.
I prepared this file...
...a week before I found the third acceleration-compatible person...
...I was looking for at Umesato—which is to say, you—in that game corner...

Pi
Pi
...WHY IS SHE TAGGING ON THAT DISCLAIMER...
PA (POP)
...HUH.........?
THIS...?
WHY...?

CHIYU ......?

Ch- Chiyu...?
She's... a Burst Linker ...?

N-no...
That's not possible!!
She's super-terrible at games, doesn't matter what kind.
And everything shows up on her face. She can't be the person who's targeting you with such total focus ...!!

......
You know her pretty well, hm?
That's... I mean.
We've been friends since we were kids.

...When she came up to us at the gates before, I was surprised.
If she is Cyan Pile, she should obviously know I'm Black Lotus.
I suspected it was some kind of strategy ...
Um...she doesn't have that kind of skill.
She's not that kind of person.
In that case, isn't it even more natural to think she is Cyan Pile?
You saw the hostility she has toward me.
NO... THAT WAS JUST...
THAT WAS JUST YOU AND ME ARE DIRECTING... AND STUFF.
WHY WOULD SHE GET MAD ABOUT THAT!?
KURASHIMA-KUN HAS A PROPER BOYFRIEND, DOESN'T SHE!?
TO CHIYU
POSSESSION?
UNDER EXCLUSIVE OWNERSHIP?
SUBORDINATE?
WELL, THAT'S JUST, UM......
IT'S HARD TO EXPLAIN !!
JUST WHAT EXACTLY IS GOING ON WITH YOU!?
IF YOU HAVE SOME-THING TO SAY—
—I...
I-I understand!!
Then— I'll check directly with her!!
PIKU (FLIK)
...You will?

But what do you intend to do exactly?
You can't simply go up to her and ask if she's a Burst Linker, you know?
Which is exactly why I've been working so hard; I have no way of confirming anything from this.
Are you trying to say you have some kind of plan?
I......
I... I'll...
I'll direct with her and see!!
!!
ガタッ
GATA (KLATTER)
She can block the duels, but if I look in her memory directly through her Neuro-linker...
...I should be able to check if she has the Brain Burst program or not.
That should satisfy you, right ...!?

▶▶▶ACCEL·WORLD

To Be Continued in the Next Stage...!!

AFTERWORD

THANK YOU SO MUCH FOR PICKING UP THE MANGA VERSION OF ACCEL WORLD. I'M THE ARTIST, HIROYUKI AIGAMO.

I FIRST CAME ACROSS ACCEL WORLD WHEN THE PLAN TO MAKE THE MANGA VERSION OF IT CAME UP.

I'M A BIT EMBARRASSED, BUT AT THE TIME, I HAD NO CONCEPTION OF THE EXISTENCE OF THE WILDLY POPULAR ACCEL WORLD. THE E-MAIL I GOT ABOUT THE PROJECT FROM THE EDITOR AT DENGEKI BUNKO SAID THAT THEY WOULD SEND ME THE BOOKS IF I WANTED, BUT IMMEDIATELY AFTER READING THE E-MAIL, I WENT OVER TO A NEARBY BOOKSTORE, BOUGHT THE FIRST VOLUME, AND HEADED STRAIGHT HOME WITH IT.

A FEW HOURS AFTER I FINISHED READING IT, I SENT AN E-MAIL IN REPLY TO THAT EDITOR WHILE THE FEELINGS THE BOOK AROUSED IN ME WERE STILL STRONG, TO THE EFFECT THAT I WOULD LOVE TO HEAR MORE ABOUT THE PROJECT. I WAS COMPLETELY WON OVER BY ACCEL WORLD, AND I REALLY WANTED TO BE GIVEN THE CHANCE TO DRAW THE MANGA! I VIVIDLY REMEMBER THAT MOMENT IN FRONT OF MY COMPUTER, FULL OF EXCITEMENT.

I HOPE THAT I CAN KEEP GIVING EVERYTHING I'VE GOT TO THIS MANGA GOING FORWARD, WITHOUT FORGETTING THOSE INITIAL IMPRESSIONS. I'D BE DELIGHTED IF YOU'D JOIN ME FOR THE RIDE.

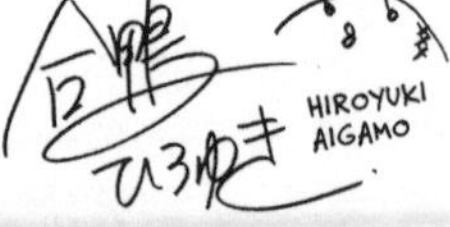

•ASSISTANTS•
Motoko Ikeda
Hio
Getsuyo
Mk=II Inoue
Momo Usagi
Kumiko Morita
Sakuraha
Shige Edo
Sayoko Kamimoto
B King Ito
Hanimaru
Kana Shibusawa
•SPECIAL THANKS•
Reki Kawahara
Akari Ryuryuu
Chie Tsuchiya
HIMA
Kazuma Miki

comment in support of "comic" accel world

CONGRATULATIONS ON THE PUBLICATION OF THE COMICS VERSION OF ACCEL WORLD 1 AND 2!
I'M LOOKING FORWARD TO THE REST OF THE BOOKS!
HIMA

original story: reki kawahara

comment

When I was writing the novel, once the scene came into my mind as a visual, I tried to portray this in text. However, at the limits of my sad abilities to turn these images into language, there were many things that I couldn't quite manage to depict in the finished text. Not only did Hiroyuki Aigamo-san manage to wonderfully resolve in this manga version of *Accel World* all my dissatisfactions—if only this scene had been more bang! pow! with a little more za-za-za-zoom—he actually created something many times more beautiful, interesting, and exciting than the images in my head. As a creator, and also as a reader, I have the very happy experience of waiting impatiently for the next issue of *Dengeki Bunko Magazine* to arrive every two months and then following along with Haruyuki and Kuroyukihime as they laugh, cry, and run with such energy and life.

I really can't wait to be able to read once again about the battles of Haru and the gang with these books finishing up the story of novel volume 1, released as collected books now (and two at the same time no less!).

Aigamo-san, congratulations on the publication of these comics! All your hard work has really paid off! I hope you keep doing this well with the serialization in the future too!!

Reki Kawahara

character design: hima

accel world

art:
hiroyuki aigamo
original story:
reki kawahara
accel world 01: kuroyukihime's return
character design:
hima

CONGRATULATIONS!!
COMICS
ON SALE!!
TWO VOLUMES COMING OUT AT ONCE, THAT'S AMAZING! EACH CHAPTER MAKES MY HEART POUND WITH ALL THE COOL ACTION!
AKARI RYURYUU

ACCEL WORLD 1

ART: HIROYUKI AIGAMO
ORIGINAL STORY: REKI KAWAHARA
CHARACTER DESIGN: HIMA

Translation: Jocelyne Allen • Lettering: Lys Blakeslee

This book is a work of fiction. Names, characters, places, and incidents are the product of the author's imagination or are used fictitiously. Any resemblance to actual events, locales, or persons, living or dead, is coincidental.

Edited by ASCII MEDIA WORKS
First published in Japan in 2011 by KADOKAWA CORPORATION, Tokyo.
English translation rights arranged with KADOKAWA CORPORATION, Tokyo, through Tuttle-Mori Agency, Inc., Tokyo.

Yen Press
Hachette Book Group
1290 Avenue of the Americ

www.HachetteBookGroup.
www.YenPress.com

Yen Press is an imprint of
and logo are trademarks of

First Yen Press Edition: September 2014

ISBN: 978-0-316-33586-7

10 9 8 7 6 5 4 3 2

BVG

Printed in the United States of America